THE CLAVERINGS

Anthony Trollope

THE CLAVERINGS

With a New Introduction by
NORMAN DONALDSON

And 16 Plates from the Original Edition by
M. E. EDWARDS

DOVER PUBLICATIONS, INC.

NEW YORK

Published in Canada by General Publishing Com-
pany, Ltd., 30 Lesmill Road, Don Mills, Toronto,
Ontario.
Published in the United Kingdom by Constable
and Company, Ltd., 10 Orange Street, London
WC2H 7EG.

This Dover edition, first published in 1977, is an
unabridged reproduction of the work as it first appeared in *The Cornhill Magazine,* February 1866 –
May 1867. The Introduction by Norman Donaldson has been prepared especially for this edition.

International Standard Book Number: 0-486-23464-9
Library of Congress Catalog Card Number: 76-46037

Manufactured in the United States of America
Dover Publications, Inc.
180 Varick Street
New York, N.Y. 10014

INTRODUCTION
TO THE DOVER EDITION

The Claverings has been authoritatively ranked as one of Anthony Trollope's three faultless books. Those admirers of the great Victorian novelist who have not so far made the acquaintance of this somewhat unfamiliar story will, of course, welcome its reappearance. New readers who wish to sample Trollope's prose without quite committing themselves to the Barsetshire series could make no better choice than this excellent independent novel. Even the lucky few who possess an entire shelf of Trollope's works would do well to secure this edition of *The Claverings,* which contains material not available since it first appeared in *The Cornhill Magazine* over a century ago.

When Anthony Trollope wrote *The Claverings* he was at the height of his success—literary, financial and social. For five years, since his return from postal duties in Ireland, he had been living with his wife Rose and their two sons at Waltham Cross, north of London, "14 miles out of town on the Norwich line of railway." This was convenient for his daily work at the General Post Office, where he had now reached the rank of Surveyor General at an annual salary of £800. Two or three times a week he loved to hunt, for which purpose he maintained his own stables. Extensive gardens surrounded his home: strawberries were grown, cows milked, butter made. The atmosphere was friendly; relatives and friends were always welcome for dinner, followed by wine and fruit under the old cedar in the twilight.

For the first time in his life, Trollope felt himself to be really popular. He had just become a member of the Garrick Club, where, if he could find a few free hours, he enjoyed a game of whist. His health, energies and prospects were at their height; in 1867, the year *The Claverings* was published, his literary earnings reached their maximum of £6000.

A greater contrast between this prosperity and his early years can scarcely be imagined. It is, in fact, difficult to understand how Trollope avoided becoming psychologically disabled by his experiences. His schooldays were an unrelieved nightmare, much more extended and degrading than the 12-year-old Dickens' stint in the blacking factory at Old Hungerford Stairs. Yet, while Dickens could never bring himself, in later life, to speak or write of his betrayal, as he considered it, Trollope in his autobiography recalls his dreadful experiences with barely a hint of bitterness.

For lack of family funds he was sent to Harrow, not as a boarder but as a despised day-boy. Awkward, untidy, big for his age, he was scorned by the masters and ridiculed by his fellow students, while at home he was ignored. His distracted mother Frances soon decamped with most of the children in what became a successful effort to salvage the family fortunes in America. Later, when his irascible, unhappy father joined her, young Tony was left quite alone, his position terrible indeed. With his fees unpaid, even his shilling-a-week "battels" were withheld from him, so that the school servants, perforce left without their statutory tips, joined masters and boys in an unbroken wall of contempt.

Anthony entered the service of the General Post Office at the age of nineteen as a junior clerk. Quite lacking in self-confidence and the ability to manage his affairs, he spent seven wretched years on the verge of dismissal, badgered by moneylenders and uncertain even of his daily food, before a dramatic improvement occurred. He applied for the post of surveyor's clerk in the west of Ireland where, though the pay was still miserably low, the traveling expenses held out prospects of a more tolerable existence. So it was that, in August 1841, his new life began in Banagher, where he arrived with official documents from his superiors attesting to his bad character.

Away from oppressive authority, he grasped control of his own destiny at last. He bought a horse and took up hunting, which became his life's chief delight; he met his future wife and began saving to get married; he also commenced his writing career. His first three novels were commercial failures. In 1851, in Salisbury, the idea of the first Barsetshire story took shape in his mind. Although this novel, *The Warden* (1855), sold only a few hundred copies, the reviews were sufficiently favorable to encourage the author to persevere in the same line. Thus it was that he went on to write *Barchester Towers* (1857) and the remaining four novels about the mythical county of Barsetshire. Though most of his greatest books came later, it was this series that made him famous in his forties. It was his achievement to create a magical land and people its towns and villages with clergymen, landed gentry and their families and neighbors. Nathaniel Hawthorne, for one, was deeply impressed, finding the effect to be "just as real as if some giant had hewn a great lump out of the earth and put it under a glass case, with all its inhabitants going about their business, and not suspecting they were made a show of." George Eliot found his books to resemble "pleasant public gardens, where people go for amusement and, whether they think it or not, get health as well." "There is a whole class of addicts," writes Clara Claiborne Park, "who would like nothing so much as to walk into the Barsetshire Arcadia and never come out."

Though his prose seldom leaps or sparkles, though even his scenes of high drama are frequently subdued, yet Trollope is an immensely enjoyable author, one whom we can read when no one else satisfies. The characters are real, the conversations true to life, so that his novels have become favorites in Britain when adapted as radio plays. It is fitting that this loyal servant of the postal service often forwards the action in his stories by means of letters—well-written, effective letters.

Barchester Towers was the book for which Anthony first devised his own special routine of writing, a routine made necessary by the demands of his official career, which at that period took him all over Ireland and was later to carry him to distant parts of the world. He would prepare a calendar for each major work which called for so many pages a day for so many weeks. By that means he could gauge his progress and press on harder if he fell behind. He did not plot his novels in advance; instead, he wrote down the names of the chief characters as they formed in his mind, and thereafter allowed them to act according to their natures, which he always understood very fully before he began.

These relentless methods of composition were the foundation of his fame and financial success, but they were to damage his reputation when his candid autobiography was published in 1883, after his death. It was deemed scandalous that an author should write at a constant, rapid rate without pausing for inspiration. A revival began in the United States in the nineties, and in the present century, especially in the harassed days of the two World Wars, his fellow countrymen have taken him to their hearts.

At Waltham House, Anthony Trollope was awakened very early each morning by an old groom who was paid an extra wage for this duty. After a cup of coffee he was at his writing table in the silent house by 5:30, reading through the previous day's work. Thereafter for the remainder of the three hours set aside for authorship he wrote steadily to meet, or more usually to exceed, the quota he had set himself. We know from the working table found among his papers that he began *The Claverings* on 24 August 1864, six days after completing a minor novel, *Miss Mackenzie.* He planned to write 35 pages of 260 words each week for 22 weeks to reach his total estimate of 770 pages, which was to be divided into 16 equal parts for publication in *The Cornhill Magazine.* In the event, though there were several interruptions along the way, he finished the book's 768 pages on the last day of the year, more than three weeks early. He did this by regularly writing 48 pages a week rather than the stipulated 35. Thus he was able to take a few days off in September to write a short story, "Malachi's Cove," for *Good Words* magazine, to spend a short time in Paris with his son Harry, and to take his wife for a long weekend at Freshwater on the Isle of Wight. A week or so after this last outing he used the quiet resort in his novel as the scene of Julia Ongar's encounter with the shady Count Pateroff. In November, several days were lost when relatives stayed, and in December two weeks of his calendar simply carry the notation "Alas!" and the word "Ramsgate," which seem to imply a short illness and a recuperative visit to the seaside.

Characteristically, he began writing other things the moment *The Claverings* was complete, and the novel was wrapped up in brown paper until the *Cornhill* required it. It was serialized from February 1866 until May 1867. An unprecedented mishap occurred when the novel was being set up in book type for publication, in accordance with the usual practice, about a month before the final installment of the serial appeared. Perhaps the copy of the magazine containing the second part of the story was defective when it reached the compositor. At any rate, from this cause or some other, the entire final page of this installment was left out of the book, whereby Chapter VI ends very abruptly in the middle of a conversation between Harry, the young hero, and the pathetic Lady Clavering, with the words "Hugh will not go to her." The remaining dialogue, as well as an important letter from Julia Ongar to Harry, and a hint of forthcoming indiscreet conduct on the latter's part, are all lost to the reader of the book. Not only was Chapter VI weakened, but a remark made by Julia a few pages later to the effect that she had already informed Harry that "the apartments had been all that she desired" must puzzle the careful reader, for that information is in the omitted letter. This important material is missing not only from the first (two-volume) book edition of 1867 but also from all subsequent single-volume editions. The text now in the reader's hands is therefore the first edition in volume form to relate the story as Trollope intended.

In *The Claverings* we meet a beautiful, flawed heroine, Julia Brabazon, and a weak vacillating hero, Harry Clavering. At least, his creator considered him weak, but not all critics have agreed. In many of his actions, indeed, Harry behaves well enough. It is his misfortune to be jilted by the masterful Julia in favor of the debauched—but very wealthy—Lord Ongar, and to be powerfully attracted to her again in her early widowhood. She is unaware that he has become betrothed in the meantime to the pleasant but rather colorless Florence Burton. Having failed to tell Julia of this commitment at once, he finds himself faced by a difficult choice: on the one hand, his clear duty; on the other, his first love, who, in her social ostracism, is deeply in need of a loyal friend. Many novelists would have resolved this impasse by allowing fate to intervene, but that is not Anthony Trollope's way. A choice must be made, and made, at last, it is.

As always, Trollope's conversations are natural and convincing, his analysis of character penetrating and just, his spare but adequate settings memorable. The novel is especially free of side issues. Even the subplot of the angular Mr. Saul's all-but-hopeless courtship of Fanny, which might otherwise be considered a diversion, plays its part by contrasting Harry's weathervane behavior with the single-hearted dignity of the impoverished curate earnestly pressing his cause without benefit of good looks, social graces or other advantages.

Trollope's skill in setting the scene is evident even in the opening paragraph. Instead of introducing us at once, by a scrap of conversation, to the two protagonists, he moves in on them from a distance, his initial wide-angled shot showing us the tyrannical Sir Hugh's somber mansion set in its "yellow, adust, harsh, and dry" park, whereby we are prepared for its owner when we meet him in due course. At the end of the paragraph, the author describes the young couple in these terms: "Over the burnt turf . . . a lady was walking, and by her side there walked a gentleman." These words portray the precise situation, for Julia has dismissed Harry, while he is determined on a final interview.

For these and many other reasons, *The Claverings* is an outstanding novel. Michael Sadleir, Trollope's chief biographer and bibliographer, has selected about a dozen of his fifty or so novels as particularly fine; of these, he considers three to be "faultless books." They are *Doctor Thorne* (1858)—the third of the six Barsetshire novels—*Harry Hotspur of Humblethwaite* (1871) and *The Claverings*. "In these," he writes, "there is not a loose end, not a patch of drowsiness, not a moment of false proportion."

A mystery remains to be unraveled. *The Claverings* introduces us to a character so completely un-Trollopian that she cannot be passed over without discussion. When Julia returns to London from Italy after the timely death of her monstrous husband, she is accompanied by a grotesque Polish-Frenchwoman, Sophie Gordeloup. Hugh Walpole was a great admirer of this strange creature, whom he calls one of the novelist's three best wicked women: "Sophie Gordeloup is *The Claverings,* and *The Claverings* is Sophie Gordeloup," he writes. Anthony himself was delighted with her, proud of the "genuine fun" he had been able to introduce into her interviews with the ne'er-do-well Archie Clavering and his agent Captain Boodle. But Trollope's autobiography gives us no hint of her genesis.

Where did Sophie come from? *The Saturday Review* was puzzled. "We should be disposed to doubt whether Mr. Trollope knows a real Gordeloup," wrote its reviewer, and we can only concur. Trollope in his fiction usually deals with only two types of person, those whom he met from day to day, and those—like the clergy in his Barchester novels—with whom he was personally unfamiliar but who sprang from the same soil and whose thoughts and feelings his wide experience and wider sympathies enabled him to imagine. So we repeat the question: Where did Sophie come from? The answer is not to be found in earlier commentaries on Trollope and *The Claverings;* we must attempt to find the truth for ourselves.

The Dublin University Magazine, published monthly in both Dublin and London, was an excellent periodical of the type an Englishman with Irish connections would be especially likely to read regularly. Indeed, it contained from time to time reviews of Trollope's works, and our author during the 1850's had occasionally contributed reviews and articles to it. In its issue of August 1864, the very month Trollope began writing *The Claverings,* appeared the first part of one of the most remarkable Gothic novels ever written, Joseph Sheridan LeFanu's *Uncle Silas.* In the first pages (which bear the original title, *Maud Ruthyn*) is introduced the diabolical, grimacing Madame de la Rougierre, who, much to Maud's consternation, has been appointed her governess.

In an early scene, Madame, accompanied by the reluctant girl, visits the tomb of Maud's mother and observes the new inscription. Asked to read it aloud, Maud moves closer.

> As I approached, I happened to look, I can't tell why, suddenly, over my shoulder; I was startled, for Madame was grimacing after me with a vile derisive distortion. She pretended to be seized with a fit of coughing. But it would not do: she saw that I had detected her, and she laughed aloud.
>
> "Come here, dear cheaile. I was just reflecting how foolish is all this thing—the tomb—the epitaph. I think I would 'av none—no, no epitaph."

A little later the frightful woman resorts to torture to extract a secret from her terrified pupil.

> "You do know, and you must tell, petite dure-tête, or I will break a your leetle finger."
>
> With which words she seized that joint and, laughing spitefully, she twisted it suddenly back.

In *The Claverings,* Sophie has accepted money from Archie, but in return has done nothing to further his wooing of the now-wealthy Julia. He therefore dispatches Captain Boodle, his horse-racing fellow-clubman in the cutaway coat, to interview the dingy Frenchwoman. Boodle, nicknamed "Doodles," introduces himself as coming originally from a small property in Warwickshire, and raises the question of the money already paid to her for her services.

"... Seventy pounds, you know, ma'am, is a smart bit of money."

"A smart bit of money, is it? That is what you think on your leetle property down in Warwickshire."

"It isn't my property, ma'am, at all. It belongs to my uncle."

"Oh, it is your uncle that has the leetle property. And what had your uncle to do with Lady Ongar? What is your uncle to your friend Archie?"

"Nothing at all, ma'am; nothing on earth."

"Then why do you tell me all this rigmarole about your uncle and his leetle property, and Warwickshire? ..."

... "Damn Warwickshire!" said Doodles, who was put beyond himself.

"With all my heart. Damn Warwickshire." And the horrid woman grinned at him as she repeated his words. "And the leetle property, and the uncle, if you wish it; and the leetle nephew,—and the leetle nephew!" She stood over him as she repeated the last words with wondrous rapidity, and grinned at him, and grimaced and shook herself, till Doodles was altogether bewildered.

There we have Trollope's Sophie and "Doodles." Let us compare this passage with the meeting of Rougierre and her shady acquaintance Dud, or "Deedle," whom LeFanu introduces as "a rather fat . . . young man [wearing a] green cutaway coat with gilt buttons."

"Ha, Deedle, you are there! an' look so well. I am here, too, quite *a*lon; but my friend, she wait outside the churchyard, byside the leetle river, for she must not think I know you—so I am come *a*lon."

"You're a quarter late, and I lost a fight by you, old girl, this morning," said the gay man, and spat on the ground; "and I wish you would not call me Diddle. I'll call you Granny if you do."

"Eh bien! *Dud,* then. . . ."

There is much play with gloves in both novels, and English county names are bandied about—Warwickshire (as we have seen) by Sophie, and Derbyshire by LeFanu's harpy. But to extend the parallel would be tiresome. Interested readers can readily obtain a copy of *Uncle Silas* for themselves; a handsome, reasonably priced edition is available.[1] Sophie is less sinister, more comic, than LeFanu's villainess, and her personality is much better analyzed. Physically, also, they differ greatly, for Rougierre is large-boned and ungainly. Moreover, Sophie is given a less outlandish accent.

But in spite of these differences, Trollope has captured the essence of LeFanu's creation with such fidelity that, even to one who has not read *Uncle Silas* for many years, the effect, as I can attest, is one of immediate, startled recognition. The ladies, in a word, share the characteristic of using a great excess of energy in every situation. In the current vernacular, they "come on very strong." Boodle, quite unlike "Dud," is a rather likeable fellow; Trollope thought enough of him to employ him—briefly—in *Phineas Redux* (1874), where, as in *The Claverings,* he imparts advice to the lovelorn by way of amusingly horsey metaphors.

Though there can remain no doubt that Trollope was strongly influenced by LeFanu's story, his great novelistic powers adapted and transmuted what he had so recently absorbed to accord with the need of his novel and his own view of life. In the lists of characters he sometimes jotted down on commencing a novel are to be found, as Sadleir has discovered, the names of real acquaintances whom he intended to use as models. While his characters survive in his books, the models are long dead and gone, so that judgments on the verisimilitude with which Trollope has portrayed them can never now be made. In the case of Sophie Gordeloup both model and portrait are available to us, and we find, as we might have expected, that what Trollope changes is outward appearance; what he adheres to is the deeper traits of character, in the analysis of which he has shown himself to be such a master.

Columbus, Ohio NORMAN DONALDSON

---

[1] J. S. LeFanu, *Uncle Silas: A Tale of Bartram-Haugh,* with an introduction by Frederick Shroyer (Dover Publications, Inc., 1966).

THE CLAVERINGS

CHAPTER I.

JULIA BRABAZON.

THE gardens of Clavering Park were removed some three hundred yards from the large, square, sombre-looking stone mansion which was the country-house of Sir Hugh Clavering, the eleventh baronet of that name; and in these gardens, which had but little of beauty to recommend them, I will introduce my readers to two of the personages with whom I wish to make them acquainted in the following story. It was now the end of August, and the parterres, beds, and bits of lawn were dry, disfigured, and almost ugly, from the effects of a long drought. In gardens to which care and labour are given abundantly, flower-beds will be pretty, and grass will be green, let the weather be what it may; but care and labour were but scantily bestowed on the Clavering Gardens, and everything was yellow, adust, harsh, and dry. Over the burnt turf towards a gate that led to the house, a lady was walking, and by her side there walked a gentleman.

"You are going in, then, Miss Brabazon," said the gentleman, and it was very manifest from his tone that he intended to convey some deep reproach in his words.

"Of course I am going in," said the lady. "You asked me to walk with you, and I refused. You have now waylaid me, and therefore I shall escape,—unless I am prevented by violence." As she spoke she stood still for a moment, and looked into his face with a smile which seemed to indicate that if such violence were used, within rational bounds, she would not feel herself driven to great anger.

But though she might be inclined to be playful, he was by no means in that mood. "And why did you refuse me when I asked you?" said he.

"For two reasons, partly because I thought it better to avoid any conversation with you."

"That is civil to an old friend."

"But chiefly," and now as she spoke she drew herself up, and dismissed the smile from her face, and allowed her eyes to fall upon the ground; "but chiefly because I thought that Lord Ongar would prefer that I should not roam alone about Clavering Park with any young gentleman while I am down here; and that he might specially object to my roaming with you, were he to know that you and I were—old acquaintances. Now I have been very frank, Mr. Clavering, and I think that that ought to be enough."

"You are afraid of him already, then?"

"I am afraid of offending any one whom I love, and especially any one to whom I owe any duty."

"Enough! indeed it is not. From what you know of me do you think it likely that that will be enough?" He was now standing in front of her, between her and the gate, and she made no effort to leave him.

"And what is it you want? I suppose you do not mean to fight Lord Ongar, and that if you did you would not come to me."

"Fight him! No; I have no quarrel with him. Fighting him would do no good."

"None in the least; and he would not fight if you were to ask him; and you could not ask him without being false to me."

"I should have had an example for that, at any rate."

"That's nonsense, Mr. Clavering. My falsehood, if you should choose to call me false, is of a very different nature, and is pardonable by all laws known in the world."

"You are a jilt,—that is all."

"Come, Harry, don't use hard words," and she put her hand kindly upon his arm. "Look at me, such as I am, and at yourself, and then say whether anything but misery could come of a match between you and me. Our ages by the register are the same, but I am ten years older than you by the world. I have two hundred a year, and I owe at this moment six hundred pounds. You have, perhaps, double as much, and would lose half of that if you married. You are an usher at a school."

" No, madam, I am not an usher at a school."

" Well, well, you know I don't mean to make you angry."

" At the present moment, I am a schoolmaster, and if I remained so, I might fairly look forward to a liberal income. But I am going to give that up."

" You will not be more fit for matrimony because you are going to give up your profession. Now Lord Ongar has—heaven knows what;—perhaps sixty thousand a year."

" In all my life I never heard such effrontery,—such barefaced shameless worldliness."

" Why should I not love a man with a large income ? "

" He is old enough to be your father."

" He is thirty-six, and I am twenty-four."

" Thirty-six ! "

" There is the Peerage for you to look at. But, my dear Harry, do you not know that you are perplexing me and yourself too, for nothing ? I was fool enough when I came here from Nice, after papa's death, to let you talk nonsense to me for a month or two."

" Did you or did you not swear that you loved me ? "

" Oh, Mr. Clavering, I did not imagine that your strength would have condescended to take such advantage over the weakness of a woman. I remember no oaths of any kind, and what foolish assertions I may have made, I am not going to repeat. It must have become manifest to you during these two years that all that was a romance. If it be a pleasure to you to look back to it, of that pleasure I cannot deprive you. Perhaps I also may sometimes look back. But I shall never speak of that time again; and you, if you are as noble as I take you to be, will not speak of it either. I know you would not wish to injure me."

" I would wish to save you from the misery you are bringing on yourself."

" In that you must allow me to look after myself. Lord Ongar certainly wants a wife, and I intend to be true to him,—and useful."

" How about love ? "

" And to love him, sir. Do you think that no man can win a woman's love, unless he is filled to the brim with poetry, and has a neck like Lord Byron, and is handsome like your worship ? You are very handsome, Harry, and you, too, should go into the market and make the best of yourself. Why should you not learn to love some nice girl that has money to assist you ? "

" Julia ! "

" No, sir; I will not be called Julia. If you do, I will be insulted, and leave you instantly. I may call you Harry, as being so much younger,—though we were born in the same month, and as a sort of cousin. But I shall never do that after to-day."

" You have courage enough, then, to tell me that you have not ill-used me ? "

" Certainly I have. Why, what a fool you would have me be ! Look at me, and tell me whether I am fit to be the wife of such a one as you. By the time you are entering the world, I shall be an old woman, and shall have lived my life. Even if I were fit to be your mate when we were living here together, am I fit, after what I have done and seen during the last two years ? Do you think it would really do any good to any one if I were to jilt, as you call it, Lord Ongar, and tell them all,—your cousin, Sir Hugh, and my sister, and your father,—that I was going to keep myself up, and marry you when you were ready for me ? "

" You mean to say that the evil is done."

" No, indeed. At the present moment I owe six hundred pounds, and I don't know where to turn for it, so that my husband may not be dunned for my debts as soon as he has married me. What a wife I should have been for you ;—should I not ? "

" I could pay the six hundred pounds for you with money that I have earned myself, though you do call me an usher ; and perhaps would ask fewer questions about it than Lord Ongar will do with all his thousands."

" Dear Harry, I beg your pardon about the usher. Of course, I know that you are a fellow of your college, and that St. Cuthbert's, where you teach the boys, is one of the grandest schools in England ; and I hope you'll be a bishop ; nay,—I think you will, if you make up your mind to try for it."

" I have given up all idea of going into the church."

" Then you'll be a judge. I know you'll be great and distinguished, and that you'll do it all yourself. You are distinguished already. If you could only know how infinitely I should prefer your lot to mine ! Oh, Harry, I envy you ! I do envy you ! You have got the ball at your feet, and the world before you, and can win everything for yourself."

" But nothing is anything without your love."

" Psha ! Love, indeed. What could I do for you but ruin you ? You know it as well as I do ; but you are selfish enough to wish to continue a romance which would be absolutely destructive to me, though for a while it might afford a pleasant relaxation to your graver studies. Harry, you can choose in the world. You have divinity, and law, and literature, and art. And if debarred from love now by the exigencies of labour, you will be as fit for love in ten years' time as you are at present."

" But I do love now."

" Be a man, then, and keep it to yourself. Love is not to be our master. You can choose, as I say ; but I have had no choice,—no choice but to be married well, or to go out like a snuff of a candle. I don't like the snuff of a candle, and, therefore, I am going to be married well."

" And that suffices ? "

" It must suffice. And why should it not suffice ? You are very uncivil, cousin, and very unlike the rest of the world. Everybody compliments me on my marriage. Lord Ongar is not only rich, but he is a man of fashion, and a man of talent."

"Are you fond of race-horses yourself?"

"Very fond of them."

"And of that kind of life?"

"Very fond of it. I mean to be fond of everything that Lord Ongar likes. I know that I can't change him, and, therefore, I shall not try."

"You are right there, Miss Brabazon."

"You mean to be impertinent, sir; but I will not take it so. This is to be our last meeting in private, and I won't acknowledge that I am insulted. But it must be over now, Harry; and here I have been pacing round and round the garden with you, in spite of my refusal just now. It must not be repeated, or things will be said which I do not mean to have ever said of me. Good-by, Harry."

"Good-by, Julia."

"Well, for that once let it pass. And remember this; I have told you all my hopes, and my one trouble. I have been thus open with you because I thought it might serve to make you look at things in a right light. I trust to your honour as a gentleman to repeat nothing that I have said to you."

"I am not given to repeat such things as those."

"I'm sure you are not. And I hope you will not misunderstand the spirit in which they have been spoken. I shall never regret what I have told you now, if it tends to make you perceive that we must both regard our past acquaintance as a romance, which must, from the stern necessity of things, be treated as a dream which we have dreamt, or a poem which we have read."

"You can treat it as you please."

"God bless you, Harry; and I will always hope for your welfare, and hear of your success with joy. Will you come up and shoot with them on Thursday?"

"What, with Hugh? No; Hugh and I do not hit it off together. If I shot at Clavering I should have to do it as a sort of head-keeper. It's a higher position, I know, than that of an usher, but it doesn't suit me."

"Oh, Harry! that is so cruel! But you will come up to the house. Lord Ongar will be there on the thirty-first; the day after to-morrow, you know."

"I must decline even that temptation. I never go into the house when Hugh is there, except about twice a year on solemn invitation—just to prevent there being a family quarrel."

"Good-by, then," and she offered him her hand.

"Good-by, if it must be so."

"I don't know whether you mean to grace my marriage?"

"Certainly not. I shall be away from Clavering, so that the marriage bells may not wound my ears. For the matter of that, I shall be at the school."

"I suppose we shall meet some day in town."

"Most probably not. My ways and Lord Ongar's will be altogether different, even if I should succeed in getting up to London. If you ever come to see Hermione here, I may chance to meet you in the house. But you will not do that often, the place is so dull and unattractive."

"It is the dearest old park."

"You won't care much for old parks as Lady Ongar."

"You don't know what I may care about as Lady Ongar; but as Julia Brabazon I will now say good-by for the last time." Then they parted, and the lady returned to the great house, while Harry Clavering made his way across the park towards the rectory.

Three years before this scene in the gardens at Clavering Park, Lord Brabazon had died at Nice, leaving one unmarried daughter, the lady to whom the reader has just been introduced. One other daughter he had, who was then already married to Sir Hugh Clavering, and Lady Clavering was the Hermione of whom mention has already been made. Lord Brabazon, whose peerage had descended to him in a direct line from the times of the Plantagenets, was one of those unfortunate nobles of whom England is burdened with but few, who have no means equal to their rank. He had married late in life, and had died without a male heir. The title which had come from the Plantagenets was now lapsed; and when the last lord died, about four hundred a year was divided between his two daughters. The elder had already made an excellent match, as regarded fortune, in marrying Sir Hugh Clavering; and the younger was now about to make a much more splendid match in her alliance with Lord Ongar. Of them I do not know that it is necessary to say much more at present.

And of Harry Clavering it perhaps may not be necessary to say much in the way of description. The attentive reader will have already gathered nearly all that should be known of him before he makes himself known by his own deeds. He was the only son of the Reverend Henry Clavering, rector of Clavering, uncle of the present Sir Hugh Clavering, and brother of the last Sir Hugh. The Reverend Henry Clavering, and Mrs. Clavering his wife, and his two daughters, Mary and Fanny Clavering, lived always at Clavering Rectory, on the outskirts of Clavering Park, at a full mile's distance from the house. The church stood in the park, about midway between the two residences. When I have named one more Clavering, Captain Clavering, Captain Archibald Clavering, Sir Hugh's brother, and when I shall have said also that both Sir Hugh and Captain Clavering were men fond of pleasure and fond of money, I shall have said all that I need now say about the Clavering family at large.

Julia Brabazon had indulged in some reminiscence of the romance of her past poetic life when she talked of cousinship between her and Harry Clavering. Her sister was the wife of Harry Clavering's first cousin, but between her and Harry there was no relationship whatever. When old Lord Brabazon had died at Nice she had come to Clavering Park, and had created some astonishment among those who knew Sir Hugh by making good her footing in his establishment. He was not the man to take up a wife's sister, and make his house her home, out of charity or from domestic love. Lady Clavering, who had been a handsome woman and fashionable withal, no doubt may have had some influence; but Sir Hugh was a man much prone to follow his own courses. It must be presumed that Julia Brabazon had made herself agreeable in the house, and probably also useful. She had been taken to London through two seasons, and had there held up her head among the bravest. And she had been taken abroad,—for Sir Hugh did not love Clavering Park, except during six weeks of partridge shooting ; and she had been at Newmarket with them, and at the house of a certain fast hunting duke with whom Sir Hugh was intimate ; and at Brighton with her sister, when it suited Sir Hugh to remain alone at the duke's ; and then again up in London, where she finally arranged matters with Lord Ongar. It was acknowledged by all the friends of the two families, and indeed I may say of the three families now—among the Brabazon people, and the Clavering people, and the Courton people,—Lord Ongar's family name was Courton,—that Julia Brabazon had been very clever. Of her and Harry Clavering together no one had ever said a word. If any words had been spoken between her and Hermione on the subject, the two sisters had been discreet enough to manage that they should go no further. In those short months of Julia's romance Sir Hugh had been away from Clavering, and Hermione had been much occupied in giving birth to an heir. Julia had now lived past her one short spell of poetry, had written her one sonnet, and was prepared for the business of the world.

CHAPTER II.

HARRY CLAVERING CHOOSES HIS PROFESSION.

HARRY CLAVERING might not be an usher, but, nevertheless, he was home for the holidays. And who can say where the usher ends and the school-master begins ? He, perhaps, may properly be called an usher, who is hired by a private schoolmaster to assist himself in his private occupation, whereas Harry Clavering had been selected by a public body out of a hundred candidates, with much real or pretended reference to certificates of qualification. He was certainly not an usher, as he was paid three hundred a year for his work,—which is quite beyond the mark of ushers. So much was certain ; but yet the word stuck in his throat and made him uncomfortable. He did not like to reflect that he was home for the holidays.

But he had determined that he would never come home for the holi-days again. At Christmas he would leave the school at which he had won his appointment with so much trouble, and go into an open pro-fession. Indeed he had chosen his profession, and his mode of entering it. He would become a civil engineer, and perhaps a land surveyor, and with this view he would enter himself as a pupil in the great house of Beilby and Burton. The terms even had been settled.• He was to pay a premium of five hundred pounds and join Mr. Burton, who was settled in the town of Stratton, for twelve months before he placed himself in Mr. Beilby's office in London. Stratton was less than twenty miles from Clavering. It was a comfort to him to think that he could pay this five hundred pounds out of his own earnings, without troubling his father. It was a comfort, even though he had earned that money by "ushering" for the last two years.

When he left Julia Brabazon in the garden, Harry Clavering did not go at once home to the rectory, but sauntered out all alone into the park, intending to indulge in reminiscences of his past romance. It was all over, that idea of having Julia Brabazon for his love; and now he had to ask himself whether he intended to be made permanently miserable by her worldly falseness, or whether he would borrow something of her worldly wisdom, and agree with himself to look back on what was past as a pleasurable excitement in his boyhood. Of course we all know that really permanent misery was in truth out of the question. Nature had not made him physically or mentally so poor a creature as to be incapable of a cure. But on this occasion he decided on permanent misery. There was about his heart,—about his actual anatomical heart, with its internal arrangement of valves and blood-vessels,—a heavy dragging feel that almost amounted to corporeal pain, and which he described to himself as agony. Why should this rich, debauched, disreputable lord have the power of taking the cup from his lip, the one morsel of bread which he coveted from his mouth, his one ingot of treasure out of his coffer? Fight him! No, he knew he could not fight Lord Ongar. The world was against such an arrangement. And in truth Harry Clavering had so much contempt for Lord Ongar, that he had no wish to fight so poor a creature. The man had had delirium tremens, and was a worn-out miserable object. So at least Harry Clavering was only too ready to believe. He did not care much for Lord Ongar in the matter. His anger was against her;—that she should have deserted him for a miserable creature, who had nothing to back him but wealth and rank!

There was wretchedness in every view of the matter. He loved her so well, and yet he could do nothing! He could take no step towards saving her or assisting himself. The marriage bells would ring within a month from the present time, and his own father would go to the church and marry them. Unless Lord Ongar were to die before then by God's hand, there could be no escape,—and of such escape Harry Clavering had no thought. He felt a weary, dragging soreness at his heart, and told himself that he must be miserable for ever,—not so miserable but what he would work, but so wretched that the world could have for him no satisfaction.

What could he do? What thing could he achieve so that she should know that he did not let her go from him without more thought than his poor words had expressed? He was perfectly aware that in their conversation she had had the best of the argument,—that he had talked almost like a boy, while she had talked quite like a woman. She had treated him de haut en bas with all that superiority which youth and beauty give to a young woman over a very young man. What could he do ? Before he returned to the rectory, he had made up his mind what he would do, and on the following morning Julia Brabazon received by the hands of her maid the following note :—

" I think I understood all that you said to me yesterday. At any rate, I understand that you have one trouble left, and that I have the means of curing it." In the first draft of his letter he said something about ushering, but that he omitted afterwards. " You may be assured that the enclosed is all my own, and that it is entirely at my own disposal. You may also be quite sure of good faith on the part of the lender.—H. C." And in this letter he enclosed a cheque for six hundred pounds. It was the money which he had saved since he took his degree, and had been intended for Messrs. Beilby and Burton. But he would wait another two years,—continuing to do his ushering for her sake. What did it matter to a man who must, under any circumstances, be permanently miserable ?

Sir Hugh was not yet at Clavering. He was to come with Lord Ongar on the eve of the partridge-shooting. The two sisters, therefore, had the house all to themselves. At about twelve they sat down to breakfast together in a little upstairs chamber adjoining Lady Clavering's own room, Julia Brabazon at that time having her lover's generous letter in her pocket. She knew that it was as improper as it was generous, and that, moreover, it was very dangerous. There was no knowing what might be the result of such a letter should Lord Ongar even know that she had received it. She was not absolutely angry with Harry, but had, to herself, twenty times called him a foolish, indiscreet, dear generous boy. But what was she to do with the cheque ? As to that, she had hardly as yet made up her mind when she joined her sister on the morning in question. Even to Hermione she did not dare to tell the fact that such a letter had been received by her.

But in truth her debts were a great torment to her; and yet how trifling they were when compared with the wealth of the man who was to become her husband in six weeks ! Let her marry him, and not pay them, and he probably would never be the wiser. They would get themselves paid almost without his knowledge, perhaps altogether without his hearing of them. But yet she feared him, knowing him to be greedy about money; and, to give her such merit as was due to her, she felt the meanness of going to her husband with debts on her shoulder. She had five thousand pounds of her own ; but the very settlement which gave her a noble dower, and which made the marriage so brilliant, made over this small sum in its entirety to her lord. She had been wrong not to tell the lawyer of her trouble when he had brought the paper for her to sign ; but she had not told him. If Sir Hugh Clavering had been her own brother there would have been no difficulty, but he was only her brother-in-law, and she feared to speak to him. Her sister, however, knew that there were debts, and on that subject she was not afraid to speak to Hermione.

"Hermy," said she, "what am I to do about this money that I owe? I got a bill from Colclugh's this morning."

"Just because he knows you're going to be married; that's all."

"But how am I to pay him?"

"Take no notice of it till next spring. I don't know what else you can do. You'll be sure to have money when you come back from the Continent."

"You couldn't lend it me; could you?"

"Who? I? Did you ever know me have any money in hand since I was married? I have the name of an allowance, but it is always spent before it comes to me, and I am always in debt."

"Would Hugh—let me have it?"

"What, give it you?"

"Well, it wouldn't be so very much for him. I never asked him for a pound yet."

"I think he would say something you wouldn't like if you were to ask him; but, of course, you can try it if you please."

"Then what am I to do?"

"Lord Ongar should have let you keep your own fortune. It would have been nothing to him."

"Hugh didn't let you keep your own fortune."

"But the money which will be nothing to Lord Ongar was a good deal to Hugh. You're going to have sixty thousand a year, while we have to do with seven or eight. Besides, I hadn't been out in London, and it wasn't likely I should owe much in Nice. He did ask me, and there was something."

"What am I to do, Hermy?"

"Write and ask Lord Ongar to let you have what you want out of your own money. Write to-day, so that he may get your letter before he comes."

"Oh, dear! oh, dear! I never wrote a word to him yet, and to begin with asking him for money!"

"I don't think he can be angry with you for that."

"I shouldn't know what to say. Would you write it for me, and let me see how it looks?"

This Lady Clavering did; and had she refused to do it, I think that poor Harry Clavering's cheque would have been used. As it was, Lady Clavering wrote the letter to "My dear Lord Ongar," and it was copied and signed by "Yours most affectionately, Julia Brabazon." The effect of this was the receipt of a cheque for a thousand pounds in a very pretty note from Lord Ongar, which the lord brought with him to Clavering, and sent up to Julia as he was dressing for dinner. It was an extremely comfortable arrangement, and Julia was very glad of the money,—feeling it to be a portion of that which was her own. And Harry's cheque had been returned to him on the day of its receipt. " Of course I cannot take it, and of course you should not have sent it." These words were written on the morsel of paper in which the money was returned. But Miss Brabazon had torn the signature off the cheque, so that it might be safe, whereas Harry Clavering had taken no precaution with it whatever. But then Harry Clavering had not lived two years in London.

During the hours that the cheque was away from him, Harry had told his father that perhaps, even yet, he might change his purpose as to going to Messrs. Beilby and Burton. He did not know, he said, but he was still in doubt. This had sprung from some chance question which his father had asked, and which had seemed to demand an answer. Mr. Clavering greatly disliked the scheme of life which his son had made. Harry's life hitherto had been prosperous and very creditable. He had gone early to Cambridge, and at twenty-two had become a fellow of his college. This fellowship he could hold for five or six years without going into orders. It would then lead to a living, and would in the meantime afford a livelihood. But, beyond this, Harry, with an energy which he certainly had not inherited from his father, had become a schoolmaster, and was already a rich man. He had done more than well, and there was a great probability that between them they might be able to buy the next presentation to Clavering, when the time should come in which Sir Hugh should determine on selling it. That Sir Hugh should give the family living to his cousin was never thought probable by any of the family at the rectory; but he might perhaps part with it under such circumstances on favourable terms. For all these reasons the father was very anxious that his son should follow out the course for which he had been intended; but that he, being unenergetic and having hitherto done little for his son, should dictate to a young man who had been energetic, and who had done much for himself, was out of the question. Harry, therefore, was to be the arbiter of his own fate. But when Harry received back the cheque from Julia Brabazon, then he again returned to his resolution respecting Messrs. Beilby and Burton, and took the first opportunity of telling his father that such was the case.

After breakfast he followed his father into his study, and there, sitting in two easy-chairs opposite to each other, they lit each a cigar. Such was the reverend gentleman's custom in the afternoon, and such also in the morning. I do not know whether the smoking of four or five cigars daily by the parson of a parish may now-a-day be considered as a vice in him, but if so, it was the only vice with which Mr. Clavering could be charged. He was a kind, soft-hearted, gracious man, tender to his wife, whom he ever regarded as the angel of his house, indulgent to his daughters, whom he idolized, ever patient with his parishioners, and awake,—though not widely awake,—to the responsibilities of his calling. The world had been too comfortable for him, and also too narrow; so that he had sunk into idleness. The world had given him much to eat and drink, but it had given him little to do, and thus he had gradually fallen away from his early purposes, till his energy hardly sufficed for the doing of that little. His living gave him eight hundred a year; his wife's fortune nearly doubled that. He had married early, and had got his living early, and had been very prosperous. But he was not a happy man. He knew that he had put off the day of action till the power of action had passed away from him. His library was well furnished, but he rarely read much else than novels and poetry; and of late years the reading even of poetry had given way to the reading of novels. Till within ten years of the hour of which I speak, he had been a hunting parson,—not hunting loudly, but following his sport as it is followed by moderate sportsmen. Then there had come a new bishop, and the new bishop had sent for him,—nay, finally had come to him, and had lectured him with blatant authority. "My lord," said the parson of Clavering, plucking up something of his past energy, as the colour rose to his face, " I think you are wrong in this. I think you are specially wrong to inter- fere with me in this way on your first coming among us. You feel it to be your duty, no doubt; but to me it seems that you mistake your duty. But, as the matter is one simply of my own pleasure, I shall give it up." After that Mr. Clavering hunted no more, and never spoke a good word to any one of the bishop of his diocese. For myself, I think it as well that clergymen should not hunt; but had I been the parson of Clavering, I should, under those circumstances, have hunted double.

Mr. Clavering hunted no more, and probably smoked a greater number of cigars in consequence. He had an increased amount of time at his disposal, but did not, therefore, give more time to his duties. Alas! what time did he give to his duties? He kept a most energetic curate, whom he allowed to do almost what he would with the parish. Every-day services he did prohibit, declaring that he would not have the parish church made ridiculous; but in other respects his curate was the pastor. Once every Sunday he read the service, and once every Sunday he preached, and he resided in his parsonage ten months every year. His wife and daughters went among the poor,—and he smoked cigars in his library. Though not yet fifty, he was becoming fat and idle,—unwilling to walk, and not caring much even for such riding as the bishop had left to him. And, to make matters worse,—far worse, he knew all this of himself, and understood it thoroughly. "I see a better path, and know how good it is, but I follow ever the worse." He was saying that to himself daily, and was saying it always without hope.

And his wife had given him up. She had given him up, not with disdainful rejection, nor with contempt in her eye, or censure in her voice, not with diminution of love or of outward respect. She had given him up as a man abandons his attempts to make his favourite dog take the water. He would fain that the dog he loves should dash into the stream as other dogs will do. It is, to his thinking, a noble instinct in a dog. But his dog dreads the water. As, however, he has learned to love the beast, he puts up with this mischance, and never dreams of banishing poor Ponto from his hearth because of this failure. And so it was with Mrs. Clavering and her husband at the rectory. He understood it all. He knew that he was so far rejected; and he acknowledged to himself the necessity for such rejection.

"It is a very serious thing to decide upon," he said, when his son had spoken to him.

"Yes ; it is serious,—about as serious a thing as a man can think of; but a man cannot put it off on that account. If I mean to make such a change in my plans, the sooner I do it the better."

"But yesterday you were in another mind."

"No, father, not in another mind. I did not tell you then, nor can I tell you all now. I had thought that I should want my money for another purpose for a year or two ; but that I have abandoned."

"Is the purpose a secret, Harry ? "

"It is a secret, because it concerns another person."

"You were going to lend your money to some one ? "

"I must keep it a secret, though you know I seldom have any secrets from you. That idea, however, is abandoned, and I mean to go over to Stratton to-morrow, and tell Mr. Burton that I shall be there after Christmas. I must be at St. Cuthbert's on Tuesday."

Then they both sat silent for a while, silently blowing out their clouds of smoke. The son had said all that he cared to say, and would have wished that there might then be an end of it; but he knew that his father had much on his mind, and would fain express, if he could express it without too much trouble, or without too evident a need of self-reproach, his own thoughts on the subject. "You have made up your mind, then, altogether that you do not like the church as a profession," he said at last.

"I think I have, father."

"And on what grounds ? The grounds which recommend it to you are very strong. Your education has adapted you for it. Your success in it is already ensured by your fellowship. In a great degree you have entered it as a profession already, by taking a fellowship. What you are doing is not choosing a line in life, but changing one already chosen. You are making of yourself a rolling stone."

"A stone should roll till it has come to the spot that suits it."

"Why not give up the school if it irks you ? "

'And become a Cambridge Don, and practise deportment among the undergraduates."

"I don't see that you need do that. You need not even live at Cambridge. Take a church in London. You would be sure to get one by holding up your hand. If that, with your fellowship, is not sufficient, I will give you what more you want."

"No, father—no. By God's blessing I will never ask you for a pound. I can hold my fellowship for four years longer without orders, and in four years' time I think I can earn my bread."

"I don't doubt that, Harry."

" Then why should I not follow my wishes in this matter? The truth is, I do not feel myself qualified to be a good clergyman."

" It is not that you have doubts, is it ? "

" I might have them if I came to think much about it,—as I must do if I took orders. And I do not wish to be crippled in doing what I think lawful by conventional rules. A rebellious clergyman is, I think, a sorry object. It seems to me that he is a bird fouling his own nest. Now, I know I should be a rebellious clergyman."

" In our church the life of a clergyman is as the life of any other gentleman,—within very broad limits."

" Then why did Bishop Proudie interfere with your hunting ? "

" Limits may be very broad, Harry, and yet exclude hunting. Bishop Proudie was vulgar and intrusive, such being the nature of his wife, who instructs him ; but if you were in orders I should be very sorry to see you take to hunting."

" It seems to me that a clergyman has nothing to do in life unless he is always preaching and teaching. Look at Saul,"—Mr. Saul was the curate of Clavering—" he is always preaching and teaching. He is doing the best he can ; and what a life of it he has. He has literally thrown off all worldly cares,—and consequently everybody laughs at him, and nobody loves him. I don't believe a better man breathes, but I shouldn't like his life."

At this point there was another pause, which lasted till the cigars had come to an end. Then, as he threw the stump into the fire, Mr. Clavering spoke again. " The truth is, Harry, that you have had, all your life, a bad example before you."

" No, father."

" Yes, my son ;—let me speak on to the end, and then you can say what you please. In me you have had a bad example on one side, and now, in poor Saul, you have a bad example on the other side. Can you fancy no life between the two, which would fit your physical nature which is larger than his, and your mental wants which are higher than mine? Yes, they are, Harry. It is my duty to say this, but it would be unseemly that there should be any controversy between us on the subject."

" If you choose to stop me in that way ——"

" I do choose to stop you in that way. As for Saul, it is impossible that you should become such a man as he. It is not that he mortifies his flesh, but that he has no flesh to mortify. He is unconscious of the flavour of venison, or the scent of roses, or the beauty of women. He is an exceptional specimen of a man, and you need no more fear, than you should venture to hope, that you could become such as he is."

At this point they were interrupted by the entrance of Fanny Clavering, who came to say that Mr. Saul was in the drawing-room. " What does he want, Fanny ? " This question Mr. Clavering asked half in a whisper, but with something of comic humour in his face, as though partly afraid that Mr. Saul should hear it, and partly intending to convey a wish that he might escape Mr. Saul, if it were possible.

"It's about the iron church, papa. He says it is come,—or part of it has come,—and he wants you to go out to Cumberly Green about the site."

"I thought that was all settled."

"He says not."

"What does it matter where it is? He can put it anywhere he likes on the Green. However, I had better go to him." So Mr. Clavering went. Cumberly Green was a hamlet in the parish of Clavering, three miles distant from the church, the people of which had got into a wicked habit of going to a dissenting chapel near to them. By Mr. Saul's energy, but chiefly out of Mr. Clavering's purse, an iron chapel had been purchased for a hundred and fifty pounds, and Mr. Saul proposed to add to his own duties the pleasing occupation of walking to Cumberly Green every Sunday morning before breakfast, and every Wednesday evening after dinner, to perform a service and bring back to the true flock as many of the erring sheep of Cumberly Green as he might be able to catch. Towards the purchase of this iron church Mr. Clavering had at first given a hundred pounds. Sir Hugh, in answer to the fifth application, had very ungraciously, through h steward, bestowed ten pounds. Among the farmers one pound nine and eightpence had been collected. Mr. Saul had given two pounds; Mrs. Clavering gave five pounds; the girls gave ten shillings each; Henry Clavering gave five pounds;—and then the parson made up the remainder. But Mr. Saul had journeyed thrice painfully to Bristol, making the bargain for the church, going and coming each time by third-class, and he had written all the letters; but Mrs. Clavering had paid the postage, and she and the girls between them were making the covering for the little altar.

"Is it all settled, Harry?" said Fanny, stopping with her brother, and hanging over his chair. She was a pretty, gay-spirited girl, with bright eyes and dark brown hair, which fell in two curls behind her ears.

"He has said nothing to unsettle it."

"I know it makes him very unhappy."

"No, Fanny, not very unhappy. He would rather that I should go into the church, but that is about all."

"I think you are quite right."

"And Mary thinks I am quite wrong."

"Mary thinks so, of course. So should I too, perhaps, if I were engaged to a clergyman. That's the old story of the fox who had lost his tail."

"And your tail isn't gone yet?"

"No, my tail isn't gone yet. Mary thinks that no life is like a clergyman's life. But, Harry, though mamma hasn't said so, I'm sure she thinks you are right. She won't say so as long as it may seem to interfere with anything papa may choose to say; but I'm sure she's glad in her heart."

"And I am glad in my heart, Fanny. And as I'm the person most concerned, I suppose that's the most material thing." Then they followed their father into the drawing-room.

" Couldn't you drive Mrs. Clavering over in the pony chair, and settle it between you," said Mr. Clavering to his curate. Mr. Saul looked disappointed. In the first place, he hated driving the pony, which was a rapid-footed little beast, that had a will of his own; and in the next place, he thought the rector ought to visit the spot on such an occasion. " Or Mrs. Clavering will drive you," said the rector, remembering Mr. Saul's objection to the pony. Still Mr. Saul looked unhappy. Mr. Saul was very tall and very thin, with a tall thin head, and weak eyes, and a sharp, well-cut nose, and, so to say, no lips, and very white teeth, with no beard, and a well-cut chin. His face was so thin that his cheekbones obtruded themselves unpleasantly. He wore a long rusty black coat, and a high rusty black waistcoat, and trousers that were brown with dirty roads and general ill-usage. Nevertheless, it never occurred to any one that Mr. Saul did not look like a gentleman, not even to himself, to whom no ideas whatever on that subject ever presented themselves. But that he was a gentleman I think he knew well enough, and was able to carry himself before Sir Hugh and his wife with quite as much ease as he could do in the rectory. Once or twice he had dined at the great house; but Lady Clavering had declared him to be a bore, and Sir Hugh had called him "that most offensive of all animals, a clerical prig." It had therefore been decided that he was not to be asked to the great house any more. It may be as well to state here, as elsewhere, that Mr. Clavering very rarely went to his nephew's table. On certain occasions he did do so, so that there might be no recognized quarrel between him and Sir Hugh ; but such visits were few and far between.

After a few more words from Mr. Saul, and a glance from his wife's eye, Mr. Clavering consented to go to Cumberly Green, though there was nothing he liked so little as a morning spent with his curate. When he had started, Harry told his mother also of his final decision. I shall go to Stratton to-morrow and settle it all."

" And what does papa say ? " asked the mother.

" Just what he has said before. It is not so much that he wishes me to be a clergyman, as that he does not wish me to have lost all my time up to this."

" It is more than that, I think, Harry," said his elder sister, a tall girl, less pretty than her sister, apparently less careful of her prettiness, very quiet, or, as some said, demure, but known to be good as gold by all who knew her well.

" I doubt it," said Harry, stoutly. " But, however that may be, a man must choose for himself."

" We all thought you had chosen," said Mary.

" If it is settled," said the mother, " I suppose we shall do no good by opposing it."

" Would you wish to oppose it, mamma ? " said Harry.

"No, my dear. I think you should judge for yourself."

"You see I could have no scope in the church for that sort of ambition which would satisfy me. Look at such men as Locke, and Stephenson, and Brassey. They are the men who seem to me to do most in the world. They were all self-educated, but surely a man can't have a worse chance because he has learned something. Look at old Beilby with a seat in Parliament, and a property worth two or three hundred thousand pounds! When he was my age he had nothing but his weekly wages."

"I don't know whether Mr. Beilby is a very happy man or a very good man," said Mary.

"I don't know, either," said Harry; "but I do know that he has thrown a single arch over a wider span of water than ever was done before, and that ought to make him happy." After saying this in a tone of high authority, befitting his dignity as a fellow of his college, Harry Clavering went out, leaving his mother and sisters to discuss the subject which to two of them was all-important. As to Mary, she had hopes of her own, vested in the clerical concerns of a neighbouring parish.

<hr>

CHAPTER III.

LORD ONGAR.

On the next morning Harry Clavering rode over to Stratton, thinking much of his misery as he went. It was all very well for him, in the presence of his own family to talk of his profession as the one subject which was to him of any importance ; but he knew very well himself that he was only beguiling them in doing so. This question of a profession was, after all, but dead leaves to him,—to him who had a canker at his heart, a perpetual thorn in his bosom, a misery within him which no profession could mitigate! Those dear ones at home guessed nothing of this, and he would take care that they should guess nothing. Why should they have the pain of knowing that he had been made wretched for ever by blighted hopes? His mother, indeed, had suspected something in those sweet days of his roaming with Julia through the park. She had once or twice said a word to warn him. But of the very truth of his deep love,—so he told himself,—she had been happily ignorant. Let her be ignorant. Why should he make his mother unhappy? As these thoughts passed through his mind, I think that he revelled in his wretchedness, and made much to himself of his misery. He sucked in his sorrow greedily, and was somewhat proud to have had occasion to break his heart. But not the less, because he was thus early blighted, would he struggle for success in the world. He would show her that, as his wife, she might have had a worthier position than Lord Ongar could give her. He, too, might probably rise the quicker in the world, as now he would have no impediment of wife or family. Then, as he rode along, he composed a sonnet, fitting to his case, the strength and rhythm of which seemed to him, as he sat on horseback, to be almost perfect. Unfortunately, when he was back at Clavering, and sat in his room with the pen in his hand, the turn of the words had escaped him.

He found Mr. Burton at home, and was not long in concluding his business. Messrs. Beilby and Burton were not only civil engineers, but were land surveyors also, and land valuers on a great scale. They were employed much by Government upon public buildings, and if not architects themselves, were supposed to know all that architects should do and should not do. In the purchase of great properties Mr. Burton's opinion was supposed to be, or to have been, as good as any in the kingdom, and therefore there was very much to be learned in the office at Stratton. But Mr. Burton was not a rich man like his partner, Mr. Beilby, nor an ambitious man. He had never soared Parliamentwards, had never speculated, had never invented, and never been great. He had been the father of a very large family, all of whom were doing as well in the world, and some of them perhaps better, than their father. Indeed, there were many who said that Mr. Burton would have been a richer man if he had not joined himself in partnership with Mr. Beilby. Mr. Beilby had the reputation of swallowing more than his share wherever he went.

When the business part of the arrangement was finished Mr. Burton talked to his future pupil about lodgings, and went out with him into the town to look for rooms. The old man found that Harry Clavering was rather nice in this respect, and in his own mind formed an idea that this new beginner might have been a more auspicious pupil, had he not already become a fellow of a college. Indeed, Harry talked to him quite as though they two were on an equality together; and, before they had parted, Mr. Burton was not sure that Harry did not patronize him. He asked the young man, however, to join them at their early dinner, and then introduced him to Mrs. Burton, and to their youngest daughter, the only child who was still living with them. "All my other girls are married, Mr. Clavering; and all of them married to men connected with my own profession." The colour came slightly to Florence Burton's cheeks as she heard her father's words, and Harry asked himself whether the old man expected that he should go through the same ordeal; but Mr. Burton himself was quite unaware that he had said anything wrong, and then went on to speak of the successes of his sons. "But they began early, Mr. Clavering; and worked hard,—very hard indeed." He was a good, kindly, garrulous old man; but Harry began to doubt whether he would learn much at Stratton. It was, however, too late to think of that now, and everything was fixed.

Harry, when he looked at Florence Burton, at once declared to himself that she was plain. Anything more unlike Julia Brabazon never appeared in the guise of a young lady. Julia was tall, with a high brow, a glorious complexion, a nose as finely modelled as though a Grecian sculptor had cut it, a small mouth, but lovely in its curves, and a chin that finished and made perfect the symmetry of her face. Her neck was long, but graceful as a swan's, her bust was full, and her whole figure like that of a goddess. Added to this, when he had first known her, had been all the charm of youth. When she had returned to Clavering the other day, the affianced bride of Lord Ongar, he had hardly known whether to admire or to deplore the settled air of established womanhood which she had assumed. Her large eyes had always lacked something of rapid glancing sparkling brightness. They had been glorious eyes to him, and in those early days he had not known that they lacked aught; but he had perceived, or perhaps fancied, that now, in her present condition they were often cold, and sometimes almost cruel. Nevertheless he was ready to swear that she was perfect in her beauty.

Poor Florence Burton was short of stature, was brown, meagre, and poor-looking. So said Harry Clavering to himself. Her small hand, though soft, lacked that wondrous charm of touch which Julia's possessed. Her face was short, and her forehead, though it was broad and open, had none of that feminine command which Julia's look conveyed. That Florence's eyes were very bright,—bright and soft as well, he allowed ; and her dark brown hair was very glossy ; but she was, on the whole, a mean-looking little thing. He could not, as he said to himself on his return home, avoid the comparison, as she was the first girl he had seen since he had parted from Julia Brabazon.

" I hope you'll find yourself comfortable at Stratton, sir," said old Mrs. Burton.

" Thank you," said Harry, " but I want very little myself in that way. Anything does for me."

" One young gentleman we had took a bedroom at Mrs. Pott's, and did very nicely without any second room at all. " Don't you remember, Mr. B. ; it was young Granger."

" Young Granger had a very short allowance," said Mr. Burton. " He lived upon fifty pounds a year all the time he was here."

" And I don't think Scarness had more when he began," said Mrs. Burton. " Mr. Scarness married one of my girls, Mr. Clavering, when he started himself at Liverpool. He has pretty nigh all the Liverpool docks under him now. I have heard him say that butcher's meat did not cost him four shillings a week all the time he was here. I've always thought Stratton one of the reasonablest places anywhere for a young man to do for himself in."

" I don't know, my dear," said the husband, " that Mr. Clavering will care very much for that."

" Perhaps not, Mr. B. ; but I do like to see young men careful about their spendings. What's the use of spending a shilling when sixpence will do as well; and sixpence saved when a man has nothing but himself, becomes pounds and pounds by the time he has a family about him."

During all this time Miss Burton said little or nothing, and Harry

Clavering himself did not say much. He could not express any intention of rivalling Mr. Scarness's economy in the article of butcher's meat, nor could he promise to content himself with Granger's solitary bedroom. But as he rode home he almost began to fear that he had made a mistake. He was not wedded to the joys of his college hall, or the college common room. He did not like the narrowness of college life. But he doubted whether the change from that to the oft-repeated hospitalities of Mrs. Burton might not be too much for him. Scarness's four shillings'-worth of butcher's meat had already made him half sick of his new profession, and though Stratton might be the "reasonablest place anywhere for a young man," he could not look forward to living there for a year with much delight. As for Miss Burton, it might be quite as well that she was plain, as he wished for none of the delights which beauty affords to young men.

On his return home, however, he made no complaint of Stratton. He was too strong-willed to own that he had been in any way wrong, and when early in the following week he started for St. Cuthbert's, he was able to speak with cheerful hope of his new prospects. If ultimately he should find life in Stratton to be unendurable, he would cut that part of his career short, and contrive to get up to London at an earlier time than he had intended.

On the 31st of August Lord Ongar and Sir Hugh Clavering reached Clavering Park, and, as has been already told, a pretty little note was at once sent up to Miss Brabazon in her bedroom. When she met Lord Ongar in the drawing-room, about an hour afterwards, she had instructed herself that it would be best to say nothing of the note; but she could not refrain from a word. "I am much obliged, my lord, by your kindness and generosity," she said, as she gave him her hand. He merely bowed and smiled, and muttered something as to his hoping that he might always find it as easy to gratify her. He was a little man, on whose behalf it certainly appeared that the Peerage must have told a falsehood; it seemed so at least to those who judged of his years from his appearance. The Peerage said that he was thirty-six, and that, no doubt, was in truth his age, but any one would have declared him to be ten years older. This look was produced chiefly by the effect of an elaborately dressed jet black wig which he wore. What misfortune had made him bald so early, —if to be bald early in life be a misfortune,—I cannot say; but he had lost the hair from the crown of his head, and had preferred wiggery to baldness. No doubt an effort was made to hide the wiggishness of his wigs, but what effect in that direction was ever made successfully? He was, moreover, weak, thin, and physically poor, and had, no doubt, increased this weakness and poorness by hard living. Though others thought him old, time had gone swiftly with him, and he still thought himself a young man. He hunted, though he could not ride. He shot, though he could not walk. And, unfortunately, he drank, though he had no capacity for drinking! His friends at last had taught him to believe that his only chance of saving himself lay in marriage, and therefore he had engaged himself to Julia Brabazon, purchasing her at the price of a brilliant settlement. If ˉLord Ongar should die before her, Ongar Park was to be hers for life, with thousands a year to maintain it. Courton Castle, the great family seat, would of course go to the heir; but Ongar Park was supposed to be the most delightful small country-seat anywhere within thirty miles of London. It lay among the Surrey hills, and all the world had heard of the charms of Ongar Park. If Julia were to survive her lord, Ongar Park was to be hers; and they who saw them both together had but little doubt that she would come to the enjoyment of this clause in her settlement. Lady Clavering had been clever in arranging the match; and Sir Hugh, though he might have been unwilling to give his sister-in-law money out of his own pocket, had performed his duty as a brother-in-law in looking to her future welfare. Julia Brabazon had no doubt that she was doing well. Poor Harry Clavering! She had loved him in the days of her romance. She, too, had written her sonnets. But she had grown old earlier in life than he had done, and had taught herself that romance could not be allowed to a woman in her position. She was highly born, the daughter of a peer, without money, and even without a home to which she had any claim. Of course she had accepted Lord Ongar, but she had not put out her hand to take all these good things without resolving that she would do her duty to her future lord. The duty would be doubtless disagreeable, but she would do it with all the more diligence on that account.

September passed by, hecatombs of partridges were slaughtered, and the day of the wedding drew nigh. It was pretty to see Lord Ongar and the self-satisfaction which he enjoyed at this time. The world was becoming young with him again, and he thought that he rather liked the respectability of his present mode of life. He gave himself but scanty allowances of wine, and no allowance of anything stronger than wine, and did not dislike his temperance. There was about him at all hours an air which seemed to say, "There; I told you all that I could do it as soon as there was any necessity." And in these halcyon days he could shoot for an hour without his pony, and he liked the gentle courteous badinage which was bestowed upon his courtship, and he liked also Julia's beauty. Her conduct to him was perfect. She was never pert, never exigeant, never romantic, and never humble. She never bored him, and yet was always ready to be with him when he wished it. She was never exalted; and yet she bore her high place as became a woman nobly born and acknowledged to be beautiful.

"I declare you have quite made a lover of him," said Lady Clavering to her sister. When a thought of the match had first arisen in Sir Hugh's London house, Lady Clavering had been eager in praise of Lord Ongar, or eager in praise rather of the position which the future Lady Ongar might hold; but since the prize had been secured, since it had become plain that Julia was to be the greater woman of the two, she had harped sometimes on the other string. As a sister she had striven for a sister's welfare, but as a woman she could not keep herself from comparisons which might tend to show that after all, well as Julia was doing, she was not doing better than her elder sister had done. Hermione had married simply a baronet, and not the richest or the most amiable among baronets; but she had married a man suitable in age and wealth, with whom any girl might have been in love. She had not sold herself to be the nurse, or not to be the nurse, as it might turn out, of a worn-out debauché. She would have hinted nothing of this, perhaps have thought nothing of this, had not Julia and Lord Ongar walked together through the Clavering groves as though they were two young people. She owed it as a duty to her sister to point out that Lord Ongar could not be a romantic young person, and ought not to be encouraged to play that part.

"I don't know that I have made anything of him," answered Julia. "I suppose he's much like other men when they're going to be married." Julia quite understood the ideas that were passing through her sister's mind, and did not feel them to be unnatural.

"What I mean is, that he has come out so strong in the Romeo line, which we hardly expected, you know. We shall have him under your bedroom window with a guitar like Don Giovanni."

"I hope not, because it's so cold. I don't think it likely, as he seems fond of going to bed early."

"And it's the best thing for him," said Lady Clavering, becoming serious and carefully benevolent. "It's quite a wonder what good hours and quiet living have done for him in so short a time. I was observing him as he walked yesterday, and he put his feet to the ground as firmly almost as Hugh does."

"Did he indeed? I hope he won't have the habit of putting his hand down firmly as Hugh does sometimes."

"As for that," said Lady Clavering, with a little tremor, "I don't think there's much difference between them. They all say that when Lord Ongar means a thing he does mean it."

"I think a man ought to have a way of his own."

"And a woman also, don't you, my dear? But, as I was saying, if Lord Ongar will continue to take care of himself he may become quite a different man. Hugh says that he drinks next to nothing now, and though he sometimes lights a cigar in the smoking-room at night, he hardly ever smokes it. You must do what you can to keep him from tobacco. I happen to know that Sir Charles Poddy said that so many cigars were worse for him even than brandy."

All this Julia bore with an even temper. She was determined to bear everything till her time should come. Indeed she had made herself understand that the hearing of such things as these was a part of the price which she was to be called upon to pay. It was not pleasant for her to hear what Sir Charles Poddy had said about the tobacco and brandy of the man she was just going to marry. She would sooner have heard of his riding sixty miles a day, or dancing all night, as she might have heard had she been contented to take Harry Clavering. But she had made her selection with her eyes open, and was not disposed to quarrel with her bargain, because that which she had bought was no better than the article which she had known it to be when she was making her purchase. Nor was she even angry with her sister. " I will do the best I can, Hermy; you may be sure of that. But there are some things which it is useless to talk about."

" But it was as well you should know what Sir Charles said."

" I know quite enough of what he says, Hermy,—quite as much, I daresay, as you do. But, never mind. If Lord Ongar has given up smoking, I quite agree with you that it's a good thing. I wish they'd all give it up, for I hate the smell of it. Hugh has got worse and worse. He never cares about changing his clothes now."

" I'll tell you what it is," said Sir Hugh to his wife that night; " sixty thousand a year is a very fine income, but Julia will find she has caught a Tartar."

" I suppose he'll hardly live long; will he?"

" I don't know or care when he lives or when he dies; but, by heaven, he is the most overbearing fellow I ever had in the house with me. I wouldn't stand him here for another fortnight,—not even to make her all safe."

" It will soon be over. They'll be gone on Thursday."

" What do you think of his having the impudence to tell Cunliffe,"— Cunliffe was the head keeper;—" before my face, that he didn't know anything about pheasants ! ' Well, my lord, I think we've got a few about the place,' said Cunliffe. ' Very few,' said Ongar, with a sneer. Now, if I haven't a better head of game here than he has at Courton, I'll eat him. But the impudence of his saying that before me !"

" Did you make him any answer?"

" ' There's about enough to suit me,' I said. Then he skulked away, knocked off his pins. I shouldn't like to be his wife; I can tell Julia that."

" Julia is very clever," said the sister.

The day of the marriage came, and everything at Clavering was done with much splendour. Four bridesmaids came down from London on the preceding day; two were already staying in the house, and the two cousins came as two more from the rectory. Julia Brabazon had never been really intimate with Mary and Fanny Clavering, but she had known them well enough to make it odd if she did not ask them to come to her wedding and to take a part in the ceremony. And, moreover, she had thought of Harry and her little romance of other days. Harry, perhaps, might be glad to know that she had shown this courtesy to his sisters. Harry, she knew, would be away at his school. Though she had asked him whether he meant to come to her wedding, she had been better pleased that he should be absent. She had not many regrets herself, but

"A PUIR FECKLESS THING, TOTTERING ALONG LIKE.—

it pleased her to think that he should have them. So Mary and Fanny Clavering were asked to attend her at the altar. Mary and Fanny would both have preferred to decline, but their mother had told them that they could not do so. "It would make ill-feeling," said Mrs. Clavering; "and that is what your papa particularly wishes to avoid."

"When you say papa particularly wishes anything, mamma, you always mean that you wish it particularly yourself," said Fanny. "But if it must be done, it must; and then I shall know how to behave when Mary's time comes."

The bells were rung lustily all the morning, and all the parish was there, round about the church, to see. There was no record of a lord ever having been married in Clavering church before; and now this lord was going to marry my lady's sister. It was all one as though she were a Clavering herself. But there was no ecstatic joy in the parish. There were to be no bonfires, and no eating and drinking at Sir Hugh's expense, —no comforts provided for any of the poor by Lady Clavering on that special occasion. Indeed, there was never much of such kindnesses between the lord of the soil and his dependants. A certain stipulated dole was given at Christmas for coals and blankets; but even for that there was generally some wrangle between the rector and the steward. "If there's to be all this row about it," the rector had said to the steward, "I'll never ask for it again." "I wish my uncle would only be as good as his word," Sir Hugh had said, when the rector's speech was repeated to him. Therefore, there was not much of real rejoicing in the parish on this occasion, though the bells were rung loudly, and though the people, young and old, did cluster round the churchyard to see the lord lead his bride out of the church. "A puir feckless thing, tottering along like,— not half the makings of a man. A stout lass like she could a'most blow him away wi' a puff of her mouth." That was the verdict which an old farmer's wife passed upon him, and that verdict was made good by the general opinion of the parish.

But though the lord might be only half a man, Julia Brabazon walked out from the church every inch a countess. Whatever price she might have paid, she had at any rate got the thing which she had intended to buy. And as she stepped into the chariot which carried her away to the railway station on her way to Dover, she told herself that she had done right. She had chosen her profession, as Harry Clavering had chosen his; and having so far succeeded, she would do her best to make her success perfect. Mercenary! Of course she had been mercenary. Were not all men and women mercenary upon whom devolved the necessity of earning their bread?

Then there was a great breakfast at the park,—for the quality,—and the rector on this occasion submitted himself to become the guest of the nephew whom he thoroughly disliked.

CHAPTER IV.

FLORENCE BURTON.

T was now Christmas time at Stratton, or rather Christmas time was near at hand ; not the Christmas next after the autumn of Lord Ongar's marriage, but the following Christmas, and Harry Clavering had finished his studies in Mr. Burton's office. He flattered himself that he had not been idle while he was there, and was now about to commence his more advanced stage of pupilage, under the great Mr. Beilby in London, with hopes which were still good, if they were not so magnificent as they once had been. When he first saw Mr. Burton in his office, and beheld the dusty pigeon-holes with dusty papers, and caught the first glimpse of things as they really were in the workshop of that man of business, he had, to say the truth, been disgusted. And Mrs. Burton's early dinner, and Florence Burton's " plain face " and plain ways, had disconcerted him.

On that day he had repented of his intention with regard to Stratton ; but he had carried out his purpose like a man, and now he rejoiced greatly that he had done so. He rejoiced greatly, though his hopes were somewhat sobered, and his views of life less grand than they had been. He was to start for Clavering early on the following morning, intending to spend his Christmas at home, and we will see him and listen to him as he bade farewell to one of the members of Mr. Burton's family.

He was sitting in a small back parlour in Mr. Burton's house, and on the table of the room there was burning a single candle. It was a dull, dingy, brown room, furnished with horsehair-covered chairs, an old horsehair sofa, and heavy rusty curtains. I don't know that there was in the room any attempt at ornament, as certainly there was no evidence of wealth. It was now about seven o'clock in the evening, and tea was over in Mrs. Burton's establishment. Harry Clavering had had his tea, and had eaten his hot muffin, at the further side from the fire of the family table, while Florence had poured out the tea, and Mrs. Burton had sat by the fire on one side with a handkerchief over her lap, and Mr. Burton had been comfortable with his arm-chair and his slippers on the other side. When tea was over, Harry had made his parting speech to Mrs. Burton, and that lady had kissed him, and bade God bless him. " I'll see you for a moment before you go, in my office, Harry," Mr. Burton had said. Then Harry had gone downstairs, and some one else had gone boldly with him, and they two were sitting together in the dingy brown room. After that I need hardly tell my reader what had become of Harry Clavering's perpetual life-enduring heart's misery.

He and Florence were sitting on the old horsehair sofa, and Florence's hand was in his. " My darling," he said, " how am I to live for the next two years ? "

" You mean five years, Harry."

" No ; I mean two,—that is two, unless I can make the time less. I believe you'd be better pleased to think it was ten."

" Much better pleased to think it was ten than to have no such hope at all. Of course we shall see each other. It's not as though you were going to New Zealand."

" I almost wish I were. One would agree then as to the necessity of this cursed delay."

" Harry, Harry ! "

" It is accursed. The prudence of the world in these latter days seems to me to be more abominable than all its other iniquities."

" But, Harry, we should have no income."

" Income is a word that I hate."

" Now you are getting on to your high horse, and you know I always go out of the way when you begin to prance on that beast. As for me, I don't want to leave papa's house where I'm sure of my bread and butter, till I'm sure of it in another."

" You say that, Florence, on purpose to torment me."

"Dear Harry, do you think I want to torment you on your last night? The truth is, I love you so well that I can afford to be patient for you."

"I hate patience, and always did. Patience is one of the worst vices I know. It's almost as bad as humility. You'll tell me you're 'umble next. If you'll only add that you're contented, you'll describe yourself as one of the lowest of God's creatures."

"I don't know about being 'umble, but I am contented. Are not you contented with me, sir?"

"No,—because you're not in a hurry to be married."

"What a goose you are. Do you know I'm not sure that if you really love a person, and are quite confident about him,—as I am of you,—that having to look forward to being married is not the best part of it all. I suppose you'll like to get my letters now, but I don't know that you'll care for them much when we've been man and wife for ten years."

"But one can't live upon letters."

"I shall expect you to live upon mine, and to grow fat on them. There;—I heard papa's step on the stairs. He said you were to go to him. Good-by, Harry;—dearest Harry! What a blessed wind it was that blew you here."

"Stop a moment;—about your getting to Clavering. I shall come for you on Easter-eve."

"Oh, no;—why should you have so much trouble and expense?"

"I tell you I shall come for you,—unless, indeed, you decline to travel with me."

"It will be so nice! And then I shall be sure to have you with me the first moment I see them. I shall think it very awful when I first meet your father."

"He's the most good-natured man, I should say, in England."

"But he'll think me so plain. You did at first, you know. But he won't be uncivil enough to tell me so, as you did. And Mary is to be married in Easter week? Oh, dear, oh, dear; I shall be so shy among them all."

"You shy! I never saw you shy in my life. I don't suppose you were ever really put out yet."

"But I must really put you out, because papa is waiting for you. Dear, dear, dearest Harry. Though I am so patient I shall count the hours till you come for me. Dearest Harry!" Then she bore with him, as he pressed her close to his bosom, and kissed her lips, and her forehead, and her glossy hair. When he was gone she sat down alone for a few minutes on the old sofa, and hugged herself in her happiness. What a happy wind that had been which had blown such a lover as that for her to Stratton!

"I think he's a good young man," said Mrs. Burton, as soon as she was left with her old husband upstairs.

"Yes, he's a good young man. He means very well."

"But he is not idle; is he?"

"No—no; he's not idle. And he's very clever;—too clever, I'm afraid. But I think he'll do well, though it may take him some time to settle."

"It seems so natural his taking to Flo; doesn't it? They've all taken one when they went away, and they've all done very well. Deary me; how sad the house will be when Flo has gone."

"Yes,—it'll make a difference that way. But what then? I wouldn't wish to keep one of 'em at home for that reason."

"No, indeed. I think I'd feel ashamed of myself to have a daughter not married, or not in the way to be married afore she's thirty. I couldn't bear to think that no young man should take a fancy to a girl of mine. But Flo's not twenty yet, and Carry, who was the oldest to go, wasn't four-and-twenty when Scarness took her." Thereupon the old lady put her handkerchief to the corner of her eyes, and wept gently.

"Flo isn't gone yet," said Mr. Burton.

"But I hope, B., it's not to be a long engagement. I don't like long engagements. It ain't good,—not for the girl; it ain't, indeed."

"We were engaged for seven years."

"People weren't so much in a hurry then at anything; but I ain't sure it was very good for me. And though we weren't just married, we were living next door and saw each other. What'll come to Flo if she's to be here and he's to be up in London, pleasuring himself?"

"Flo must bear it as other girls do," said the father, as he got up from his chair.

"I think he's a good young man; I think he is," said the mother. "But don't stand out for too much for 'em to begin upon. What matters? Sure if they were to be a little short you could help 'em." To such a suggestion as this Mr. Burton thought it as well to make no answer, but with ponderous steps descended to his office.

"Well, Harry," said Mr. Burton, "so you're to be off in the morning?"

"Yes, sir; I shall breakfast at home to-morrow."

"Ah,—when I was your age I always used to make an early start. Three hours before breakfast never does any hurt. But it shouldn't be more than that. The wind gets into the stomach." Harry had no remark to make on this, and waited, therefore, till Mr. Burton went on. "And you'll be up in London by the 10th of next month?"

"Yes, sir; I intend to be at Mr. Beilby's office on the 11th."

"That's right. Never lose a day. In losing a day now, you don't lose what you might earn now in a day, but what you might be earning when you're at your best. A young man should always remember that. You can't dispense with a round in the ladder going up. You only make your time at the top so much the shorter."

"I hope you'll find that I'm all right, sir. I don't mean to be idle."

"Pray don't. Of course, you know, I speak to you very differently from what I should do if you were simply going away from my office. What I shall have to give Florence will be very little,—that is, compa-

ratively little.   She shall have a hundred a year, when she marries, till I
die; and after my death and her mother's she will share with the others.
But a hundred a year will be nothing to you."

"Won't it, sir?   I think a very great deal of a hundred a year.   I'm
to have a hundred and fifty from the office; and I should be ready to
marry on that to-morrow."

"You couldn't live on such an income,—unless you were to alter your
habits very much."

"But I will alter them."

"We shall see.   You are so placed that by marrying you would lose
a considerable income; and I would advise you to put off thinking of it
for the next two years."

"My belief is, that settling down would be the best thing in the world
to make me work."

"We'll try what a year will do.   So Florence is to go to your father's
house at Easter?"

"Yes, sir; she has been good enough to promise to come, if you have
no objection."

"It is quite as well that they should know her early.   I only hope
they will like her as well as we like you.   Now I'll say good-night,—and
good-by."   Then Harry went, and walking up and down the High Street
of Stratton, thought of all that he had done during the past year.

On his arrival at Stratton that idea of perpetual misery arising from
blighted affection was still strong within his breast.   He had given all his
heart to a false woman who had betrayed him.   He had risked all his
fortune on one cast of the die, and, gambler-like, had lost everything.
On the day of Julia's marriage he had shut himself up at the school,—
luckily it was a holiday,—and had flattered himself that he had gone
through some hours of intense agony.   No doubt he did suffer somewhat,
for in truth he had loved the woman ; but such sufferings are seldom
perpetual, and with him they had been as easy of cure as with most others.
A little more than a year had passed, and now he was already engaged
to another woman.   As he thought of this he did not by any means
accuse himself of inconstancy or of weakness of heart.   It appeared to him
now the most natural thing in the world that he should love Florence
Burton.   In those old days he had never seen Florence, and had hardly
thought seriously of what qualities a man really wants in a wife.   As he
walked up and down the hill of Stratton Street with the kiss of the dear,
modest, affectionate girl still warm upon his lips, he told himself that a
marriage with such a one as Julia Brabazon would have been altogether
fatal to his chance of happiness.

And things had occurred and rumours had reached him which assisted
him much in adopting this view of the subject.   It was known to all the
Claverings,—and even to all others who cared about such things,—that
Lord and Lady Ongar were not happy together, and it had been already
said that Lady Ongar had misconducted herself.   There was a

certain count whose name had come to be mingled with hers in a way that was, to say the least of it, very unfortunate. Sir Hugh Clavering had declared, in Mrs. Clavering's hearing, though but little disposed in general to make many revelations to any of the family at the rectory, "that he did not intend to take his sister-in-law's part. She had made her own bed, and she must lie upon it. She had known what Lord Ongar was before she had married him, and the fault was her own." So much Sir Hugh had said, and, in saying it, had done all that in him lay to damn his sister-in-law's fair fame. Harry Clavering, little as he had lived in the world during the last twelve months, still knew that some people told a different story. The earl too and his wife had not been in England since their marriage;—so that these rumours had been filtered to them at home through a foreign medium. During most of their time they had been in Italy, and now, as Harry knew, they were at Florence. He had heard that Lord Ongar had declared his intention of suing for a divorce; but that he supposed to be erroneous, as the two were still living under the same roof. Then he heard that Lord Ongar was ill; and whispers were spread abroad darkly and doubtingly, as though great misfortunes were apprehended.

Harry could not fail to tell himself that had Julia become his wife, as she had once promised, these whispers and this darkness would hardly have come to pass. But not on that account did he now regret that her early vows had not been kept. Living at Stratton, he had taught himself to think much of the quiet domesticities of life, and to believe that Florence Burton was fitter to be his wife than Julia Brabazon. He told himself that he had done well to find this out, and that he had been wise to act upon it. His wisdom had in truth consisted in his capacity to feel that Florence was a nice girl, clever, well-minded, high-principled, and full of spirit,—and in falling in love with her as a consequence. All his regard for the quiet domesticities had come from his love, and had had no share in producing it. Florence was bright-eyed. No eyes were ever brighter, either in tears or in laughter. And when he came to look at her well he found that he had been an idiot to think her plain. " There are things that grow to beauty as you look at them,—to exquisite beauty ; and you are one of them," he had said to her. " And there are men," she had answered, " who grow to flattery as you listen to them,—to impudent flattery ; and you are one of them." " I thought you plain the first day I saw you. That's not flattery." " Yes, sir, it is ; and you mean it for flattery. But after all, Harry, it comes only to this, that you want to tell me that you have learned to love me." He repeated all this to himself as he walked up and down Stratton, and declared to himself that she was very lovely. It had been given to him to ascertain this, and he was rather proud of himself. But he was a little diffident about his father. He thought that, perhaps, his father might see Florence as he himself had first seen her, and might not have discernment enough to ascertain his mistake as he had done. But Florence was not going to

Clavering at once, and he would be able to give beforehand his own account of her. He had not been home since his engagement had been a thing settled; but his position with regard to Florence had been declared by letter, and his mother had written to the young lady asking her to come to Clavering.

When Harry got home all the family received him with congratulations. " I am so glad to think that you should marry early," his mother said to him in a whisper. " But I am not married yet, mother," he answered.

"Do show me a lock of her hair," said Fanny, laughing. " It's twice prettier hair than yours, though she doesn't think half so much about it as you do," said her brother, pinching Fanny's arm. " But you'll show me a lock, won't you," said Fanny.

" I'm so glad she's to be here at my marriage," said Mary, " because then Edward will know her. I'm so glad that he will see her." " Edward will have other fish to fry, and won't care much about her," said Harry.

" It seems you're going to do the regular thing," said his father, " like all the good apprentices. Marry your master's daughter, and then become Lord Mayor of London." This was not the view in which it had pleased Harry to regard his engagement. All the other " young men" that had gone to Mr. Burton's had married Mr. Burton's daughters,—or, at least, enough had done so to justify the Stratton assertion that all had fallen into the same trap. The Burtons, with their five girls, were supposed in Stratton to have managed their affairs very well, and something of these hints had reached Harry's ears. He would have preferred that the thing should not have been made so common, but he was not fool enough to make himself really unhappy on that head. " I don't know much about becoming Lord Mayor," he replied. " That promotion doesn't lie exactly in our line." " But marrying your master's daughter does, it seems," said the Rector. Harry thought that this as coming from his father was almost ill-natured, and therefore dropped the conversation.

" I'm sure we shall like her," said Fanny.

" I think that I shall like Harry's choice," said Mrs. Clavering.

" I do hope Edward will like her," said Mary.

" Mary," said her sister, " I do wish you were once married. When you are, you'll begin to have a self of your own again. Now you're no better than an unconscious echo."

" Wait for your own turn, my dear," said the mother.

Harry had reached home on a Saturday, and the following Monday was Christmas-day. Lady Clavering, he was told, was at home at the park, and Sir Hugh had been there lately. No one from the house except the servants were seen at church either on the Sunday or on Christmas-day. " But that shows nothing," said the Rector, speaking in anger. " He very rarely does come, and when he does, it would be better that he should be away. I think that he likes to insult me by misconducting himself. They say that she is not well, and I can easily believe that all this about her sister makes her unhappy. If I were you I would go up and call. Your mother was there the other day, but did not see them. I think you'll find that he's away, hunting somewhere. I saw the groom going off with three horses on Sunday afternoon. He always sends them by the church gate just as we're coming out."

So Harry went up to the house, and found Lady Clavering at home. She was looking old and careworn, but she was glad to see him. Harry was the only one of the rectory family who had been liked at the great house since Sir Hugh's marriage, and he, had he cared to do so, would have been made welcome there. But, as he had once said to Sir Hugh's sister-in-law, if he shot the Clavering game, he would be expected to do so in the guise of a head gamekeeper, and he did not choose to play that part. It would not suit him to drink Sir Hugh's claret, and be bidden to ring the bell, and to be asked to step into the stable for this or that. He was a fellow of his college, and quite as big a man, he thought, as Sir Hugh. He would not be a hanger-on at the park, and, to tell the truth, he disliked his cousin quite as much as his father did. But there had even been a sort of friendship,—nay, occasionally almost a confidence, between him and Lady Clavering, and he believed that by her he was really liked.

Lady Clavering had heard of his engagement, and of course congratulated him. "Who told you?" he asked,—"was it my mother?"

"No; I have not seen your mother I don't know when. I think it was my maid told me. Though we somehow don't see much of you all at the rectory, our servants are no doubt more gracious with the rectory servants. I'm sure she must be nice, Harry, or you would not have chosen her. I hope she has got some money."

"Yes, I think she is nice. She is coming here at Easter."

"Ah, we shall be away then, you know; and about the money?"

"She will have a little, but very little;—a hundred a year."

"Oh, Harry, is not that rash of you? Younger brothers should always get money. You're the same as a younger brother, you know."

"My idea is to earn my own bread. It's not very aristocratic, but, after all, there are a great many more in the same boat with me."

"Of course you will earn your bread, but having a wife with money would not hinder that. A girl is not the worse because she can bring some help. However, I'm sure I hope you'll be happy."

"What I meant was that I think it best when the money comes from the husband."

"I'm sure I ought to agree with you, because we never had any." Then there was a pause. "I suppose you've heard about Lord Ongar," she said.

"I have heard that he is very ill."

"Very ill. I believe there was no hope when we heard last; but Julia never writes now."

"I'm sorry that it is so bad as that," said Harry, not well knowing what else to say.

"As regards Julia, I do not know whether it may not be for the best.

It seems to be a cruel thing to say, but of course I cannot but think most of her. You have heard, perhaps, that they have not been happy ? "

" Yes; I had heard that."

" Of course ; and what is the use of pretending anything with you ? You know what people have said of her."

" I have never believed it."

" You always loved her, Harry. Oh, dear, I remember how unhappy that made me once, and I was so afraid that Hugh would suspect it. She would never have done for you ;—would she, Harry ? "

" She did a great deal better for herself," said Harry.

" If you mean that ironically, you shouldn't say it now. If he dies, she will be well off, of course, and people will in time forget what has been said,—that is, if she will live quietly. The worst of it is that she fears nothing."

" But you speak as though you thought she had been—been—"

" I think she was probably imprudent, but I believe nothing worse than that. But who can say what is absolutely wrong, and what only impru- dent ? I think she was too proud to go really astray. And then with such a man as that, so difficult and so ill-tempered—— ! Sir Hugh thinks——" But at that moment the door was opened and Sir Hugh came in.

" What does Sir Hugh think ? " said he.

" We were speaking of Lord Ongar," said Harry, sitting up and shaking hands with his cousin.

" Then, Harry, you were speaking on a subject that I would rather not have discussed in this house. Do you understand that, Hermione ? I will have no talking about Lord Ongar or his wife. We know very little, and what we hear is simply uncomfortable. Will you dine here to-day, Harry ? "

" Thank you, no; I have only just come home."

" And I am just going away. That is, I go to-morrow. I cannot stand this place. I think it the dullest neighbourhood in all England, and the most gloomy house I ever saw. Hermione likes it."

To this last assertion Lady Clavering expressed no assent; nor did she venture to contradict him.

CHAPTER V.

Lady Ongar's Return.

But Sir Hugh did not get away from Clavering Park on the next morning as he had intended. There came to him that same afternoon a message by telegraph, to say that Lord Ongar was dead. He had died at Florence on the afternoon of Christmas-day, and Lady Ongar had expressed her inten- tion of coming at once to England.

" Why the devil doesn't she stay where she is ? " said Sir Hugh, to his wife. " People would forget her there, and in twelve months time the row would be all over."

"Perhaps she does not want to be forgotten," said Lady Clavering.

"Then she should want it. I don't care whether she has been guilty or not. When a woman gets her name into such a mess as that, she should keep in the background."

"I think you are unjust to her, Hugh."

"Of course you do. You don't suppose that I expect anything else. But if you mean to tell me that there would have been all this row, if she had been decently prudent, I tell you that you're mistaken."

"Only think what a man he was."

"She knew that when she took him, and should have borne with him while he lasted. A woman isn't to have seven thousand a year for nothing."

"But you forget that not a syllable has been proved against her, or been attempted to be proved. She has never left him, and now she has been with him in his last moments. I don't think you ought to be the first to turn against her."

"If she would remain abroad, I would do the best I could for her. She chooses to return home; and as I think she's wrong, I won't have her here;—that's all. You don't suppose that I go about the world accusing her?"

"I think you might do something to fight her battle for her."

"I will do nothing,—unless she takes my advice and remains abroad. You must write to her now, and you will tell her what I say. It's an infernal bore, his dying at this moment; but I suppose people won't expect that I'm to shut myself up."

For one day only did the baronet shut himself up, and on the following, he went whither he had before intended.

Lady Clavering thought it proper to write a line to the rectory, informing the family there that Lord Ongar was no more. This she did in a note to Mrs. Clavering; and when it was received, there came over the faces of them all that lugubrious look, which is, as a matter of course, assumed by decorous people when tidings come of the death of any one who has been known to them, even in the most distant way. With the exception of Harry, all the rectory Claverings had been introduced to Lord Ongar, and were now bound to express something approaching to sorrow. Will any one dare to call this hypocrisy? If it be so called, who in the world is not a hypocrite? Where is the man or woman who has not a special face for sorrow before company? The man or woman who has no such face, would at once be accused of heartless impropriety.

"It is very sad," said Mrs. Clavering; "only think, it is but little more than a year since you married them!"

"And twelve such months as they have been for her!" said the Rector, shaking his head. His face was very lugubrious, for though as a parson he was essentially a kindly, easy man, to whom humbug was odious, and who dealt little in the austerities of clerical denunciation, still he had his face of pulpit sorrow for the sins of the people,—what I may perhaps call his clerical knack of gentle condemnation,—and could therefore assume a solemn look, and a little saddened motion of his head, with more ease than people who are not often called upon for such action.

"Poor woman !" said Fanny, thinking of the woman's married sorrows, and her early widowhood.

"Poor man," said Mary, shuddering as she thought of the husband's fate.

"I hope," said Harry, almost sententiously, "that no one in this house will condemn her upon such mere rumours as have been heard."

"Why should any one in this house condemn her," said the Rector, "even if there were more than rumours ? My dears, judge not, lest ye be judged. As regards her, we are bound by close ties not to speak ill of her—or even to think ill, unless we cannot avoid it. As far as I know, we have not even any reason for thinking ill." Then he went out, changed the tone of his countenance among the rectory stables, and lit his cigar.

Three days after that a second note was brought down from the great house to the rectory, and this was from Lady Clavering to Harry. "Dear Harry," ran the note,—" Could you find time to come up to me this morning ? Sir Hugh has gone to North Priory.—Ever yours, H. C." Harry, of course, went, and as he went, he wondered how Sir Hugh could have had the heart to go to North Priory at such a moment. North Priory was a hunting seat some thirty miles from Clavering, belonging to a great nobleman with whom Sir Hugh much consorted. Harry was grieved that his cousin had not resisted the temptation of going at such a time, but he was quick enough to perceive that Lady Clavering alluded to the absence of her lord as a reason why Harry might pay his visit to the house with satisfaction.

"I'm so much obliged to you for coming," said Lady Clavering. "I want to know if you can do something for me" As she spoke, she had a paper in her hand which he immediately perceived to be a letter from Italy.

"I'll do anything I can, of course, Lady Clavering."

"But I must tell you, that I hardly know whether I ought to ask you. I'm doing what would make Hugh very angry. But he is so unreasonable, and so cruel about Julia. He condemns her simply because, as he says, there is no smoke without fire. That is such a cruel thing to say about a woman ;—is it not ? "

Harry thought that it was a cruel thing, but as he did not wish to speak evil of Sir Hugh before Lady Clavering, he held his tongue.

"When we got the first news by telegraph, Julia said that she intended to come home at once. Hugh thinks that she should remain abroad for some time, and indeed I am not sure but that would be best. At any rate he made me write to her, and advise her to stay. He declared that if she came at once he would do nothing for her. The truth is, he does not want to have her here, for if she were again in the house he would have to take her part, if ill-natured things were said."

"That's cowardly," said Harry, stoutly.

"Don't say that, Harry, till you have heard it all. If he believes these things, he is right not to wish to meddle. He is very hard, and always believes evil. But he is not a coward. If she were here, living with him as my sister, he would take her part, whatever he might himself think."

"But why should he think ill of his own sister-in-law? I have never thought ill of her."

"You loved her, and he never did;—though I think he liked her too in his way. But that's what he told me to do, and I did it. I wrote to her, advising her to remain at Florence till the warm weather comes, saying that as she could not specially wish to be in London for the season, I thought she would be more comfortable there than here;—and then I added that Hugh also advised her to stay. Of course I did not say that he would not have her here,—but that was his threat."

"She is not likely to press herself where she is not wanted."

"No,—and she will not forget her rank and her money;—for that must now be hers. Julia can be quite as hard and as stubborn as he can. But I did write as I say, and I think that if she had got my letter before she had written herself, she would perhaps have stayed. But here is a letter from her, declaring that she will come at once. She will be starting almost as soon as my letter gets there, and I am sure she will not alter her purpose now."

"I don't see why she should not come if she likes it."

"Only that she might be more comfortable there. But read what she says. You need not read the first part. Not that there is any secret; but it is about him and his last moments, and it would only pain you."

Harry longed to read the whole, but he did as he was bid, and began the letter at the spot which Lady Clavering marked for him with her finger. "I have to start on the third, and as I shall stay nowhere except to sleep at Turin and Paris, I shall be home by the eighth;—I think on the evening of the eighth. I shall bring only my own maid, and one of his men who desires to come back with me. I wish to have apartments taken for me in London. I suppose Hugh will do as much as this for me?"

"I am quite sure Hugh won't," said Lady Clavering, who was watching his eye as he read.

Harry said nothing, but went on reading. "I shall only want two sitting-rooms and two bedrooms,—one for myself and one for Clara, and should like to have them somewhere near Piccadilly,—in Clarges Street, or about there. You can write me a line, or send me a message to the Hôtel Bristol, at Paris. If anything fails, so that I should not hear, I shall go to the Palace Hotel; and, in that case, should telegraph for rooms from Paris."

"Is that all I'm to read?" Harry asked.

"You can go on and see what she says as to her reason for coming."

So Harry went on reading. " I have suffered much, and of course I know that I must suffer more ; but I am determined that I will face the worst of it at once. It has been hinted to me that an attempt will be made to interfere with the settlement——" " Who can have hinted that ? " said Harry. Lady Clavering suspected who might have done so, but she made no answer. " I can hardly think it possible; but, if it is done, I will not be out of the way. I have done my duty as best I could, and have done it under circumstances that I may truly say were terrible ;—and I will go on doing it. No one shall say that I am ashamed to show my face and claim my own. You will be surprised when you see me. I have aged so much ;——"

" You need not go on," said Lady Clavering. " The rest is about nothing that signifies."

Then Harry refolded the letter and gave it back to his companion.

" Sir Hugh is gone, and therefore I could not show him that in time to do anything ; but if I were to do so, he would simply do nothing, and let her go to the hotel in London. Now that would be unkind;—would it not ? "

" Very unkind, I think."

" It would seem so cold to her on her return."

" Very cold. Will you not go and meet her ? "

Lady Clavering blushed as she answered. Though Sir Hugh was a tyrant to his wife, and known to be such, and though she knew that this was known, she had never said that it was so to any of the Claverings ; but now she was driven to confess it. " He would not let me go, Harry. I could not go without telling him, and if I told him he would forbid it."

" And she is to be all alone in London, without any friend ? "

" I shall go to her as soon as he will let me. I don't think he will .orbid my going to her, perhaps after a day or two ; but I know he would not let me go on purpose to meet her."

" It does seem hard."

" But about the apartments, Harry ? I thought that perhaps you would see about them. After all that has passed I could not have asked you, only that now, as you are engaged yourself, it is nearly the same as though you were married. I would ask Archibald, only then there would be a fuss between Archibald and Hugh ; and somehow I look on you more as a brother-in-law than I do Archibald."

" Is Archie in London ? "

" His address is at his club, but I daresay he is at North Priory also. At any rate, I shall say nothing to him."

" I was thinking he might have met her."

" Julia never liked him. And, indeed, I don't think she will care so much about being met. She was always independent in that way, and would go over the world alone better than many men. But couldn't you run up and manage about the apartments? A woman coming home as a widow,—and in her position,—feels an hotel to be so public."

" I will see about the apartments."

" I knew you would. And there will be time for you to send to me, so that I can write to Paris ;—will there not ? There is more than a week, you know."

But Henry did not wish to go to London on this business immediately. He had made up his mind that he would not only take the rooms, but that he would also meet Lady Ongar at the station. He said nothing of this to Lady Clavering, as, perhaps, she might not approve ; but such was his intention. He was wrong no doubt. A man in such cases should do what he is asked to do, and do no more. But he repeated to himself the excuse that Lady Clavering had made,—namely, that he was already the same as a married man, and that, therefore, no harm could come of his courtesy to his cousin's wife's sister. But he did not wish to make two journeys to London, nor did he desire to be away for a full week out of his holidays. Lady Clavering could not press him to go at once, and, therefore, it was settled as he proposed. She would write to Paris immediately, and he would go up to London after three or four days. " If we only knew of any apartments, we could write," said Lady Clavering. " You could not know that they were comfortable," said Harry ; " and you will find that I will do it in plenty of time." Then he took his leave ; but Lady Clavering had still one other word to say to him. " You had better not say anything about all this at the rectory ; had you ? " Harry, without considering much about it, said that he would not mention it.

Then he went away and walked again about the park, thinking of it all. He had not seen her since he had walked round the park, in his misery, after parting with her in the garden. How much had happened since then ! She had been married in her glory, had become a countess, and then a widow, and was now returning with a tarnished name, almost repudiated by those who had been her dearest friends ; but with rank and fortune at her command,—and again a free woman. He could not but think what might have been his chance were it not for Florence Burton ! But much had happened to him also. He had almost perished in his misery ;—so he told himself ;—but had once more " tricked his beams,"—that was his expression to himself,—and was now " flaming in the forehead " of a glorious love. And even if there had been no such love, would a widowed countess with a damaged name have suited his ambition, simply because she had the rich dower of the poor wretch to whom she had sold herself ? No, indeed. There could be no question of renewed vows between them now ;—there could have been no such question even had there been no " glorious love," which had accrued to him almost as his normal privilege in right of his pupilage in Mr. Burton's office. No ;—there could be, there could have been, nothing now between him and the widowed Countess of Ongar. But, nevertheless, he liked the idea of meeting her in London. He felt some triumph in the thought that he should be the first to touch her hand on her return after all that she had suffered. He would be very courteous to her, and would spare no trouble that would give her any ease. As for her rooms, he would see to everything of which he could think that might add to her comfort; and a wish crept upon him, uninvited, that she might be conscious of what he had done for her.

Would she be aware, he wondered, that he was engaged? Lady Clavering had known it for the last three months, and would probably have mentioned the circumstance in a letter. But perhaps not. The sisters, he knew, had not been good correspondents; and he almost wished that she might not know it. "I should not care to be talking to her about Florence," he said to himself.

It was very strange that they should come to meet in such a way, after all that had passed between them in former days. Would it occur to her that he was the only man she had ever loved?—for, of course, as he well knew, she had never loved her husband. Or would she now be too callous to everything but the outer world to think at all of such a subject? She had said that she was aged, and he could well believe it. Then he pictured her to himself in her weeds, worn, sad, thin, but still proud and handsome. He had told Florence of his early love for the woman whom Lord Ongar had married, and had described with rapture his joy that that early passion had come to nothing. Now he would have to tell Florence of this meeting; and he thought of the comparison he would make between her bright young charms and the shipwrecked beauty of the widow. On the whole, he was proud that he had been selected for the commission, as he liked to think of himself as one to whom things happened which were out of the ordinary course. His only objection to Florence was that she had come to him so much in the ordinary course.

"I suppose the truth is you are tired of our dulness," said his father to him, when he declared his purpose of going up to London, and, in answer to certain questions that were asked him, had hesitated to tell his business.

"Indeed, it is not so," said Harry, earnestly; "but I have a commission to execute for a certain person, and I cannot explain what it is."

"Another secret ;—eh, Harry ? "

"I am very sorry,—but it is a secret. It is not one of my own seeking; that is all I can say." His mother and sisters also asked him a question or two; but when he became mysterious, they did not persevere. "Of course it is something about Florence," said Fanny. "I'll be bound he is going to meet her. What will you bet me, Harry, you don't go to the play with Florence before you come home ? " To this Henry deigned no answer ; and after that no more questions were asked.

He went up to London and took rooms in Bolton Street. There was a pretty fresh-looking light drawing-room, or, indeed, two drawing-rooms, and a small dining-room, and a large bed-room looking over upon the trees of some great nobleman's garden. As Harry stood at the window it seemed so odd to him that he should be there. And he was busy about everything in the chamber, seeing that all things were clean and well ordered. Was the woman of the house sure of her cook? Sure; of course she was sure. Had not old Lady Dimdaff lived there for two years, and nobody ever was so particular about her victuals as Lady Dimdaff. "And would Lady Ongar keep her own carriage?" As to this Harry could say nothing. Then came the question of price, and Harry found his commission very difficult. The sum asked seemed to be enormous. "Seven guineas a week at that time of the year!" Lady Dimdaff had always paid seven guineas. "But that was in the season," suggested Harry. To this the woman replied that it was the season now. Harry felt that he did not like to drive a bargain for the Countess, who would probably care very little what she paid, and therefore assented. But a guinea a day for lodgings did seem a great deal of money. He was prepared to marry and commence housekeeping upon a less sum for all his expenses. However, he had done his commission, had written to Lady Clavering, and had telegraphed to Paris. He had almost brought himself to write to Lady Ongar, but when the moment came he abstained. He had sent the telegram as from H. Clavering. She might think that it came from Hugh if she pleased.

He was unable not to attend specially to his dress when he went to meet her at the Victoria Station. He told himself that he was an ass,—but still he went on being an ass. During the whole afternoon he could do nothing but think of what he had in hand. He was to tell Florence everything, but had Florence known the actual state of his mind, I doubt whether she would have been satisfied with him. The train was due at 8 p.m. He dined at the Oxford and Cambridge Club at six, and then went to his lodgings to take one last look at his outer man. The evening was very fine, but he went down to the station in a cab, because he would not meet Lady Ongar in soiled boots. He told himself again that he was an ass; and then tried to console himself by thinking that such an occasion as this seldom happened once to any man,—could hardly happen more than once to any man. He had hired a carriage for her, not thinking it fit that Lady Ongar should be taken to her new home in a cab; and when he was at the station, half an hour before the proper time, was very fidgety because it had not come. Ten minutes before eight he might have been seen standing at the entrance to the station looking out anxiously for the vehicle. The man was there, of course, in time, but Harry made himself angry because he could not get the carriage so placed that Lady Ongar might be sure of stepping into it without leaving the platform. Punctually to the moment the coming train announced itself by its whistle, and Harry Clavering felt himself to be in a flutter.

The train came up along the platform, and Harry stood there expecting to see Julia Brabazon's head projected from the first window that caught his eye. It was of Julia Brabazon's head, and not of Lady Ongar's, that he was thinking. But he saw no sign of her presence while the carriages were coming to a stand-still, and the platform was covered with passengers before he discovered her whom he was seeking. At last he encountered in the crowd a man in livery, and found from him that he was Lady Ongar's servant. "I have come to meet Lady Ongar," said Harry, "and have got a carriage for her." Then the servant found his mistress, and Harry offered his hand to a tall woman in black. She wore a black straw hat with a veil, but the veil was so thick that Harry could not at all see her face.

"Is that Mr. Clavering?" said she.

"Yes," said Harry, "it is I. Your sister asked me to take rooms for you, and as I was in town I thought I might as well meet you to see if you wanted anything. Can I get the luggage?"

"Thank you;—the man will do that. He knows where the things are."

"I ordered a carriage;—shall I show him where it is? Perhaps you will let me take you to it? They are so stupid here. They would not let me bring it up."

"It will do very well I'm sure. It's very kind of you. The rooms are in Bolton Street. I have the number here. Oh! thank you." But she would not take his arm. So he led the way, and stood at the door while she got into the carriage with her maid. "I'd better show the man where you are now." This he did, and afterwards shook hands with her through the carriage window. This was all he saw of her, and the words which have been repeated were all that were spoken. Of her face he had not caught a glimpse.

As he went home to his lodgings he was conscious that the interview had not been satisfactory. He could not say what more he wanted, but he felt that there was something amiss. He consoled himself, however, by reminding himself that Florence Burton was the girl whom he had really loved, and not Julia Brabazon. Lady Ongar had given him no invitation to come and see her, and therefore he determined that he would return home on the following day without going near Bolton Street. He had pictured to himself beforehand the sort of description he would give to Lady Clavering of her sister; but, seeing how things had turned out, he made up his mind that he would say nothing of the meeting. Indeed, he would not go up to the great house at all. He had done Lady Clavering's commission,—at some little trouble and expense to himself, and there should be an end of it. Lady Ongar would not mention that she had seen him. He doubted, indeed, whether she would remember whom she had seen. For any good that he had done, or for any sentiment that there had been, his cousin Hugh's butler might as well have gone to the train. In this mood he returned home, consoling himself with the fitness of things which had given him Florence Burton instead of Julia Brabazon for a wife.

CHAPTER VI.

The Rev. Samuel Saul.

During Harry's absence in London, a circumstance had occurred at the rectory which had surprised some of them and annoyed others a good deal. Mr. Saul, the curate, had made an offer to Fanny. The Rector and Fanny declared themselves to be both surprised and annoyed. That the Rector was in truth troubled by the thing was very evident. Mrs. Clavering said that she had almost suspected it,—that she was at any rate not surprised; as to the offer itself, of course she was sorry that it should have been made, as it could not suit Fanny to accept it. Mary was surprised, as she had thought Mr. Saul to be wholly intent on other things; but she could not see any reason why the offer should be regarded as being on his part unreasonable.

"How can you say so, mamma?" Such had been Fanny's indignant exclamation when Mrs. Clavering had hinted that Mr. Saul's proceeding had been expected by her.

"Simply because I saw that he liked you, my dear. Men under such circumstances have different ways of showing their liking."

Fanny, who had seen all of Mary's love-affair from the beginning to the end, and who had watched the Reverend Edward Fielding in all his very conspicuous manœuvres, would not agree to this. Edward Fielding from the first moment of his intimate acquaintance with Mary had left no doubt of his intentions on the mind of any one. He had talked to Mary and walked with Mary whenever he was allowed or found it possible to do so. When driven to talk to Fanny, he had always talked about Mary. He had been a lover of the good, old, plainspoken stamp, about whom there had been no mistake. From the first moment of his coming much about Clavering Rectory the only question had been about his income. "I don't think Mr. Saul ever said a word to me except about the poor people and the church services," said Fanny. "That was merely his way," said Mrs. Clavering. "Then he must be a goose," said Fanny. "I am very sorry if I have made him unhappy, but he had no business to come to me in that way."

"I suppose I shall have to look for another curate," said the Rector. But this was said in private to his wife.

"I don't see that at all," said Mrs. Clavering. "With many men it would be so; but I think you will find that he will take an answer, and that there will be an end of it."

Fanny, perhaps, had a right to be indignant, for certainly Mr. Saul had given her no fair warning of his intention. Mary had for some months been intent rather on Mr. Fielding's church matters than on those going on in her own parish, and therefore there had been nothing singular in the fact that Mr. Saul had said more on such matters to Fanny than to her sister. Fanny was eager and active, and as Mr. Saul was very eager and very active, it was natural that they should have had some interests in common. But there had been no private walkings, and no talkings that could properly be called private. There was a certain book which Fanny kept, containing the names of all the poor people in the parish, to which Mr. Saul had access equally with herself; but its contents were of a most prosaic nature, and when she had sat over it in the rectory drawing-room, with Mr. Saul by her side, striving to extract more than twelve pennies out of charity shillings, she had never thought that it would lead to a declaration of love.

He had never called her Fanny in his life,—not up to the moment when she declined the honour of becoming Mrs. Saul. The offer itself was made in this wise. She had been at the house of old Widow Tubb, half-way between Cumberly Green and the little village of Clavering, striving to make that rheumatic old woman believe that she had not been cheated by a general conspiracy of the parish in the matter of a distribution of coal, when, just as she was about to leave the cottage, Mr. Saul came up. It was then past four, and the evening was becoming dark, and there was, moreover, a slight drizzle of rain. It was not a tempting evening for a walk of a mile and a half through a very dirty lane; but Fanny Clavering did not care much for such things, and was just stepping out into the mud and moisture, with her dress well looped up, when Mr. Saul accosted her.

"I'm afraid you'll be very wet, Miss Clavering."

"That will be better than going without my cup of tea, Mr. Saul, which I should have to do if I stayed any longer with Mrs. Tubb. And I have got an umbrella."

"But it is so dark and dirty," said he.

"I'm used to that, as you ought to know."

"Yes; I do know it," said he, walking on with her. "I do know that nothing ever turns you away from the good work."

There was something in the tone of his voice which Fanny did not like. He had never complimented her before. They had been very intimate and had often scolded each other. Fanny would accuse him of exacting too much from the people, and he would retort upon her that she coddled them. Fanny would often decline to obey him, and he would make angry hints as to his clerical authority. In this way they had worked together pleasantly, without any of the awkwardness which on other terms would have arisen between a young man and a young woman. But now that he began to praise her with some pecu-liar intention of meaning in his tone, she was confounded. She had made no immediate answer to him, but walked on rapidly through the mud and slush.

"You are very constant," said he; "I have not been two years at Clavering without finding that out." It was becoming worse and worse. It was not so much his words which provoked her as the tone in which they were uttered. And yet she had not the slightest idea of what was

Mr. Saul Proposes.

coming. If, thoroughly admiring her devotion and mistaken as to her character, he were to ask her to become a Protestant nun, or suggest to her that she should leave her home and go as nurse into a hospital, then there would have occurred the sort of folly of which she believed him to be capable. Of the folly which he now committed, she had not believed him to be capable.

It had come on to rain hard, and she held her umbrella low over her head. He also was walking with an open umbrella in his hand, so that they were not very close to each other. Fanny, as she stepped on impetuously, put her foot into the depth of a pool, and splashed herself thoroughly.

"Oh dear, oh dear," said she; "this is very disagreeable."

"Miss Clavering," said he, "I have been looking for an opportunity to speak to you, and I do not know when I may find another so suitable as this." She still believed that some proposition was to be made to her which would be disagreeable, and perhaps impertinent,—but it never occurred to her that Mr. Saul was in want of a wife.

"Doesn't it rain too hard for talking?" she said.

"As I have begun I must go on with it now," he replied, raising his voice a little, as though it were necessary that he should do so to make her hear him through the rain and darkness. She moved a little further away from him with unthinking irritation; but still he went on with his purpose. "Miss Clavering, I know that I am ill-suited to play the part of a lover;—very ill suited." Then she gave a start and again splashed herself sadly. "I have never read how it is done in books, and have not allowed my imagination to dwell much on such things."

"Mr. Saul, don't go on; pray don't." Now she did understand what was coming.

"Yes, Miss Clavering, I must go on now; but not on that account would I press you to give me an answer to-day. I have learned to love you, and if you can love me in return, I will take you by the hand, and you shall be my wife. I have found that in you which I have been unable not to love,—not to covet that I may bind it to myself as my own for ever. Will you think of this, and give me an answer when you have considered it fully?"

He had not spoken altogether amiss, and Fanny, though she was very angry with him, was conscious of this. The time he had chosen might not be considered suitable for a declaration of love, nor the place; but having chosen them, he had, perhaps, made the best of them. There had been no hesitation in his voice, and his words had been perfectly audible.

"Oh, Mr. Saul, of course I can assure you at once," said Fanny. "There need not be any consideration. I really have never thought ——" Fanny, who knew her own mind on the matter thoroughly, was hardly able to express herself plainly and without incivility. As soon as that phrase "of course" had passed her lips, she felt that it should not have been spoken. There was no need that she should insult him by telling him that such a proposition from him could have but one answer.

"No, Miss Clavering; I know you have never thought of it, and therefore it would be well that you should take time. I have not been able to make manifest to you by little signs, as men do who are less awkward, all the love that I have felt for you. Indeed, could I have done so, I should still have hesitated till I had thoroughly resolved that I might be better with a wife than without one; and had resolved also, as far as that might be possible for me, that you also would be better with a husband."

"Mr. Saul, really that should be for me to think of."

"And for me also. Can any man offer to marry a woman,—to bind a woman for life to certain duties, and to so close an obligation without thinking whether such bonds would be good for her as well as for himself? Of course you must think for yourself;—and so have I thought for you. You should think for yourself, and you should think also for me."

Fanny was quite aware that as regarded herself, the matter was one which required no more thinking. Mr. Saul was not a man with whom she could bring herself to be in love. She had her own ideas as to what was loveable in men, and the eager curate, splashing through the rain by her side, by no means came up to her standard of excellence. She was unconsciously aware that he had altogether mistaken her character, and given her credit for more abnegation of the world than she pretended to possess, or was desirous of possessing. Fanny Clavering was in no hurry to get married. I do not know that she had even made up her mind that marriage would be a good thing for her; but she had an untroubled conviction that if she did marry, her husband should have a house and an income. She had no reliance on her own power of living on a potato, and with one new dress every year. A comfortable home, with nice, comfortable things around her, ease in money matters, and elegance in life, were charms with which she had not quarrelled, and, though she did not wish to be hard upon Mr. Saul on account of his mistake, she did feel that in making his proposition he had blundered. Because she chose to do her duty as a parish clergyman's daughter, he thought himself entitled to regard her as devotée, who would be willing to resign everything to become the wife of a clergyman, who was active, indeed, but who had not one shilling of income beyond his curacy. "Mr. Saul," she said, "I can assure you I need take no time for further thinking. It cannot be as you would have it."

"Perhaps I have been abrupt. Indeed, I feel that it is so, though I did not know how to avoid it."

"It would have made no difference. Indeed, indeed, Mr. Saul, nothing of that kind could have made a difference."

"Will you grant me this;—that I may speak to you again on the same subject after six months?"

"It cannot do any good."

"It will do this good;—that for so much time you will have had the idea before you." Fanny thought that she would have Mr. Saul himself before her, and that that would be enough. Mr. Saul, with his rusty clothes and his thick, dirty shoes, and his weak, blinking eyes, and his mind always set upon the one wish of his life, could not be made to present himself to her in the guise of a lover. He was one of those men of whom women become very fond with the fondness of friendship, but from whom young women seem to be as far removed in the way of love as though they belonged to some other species. "I will not press you further," said he, "as I gather by your tone that it distresses you."

"I am so sorry if I distress you, but really, Mr. Saul, I could give you,—I never could give you any other answer."

Then they walked on silently through the rain,—silently, without a single word,—for more than half a mile, till they reached the rectory gate. Here it was necessary that they should, at any rate, speak to each other, and for the last three hundred yards Fanny had been trying to find the words which would be suitable. But he was the first to break the silence. "Good-night, Miss Clavering," he said, stopping and putting out his hand.

"Good-night, Mr. Saul."

"I hope that there may be no difference in our bearing to each other, because of what I have to-day said to you?"

"Not on my part ;—that is, if you will forget it."

"No, Miss Clavering ; I shall not forget it. If it had been a thing to be forgotten, I should not have spoken. I certainly shall not forget it."

"You know what I mean, Mr. Saul."

"I shall not forget it even in the way that you mean. But still I think you need not fear me, because you know that I love you. I think I can promise that you need not withdraw yourself from me, because of what has passed. But you will tell your father and your mother, and of course will be guided by them. And now, good-night." Then he went, and she was astonished at finding that he had had much the best of it in his manner of speaking and conducting himself. She had refused him very curtly, and he had borne it well. He had not been abashed, nor had he become sulky, nor had he tried to melt her by mention of his own misery. In truth he had done it very well,—only that he should have known better than to make any such attempt at all.

Mr. Saul had been right in one thing. Of course she told her mother, and of course her mother told her father. Before dinner that evening the whole affair was being debated in the family conclave. They all agreed that Fanny had had no alternative but to reject the proposition at once. That, indeed, was so thoroughly taken for granted, that the point was not discussed. But there came to be a difference between the Rector and Fanny on one side, and Mrs. Clavering and Mary on the other. "Upon

my word," said the Rector, " I think it was very impertinent." Fanny
would not have liked to use that word herself, but she loved her father
for using it.

" I do not see that," said Mrs. Clavering. " He could not know what
Fanny's views in life might be. Curates very often marry out of the
houses of the clergymen with whom they are placed, and I do not see why
Mr. Saul should be debarred from the privilege of trying."

" If he had got to like Fanny what else was he to do ? " said Mary.

" Oh, Mary, don't talk such nonsense," said Fanny. " Got to like !
People shouldn't get to like people unless there's some reason for it."

" What on earth did he intend to live on ? " demanded the Rector.

" Edward had nothing to live on, when you first allowed him to come
here," said Mary.

" But Edward had prospects, and Saul, as far as I know, has none.
He had given no one the slightest notice. If the man in the moon had
come to Fanny I don't suppose she would have been more surprised."

" Not half so much, papa."

Then it was that Mrs. Clavering had declared that she was not
surprised,—that she had suspected it, and had almost made Fanny angry
by saying so. When Harry came back two days afterwards, the family
news was imparted to him, and he immediately ranged himself on his
father's side. " Upon my word I think that he ought to be forbidden
the house," said Harry. " He has forgotten himself in making such a
proposition."

" That's nonsense, Harry," said his mother. " If he can be comfortable coming here, there can be no reason why he should be uncomfortable. It would be an injustice to him to ask him to go, and a great
trouble to your father to find another curate that would suit him so well."
There could be no doubt whatever as to the latter proposition, and therefore it was quietly argued that Mr. Saul's fault, if there had been a fault,
should be condoned. On the next day he came to the rectory, and they
were all astonished at the ease with which he bore himself. It was not
that he affected any special freedom of manner, or that he altogether
avoided any change in his mode of speaking to them. A slight blush
came upon his sallow face as he first spoke to Mrs. Clavering, and he
hardly did more than say a single word to Fanny. But he carried himself as though conscious of what he had done, but in no degree ashamed
of the doing it. The Rector's manner to him was stiff and formal ;—seeing
which Mrs. Clavering spoke to him gently, and with a smile. " I saw you
were a little hard on him, and therefore I tried to make up for it," said
she afterwards. " You were quite right," said the husband. " You always
are. But I wish he had not made such a fool of himself. It will never
be the same thing with him again." Harry hardly spoke to Mr. Saul the
first time he met him, all of which Mr. Saul understood perfectly.

" Clavering," he said to Harry, a day or two after this, " I hope there
is to be no difference between you and me."

"Difference! I don't know what you mean by difference."

"We were good friends, and I hope that we are to remain so. No doubt you know what has taken place between me and your sister."

"Oh, yes;—I have been told, of course."

"What I mean is, that I hope you are not going to quarrel with me on that account? What I did, is it not what you would have done in my position?—only you would have done it successfully?"

"I think a fellow should have some income, you know."

"Can you say that you would have waited for income before you spoke of marriage?"

"I think it might have been better that you should have gone to my father."

"It may be that that is the rule in such things, but if so I do not know it. Would she have liked that better?"

"Well;—I can't say."

"You are engaged? Did you go to the young lady's family first?"

"I can't say I did; but I think I had given them some ground to expect it. I fancy they all knew what I was about. But it's over now, and I don't know that we need say anything more about it."

"Certainly not. Nothing can be said that would be of any use; but I do not think I have done anything that you should resent."

"Resent is a strong word. I don't resent it, or, at any rate, I won't; and there may be an end of it." After this, Harry was more gracious with Mr. Saul, having an idea that the curate had made some sort of apology for what he had done. But that, I fancy, was by no means Mr. Saul's view of the case. Had he offered to marry the daughter of the Archbishop of Canterbury, instead of the daughter of the Rector of Clavering, he would not have imagined that his doing so needed an apology.

The day after his return from London Lady Clavering sent for Harry up to the house. "So you saw my sister in London?" she said.

"Yes," said Harry blushing; "as I was in town, I thought that I might as well meet her. But, as you said, Lady Ongar is able to do without much assistance of that kind. I only just saw her."

"Julia took it so kindly of you; but she seems surprised that you did not come to her the following day. She thought you would have called."

"Oh, dear, no. I fancied that she would be too tired and too busy to wish to see any mere acquaintance."

"Ah, Harry, I see that she has angered you," said Lady Clavering; "otherwise you would not talk about mere acquaintance."

"Not in the least. Angered me! How could she anger me? What I meant was that at such a time she would probably wish to see no one but people on business,—unless it was some one near to her, like yourself or Hugh."

"Hugh will not go to her."

" But you will do so ; will you not ? "

" Before long I will. You don't seem to understand, Harry,—and, perhaps, it would be odd if you did,—that I can't run up to town and back as I please. I ought not to tell you this, I dare say, but one feels as though one wanted to talk to some one about one's affairs. At the present moment, I have not the money to go,—even if there were no other reason." These last words she said almost in a whisper, and then she looked up into the young man's face, to see what he thought of the communication she had made him.

" Oh, money ! " he said. " You could soon get money. But I hope it won't be long before you go."

On the next morning but one a letter came by the post for him from Lady Ongar. When he saw the handwriting, which he knew, his heart was at once in his mouth, and he hesitated to open his letter at the breakfast-table. He did open it and read it, but, in truth, he hardly understood it or digested it till he had taken it away with him up to his own room. The letter, which was very short, was as follows :—

DEAR FRIEND,

I FELT your kindness in coming to me at the station so much !—the more, perhaps, because others, who owed me more kindness, have paid me less. Don't suppose that I allude to poor Hermione, for, in truth, I have no intention to complain of her. I thought, perhaps, you would have come to see me before you left London ; but I suppose you were hurried. I hear from Clavering that you are to be up about your new profession in a day or two. Pray come and see me before you have been many days in London. I shall have so much to say to you ! The rooms you have taken are everything that I wanted, and I am so grateful !

Yours ever,
J. O.

When Harry had read and had digested this, he became aware that he was again fluttered. " Poor creature ! " he said to himself ; " it is sad to think how much she is in want of a friend."

CHAPTER VII.

SOME SCENES IN THE LIFE OF A COUNTESS.

BOUT the middle of January Harry Clavering went up to London, and settled himself to work at Mr. Beilby's office. Mr. Beilby's office consisted of four or five large chambers, overlooking the river from the bottom of Adam Street in the Adelphi, and here Harry found a table for himself in the same apartment with three other pupils. It was a fine old room, lofty, and with large windows, ornamented on the ceiling with Italian scroll-work, and a flying goddess in the centre. In days gone by the house had been the habitation of some great rich man, who had there enjoyed the sweet breezes from the river before London had become the London of the present days, and when no embankment had been needed for the Thames. Nothing could be nicer than his room, or more pleasant than the table and seat which he was to occupy near a window; but there was something in the tone of the other men towards him which did not quite satisfy him. They probably did not know that he was a fellow of a college, and treated him almost as they might have done had he come to them direct from King's College, in the Strand, or from the London University. Down at Stratton, a certain amount of honour had been paid to him. They had known there who he was, and had felt some deference for him. They had not slapped him on the back, or poked him in the ribs, or even called him old fellow, before some length of acquaintance justified such appellation. But up at Mr. Beilby's, in the Adelphi, one young man, who was certainly his junior in age, and who did not seem as yet to have attained any high position in the science of engineering, manifestly thought that he was acting in a friendly and becoming way by declaring the stranger to be a lad of wax on the second day of his appearance. Harry Clavering was not disinclined to believe that he was a " lad of wax," or "a brick," or " a trump," or " no small beer." But he desired that such complimentary and endearing appellations should be used to him only by those who had known him long enough to be aware that he deserved them. Mr. Joseph Walliker certainly was not as yet among this number.

There was a man at Mr. Beilby's, who was entitled to greet him with endearing terms, and to be so greeted himself, although Harry had never seen him till he attended for the first time at the Adelphi. This was Theodore Burton, his future brother-in-law, who was now the leading man in the London house ;—the leading man as regarded business, though he was not as yet a partner. It was understood that this Mr. Burton was to come in when his father went out ; and in the meantime he received a salary of a thousand a year as managing clerk. A very hard-working, steady, intelligent man was Mr. Theodore Burton, with a bald head, a high forehead, and that look of constant work about him which such men obtain. Harry Clavering could not bring himself to take a liking to him, because he wore cotton gloves and had an odious habit of dusting his shoes with his pocket-handkerchief. Twice Harry saw him do this on the first day of their acquaintance, and he regretted it exceedingly. The cotton gloves too were offensive, as were also the thick shoes which had been dusted ; but the dusting was the great sin.

And there was something which did not quite please Harry in Mr. Theodore Burton's manner, though the gentleman had manifestly intended to be very kind to him. When Burton had been speaking to him for a minute or two, it flashed across Harry's mind that he had not bound himself to marry the whole Burton family, and that, perhaps, he must take some means to let that fact be known. "Theodore," as he had so often heard the younger Mr. Burton called by loving lips, seemed to claim him as his own, called him Harry, and upbraided him with friendly warmth for not having come direct to his,—Mr. Burton's,—house in Onslow Crescent. "Pray feel yourself at home there," said Mr. Burton. "I hope you'll like my wife. You needn't be afraid of being made to be idle if you spend your evenings there, for we are all reading people. Will you

come and dine to-day?" Florence had told him that she was her brother
Theodore's favourite sister, and that Theodore as a husband and a
brother, and a man, was perfect. But Theodore had dusted his boots with
his handkerchief, and Harry Clavering would not dine with him on that day.

And then it was painfully manifest to him that every one in the office
knew his destiny with reference to old Burton's daughter. He had been
one of the Stratton men, and no more than any other had he gone unscathed
through the Stratton fire. He had been made to do the regular thing, as
Granger, Scarness, and others had done it. Stratton would be safer ground
now, as Clavering had taken the last. That was the feeling on the matter
which seemed to belong to others. It was not that Harry thought in this
way of his own Florence. He knew well enough what a lucky fellow he
was to have won such a girl. He was well aware how widely his Florence
differed from Carry Scarness. He denied to himself indignantly that he had
any notion of repenting what he had done. But he did wish that these
private matters might have remained private, and that all the men at
Beilby's had not known of his engagement. When Walliker, on the fourth
day of their acquaintance, asked him if it was all right at Stratton, he
made up his mind that he hated Walliker, and that he would hate Walliker
to the last day of his life. He had declined the first invitation given to
him by Theodore Burton; but he could not altogether avoid his future
brother-in-law, and had agreed to dine with him on this day.

On that same afternoon Harry, when he left Mr. Beilby's office, went
direct to Bolton Street, that he might call on Lady Ongar. As he went
thither he bethought himself that these Wallikers and the like had had no
such events in life as had befallen him! They laughed at him about
Florence Burton, little guessing that it had been his lot to love, and to be
loved by such a one as Julia Brabazon had been,—such a one as Lady
Ongar now was. But things had gone well with him. Julia Brabazon
could have made no man happy, but Florence Burton would be the
sweetest, dearest, truest little wife that ever man ever took to his home.
He was thinking of this, and determined to think of it more and more
daily, as he knocked at Lady Ongar's door. "Yes; her ladyship was at
home," said the servant whom he had seen on the railway platform; and
in a few moments' time he found himself in the drawing-room which he
had criticized so carefully when he was taking it for its present occupant.

He was left in the room for five or six minutes, and was able to make
a full mental inventory of its contents. It was very different in its
present aspect from the room which he had seen not yet a month since.
She had told him that the apartments had been all that she desired; but
since then everything had been altered, at least in appearance. A new
piano had been brought in, and the chintz on the furniture was surely
new. And the room was crowded with small feminine belongings, indicative of wealth and luxury. There were ornaments about, and pretty
toys, and a thousand knickknacks which none but the rich can possess,
and which none can possess even among the rich unless they can give

taste as well as money to their acquisition. Then he heard a light step ; the door opened, and Lady Ongar was there.

He expected to see the same figure that he had seen on the railway platform, the same gloomy drapery, the same quiet, almost deathlike demeanour, nay, almost the same veil over her features ; but the Lady Ongar whom he now saw was as unlike that Lady Ongar as she was unlike that Julia Brabazon whom he had known in old days at Clavering Park. She was dressed, no doubt, in black ; nay, no doubt, she was dressed in weeds ; but in spite of the black and in spite of the weeds there was nothing about her of the weariness or of the solemnity of woe. He hardly saw that her dress was made of crape, or that long white pendants were hanging down from the cap which sat so prettily upon her head. But it was her face at which he gazed. At first he thought that she could hardly be the same woman, she was to his eyes so much older than she had been ! And yet as he looked at her, he found that she was as handsome as ever,—more handsome than she had ever been before. There was a dignity about her face and figure which became her well, and which she carried as though she knew herself to be in very truth a countess. It was a face which bore well such signs of age as those which had come upon it. She seemed to be a woman fitter for woman-hood than for girlhood. Her eyes were brighter than of yore, and, as Harry thought, larger ; and her high forehead and noble stamp of counte-nance seemed fitted for the dress and headgear which she wore.

" I have been expecting you," said she, stepping up to him. " Hermione wrote me word that you were to come up on Monday. Why did you not come sooner ? " There was a smile on her face as she spoke, and a confidence in her tone which almost confounded him.

" I have had so many things to do," said he lamely.

" About your new profession. Yes, I can understand that. And so you are settled in London now ? Where are you living ;—that is, if you are settled yet ? " In answer to this, Harry told her that he had taken lodgings in Bloomsbury Square, blushing somewhat as he named so unfashionable a locality. Old Mrs. Burton had recommended him to the house in which he was located, but he did not find it necessary to explain that fact to Lady Ongar.

" I have to thank you for what you did for me," continued she. " You ran away from me in such a hurry on that night that I was unable to speak to you. But to tell the truth, Harry, I was in no mood then to speak to any one. Of course you thought that I treated you ill."

" Oh, no," said he.

" Of course you did. If I thought you did not, I should be angry with you now. But had it been to save my life I could not have helped it. Why did not Sir Hugh Clavering come to meet me ? Why did not my sister's husband come to me ? " To this question Harry could make no answer. He was still standing with his hat in his hand, and now turned his face away from her and shook his head.

" Sit down, Harry," she said, " and let me talk to you like a friend ; —unless you are in a hurry to go away."

" Oh, no," said he, seating himself.

" Or unless you, too, are afraid of me."

" Afraid of you, Lady Ongar ? "

" Yes, afraid ; but I don't mean you. I don't believe that you are coward enough to desert a woman who was once your friend because misfortune has overtaken her, and calumny has been at work with her name."

" I hope not," said he.

" No, Harry ; I do not think it of you. But if Sir Hugh be not a coward, why did he not come and meet me ? Why has he left me to stand alone, now that he could be of service to me ? I knew that money was his god, but I have never asked him for a shilling and should not have done so now. Oh, Harry, how wicked you were about that cheque ! Do you remember ? "

" Yes ; I remember."

" So shall I ; always, always. If I had taken that money how often should I have heard of it since ? "

" Heard of it ? " he asked. " Do you mean from me ? "

" Yes ; how often from you ? Would you have dunned me, and told me of it once a week ? Upon my word, Harry, I was told of it more nearly every day. Is it not wonderful that men should be so mean ? "

It was clear to him now that she was talking of her husband who was dead, and on that subject he felt himself at present unable to speak a word. He little dreamed at that moment how openly she would soon speak to him of Lord Ongar and of Lord Ongar's faults !

" Oh, how I have wished that I had taken your money ! But never mind about that now, Harry. Wretched as such taunts were, they soon became a small thing. But it has been cowardly in your cousin, Hugh ; has it not ? If I had not lived with him as one of his family, it would not have mattered. People would not have expected it. It was as though my own brother had cast me forth."

" Lady Clavering has been with you ; has she not ? "

" Once, for half-an-hour. She came up for one day, and came here by herself, cowering as though she were afraid of me. Poor Hermy ! She has not a good time of it either. You lords of creation lead your slaves sad lives when it pleases you to change your billing and cooing for matter-of-fact masterdom and rule. I don't blame Hermy. I suppose she did all she could, and I did not utter one word of reproach of her. Nor should I to him. Indeed, if he came now the servant would deny me to him. He has insulted me, and I shall remember the insult."

Harry Clavering did not clearly understand what it was that Lady Ongar had desired of her brother-in-law,—what aid she had required ; nor did he know whether it would be fitting for him to offer to act in Sir Hugh's place. Anything that he could do, he felt himself at that moment willing to do, even though the necessary service should demand some sacrifice greater than prudence could approve. "If I had thought that anything was wanted, I should have come to you sooner," said he.

"Everything is wanted, Harry. Everything is wanted;—except that cheque for six hundred pounds which you sent me so treacherously. Did you ever think what might have happened if a certain person had heard of that? All the world would have declared that you had done it for your own private purposes;—all the world, except one."

Harry, as he heard this, felt that he was blushing. Did Lady Ongar know of his engagement with Florence Burton? Lady Clavering knew it, and might probably have told the tidings; but then, again, she might not have told them. Harry at this moment wished that he knew how it was. All that Lady Ongar said to him would come with so different a meaning according as she did, or did not know that fact. But he had no mind to tell her of the fact himself. He declared to himself that he hoped she knew it, as it would serve to make them both more comfortable together; but he did not think that it would do for him to bring forward the subject, neck and heels as it were. The proper thing would be that she should congratulate him, but this she did not do. "I certainly meant no ill," he said, in answer to the last words she had spoken.

"You have never meant ill to me, Harry; though you know you have abused me dreadfully before now. I daresay you forget the hard names you have called me. You men do forget such things."

"I remember calling you one name."

"Do not repeat it now, if you please. If I deserved it, it would shame me; and if I did not, it should shame you."

"No; I will not repeat it."

"Does it not seem odd, Harry, that you and I should be sitting, talking together in this way?" She was leaning now towards him, across the table, and one hand was raised to her forehead while her eyes were fixed intently upon his. The attitude was one which he felt to express extreme intimacy. She would not have sat in that way, pressing back her hair from her brow, with all appearance of widowhood banished from her face, in the presence of any but a dear and close friend. He did not think of this, but he felt that it was so, almost by instinct. "I have such a tale to tell you," she said; "such a tale!"

Why should she tell it to him? Of course he asked himself this question. Then he remembered that she had no brother,—remembered also that her brother-in-law had deserted her, and he declared to himself that, if necessary, he would be her brother. "I fear that you have not been happy," said he, "since I saw you last."

"Happy!" she replied. "I have lived such a life as I did not think any man or woman could be made to live on this side the grave. I will be honest with you, Harry. Nothing but the conviction that it could not be for long, has saved me from destroying myself. I knew that he must die!"

"Oh, Lady Ongar!"

"Yes, indeed; that is the name he gave me; and because I con-

A Friendly Talk.

sented to take it from him, he treated me;—O heavens! how am I to find words to tell you what he did, and the way in which he treated me. A woman could not tell it to a man. Harry, I have no friend that I trust but you, but to you I cannot tell it. When he found that he had been wrong in marrying me, that he did not want the thing which he had thought would suit him, that I was a drag upon him rather than a comfort,—what was his mode, do you think, of ridding himself of the burden?" Clavering sat silent looking at her. Both her hands were now up to her forehead, and her large eyes were gazing at him till he found himself unable to withdraw his own for a moment from her face. "He strove to get another man to take me off his hands; and when he found that he was failing,—he charged me with the guilt which he himself had contrived for me."

"Lady Ongar!"

"Yes; you may well stare at me. You may well speak hoarsely and look like that. It may be that even you will not believe me;—but by the God in whom we both believe, I tell you nothing but the truth. He attempted that and he failed,—and then he accused me of the crime which he could not bring me to commit."

"And what then?"

"Yes; what then? Harry, I had a thing to do, and a life to live, that would have tried the bravest; but I went through it. I stuck to him to the last! He told me before he was dying,—before that last frightful illness, that I was staying with him for his money. ' For your money, my lord,' I said, ' and for my own name.' And so it was. Would it have been wise in me, after all that I had gone through, to have given up that for which I had sold myself? I had been very poor, and had been so placed that poverty, even such poverty as mine, was a curse to me. You know what I gave up because I feared that curse. Was I to be foiled at last, because such a creature as that wanted to shirk out of his bargain? I knew there were some who would say I had been false. Hugh Clavering says so now, I suppose. But they never should say I had left him to die alone in a foreign land."

"Did he ask you to leave him?"

"No;—but he called me that name which no woman should hear and stay. No woman should do so unless she had a purpose such as mine. He wanted back the price that he had paid, and I was determined to do nothing that should assist him in his meanness! And then, Harry, his last illness! Oh, Harry, you would pity me if you could know all!"

"It was his own intemperance!"

"Intemperance! It was brandy,—sheer brandy. He brought himself to such a state that nothing but brandy would keep him alive, and in which brandy was sure to kill him;—and it did kill him. Did you ever hear of the horrors of drink?"

"Yes; I have heard of such a state."

"I hope you may never live to see it. It is a sight that would stick by you for ever. But I saw it, and tended him through the whole, as though I had been his servant. I remained with him when that man who opened the door for you could no longer endure the room. I was with him when the strong woman from the hospital, though she could not understand his words, almost fainted at what she saw and heard. He was punished, Harry. I need wish no farther vengeance on him, even for all his cruelty, his injustice, his unmanly treachery. Is it not fearful to think that any man should have the power of bringing himself to such an end as that?"

Harry was thinking rather how fearful it was that a man should have it in his power to drag any woman through such a Gehenna as that which this lord had created. He felt that had Julia Brabazon been his, as she had once promised him, he never would have allowed himself to speak a harsh word to her, to have looked at her except with loving eyes. But she had chosen to join herself to a man who had treated her with a cruelty exceeding all that his imagination could have conceived. "It is a mercy that he has gone," said he at last.

"It is a mercy for both. Perhaps you can understand now something of my married life. And through it all I had but one friend;—if I may call him a friend who had come to terms with my husband, and was to have been his agent in destroying me. But when this man understood from me that I was not what he had been taught to think me,—which my husband had told him I was,—he relented."

"May I ask what was that man's name?"

"His name is Pateroff. He is a Pole, but he speaks English like an Englishman. In my presence he told Lord Ongar that he was false and brutal. Lord Ongar laughed, with that little, low, sneering laughter which was his nearest approach to merriment, and told Count Pateroff that that was of course his game before me. There, Harry,—I will tell you nothing more of it. You will understand enough to know what I have suffered; and if you can believe that I have not sinned——"

"Oh, Lady Ongar!"

"Well, I will not doubt you again. But as far as I can learn you are nearly alone in your belief. What Hermy thinks I cannot tell, but she will soon come to think as Hugh may bid her. And I shall not blame her. What else can she do, poor creature?"

"I am sure she believes no ill of you."

"I have one advantage, Harry,—one advantage over her and some others. I am free. The chains have hurt me sorely during my slavery; but I am free, and the price of my servitude remains. He had written home,—would you believe that?—while I was living with him he had written home to say that evidence should be collected for getting rid of me. And yet he would sometimes be civil, hoping to cheat me into inadvertencies. He would ask that man to dine, and then of a sudden would be absent; and during this he was ordering that evidence should be collected! Evidence, indeed! The same servants have lived with me through it all. If I could now bring forward evidence I could make it all clear as the day. But there needs no care for a woman's honour, though a man may have to guard his by collecting evidence !"

"But what he did cannot injure you."

"Yes, Harry, it has injured me ; it has all but destroyed me. Have not reports reached even you ? Speak out like a man, and say whether it is not so ?"

"I have heard something."

"Yes, you have heard something ! If you heard something of your sister where would you be ? All the world would be a chaos to you till you had pulled out somebody's tongue by the roots. Not injured me ! For two years your cousin Hugh's house was my home. I met Lord Ongar in his house. I was married from his house. He is my brother-in-law, and it so happens that of all men he is the nearest to me. He stands well before the world, and at this time could have done me real service. How is it that he did not welcome me home ;—that I am not now at his house with my sister ; that he did not meet me so that the world might know that I was received back among my own people ? Why is it, Harry, that I am telling this to you ;—to you, who are nothing to me ; my sister's husband's cousin ; a young man, from your position not fit to be my confidant ? Why am I telling this to you, Harry ? "

"Because we are old friends," said he, wondering again at this moment whether she knew of his engagement with Florence Burton.

"Yes, we are old friends, and we have always liked each other ; but you must know that, as the world judges, I am wrong to tell all this to you. I should be wrong,—only that the world has cast me out, so that I am no longer bound to regard it. I am Lady Ongar, and I have my share of that man's money. They have given me up Ongar Park, having satisfied themseves that it is mine by right, and must be mine by law. But he has robbed me of every friend I had in the world, and yet you tell me he has not injured me !"

"Not every friend."

"No, Harry, I will not forget you, though I spoke so slightingly of you just now. But your vanity need not be hurt. It is only the world,— Mrs. Grundy, you know, that would deny me such friendship as yours ; not my own taste or choice. Mrs. Grundy always denies us exactly those things which we ourselves like best. You are clever enough to understand that."

He smiled and looked foolish, and declared that he only offered his assistance because perhaps it might be convenient at the present moment. What could he do for her ? How could he show his friendship for her now at once ?

"You have done it, Harry, in listening to me and giving me your sympathy. It is seldom that we want any great thing from our friends. I want nothing of that kind. No one can hurt me much further now. My money and my rank are safe ; and, perhaps, by degrees, acquaintances, if not friends, will form themselves round me again. At present, of course, I see no one ; but because I see no one, I wanted some one to whom I could speak. Poor Hermy is worse than no one. Good-by, Harry ; you look surprised and bewildered now, but you will soon get over that. Don't be long before I see you again."

Then, feeling that he was bidden to go, he wished her good-by, and went.

CHAPTER VIII.

The House in Onslow Crescent.

HARRY, as he walked away from the house in Bolton Street, hardly knew whether he was on his heels or his head. Burton had told him not to dress—"We don't give dress dinner parties, you know. It's all in the family way with us,"—and Harry, therefore, went direct from Bolton Street to Onslow Crescent. But, though he managed to keep the proper course down Piccadilly, he was in such confusion of mind that he hardly knew whither he was going. It seemed as though a new form of life had been opened to him, and that it had been opened in such a way as almost necessarily to engulph him. It was not only that Lady Ongar's history was so terrible, and her life so strange, but that he himself was called upon to form a part of that history, and to join himself in some sort to that life. This countess with her wealth, her rank, her beauty, and her bright intellect had called him to her, and told him that he was her only friend. Of course he had promised his friendship. How could he have failed to give such a promise to one whom he had loved so well ? But to what must such a promise lead, or rather to what must it not have led had it not been for Florence Burton ? She was young, free, and rich. She made no pretence of regret for the husband she had lost, speaking of him as though in truth she hardly regarded herself as his wife. And she was the same Julia whom he had loved, who had loved him, who had jilted him, and in regret for whom he had once resolved to lead a wretched, lonely life ! Of course she must expect that he would renew it all ;—unless, indeed, she knew of his engagement. But if she knew it, why had she not spoken of it ?

And could it be that she had no friends,—that everybody had deserted her, that she was all alone in the world ? As he thought of it all, the whole thing seemed to him to be too terrible for reality. What a tragedy was that she had told him ! He thought of the man's insolence to the woman whom he had married and sworn to love, then of his cruelty, his fiendish, hellish cruelty,—and lastly of his terrible punishment. " I stuck to him through it all," she had said to him ; and then he endeavoured to picture to himself that bedside by which Julia Brabazon, his Julia Brabazon, had remained firm, when hospital attendants had been scared by the horrors they had witnessed, and the nerves of a strong man,—of a man paid for such work, had failed him !

The truth of her word throughout he never doubted; and, indeed, no man or woman who heard her could have doubted. One hears stories told that to oneself, the hearer, are manifestly false; and one hears stories as to the truth or falsehood of which one is in doubt; and stories again which seem to be partly true and partly untrue. But one also hears that of the truth of which no doubt seems to be possible. So it had been with the tale which Lady Ongar had told. It had been all as she had said; and had Sir Hugh heard it,—even Sir Hugh, who doubted all men and regarded all women as being false beyond doubt,—even he, I think, would have believed it.

But she had deserved the sufferings which had come upon her. Even Harry, whose heart was very tender towards her, owned as much as that. She had sold herself, as she had said of herself more than once. She had given herself to a man whom she regarded not at all, even when her heart belonged to another,—to a man whom she must have loathed and despised when she was putting her hand into his before the altar. What scorn had there been upon her face when she spoke of the beginning of their married miseries! With what eloquence of expression had she pronounced him to be vile, worthless, unmanly; a thing from which a woman must turn with speechless contempt! She had now his name, his rank, and his money, but she was friendless and alone. Harry Clavering declared to himself that she had deserved it,—and, having so declared, forgave her all her faults. She had sinned, and then had suffered; and, therefore, should now be forgiven. If he could do aught to ease her troubles, he would do it,—as a brother would for a sister.

But it would be well that she should know of his engagement. Then he thought of the whole interview, and felt sure that she must know it. At any rate he told himself that he was sure. She could hardly have spoken to him as she had done, unless she had known. When last they had been together, sauntering round the gardens at Clavering, he had rebuked her for her treachery to him. Now she came to him almost open-armed, free, full of her cares, swearing to him that he was her only friend! All this could mean but one thing,—unless she knew that that one thing was barred by his altered position.

But it gratified him to think that she had chosen him for the repositary of her tale; that she had told her terrible history to him. I fear that some small part of this gratification was owing to her rank and wealth. To be the one friend of a widowed countess, young, rich, and beautiful, was something much out of the common way. Such confidence lifted him far above the Wallikers of the world. That he was pleased to be so trusted by one that was beautiful, was, I think, no disgrace to him; —although I bear in mind his condition as a man engaged. It might be dangerous, but that danger in such case it would be his duty to overcome. But in order that it might be overcome, it would certainly be well that she should know his position.

I fear he speculated as he went along as to what might have been his condition in the world had he never seen Florence Burton. First he asked himself, whether under any circumstances, he would have wished to marry a widow, and especially a widow by whom he had already been jilted. Yes; he thought that he could have forgiven her even that, if his own heart had not changed; but he did not forget to tell himself again how lucky it was for him that his heart was changed. What countess in the world, let her have what park she might, and any imaginable number of thousands a year, could be so sweet, so nice, so good, so fitting for him as his own Florence Burton? Then he endeavoured to reflect what happened when a commoner married the widow of a peer. She was still called, he believed, by her old title, unless she should choose to abandon it. Any such arrangement was now out of the question; but he thought that he would prefer that she should have been called Mrs. Clavering, if such a state of things had come about. I do not know that he pictured to himself any necessity, either on her part or on his, of abandoning anything else that came to her from her late husband.

At half-past six, the time named by Theodore Burton, he found himself at the door in Onslow Crescent, and was at once shown up into the drawing-room. He knew that Mr. Burton had a family, and he had pictured to himself an untidy, ugly house, with an untidy, motherly woman going about with a baby in her arms. Such would naturally be the home of a man who dusted his shoes with his pocket-handkerchief. But to his surprise he found himself in as pretty a drawing-room as he remembered to have seen; and seated on a sofa, was almost as pretty a woman as he remembered. She was tall and slight, with large brown eyes and well-defined eyebrows, with an oval face, and the sweetest, kindest mouth that ever graced a woman. Her dark brown hair was quite plain, having been brushed simply smooth across the forehead, and then collected in a knot behind. Close beside her, on a low chair, sat a little fair-haired girl, about seven years old, who was going through some pretence at needlework; and kneeling on a higher chair, while she sprawled over the drawing-room table, was another girl, some three years younger, who was engaged with a puzzle-box.

"Mr. Clavering," said she, rising from her chair; "I am so glad to see you, though I am almost angry with you for not coming to us sooner. I have heard so much about you; of course you know that." Harry explained that he had only been a few days in town, and declared that he was happy to learn that he had been considered worth talking about.

"If you were worth accepting you were worth talking about."

"Perhaps I was neither," said he.

"Well; I am not going to flatter you yet. Only as I think our Flo is without exception the most perfect girl I ever saw, I don't suppose she would be guilty of making a bad choice. Cissy, dear, this is Mr. Clavering."

Cissy got up from her chair, and came up to him. "Mamma says I am to love you very much," said Cissy, putting up her face to be kissed.

"But I did not tell you to say I had told you," said Mrs. Burton, laughing.

"And I will love you very much," said Harry, taking her up in his arms.

"But not so much as Aunt Florence,—will you?"

They all knew it. It was clear to him that everybody connected with the Burtons had been told of the engagement, and that they all spoke of it openly, as they did of any other everyday family occurrence. There was not much reticence among the Burtons. He could not but feel this, though now, at the present moment, he was disposed to think specially well of the family because Mrs. Burton and her children were so nice.

"And this is another daughter?"

"Yes; another future niece, Mr. Clavering. But I suppose I may call you Harry; may I not? My name is Cecilia. Yes, that is Miss Pert."

"I'm not Miss Pert," said the little soft round ball of a girl from the chair. "I'm Sophy Burton. Oh! you musn't tittle."

Harry found himself quite at home in ten minutes; and before Mr. Burton had returned, had been taken upstairs into the nursery to see Theodore Burton Junior in his cradle, Theodore Burton Junior being as yet only some few months old. "Now you've seen us all," said Mrs. Burton, "and we'll go downstairs and wait for my husband. I must let you into a secret, too. We don't dine till past seven; you may as well remember that for the future. But I wanted to have you for half-an-hour to myself before dinner, so that I might look at you, and make up my mind about Flo's choice. I hope you won't be angry with me?"

"And how have you made up your mind?"

"If you want to find that out, you must get it through Florence. You may be quite sure I shall tell her; and, I suppose, I may be quite sure she will tell you. Does she tell you everything?"

"I tell her everything," said Harry, feeling himself, however, to be a little conscience-smitten at the moment, as he remembered his interview with Lady Ongar. Things had occurred this very day which he certainly could not tell her.

"Do;—do; always do that," said Mrs. Burton, laying her hand affectionately on his arm. "There is no way so certain to bind a woman to you, heart and soul, as to show her that you trust her in everything. Theodore tells me everything. I don't think there's a drain planned under a railway-bank, but that he shows it me in some way; and I feel so grateful for it. It makes me know that I can never do enough for him. I hope you'll be as good to Flo, as he is to me."

"We can't both be perfect, you know."

"Ah, well! of course you'll laugh at me. Theodore always laughs at me when I get on what he calls a high horse. I wonder whether you are as sensible as he is?"

Harry reflected that he never wore cotton gloves. "I don't think I am very sensible," said he. "I do a great many foolish things, and the worst is, that I like them."

"So do I. I like so many foolish things?"

"Oh, mamma!" said Cissy.

"I shall have that quoted against me, now, for the next six months, whenever I am preaching wisdom in the nursery. But Florence is nearly as sensible as her brother."

"Much more so than I am."

"All the Burtons are full up to their eyes with good sense. And what a good thing it is! Who ever heard of any of them coming to sorrow? Whatever they have to live on, they always have enough. Did you ever know a woman who has done better with her children, or has known how to do better, than Theodore's mother? She is the dearest old woman." Harry had heard her called a very clever old woman by certain persons in Stratton, and could not but think of her matrimonial successes as her praises were thus sung by her daughter-in-law.

They went on talking, while Sophy sat in Harry's lap, till there was heard the sound of the key in the latch of the front-door, and the master of the house was known to be there. "It's Theodore," said his wife, jumping up and going out to meet him. "I'm so glad that you have been here a little before him, because now I feel that I know you. When he's here I shan't get in a word." Then she went down to her husband, and Harry was left to speculate how so very charming a woman could ever have been brought to love a man who cleaned his boots with his pocket-handkerchief.

There were soon steps again upon the stairs, and Burton returned bringing with him another man whom he introduced to Harry as Mr. Jones. "I didn't know my brother was coming," said Mrs. Burton, "but it will be very pleasant, as of course I shall want you to know him." Harry became a little perplexed. How far might these family ramifications be supposed to go? Would he be welcomed, as one of the household, to the hearth of Mrs. Jones; and if of Mrs. Jones, then of Mrs. Jones's brother? His mental inquiries, however, in this direction, were soon ended by his finding that Mr. Jones was a bachelor.

Jones, it appeared, was the editor, or sub-editor, or co-editor, of some influential daily newspaper. "He is a·night bird, Harry——," said Mrs. Burton. She had fallen into the way of calling him Harry at once, but he could not on that occasion bring himself to call her Cecilia. He might have done so had not her husband been present, but he was ashamed to do it before him. "He is a night bird, Harry," said she, speaking of her brother, "and flies away at nine o'clock, that he may go and hoot like an owl in some dark city haunt that he has. Then, when he is himself asleep at breakfast-time, his hootings are being heard round the town."

Harry rather liked the idea of knowing an editor. Editors were, he thought, influential people, who had the world very much under their feet,—being, as he conceived, afraid of no men, while other men are very much afraid of them. He was glad enough to shake Jones by the hand, when he found that Jones was an editor. But Jones, though he had the face and forehead of a clever man, was very quiet, and seemed almost submissive to his sister and brother-in-law.

The dinner was plain, but good, and Harry after a while became happy and satisfied, although he had come to the house with something almost like a resolution to find fault. Men, and women also, do frequently go about in such a mood, having unconscionably from some small circumstance, prejudged their acquaintances, and made up their mind that their acquaintances should be condemned. Influenced in this way, Harry had not intended to pass a pleasant evening, and would have stood aloof and been cold, had it been possible to him; but he found that it was not possible; and after a little while he was friendly and joyous, and the dinner went off very well. There was some wild-fowl, and he was agreeably surprised as he watched the mental anxiety and gastronomic skill with which Burton went through the process of preparing the gravy, with lemon and pepper, having in the room a little silver-pot and an apparatus of fire for the occasion. He would as soon have expected the Archbishop of Canterbury himself to go through such an operation in the dining-room at Lambeth as the hard-working man of business whom he had known in the chambers at the Adelphi.

"Does he always do that, Mrs. Burton?" Harry asked.

"Always," said Burton, "when I can get the materials. One doesn't bother oneself about a cold leg of mutton, you know, which is my usual dinner when we are alone. The children have it hot in the middle of the day."

"Such a thing never happened to him yet, Harry," said Mrs. Burton.

"Gently with the pepper," said the editor. It was the first word he had spoken for some time.

"Be good enough to remember that, yourself, when you are writing your article to-night."

"No, none for me, Theodore," said Mrs Burton.

"Cissy!"

"I have dined really. If I had remembered that you were going to display your cookery, I would have kept some of my energy, but I forgot it."

"As a rule," said Burton, "I don't think women recognize any difference in flavours. I believe wild duck and hashed mutton would be quite the same to my wife if her eyes were blinded. I should not mind this, if it were not that they are generally proud of the deficiency. They think it grand."

"Just as men think it grand not to know one tune from another," said his wife.

When dinner was over, Burton got up from his seat. "Harry," said he, "do you like good wine?" Harry said that he did. Whatever women may say about wild-fowl, men never profess an indifference to good wine, although there is a theory about the world, quite as incorrect as it is general, that they have given up drinking it. "Indeed, I do," said Harry. "Then I'll give you a bottle of port," said Burton, and so saying he left the room.

"I'm very glad you have come to-day," said Jones, with much gravity. "He never gives me any of that when I'm alone with him; and he never, by any means, brings it out for company."

"You don't mean to accuse him of drinking it alone, Tom?" said his sister, laughing.

"I don't know when he drinks it; I only know when he doesn't."

The wine was decanted with as much care as had been given to the concoction of the gravy, and the clearness of the dark liquid was scrutinized with an eye that was full of anxious care. "Now, Cissy, what do you think of that? She knows a glass of good wine when she gets it, as well as you do, Harry; in spite of her contempt for the duck."

As they sipped the old port they sat round the dining-room fire, and Harry Clavering was forced to own to himself that he had never been more comfortable.

"Ah," said Burton, stretching out his slippered feet, "why can't it all be after-dinner, instead of that weary room at the Adelphi?"

"And all old port?" said Jones.

"Yes, and all old port. You are not such an ass as to suppose that a man in suggesting to himself a continuance of pleasure suggests to himself also the evils which are supposed to accompany such pleasure. If I took much of the stuff I should get cross and sick, and make a beast of myself; but then what a pity it is that it should be so."

"You wouldn't like much of it, I think," said his wife.

"That is it," said he. "We are driven to work because work never palls on us, whereas pleasure always does. What a wonderful scheme it is when one looks at it all. No man can follow pleasure long continually. When a man strives to do so, he turns his pleasure at once into business, and works at that. Come, Harry, we mustn't have another bottle, as Jones would go to sleep among the type." Then they all went upstairs together. Harry, before he went away, was taken again up into the nursery, and there kissed the two little girls in their cots. When he was outside the nursery door, on the top of the stairs, Mrs. Burton took him by the hand. "You'll come to us often," said she, "and make yourself at home here, will you not?" Harry could not but say that he would. Indeed he did so without hesitation, almost with eagerness, for he had liked her and had liked her house. "We think of you, you know," she continued, "quite as one of ourselves. How could it be otherwise when Flo is the dearest to us of all beyond our own?"

"It makes me so happy to hear you say so," said he.

"Then come here and talk about her. I want Theodore to feel that you are his brother; it will be so important to you in the business that it should be so." After that he went away, and as he walked back along

Piccadilly, and then up through the regions of St. Giles to his home in Bloomsbury Square, he satisfied himself that the life of Onslow Crescent was a better manner of life than that which was likely to prevail in Bolton Street.

When he was gone his character was of course discussed between the husband and wife in Onslow Crescent. " What do you think of him ? " said the husband.

" I like him so much ! He is so much nicer than you told me,—so much pleasanter and easier; and I have no doubt he is as clever, though I don't think he shows that at once."

" He is clever enough ; there's no doubt about that."

" And did you not think he was pleasant ? "

" Yes ; he was pleasant here. He is one of those men who get on best with women. You'll make much more of him for awhile than I shall. He'll gossip with you and sit idling with you for the hour together, if you'll let him. There's nothing wrong about him, and he'd like nothing better than that."

" You don't believe that he's idle by disposition ? Think of all that he has done already."

" That's just what is most against him. He might do very well with us if he had not got that confounded fellowship ; but having got that, he thinks the hard work of life is pretty well over with him."

" I don't suppose he can be so foolish as that, Theodore."

" I know well what such men are, and I know the evil that is done to them by the cramming they endure. They learn many names of things,— high-sounding names, and they come to understand a great deal about words. It is a knowledge that requires no experience and very little real thought. But it demands much memory ; and when they have loaded themselves in this way, they think that they are instructed in all things. After all, what can they do that is of real use to mankind ? What can they create ? "

" I suppose they are of use."

" I don't know it. A man will tell you, or pretend to tell you,—for the chances are ten to one that he is wrong,—what sort of lingo was spoken in some particular island or province six hundred years before Christ. What good will that do any one, even if he were right ? And then see the effect upon the men themselves ! At four-and-twenty a young fellow has achieved some wonderful success, and calls himself by some outlandish and conceited name—a double first, or something of the kind. Then he thinks he has completed everything, and is too vain to learn anything afterwards. The truth is, that at twenty-four no man has done more than acquire the rudiments of his education. The system is bad from begin- ning to end. All that competition makes false and imperfect growth. Come, I'll go to bed."

What would Harry have said if he had heard all this from the man who dusted his boots with his handkerchief?

CHAPTER IX.

Too Prudent by Half.

FLORENCE BURTON thought herself the happiest girl in the world. There was nothing wanting to the perfection of her bliss. She could perceive, though she never allowed her mind to dwell upon the fact, that her lover was superior in many respects, to the men whom her sisters had married. He was better educated, better looking, in fact more fully a gentleman at all points than either Scarness or any of the others. She liked her sisters' husbands very well, and in former days, before Harry Clavering had come to Stratton, she had never taught herself to think that she, if she married, would want anything different from that which Providence had given to them. She had never thrown up her head, or even thrown up her nose, and told herself that she would demand something better than that. But not the less was she alive to the knowledge that something better had come in her way, and that that something better was now her own. She was very proud of her lover, and, no doubt, in some gently feminine way showed that she was so as she made her way about among her friends at Stratton. Any idea that she herself was better educated, better looking, or more clever than her elder sisters, and that, therefore, she was deserving of a higher order of husband, had never entered her mind. The Burtons in London,—Theodore Burton and his wife,—who knew her well, and who, of all the family, were best able to appreciate her worth, had long been of opinion that she deserved some specially favoured lot in life. The question with them would be, whether Harry Clavering was good enough for her.

Everybody at Stratton knew that she was engaged, and when they wished her joy she made no coy denials. Her sisters had all been engaged in the same way, and their marriages had gone off in regular sequence to their engagements. There had never been any secret with them about their affairs. On this matter the practice is very various among different people. There are families who think it almost indelicate to talk about marriage, as a thing actually in prospect for any of their own community. An ordinary acquaintance would be considered to be impertinent in even hinting at such a thing, although the thing were an established fact. The engaged young ladies only whisper the news through the very depths of their pink note-paper, and are supposed to blush as they communicate the tidings by their pens, even in the retirement of their own rooms. But there are other families in which there is no vestige of such mystery, in which an engaged couple are spoken of together as openly as though they were already bound in some sort of public partnership. In these families the young ladies talk openly of their lovers, and generally prefer that subject of conversation to any other. Such a family,—so little mysterious, —so open in their arrangements, was that of the Burtons at Stratton. The reserve in the reserved families is usually atoned for by the magnificence of the bridal arrangements, when the marriage is at last solemnized; whereas, among the other set,—the people who have no reserve,—the marriage when it comes, is customarily an affair of much less outward ceremony. They are married without blast of trumpet, with very little profit to the confectioner, and do their honeymoon, if they do it at all, with prosaic simplicity.

Florence had made up her mind that she would be in no hurry about it. Harry was in a hurry; but that was a matter of course. He was a quick-blooded, impatient, restless being. She was slower, and more given to consideration. It would be better that they should wait, even if it were for five or six years. She had no fear of poverty for herself. She had lived always in a house in which money was much regarded, and among people who were of inexpensive habits. But such had not been his lot, and it was her duty to think of the mode of life which might suit him. He would not be happy as a poor man,—without comforts around him, which would simply be comforts to him though they would be luxuries to her. When her mother told her, shaking her head rather sorrowfully as she heard Florence talk, that she did not like long engage-ments, Florence would shake hers too, in playful derision, and tell her mother not to be so suspicious. "It is not you that are going to marry him, mamma."

"No, my dear; I know that. But long engagements never are good. And I can't think why young people should want so many things, now, that they used to do without very well when I was married. When I went into housekeeping, we only had one girl of fifteen to do everything; and we hadn't a nursemaid regular till Theodore was born; and there were three before him."

Florence could not say how many maid-servants Harry might wish to have under similar circumstances, but she was very confident that he would want much more attendance than her father and mother had done, or even than some of her brothers and sisters. Her father, when he first married, would not have objected, on returning home, to find his wife in the kitchen, looking after the progress of the dinner; nor even would her brother Theodore have been made unhappy by such a circumstance. But Harry, she knew, would not like it; and therefore Harry must wait. "It will do him good, mamma," said Florence. "You can't think that I mean to find fault with him; but I know that he is young in his ways. He is one of those men who should not marry till they are twenty-eight, or thereabouts."

"You mean that he is unsteady?"

"No,—not unsteady. I don't think him a bit unsteady; but he will be happier single for a year or two. He hasn't settled down to like his tea and toast when he is tired of his work, as a married man should do. Do you know that I am not sure that a little flirtation would not be very good for him?"

"Oh, my dear!"

" It should be very moderate, you know."

" But then, suppose it wasn't moderate. I don't like to see engaged young men going on in that way. I suppose I'm very old-fashioned; but I think when a young man is engaged, he ought to remember it and to show it. It ought to make him a little serious, and he shouldn't be going about like a butterfly, that may do just as it pleases in the sunshine."

During the three months which Henry remained in town before the Easter holidays he wrote more than once to Florence, pressing her to name an early day for their marriage. These letters were written, I think, after certain evenings spent under favourable circumstances in Onslow Crescent, when he was full of the merits of domestic comfort, and perhaps also owed some of their inspiration to the fact that Lady Ongar had left London without seeing him. He had called repeatedly in Bolton Street, having been specially pressed to do so by Lady Ongar, but he had only once found her at home, and then a third person had been present. This third person had been a lady who was not introduced to him, but he had learned from her speech that she was a foreigner. On that occasion Lady Ongar had made herself gracious and pleasant, but nothing had passed which interested him, and, most unreasonably, he had felt himself to be provoked. When next he went to Bolton Street he found that Lady Ongar had left London. She had gone down to Ongar Park, and, as far as the woman at the house knew, intended to remain there till after Easter. Harry had some undefined idea that she should not have taken such a step without telling him. Had she not declared to him that he was her only friend? When a friend is going out of town, leaving an only friend behind, that friend ought to tell her only friend what she is going to do, otherwise such a declaration of only-friend-ship means nothing. Such was Harry Clavering's reasoning, and having so reasoned, he declared to himself that it did mean nothing, and was very pressing to Florence Burton to name an early day. He had been with Cecilia, he told her,—he had learned to call Mrs. Burton Cecilia in his letters,—and she quite agreed with him that their income would be enough. He was to have two-hundred a year from his father, having brought himself to abandon that high-toned resolve which he had made some time since that he would never draw any part of his income from the parental coffers. His father had again offered it, and he had accepted it. Old Mr. Burton was to add a hundred, and Harry was of opinion that they could do very well. Cecilia thought the same, he said, and therefore Florence surely would not refuse. But Florence received, direct from Onslow Crescent, Cecilia's own version of her thoughts, and did refuse. It may be surmised that she would have refused even without assistance from Cecilia, for she was a young lady not of a fickle or changing disposition. So she wrote to Harry with much care, and as her letter had some influence on the story to be told, the reader shall read it,—if the reader so pleases.

DEAR HARRY,— *Stratton. March*, 186–.

I RECEIVED your letter this morning, and answer it at once, because I know you will be impatient for an answer. You are impatient about things,—are you not? But it was a kind, sweet, dear, generous letter, and I need not tell you now that I love the writer of it with all my heart. I am so glad you like Cecilia. I think she is the perfection of a woman. And Theodore is every bit as good as Cecilia, though I know you don't think so, because you don't say so. I am always happy when I am in Onslow Crescent. I should have been there this spring, only that a certain person who chooses to think that his claims on me are stronger than those of any other person wishes me to go elsewhere. Mamma wishes me to go to London also for a week, but I don't want to be away from the old house too much before the final parting comes at last.

And now about the final parting ; for I may as well rush at it at once. I need hardly tell you that no care for father or mother shall make me put off my marriage. Of course I owe everything to you now ; and as they have approved it, I have no right to think of them in opposition to you. And you must not suppose that they ask me to stay. On the contrary, mamma is always telling me that early marriages are best. She has sent all the birds out of the nest but one ; and is impatient to see that one fly away, that she may be sure that there is no lame one in the brood. You must not therefore think that it is mamma; nor is it papa, as regards himself,—though papa agrees with me in thinking that we ought to wait a little.

Dear Harry, you must not be angry, but I am sure that we ought to wait. We are, both of us, young, and why should we be in a hurry? I know what you will say, and of course I love you the more because you love me so well ; but I fancy that I can be quite happy if I can see you two or three times in the year, and hear from you constantly. It is so good of you to write such nice letters, and the longer they are the better I like them. Whatever you put in them, I like them to be full. I know I can't write nice letters myself, and it makes me unhappy. Unless I have got something special to say, I am dumb.

But now I have something special to say. In spite of all that you tell me about Cecilia, I do not think it would do for us to venture upon marrying yet. I know that you are willing to sacrifice everything, but I ought not on that account to accept a sacrifice. I could not bear to see you poor and uncomfortable ; and we should be very poor in London now-a-days with such an income as we should have. If we were going to live here at Stratton perhaps we might manage, but I feel sure that it would be imprudent in London. You ought not to be angry with me for saying this, for I am quite as anxious to be with you as you can possibly be to be with me ; only I can bear to look forward, and have a pleasure in feeling that all my happiness is to come. I know I am right in this. Do write me one little line to say that you are not angry with your little girl.

I shall be quite ready for you by the 29th. I got such a dear little note from Fanny the other day. She says that you never write to them, and she supposes that I have the advantage of all your energy in that way. I have told her that I do get a good deal. My brother writes to me very seldom, I know ; and I get twenty letters from Cecilia for one scrap that Theodore ever sends me. Perhaps some of these days I shall be the chief correspondent with the rectory. Fanny told me all about the dresses, and I have my own quite ready. I've been bridesmaid to four of my own sisters, so I ought to know what I'm about. I'll never be bridesmaid to anybody again, after Fanny; but whom on earth shall I have for myself? I think we must wait till Cissy and Sophy are ready. Cissy wrote me word that you were a darling man. I don't know how much of that came directly from Cissy, or how much from Cecilia.

God bless you, dear, dearest Harry. Let me have one letter before you come to fetch me, and acknowledge that I am right, even if you say that I am disagreeable. Of course I like to think that you want to have me ; but, you see, one has to pay the penalty of being civilized.—Ever and always your own affectionate

FLORENCE BURTON.

Harry Clavering was very angry when he got this letter. The primary cause of his anger was the fact that Florence should pretend to know what was better for him than he knew himself. If he was willing to encounter life in London on less than four hundred a year, surely she might be contented to try the same experiment. He did not for a moment suspect that she feared for herself, but he was indignant with her because of her fear for him. What right had she to accuse him of wanting to be comfortable? Had he not for her sake consented to be very uncomfortable at that old house at Stratton? Was he not willing to give up his fellowship, and the society of Lady Ongar, and everything else, for her sake? Had he not shown himself to be such a lover as there is not one in a hundred? And yet she wrote and told him that it wouldn't do for him to be poor and uncomfortable! After all that he had done in the world, after all that he had gone through, it would be odd if, at this time of day, he did not know what was good for himself! It was in that way that he regarded Florence's pertinacity.

He was rather unhappy at this period. It seemed to him that he was somewhat slighted on both sides,—or, if I may say so, less thought of on both sides than he deserved. Had Lady Ongar remained in town, as she ought to have done, he would have solaced himself, and at the same time have revenged himself upon Florence, by devoting some of his spare hours to that lady. It was Lady Ongar's sudden departure that had made him feel that he ought to rush at once into marriage. Now he had no consolation, except that of complaining to Mrs. Burton, and going frequently to the theatre. To Mrs. Burton he did complain a great deal, pulling her worsteds and threads about the while, sitting in idleness while she was working, just as Theodore Burton had predicted that he would do.

" I won't have you so idle, Harry," Mrs. Burton said to him one day. " You know you ought to be at your office now." It must be admitted on behalf of Harry Clavering, that they who liked him, especially women, were able to become intimate with him very easily. He had comfortable, homely ways about him, and did not habitually give himself airs. He had become quite domesticated at the Burtons' house during the ten weeks that he had been in London, and knew his way to Onslow Crescent almost too well. It may, perhaps, be surmised correctly that he would not have gone there so frequently if Mrs. Theodore Burton had been an ugly woman.

" It's all her fault," said he, continuing to snip a piece of worsted with a pair of scissors as he spoke. " She's too prudent by half."

" Poor Florence!"

" You can't but know that I should work three times as much if she had given me a different answer. It stands to reason any man would work under such circumstances as that. Not that I am idle, I believe. I do as much as any other man about the place."

" I won't have my worsted destroyed all the same. Theodore says that Florence is right."

" Of course he does; of course he'll say I'm wrong. I won't ask her again,—that's all."

" Oh, Harry! don't say that. You know you'll ask her. You would to-morrow, if she were here."

" You don't know me, Cecilia, or you would not say so. When I have made up my mind to a thing, I am generally firm about it. She said something about two years, and I will not say a word to alter that decision. If it be altered, it shall be altered by her."

In the meantime he punished Florence by sending her no special answer to her letter. He wrote to her as usual; but he made no reference to his last proposal, nor to her refusal. She had asked him to tell her that he was not angry, but he would tell her nothing of the kind. He told her when and where and how he would meet her, and convey her from Stratton to Clavering; gave her some account of a play he had seen; described a little dinner-party in Onslow Crescent; and told her a funny story about Mr. Walliker and the office at the Adelphi. But he said no word, even in rebuke, as to her decision about their marriage. He intended that this should be felt to be severe, and took pleasure in the pain that he would be giving. Florence, when she received her letter, knew that he was sore, and understood thoroughly the working of his mind. " I will comfort him when we are together," she said to herself. " I will make him reasonable when I see him." It was not the way in which he expected that his anger would be received.

One day on his return home he found a card on his table which surprised him very much. It contained a name but no address, but over the name there was a pencil memorandum, stating that the owner of the card would call again on his return to London after Easter. The name on the card was that of Count Pateroff. He remembered the name well as soon as he saw it, though he had never thought of it since the solitary occasion on which it had been mentioned to him. Count Pateroff was the man who had been Lord Ongar's friend, and respecting whom Lord Ongar had brought a false charge against his wife. Why should Count Pateroff call on him? Why was he in England? Whence had he learned the address in Bloomsbury Square? To that last question he had no difficulty in finding an answer. Of course he must have heard it from Lady Ongar. Count Pateroff had now left London! Had he gone to Ongar Park? Harry Clavering's mind was instantly filled with suspicion, and he became jealous in spite of Florence Burton. Could it be that Lady Ongar, not yet four months a widow, was receiving at her house in the country this man with whose name her own had been so fatally joined? If so, what could he think of such behaviour? He was very angry. He knew that he was angry, but he did not at all know that he was jealous. Was he not, by her own declaration to him, her only friend ; and as such could he entertain such a suspicion without anger? " Her friend ! " he said to himself. " Not if she has any dealings whatever with that man after what she has told me of him ! " He remembered at last that perhaps the count might not be at Ongar Park; but he must, at any rate, have had some dealing with Lady Ongar or he would not have known the address in Bloomsbury Square. " Count Pateroff! " he said, repeating the name, " I shouldn't wonder if I have to quarrel with that man." During the whole of that night he was thinking of Lady Ongar. As regarded himself, he knew that he had nothing to offer to Lady Ongar but a brotherly friendship; but, nevertheless, it was an injury to him that she should be acquainted intimately with any unmarried man but himself.

On the next day he was to go to Stratton, and in the morning a letter was brought to him by the postman; a letter, or rather a very short note. Guildford was the postmark, and he knew at once that it was from Lady Ongar.

Dear Mr. Clavering (the note said),—
        I was so sorry to leave London without seeing you; I shall be back by the end of April, and am keeping on the same rooms. Come to me, if you can, on the evening of the 30th, after dinner. He at last bade Hermy to write and ask me to go to Clavering for the Easter week. Such a note! I'll show it you when we meet. Of course I declined.
        But I write on purpose to tell you that I have begged Count Pateroff to see you. I have not seen him, but I have had to write to him about things that happened in Florence. He has come to England chiefly with reference to the affairs of Lord Ongar. I want you to hear his story. As far as I have known him he is a truth-telling man, though I do not know that I am able to say much more in his favour.
                                                Ever yours, J. O.

When he had read this he was quite an altered man. See Count Pateroff! Of course he would see him. What task could be more fitting for a friend than this, of seeing such a man under such circumstances. Before he left London he wrote a note for Count Pateroff, to be given to the count by the people at the lodgings should he call during Harry's absence from London. In this he explained that he would be at Clavering for a fortnight, but expressed himself ready to come up to London at a day's notice should Count Pateroff be necessitated again to leave London before the day named.

As he went about his business that day, and as he journeyed down to Stratton, he entertained much kinder ideas about Lady Ongar than he had previously done since seeing Count Pateroff's card.

CHAPTER X.

FLORENCE BURTON AT THE RECTORY.

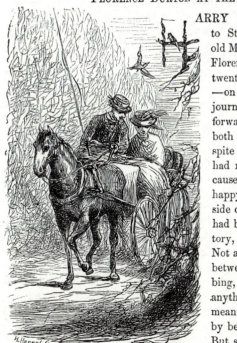

ARRY CLAVERING went down to Stratton, slept one night at old Mr. Burton's house, and drove Florence over to Clavering,— twenty miles across the country, —on the following day. This journey together had been looked forward to with great delight by both of them, and Florence, in spite of the snubbing which she had received from her lover because of her prudence, was very happy as she seated herself alongside of him in the vehicle which had been sent over from the rectory, and which he called a trap. Not a word had as yet been said between them as to that snubbing, nor was Harry minded that anything should be said. He meant to carry on his revenge by being dumb on that subject. But such was not Florence's intention. She desired not only to have her own way in this matter, but desired also that he should assent to her arrangements.

It was a charming day for such a journey. It was cold, but not cold enough to make them uncomfortable. There was a wind, but not wind enough to torment them. Once there came on a little shower, which just sufficed to give Harry an opportunity of wrapping his companion very closely, but he had hardly completed the ceremony before the necessity for it was over. They both agreed that this mode of travelling was infinitely preferable to a journey by railroad, and I myself should be of the same opinion if one could always make one's journeys under the same circumstances. And it must be understood that Harry, though no doubt he was still taking his revenge on Florence by abstaining from all allusion to her letter, was not disposed to make himself otherwise disagreeable. He played his part of lover very well, and Florence was supremely happy.

"Harry," she said, when the journey was more than half completed, "you never told me what you thought of my letter."

"Which letter?" But he knew very well which was the letter in question.

"My prudent letter,—written in answer to yours that was very imprudent."

"I thought there was nothing more to be said about it."

"Come, Harry, don't let there be any subject between us that we don't care to think about and discuss. I know what you meant by not answering me. You meant to punish me,—did you not, for having an opinion different from yours? Is not that true, Harry?"

"Punish you,—no; I did not want to punish you. It was I that was punished, I think."

"But you know I was right. Was I not right?"

"I think you were wrong, but I don't want to say anything more about it now."

"Ah, but, Harry, I want you to talk about it. Is it not everything to me,—everything in this world,—that you and I should agree about this? I have nothing else to think of but you. I have nothing to hope for but that I may live to be your wife. My only care in the world is my care for you! Come, Harry, don't be glum with me."

"I am not glum."

"Speak a nice word to me. Tell me that you believe me when I say that it is not of myself I am thinking, but of you."

"Why can't you let me think for myself in this?"

"Because you have got to think for me."

"And I think you'd do very well on the income we've got. If you'll consent to marry, this summer, I won't be glum, as you call it, a moment longer."

"No, Harry; I must not do that. I should be false to my duty to you if I did."

"Then it's no use saying anything more about it."

"Look here, Harry, if an engagement for two years is tedious to you——"

" Of course it is tedious. Is not waiting for anything always tedious ?
There's nothing I hate so much as waiting."

" But listen to me," said she, gravely. " If it is too tedious, if it is
more than you think you can bear without being unhappy, I will release
you from your engagement."

" Florence ! "

" Hear me to the end. It will make no change in me ; and then if
you like to come to me again at the end of the two years, you may be
sure of the way in which I shall receive you."

" And what good would that do ? "

" Simply this good, that you would not be bound in a manner that
makes you unhappy. If you did not intend that when you asked me to
be your wife —— Oh, Harry, all I want is to make you happy. That
is all that I care for, all that I think about ! "

Harry swore to her with ten thousand oaths that he would not release
her from any part of her engagement with him, that he would give her
no loophole of escape from him, that he intended to hold her so firmly
that if she divided herself from him, she should be accounted among
women a paragon of falseness. He was ready, he said, to marry her to-
morrow. That was his wish, his idea of what would be best for both of
them ;—and after that, if not to-morrow, then on the next day, and so on
till the day should come on which she should consent to become his wife.
He went on also to say that he should continue to torment her on the
subject about once a week till he had induced her to give way ; and then
he quoted a Latin line to show that a constant dropping of water will
hollow a stone. This was somewhat at variance with a declaration he
had made to Mrs. Burton, in Onslow Crescent, to the effect that he would
never speak to Florence again upon the subject; but then men do
occasionally change their minds, and Harry Clavering was a man who
often changed his.

Florence, as he made the declaration above described, thought that he
played his part of lover very well, and drew herself a little closer to him
as she thanked him for his warmth. " Dear Harry, you are so good and
so kind, and I do love you so truly ! " In this way the journey was
made very pleasantly, and when Florence was driven up to the rectory
door she was quite contented with her coachman.

Harry Clavering, who is the hero of our story, will not, I fear, have
hitherto presented himself to the reader as having much of the heroic
nature in his character. It will, perhaps, be complained of him that he
is fickle, vain, easily led, and almost as easily led to evil as to good. But
it should be remembered that hitherto he has been rather hardly dealt with
in these pages, and that his faults and weaknesses have been exposed
almost unfairly. That he had such faults and was subject to such weaknesses may be believed of him ; but there may be a question whether as
much evil would not be known of most men, let them be heroes or not be
heroes, if their characters were, so to say, turned inside out before our eyes.

Harry Clavering, fellow of his college, six feet high, with handsome face and person, and with plenty to say for himself on all subjects, was esteemed highly and regarded much by those who knew him, in spite of those little foibles which marred his character; and I must beg the reader to take the world's opinion about him, and not to estimate him too meanly thus early in this history of his adventures.

If this tale should ever be read by any lady who, in the course of her career, has entered a house under circumstances similar to those which had brought Florence Burton to Clavering rectory, she will understand how anxious must have been that young lady when she encountered the whole Clavering family in the hall. She had been blown about by the wind, and her cloaks and shawls were heavy on her, and her hat was a little out of shape,—from some fault on the part of Harry, as I believe,—and she felt herself to be a dowdy as she appeared among them. What would they think of her, and what would they think of Harry in that he had chosen such an one to be his wife? Mrs. Clavering had kissed her before she had seen that lady's face; and Mary and Fanny had kissed her before she knew which was which; and then a stout, clerical gentleman kissed her who, no doubt, was Mr. Clavering, senior. After that, another clerical gentleman, very much younger and very much slighter, shook hands with her. He might have kissed her, too, had he been so minded, for Florence was too confused to be capable of making any exact reckoning in the matter. He might have done so —that is, as far as Florence was concerned. It may be a question whether Mary Clavering would not have objected; for this clerical gentleman was the Rev. Edward Fielding who was to become her husband in three days' time.

"Now, Florence," said Fanny, "come upstairs into mamma's room and have some tea, and we'll look at you. Harry, you needn't come. You've had her to yourself for a long time, and can have her again in the evening."

Florence, in this way, was taken upstairs and found herself seated by a fire, while three pairs of hands were taking from her her shawls and hat and cloak, almost before she knew where she was.

"It is so odd to have you here," said Fanny. "We have only one brother, so, of course, we shall make very much of you. Isn't she nice, mamma?"

"I'm sure she is; very nice. But I shouldn't have told her so before her face, if you hadn't asked the question."

"That's nonsense, mamma. You mustn't believe mamma when she pretends to be grand and sententious. It's only put on as a sort of company air, but we don't mean to make company of you."

"Pray don't," said Florence.

"I'm so glad you are come just at this time," said Mary. "I think so much of having Harry's future wife at my wedding. I wish we were both going to be married the same day."

"But we are not going to be married for ever so long. Two years hence has been the shortest time named."

"Don't be sure of that, Florence," said Fanny. "We have all of us received a special commission from Harry to talk you out of that heresy; have we not, mamma?"

"I think you had better not tease Florence about that immediately on her arrival. It's hardly fair." Then, when they had drunk their tea, Florence was taken away to her own room, and before she was allowed to go downstairs she was intimate with both the girls, and had so far overcome her awe of Harry's mother as to be able to answer her without confusion.

"Well, sir, what do you think of her?" said Harry to his father, as soon as they were alone.

"I have not had time to think much of her yet. She seems to be very pretty. She isn't so tall as I thought she would be."

"No; she's not tall," said Harry, in a voice of disappointment.

"I've no doubt we shall like her very much. What money is she to have?"

"A hundred a year while her father lives."

"That's not much."

"Much or little, it made no difference with me. I should never have thought of marrying a girl for her money. It's a kind of thing that I hate. I almost wish she was to have nothing."

"I shouldn't refuse it if I were you."

"Of course, I shan't refuse it; but what I mean is that I never thought about it when I asked her to have me; and I shouldn't have been a bit more likely to ask her if she had ten times as much."

"A fortune with one's wife isn't a bad thing for a poor man, Harry."

"But a poor man must be poor in more senses than one when he looks about to get a fortune in that way."

"I suppose you won't marry just yet," said the father. "Including everything, you would not have five hundred a year, and that would be very close work in London."

"It's not quite decided yet, sir. As far as I am myself concerned, I think that people are a great deal too prudent about money. I believe I could live as a married man on a hundred a year, if I had no more; and as for London, I don't see why London should be more expensive than any other place. You can get exactly what you want in London, and make your halfpence go farther there than anywhere else."

"And your sovereigns go quicker," said the rector.

"All that is wanted," said Harry, "is the will to live on your income, and a little firmness in carrying out your plans."

The rector of Clavering, as he heard all this wisdom fall from his son's lips, looked at Harry's expensive clothes, at the ring on his finger, at the gold chain on his waistcoat, at the studs in his shirt, and smiled gently. He was by no means so clever a man as his son, but he knew something more of the world, and though not much given to general reading, he had read his son's character. "A great deal of firmness and of fortitude also is wanted for that kind of life," he said. "There are men who can go through it without suffering, but I would not advise any young man to commence it in a hurry. If I were you I should wait a year or two. Come, let's have a walk; that is, if you can tear yourself away from your lady-love for an hour. If there is not Saul coming up the avenue! Take your hat, Harry, and we'll get out the other way. He only wants to see the girls about the school, but if he catches us he'll keep us for an hour." Then Harry asked after Mr. Saul's love-affairs. "I've not heard one single word about it since you went away," said the rector. "It seems to have passed off like a dream. He and Fanny go on the same as ever, and I suppose he knows that he made a fool of himself." But in this matter the rector of Clavering was mistaken. Mr. Saul did not by any means think that he had made a fool of himself.

"He has never spoken a word to me since," said Fanny to her brother that evening; "that is, not a word as to what occurred then. Of course it was very embarrassing at first, though I don't think he minded it much. He came after a day or two just the same as ever, and he almost made me think that he had forgotten it."

"And he wasn't confused?"

"Not at all. He never is. The only difference is that I think he scolds me more than he used to do."

"Scold you!"

"Oh dear, yes; he always scolded me if he thought there was anything wrong, especially about giving the children holidays. But he does it now more than ever."

"And how do you bear it?"

"In a half-and-half sort of way. I laugh at him, and then do as I'm bid. He makes everybody do what he bids them at Clavering,—except papa, sometimes. But he scolds him, too. I heard him the other day in the library."

"And did my father take it from him?"

"He did, in a sort of a way. I don't think papa likes him; but then he knows, and we all know, that he is so good. He never spares himself in anything. He has nothing but his curacy, and what he gives away is wonderful."

"I hope he won't take to scolding me," said Harry, proudly.

"As you don't concern yourself about the parish, I should say that you're safe. I suppose he thinks mamma does everything right, for he never scolds her."

"There is no talk of his going away."

"None at all. I think we should all be sorry, because he does so much good."

Florence reigned supreme in the estimation of the rectory family all the evening of her arrival and till after breakfast the next morning, but then the bride elect was restored to her natural pre-eminence. This, however, lasted only for two days, after which the bride was taken away. The wedding was very nice, and pretty, and comfortable; and the people of Clavering were much better satisfied with it than they had been with that other marriage which has been mentioned as having been celebrated in Clavering Church. The rectory family was generally popular, and everybody wished well to the daughter who was being given away. When they were gone there was a breakfast at the rectory, and speeches were made with much volubility. On such an occasion the rector was a great man, and Harry also shone in conspicuous rivalry with his father. But Mr. Saul's spirit was not so well tuned to the occasion as that of the rector or his son, and when he got upon his legs, and mournfully expressed a hope that his friend Mr. Fielding might be enabled to bear the trials of this life with fortitude, it was felt by them all that the speaking had better be brought to an end.

"You shouldn't laugh at him, Harry," Fanny said to her brother afterwards, almost seriously. "One man can do one thing and one another. You can make a speech better than he can, but I don't think you could preach so good a sermon."

"I declare I think you're getting fond of him after all," said Harry. Upon hearing this Fanny turned away with a look of great offence. "No one but a brother," said she, "would say such a thing as that to me, because I don't like to hear the poor man ridiculed without cause." That evening, when they were alone, Fanny told Florence the whole story about Mr. Saul. "I tell you, you know, because you're like one of ourselves now. It has never been mentioned to any one out of the family."

Florence declared that the story would be sacred with her.

"I'm sure of that, dear, and therefore I like you to know it. Of course such a thing was quite out of the question. The poor fellow has no means at all,—literally none. And then, independently of that——"

"I don't think I should ever bring myself to think of that as the first thing," said Florence.

"No, nor would I. If I really were attached to a man, I think I would tell him so, and agree to wait, either with hope or without it."

"Just so, Fanny."

"But there was nothing of that kind; and, indeed, he's the sort of man that no girl would think of being in love with,—isn't he? You see he will hardly take the trouble to dress himself decently."

"I have only seen him at a wedding, you know."

"And for him he was quite bright. But you will see plenty of him if you will go to the schools with me. And indeed he comes here a great deal, quite as much as he did before that happened. He is so good, Florence!"

"Poor man!"

"I can't in the least make out from his manner whether he has given up thinking about it. I suppose he has. Indeed, of course he has, because he must know that it would be of no sort of use. But he is one of those men of whom you can never say whether they are happy or not; and you never can be quite sure what may be in his mind."

"He is not bound to the place at all,—not like your father?"

"Oh, no," said Fanny, thinking perhaps that Mr. Saul might find himself to be bound to the place, though not exactly with bonds similar to those which kept her father there.

"If he found himself to be unhappy, he could go," said Florence.

"Oh, yes; he could go if he were unhappy," said Fanny. "That is, he could go if he pleased."

Lady Clavering had come to the wedding; but no one else had been present from the great house. Sir Hugh, indeed, was not at home; but, as the rector truly observed, he might have been at home if he had so pleased. "But he is a man," said the father to the son, "who always does a rude thing if it be in his power. For myself, I care nothing for him, as he knows. But he thinks that Mary would have liked to have seen him as the head of the family, and therefore he does not come. He has greater skill in making himself odious than any man I ever knew. As for her, they say he's leading her a terrible life. And he's becoming so stingy about money, too!"

"I hear that Archie is very heavy on him."

"I don't believe that he would allow any man to be heavy on him, as you call it. Archie has means of his own, and I suppose has not run through them yet. If Hugh has advanced him money, you may be sure that he has security. As for Archie, he will come to an end very soon, if what I hear is true. They tell me he is always at Newmarket, and that he always loses."

But though Sir Hugh was thus uncourteous to the rector and to the rector's daughter, he was so far prepared to be civil to his cousin Harry, that he allowed his wife to ask all the rectory family to dine up at the house, in honour of Harry's sweetheart. Florence Burton was specially invited with Lady Clavering's sweetest smile. Florence, of course, referred the matter to her hostess, but it was decided that they should all accept the invitation. It was given, personally, after the breakfast, and it is not always easy to decline invitations so given. It may, I think, be doubted whether any man or woman has a right to give an invitation in this way, and whether all invitations so given should not be null and void, from the fact of the unfair advantage that has been taken. The man who fires at a sitting bird is known to be no sportsman. Now, the dinner-giver who catches his guest in an unguarded moment, and bags him when he has had no chance to rise upon his wing, does fire at a sitting bird. In this instance, however, Lady Clavering's little speeches were made only to Mrs. Clavering and to Florence. She said nothing personally to the rector, and he therefore might have escaped. But his wife talked him over.

"I think you should go for Harry's sake," said Mrs. Clavering.

"I don't see what good it will do Harry."

" It will show that you approve of the match."

" I don't approve or disapprove of it. He's his own master."

" But you do approve, you know, as you countenance it; and there cannot possibly be a sweeter girl than Florence Burton. We all like her, and I'm sure you seem to take to her thoroughly."

" Take to her ; yes, I take to her very well. She's ladylike, and though she's no beauty, she looks pretty, and is spirited. And I daresay she's clever."

" And so good."

" If she's good, that's better than all. Only I don't see what they're to live on."

" But as she is here, you will go with us to the great house ? "

Mrs. Clavering never asked her husband anything in vain, and the rector agreed to go. He apologized for this afterwards to his son by explaining that he did it as a duty. " It will serve for six months," he said. " If I did not go there about once in six months, there would be supposed to be a family quarrel, and that would be bad for the parish."

Harry was to remain only a week at Clavering, and the dinner was to take place the evening before he went away. On that morning he walked all round the park with Florence,—as he had before often walked with Julia,—and took that occasion of giving her a full history of the Clavering family. " We none of us like my cousin Hugh," he had said. " But she is at least harmless, and she means to be good-natured. She is very unlike her sister, Lady Ongar."

" So I should suppose, from what you have told me."

" Altogether an inferior being."

" And she has only one child."

" Only one,—a boy now two years old. They say he's anything but strong."

" And Sir Hugh has one brother."

" Yes ; Archie Clavering. I think Archie is a worse fellow even than Hugh. He makes more attempts to be agreeable, but there is something in his eye which I always distrust. And then he is a man who does no good in the world to anybody."

" He's not married ? "

" No ; he's not married, and I don't suppose he ever will marry. It's on the cards, Florence, that the future baronet may be ——" Then she frowned on him, walked on quickly, and changed the conversation.

CHAPTER XI.

Sir Hugh and his Brother Archie.

There was a numerous gathering of Claverings in the drawing-room of the Great House when the family from the rectory arrived comprising three generations; for the nurse was in the room holding the heir in her arms. Mrs. Clavering and Fanny of course inspected the child at once, as they were bound to do, while Lady Clavering welcomed Florence Burton. Archie spoke a word or two to his uncle, and Sir Hugh vouch-safed to give one finger to his cousin Harry by way of shaking hands with him. Then there came a feeble squeak from the infant, and there was a cloud at once upon Sir Hugh's brow. "Hermione," he said, "I wish you wouldn't have the child in here. It's not the place for him. He's always cross. I've said a dozen times I wouldn't have him down here just before dinner." Then a sign was made to the nurse, and she walked off with her burden. It was a poor, rickety, unalluring bairn, but it was all that Lady Clavering had, and she would fain have been allowed to show it to her relatives, as other mothers are allowed to do.

"Hugh," said his wife, "shall I introduce you to Miss Burton?"

Then Sir Hugh came forward and shook hands with his new guest, with some sort of apology for his remissness, while Harry stood by, glowering at him, with offence in his eye. "My father is right," he had said to himself when his cousin failed to notice Florence on her first entrance into the room; "he is impertinent as well as disagreeable. I don't care for quarrels in the parish, and so I shall let him know."

"Upon my word she's a doosed good-looking little thing," said Archie, coming up to him, after having also shaken hands with her;— "doosed good-looking, I call her."

"I'm glad you think so," said Harry, drily.

"Let's see; where was it you picked her up? I did hear, but I forget."

"I picked her up, as you call it, at Stratton, where her father lives."

"Oh, yes; I know. He's the fellow that coached you in your new business, isn't he? By-the-by, Harry, I think you've made a mess of it in changing your line. I'd have stuck to my governor's shop if I'd been you. You'd got through all the d—d fag of it, and there's the living that has always belonged to a Clavering."

"What would your brother have said if I had asked him to give it to me?"

"He wouldn't have given it of course. Nobody does give anything to anybody now-a-days. Livings are a sort of thing that people buy. But you'd have got it under favourable circumstances."

"The fact is, Archie, I'm not very fond of the church, as a pro-fession."

"I should have thought it easy work. Look at your father. He keeps a curate and doesn't take any trouble himself. Upon my word, if I'd known as much then as I do now, I'd have had a shy for it myself. Hugh couldn't have refused it to me."

"But Hugh can't give it while his uncle holds it."

"That would have been against me to be sure, and your governor's life is pretty nearly as good as mine. I shouldn't have liked waiting ; so I suppose it's as well as it is."

There may perhaps have been other reasons why Archie Clavering's regrets that he did not take holy orders were needless. He had never succeeded in learning anything that any master had ever attempted to teach him, although he had shown considerable aptitude in picking up acquirements for which no regular masters are appointed. He knew the fathers and mothers,—sires and dams I ought perhaps to say,—and grandfathers and grandmothers, and so back for some generations, of all the horses of note living in his day. He knew also the circumstances of all races,—what horses would run at them, and at what ages, what were the stakes, the periods of running, and the special interests of each affair. But not, on that account, should it be thought that the turf had been profitable to him. That it might become profitable at some future time, was possible; but Captain Archibald Clavering had not yet reached the profitable stage in the career of a betting-man, though perhaps he was beginning to qualify himself for it. He was not bad-looking, though his face was unprepossessing to a judge of character. He was slight and well made, about five feet nine in height, with light brown hair, which had already left the top of his head bald, with slight whiskers, and a well-formed moustache. But the peculiarity of his face was in his eyes. His eyebrows were light-coloured and very slight, and this was made more apparent by the skin above the eyes, which was loose and hung down over the outside corners of them, giving him a look of cunning which was disagreeable. He seemed always to be speculating, counting up the odds, and calculating whether anything could be done with the events then present before him. And he was always ready to make a bet, being ever provided with a book for that purpose. He would take the odds that the sun did not rise on the morrow, and would either win the bet or wrangle in the losing of it. He would wrangle, but would do so noiselessly, never on such occasions damaging his cause by a loud voice. He was now about thirty-three years of age, and was two years younger than the baronet. Sir Hugh was not a gambler like his brother, but I do not know that he was therefore a more estimable man. He was greedy and anxious to increase his store, never willing to lose that which he possessed, fond of pleasure, but very careful of himself in the enjoyment of it, handsome, every inch an English gentleman in appearance, and therefore popular with men and women of his own class who were not near enough to him to know him well, given to but few words, proud of his name, and rank, and place, well versed in the business of the world, a match for most men in money matters, not ignorant, though he rarely opened a book, selfish, and utterly regardless of the feelings of all those with whom he came in contact. Such were Sir Hugh Clavering, and his brother the captain.

Sir Hugh took Florence in to dinner, and when the soup had been eaten made an attempt to talk to her. "How long have you been here, Miss Burton?"

"Nearly a week," said Florence.

" Ah ;—you came to the wedding ; I was sorry I couldn't be here. It went off very well, I suppose ? "

" Very well indeed, I think."

" They're tiresome things in general,—weddings. Don't you think so ? "

" Oh dear, no,—except that some person one loves is always being taken away."

" You'll be the next person to be taken away yourself, I suppose ? "

" I must be the next person at home, because I am the last that is left. All my sisters are married."

" And how many are there ? "

" There are five married."

" Good heavens—Five ! "

" And they are all married to men in the same profession as Harry."

" Quite a family affair," said Sir Hugh. Harry, who was sitting on the other side of Florence, heard this, and would have preferred that Florence should have said nothing about her sisters. " Why, Harry," said the baronet, " if you will go into partnership with your father-in-law and all your brothers-in-law you could stand against the world."

" You might add my four brothers," said Florence, who saw no shame in the fact that they were all engaged in the same business.

" Good heaven ! " exclaimed Sir Hugh, and after that he did not say much more to Florence.

The rector had taken Lady Clavering into dinner, and they two did manage to carry on between them some conversation respecting the parish affairs. Lady Clavering was not active among the poor,—nor was the rector himself, and perhaps neither of them knew how little the other did ; but they could talk Clavering talk, and the parson was willing to take for granted his neighbour's good will to make herself agreeable. But Mrs. Clavering, who sat between Sir Hugh and Archie, had a very bad time of it. Sir Hugh spoke to her once during the dinner, saying that he hoped she was satisfied with her daughter's marriage ; but even this he said in a tone that seemed to imply that any such satisfaction must rest on very poor grounds. " Thoroughly satisfied," said Mrs. Clavering, drawing herself up and looking very unlike the usual Mrs. Clavering of the rectory. After that there was no further conversation between her and Sir Hugh. " The worst of him to me is always this," she said that evening to her husband, " that he puts me so much out of conceit with myself. If I were with him long I should begin to find myself the most disagreeable woman in England ! " " Then pray don't be with him long," said the rector.

But Archie made conversation throughout dinner, and added greatly to Mrs. Clavering's troubles by doing so. There was nothing in common between them, but still Archie went on laboriously with his work. It was a duty which he recognized, and at which he would work hard. When he had used up Mary's marriage, a subject which he economized

carefully, so that he brought it down to the roast saddle of mutton, he
began upon Harry's match. When was it to be? Where were they to
live? Was there any money? What manner of people were the Burtons?
Perhaps he might get over it? This he whispered very lowly, and it was
the question next in sequence to that about the money. When, in answer
to this, Mrs. Clavering with considerable energy declared that anything of
that kind would be a misfortune of which there seemed to be no chance
whatever, he recovered himself as he thought very skilfully. "Oh, yes;
of course; that's just what I meant;—a doosed nice girl I think her;—a
doosed nice girl, all round." Archie's questions were very laborious to his
fellow-labourer in his conversation because he never allowed one of them
to pass without an answer. He always recognized the fact that he was
working hard on behalf of society, and, as he used to say himself, that he
had no idea of pulling all the coach up the hill by his own shoulders.
Whenever therefore he had made his effort he waited for his companion's,
looking closely into her face, cunningly driving her on, so that she also
should pull her share of the coach. Before dinner was over Mrs.
Clavering found the hill to be very steep, and the coach to be very heavy.
"I'll bet you seven to one," said he,—and this was his parting speech as
Mrs. Clavering rose up at Lady Clavering's nod,—"I'll bet you seven to one,
that the whole box and dice of them are married before me,—or at any
rate as soon; and I don't mean to remain single much longer, I can tell
you." The "box and dice of them" was supposed to comprise Harry,
Florence, Fanny, and Lady Ongar, of all of whom mention had been
made, and that saving clause,—"at any rate as soon,"—was cunningly put
in, as it had occurred to Archie that he perhaps might be married on the
same day as one of those other persons. But Mrs. Clavering was not
compelled either to accept or reject the bet, as she was already moving
before the terms had been fully explained to her.

Lady Clavering as she went out of the room stopped a moment behind
Harry's chair and whispered a word to him. "I want to speak to you
before you go to-night." Then she passed on.

"What's that Hermione was saying?" asked Sir Hugh, when he had
shut the door.

"She only told me that she wanted to speak to me."

"She has always got some cursed secret," said Sir Hugh. "If there
is anything I hate, it's a secret." Now this was hardly fair, for Sir Hugh
was a man very secret in his own affairs, never telling his wife anything
about them. He kept two banker's accounts so that no banker's clerk
might know how he stood as regarded ready money, and hardly treated
even his lawyer with confidence.

He did not move from his own chair, so that, after dinner, his uncle
was not next to him. The places left by the ladies were not closed up,
and the table was very uncomfortable.

"I see they're going to have another week after this with the Pytch-
ley," said Sir Hugh to his brother.

"I suppose they will,—or ten days. Things ain't very early this year."

"I think I shall go down. It's never any use trying to hunt here after the middle of March."

"You're rather short of foxes, are you not?" said the rector, making an attempt to join the conversation.

"Upon my word I don't know anything about it," said Sir Hugh.

"There are foxes at Clavering," said Archie, recommencing his duty. "The hounds will be here on Saturday, and I'll bet three to one I find a fox before twelve o'clock, or, say, half-past twelve,—that is, if they'll draw punctually and let me do as I like with the pack. I'll bet a guinea we find, and a guinea we run, and a guinea we kill; that is, you know, if they'll really look for a fox."

The rector had been willing to fall into a little hunting talk for the sake of society, but he was not prepared to go the length that Archie proposed to take him, and therefore the subject dropped.

"At any rate I shan't stay here after to-morrow," said Sir Hugh, still addressing himself to his brother. "Pass the wine, will you, Harry; that is, if your father is drinking any."

"No more wine for me," said the rector, almost angrily.

"Liberty Hall," said Sir Hugh; "everybody does as they like about that I mean to have another bottle of claret. Archie, ring the bell, will you?" Captain Clavering, though he was further from the bell than his elder brother, got up and did as he was bid. The claret came, and was drunk almost in silence. The rector, though he had a high opinion of the cellar of the great house, would take none of the new bottle, because he was angry. Harry filled his glass, and attempted to say something. Sir Hugh answered him by a monosyllable, and Archie offered to bet him two to one that he was wrong.

"I'll go into the drawing-room," said the rector, getting up.

"All right," said Sir Hugh; "you'll find coffee there, I daresay. Has your father given up wine?" he asked, as soon as the door was closed.

"Not that I know of," said Harry.

"He used to take as good a whack as any man I know. The bishop hasn't put his embargo on that as well as the hunting, I hope?" To this Harry made no answer.

"He's in the blues, I think," said Archie. "Is there anything the matter with him, Harry?"

"Nothing as far as I know."

"If I were left at Clavering all the year, with nothing to do, as he is, I think I should drink a good deal of wine," said Sir Hugh. "I don't know what it is,—something in the air, I suppose,—but everybody always seems to me to be dreadfully dull here. You ain't taking any wine either. Don't stop here out of ceremony, you know, if you want to go after Miss Burton." Harry took him at his word, and went after Miss Burton, leaving the brothers together over their claret.

The two brothers remained drinking their wine, but they drank it in an uncomfortable fashion, not saying much to each other for the first ten minutes after the other Claverings were gone. Archie was in some degree afraid of his brother, and never offered to make any bets with him. Hugh had once put a stop to this altogether. "Archie," he had said, "pray understand that there is no money to be made out of me, at any rate not by you. If you lost money to me, you wouldn't think it necessary to pay ; and I certainly shall lose none to you." The habit of proposing to bet had become with Archie so much a matter of course, that he did not generally intend any real speculation by his offers ; but with his brother he had dropped even the habit. And he seldom began any conversation with Hugh unless he had some point to gain,—an advance of money to ask, or some favour to beg in the way of shooting, or the loan of a horse. On such occasions he would commence the negotiation with his usual diplomacy, not knowing any other mode of expressing his wishes ; but he was aware that his brother would always detect his manœuvres, and expose them before he had got through his first preface ; and, therefore, as I have said, he was afraid of Hugh.

"I don't know what's come to my uncle of late," said Hugh, after a while. "I think I shall have to drop them at the rectory altogether."

"He never had much to say for himself."

"But he has a mode of expressing himself without speaking, which I do not choose to put up with at my table. The fact is they are going to the mischief at the rectory. His eldest girl has just married a curate."

"Fielding has got a living."

"It's something very small then, and I suppose Fanny will marry that prig they have here. My uncle himself never does any of his own work, and now Harry is going to make a fool of himself. I used to think he would fall on his legs."

"He is a clever fellow."

"Then why is he such a fool as to marry such a girl as this, without money, good looks, or breeding ? It's well for you he is such a fool, or else you wouldn't have a chance."

"I don't see that at all," said Archie.

"Julia always had a sneaking fondness for Harry, and if he had waited would have taken him now. She was very near making a fool of herself with him once, before Lord Ongar turned up."

To this Archie said nothing, but he changed colour, and it may almost be said of him that he blushed. Why he was affected in so singular a manner by his brother's words will be best explained by a statement of what took place in the back drawing-room a little later in the evening.

When Harry reached the drawing-room he went up to Lady Clavering, but she said nothing to him then of especial notice. She was talking to Mrs. Clavering while the rector was reading,—or pretending to read,—a review, and the two girls were chattering together in another part of the room. Then they had coffee, and after awhile the two other men came in from their wine. Lady Clavering did not move at once, but she took the first opportunity of doing so, when Sir Hugh came up to Mrs. Clavering and spoke a word to her. A few minutes after that Harry found himself closeted with Lady Clavering, in a little room detached from the others, though the doors between the two were open.

"Do you know," said Lady Clavering, "that Sir Hugh has asked Julia to come here?" Harry paused a moment, and then acknowledged that he did know it.

"I hope you did not advise her to refuse."

"I advise her! Oh dear, no. She did not ask me anything about it."

"But she has refused. Don't you think she has been very wrong!"

"It is hard to say," said Harry. "You know I thought it very cruel that Hugh did not receive her immediately on her return. If I had been him I should have gone to Paris to meet her."

"It's no good talking of that now, Harry. Hugh is hard, and we all know that. Who feels it most, do you think; Julia or I? But as he has come round, what can she gain by standing off? Will it not be the best thing for her to come here?"

"I don't know that she has much to gain by it."

"Harry,—do you know that we have a plan?" "Who is we?" Harry asked; but she went on without noticing his question. "I tell you, because I believe you can help us more than any one, if you will. Only for your engagement with Miss Burton I should not mention it to you; and, but for that, the plan would, I daresay, be of no use."

"What is the plan?" said Harry, very gravely. A vague idea of what the plan might be had come across Harry's mind during Lady Clavering's last speech.

"Would it not be a good thing if Julia and Archie were to be married?" She asked the question in a quick, hesitating voice, looking at first eagerly up into his face, and then turning away her eyes, as though she were afraid of the answer she might read there. "Of course I know that you were fond of her, but all that can be nothing now."

"No," said Harry, "that can be nothing now."

"Then why shouldn't Archie have her? It would make us all so much more comfortable together. I told Archie that I should speak to you, because I know that you have more weight with her than any of us; but Hugh doesn't know that I mean it."

"Does Sir Hugh know of the,—the plan?"

"It was he who proposed it. Archie will be very badly off when he has settled with Hugh about all their money dealings. Of course Julia's money would be left in her own hands; there would be no intention to interfere with that. But the position would be so good for him; and it would, you know, put him on his legs."

"Yes," said Harry, "it would put him on his legs, I daresay."

"And why shouldn't it be so? She can't live alone by herself always. Of course she never could have really loved Lord Ongar."

"Never, I should think," said Harry.

"And Archie is good-natured, and good-tempered, and—and—and—good-looking. Don't you think so? I think it would just do for her. She'd have her own way, for he's not a bit like Hugh, you know. He's not so clever as Hugh, but he is much more good-natured. Don't you think it would be a good arrangement, Harry?" Then again she looked up into his face anxiously.

Nothing in the whole matter surprised him more than her eagerness in advocating the proposal. Why should she desire that her sister should be sacrificed in this way? But in so thinking of it he forgot her own position, and the need that there was to her for some friend to be near to her,—for some comfort and assistance. She had spoken truly in saying that the plan had originated with her husband; but since it had been suggested to her, she had not ceased to think of it, and to wish for it.

"Well, Harry, what do you say?" she asked.

"I don't see that I have anything to say."

"But I know you can help us. When I was with her the last time she declared that you were the only one of us she ever wished to see again. She meant to include me then especially, but of course she was not thinking of Archie. I know you can help us if you will."

"Am I to ask her to marry him?"

"Not exactly that; I don't think that would do any good. But you might persuade her to come here. I think she would come if you advised her; and then, after a bit, you might say a good word for Archie."

"Upon my word I could not."

"Why not, Harry?"

"Because I know he would not make her happy. What good would such a marriage do her?"

"Think of her position. No one will visit her unless she is first received here, or at any rate unless she comes to us in town. And then it would be up-hill work. Do you know Lord Ongar had absolutely determined at one time to—to get a divorce?"

"And do you believe that she was guilty?"

"I don't say that. No; why should I believe anything against my own sister when nothing is proved. But that makes no difference, if the world believes it. They say now that if he had lived three months longer she never would have got the money."

"Then they say lies. Who is it says so? A parcel of old women who delight in having some one to run down and backbite. It is all false, Lady Clavering."

"But what does it signify, Harry? There she is, and you know how people are talking. Of course it would be best for her to marry again; and if she would take Archie,—Sir Hugh's brother, my brother-in-law, nothing further would be said. She might go anywhere then. As her sister, I feel sure that it is the best thing she could do."

Harry's brow became clouded, and there was a look of anger on his face as he answered her.

"Lady Clavering," he said, "your sister will never marry my cousin Archie. I look upon the thing as impossible."

"Perhaps it is, Harry, that you,—you yourself would not wish it."

"Why should I wish it?"

"He is your own cousin."

"Cousin indeed! Why should I wish it, or why should I not wish it? They are neither of them anything to me."

"She ought not to be anything to you."

"And she is nothing. She may marry Archie, if she pleases, for me. I shall not set her against him. But, Lady Clavering, you might as well tell him to get one of the stars. I don't think you can know your sister when you suppose such a match to be possible."

"Hermione!" shouted Sir Hugh,—and the shout was uttered in a voice that always caused Lady Clavering to tremble.

"I am coming," she said, rising from her chair. "Don't set yourself against it, Harry," and then, without waiting to hear him further, she obeyed her husband's summons. "What the mischief keeps you in there?" he said. It seemed that things had not been going well in the larger room. The rector had stuck to his review, taking no notice of Sir Hugh when he entered. "You seem to be very fond of your book, all of a sudden," Sir Hugh had said, after standing silent on the rug for a few minutes.

"Yes, I am," said the rector,—"just at present."

"It's quite new with you, then," said Sir Hugh, "or else you're very much belied."

"Hugh," said Mr. Clavering, rising slowly from his chair, "I don't often come into my father's house, but when I do, I wish to be treated with respect. You are the only person in this parish that ever omits to do so."

"Bosh!" said Sir Hugh.

The two girls sat cowering in their seats, and poor Florence must have begun to entertain an uncomfortable idea of her future connexions. Archie made a frantic attempt to raise some conversation with Mrs. Clavering about the weather. Mrs. Clavering, paying no attention to Archie whatever, looked at her husband with beseeching eyes. "Henry," she said, "do not allow yourself to be angry; pray do not. What is the use?"

"None on earth," he said, returning to his book. "No use on earth;—and worse than none in showing it."

Then it was that Sir Hugh had made a diversion by calling to his wife. "I wish you'd stay with us, and not go off alone with one person in particular, in that way." Lady Clavering looked round and immediately saw that things were unpleasant. "Archie," she said, "will you ring for tea?" And Archie did ring. The tea was brought, and a cup was taken all round, almost in silence.

Harry in the meantime remained by himself thinking of what he had heard from Lady Clavering. Archie Clavering marry Lady Ongar,—marry his Julia! It was impossible. He could not bring himself even to think of such an arrangement with equanimity. He was almost frantic with anger as he thought of this proposition to restore Lady Ongar to the position in the world's repute which she had a right to claim, by such a marriage as that. "She would indeed be disgraced then," said Harry to himself. But he knew that it was impossible. He could see what would be the nature of Julia's countenance if Archie should ever get near enough to her to make his proposal! Archie indeed! There was no one for whom, at that moment, he entertained so thorough a contempt as he did for his cousin, Archie Clavering.

Let us hope that he was no dog in the manger;—that the feelings which he now entertained for poor Archie would not have been roused against any other possible suitor who might have been named as a fitting husband for Lady Ongar. Lady Ongar could be nothing to him!

But I fear that he was a dog in the manger, and that any marriage contemplated for Lady Ongar, either by herself or by others for her, would have been distasteful to him,—unnaturally distasteful. He knew that Lady Ongar could be nothing to him; and yet, as he came out of the small room into the larger room, there was something sore about his heart, and the soreness was occasioned by the thought that any second marriage should be thought possible for Lady Ongar. Florence smiled on him as he went up to her, but I doubt whether she would have smiled had she known all his heart.

Soon after that Mrs. Clavering rose to return home, having swallowed a peace-offering in the shape of a cup of tea. But though the tea had quieted the storm then on the waters, there was no true peace in the rector's breast. He shook hands cordially with Lady Clavering, without animosity with Archie, and then held out three fingers to the baronet. The baronet held out one finger. Each nodded at the other, and so they parted. Harry, who knew nothing of what had happened, and who was still thinking of Lady Ongar, busied himself with Florence, and they were soon out of the house, walking down the broad road from the front door.

"I will never enter that house again, when I know that Hugh Clavering is in it," said the rector.

"Don't make rash assertions, Henry," said his wife.

"I hope it is not rash, but I make that assertion," he said. "I will never again enter that house as my nephew's guest. I have borne a great deal for the sake of peace, but there are things which a man cannot bear."

Then, as they walked home, the two girls explained to Harry what had occurred in the larger room, while he was talking to Lady Clavering in the smaller one. But he said nothing to them of the subject of that conversation.

CHAPTER XII.

Lady Ongar takes Possession.

I do not know that there is in England a more complete gentleman's residence than Ongar Park, nor could there be one in better repair, or more fit for immediate habitation than was that house when it came into the hands of the young widow. The park was not large, containing about sixty or seventy acres. But there was a home-farm attached to the place, which also now belonged to Lady Ongar for her life, and which gave to the park itself an appearance of extent which it would otherwise have wanted. The house, regarded as a nobleman's mansion, was moderate in size, but it was ample for the requirements of any ordinarily wealthy family. The dining-room, library, drawing-rooms, and breakfast-room, were all large and well-arranged. The hall was handsome and spacious, and the bed-rooms were sufficiently numerous to make an auctioneer's mouth water. But the great charm of Ongar Park lay in the grounds immediately round the house, which sloped down from the terrace before the windows to a fast-running stream which was almost hidden, —but was not hidden,—by the shrubs on its bank. Though the domain itself was small, the shrubberies and walks were extensive. It was a place costly to maintain in its present perfect condition, but when that was said against it, all was said against it which its bitterest enemies could allege.

But Lady Ongar, with her large jointure, and with no external expenses whatever, could afford this delight without imprudence. Everything in and about the place was her own, and she might live there happily, even in the face of the world's frowns, if she could teach herself to find happiness in rural luxuries. On her immediate return to England, her lawyer had told her that he found there would be opposition to her claim, and that an attempt would be made to keep the house out of her hands. Lord Ongar's people would, he said, bribe her to submit to this by immediate acquiescence as to her income. But she had declared that she would not submit,—that she would have house and income and all ; and she had been successful. "Why should I surrender what is my own?" she had said, looking the lawyer full in the face. The lawyer had not dared to tell her that her opponents,—Lord Ongar's heirs,—had calculated on her anxiety to avoid exposure ; but she knew that that was meant. "I have nothing to fear from them," she said, "and mean to claim what is my own by my settlement." There had, in truth, been no ground for disputing her right, and the place was given up to her before she had been three months in England. She at once went down and took possession, and there she was, alone, when her sister was communicating to Harry Clavering her plan about Captain Archie.

She had never seen the place till she reached it on this occasion ; nor had she ever seen, nor would she now probably ever see, Lord Ongar's larger house, Courton Castle. She had gone abroad with him immediately on their marriage, and now she had returned a widow to take possession of his house. There she was in possession of it all. The furniture in the rooms, the books in the cases, the gilded clocks and grand mirrors about the house, all the implements of wealthy care about the gardens, the corn in the granaries and the ricks in the hay-yard, the horses in the stable, and the cows lowing in the fields,—they were all hers. She had performed her part of the bargain, and now the price was paid to her into her hands. When she arrived she did not know what was the extent of her riches in this world's goods; nor, in truth, had she at once the courage to ask questions on the subject. She saw cows, and was told of horses; and words came to her gradually of sheep and oxen, of poultry, pigs, and growing calves. It was as though a new world had opened itself before her eyes, full of interest, and as though all that world were her own. She looked at it, and knew that it was the price of her bargain. Upon the whole she had been very lucky. She had, indeed, passed through a sharp agony,—an agony sharp almost to death; but the agony had been short, and the price was in her hand.

A close carriage had met her at the station, and taken her with her maid to the house. She had so arranged that she had reached the station after dark, and even then had felt that the eyes of many were upon her as she went out to her carriage, with her face covered by a veil. She was all alone, and there would be no one at the house to whom she could speak;—but the knowledge that the carriage was her own perhaps consoled her. The housekeeper who received her was a stout, elderly, comfortable body, to whom she could perhaps say a few words beyond those which might be spoken to an ordinary servant; but she fancied at once that the housekeeper was cold to her, and solemn in her demeanour. "I hope you have good fires, Mrs. Button." "Yes, my lady." "I think I will have some tea; I don't want anything else to-night." "Very well, my lady." Mrs. Button, maintaining a solemn countenance, would not go beyond this; and yet Mrs. Button looked like a woman who could have enjoyed a gossip, had the lady been a lady to her mind. Perhaps Mrs. Button did not like serving a lady as to whom such sad stories were told. Lady Ongar, as she thought of this, drew herself up unconsciously, and sent Mrs. Button away from her.

The next morning, after an early breakfast, Lady Ongar went out. She was determined that she would work hard; that she would understand the farm; that she would know the labourers; that she would assist the poor; that she would have a school; and, above all, that she would make all the privileges of ownership her own. Was not the price in her hand, and would she not use it? She felt that it was very good that something of the price had come to her thus in the shape of land, and beeves, and wide, heavy outside garniture. From them she would pluck an interest which mere money could not have given her. She was out early, therefore, that she might look round upon the things that were her own.

And there came upon her a feeling that she would not empty this sweet cup at one draught, that she would dally somewhat with the rich banquet that was spread for her. She had many griefs to overcome, much sorrow to conquer, perhaps a long period of desolation to assuage, and she would not be prodigal of her resources. As she looked around her while she walked, almost furtively, lest some gardener as he spied her might guess her thoughts and tell how my lady was revelling in her pride of possession,—it appeared to her that those novelties in which she was to find her new interest were without end. There was not a tree there, not a shrub, not a turn in the walks, which should not become her friend. She did not go far from the house, not even down to the water. She was husbanding her resources. But yet she lost herself amidst the paths, and tried to find a joy in feeling that she had done so. It was all her own. It was the price of what she had done ; and the price was even now being paid into her hand,—paid with current coin and of full weight.

As she sat down alone to her breakfast, she declared to herself that this should be enough for her,—that it should satisfy her. She had made her bargain with her eyes open, and would not now ask for things which had not been stipulated in the contract. She was alone, and all the world was turning its back on her. The relatives of her late husband would, as a matter of course, be her enemies. Them she had never seen, and that they should speak evil of her seemed to be only natural. But her own relatives were removed from her by a gulf nearly equally wide. Of Brabazon cousins she had none nearer than the third or fourth degree of cousinship, and of them she had never taken heed, and expected no heed from them. Her set of friends would naturally have been the same as her sister's, and would have been made up of those she had known when she was one of Sir Hugh's family. But from Sir Hugh she was divided now as widely as from the Ongar people, and,—for any purposes of society, —from her sister also. Sir Hugh had allowed his wife to invite her to Clavering, but to this she would not submit after Sir Hugh's treatment to her on her return. Though she had suffered much, her spirit was unbroken. Sir Hugh was, in truth, responsible for her reception in England. Had he come forward like a brother, all might have been well. But it was too late now for Sir Hugh Clavering to remedy the evil he had done, and he should be made to understand that Lady Ongar would not become a suppliant to him for mercy. She was striving to think how "rich she was in horses, how rich in broidered garments and in gold," as she sat solitary over her breakfast ; but her mind would run off to other things, cumbering itself with unnecessary miseries and useless indignation. Had she not her price in her hand ?

Would she see the steward that morning ? No,—not that morning. Things outside could go on for a while in their course as heretofore. She feared to seem to take possession with pride, and then there was that conviction that it would be well to husband her resources. So she sent for Mrs. Button, and asked Mrs. Button to walk through the rooms with her. Mrs. Button came, but again declined to accept her lady's condescension. Every spot about the house, every room, closet, and wardrobe, she was ready to open with zeal ; the furniture she was prepared to describe, if Lady Ongar would listen to her ; but every word was spoken in a solemn voice, very far removed from gossiping. Only once was Mrs. Button moved to betray any emotion. "That, my lady, was my lord's mother's room, after my lord died,—my lord's father that was ; may God bless her." Then Lady Ongar reflected that from her husband she had never heard a word either of his father or his mother. She wished that she could seat herself with that woman in some small upstairs room, and then ask question after question about the family. But she did not dare to make the attempt. She could not bring herself to explain to Mrs. Button that she had never known anything of the belongings of her own husband.

When she had seen the upper part of the house, Mrs. Button offered to convoy her through the kitchens and servants' apartments, but she declined this for the present. She had done enough for the day. So she dismissed Mrs. Button, and took herself to the library. How often had she heard that books afforded the surest consolation to the desolate. She would take to reading ; not on this special day, but as the resource for many days and months, and years to come. But this idea had faded and become faint, before she had left the gloomy, damp-feeling, chill room, in which some former Lord Ongar had stored the musty volumes which he had thought fit to purchase. The library gave her no ease, so she went out again among the lawns and shrubs. For some time to come her best resources must be those which she could find outside the house.

Peering about, she made her way behind the stables, which were attached to the house, to a farmyard gate, through which the way led to the head-quarters of the live-stock. She did not go through, but she looked over the gate, telling herself that those barns and sheds, that wealth of straw-yard, those sleeping pigs and idle dreaming calves, were all her own. As she did so, her eye fell upon an old labourer, who was sitting close to her, on a felled tree, under the shelter of a paling, eating his dinner. A little girl, some six years old, who had brought him his meal tied up in a handkerchief, was crouching near his feet. They had both seen her before she had seen them, and when she noticed them, were staring at her with all their eyes. She and they were on the same side of the farmyard paling, and so she could reach them and speak to them without difficulty. There was apparently no other person near enough to listen, and it occurred to her that she might at any rate make a friend of this old man. His name, he said, was Enoch Gubby, and the girl was his grandchild. Her name was Patty Gubby. Then Patty got up and had her head patted by her ladyship and received sixpence. They neither of them, however, knew who her ladyship was, and, as far as Lady Ongar could ascertain without a question too direct to be asked, had never heard of her. Enoch Gubby said he worked for Mr. Giles, the steward,—that was

Was not the Price in her Hand?

for my lord, and as he was old and stiff with rheumatism he only got eight shillings a week. He had a daughter, the mother of Patty, who worked in the fields, and got six shillings a week. Everything about the poor Gubbys seemed to be very wretched and miserable. Sometimes he could hardly drag himself about, he was so bad with the rheumatics. Then she thought that she would make one person happy, and told him that his wages should be raised to ten shillings a week. No matter whether he earned it or not, or what Mr. Giles might say, he should have ten shillings a week. Enoch Gubby bowed, and rubbed his head, and stared, and was in truth thankful because of the sixpence in ready money; but he believed nothing about the ten shillings. He did not especially disbelieve, but simply felt confident that he understood nothing that was said to him. That kindness was intended, and that the sixpence was there, he did understand.

But Enoch Gubby got his weekly ten shillings, though Lady Ongar hardly realized the pleasure that she had expected from the transaction. She sent that afternoon for Mr. Giles, the steward, and told him what she had done. Mr. Giles did not at all approve, and spoke his disapproval very plainly, though he garnished his rebuke with a great many "my lady's." The old man was a hanger-on about the place, and for years had received eight shillings a week, which he had not half earned. "Now he will have ten, that is all," said Lady Ongar. Mr. Giles acknowledged that if her ladyship pleased, Enoch Gubby must have the ten shillings, but declared that the business could not be carried on in that way. Everybody about the place would expect an addition, and those people who did earn what they received, would think themselves cruelly used in being worse treated than Enoch Gubby, who, according to Mr. Giles, was by no means the most worthy old man in the parish. And as for his daughter—oh! Mr. Giles could not trust himself to talk about the daughter to her ladyship. Before he left her, Lady Ongar was convinced that she had made a mistake. Not even from charity will pleasure come, if charity be taken up simply to appease remorse.

The price was in her hand. For a fortnight the idea clung to her, that gradually she would realize the joys of possession ; but there was no moment in which she could tell herself that the joy was hers. She was now mistress of the geography of the place. There was no more losing herself amidst the shrubberies, no thought of economizing her resources. Of Mr. Giles and his doings she still knew very little, but the desire of knowing much had faded. The ownership of the haystacks had become a thing tame to her, and the great cart-horses, as to every one of which she had intended to feel an interest, were matters of indifference to her. She observed that since her arrival a new name in new paint,—her own name,—was attached to the carts, and that the letters were big and glaring. She wished that this had not been done, or, at any rate, that the letters had been smaller. Then she began to think that it might be well for her to let the farm to a tenant; not that she might thus get more money, but because she felt

that the farm would be a trouble.   The apples had indeed quickly turned
to ashes between her teeth !

On the first Sunday that she was at Ongar Park she went to the
parish church.   She had resolved strongly that she would do this, and
she did it ; but when the moment for starting came, her courage almost
failed her.   The church was but a few yards from her own gate, and she
walked there without any attendant.   She had, however, sent word to the
sexton to say that she would be there, and the old man was ready to show
her into the family pew.   She wore a thick veil, and was dressed, of
course, in all the deep ceremonious woe of widowhood.   As she walked
up the centre of the church she thought of her dress, and told herself that
all there would know how it had been between her and her husband.
She was pretending to mourn for the man to whom she had sold herself ;
for the man who through happy chance had died so quickly, leaving her
with the price in her hand !   All of course knew that, and all thought
that they knew, moreover, that she had been foully false to her bargain,
and had not earned the price !   That, also, she told herself.   But she
went through it, and walked out of the church among the village crowd
with her head on high.

Three days afterwards she wrote to the clergyman, asking him to call
on her.   She had come, she said, to live in the parish, and hoped to be
able, with his assistance, to be of some use among the people.   She would
hardly know how to act without some counsel from him.   The schools
might be all that was excellent, but if there was anything required she
hoped he would tell her.   On the following morning the clergyman called,
and, with many thanks for her generosity, listened to her plans, and
accepted her subsidies.   But he was a married man, and he said nothing
of his wife, nor during the next week did his wife come to call on her.   She
was to be left desolate by all, because men had told lies of her !

She had the price in her hands, but she felt herself tempted to do as
Judas did,—to go out and hang herself.

CHAPTER XIII.

A VISITOR CALLS AT ONGAR PARK.

IT will be remembered that Harry Clavering, on returning one evening to his lodgings in Bloomsbury Square, had been much astonished at finding there the card of Count Pateroff, a man of whom he had only heard, up to that moment, as the friend of the late Lord Ongar. At first he had been very angry with Lady Ongar, thinking that she and this count were in some league together, some league of which he would greatly disapprove; but his anger had given place to a new interest when he learned direct from herself that she had not seen the count, and that she was simply anxious that he, as her friend, should have an interview with the man. He had then become very eager in the matter, offering to subject himself to any amount of inconvenience so that he might effect that which Lady Ongar asked of him. He was not, however, called upon to endure

any special trouble or expense, as he heard nothing more from Count
Pateroff till he had been back in London for two or three weeks.

Lady Ongar's statement to him had been quite true. It had been even
more than true; for when she had written she had not even heard directly
from the count. She had learned by letter from another person that
Count Pateroff was in London, and had then communicated the fact to her
friend. This other person was a sister of the count's, who was now living
in London, one Madame Gordeloup,—Sophie Gordeloup,—a lady whom
Harry had found sitting in Lady Ongar's room when last he had seen her
in Bolton Street. He had not then heard her name; nor was he aware
then, or for some time subsequently, that Count Pateroff had any relative
in London.

Lady Ongar had been a fortnight in the country before she received
Madame Gordeloup's letter. In that letter the sister had declared herself to
be most anxious that her brother should see Lady Ongar. The letter had
been in French, and had been very eloquent,—more eloquent in its cause
than any letter with the same object could have been if written by an
Englishwoman in English; and the eloquence was less offensive than it
might, under all concurrent circumstances, have been had it reached
Lady Ongar in English. The reader must not, however, suppose that
the letter contained a word that was intended to support a lover's suit.
It was very far indeed from that, and spoke of the count simply as a
friend; but its eloquence went to show that nothing that had passed
should be construed by Lady Ongar as offering any bar to a fair friendship.
What the world said!—Bah! Did not she know,—she, Sophie,—and did
not her friend know,—her friend Julie,—that the world was a great liar?
Was it not even now telling wicked venomous lies about her friend Julie?
Why mind what the world said, seeing that the world could not be brought
to speak one word of truth? The world indeed! Bah!

But Lady Ongar, though she was not as yet more than half as old as
Madame Gordeloup, knew what she was about almost as well as that lady
knew what Sophie Gordeloup was doing. Lady Ongar had known the
count's sister in France and Italy, having seen much of her in one of
those sudden intimacies to which English people are subject when
abroad; and she had been glad to see Madame Gordeloup in London,—
much more glad than she would have been had she been received there
on her return by a crowd of loving native friends. But not on that
account was she prepared to shape her conduct in accordance with her
friend Sophie's advice, and especially not so when that advice had reference
to Sophie's brother. She had, therefore, said very little in return to the
lady's eloquence, answering the letter on that matter very vaguely; but,
having a purpose of her own, had begged that Count Pateroff might be
asked to call upon Harry Clavering. Count Pateroff did not feel himself
to care very much about Harry Clavering, but wishing to do as he was
bidden, did leave his card in Bloomsbury Square.

And why was Lady Ongar anxious that the young man who was her friend should see the man who had been her husband's friend, and whose name had been mixed with her own in so grievous a manner? She had called Harry her friend, and it might be that she desired to give this friend every possible means of testing the truth of that story which she herself had told. The reader, perhaps, will hardly have believed in Lady Ongar's friendship;—will, perhaps, have believed neither the friendship nor the story. If so, the reader will have done her wrong, and will not have read her character aright. The woman was not heartless because she had once, in one great epoch of her life, betrayed her own heart; nor was she altogether false because she had once lied; nor altogether vile, because she had once taught herself that, for such an one as her, riches were a necessity. It might be that the punishment of her sin could meet with no remission in this world, but not on that account should it be presumed that there was no place for repentance left to her.

As she walked alone through the shrubberies at Ongar Park she thought much of those other paths at Clavering, and of the walks in which she had not been alone; and she thought of that interview in the garden when she had explained to Harry,—as she had then thought so successfully,—that they two, each being poor, were not fit to love and marry each other. She had brooded over all that, too, during the long hours of her sad journey home to England. She was thinking of it still when she had met him, and had been so cold to him on the platform of the railway station, when she had sent him away angry because she had seemed to slight him. She had thought of it as she had sat in her London room, telling him the terrible tale of her married life, while her eyes were fixed on his and her head was resting on her hands. Even then, at that moment, she was asking herself whether he believed her story, or whether, within his breast, he was saying that she was vile and false. She knew that she had been false to him, and that he must have despised her when, with her easy philosophy, she had made the best of her own mercenary perfidy. He had called her a jilt to her face, and she had been able to receive the accusation with a smile. Would he now call her something worse, and with a louder voice, within his own bosom? And if she could convince him that to that accusation she was not fairly subject, might the old thing come back again? Would he walk with her again, and look into her eyes as though he only wanted her commands to show himself ready to be her slave? She was a widow, and had seen many things, but even now she had not reached her six-and-twentieth year.

The apples at her rich country-seat had quickly become ashes between her teeth, but something of the juice of the fruit might yet reach her palate if he would come and sit with her at the table. As she complained to herself of the coldness of the world, she thought that she would not care how cold might be all the world if there might be but one whom she could love, and who would 'love her. And him she had loved. To him, in old days,—in days which now seemed to her to be very old,—she had made confession of her love. Old as were those days, it could not be but he should still remember them. She had loved him, and him only. To none other had she ever pretended love. From none other had love been offered to her. Between her and that wretched being to whom she had sold herself, who had been half dead before she had seen him, there had been no pretence of love. But Harry Clavering she had loved. Harry Clavering was a man, with all those qualities which she valued, and also with those foibles which saved him from being too perfect for so slight a creature as herself. Harry had been offended to the quick, and had called her a jilt; but yet it might be possible that he would return to her.

It should not be supposed that since her return to England she had had one settled, definite object before her eyes with regard to this renewal of her love. There had been times in which she had thought that she would go on with the life which she had prepared for herself, and that she would make herself contented, if not happy, with the price which had been paid to her. And there were other times, in which her spirits sank low within her, and she told herself that no contentment was any longer possible to her. She looked at herself in the glass, and found herself to be old and haggard. Harry, she said, was the last man in the world to sell himself for wealth, when there was no love remaining. Harry would never do as she had done with herself! Not for all the wealth that woman ever inherited,—so she told herself,—would he link himself to one who had made herself vile and tainted among women! In this, I think, she did him no more than justice, though it may be that in some other matters she rated his character too highly. Of Florence Burton she had as yet heard nothing, though had she heard of her, it may well be that she would not on that account have desisted. Such being her thoughts and her hopes, she had written to Harry, begging him to see this man who had followed her,—she knew not why,—from Italy ; and had told the sister simply that she could not do as she was asked, because she was away from London, alone in a country house.

And quite alone she was sitting one morning, counting up her misery, feeling that the apples were, in truth, ashes, when a servant came to her, telling her that there was a gentleman in the hall desirous of seeing her. The man had the visitor's card in his hand, but before she could read the name, the blood had mounted into her face as she told herself that it was Harry Clavering. There was joy for a moment at her heart; but she must not show it,—not as yet. She had been but four months a widow, and he should not have come to her in the country. She must see him and in some way make him understand this,—but she would be very gentle with him. Then her eye fell upon the card, and she saw, with grievous disappointment, that it bore the name of Count Pateroff. No :—she was not going to be caught in that way. Let the result be what it might, she would not let Sophie Gordeloup, or Sophie's brother, get the better of her by such a ruse as that ! " Tell the gentleman, with my compliments," she said, as she handed back the card, " that I regret it greatly, but I can see no one now." Then the servant went away, and she sat wondering whether the count would be able

to make his way into her presence. She felt rather than knew that she had
some reason to fear him. All that had been told of him and of her had been
false. No accusation brought against her had contained one spark of truth.
But there had been things between Lord Ongar and this man which she
would not care to have told openly in England. And though, in his conduct
to her, he had been customarily courteous, and on one occasion had been
generous, still she feared him. She would much rather that he should
have remained in Italy. And though, when all alone in Bolton Street, she
had in her desolation welcomed his sister Sophie, she would have preferred
that Sophie should not have come to her, claiming to renew their friendship. But with the count she would hold no communion now, even
though he should find his way into the room.

A few minutes passed before the servant returned, and then he
brought a note with him. As the door opened Lady Ongar rose, ready
to leave the room by another passage ; but she took the note and read it.
It was as follows :—" I cannot understand why you should refuse to see
me, and I feel aggrieved. My present purpose is to say a few words to
you on private matters connected with papers that belonged to Lord
Ongar. I still hope that you will admit me.—P." Having read these
words while standing, she made an effort to think what might be the best
course for her to follow. As for Lord Ongar's papers, she did not believe
in the plea. Lord Ongar could have had no papers interesting to her in
such a manner as to make her desirous of seeing this man or of hearing
of them in private. Lord Ongar, though she had nursed him to the hour
of his death, earning her price, had been her bitterest enemy; and though
there had been something about this count that she had respected, she had
known him to be a man of intrigue and afraid of no falsehoods in his
intrigues,—a dangerous man, who might perhaps now and again do a
generous thing, but one who would expect payment for his generosity.
Besides, had he not been named openly as her lover ? She wrote to him,
therefore, as follows :—" Lady Ongar presents her compliments to Count
Pateroff, and finds it to be out of her power to see him at present." This
answer the visitor took and walked away from the front door without
showing any disgust to the servant, either by his demeanour or in his
countenance. On that evening she received from him a long letter,
written at the neighbouring inn, expostulating with her as to her conduct
towards him, and saying in the last line, that it was "impossible now
that they should be strangers to each other." " Impossible, that we
should be strangers," she said almost out loud. " Why impossible ? I
know no such impossibility." After that she carefully burned both the
letter and the note.

She remained at Ongar Park something over six weeks, and then,
about the beginning of May, she went back to London. No one had
been to see her, except Mr. Sturm, the clergyman of the parish ; and he,
though something almost approaching to an intimacy had sprung up
between them, had never yet spoken to her of his wife. She was not

quite sure whether her rank might not deter him,—whether under such
circumstances as those now in question, the ordinary social rules were not
ordinarily broken,—whether a countess should not call on a clergyman's
wife first, although the countess might be the stranger ; but she did not
dare to do as she would have done, had no blight attached itself to her
name. She gave, therefore, no hint ; she said no word of Mrs. Sturm,
though her heart was longing for a kind word from some woman's mouth.
But she allowed herself to feel no anger against the husband, and went
through her parish work, thanking him for his assistance.

Of Mr. Giles she had seen very little, and since her misfortune with
Enoch Gubby, she had made no further attempt to interfere with the wages
of the persons employed. Into the houses of some of the poor she had
made her way, but she fancied that they were not glad to see her. They
might, perhaps, have all heard of her reputation, and Gubby's daughter
may have congratulated herself that there was another in the parish as
bad as herself, or perhaps, happily, worse. The owner of all the wealth
around strove to make Mrs. Button become a messenger of charity
between herself and some of the poor ; but Mrs. Button altogether
declined the employment, although, as her mistress had ascertained, she
herself performed her own little missions of charity with zeal. Before
the fortnight was over, Lady Ongar was sick of her house and her park,
utterly disregardful of her horses and oxen, and unmindful even of the
pleasant stream which in these spring days rippled softly at the bottom of
her gardens.

She had undertaken to be back in London early in May, by appointment with her lawyer, and had unfortunately communicated the fact to
Madame Gordeloup. Four or five days before she was due in Bolton
Street, her mindful Sophie, with unerring memory, wrote to her, declaring
her readiness to do all and anything that the most diligent friendship
could prompt. Should she meet her dear Julie at the station in London ?
Should she bring any special carriage? Should she order any special
dinner in Bolton Street? She herself would of course come to Bolton
Street, if not allowed to be present at the station. It was still chilly in
the evenings, and she would have fires lit. Might she suggest a roast
fowl and some bread sauce, and perhaps a sweetbread,—and just one glass
of champagne? And might she share the banquet? There was not a
word in the note about the too obtrusive brother, either as to the offence
committed by him, or the offence felt by him.

The little Franco-Polish woman was there in Bolton Street, of course,
—for Lady Ongar had not dared to refuse her. A little, dry, bright woman
she was, with quick eyes, and thin lips, and small nose, and mean forehead, and scanty hair drawn back quite tightly from her face and head ;
very dry, but still almost pretty with her quickness and her brightness.
She was fifty, was Sophie Gordeloup, but she had so managed her years
that she was as active on her limbs as most women are at twenty-five.
And the chicken and the bread-sauce, and the sweetbread, and the cham-

pagne were there, all very good of their kind; for Sophie Gordeloup liked such things to be good, and knew how to indulge her own appetite, and to coax that of another person.

Some little satisfaction Lady Ongar received from the fact that she was not alone ; but the satisfaction was not satisfactory. When Sophie had left her at ten o'clock, running off by herself to her lodgings in Mount Street, Lady Ongar, after but one moment's thought, sat down and wrote a note to Harry Clavering.

"DEAR HARRY,—I am back in town. Pray come and see me to-morrow evening.
Yours ever,
"J. O."

CHAPTER XIV.

COUNT PATEROFF AND HIS SISTER.

AFTER an interval of some weeks, during which Harry had been down at Clavering and had returned again to his work at the Adelphi, Count Pateroff called again in Bloomsbury Square;—but Harry was at Mr. Beilby's office. Harry at once returned the count's visit at the address given in Mount Street. Madame was at home, said the servant-girl, from which Harry was led to suppose that the count was a married man ; but Harry felt that he had no right to intrude upon madame, so he simply left his card. Wishing; however, really to have this interview, and having been lately elected at a club of which he was rather proud, he wrote to the count asking him to dine with him at the Beaufort. He explained that there was a strangers' room,—which Pateroff knew very well, having often dined at the Beaufort,—and said something as to a private little dinner for two, thereby apologizing for proposing to the count to dine without other guests. Pateroff accepted the invitation, and Harry, never having done such a thing before, ordered his dinner with much nervousness.

The count was punctual, and the two men introduced themselves. Harry had expected to see a handsome foreigner, with black hair, polished whiskers, and probably a hook nose,—forty years of age or thereabouts, but so got up as to look not much more than thirty. But his guest was by no means a man of that stamp. Excepting that the count's age was alto-gether uncertain, no correctness of guess on that matter being possible by means of his appearance, Harry's preconceived notion was wrong in every point. He was a fair man, with a broad fair face, and very light blue eyes ; his forehead was low, but broad ; he wore no whiskers, but bore on his lip a heavy moustache which was not grey, but perfectly white—white it was with years of course, but yet it gave no sign of age to his face. He was well made, active, and somewhat broad in the shoulders, though rather below the middle height. But for a certain ease of manner which he possessed, accompanied by something of restlessness in his eye, any one would have taken him for an Englishman. And his speech hardly betrayed that he was not English. Harry, knowing that he was a foreigner, noticed now and again some little acquired distinctness of speech which is hardly natural to a native; but otherwise there was nothing in his tongue to betray him.

"I am sorry that you should have had so much trouble," he said, shaking hands with Harry. Clavering declared that he had incurred no trouble, and declared also that he would be only too happy to have taken any trouble in obeying a behest from his friend Lady Ongar. Had he been a Pole as was the count, he would not have forgotten to add that he would have been equally willing to exert himself with the view of making the count's acquaintance; but being simply a young Englishman, he was much too awkward for any such courtesy as that. The count observed the omission, smiled, and bowed. Then he spoke of the weather, and said that London was a magnificent city. Oh, yes, he knew London well,—had known it these twenty years;—had been for fifteen years a member of the Travellers';—he liked everything English, except hunting. English hunting he had found to be dull work. But he liked shooting for an hour or two. He could not rival, he said, the intense energy of an Englishman, who would work all day with his guns harder than ploughmen with their ploughs. Englishmen sported, he said, as though more than their bread, —as though their honour, their wives, their souls, depended on it. It was very fine! He often wished that he was an Englishman. Then he shrugged his shoulders.

Harry was very anxious to commence a conversation about Lady Ongar, but he did not know how at first to introduce her name. Count Pateroff had come to him at Lady Ongar's request, and therefore, as he thought, the count should have been the first to mention her. But the count seemed to be enjoying his dinner without any thought either of Lady Ongar or of her late husband. At this time he had been down to Ongar Park, on that mission which had been, as we know, futile; but he said no word of that to Harry. He seemed to enjoy his dinner thoroughly, and made himself very agreeable. When the wine was discussed he told Harry that a certain vintage of Moselle was very famous at the Beaufort. Harry ordered the wine of course, and was 'delighted to give his guest the best of everything; but he was a little annoyed at finding that the stranger knew his club better than he knew it himself. Slowly the count ate his dinner, enjoying every morsel that he took with that thoughtful, conscious pleasure which young men never attain in eating and drinking, and which men as they grow older so often forget to acquire. But the count never forgot any of his own capacities for pleasure, and in all things made the most of his own resources. To be rich is not to have one or ten thousand a year, but to be able to get out of that one or ten thousand all that every pound, and every shilling, and every penny will give you. After this fashion the count was a rich man.

"You don't sit after dinner here, I suppose," said the count, when he had completed an elaborate washing of his mouth and moustache. "I like this club because we who are strangers have so charming a room for our smoking. It is the best club in London for men who do not belong to it."

It occurred to Harry that in the smoking-room there could be no privacy. Three or four men had already spoken to the count, showing that he was well known, giving notice, as it were, that Pateroff would become a public man when once he was placed in a public circle. To have given a dinner to the count, and to have spoken no word to him about Lady Ongar, would be by no means satisfactory to Harry's feelings, though, as it appeared, it might be sufficiently satisfactory to the guest. Harry therefore suggested one bottle of claret. The count agreed, expressing an opinion that the 51 Lafitte was unexceptional. The 51 Lafitte was ordered, and Harry, as he filled his glass, considered the way in which his subject should be introduced.

"You knew Lord Ongar, I think, abroad?"

"Lord Ongar,—abroad! Oh, yes, very well ; and for many years here in London ; and at Vienna ; and very early in life at St. Petersburg. I knew Lord Ongar first in Russia when he was attached to the embassy as Frederic Courton. His father, Lord Courton, was then alive, as was also his grandfather. He was a nice, good-looking lad then."

"As regards his being nice, he seems to have changed a good deal before he died." This the count noticed by simply shrugging his shoulders and smiling as he sipped his wine. "By all that I can hear he became a horrid brute when he married," said Harry, energetically.

"He was not pleasant when he was ill at Florence," said the count.

"She must have had a terrible time with him," said Harry.

The count put up his hands, again shrugged his shoulders, and then shook his head. "She knew he was no longer an Adonis when he married her."

"An Adonis! No ; she did not expect an Adonis ; but she thought he would have something of the honour and feelings of a man."

"She found it uncomfortable, no doubt. He did too much of this, you know," said the count, raising his glass to his lips ; "and he didn't do it with 51 Lafitte. That was Ongar's fault. All the world knew it for the last ten years. No one knew it better than Hugh Clavering."

"But——" said Harry, and then he stopped. He hardly knew what it was that he wished to learn from the man, though he certainly did wish to learn something. He had thought that the count would himself have talked about Lady Ongar and those Florentine days, but this he did not seem disposed to do. "Shall we have our cigars now?" said Count Pateroff.

"One moment, if you don't mind."

"Certainly, certainly. There is no hurry."

"You will take no more wine?"

"No more wine. I take my wine at dinner, as you saw."

"I want to ask you one special question,—about Lady Ongar."

"I will say anything in her favour that you please. I am always ready to say anything in the favour of any lady, and, if needs be, to swear it. But anything against any lady nobody ever heard me say."

Harry was sharp enough to perceive that any assertion made under such a stipulation was worse than nothing. It was as when a man, in denying the truth of a statement, does so with an assurance that on that subject he should consider himself justified in telling any number of lies. "I did not write the book,—but you have no right to ask the question ; and I should say that I had not, even if I had." Pateroff was speaking of Lady Ongar in this way, and Harry hated him for doing so.

"I don't want you to say any good of her," said he, "or any evil."

"I certainly shall say no evil of her."

"But I think you know that she has been most cruelly treated."

"Well, there is about seven—thousand—pounds a year, I think ! Seven—thousand—a year ! Not francs, but pounds ! We poor foreigners lose ourselves in amazement when we hear about your English fortunes. Seven thousand pounds a year for a lady all alone, and a beau-tiful house ! A house so beautiful, they tell me !"

"What has that to do with it ?" said Harry ; whereupon the count again shrugged his shoulders. "What has that to do with it ? Because the man was rich he was not justified in ill-treating his wife. Did he not bring false accusations against her, in order that he might rob her after his death of all that of which you think so much ? Did he not bear false witness against her, to his own dishonour ?"

"She has got the money, I think,—and the beautiful house."

"But her name has been covered with lies."

"What can I do ? Why do you ask me ? I know nothing. Look here, Mr. Clavering, if you want to make any inquiry you had better go to my sister. I don't see what good it will do, but she will talk to you by the hour together, if you wish it. Let us smoke."

"Your sister ? "

"Yes, my sister. Madame Gordeloup is her name. Has not Lady Ongar mentioned my sister ? They are inseparables. My sister lives in Mount Street."

"With you ?"

"No, not with me ; I do not live in Mount Street. I have my address sometimes at her house."

"Madame Gordeloup ? "

"Yes, Madame Gordeloup. She is Lady Ongar's friend. She will talk to you."

"Will you introduce me, Count Pateroff?"

"Oh, no ; it is not necessary. You can go to Mount Street, and she will be delighted. There is the card. And now we will smoke." Harry felt that he could not, with good-breeding, detain the count any longer, and, therefore, rising from his chair, led the way into the smoking-room. When there, the man of the world separated himself from his young friend, of whose enthusiasm he had perhaps had enough, and was soon engaged in conversation with sundry other men of his own standing. Harry soon perceived that his guest had no further need of his coun-

"Did he not bear false witness against her?"

tenance, and went home to Bloomsbury Square by no means satisfied with
his new acquaintance.

On the next day he dined in Onslow Crescent with the Burtons, and
when there he said nothing about Lady Ongar or Count Pateroff. He
was not aware that he had any special reason for being silent on the
subject, but he made up his mind that the Burtons were people so far
removed in their sphere of life from Lady Ongar, that the subject would
not be suitable in Onslow Crescent. It was his lot in life to be concerned
with people of the two classes. He did not at all mean to say,—even to
himself,—that he liked the Ongar class the better ; but still, as such was
his lot, he must take it as it came, and entertain both subjects of interest,
without any commingling of them one with another. Of Lady Ongar and
his early love he had spoken to Florence at some length, but he did not
find it necessary in his letters to tell her anything of Count Pateroff and
his dinner at the Beaufort. Nor did he mention the dinner to his dear
friend Cecilia. On this occasion he made himself very happy in Onslow
Crescent, playing with the children, chatting with his friend, and enduring, with a good grace, Theodore Burton's sarcasm, when that ever-
studious gentleman told him that he was only fit to go about tied to a
woman's apron-string.

On the following day, about five o'clock, he called in Mount Street.
He had doubted much as to this, thinking that at any rate he ought, in the
first place, to write and ask permission. But at last he resolved that he
would take the count at his word, and presenting himself at the door, he
sent up his name. Madame Gordeloup was at home, and in a few moments
he found himself in the room in which the lady was sitting, and recognized
her whom he had seen with Lady Ongar in Bolton Street. She got up at
once, having glanced at the name upon the card, and seemed to know all
about him. She shook hands with him cordially, almost squeezing his
hand, and bade him sit down near her on the sofa. " She was so glad to
see him, for her dear Julie's sake. Julie, as of course he knew, was at
' Ongere' Park. Oh ! so happy,"—which, by the by, he did not know,—
" and would be up in the course of next week. So many things to do, of
course, Mr. Clavering. The house, and the servants, and the park, and
the beautiful things of a large country establishment ! But it was delightful, and Julie was quite happy ! "

No people could be more unlike to each other than this brother and
his sister. No human being could have taken Madame Gordeloup for an
Englishwoman, though it might be difficult to judge, either from her
language or her appearance, of the nationality to which she belonged.
She spoke English with great fluency, but every word uttered declared
her not to be English. And when she was most fluent she was most
incorrect in her language. She was small, eager, and quick, and appeared
quite as anxious to talk as her brother had been to hold his tongue. She
lived in a small room on the first floor of a small house ; and it seemed to
Harry that she lived alone. But he had not been long there before she

had told him all her history, and explained to him most of her circumstances. That she kept back something is probable; but how many are there who can afford to tell everything?

Her husband was still living, but he was at St. Petersburg. He was a Frenchman by family, but had been born in Russia. He had been attached to the Russian embassy in London, but was now attached to diplomacy in general in Russia. She did not join him because she loved England,—oh, so much! And, perhaps, her husband might come back again some day. She did not say that she had not seen him for ten years, and was not quite sure whether he was dead or alive; but had she made a clean breast in all things, she might have done so. She said that she was a good deal still at the Russian embassy; but she did not say that she herself was a paid spy. Nor do I say so now, positively; but that was the character given to her by many who knew her. She called her brother Edouard, as though Harry had known the count all his life; and always spoke of Lady Ongar as Julie. She uttered one or two little hints which seemed to imply that she knew everything that had passed between "Julie" and Harry Clavering in early days; and never mentioned Lord Ongar without some term of violent abuse.

"Horrid wretch!" she said, pausing over all the r's in the name she had called him. "It began, you know, from the very first. Of course he had been a fool. An old roué is always a fool to marry. What does he get, you know, for his money? A pretty face. He's tired of that as soon as it's his own. Is it not so, Mr. Clavering? But other people ain't tired of it, and then he becomes jealous. But Lord Ongar was not jealous. He was not man enough to be jealous. Hor-r-rid wr-retch!" She then went on telling many things which, as he listened, almost made Harry Clavering's hair stand on end, and which must not be repeated here. She herself had met her brother in Paris, and had been with him when they encountered the Ongars in that capital. According to her showing, they had, all of them, been together nearly from that time to the day of Lord Ongar's death. But Harry soon learned to feel that he could not believe all that the little lady told him.

"Edouard was always with him. Poor Edouard!" she said. "There was some money matter between them about écarté. When that wr-retch got to be so bad, he did not like parting with his money,—not even when he had lost it! And Julie had been so good always! Julie and Edouard had done everything for the nasty wr-retch." Harry did not at all like this mingling of the name of Julie and Edouard, though it did not for a moment fill his mind with any suspicion as to Lady Ongar. It made him feel, however, that this woman was dangerous, and that her tongue might be very mischievous if she talked to others as she did to him. As he looked at her,—and being now in her own room she was not dressed with scrupulous care,—and as he listened to her, he could not conceive what Lady Ongar had seen in her that she should have made a friend of her. Her brother, the count, was undoubtedly a gentleman in his manners and way of life, but he did not know by what name to call this woman, who called Lady Ongar Julie. She was altogether unlike any ladies whom he had known.

"You know that Julie will be in town next week?"

"No; I did not know when she was to return."

"Oh, yes; she has business with those people in South Audley Street on Thursday. Poor dear! Those lawyers are so harassing! But when people have seven—thousand—pounds a year, they must put up with lawyers." As she pronounced those talismanic words, which to her were almost celestial, Harry perceived for the first time that there was some sort of resemblance between her and the count. He could see that they were brother and sister. "I shall go to her directly she comes, and of course I will tell her how good you have been to come to me. And Edouard has been dining with you? How good of you. He told me how charming you are,"—Harry was quite sure then that she was fibbing,—"and that it was so pleasant! Edouard is very much attached to Julie; very much. Though, of course, all that was mere nonsense; just lies told by that wicked lord. Bah! what did he know?" Harry by this time was beginning to wish that he had never found his way to Mount Street.

"Of course they were lies," he said roughly.

"Of course, mon cher. Those things always are lies, and so wicked! What good do they do?"

"Lies never do any good," said Harry.

To so wide a proposition as this madame was not prepared to give an unconditional assent; she therefore shrugged her shoulders and once again looked like her brother.

"Ah!" she said. "Julie is a happy woman now. Seven—thousand —pounds a year! One does not know how to believe it; does one?"

"I never heard the amount of her income," said Harry.

"It is all that," said the Franco-Pole, energetically, "every franc of it, besides the house! I know it. She told me herself. Yes. What woman would risk that, you know; and his life, you may say, as good as gone? Of course they were lies."

"I don't think you understand her, Madame Gordeloup."

"Oh, yes; I know her, so well. And love her—oh, Mr. Clavering, I love her so dearly! Is she not charming? So beautiful you know, and grand. Such a will, too! That is what I like in a woman. Such a courage! She never flinched in those horrid days, never. And when he called her,—you know what,—she only looked at him, just looked at him, miserable object. Oh, it was beautiful!" And Madame Gordeloup, rising in her energy from her seat for the purpose, strove to throw upon Harry such another glance as the injured, insulted wife had thrown upon her foul-tongued, dying lord.

"She will marry," said Madame Gordeloup, changing her tone with a suddenness that made Harry start; "yes, she will marry of course.

Your English widows always marry if they have money. They are wrong, and she will be wrong; but she will marry."

"I do not know how that may be," said Harry, looking foolish.

"I tell you I know she will marry, Mr. Clavering; I told Edouard so yesterday. He merely smiled. It would hardly do for him, she has so much will. Edouard has a will also."

"All men have, I suppose."

"Ah, yes; but there is a difference. A sum of money down, if a man is to marry, is better than a widow's dower. If she dies, you know, he looks so foolish. And she is grand and will want to spend everything. Is she much older than you, Mr. Clavering? Of course I know Julie's age, though perhaps you do not. What will you give me to tell?" And the woman leered at him with a smile which made Harry think that she was almost more than mortal. He found himself quite unable to cope with her in conversation, and soon after this got up to take his leave. "You will come again," she said. "Do. I like you so much. And when Julie is in town, we shall be able to see her together, and I will be your friend. Believe me."

Harry was very far from believing her, and did not in the least require her friendship. Her friendship indeed! How could any decent English man or woman wish for the friendship of such a creature as that? It was thus that he thought of her as he walked away from Mount Street, making heavy accusations, within his own breast, against Lady Ongar as he did so. Julia! He repeated the name over to himself a dozen times, thinking that the flavour of it was lost since it had been contaminated so often by that vile tongue. But what concern was it of his? Let her be Julia to whom she would, she could never be Julia again to him. But she was his friend—Lady Ongar, and he told himself plainly that his friend had been wrong in having permitted herself to hold any intimacy with such a woman as that. No doubt Lady Ongar had been subjected to very trying troubles in the last months of her husband's life, but no circumstances could justify her, if she continued to endorse the false cordiality of that horribly vulgar and evil-minded little woman. As regarded the grave charges brought against Lady Ongar, Harry still gave no credit to them, still looked upon them as calumnies, in spite of the damning advocacy of Sophie and her brother; but he felt that she must have dabbled in very dirty water to have returned to England with such claimants on her friendship as these. He had not much admired the count, but the count's sister had been odious to him. "I will be your friend. Believe me." Harry Clavering stamped upon the pavement as he thought of the little Pole's offer to him. She be his friend! No, indeed;—not if there were no other friend for him in all London.

Sophie, too, had her thoughts about him. Sophie was very anxious in this matter, and was resolved to stick as close to her Julie as possible. "I will be his friend or his enemy;—let him choose." That had been Sophie's reflection on the matter when she was left alone.

CHAPTER XV.

AN EVENING IN BOLTON STREET.

TEN days after his visit in Mount Street, Harry received the note which Lady Ongar had written to him on the night of her arrival in London. It was brought to Mr. Beilby's office by her own footman early in the morning; but Harry was there at the time, and was thus able to answer it, telling Lady Ongar that he would come as she had desired. She had commenced her letter " Dear Harry," and he well remembered that when she had before written she had called him " Dear Mr. Clavering." And though the note contained only half-a-dozen ordinary words, it seemed to him to be affectionate, and almost loving. Had she not been eager to see him, she would hardly thus have written to him on the very instant of her return. " Dear Lady Ongar," he wrote, " I shall dine at my club, and be with you about eight. Yours always, H. C." After that he could hardly bring himself to work satisfactorily during the whole day. Since his interview with the Franco-Polish lady he had thought a good deal about himself, and had resolved to work harder and to love Florence Burton more devotedly than ever. The nasty little woman had said certain words to him which had caused him to look into his own breast and to tell himself that this was necessary. As the love was easier than the work, he began his new tasks on the following morning by writing a long and very affectionate letter to his own Flo, who was still staying at Clavering rectory;—a letter so long and so affectionate that Florence, in her ecstasy of delight, made Fanny read it, and confess that, as a love-letter, it was perfect.

" It's great nonsense, all the same," said Fanny.

" It isn't nonsense at all," said Florence; " and if it were, it would not signify. Is it true? That's the question."

" I'm sure it's true," said Fanny.

" And so am I," said Florence. " I don't want any one to tell me that."

" Then why did you ask, you simpleton?" Florence indeed was having a happy time of it at Clavering rectory. When Fanny called her a simpleton, she threw her arms round Fanny's neck and kissed her.

And Harry kept his resolve about the work too, investigating plans with a resolution to understand them which was almost successful. During those days he would remain at his office till past four o'clock, and would then walk away with Theodore Burton, dining sometimes in Onslow Crescent, and going there sometimes in the evening after dinner. And when there he would sit and read; and once when Cecilia essayed to talk to him, he told her to keep her apron-strings to herself. Then Theodore laughed and apologized, and Cecilia said that too much work made Jack a dull boy; and then Theodore laughed again, stretching out his legs and arms as he rested a moment from his own study, and declared that, under those circumstances, Harry never would be dull. And Harry, on those evenings, would be taken upstairs to see the bairns in their cots ; and as he stood with their mother looking down upon the children, pretty words would be said about Florence and his future life ; and all was going merry as a marriage bell. But on that morning, when the note had come from Lady Ongar, Harry could work no more to his satisfaction. He scrawled upon his blotting-paper, and made no progress whatsoever towards the understanding of anything. It was the day on which, in due course, he would write to Florence ; and he did write to her. But Florence did not show this letter to Fanny, claiming for it any meed of godlike perfection. It was a stupid, short letter, in which he declared that he was very busy, and that his head ached. In a postscript he told her that he was going to see Lady Ongar that evening. This he communicated to her under an idea that by doing so he made everything right. And I think that the telling of it did relieve his conscience.

He left the office soon after three, having brought himself to believe in the headache, and sauntered down to his club. He found men playing whist there, and, as whist might be good for his head, he joined them. They won his money, and scolded him for playing badly till he was angry, and then he went out for a walk by himself. As he went along Piccadilly, he saw Sophie Gordeloup coming towards him, trotting along, with her dress held well up over her ankles, eager, quick, and, as he said to himself, clearly intent upon some mischief. He endeavoured to avoid her by turning up the Burlington Arcade, but she was too quick for him, and was walking up the arcade by his side before he had been able to make up his mind as to the best mode of ridding himself of such a companion.

" Ah, Mr. Clavering, I am so glad to see you. I was with Julie last night. She was fagged, very much fagged ; the journey, you know, and the business. But yet so handsome ! And we talked of you. Yes, Mr. Clavering ; and I told her how good you had been in coming to me. She said you were always good ; yes, she did. When shall you see her ? "

Harry Clavering was a bad hand at fibbing, and a bad hand also at leaving a question unanswered. When questioned in this way he did not know what to do but to answer the truth. He would much rather not have said that he was going to Bolton Street that evening, but he could find no alternative. " I believe I shall see her this evening," he said, simply venturing to mitigate the evil of making the communication by rendering it falsely doubtful. There are men who fib with so bad a grace and with so little tact that they might as well not fib at all. They not only never arrive at success, but never even venture to expect it.

" Ah, this evening. Let me see. I don't think I can be there to-night ; Madame Berenstoff receives at the embassy."

" Good afternoon," said Harry, turning into Truefit's, the hair-dresser's, shop.

" Ah, very well," said Sophie to herself ; " just so. It will be better, much better. He is simply one lout, and why should he have it all? My God, what fools, what louts, are these Englishmen!" Now having read Sophie's thoughts so far, we will leave her to walk up the remainder of the arcade by herself.

I do not know that Harry's visit to Truefit's establishment had been in any degree caused by his engagement for the evening. I fancy that he had simply taken to ground at the first hole, as does a hunted fox. But now that he was there he had his head put in order, and thought that he looked the better for the operation. He then went back to his club, and when he sauntered into the card-room one old gentleman looked askance at him, as though inquiring angrily whether he had come there to make fresh misery. "Thank you; no,—I won't play again," said Harry. Then the old gentleman was appeased, and offered him a pinch of snuff. "Have you seen the new book about whist?" said the old gentleman. "It is very useful,—very useful. I'll send you a copy if you will allow me." Then Harry left the room, and went down to dinner.

It was a little past eight when he knocked at Lady Ongar's door. I fear he had calculated that if he were punctual to the moment, she would think that he thought the matter to be important. It was important to him, and he was willing that she should know that it was so. But there are degrees in everything, and therefore he was twenty minutes late. He was not the first man who has weighed the diplomatic advantage of being after his time. But all those ideas went from him at once when she met him almost at the door of the room, and, taking him by the hand, said that she was "so glad to see him,—so very glad. Fancy, Harry, I haven't seen an old friend since I saw you last. You don't know how hard all that seems."

"It is hard," said he; and when he felt the pressure of her hand, and saw the brightness of her eye, and when her dress rustled against him as he followed her to her seat, and he became sensible of the influence of her presence, all his diplomacy vanished, and he was simply desirous of devoting himself to her service. Of course, any such devotion was to be given without detriment to that other devotion which he owed to Florence Burton. But this stipulation, though it was made, was made quickly, and with a confused brain.

"Yes,—it is hard," she said. "Harry, sometimes I think I shall go mad. It is more than I can bear. I could bear it if it hadn't been my own fault,—all my own fault."

There was a suddenness about this which took him quite by surprise. No doubt it had been her own fault. He also had told himself that; though, of course, he would make no such charge to her. "You have not recovered yet," he said, "from what you have suffered lately. Things will look brighter to you after a while."

"Will they? Ah,—I do not know. But come, Harry; come and sit down, and let me get you some tea. There is no harm, I suppose, in having you here,—is there?"

" Harm, Lady Ongar ? "

" Yes,—harm, Lady Ongar." As she repeated her own name after him, nearly in his tone, she smiled once again; and then she looked as she used to look in the old days, when she would be merry with him. " It is hard to know what a woman may do, and what she may not. When my husband was ill and dying, I never left his bedside. From the moment of my marrying him till his death, I hardly spoke to a man but in his presence ; and when once I did, it was he that had sent him. And for all that people have turned their backs upon me. You and I were old friends, Harry, and something more once,—were we not ? But I jilted you, as you were man enough to tell me. How I did respect you when you dared to speak the truth to me. Men don't know women, or they would be harder to them."

" I did not mean to be hard to you."

" If you had taken me by the shoulders and shaken me, and have declared that before God you would not allow such wickedness, I should have obeyed you. I know I should." Harry thought of Florence, and could not bring himself to say that he wished it had been so. " But where would you have been then, Harry ? I was wrong and false and a beast to marry that man; but I should not, therefore, have been right to marry you and ruin you. It would have been ruin, you know, and we should simply have been fools."

" The folly was very pleasant," said he.

" Yes, yes ; I will not deny that. But then the wisdom and the prudence afterwards ! Oh, Harry, that was not pleasant. That was not pleasant ! But what was I saying ? Oh ! about the propriety of your being here. It is so hard to know what is proper. As I have been married, I suppose I may receive whom I please. Is not that the law ? "

" You may receive me, I should think. Your sister is my cousin's wife." Harry's matter-of-fact argument did as well as anything else, for it turned her thought at the moment.

" My sister, Harry ! If there was nothing to make us friends but our connection through Sir Hugh Clavering, I do not know that I should be particularly anxious to see you. How unmanly he has been, and how cruel."

" Very cruel," said Harry. Then he thought of Archie and Archie's suit. " But he is willing to change all that now. Hermione asked me the other day to persuade you to go to Clavering."

" And have you come here to use your eloquence for that purpose ? I will never go to Clavering again, Harry, unless it should be yours and your wife should offer to receive me. Then I'd pack up for the dear, dull, solemn old place though I was on the other side of Europe."

" It will never be mine."

" Probably not, and probably, therefore, I shall never be there again. No ; I can forgive an injury, but not an insult,—not an insult such as that. I will not go to Clavering; so, Harry, you may save your eloquence.

Hermione I shall be glad to see whenever she will come to me. If you can persuade her to that, you will persuade her to a charity."

" She goes nowhere, I think, without his—his——"

" Without his permission. Of course she does not. That, I suppose, is all as it should be. And he is such a tyrant that he will give no such permission. He would tell her, I suppose, that her sister was no fit companion for her."

" He could not say that now, as he has asked you there."

" Ah, I don't know that. He would say one thing first and another after, just as it would suit him. He has some object in wishing that I should go there, I suppose." Harry, who knew the object, and who was too faithful to betray Lady Clavering, even though he was altogether hostile to his cousin Archie's suit, felt a little proud of his position, but said nothing in answer to this. " But I shall not go ; nor will I see him, or go to his house when he comes up to London. When do they come, Harry ? "

" He is in town now."

" What a nice husband, is he not ? And when does Hermione come ? "

" I do not know ; she did not say. Little Hughy is ill, and that may keep her."

" After all, Harry, I may have to pack up and go to Clavering even yet,—that is, if the mistress of the house will have me."

" Never in the way you mean, Lady Ongar. Do not propose to kill all my relations in order that I might have their property. Archie intends to marry, and have a dozen children."

" Archie marry ! Who will have him ? But such men as he are often in the way by marrying some cookmaid at last. Archie is Hugh's body-slave. Fancy being body-slave to Hugh Clavering ! He has two, and poor Hermy is the other ; only he prefers not to have Hermy near him, which is lucky for her. Here is some tea. Let us sit down and be comfortable, and talk no more about our horrid relations. I don't know what made me speak of them. I did not mean it."

Harry sat down and took the cup from her hand, as she had bidden the servant to leave the tray upon the table.

" So you saw Count Pateroff," she said.

" Yes, and his sister."

" So she told me. What do you think of them ? " To this question Harry made no immediate answer. " You may speak out. Though I lived abroad with such as them for twelve months, I have not forgotten the sweet scent of our English hedgerows, nor the wholesomeness of English household manners. What do you think of them ? "

" They are not sweet or wholesome," said he.

" Oh, Harry, you are so honest ! Your honesty is beautiful. A spade will ever be a spade with you."

He thought that she was laughing at him, and coloured.

" You pressed me to speak," he said, " and I did but use your own words."

" Yes, but you used them with such straightforward violence ! Well, you shall use what words you please, and how you please, because a word of truth is so pleasant after living in a world of lies. I know you will not lie to me, Harry. You never did."

He felt that now was the moment in which he should tell her of his engagement, but he let the moment pass without using it. And, indeed, it would have been hard for him to tell. In telling such a story he would have been cautioning her that it was useless for her to love him,—and this he could not bring himself to do. And he was not sure even now that she had not learned the fact from her sister. " I hope not," he said. In all that he was saying he knew that his words were tame and impotent in comparison with hers, which seemed to him to mean so much. But then his position was so unfortunate ! Had it not been for Florence Burton he would have been long since at her feet ; for, to give Harry Clavering his due, he could be quick enough at swearing to a passion. He was one of those men to whom love-making comes so readily that it is a pity that they should ever marry. He was ever making love to women, usually meaning no harm. He made love to Cecilia Burton over her children's beds, and that discreet matron liked it. But it was a love-making without danger. It simply signified on his part the pleasure he had in being on good terms with a pretty woman. He would have liked to have made love in the same way to Lady Ongar ; but that was impossible, and in all love-making with Lady Ongar there must be danger. There was a pause after the expression of his last hopes, during which he finished his tea, and then looked at his boots.

" You do not ask me what I have been doing at my country-house."

" And what have you been doing there ? "

" Hating it."

" That is wrong."

" Everything is wrong that I do ; everything must be wrong. That is the nature of the curse upon me."

" You think too much of all that now."

" Ah, Harry, that is so easily said. People do not think of such things if they can help themselves. The place is full of him and his memories ; full of him, though I do not as yet know whether he ever put his foot in it. Do you know, I have a plan, a scheme, which would, I think, make me happy for one half-hour. It is to give everything back to the family. Everything ! money, house, and name ; to call myself Julia Brabazon, and let the world call me what it pleases. Then I would walk out into the streets, and beg some one to give me my bread. Is there one in all the wide world that would give me a crust ? Is there one, except yourself, Harry—one, except yourself ? "

Poor Florence ! I fear it fared badly with her cause at this moment. How was it possible that he should not regret, that he should not look back upon Stratton with something akin to sorrow ? Julia had been his first love, and to her he could have been always true. I fear he thought

of this now. I fear that it was a grief to him that he could not place himself close at her side, bid her do as she had planned, and then come to him,
and share all his crusts. Had it been open to him to play that part, he
would have played it well, and would have gloried in the thoughts of her
poverty. The position would have suited him exactly. But Florence was
in the way, and he could not do it. How was he to answer Lady Ongar?
It was more difficult now than ever to tell her of Florence Burton.

His eyes were full of tears, and she accepted that as his excuse for not
answering her. " I suppose they would say that I was a romantic fool.
When the price has been taken one cannot cleanse oneself of the stain.
With Judas, you know, it was not sufficient that he gave back the money.
Life was too heavy for him, and so he went out and hanged himself."

" Julia," he said, getting up from his chair, and going over to where
she sat on a sofa, " Julia, it is horrid to hear you speak of yourself in
that way. I will not have it. You are not such a one as the Iscariot."
And as he spoke to her, he found her hand in his.

" I wish you had my burden, Harry, for one half day, so that you
might know its weight."

" I wish I could bear it for you—for life."

" To be always alone, Harry; to have none that come to me and
scold me, and love me, and sometimes make me smile! You will scold me
at any rate; will you not? It is terrible to have no one near one that
will speak to one with the old easiness of familiar affection. And then the
pretence of it where it does not, cannot, could not, exist! Oh, that
woman, Harry;—that woman who comes here and calls me Julie!
And she has got me to promise too that I would call her Sophie! I know
that you despise me because she comes here. Yes; I can see it. You said
at once that she was not wholesome, with your dear outspoken honesty."

" It was your word."

" And she is not wholesome, whosever word it was. She was there,
hanging about him when he was so bad, before the worst came. She read
novels to him,—books that I never saw, and played ecarté with him for
what she called gloves. I believe in my heart she was spying me, and I
let her come and go as she would, because I would not seem to be afraid
of her. So it grew. And once or twice she was useful to me. A
woman, Harry, wants to have a woman near her sometimes,—even
though it be such an unwholesome creature as Sophie Gordeloup. You
must not think too badly of me on her account."

" I will not ;—I will not think badly of you at all."

" He is better, is he not? I know little of him or nothing, but he has
a more reputable outside than she has. Indeed I liked him. He had
known Lord Ongar well; and though he did not toady him nor was afraid
of him, yet he was gentle and considerate. Once to me he said words
that I was called on to resent ;—but he never repeated them, and I know
that he was prompted by him who should have protected me. It is too
bad, Harry, is it not? Too bad almost to be believed by such as you."

" It is very bad," said Harry.

" After that he was always courteous ; and when the end came and things were very terrible, he behaved well and kindly. He went in and out quietly, and like an old friend. He paid for everything, and was useful. I know that even this made people talk ;—yes, Harry, even at such a moment as that ! But in spite of the talking I did better with him then than I could have done without him."

" He looks like a man who could be kind if he chooses."

" He is one of those, Harry, who find it easy to be good-natured, and who are soft by nature, as cats are,—not from their heart, but through instinctive propensity to softness. When it suits them, they scratch, even though they have been ever so soft before. Count Pateroff is a cat. You, Harry, I think are a dog." She perhaps expected that he would promise to her that he would be her dog,—a dog in constancy and affection ; but he was still mindful in part of Florence, and restrained himself.

" I must tell you something further," she said. " And indeed it is this that I particularly want to tell you. I have not seen him, you know, since I parted with him at Florence."

" I did not know," said Harry.

" I thought I had told you. However, so it is. And now, listen :— He came down to Ongar Park the other day while I was there, and sent in his card. When I refused to receive him, he wrote to me pressing his visit. I still declined, and he wrote again. I burned his note, because I did not choose that anything from him should be in my possession. He told some story about papers of Lord Ongar. I have nothing to do with Lord Ongar's papers. Everything of which I knew was sealed up in the count's presence and in mine, and was sent to the lawyers for the executors. I looked at nothing ; not at one word in a single letter. What could he have to say to me of Lord Ongar's papers ? "

" Or he might have written ? "

" At any rate he should not have come there, Harry. I would not see him, nor, if I can help it, will I see him here. I will be open with you, Harry. I think that perhaps it might suit him to make me his wife. Such an arrangement, however, would not suit me. I am not going to be frightened into marrying a man, because he has been falsely called my lover. If I cannot escape the calumny in any other way, I will not escape it in that way."

" Has he said anything ? "

" No ; not a word. I have not seen him since the day after Lord Ongar's funeral. But I have seen his sister."

" And has she proposed such a thing ? "

" No, she has not proposed it. But she talks of it, saying that it would not do. Then, when I tell her that of course it would not do, she shows me all that would make it expedient. She is so sly and so false, that with all my eyes open I cannot quite understand her, or quite know what she is doing. I do not feel sure that she wishes it herself."

" She told me that it would not do."

" She did, did she? If she speaks of it again, tell her that she is right, that it will never do. Had he not come down to Ongar Park, I should not have mentioned this to you. I should not have thought that he had in truth any such scheme in his head. He did not tell you that he had been there? "

" He did not mention it. Indeed, he said very little about you at all."

" No, he would not. He is cautious. He never talks of anybody to anybody. He speaks only of the outward things of the world. Now, Harry, what you must do for me is this." As she was speaking to him she was leaning again upon the table, with her forehead resting upon her hands. Her small widow's cap had become thus thrust back, and was now nearly off her head, so that her rich brown hair was to be seen in its full luxuriance, rich and lovely as it had ever been. Could it be that she felt,—half thought, half felt, without knowing that she thought it,— that while the signs of her widowhood were about her, telling in their too plain language the tale of what she had been, he could not dare to speak to her of his love? She was indeed a widow, but not as are other widows. She had confessed, did hourly confess to herself, the guilt which she had committed in marrying that man; but the very fact of such confessions, of such acknowledgment, absolved her from the necessity of any show of sorrow. When she declared how she had despised and hated her late lord, she threw off mentally all her weeds. Mourning, the appearance even of mourning, became impossible to her, and the cap upon her head was declared openly to be a sacrifice to the world's requirements. It was now pushed back, but I fancy that nothing like a thought on the matter had made itself plain to her mind. " What you must do for me is this," she continued. " You must see Count Pateroff again, and tell him from me,—as my friend,—that I cannot consent to see him. Tell him that if he will think of it, he must know the reason why."

" Of course he will know."

" Tell him what I say, all the same; and tell him that as I have hitherto had cause to be grateful to him for his kindness, so also I hope he will not put an end to that feeling by anything now, that would not be kind. If there be papers of Lord Ongar's, he can take them either to my lawyers, if that be fit, or to those of the family. You can tell him that, can you not? "

" Oh, yes; I can tell him."

" And have you any objection? "

" None for myself. The question is,—would it not come better from some one else? "

" Because you are a young man, you mean? Whom else can I trust, Harry? To whom can I go? Would you have me ask Hugh to do this? Or, perhaps you think Archie Clavering would be a proper messenger. Who else have I got? "

" Would not his sister be better ? "

" How should I know that she had told him ? She would tell him her own story,—what she herself wished. And whatever story she told, he would not believe it. They know each other better than you and I know them. It must be you, Harry, if you will do it."

" Of course I will do it. I will try and see him to-morrow. Where does he live ? "

" How should I know ? Perhaps nobody knows ; no one, perhaps, of all those with whom he associates constantly. They do not live after our fashion, do they, these foreigners ? But you will find him at his club, or hear of him at the house in Mount Street. You will do it ; eh, Harry ? "

" I will."

" That is my good Harry. But I suppose you would do anything I asked you. Ah, well ; it is good to have one friend, if one has no more. Look, Harry ! if it is not near eleven o'clock ! Did you know that you had been here nearly three hours ? And I have given you nothing but a cup of tea ! "

" What else do you think I have wanted ? "

" At your club you would have had cigars and brandy-and-water, and billiards, and broiled bones, and oysters, and tankards of beer. I know all about it. You have been very patient with me. If you go quick perhaps you will not be too late for the tankards and the oysters."

" I never have any tankards or any oysters."

" Then it is cigars and brandy-and-water. Go quick, and perhaps you may not be too late."

" I will go, but not there. One cannot change one's thoughts so suddenly."

" Go, then ; and do not change your thoughts. Go and think of me, and pity me. Pity me for what I have got, but pity me most for what I have lost." Harry did not say another word, but took her hand, and kissed it, and then left her.

Pity her for what she had lost ! What had she lost ? What did she mean by that ? He knew well what she meant by pitying her for what she had got. What had she lost ? She had lost him. Did she intend to evoke his pity for that loss ? She had lost him. Yes, indeed. Whether or no the loss was one to regret, he would not say to himself; or rather, he, of course, declared that it was not ; but such as it was, it had been incurred. He was now the property of Florence Burton, and, whatever happened, he would be true to her.

Perhaps he pitied himself also. If so, it is to be hoped that Florence may never know of such pity. Before he went to bed, when he was praying on his knees, he inserted it in his prayers that the God in whom he believed might make him true in his faith to Florence Burton.

CHAPTER XVI.

THE RIVALS.

LADY ONGAR sat alone, long into the night, when Harry Clavering had left her. She sat there long, getting up occasionally from her seat, once or twice attempting to write at her desk, looking now and then at a paper or two, and then at a small picture which she had, but passing the long hours in thinking,—in long, sad, solitary thoughts. What should she do with herself,—with herself, her title, and her money? Would it be still well that she should do something, that she should make some attempt; or should she, in truth, abandon all, as the arch-traitor did, and acknowledge that for her foot there could no longer be a resting-place on the earth? At six-and-twenty, with youth, beauty, and wealth at her command, must she despair? But her youth had been stained, her beauty had lost its freshness; and as for her wealth, had she not stolen it? Did not the weight of the theft sit so heavy on her, that her brightest thought was one which prompted her to abandon it?

As to that idea of giving up her income and her house, and calling herself again Julia Brabazon, though there was something in the poetry of it which would now and again for half an hour relieve her, yet she hardly proposed such a course to herself as a reality. The world in which she had lived had taught her to laugh at romance, to laugh at it even while she liked its beauty; and she would tell herself that for such a one as her to do such a thing as this, would be to insure for herself the ridicule of all who knew her name. What would Sir Hugh say, and her sister? What Count Pateroff and the faithful Sophie? What all the Ongar tribe, who would reap the rich harvest of her insanity? These latter would offer to provide her a place in some convenient asylum, and the others would all agree that such would be her fitting destiny. She could bear the idea of walking forth, as she had said, penniless into the street, without a crust; but she could not bear the idea of being laughed at when she got there.

To her, in her position, her only escape was by marriage. It was the solitude of her position which maddened her;—its solitude, or the necessity of breaking that solitude by the presence of those who were odious to her. Whether it were better to be alone, feeding on the bitterness of her own thoughts, or to be comforted by the fulsome flatteries and odious falsenesses of Sophie Gordeloup, she could not tell. She hated herself for her loneliness, but she hated herself almost worse for submitting herself to the society of Sophie Gordeloup. Why not give all that she possessed to Harry Clavering—herself, her income, her rich pastures and horses and oxen, and try whether the world would not be better to her when she had done so?

She had learned to laugh at romance, but still she believed in love. While that bargain was going on as to her settlement, she had laughed at romance, and had told herself that in this world worldly prosperity was everything. Sir Hugh then had stood by her with truth, for he had well understood the matter, and could enter into it with zest. Lord Ongar, in his state of health, had not been in a position to make close stipulations as to the dower in the event of his proposed wife becoming a widow. " No, no; we won't stand that," Sir Hugh had said to the lawyers. " We all hope, of course, that Lord Ongar may live long; no doubt he'll turn over a new leaf, and die at ninety. But in such a case as this the widow must not be fettered." The widow had not been fettered, and Julia had been made to understand the full advantage of such an arrangement. But still she had believed in love when she had bade farewell to Harry in the garden. She had told herself then, even then, that she would have better liked to have taken him and his love,—if only she could have afforded it. He had not dreamed that on leaving him she had gone from him to her room, and taken out his picture,—the same that she had with her now in Bolton Street,—and had kissed it, bidding him farewell there with a passion which she could not display in his presence. And she had thought of his offer about the money over and over again. "Yes," she would say; "that man loved me. He would have given me all he had to relieve me, though nothing was to come to him in return." She had, at any rate, been loved once; and she almost wished that she had taken the money, that she might now have an opportunity of repaying it.

And she was again free, and her old lover was again by her side. Had that fatal episode in her life been so fatal that she must now regard herself as tainted and unfit for him? There was no longer anything to separate them,—anything of which she was aware, unless it was that. And as for his love,—did he not look and speak as though he loved her still? Had he not pressed her hand passionately, and kissed it, and once more called her Julia? How should it be that he should not love her? In such a case as his, love might have been turned to hatred or to enmity; but it was not so with him. He called himself her friend. How could there be friendship between them without love?

And then she thought how much with her wealth she might do for him. With all his early studies and his talent Harry Clavering was not the man, she thought, to make his way in the world by hard work; but with such an income as she could give him, he might shine among the proud ones of his nation. He should go into Parliament, and do great things. He should be lord of all. It should all be his without a word of reserve. She had been mercenary once, but she would atone for that now by open-handed, undoubting generosity. She herself had learned to hate the house and fields and widespread comforts of Ongar Park. She had walked among it all alone, and despised. But it would be a glory to her to see him go forth, with Giles at his heels, boldly giving his orders, changing this and improving that. He would be rebuked for no errors, let him do with Enoch Gubby and the rest of them what he pleased! And then the parson's wife would be glad enough to come to her, and the house would be full of smiling faces. And it might be that God would be good to her, and that she would have treasures, as other women had them, and that the flavour would come back to the apples, and that the ashes would cease to grate between her teeth.

She loved him, and why should it not be so? She could go before God's altar with him without disgracing herself with a lie. She could put her hand in his, and swear honestly that she would worship him and obey him. She had been dishonest;—but if he would pardon her for that, could she not reward him richly for such pardon? And it seemed to her that he had pardoned her. He had forgiven it all and was gracious to her,—coming at her beck and call, and sitting with her as though he liked her presence. She was woman enough to understand this, and she knew that he liked it. Of course he loved her. How could it be otherwise?

But yet he spoke nothing to her of his love. In the old days there had been with him no bashfulness of that kind. He was not a man to tremble and doubt before a woman. In those old days he had been ready enough,—so ready, that she had wondered that one who had just come from his books should know so well how to make himself master of a girl's heart. Nature had given him that art, as she does give it to some, with-holding it from many. But now he sat near her, dropping once and again half words of love, hearing her references to the old times;—and yet he said nothing.

But how was he to speak of love to one who was a widow but of four months' standing? And with what face could he now again ask for her hand, knowing that it had been filled so full since last it was refused to him? It was thus she argued to herself when she excused him in that he did not speak to her. As to her widowhood, to herself it was a thing of scorn. Thinking of it, she cast her weepers from her, and walked about the room, scorning the hypocrisy of her dress. It needed that she should submit herself to this hypocrisy before the world; but he might know,—for had she not told him?—that the clothes she wore were no index of her feeling or of her heart. She had been mean enough, base enough, vile enough, to sell herself to that wretched lord. Mean, base, and vile she had been, and she now confessed it; but she was not false enough to pretend that she mourned the man as a wife mourns. Harry might have seen enough to know, have understood enough to perceive, that he need not regard her widowhood.

And as to her money! If that were the stumbling-block, might it not be well that the first overture should come from her? Could she not find words to tell him that it might all be his? Could she not say to him, "Harry Clavering, all this is nothing in my hands. Take it into your hands, and it will prosper." Then it was that she went to her desk, and attempted to write to him. She did write to him a completed note, offering herself and all that was hers for his acceptance. In doing so, she strove hard to be honest and yet not over bold; to be affectionate and yet not unfeminine. Long she sat, holding her head with one hand, while the other attempted to use the pen which would not move over the paper. At length, quickly it flew across the sheet, and a few lines were there for her to peruse.

"Harry Clavering," she had written, "I know I am doing what men and women say no woman should do. You may, perhaps, say so of me now; but if you do, I know you so well, that I do not fear that others will be able to repeat it. Harry, I have never loved any one but you. Will you be my husband? You well know that I should not make you this offer if I did not intend that everything I have should be yours. It will be pleasant to me to feel that I can make some reparation for the evil I have done. As for love, I have never loved any one but you. You yourself must know that well. Yours, altogether if you will have it so,—JULIA."

She took the letter with her, back across the room to her seat by the fire, and took with her at the same time the little portrait; and there she sat, looking at the one and reading the other. At last she slowly folded the note up into a thin wisp of paper, and, lighting the end of it, watched it till every shred of it was burnt to an ash. "If he wants me," she said, "he can come and take me,—as other men do." It was a fearful attempt, that which she had thought of making. How could she have looked him in the face again had his answer to her been a refusal?

Another hour went by before she took herself to her bed, during which her cruelly-used maiden was waiting for her half asleep in the chamber above; and during that time she tried to bring herself to some

steady resolve. She would remain in London for the coming months, so
that he might come to her if he pleased. She would remain there, even
though she were subject to the daily attacks of Sophie Gordeloup. She
hardly knew why, but in part she was afraid of Sophie. She had done
nothing of which Sophie knew the secret. She had no cause to tremble
because Sophie might be offended. The woman had seen her in some of
her saddest moments, and could indeed tell of indignities which would
have killed some women. But these she had borne, and had not disgraced herself in the bearing of them. But still she was afraid of Sophie,
and felt that she could not bring herself absolutely to dismiss her friend
from her house. Nevertheless, she would remain;—because Harry Clavering was in London and could come to her there. To her house at
Ongar Park she would never go again, unless she went as his wife. The
place had become odious to her. Bad as was her solitude in London, with
Sophie Gordeloup to break it,—and perhaps with Sophie's brother to
attack her, it was not so bad as the silent desolation of Ongar Park.
Never again would she go there, unless she went there, in triumph,—as
Harry's wife. Having so far resolved she took herself at last to her room,
and dismissed her drowsy Phœbe to her rest.

And now the reader must be asked to travel down at once into the
country, that he may see how Florence Burton passed the same evening
at Clavering Rectory. It was Florence's last night there, and on the
following morning she was to return to her father's house at Stratton.
Florence had not as yet received her unsatisfactory letter from Harry.
That was to arrive on the following morning. At present she was, as
regarded her letters, under the influence of that one which had been satisfactory in so especial a degree. Not that the coming letter,—the one now
on its route,—was of a nature to disturb her comfort permanently, or to
make her in any degree unhappy. "Dear fellow; he must be careful, he
is overworking himself." Even the unsatisfactory letter would produce
nothing worse than this from her; but now, at the moment of which I am
writing, she was in a paradise of happy thoughts.

Her visit to Clavering had been in every respect successful. She had
been liked by every one, and every one in return had been liked by her.
Mrs. Clavering had treated her as though she were a daughter. The rector
had made her pretty presents, had kissed her, and called her his child. With
Fanny she had formed a friendship which was to endure for ever, let destiny separate them how it might. Dear Fanny! She had had a wonderful
interview respecting Fanny on this very day, and was at this moment dis-
quieting her mind because she could not tell her friend what had happened without a breach of confidence! She had learned a great deal at
Clavering, though in most matters of learning she was a better instructed
woman than they were whom she had met. In general knowledge and in
intellect she was Fanny's superior, though Fanny Clavering was no fool;
but Florence, when she came thither, had lacked something which living
in such a house had given to her;—or, I should rather say, something had

been given to her of which she would greatly feel the want, if it could be again taken from her. Her mother was as excellent a woman as had ever sent forth a family of daughters into the world, and I do not know that any one ever objected to her as being ignorant, or specially vulgar; but the house in Stratton was not like Clavering Rectory in the little ways of living, and this Florence Burton had been clever enough to understand. She knew that a sojourn under such a roof, with such a woman as Mrs. Clavering, must make her fitter to be Harry's wife; and, therefore, when they pressed her to come again in the autumn, she said that she thought she would. She could understand, too, that Harry was different in many things from the men who had married her sisters, and she rejoiced that it was so. Poor Florence ! Had he been more like them it might have been safer for her.

But we must return for a moment to the wonderful interview which has been mentioned. Florence, during her sojourn at Clavering, had become intimate with Mr. Saul, as well as with Fanny. She had given herself for the time heartily to the schools, and matters had so far progressed with her that Mr. Saul had on one occasion scolded her soundly. " It's a great sign that he thinks well of you," Fanny had said. " It was the only sign he ever gave me, before he spoke to me in that sad strain." On the afternoon of this, her last day at Clavering, she had gone over to Cumberly Green with Fanny, to say farewell to the children, and walked back by herself, as Fanny had not finished her work. When she was still about half a mile from the rectory, she met Mr. Saul, who was on his way out to the Green. " I knew I should meet you," he said, " so that I might say good-by."

" Yes, indeed, Mr. Saul,—for I am going in truth, to-morrow."

" I wish you were staying. I wish you were going to remain with us. Having you here is very pleasant, and you do more good here, perhaps, than you will elsewhere."

" I will not allow that. You forget that I have a father and mother."

" Yes; and you will have a husband soon."

" No, not soon ; some day, perhaps, if all goes well. But I mean to be back here often before that. I mean to be here in October, just for a little visit, if mamma can spare me."

" Miss Burton," he said, speaking in a very serious tone——. All his tones were serious, but that which he now adopted was more solemn than usual. " I wish to consult you on a certain matter, if you can give me five minutes of your time."

" To consult me, Mr. Saul ? "

" Yes, Miss Burton. I am hard pressed at present, and I know no one else of whom I can ask a certain question, if I cannot ask it of you. I think that you will answer me truly, if you answer me at all. I do not think you would flatter me, or tell me an untruth."

" Flatter you ! how could I flatter you ? "

"By telling me——; but I must ask you my question first. You and Fanny Clavering are dear friends now. You tell each other everything."

"I do not know," said Florence, doubting as to what she might best say, but guessing something of that which was coming.

"She will have told you, perhaps, that I asked her to be my wife. Did she ever tell you that?" Florence looked into his face for a few moments without answering him, not knowing how to answer such a question. "I know that she has told you," said he. "I can see that it is so."

"She has told me," said Florence.

"Why should she not? How could she be with you so many hours, and not tell you that of which she could hardly fail to have the remembrance often present with her. If I were gone from here, if I were not before her eyes daily, it might be otherwise; but seeing me as she does from day to day, of course she has spoken of me to her friend."

"Yes, Mr. Saul; she has told me of it."

"And now, will you tell me whether I may hope."

"Mr. Saul!"

"I want you to betray no secret, but I ask you for your advice. Can I hope that she will ever return my love?"

"How am I to answer you?"

"With the truth. Only with the truth."

"I should say that she thinks that you have forgotten it."

"Forgotten it! No, Miss Burton; she cannot think that. Do you believe that men or women can forget such things as that? Can you ever forget her brother? Do you think people ever forget when they have loved? No, I have not forgotten her. I have not forgotten that walk which we had down this lane together. There are things which men never forget." Then he paused for an answer.

Florence was by nature steady and self-collected, and she at once felt that she was bound to be wary before she gave him any answer. She had half fancied once or twice that Fanny thought more of Mr. Saul than she allowed even herself to know. And Fanny, when she had spoken of the impossibility of such a marriage, had always based the impossibility on the fact that people should not marry without the means of living,—a reason which to Florence, with all her prudence, was not sufficient. Fanny might wait as she also intended to wait. Latterly, too, Fanny had declared more than once to Florence her conviction that Mr. Saul's passion had been a momentary insanity which had altogether passed away; and in these declarations Florence had half fancied that she discovered some tinge of regret. If it were so, what was she now to say to Mr. Saul?

"You think then, Miss Burton," he continued, "that I have no chance of success? I ask the question because if I felt certain that this was so,—quite certain, I should be wrong to remain here. It has been my first and only parish, and I could not leave it without bitter sorrow. But if I were to remain here hopelessly, I should become unfit for my work. I am becoming so, and shall be better away."

"But why ask me, Mr. Saul?"

"Because I think that you can tell me."

"But why not ask herself? Who can tell you so truly as she can do?"

"You would not advise me to do that if you were sure that she would reject me?"

"That is what I would advise."

"I will take your advice, Miss Burton. Now, good-by, and may God bless you. You say you will be here in the autumn; but before the autumn I shall probably have left Clavering. If so our farewells will be for very long, but I shall always remember our pleasant intercourse here." Then he went on towards Cumberly Green; and Florence, as she walked into the vicarage grounds, was thinking that no girl had ever been loved by a more single-hearted, pure-minded gentleman than Mr. Saul.

As she sat alone in her bed-room, five or six hours after this interview, she felt some regret that she should leave Clavering without a word to Fanny on the subject. Mr. Saul had exacted no promise of secrecy from her; he was not a man to exact such promises. But she felt not the less that she would be betraying confidence to speak, and it might even be that her speaking on the matter would do more harm than good. Her sympathies were doubtless with Mr. Saul, but she could not therefore say that she thought Fanny ought to accept his love. It would be best to say nothing of the matter, and to allow Mr. Saul to fight his own battle.

Then she turned to her own matters, and there she found that everything was pleasant. How good the world had been to her to give her such a lover as Harry Clavering! She owned with all her heart the excellence of being in love, when a girl might be allowed to call such a man her own. She could not but make comparisons between him and Mr. Saul, though she knew that she was making them on points that were hardly worthy of her thoughts. Mr. Saul was plain, uncouth, with little that was bright about him except the brightness of his piety. Harry was like the morning star. He looked and walked and spoke, as though he were something more godlike than common men. His very voice created joy, and the ring of his laughter was to Florence as the music of the heavens. What woman would not have loved Harry Clavering? Even Julia Brabazon,—a creature so base that she had sold herself to such a thing as Lord Ongar for money and a title, but so grand in her gait and ways, so Florence had been told, that she seemed to despise the earth on which she trod,—even she had loved him. Then as Florence thought of what Julia Brabazon might have had and of what she had lost, she wondered that there could be women born so sadly vicious.

But that woman's vice had given her her success, her joy, her great

triumph! It was surely not for her to deal hardly with the faults of
Julia Brabazon,—for her who was enjoying all the blessings of which
those faults had robbed the other! Julia Brabazon had been her very
good friend.

But why had this perfect lover come to her, to one so small, so trifling,
so little in the world's account as she, and given to her all the treasure
of his love? Oh, Harry,—dear Harry! what could she do for him that
would be a return good enough for such great goodness? Then she took
out his last letter, that satisfactory letter, that letter that had been
declared to be perfect, and read it and read it again. No; she did not
want Fanny or any one else to tell her that he was true. Honesty
and truth were written on every line of his face, were to be heard
in every tone of his voice, could be seen in every sentence that came
from his hand. Dear Harry; dearest Harry! She knew well that he
was true.

Then she also sat down and wrote to him, on that her last night
beneath his father's roof,—wrote to him when she had nearly prepared
herself for her bed; and honestly, out of her full heart, thanked him for
his love. There was no need that she should be coy with him now, for
she was his own. " Dear Harry, when I think of all that you have done
for me in loving me and choosing me for your wife, I know that I can
never pay you all that I owe you."

Such were the two rival claimants for the hand of Harry Clavering.

<hr/>

CHAPTER XVII.

Let her Know that you're There.

A week had passed since the evening which Harry had spent in Bolton
Street, and he had not again seen Lady Ongar. He had professed to himself that his reason for not going there was the non-performance of the
commission which Lady Ongar had given him with reference to Count
Pateroff. He had not yet succeeded in catching the count, though he had
twice asked for him in Mount Street and twice at the club in Pall Mall.
It appeared that the count never went to Mount Street, and was very
rarely seen at the club. There was some other club which he frequented,
and Harry did not know what club. On both the occasions of Harry's
calling in Mount Street, the servant had asked him to go up and see
madame; out he had declined to do so, pleading that he was hurried. He
was, however, driven to resolve that he must go direct to Sophie, as otherwise he could find no means of doing as he had promised. She probably
might put him on the scent of her brother.

But there had been another reason why Harry had not gone to Bolton
Street, though he had not acknowledged it to himself. He did not dare
to trust himself with Lady Ongar. He feared that he would be led on to

betray himself and to betray Florence,—to throw himself at Julia's feet and sacrifice his honesty, in spite of all his resolutions to the contrary. He felt when there as the accustomed but repentant dram-drinker might feel, when having resolved to abstain, he is called upon to sit with the full glass offered before his lips. From such temptation as that the repentant dram-drinker knows that he must fly. But though he did not go after the fire-water of Bolton Street, neither was he able to satisfy himself with the cool fountain of Onslow Crescent. He was wretched at this time,— ill-satisfied with himself and others, and was no fitting companion for Cecilia Burton. The world, he thought, had used him ill. He could have been true to Julia Brabazon when she was well-nigh penniless. It was not for her money that he had regarded her. Had he been now a free man,—free from those chains with which he had fettered himself at Stratton, he would again have asked this woman for her love, in spite of her past treachery ; but it would have been for her love and not for her money that he would have sought her. Was it his fault that he had loved her, that she had been false to him, and that she had now come back and thrown herself before him ? Or had he been wrong because he had ventured to think that he loved another when Julia had deserted him ? Or could he help himself if he now found that his love in truth belonged to her whom he had known first ? The world had been very cruel to him, and he could not go to Onslow Crescent and behave there prettily, hearing the praises of Florence with all the ardour of a discreet lover.

He knew well what would have been his right course, and yet he did not follow it. Let him but once communicate to Lady Ongar the fact of his engagement, and the danger would be over, though much, perhaps, of the misery might remain. Let him write to her and mention the fact, bringing it up as some little immaterial accident, and she would under- stand what he meant. But this he abstained from doing. Though he swore to himself that he would not touch the dram, he would not dash down the full glass that was held to his lips. He went about the town very wretchedly, looking for the count, and regarding himself as a man specially marked out for sorrow by the cruel hand of misfortune. Lady Ongar, in the meantime, was expecting him, and was waxing angry and becoming bitter towards him because he came not.

Sir Hugh Clavering was now up in London, and with him was his brother Archie. Sir Hugh was a man who strained an income, that was handsome and sufficient for a country gentleman, to the very utmost, wanting to get out of it more than it could be made to give. He was not a man to be in debt, or indulge himself with present pleasures to be paid for out of the funds of future years. He was possessed of a worldly wisdom which kept him from that folly, and taught him to appreciate fully the value of independence. But he was ever remembering how many shillings there are in a pound, and how many pence in a shilling. He had a great eye to discount, and looked very closely into his bills.

He searched for cheap shops;—and some men began to say of him that he had found a cheap establishment for such wines as he did not drink himself! In playing cards and in betting he was very careful, never playing high, never risking much, but hoping to turn something by the end of the year, and angry with himself if he had not done so. An unamiable man he was, but one whose heir would probably not quarrel with him,—if only he would die soon enough. He had always had a house in town, a moderate house in Berkeley Square, which belonged to him and had belonged to his father before him. Lady Clavering had usually lived there during the season ; or, as had latterly been the case, during only a part of the season. And now it had come to pass, in this year, that Lady Clavering was not to come to London at all, and that Sir Hugh was meditating whether the house in Berkeley Square might not be let. The arrangement would make the difference of considerably more than a thousand a year to him. For himself, he would take lodgings. He had no idea of giving up London in the spring and early summer. But why keep up a house in Berkeley Square, as Lady Clavering did not use it ?

He was partly driven to this by a desire to shake off the burden of his brother. When Archie chose to go to Clavering the house was open to him. That was the necessity of Sir Hugh's position, and he could not avoid it unless he made it worth his while to quarrel with his brother. Archie was obedient, ringing the bell when he was told, looking after the horses, spying about, and perhaps saving as much money as he cost. But the matter was very different in Berkeley Square. No elder brother is bound to find breakfast and bed for a younger brother in London. And yet from his boyhood upwards Archie had made good his footing in Berkeley Square. In the matter of the breakfast, Sir Hugh had indeed of late got the better of him. The servants were kept on board wages, and there were no household accounts. But there was Archie's room, and Sir Hugh felt this to be a hardship.

The present was not the moment for actually driving forth the intruder, for Archie was now up in London, especially under his brother's auspices. And if the business on which Captain Clavering was now intent could be brought to a successful issue, the standing in the world of that young man would be very much altered. Then he would be a brother of whom Sir Hugh might be proud ; a brother who would pay his way, and settle his points at whist if he lost them, even to a brother. If Archie could induce Lady Ongar to marry him, he would not be called upon any longer to ring the bells and look after the stable. He would have bells of his own, and stables too, and perhaps some captain of his own to ring them and look after them. The expulsion, therefore, was not to take place till Archie should have made his attempt upon Lady Ongar.

But Sir Hugh would admit of no delay, whereas Archie himself seemed to think that the iron was not yet quite hot enough for striking. It would be better, he had suggested, to postpone the work till Julia could be coaxed down to Clavering in the autumn. He could do the work better, he thought, down at Clavering than in London. But Sir Hugh was altogether of a different opinion. Though he had already asked his sister-in-law to Clavering, when the idea had first come up, he was glad that she had declined the visit. Her coming might be very well if she accepted Archie; but he did not want to be troubled with any renewal of his responsibility respecting her, if, as was more probable, she should reject him. The world still looked askance at Lady Ongar, and Hugh did not wish to take up the armour of a paladin in her favour. If Archie married her, Archie would be the paladin; though, indeed, in that case, no paladin would be needed.

"She has only been a widow, you know, four months," said Archie, pleading for delay. "It won't be delicate; will it?"

"Delicate!" said Sir Hugh. "I don't know whether there is much of delicacy in it at all."

"I don't see why she isn't to be treated like any other woman. If you were to die, you'd think it very odd if any fellow came up to Hermy before the season was over."

"Archie, you are a fool," said Sir Hugh; and Archie could see by his brother's brow that Hugh was angry. "You say things that for folly and absurdity are beyond belief. If you can't see the peculiarities of Julia's position, I am not going to point them out to you."

"She is peculiar, of course,—having so much money, and that place near Guildford, all her own for her life. Of course it's peculiar. But four months, Hugh!"

"If it had been four days it need have made no difference. A home, with some one to support her, is everything to her. If you wait till lots of fellows are buzzing round her you won't have a chance. You'll find that by this time next year she'll be the top of the fashion; and if not engaged to you, she will be to some one else. I shouldn't be surprised if Harry were after her again."

"He's engaged to that girl we saw down at Clavering."

"What matters that? Engagements can be broken as well as made. You have this great advantage over every one, except him, that you can go to her at once without doing anything out of the way. That girl that Harry has in tow may perhaps keep him away for some time."

"I tell you what, Hugh, you might as well call with me the first time."

"So that I may quarrel with her, which I certainly should do,—or, rather, she with me. No, Archie; if you're afraid to go alone, you'd better give it up."

"Afraid! I'm not afraid!"

"She can't eat you. Remember that with her you needn't stand on your p's and q's, as you would with another woman. She knows what she is about, and will understand what she has to get as well as what she is expected to give. All I can say is, that if she accepts you, Hermy will consent that she shall go to Clavering as much as she pleases till the marriage takes place. It couldn't be done, I suppose, till after a year; and in that case she shall be married at Clavering."

Here was a prospect for Julia Brabazon;—to be led to the same altar, at which she had married Lord Ongar, by Archie Clavering, twelve months after her first husband's death, and little more than two years after her first wedding! The peculiarity of the position did not quite make itself apparent either to Hugh or to Archie; but there was one point which did suggest itself to the younger brother at that moment.

"I don't suppose there was anything really wrong, eh?"

"Can't say, I'm sure," said Sir Hugh.

"Because I shouldn't like——"

"If I were you I wouldn't trouble myself about that. Judge not, that you be not judged."

"Yes, that's true, to be sure," said Archie; and on that point he went forth satisfied.

But the job before him was a peculiar job, and that Archie well knew. In some inexplicable manner he put himself into the scales and weighed himself, and discovered his own weight with fair accuracy. And he put her into the scales, and he found that she was much the heavier of the two. How he did this,—how such men as Archie Clavering do do it, —I cannot say; but they do weigh themselves, and know their own weight, and shove themselves aside as being too light for any real service in the world. This they do, though they may fluster with their voices, and walk about with their noses in the air, and swing their canes, and try to look as large as they may. They do not look large, and they know it; and consequently they ring the bells, and look after the horses, and shove themselves on one side, so that the heavier weights may come forth and do the work. Archie Clavering, who had duly weighed himself, could hardly bring himself to believe that Lady Ongar would be fool enough to marry him! Seven thousand a year, with a park and farm in Surrey, and give it all to him,—him, Archie Clavering, who had, so to say, no weight at all! Archie Clavering, for one, could not bring himself to believe it.

But yet Hermy, her sister, thought it possible; and though Hermy was, as Archie had found out by his invisible scales, lighter than Julia, still she must know something of her sister's nature. And Hugh, who was by no means light,—who was a man of weight, with money and position and firm ground beneath his feet,—he also thought that it might be so. "Faint heart never won a fair lady," said Archie to himself a dozen times, as he walked down to the Rag. The Rag was his club, and there was a friend there whom he could consult confidentially. No; faint heart never won a fair lady; but they who repeat to themselves that adage, trying thereby to get courage, always have faint hearts for such work. Harry Clavering never thought of the proverb when he went a-wooing.

But Captain Boodle of the Rag,—for Captain Boodle always lived at the Rag when he was not at Newmarket, or at other racecourses, or in the neighbourhood of Market Harborough,—Captain Boodle knew a thing or two, and Captain Boodle was his fast friend. He would go to Boodle and arrange the campaign with him. Boodle had none of that hectoring, domineering way which Hugh never quite threw off in his intercourse with his brother. And Archie, as he went along, resolved that when Lady Ongar's money was his, and when he had a countess for his wife, he would give his elder brother a cold shoulder.

Boodle was playing pool at the Rag, and Archie joined him; but pool is a game which hardly admits of confidential intercourse as to proposed wives, and Archie was obliged to remain quiet on that subject all the afternoon. He cunningly, however, lost a little money to Boodle, for Boodle liked to win,—and engaged himself to dine at the same table with his friend. Their dinner they ate almost in silence,—unless when they abused the cook, or made to each other some pithy suggestion as to the expediency of this or that delicacy,—bearing always steadily in view the cost as well as desirability of the viands. Boodle had no shame in not having this or that because it was dear. To dine with the utmost luxury at the smallest expense was a proficiency belonging to him, and of which he was very proud.

But after a while the cloth was gone, and the heads of the two men were brought near together over the small table. Boodle did not speak a word till his brother captain had told his story, had pointed out all the advantages to be gained, explained in what peculiar way the course lay open to himself, and made the whole thing clear to his friend's eye.

"They say she's been a little queer, don't they?" said the friendly counsellor.

"Of course people talk, you know."

"Talk, yes; they're talking a doosed sight, I should say. There's no mistake about the money, I suppose?"

"Oh, none," said Archie, shaking his head vigorously. "Hugh managed all that for her, so I know it."

"She don't lose any of it because she enters herself for running again, does she?"

"Not a shilling. That's the beauty of it."

"Was you ever sweet on her before?"

"What! before Ongar took her? O laws, no. She hadn't a rap, you know;—and knew how to spend money as well as any girl in London."

"It's all to begin then, Clavvy; all the uphill work to be done?"

"Well, yes; I don't know about up-hill, Doodles. What do you mean by up-hill?"

"I mean that seven thousand a year ain't usually to be picked up merely by trotting easy along the flat. And this sort of work is very up-hill generally, I take it;—unless, you know, a fellow has a fancy for it. If a fellow is really sweet on a girl, he likes it, I suppose."

" She's a doosed handsome woman, you know, Doodles."

" I don't know anything about it, except that I suppose Ongar wouldn't have taken her if she hadn't stood well on her pasterns, and had some breeding about her. I never thought much of her sister,— your brother's wife, you know,—that is in the way of looks. No doubt she runs straight, and that's a great thing. She won't go the wrong side of the post."

" As for running straight, let me alone for that."

" Well, now, Clavvy, I'll tell you what my ideas are. When a man's trying a young filly, his hands can't be too light. A touch too much will bring her on her haunches, or throw her out of her step. She should hardly feel the iron in her mouth. That's the sort of work which requires a man to know well what he's about. But when I've got to do with a trained mare, I always choose that she shall know that I'm there ! Do you understand me ? "

" Yes ; I understand you, Doodles."

" I always choose that she shall know that I'm there." And Captain Boodle, as he repeated these manly words with a firm voice, put out his hands as though he were handling the horse's rein. " Their mouths are never so fine then, and they generally want to be brought up to the bit, d'ye see ?—up to the bit. When a mare has been trained to her work, and knows what she's at in her running, she's all the better for feeling a fellow's hands as she's going. She likes it rather. It gives her confidence, and makes her know where she is. And look here, Clavvy, when she comes to her fences, give her her head ; but steady her first, and make her know that you're there. Damme ; whatever you do, let her know that you're there. There's nothing like it. She'll think all the more of the fellow that's piloting her. And look here, Clavvy ; ride her with spurs. Always ride a trained mare with spurs. Let her know that they're on ; and if she tries to get her head, give 'em her. Yes, by George, give 'em her." And Captain Boodle in his energy twisted himself in his chair, and brought his heel round, so that it could be seen by Archie. Then he produced a sharp click with his tongue, and made the peculiar jerk with the muscle of his legs, whereby he was accustomed to evoke the agility of his horses. After that he looked triumphantly at his friend. " Give 'em her, Clavvy, and she'll like you the better for it. She'll know then that you mean it."

It was thus that Captain Boodle instructed his friend Archie Clavering how to woo Lady Ongar ; and Archie, as he listened to his friend's words of wisdom, felt that he had learned a great deal. " That's the way I'll do it, Doodles," he said, " and upon my word I'm very much obliged to you."

" That's the way, you may depend on it. Let her know that you're there.—Let her know that you're there. She's done the filly work before, you see ; and it's no good trying that again."

Captain Clavering really believed that he had learned a good deal, and that he now knew the way to set about the work before him. What sort of spurs he was to use, and how he was to put them on, I don't think he did know ; but that was a detail as to which he did not think it necessary to consult his adviser. He sat the whole evening in the smoking-room, very silent, drinking slowly iced gin-and-water ; and the more he drank the more assured he felt that he now understood the way in which he was to attempt the work before him. "Let her know I'm there," he said to himself, shaking his head gently, so that no one should observe him ; "yes, let her know I'm there." At this time Captain Boodle, or Doodles as he was familiarly called, had again ascended to the billiard-room and was hard at work. "Let her know that I'm there," repeated Archie, mentally. Everything was contained in that precept. And he, with his hands before him on his knees, went through the process of steadying a horse with the snaffle-rein, just touching the curb, as he did so, for security. It was but a motion of his fingers and no one could see it, but it made him confident that he had learned his lesson. "Up to the bit," he repeated ; "by George, yes ; up to the bit. There's nothing like it for a trained mare. Give her head, but steady her." And Archie, as the words passed across his memory and were almost pronounced, seemed to be flying successfully over some prodigious fence. He leaned himself back a little in the saddle, and seemed to hold firm with his legs. That was the way to do it. And then the spurs ! He would not forget the spurs. She should know that he wore a spur, and that, if necessary, he would use it. Then he, too, gave a little click with his tongue, and an acute observer might have seen the motion of his heel.

Two hours after that he was still sitting in the smoking-room, chewing the end of a cigar, when Doodles came down victorious from the billiard-room. Archie was half asleep, and did not notice the entrance of his friend. "Let her know that you're there," said Doodles, close into Archie Clavering's ear,—"damme, let her know that you're there." Archie started and did not like the surprise, or the warm breath in his ear ; but he forgave the offence for the wisdom of the words that had been spoken.

Then he walked home by himself, repeating again and again the invaluable teachings of his friend.

CHAPTER XVIII.

CAPTAIN CLAVERING MAKES HIS FIRST ATTEMPT.

DURING breakfast on the following day,—which means from the hour of one till two, for the glasses of iced gin-and-water had been many,—Archie Clavering was making up his mind that he would begin at once. He would go to Bolton Street on that day, and make an attempt to be admitted. If not admitted to-day he would make another attempt to-morrow, and, if still unsuccessful, he would write a letter; not a letter containing an offer, which according to Archie's ideas would not be letting her know that he was there in a manner sufficiently potential,—but a letter in which he would explain that he had very grave reasons for wishing to see his near and dear connexion, Lady Ongar. Soon after two he sallied out, and he also went to a hairdresser's. He was aware that in doing so he was hardly obeying his friend to the letter, as this sort of operation would come rather under the head of handling a filly with a light touch; but he thought that he could in this way, at any rate, do no harm, if he would only remember the instructions he had received when in presence of the trained mare. It was nearly three when he found himself in Bolton Street, having calculated that Lady Ongar might be more probably found at home then than at a later hour. But when he came to the door, instead of knocking, he passed by it. He began to remember that he had not yet made up his mind by what means he would bring it about that she should certainly know that he was there. So he took a little turn up the street, away from Piccadilly, through a narrow passage that there is in those parts, and by some stables, and down into Piccadilly, and again to Bolton Street; during which little tour he had made up his mind that it could hardly become his duty to teach her that great lesson on this occasion. She must undoubtedly be taught to know that he was there, but not so taught on this, his first visit. That lesson should quickly precede his offer; and, although he had almost hoped in the interval between two of his beakers of gin-and-water on the preceding evening that he might ride the race and win it altogether during this very morning visit he was about to make, in his cooler moments he had begun to reflect that that would hardly be practicable. The mare must get a gallop before she would be in a condition to be brought out. So Archie knocked at the door, intending merely to give the mare a gallop if he should find her in to-day.

He gave his name, and was shown at once up into Lady Ongar's drawing-room. Lady Ongar was not there, but she soon came down, and entered the room with a smile on her face and with an outstretched hand. Between the man-servant who took the captain's name, and the maid-servant who carried it up to her mistress,—but who did not see the gentleman before she did so, there had arisen some mistake, and Lady Ongar, as she came down from her chamber above expected that she was to meet another man. Harry Clavering, she thought, had come to her at last. "I'll be down at once," Lady Ongar had said, dismissing the girl and then standing for a moment before her mirror as she smoothed her hair, obliterated as far as it might be possible the ugliness of her cap, and shook out the folds of her dress. A countess, a widow, a woman of the world who had seen enough to make her composed under all circumstances, one would say,—a trained mare as Doodles had called her,—she stood before her glass doubting and trembling like a girl, when she heard that Harry

Clavering was waiting for her below. We may surmise that she would
have spared herself some of this trouble had she known the real name of
her visitor. Then, as she came slowly down the stairs, she reflected how
she would receive him. He had stayed away from her, and she would
be cold to him,—cold and formal as she had been on the railway platform.
She knew well how to play that part. Yes; it was his turn now to show
some eagerness of friendship, if there was ever to be anything more than
friendship between them. But she changed all this as she put her hand
upon the lock of the door. She would be honest to him,—honest and true.
She was in truth glad to see him, and he should know it. What cared
she now for the common ways of women and the usual coynesses of
feminine coquetry. She told herself also, in language somewhat differing
from that which Doodles had used, that her filly days were gone by,
and that she was now a trained mare. All this passed through her
mind as her hand was on the door; and then she opened it, with a smiling
face and ready hand, to find herself in the presence of—Captain Archie
Clavering.

The captain was sharp-sighted enough to observe the change in her
manner. The change, indeed, was visible enough, and was such that it at
once knocked out of Archie's breast some portion of the courage with
which his friend's lessons had inspired him. The outstretched hand fell
slowly to her side, the smile gave place to a look of composed dignity
which made Archie at once feel that the fate which called upon him to
woo a countess, was in itself hard. And she walked slowly into the room
before she spoke to him, or he to her.

"Captain Clavering!" she said at last, and there was much more of
surprise than of welcome in her words as she uttered them.

"Yes, Lady On—, Julia, that is; I thought I might as well come and
call, as I found we weren't to see you at Clavering when we were all there
at Easter." When she had been living in his brother's house as one of
the family he had called her Julia, as Hugh had done. The connection
between them had been close, and it had come naturally to him to do so.
He had thought much of this since his present project had been initiated,
and had strongly resolved not to lose the advantage of his former
familiarity. He had very nearly broken down at the onset, but, as the
reader will have observed, had recovered himself.

"You are very good," she said; and then as he had been some time
standing with his right hand presented to her, she just touched it with her
own.

"There's nothing I hate so much as stuff and nonsense," said Archie.
To this remark she simply bowed, remaining awfully quiet. Captain
Clavering felt that her silence was in truth awful. She had always been
good at talking, and he had paused for her to say something; but when
she bowed to him in that stiff manner,—"doosed stiff she was; doosed
stiff, and impudent too," he told Doodles afterwards;—he knew that he
must go on himself. "Stuff and nonsense is the mischief, you know."

CAPTAIN CLAVERING MAKES HIS FIRST ATTEMPT.

Then she bowed again. "There's been something the matter with them all down at Clavering since you came home, Julia; but hang me if I can find out what it is!" Still she was silent. "It ain't Hermy; that I must say. Hermy always speaks of you as though there had never been anything wrong." This assurance, we may say, must have been flattering to the lady whom he was about to court.

"Hermy was always too good to me," said Lady Ongar, smiling.

"By George, she always does. If there's anything wrong it's been with Hugh; and, by George, I don't know what it is he was up to when you first came home. It wasn't my doing;—of course you know that."

"I never thought that anything was your doing, Captain Clavering."

"I think Hugh had been losing money; I do indeed. He was like a bear with a sore head just at that time. There was no living in the house with him. I daresay Hermy may have told you all about that."

"Hermione is not by nature so communicative as you are, Captain Clavering."

"Isn't she? I should have thought between sisters—; but of course that's no business of mine." Again she was silent, awfully silent, and he became aware that he must either get up and go away or carry on the conversation himself. To do either seemed to be equally difficult, and for a while he sat there almost gasping in his misery. He was quite aware that as yet he had not made her know that he was there. He was not there, as he well knew, in his friend Doodles' sense of the word. "At any rate there isn't any good in quarrelling, is there, Julia?" he said at last. Now that he had asked a question, surely she must speak.

"There is great good sometimes I think," said she, "in people remaining apart and not seeing each other. Sir Hugh Clavering has not quarrelled with me, that I am aware. Indeed, since my marriage there have been no means of quarrelling between us. But I think it quite as well that he and I should not come together."

"But he particularly wants you to go to Clavering."

"Has he sent you here as his messenger?"

"Sent me! oh dear no; nothing of that sort. I have come altogether on my own hook. If Hugh wants a messenger he must find some one else. But you and I were always friends you know,"—at this assertion she opened her large eyes widely, and simply smiled;—"and I thought that perhaps you might be glad to see me if I called. That was all."

"You are very good, Captain Clavering."

"I couldn't bear to think that you should be here in London, and that one shouldn't see anything of you or know anything about you. Tell me now; is there anything I can do for you? Do you want anybody to settle anything for you in the city?"

"I think not, Captain Clavering; thank you very much."

"Because I should be so happy; I should indeed. There's nothing I should like so much as to make myself useful in some way. Isn't there anything now ?　There must be so much to be looked after,—about money and all that."

" My lawyer does all that, Captain Clavering."

" Those fellows are such harpies.　There is no end to their charges ; and all for doing things that would only be a pleasure to me."

" I'm afraid I can't employ you in any matter that would suit your tastes."

" Can't you indeed, now ? "　Then again there was a silence, and Captain Clavering was beginning to think that he must go.　He was willing to work hard at talking or anything else ; but he could not work if no ground for starting were allowed to him.　He thought he must go, though he was aware that he had not made even the slightest preparation for future obedience to his friend's precepts.　He began to feel that he had commenced wrongly.　He should have made her know that he was there from the first moment of her entrance into the room.　He must retreat now in order that he might advance with more force on the next occasion. He had just made up his mind to this and was doubting how he might best get himself out of his chair with the purpose of going, when sudden relief came in the shape of another visitor.　The door was thrown open and Madam Gordeloup was announced.

" Well, my angel," said the little woman, running up to her friend and kissing her on either side of her face.　Then she turned round as though she had only just seen the strange gentleman, and curtseyed to him. Captain Clavering holding his hat in both his hands bowed to the little woman.

" My sister's brother-in-law, Captain Clavering," said Lady Ongar. " Madam Gordeloup."

Captain Clavering bowed again.　" Ah, Sir Oo's brother," said Madam Gordeloup.　" I am very glad to see Captain Clavering ; and is your sister come ? "

" No ; my sister is not come."

" Lady Clavering is not in town this spring," said the captain.

" Ah, not in town !　Then I do pity her.　There is only de one place to live in, and that is London, for April, May, and June.　Lady Clavering is not coming to London ? "

" Her little boy isn't quite the thing," said the captain.

" Not quite de ting ? " said the Franco-Pole in an inquiring voice, not exactly understanding the gentleman's language.

" My little nephew is ill, and my sister does not think it wise to bring him to London."

" Ah ; that is a pity.　And Sir Oo ?　Sir Oo is in London ? "

" Yes," said the captain ; " my brother has been up some time."

" And his lady left alone in the country ?　Poor lady !　But your English ladies like the country.　They are fond of the fields and the daisies.　So they say ; but I think often they lie.　Me ; I like the houses, and the people, and the pavé.　The fields are damp, and I love not rheumatism at all." Then the little woman shrugged her shoulders and shook herself. "Tell us the truth, Julie; which do you like best, the town or the country?"

"Whichever I'm not in, I think."

"Ah, just so. Whichever you are not in at present. That is because you are still idle. You have not settled yourself!" At this reference to the possibility of Lady Ongar settling herself, Captain Clavering pricked up his ears, and listened eagerly for what might come next. He only knew of one way in which a young woman without a husband could settle herself. "You must wait, my dear, a little longer, just a little longer, till the time of your trouble has passed by."

"Don't talk such nonsense, Sophie," said the countess.

"Ah, my dear, it is no nonsense. I am always telling her, Captain Clavering, that she must go through this black, troublesome time as quick as she can ; and then nobody will enjoy the town so much as de rich and beautiful Lady Ongar. Is it not so, Captain Clavering?"

Archie thought that the time had now come for him to say something pretty, so that his love might begin to know that he was there. "By George, yes, there'll be nobody so much admired when she comes out again. There never was anybody so much admired before,—before,—that is, when you were Julia Brabazon, you know ; and I shouldn't wonder if you didn't come out quite as strong as ever."

"As strong!" said the Franco-Pole. "A woman that has been married is always more admired than a meess."

"Sophie, might I ask you and Captain Clavering to be a little less personal."

"There is noting I hate so much as your meesses," continued Madame Gordeloup; "noting! Your English meesses give themselves such airs. Now in Paris, or in dear Vienna, or in St. Petersburg, they are not like that at all. There they are nobodies—they are nobodies ; but then they will be something very soon, which is to be better. Your English meess is so much and so grand ; she never can be greater and grander. So when she is a mamma, she lives down in the country by herself, and looks after de pills and de powders. I don't like that. I don't like that at all. No ; if my husband had put me into the country to look after de pills and de powders, he should have had them all, all—himself, when he came to see me." As she said this with great energy, she opened her eyes wide, and looked full into Archie's face.

Captain Clavering, who was sitting with his hat in his two hands between his knees, stared at the little foreigner. He had heard before of women poisoning their husbands, but never had heard a woman advocate the system as expedient. Nor had he often heard a woman advocate any system with the vehemence which Madame Gordeloup now displayed on this matter, and with an allusion which was so very pointed to the special position of his own sister-in-law. Did Lady Ongar agree with her? He felt as though he should like to know his Julia's opinions on that matter.

"Sophie, Captain Clavering will think you are in earnest," said the countess, laughing.

"So I am—in earnest. It is all wrong. You boil all the water out of de pot before you put the gigot into it. So the gigot is no good, is tough and dry, and you shut it up in an old house in the country. Then, to make matters pretty, you talk about de fields and de daisies. I know. 'Thank you,' I should say. 'De fields and de daisies are so nice and so good! Suppose you go down, my love, and walk in de fields, and pick de daisies, and send them up to me by de railway!' Yes, that is what I would say."

Captain Clavering was now quite in the dark, and began to regard the little woman as a lunatic. When she spoke of the pot and the gigot he vainly endeavoured to follow her; and now that she had got among the daisies he was more at a loss than ever. Fruit, vegetables, and cut flowers came up, he knew, to London regularly from Clavering, when the family was in town;—but no daisies. In France it must, he supposed, be different. He was aware, however, of his ignorance, and said nothing.

"No one ever did try to shut you up, Sophie!"

"No, indeed; M. Gordeloup knew better. What would he do if I were shut up? And no one will ever shut you up, my dear. If I were you, I would give no one a chance."

"Don't say that," said the captain, almost passionately; "don't say that."

"Ha, ha! but I do say it. Why should a woman who has got everything marry again? If she wants de fields and de daisies she has got them of her own—yes, of her own. If she wants de town, she has got that too. Jewels,—she can go and buy them. Coaches,—there they are. Parties,—one, two, three, every night, as many as she please. Gentlemen who will be her humble slaves; such a plenty,—all London. Or, if she want to be alone, no one can come near her. Why should she marry? No."

"But she might be in love with somebody," said the captain, in a surprised but humble tone.

"Love! Bah! Be in love, so that she may be shut up in an old barrack with de powders!" The way in which that word barrack was pronounced, and the middle letters sounded, almost lifted the captain off his seat. "Love is very pretty at seventeen, when the imagination is telling a parcel of lies, and when life is one dream. To like people,—oh, yes; to be very fond of your friends,—oh, yes; to be most attached,—as I am to my Julie,"—here she got hold of Lady Ongar's hand,—"it is the salt of life! But what you call love, booing and cooing, with rhymes and verses about de moon, it is to go back to pap and panade, and what you call bibs. No; if a woman wants a house, and de something to live on, let her marry a husband; or if a man want to have children, let him marry a wife. But to be shut up in a country house, when everything you have got of your own,—I say it is bad."

Captain Clavering was heartily sorry that he had mentioned the fact of his sister-in-law being left at home at Clavering Park. It was most unfortunate. How could he make it understood that if he were married he would not think of shutting his wife up at Ongar Park? "Lady Clavering, you know, does come to London generally," he said.

"Bah!" exclaimed the little Franco-Pole.

"And as for me, I never should be happy, if I were married, unless I had my wife with me everywhere," said Captain Clavering.

"Bah-ah-ah!" ejaculated the lady.

Captain Clavering could not endure this any longer. He felt that the manner of the lady was, to say the least of it, unpleasant, and he perceived that he was doing no good to his own cause. So he rose from his chair and muttered some words with the intention of showing his purpose of departure.

"Good-by, Captain Clavering," said Lady Ongar. "My love to my sister when you see her."

Archie shook hands with her and then made his bow to Madame Gordeloup.

"Au revoir, my friend," she said, "and you remember all I say. It is not good for de wife to be all alone in the country, while de husband walk about in the town and make an eye to every lady he see." Archie would not trust himself to renew the argument, but bowing again, made his way off.

"He was come for one admirer," said Sophie, as soon as the door was closed.

"An admirer of whom?"

"Not of me;—oh, no; I was not in danger at all."

"Of me? Captain Clavering! Sophie, you get your head full of the strangest nonsense."

"Ah; very well. You see. What will you give me if I am right? Will you bet? Why had he got on his new gloves, and had his head all smelling with stuff from de hair-dresser? Does he come always perfumed like that? Does he wear shiny little boots to walk about in de morning, and make an eye always? Perhaps yes."

"I never saw his boots or his eyes."

"But I see them. I see many things. He come to have Ongere Park for his own. I tell you, yes. Ten thousand will come to have Ongere Park. Why not? To have Ongere Park and all de money a man will make himself smell a great deal."

"You think much more about all that than is necessary."

"Do I, my dear? Very well. There are three already. There is Edouard, and there is this Clavering who you say is a captain; and there is the other Clavering who goes with his nose in the air, and who think himself a clever fellow because he learned his lesson at school and did not get himself whipped. He will be whipped yet some day,—perhaps."

"Sophie, hold your tongue. Captain Clavering is my sister's brother-in-law, and Harry Clavering is my friend."

"Ah, friend! I know what sort of friend he wants to be. How much better to have a park and plenty of money than to work in a ditch and make a railway! But he do not know the way with a woman. Perhaps he may be more at home, as you say, in the ditch. I should say to him, ' My friend, you will do well in de ditch if you work hard ;—suppose you stay there.' "

"You don't seem to like my cousin, and if you please, we will talk no more about him."

"Why should I not like him? He don't want to get any money from me."

"That will do, Sophie."

"Very well; it shall do for me. But this other man that come here to-day. He is a fool."

"Very likely."

"He did not learn his lesson without whipping."

"Nor with whipping either."

"No; he have learned nothing. He does not know what to do with his hat. He is a fool. Come, Julie, will you take me out for a drive. It is melancholy for you to go alone; I came to ask you for a drive. Shall we go?" And they did go, Lady Ongar and Sophie Gordeloup together. Lady Ongar, as she submitted, despised herself for her submission; but what was she to do? It is sometimes very difficult to escape from the meshes of friendship.

Captain Clavering, when he left Bolton Street, went down to his club, having first got rid of his shining boots and new gloves. He sauntered up into the billiard-room knowing that his friend would be there, and there he found Doodles with his coat off, the sleeves of his shirt turned back, and armed with his cue. His brother captain, the moment that he saw him, presented the cue at his breast. "Does she know you're there, old fellow; I say, does she know you're there?" The room was full of men, and the whole thing was done so publicly that Captain Clavering was almost offended.

"Come, Doodles, you go on with your game," said he; "it's you to play." Doodles turned to the table, and scientifically pocketed the ball on which he played; then he laid his own ball close under the cushion, picked up a shilling and put it into his waistcoat pocket, holding a lighted cigar in his mouth the while, and then he came back to his friend. "Well, Clavvy, how has it been?"

"Oh, nothing as yet, you know."

"Haven't you seen her?"

"Yes, I've seen her, of course. I'm not the fellow to let the grass grow under my feet. I've only just come from her house."

"Well, well?"

"That's nothing much to tell the first day, you know."

" Did you let her know you were there ? That's the chat. Damme, did you let her know you were there ? "

In answer to this Archie attempted to explain that he was not as yet quite sure that he had been successful in that particular; but in the middle of his story Captain Doodles was called off to exercise his skill again, and on this occasion to pick up two shillings. " I'm sorry for you, Griggs," he said, as a very young lieutenant, whose last life he had taken, put up his cue with a look of ineffable disgust, and whose shilling Doodles had pocketed; " I'm sorry for you, very; but a fellow must play the game, you know." Whereupon Griggs walked out of the room with a gait that seemed to show that he had his own ideas upon that matter, though he did not choose to divulge them. Doodles instantly returned to his friend. " With cattle of that kind it's no use trying the waiting dodge," said he. " You should make your running at once, and trust to bottom to carry you through."

" But there was a horrid little Frenchwoman came in ? "

" What; a servant ? "

" No ; a friend. Such a creature ! You should have heard her talk. A kind of confidential friend she seemed, who called her Julie. I had to go away and leave her there, of course."

" Ah ! you'll have to tip that woman."

" What, with money ? "

" I shouldn't wonder."

" It would come very expensive."

" A tenner now and then, you know. She would do your business for you. Give her a brooch first, and then offer to lend her the money. You'd find she'll rise fast enough, if you're any hand for throwing a fly."

" Oh ! I could do it, you know."

" Do it then, and let 'em both know that you're there. Yes, Parkyns, I'll divide. And, Clavvy, you can come in now in Griggs' place." Then Captain Clavering stripped himself for the battle.

CHAPTER XIX.

THE BLUE POSTS.

II; so you 'ave come to see me. I am so glad." With these words Sophie Gordeloup welcomed Harry Clavering to her room in Mount Street early one morning not long after her interview with Captain Archie in Lady Ongar's presence. On the previous evening Harry had received a note from Lady Ongar, in which she upbraided him for having left unperformed her commission with reference to Count Pateroff. The letter had begun quite abruptly. "I think it unkind of you that you do not come to me. I asked you to see a certain person on my behalf, and you have not done so. Twice he has been here. Once I was in truth out. He came again the next evening at nine, and I was then ill, and had gone to bed. You understand it all, and must know how this annoys me. I thought you would have done this for me, and I thought I should have seen you.—J." This note he found at his lodgings when he returned home at night, and on the following morning he went in his despair direct to Mount Street, on his way to the Adelphi. It was not yet ten o'clock when he was shown into Madame Gordeloup's presence, and as regarded her dress he did not find her to be quite prepared for morning visitors. But he might well be indifferent on that matter as the lady seemed to disregard the circumstances altogether. On her head she wore what he took to be a nightcap, though I will not absolutely undertake to

say that she had slept in that very head-dress. There were frills to
it, and a certain attempt at prettinesses had been made; but then the
attempt had been made so long ago, and the frills were so ignorant
of starch and all frillish propensities, that it hardly could pretend to
decency. A great white wrapper she also wore, which might not have
been objectionable had it not been so long worn that it looked like a
university college surplice at the end of the long vacation. Her slippers
had all the ease which age could give them, and above the slippers, neat-
ness, to say the least of it, did not predominate. But Sophie herself seemed
to be quite at her ease in spite of these deficiencies, and received our
hero with an eager pointed welcome, which I can hardly describe as
affectionate, and which Harry did not at all understand.

"I have to apologize for troubling you," he began.

"Trouble, what trouble? Bah! You give me no trouble. It is you
have the trouble to come here. You come early and I have not got
my crinoline. If you are contented, so am I." Then she smiled, and sat
herself down suddenly, letting herself almost fall into her special corner
in the sofa. "Take a chair, Mr. Harry; then we can talk more
comfortable."

"I want especially to see your brother. Can you give me his
address?"

"What? Edouard—certainly; Travellers' Club."

"But he is never there."

"He sends every day for his letters. You want to see him.
Why?"

Harry was at once confounded, having no answer. "A little private
business," he said.

"Ah; a little private business. You do not owe him a little money,
I am afraid, or you would not want to see him. Ha, ha! You write to
him, and he will see you. There;—there is paper and pen and ink. He
shall get your letter this day."

Harry, nothing suspicious, did as he was bid, and wrote a note in
which he simply told the count that he was specially desirous of seeing
him.

"I will go to you anywhere," said Harry, "if you will name a
place."

We, knowing Madame Gordeloup's habits, may feel little doubt but
that she thought it her duty to become acquainted with the contents of
the note before she sent it out of her house, but we may also know that
she learned very little from it.

"It shall go, almost immediately," said Sophie, when the envelope
was closed.

Then Harry got up to depart, having done his work. "What, you
are going in that way at once? You are in a hurry?"

"Well, yes; I am in a hurry, rather, Madame Gordeloup. I have got to be at my office, and I only just came up here to find out your brother's address." Then he rose and went, leaving the note behind him.

Then Madame Gordeloup, speaking to herself in French, called Harry Clavering a lout, a fool, an awkward overgrown boy, and a pig. She declared him to be a pig nine times over, then shook herself in violent disgust, and after that betook herself to the letter.

The letter was at any rate duly sent to the count, for before Harry had left Mr. Beilby's chambers on that day, Pateroff came to him there. Harry sat in the same room with other men, and therefore went out to see his acquaintance in a little antechamber that was used for such purposes. As he walked from one room to the other, he was conscious of the delicacy and difficulty of the task before him, and the colour was high in his face as he opened the door. But when he had done so, he saw that the count was not alone. A gentleman was with him, whom he did not introduce to Harry, and before whom Harry could not say that which he had to communicate.

"Pardon me," said the count, "but we are in railroad hurry. Nobody ever was in such a haste as I and my friend. You are not engaged to-morrow? No, I see. You dine with me and my friend at the Blue Posts. You know the Blue Posts?"

Harry said he did not know the Blue Posts.

"Then you shall know the Blue Posts. I will be your instructor. You drink claret. Come and see. You eat beefsteaks. Come and try. You love one glass of port wine with your cheese. No. But you shall love it when you have dined with me at the Blue Posts. We will dine altogether after the English way;—which is the best way in the world when it is quite good. It is quite good at the Blue Posts;— quite good! Seven o'clock. You are fined when a minute late; an extra glass of port wine a minute. Now I must go. Ah; yes. I am ruined already."

Then Count Pateroff, holding his watch in his hand, bolted out of the room before Harry could say a word to him.

He had nothing for it but to go to the dinner, and to the dinner he went. On that same evening, the evening of the day on which he had seen Sophie and her brother, he wrote to Lady Ongar, using to her the same manner of writing that she had used to him, and telling her that he had done his best, that he had now seen him whom he had been desired to see, but that he had not been able to speak to him. He was, however, to dine with him on the following day,—and would call in Bolton Street as soon as possible after that interview.

Exactly at seven o'clock, Harry, having the fear of the threatened fine before his eyes, was at the Blue Posts; and there, standing in the middle of the room, he saw Count Pateroff. With Count Pateroff was the same gentleman whom Harry had seen at the Adelphi, and whom the

count now introduced as Colonel Schmoff; and also a little Englishman
with a knowing eye and a bull-dog neck, and whiskers cut very short and
trim,—a horsey little man, whom the count also introduced. "Captain
Boodle; says he knows a cousin of yours, Mr. Clavering."

Then Colonel Schmoff bowed, never yet having spoken a word in
Harry's hearing, and our old friend Doodles with glib volubility told
Harry how intimate he was with Archie, and how he knew Sir Hugh,
and how he had met Lady Clavering, and how "doosed" glad he was
to meet Harry himself on this present occasion.

"And now, my boys, we'll set down," said the count. "There's just
a little soup, printanier; yes, they can make soup here; then a cut of
salmon; and after that the beefsteak. Nothing more. Schmoff, my
boy, can you eat beefsteak?"

Schmoff neither smiled nor spoke, but simply bowed his head gravely,
and sitting down, arranged with slow exactness his napkin over his waistcoat and lap.

"Captain Boodle, can you eat beefsteak," said the count; "Blue
Posts' beefsteak?"

"Try me," said Doodles. "That's all. Try me."

"I will try you, and I will try Mr. Clavering. Schmoff would eat
a horse if he had not a bullock, and a piece of a jackass if he had not
a horse."

"I did eat a horse in Hamboro' once. We was besieged."

So much said Schmoff, very slowly, in a deep bass voice, speaking
from the bottom of his chest, and frowning very heavily as he did
so. The exertion was so great that he did not repeat it for a considerable
time.

"Thank God we are not besieged now," said the count, as the soup
was handed round to them. "Ah, Albert, my friend, that is good soup;
very good soup. My compliments to the excellent Stubbs. Mr. Clavering,
the excellent Stubbs is the cook. I am quite at home here and they do
their best for me. You need not fear you will have any of Schmoff's
horse."

This was all very pleasant, and Harry Clavering sat down to his
dinner prepared to enjoy it; but there was a sense about him during the
whole time that he was being taken in and cheated, and that the count
would cheat him and actually escape away from him on that evening
without his being able to speak a word to him. They were dining in
a public room, at a large table which they had to themselves, while others
were dining at small tables round them. Even if Schmoff and Boodle
had not been there, he could hardly have discussed Lady Ongar's private
affairs in such a room as that. The count had brought him there to dine
in this way with a premeditated purpose of throwing him over, pretending
to give him the meeting that had been asked for, but intending that it
should pass by and be of no avail. Such was Harry's belief, and he

resolved that, though he might have to seize Pateroff by the tails of his coat, the count should not escape him without having been forced at any rate to hear what he had to say. In the meantime the dinner went on very pleasantly.

"Ah," said the count, "there is no fish like salmon early in the year; but not too early. And it should come alive from Grove, and be cooked by Stubbs."

"And eaten by me," said Boodle.

"Under my auspices," said the count, "and then all is well. Mr. Clavering, a little bit near the head? Not care about any particular part? That is wrong. Everybody should always learn what is the best to eat of everything, and get it if they can."

"By George, I should think so," said Doodles. "I know I do."

"Not to know the bit out of the neck of the salmon from any other bit, is not to know a false note from a true one. Not to distinguish a '51 wine from a '58, is to look at an arm or a leg on the canvas, and to care nothing whether it is in drawing, or out of drawing. Not to know Stubbs' beefsteak from other beefsteaks, is to say that every woman is the same thing to you. Only, Stubbs will let you have his beef-steak if you will pay him,—him or his master. With the beautiful woman it is not always so;—not always. Do I make myself understood?"

"Clear as mud," said Doodles. "I'm quite along with you there. Why should a man be ashamed of eating what's nice. Everybody does it."

"No, Captain Boodle; not everybody. Some cannot get it, and some do not know it when it comes in their way. They are to be pitied. I do pity them from the bottom of my heart. But there is one poor fellow I do pity more even than they."

There was something in the tone of the count's words,—a simple pathos, and almost a melody, which interested Harry Clavering. No one knew better than Count Pateroff how to use all the inflexions of his voice, and produce from the phrases he used the very highest interest which they were capable of producing. He now spoke of his pity in a way that might almost have made a sensitive man weep. "Who is it that you pity so much?" Harry asked.

"The man who cannot digest," said the count, in a low clear voice. Then he bent down his head over the morsel of food on his plate, as though he were desirous of hiding a tear. "The man who cannot digest!" As he repeated the words he raised his head again, and looked round at all their faces.

"Yes, yes;—mein Gott, yes," said Schmoff, and even he appeared as though he were almost moved from the deep quietude of his inward indifference.

"Ah; talk of blessings! What a blessing is digestion!" said the count. "I do not know whether you have ever thought of it, Captain Boodle? You are young, and perhaps not. Or you, Mr. Clavering? It is a subject worthy of your thoughts. To digest! Do you know what it means. It is to have the sun always shining, and the shade always ready for you. It is to be met with smiles, and to be greeted with kisses. It is to hear sweet sounds, to sleep with sweet dreams, to be touched ever by gentle, soft, cool hands. It is to be in paradise. Adam and Eve were in paradise. Why? Their digestion was good. Ah! then they took liberties, eat bad fruit,—things they could not digest. They what we call, ruined their constitutions, destroyed their gastric juices, and then they were expelled from paradise by an angel with a flaming sword. The angel with the flaming sword, which turned two ways, was indigestion! There came a great indigestion upon the earth because the cooks were bad, and they called it a deluge. Ah, I thank God there is to be no more deluges. All the evils come from this. Macbeth could not sleep. It was the supper, not the murder. His wife talked and walked. It was the supper again. Milton had a bad digestion because he is always so cross; and your Carlyle must have the worst digestion in the world, because he never says any good of anything. Ah, to digest is to be happy! Believe me, my friends, there is no other way not to be turned out of paradise by a fiery two-handed turning sword."

"It is true," said Schmoff; "yes, it is true."

"I believe you," said Doodles. "And how well the count describes it, don't he, Mr. Clavering. I never looked at it in that light; but, after all, digestion is everything. What is a horse worth, if he won't feed?"

"I never thought much about it," said Harry.

"That is very good," said the great preacher. "Not to think about it ever is the best thing in the world. You will be made to think about it if there be necessity. A friend of mine told me he did not know whether he had a digestion. My friend, I said, you are like the husbandmen; you do not know your own blessings. A bit more steak, Mr. Clavering; see, it has come up hot, just to prove that you have the blessing."

There was a pause in the conversation for a minute or two, during which Schmoff and Doodles were very busy giving the required proof; and the count was leaning back in his chair, with a smile of conscious wisdom on his face, looking as though he were in deep consideration of the subject on which he had just spoken with so much eloquence. Harry did not interrupt the silence, as, foolishly, he was allowing his mind to carry itself away from the scene of enjoyment that was present, and trouble itself with the coming battle which he would be obliged to fight with the count. Schmoff was the first to speak. "When I was eating a horse at Hamboro'——" he began.

"Schmoff," said the count, "if we allow you to get behind the ramparts of that besieged city, we shall have to eat that horse for the rest of the evening. Captain Boodle, if you will believe me, I eat that horse once for two hours. Ah, here is the port wine. Now, Mr. Clavering, this is the wine for cheese;—'34. No man should drink above two glasses of '34. If you want port after that, then have '20."

Schmoff had certainly been hardly treated. He had scarcely spoken a word during dinner, and should, I think, have been allowed to say something of the flavour of the horse. It did not, however, appear from his countenance that he had felt, or that he resented the interference; though he did not make any further attempt to enliven the conversation.

They did not sit long over their wine, and the count, in spite of what he had said about the claret, did not drink any. "Captain Boodle," he said, "you must respect my weakness as well as my strength. I know what I can do, and what I cannot. If I were a real hero, like you English,—which means, if I had an ostrich in my inside,—I would drink till twelve every night, and eat broiled bones till six every morning. But alas! the ostrich has not been given to me. As a common man I am pretty well, but I have no heroic capacities. We will have a little chasse, and then we will smoke.

Harry began to be very nervous. How was he to do it? It had become clearer and clearer to him through every ten minutes of the dinner, that the count did not intend to give him any moment for private conversation. He felt that he was cheated and ill-used, and was waxing angry. They were to go and smoke in a public room, and he knew, or thought he knew, what that meant. The count would sit there till he went, and had brought the Colonel Schmoff with him, so that he might be sure of some ally to remain by his side and ensure silence. And the count, doubtless, had calculated that when Captain Boodle went, as he soon would go, to his billiards, he, Harry Clavering, would feel himself compelled to go also. No! It should not result in that way. Harry resolved that he would not go. He had his mission to perform and he would perform it, even if he were compelled to do so in the presence of Colonel Schmoff.

Doodles soon went. He could not sit long with the simple gratification of a cigar, without gin-and-water or other comfort of that kind, even though the eloquence of Count Pateroff might be excited in his favour. He was a man, indeed, who did not love to sit still, even with the comfort of gin-and-water. An active little man was Captain Boodle, always doing something or anxious to do something in his own line of business. Small speculations in money, so concocted as to leave the risk against him smaller than the chance on his side, constituted Captain Boodle's trade; and in that trade he was indefatigable, ingenious, and, to a certain extent, successful. The worst of the trade was this; that though he worked at it above twelve hours a day, to the exclusion of all other interests in life, he could only make out of it an income which would have been considered a beggarly failure at any other profession. When he netted a pound a day he considered himself to have done very well; but he could not do that every day in the week. To do it often required unremitting exertion. And then, in spite of all his care, misfortunes would come. "A cursed garron, of whom nobody had ever heard the name! If a man mayn't take a liberty with such a brute as that, when is he to take a liberty?" So had he expressed himself plaintively, endeavouring to excuse himself, when on some occasion a race had been won by some outside horse which Captain Boodle had omitted to make safe in his betting-book. He was regarded by his intimate friends as a very successful man; but I think myself that his life was a mistake. To live with one's hands ever daubed with chalk from a billiard-table, to be always spying into stables and rubbing against grooms, to put up with the narrow lodgings which needy men encounter at race meetings, to be day after day on the rails running after platers and steeplechasers, to be conscious on all occasions of the expediency of selling your beast when you are hunting, to be counting up little odds at all your spare moments;—these things do not, I think, make a satisfactory life for a young man. And for a man that is not young, they are the very devil! Better have no digestion when you are forty than find yourself living such a life as that! Captain Boodle would, I think, have been happier had he contrived to get himself employed as a tax-gatherer or an attorney's clerk.

On this occasion Doodles soon went, as had been expected, and Harry found himself smoking with the two foreigners. Pateroff was no longer eloquent, but sat with his cigar in his mouth as silent as Colonel Schmoff himself. It was evidently expected of Harry that he should go.

"Count," he said at last, "you got my note?" There were seven or eight persons sitting in the room besides the party of three to which Harry belonged.

"Your note, Mr. Clavering! which note? Oh, yes; I should not have had the pleasure of seeing you here to-day but for that."

"Can you give me five minutes in private?"

"What! now! here! this evening! after dinner? Another time I will talk with you by the hour together."

"I fear I must trouble you now. I need not remind you that I could not keep you yesterday morning; you were so much hurried."

"And now I am having my little moment of comfort! These special business conversations after dinner are so bad for the digestion!"

"If I could have caught you before dinner, Count Pateroff, I would have done so."

"If it must be, it must. Schmoff, will you wait for me ten minutes? I will not be more than ten minutes." And the count as he made this promise looked at his watch. "Waiter," he said, speaking in a sharp tone which Harry had not heard before, "show this gentleman and me into a private room." Harry got up and led the way out, not forgetting to assure himself that he cared nothing for the sharpness of the count's voice.

"Now, Mr. Clavering, what is it?" said the count, looking full into Harry's eye.

"I will tell you in two words."

"In one if you can."

"I came with a message to you from Lady Ongar."

"Why are you a messenger from Lady Ongar?"

"I have known her long and she is connected with my family."

"Why does she not send her messages by Sir Hugh,—her brother-in-law?"

"It is hardly for you to ask that?"

"Yes; it is for me to ask that. I have known Lady Ongar well, and have treated her with kindness. I do not want to have messages by anybody. But go on. If you are a messenger, give your message."

"Lady Ongar bids me tell you that she cannot see you."

"But she must see me. She shall see me!"

"I am to explain to you that she declines to do so. Surely, Count Pateroff, you must understand——"

"Ah, bah; I understand everything;—in such matters as these, better, perhaps, than you, Mr. Clavering. You have given your message. Now, as you are a messenger, will you give mine?"

"That will depend altogether on its nature."

"Sir, I never send uncivil words to a woman, though sometimes I may be tempted to speak them to a man; when, for instance, a man interferes with me; do you understand? My message is this :—tell her ladyship, with my compliments, that it will be better for her to see me,—better for her, and for me. When that poor lord died,—and he had been, mind, my friend for many years before her ladyship had heard his name,—I was with him; and there were occurrences of which you know nothing and need know nothing. I did my best then to be courteous to Lady Ongar, which she returns by shutting her door in my face. I do not mind that. I am not angry with a woman. But tell her that when she has heard what I now say to her by you, she will, I do not doubt, think better of it; and therefore I shall do myself the honour of presenting myself at her door again. Good-night, Mr. Clavering; au revoir; we will have another of Stubbs' little dinners before long." As he spoke these last words the count's voice was again changed, and the old smile had returned to his face.

Harry shook hands with him and walked away homewards, not without a feeling that the count had got the better of him, even to the end. He had, however, learned how the land lay, and could explain to Lady Ongar that Count Pateroff now knew her wishes and was determined to disregard them.

CHAPTER XX.

DESOLATION.

IN the meantime there was grief down at the great house of Clavering; and grief, we must suppose also, at the house in Berkeley Square, as soon as the news from his country home had reached Sir Hugh Clavering. Little Hughy, his heir, was dead. Early one morning, Mrs. Clavering, at the rectory, received a message from Lady Clavering, begging that she would go up to the house, and, on arriving there, she found that the poor child was very ill. The doctor was then at Clavering, and had recommended that a message should be sent to the father in London, begging him to come down. This message had been already despatched when Mrs. Clavering arrived. The poor mother was in a state of terrible agony, but at that time there was yet hope. Mrs. Clavering then remained with Lady Clavering for two or three hours; but just before dinner on the same day another messenger came across to say that hope was past, and that the child had gone. Could Mrs. Clavering come over again, as Lady Clavering was in a sad way?

"You'll have your dinner first?" said the rector.

"No, I think not. I shall wish to make her take something, and I can do it better if I ask for tea for myself. I will go at once. Poor dear little boy."

"It was a blow I always feared," said the rector to his daughter as soon as his wife had left them. "Indeed, I knew that it was coming."

"And she was always fearing it," said Fanny. "But I do not think he did. He never seems to think that evil will come to him."

"He will feel this," said the rector.

"Feel it, papa! Of course he will feel it."

"I do not think he would,—not deeply, that is,—if there were four or five of them. He is a hard man;—the hardest man I ever knew. Who ever saw him playing with his own child, or with any other? Who ever heard him say a soft word to his wife? But he will be hit now, for this child was his heir. He will be hit hard now, and I pity him."

Mrs. Clavering went across the park alone, and soon found herself in the poor bereaved mother's room. She was sitting by herself, having driven the old housekeeper away from her; and there were no traces of tears then on her face, though she had wept plentifully when Mrs. Clavering had been with her in the morning. But there had come upon her suddenly a look of age, which nothing but such sorrow as this can produce. Mrs. Clavering was surprised to see that she had dressed herself carefully since the morning, as was her custom to do daily, even when alone; and that she was not in her bedroom, but in a small sitting-room which she generally used when Sir Hugh was not at the park.

"My poor Hermione," said Mrs. Clavering, coming up to her, and taking her by the hand.

"Yes, I am poor; poor enough. Why have they troubled you to come across again?"

"Did you not send for me? But it was quite right, whether you sent or no. Of course I should come when I heard it. It cannot be good for you to be all alone."

"I suppose he will be here to-night?"

"Yes, if he got your message before three o'clock."

"Oh, he will have received it, and I suppose he will come. You think he will come, eh?"

"Of course he will come."

"I do not know. He does not like coming to the country."

"He will be sure to come now, Hermione."

"And who will tell him? Some one must tell him before he comes to me. Should there not be some one to tell him? They have sent another message."

"Hannah shall be at hand to tell him." Hannah was the old house-keeper, who had been in the family when Sir Hugh was born. "Or, if you wish it, Henry shall come down and remain here. I am sure he will do so, if it will be a comfort."

"No; he would, perhaps, be rough to Mr. Clavering. He is so very hard. Hannah shall do it. Will you make her understand?" Mrs. Clavering promised that she would do this, wondering, as she did so, at the wretched, frigid immobility of the unfortunate woman before her. She knew Lady Clavering well;—knew her to be in many things weak, to be worldly, listless, and perhaps somewhat selfish; but she knew also that she had loved her child as mothers always love. Yet, at this moment, it seemed that she was thinking more of her husband than of the bairn she had lost. Mrs. Clavering had sat down by her and taken her hand, and was still so sitting in silence when Lady Clavering spoke again. "I suppose he will turn me out of his house now," she said.

"Who will do so? Hugh? Oh, Hermione, how can you speak in such a way?"

"He scolded me before because my poor darling was not strong. My darling! How could I help it? And he scolded me because there was none other but he. He will turn me out altogether now. Oh, Mrs. Clavering, you do not know how hard he is."

Anything was better than this, and therefore Mrs. Clavering asked the poor woman to take her into the room where the little body lay in its little cot. If she could induce the mother to weep for the child, even that would be better than this hard persistent fear as to what her husband would say and do. So they both went and stood together over the little fellow whose short sufferings had thus been brought to an end. "My poor dear, what can I say to comfort you?" Mrs. Clavering, as she asked this, knew well that no comfort could be spoken in words; but—if she could only make the sufferer weep!

"Comfort!" said the mother. "There is no comfort now, I believe, in anything. It is long since I knew any comfort;—not since Julia went."

"Have you written to Julia?"

"No; I have written to no one. I cannot write. I feel as though if it were to bring him back again I could not write of it. My boy! my boy! my boy!" But still there was not a tear in her eye.

"I will write to Julia," said Mrs. Clavering; "and I will read to you my letter."

"No, do not read it me. What is the use? He has made her quarrel with me. Julia cares nothing now for me, or for my angel. Why should she care? When she came home we would not see her. Of course she will not care. Who is there that will care for me?"

"Do not I care for you, Hermione?"

"Yes, because you are here; because of the nearness of the houses. If you lived far away you would not care for me. It is just the custom of the thing." There was something so true in this that Mrs. Clavering could make no answer to it. Then they turned to go back into the sitting-room, and as they did so Lady Clavering lingered behind for a moment; but when she was again with Mrs. Clavering her cheek was still dry.

"He will be at the station at nine," said Lady Clavering. "They must send the brougham for him, or the dog-cart. He will be very angry if he is made to come home in the fly from the public-house." Then the elder lady left the room and gave orders that Sir Hugh should be met by his carriage. What must the wife think of her husband, when she feared that he would be angered by little matters at such a time as this! "Do you think it will make him very unhappy?" Lady Clavering asked.

"Of course it will make him unhappy. How should it be otherwise?"

"He had said so often that the child would die. He will have got used to the fear."

"His grief will be as fresh now as though he had never thought so, and never said so."

"He is so hard; and then he has such will, such power. He will thrust it off from him and determine that it shall not oppress him. I know him so well."

"We should all make some exertion like that in our sorrow, trusting to God's kindness to relieve us. You too, Hermione, should determine also; but not yet, my dear. At first it is better to let sorrow have its way."

"But he will determine at once. You remember when Meeny went." Meeny had been a little girl who had been born before the boy, and who had died when little more than twelve months old. "He did not expect that ; but then he only shook his head, and went out of the room. He has never spoken to me one word of her since that. I think he has forgotten Meeny altogether,—even that she was ever here."

"He cannot forget the boy who was his heir."

"Ah, that is where it is. He will say words to me which would make you creep if you could hear them. Yes, my darling was his heir. Archie will marry now, and will have children, and his boy will be the heir. There will be more division and more quarrels, for Hugh will hate his brother now."

"I do not understand why."

"Because he is so hard. It is a pity he should ever have married, for he wants nothing that a wife can do for him. He wanted a boy to come after him in the estate, and now that glory has been taken from him. Mrs. Clavering, I often wish that I could die."

It would be bootless here to repeat the words of wise and loving counsel with which the elder of the two ladies endeavoured to comfort the younger, and to make her understand what were the duties which still remained to her, and which, if they were rightly performed, would in their performance, soften the misery of her lot. Lady Clavering listened with that dull, useless attention which on such occasions sorrow always gives to the prudent counsels of friendship ; but she was thinking ever and always of her husband, and watching the moment of his expected return. In her heart she wished that he might not come on that evening. At last, at half-past nine, she exerted herself to send away her visitor.

"He will be here soon, if he comes to-night," Lady Clavering said, "and it will be better that he should find me alone."

"Will it be better ? "

"Yes, yes. Cannot you see how he would frown and shake his head if you were here ? I would sooner be alone when he comes. Good-night. You have been very kind to me ; but you are always kind. Things are done kindly always at your house, because there is so much love there. You will write to Julia for me. Good-night." Then Mrs. Clavering kissed her and went, thinking as she walked home in the dark to the rectory, how much she had to be thankful in that these words had been true which her poor neighbour had spoken. Her house was full of love.

For the next half hour Lady Clavering sat alone listening with eager ear for the sound of her husband's wheels, and at last she had almost told herself that the hour for his coming had gone by, when she heard the rapid grating on the gravel as the dog-cart was driven up to the door. She ran out on to the corridor, but her heart sank within her as she did so, and she took tightly hold of the balustrade to support herself. For a moment she had thought of running down to meet him ;—of trusting to the sadness of the moment to produce in him, if it were but for a minute something of tender solicitude; but she remembered that the servants would be there, and knew that he would not be soft before them. She remembered also that the housekeeper had received her instructions, and she feared to disarrange the settled programme. So she went back to the open door of the room, that her retreating step might not be heard by him as he should come up to her, and standing there she still listened. The house was silent and her ears were acute with sorrow. She could hear the movement of the old woman as she gently, trembling, as Lady Clavering knew, made her way down the hall to meet her master. Sir Hugh of course had learned his child's fate already from the servant who met him; but it was well that the ceremony of such telling should be performed. She felt the cold air come in from the opened front door, and she heard her husband's heavy quick step as he entered. Then she heard the murmur of Hannah's voice; but the first word she heard was in her husband's tones, "Where is Lady Clavering?" Then the answer was given, and the wife knowing that he was coming, retreated back to her chair.

But still he did not come quite at once. He was pulling off his coat and laying aside his hat and gloves. Then came upon her a feeling that at such a time any other husband and wife would have been at once in each other's arms. And at the moment she thought of all that they had lost. To her her child had been all and everything. To him he had been his heir and the prop of his house. The boy had been the only link that had still bound them together. Now he was gone, and there was no longer any link between them. He was gone and she had nothing left to her. He was gone, and the father was also alone in the world, without any heir and with no prop to his house. She thought of all this as she heard his step coming slowly up the stairs. Slowly he came along the passage, and though she dreaded his coming it almost seemed as though he would never be there.

When he had entered the room she was the first to speak. "Oh, Hugh!" she exclaimed, "oh, Hugh!" He had closed the door before he uttered a word, and then he threw himself into a chair. There were candles near to him and she could see that his countenance also was altered. He had indeed been stricken hard, and his half-stunned face showed the violence of the blow. The harsh, cruel, selfish man had at last been made to suffer. Although he had spoken of it and had expected it, the death of his heir hit him hard, as the rector had said.

"When did he die?" asked the father.

"It was past four I think." Then there was again silence, and Lady Clavering went up to her husband and stood close by his shoulder. At last she ventured to put her hand upon him. With all her own misery heavy upon her, she was chiefly thinking at this moment how she might soothe him. She laid her hand upon his shoulder, and by degrees she moved it softly to his breast. Then he raised his own hand and with it moved hers from his person. He did it gently;—but what was the use of such nonsense as that?

"The Lord giveth," said the wife, "and the Lord taketh away." Hearing this Sir Hugh made with his head a gesture of impatience. "Blessed be the name of the Lord," continued Lady Clavering. Her voice was low and almost trembling, and she repeated the words as though they were a task which she had set herself.

"That's all very well in its way," said he, "but what's the special use of it now. I hate twaddle. One must bear one's misfortune as one best can. I don't believe that kind of thing ever makes it lighter."

"They say it does, Hugh."

"Ah! they say! Have they ever tried? If you have been living up to that kind of thing all your life, it may be very well;—that is as well at one time as another. But it won't give me back my boy."

"No, Hugh; he will never come back again; but we may think that he's in Heaven."

"If that is enough for you, let it be so. But don't talk to me of it. I don't like it. It doesn't suit me. I had only one, and he has gone. It is always the way." He spoke of the child as having been his—not his and hers. She felt this, and understood the want of affection which it conveyed; but she said nothing of it.

"Oh, Hugh; what could we do? It was not our fault."

"Who is talking of any fault? I have said nothing as to fault. He was always poor and sickly. The Claverings, generally, have been so strong. Look at myself, and Archie, and my sisters. Well, it cannot be helped. Thinking of it will not bring him back again. You had better tell some one to get me something to eat. I came away, of course, without any dinner."

She herself had eaten nothing since the morning, but she neither spoke nor thought of that. She rang the bell, and going out into the passage gave the servant the order on the stairs.

"It is no good my staying here," he said. "I will go and dress. It is the best not to think of such things,—much the best. People call that heartless, of course, but then people are fools. If I were to sit still, and think of it for a week together, what good could I do?"

"But how not to think of it? that is the thing."

"Women are different, I suppose. I will dress and then go down to the breakfast-room. Tell Saunders to get me a bottle of champagne. You will be better also if you will take a glass of wine."

It was the first word he had spoken which showed any care for her, and she was grateful for it. As he arose to go, she came close to him again, and put her hand very gently on his arm. "Hugh," she said, "will you not see him?"

"What good will that do?"

"I think you would regret it if you were to let them take him away

"The Lord giveth, and the Lord taketh away"

without looking at him. He is so pretty as he lays in his little bed. I thought you would come with me to see him." He was more gentle with her than she had expected, and she led him away to the room which had been their own, and in which the child had died.

"Why here?" he said, almost angrily, as he entered.

"I have had him here with me since you went."

"He should not be here now," he said, shuddering. "I wish he had been moved before I came. I will not have this room any more ; remember that." She led him up to the foot of the little cot, which stood close by the head of her own bed, and then she removed a handkerchief which lay upon the child's face.

"Oh, Hugh ! oh, Hugh !" she said, and, throwing her arms round his neck, she wept violently upon his breast. For a few moments he did not disturb her, but stood looking at his boy's face. "Hugh, Hugh," she repeated, "will you not be kind to me? Do be kind to me. It is not my fault that we are childless."

Still he endured her for a few moments longer. He spoke no word to her, but he let her remain there, with her head upon his breast.

"Dear Hugh, I love you so truly !"

"This is nonsense," said he, "sheer nonsense." His voice was low and very hoarse. "Why do you talk of kindness now?"

"Because I am so wretched."

"What have I done to make you wretched?"

"I do not mean that; but if you will be gentle with me, it will comfort me. Do not leave me here all alone, now my darling has been taken from me."

Then he shook her from him, not violently, but with a persistent action.

"Do you mean that you want to go up to town?" he said.

"Oh, no; not that."

"Then what is it you want? Where would you live, if not here?"

"Anywhere you please, only that you should stay with me."

"All that is nonsense. I wonder that you should talk of such things now. Come away from this, and let me go to my room. All this is trash and nonsense, and I hate it." She put back with careful hands the piece of cambric which she had moved, and then, seating herself on a chair, wept violently, with her hands closed upon her face. "That comes of bringing me here," he said. "Get up, Hermione. I will not have you so foolish. Get up, I say. I will have the room closed till the men come."

"Oh, no !"

"Get up, I say, and come away." Then she rose, and followed him out of the chamber, and when he went to change his clothes she returned to the room in which he had found her. There she sat and wept, while he went down and dined and drank alone. But the old housekeeper brought her up a morsel of food and a glass of wine, saying that her master desired that she would take it.

"I will not leave you, my lady, till you have done so," said Hannah. "To fast so long must be bad always."

Then she eat the food, and drank a drop of wine, and allowed the old woman to take her away to the bed that had been prepared for her. Of her husband she saw no more for four days. On the next morning a note was brought to her, in which Sir Hugh told her that he had returned to London. It was necessary, he said, that he should see his lawyer and his brother. He and Archie would return for the funeral. With reference to that he had already given orders.

During the next three days, and till her husband's return, Lady Clavering remained at the rectory, and in the comfort of Mrs. Clavering's presence she almost felt that it would be well for her if those days could be prolonged. But she knew the hour at which her husband would return, and she took care to be at home when he arrived. "You will come and see him?" she said to the rector, as she left the parsonage. "You will come at once;—in an hour or two?" Mr. Clavering remembered the circumstances of his last visit to the house, and the declaration he had then made that he would not return there. But all that could not now be considered.

"Yes," he said, "I will come across this evening. But you had better tell him, so that he need not be troubled to see me if he would rather be alone."

"Oh, he will see you. Of course he will see you. And you will not remember that he ever offended you?"

Mrs. Clavering had written both to Julia and to Harry, and the day of the funeral had been settled. Harry had already communicated his intention of coming down; and Lady Ongar had replied to Mrs. Clavering's letter, saying that she could not now offer to go to Clavering Park, but that if her sister would go elsewhere with her,—to some place, perhaps, on the sea-side,—she would be glad to accompany her; and she used many arguments in her letter to show that such an arrangement as this had better be made.

"You will be with my sister," she had said; "and she will understand why I do not write to her myself, and will not think that it comes from coldness." This had been written before Lady Ongar saw Harry Clavering.

Mr. Clavering, when he got to the great house, was immediately shown into the room in which the baronet and his younger brother were sitting. They had, some time since, finished dinner, but the decanters were still on the table before them. "Hugh," said the rector, walking up to his elder nephew, briskly, "I grieve for you. I grieve for you from the bottom of my heart."

"Yes," said Hugh, "it has been a heavy blow. Sit down, uncle.

There is a clean glass there; or Archie will fetch you one." Then Archie looked out a clean glass and passed the decanter; but of this the rector took no direct notice.

"It has been a blow, my poor boy,—a heavy blow," said the rector. "None heavier could have fallen. But our sorrows come from Heaven, as do our blessings, and must be accepted."

"We are all like grass," said Archie, "and must be cut down in our turns." Archie, in saying this, intended to put on his best behaviour. He was as sincere as he knew how to be.

"Come, Archie, none of that," said his brother. "It is my uncle's trade."

"Hugh," said the rector, "unless you can think of it so, you will find no comfort."

"And I expect none, so there is an end of that. Different people think of these things differently, you know, and it is of no more use for me to bother you than it is for you to bother me. My boy has gone, and I know that he will not come back to me. I shall never have another, and it is hard to bear. But, meaning no offence to you, I would sooner be left to bear it in my own way. If I were to talk about the grass as Archie did just now, it would be humbug, and I hate humbug. No offence to you. Take some wine, uncle."

But the rector could not drink wine in that presence, and therefore he escaped as soon as he could. He spoke one word of intended comfort to Lady Clavering, and then returned to the rectory.

CHAPTER XXI.

Yes; Wrong;—Certainly Wrong.

HARRY CLAVERING had heard the news of his little cousin's death before he went to Bolton Street to report the result of his negotiation with the count. His mother's letter with the news had come to him in the morning, and on the same evening he called on Lady Ongar. She also had then received Mrs. Clavering's letter, and knew what had occurred at the park. Harry found her alone, having asked the servant whether Madame Gordeloup was with his mistress. Had such been the case he would have gone away, and left his message untold.

As he entered the room his mind was naturally full of the tidings from Clavering. Count Pateroff and his message had lost some of their importance through this other event, and the emptiness of the childless house was the first subject of conversation between him and Lady Ongar. "I pity my sister greatly," said she. "I feel for her as deeply as I should have done had nothing occurred to separate us;—but I cannot feel for him."

"I do," said Harry.

"He is your cousin, and perhaps has been your friend?"

"No, not especially. He and I have never pulled well together; but still I pity him deeply."

"He is not my cousin, but I know him better than you do, Harry. He will not feel much himself, and his sorrow will be for his heir, not for his son. He is a man whose happiness does not depend on the life or death of any one. He likes some people, as he once liked me; but I do not think that he ever loved any human being. He will get over it, and he will simply wish that Hermy may die, that he may marry another wife. Harry, I know him so well!"

"Archie will marry now," said Harry.

"Yes; if he can get any one to have him. There are very few men who can't get wives, but I can fancy Archie Clavering to be one of them. He has not humility enough to ask the sort of girl who would be glad to take him. Now, with his improved prospects, he will want a royal princess or something not much short of it. Money, rank, and blood might have done before, but he'll expect youth, beauty, and wit now, as well as the other things. He may marry after all, for he is just the man to walk out of a church some day with the cookmaid under his arm as his wife."

"Perhaps he may find something between a princess and a cookmaid."

"I hope, for your sake, he may not;—neither a princess nor a cookmaid, nor anything between."

"He has my leave to marry to-morrow, Lady Ongar. If I had my wish, Hugh should have his house full of children."

"Of course that is the proper thing to say, Harry."

"I won't stand that from you, Lady Ongar. What I say, I mean; and no one knows that better than you."

"Won't you, Harry? From whom, then, if not from me? But come, I will do you justice, and believe you to be simple enough to wish anything of the kind. The sort of castle in the air which you build, is not one to be had by inheritance, but to be taken by storm. You must fight for it."

"Or work for it."

"Or win it in some way off your own bat; and no lord ever sat prouder in his castle than you sit in those that you build from day to day in your imagination. And you sally forth and do all manner of magnificent deeds. You help distressed damsels,—poor me, for instance; and you attack enormous dragons;—shall I say that Sophie Gordeloup is the latest dragon?—and you wish well to your enemies, such as Hugh and Archie; and you cut down enormous forests, which means your coming miracles as an engineer;—and then you fall gloriously in love. When is that last to be, Harry?"

"I suppose, according to all precedent, that must be done with the distressed damsel," he said,—fool that he was.

"No, Harry, no ; you shall take your young fresh generous heart to a better market than that ; not but that the distressed damsel will ever remember what might once have been."

He knew that he was playing on the edge of a precipice,—that he was fluttering as a moth round a candle. He knew that it behoved him now at once to tell her all his tale as to Stratton and Florence Burton ;—that if he could tell it now, the pang would be over and the danger gone. But he did not tell it. Instead of telling it he thought of Lady Ongar's beauty, of his own early love, of what might have been his had he not gone to Stratton. I think he thought, if not of her wealth, yet of the power and place which would have been his were it now open to him to ask her for her hand. When he had declared that he did not want his cousin's inheritance, he had spoken the simple truth. He was not covetous of another's money. Were Archie to marry as many wives as Henry, and have as many children as Priam, it would be no offence to him. His desires did not lie in that line. But in this other case, the woman before him who would so willingly have endowed him with all that she possessed, had been loved by him before he had ever seen Florence Burton. In all his love for Florence,—so he now told himself, but so told himself falsely,—he had ever remembered that Julia Brabazon had been his first love, the love whom he had loved with all his heart. But things had gone with him most unfortunately,—with a misfortune that had never been paralleled. It was thus he was thinking instead of remembering that now was the time in which his tale should be told.

Lady Ongar, however, soon carried him away from the actual brink of the precipice. "But how about the dragon," said she, "or rather about the dragon's brother, at whom you were bound to go and tilt on my behalf? Have you tilted, or are you a recreant knight ? "

"I have tilted," said he, "but the he-dragon professes that he will not regard himself as killed. In other words he declares that he will see you."

"That he will see me ? " said Lady Ongar, and as she spoke there came an angry spot on each cheek. "Does he send me that message as a threat ? "

"He does not send it as a threat, but I think he partly means it so."

"He will find, Harry, that I will not see him ; and that should he force himself into my presence, I shall know how to punish such an outrage. If he sent me any message, let me know it."

"To tell the truth he was most unwilling to speak to me at all, though he was anxious to be civil to me. When I had inquired for him some time in vain, he came to me with another man, and asked me to dinner.

So I went, and as there were four of us, of course I could not speak to him then. He still had the other man, a foreigner—"

"Colonel Schmoff, perhaps?"

"Yes; Colonel Schmoff. He kept Colonel Schmoff by him, so as to guard him from being questioned."

"That is so like him. Everything he does he does with some design,—with some little plan. Well, Harry, you might have ignored Colonel Schmoff for what I should have cared."

"I got the count to come out into another room at last, and then he was very angry,—with me, you know,—and talked of what he would do to men who interfered with him."

"You will not quarrel with him, Harry? Promise me that there shall be no nonsense of that sort,—no fighting."

"Oh, no; we were friends again very soon. But he bade me tell you that there was something important for him to say and for you to hear, which was no concern of mine, and which required an interview."

"I do not believe him, Harry."

"And he said that he had once been very courteous to you—"

"Yes; once insolent,—and once courteous. I have forgiven the one for the other."

"He then went on to say that you made him a poor return for his civility by shutting your door in his face, but that he did not doubt you would think better of it when you had heard his message. There-fore, he said, he should call again. That, Lady Ongar, was the whole of it."

"Shall I tell you what his intention was, Harry?" Again her face became red as she asked this question; but the colour which now came to her cheeks was rather that of shame than of anger.

"What was his intention?"

"To make you believe that I am in his power; to make you think that he has been my lover; to lower me in your eyes, so that you might believe all that others have believed,—all that Hugh Clavering has pre-tended to believe. That has been his object, Harry, and perhaps you will tell me what success he has had."

"Lady Ongar!"

"You know the old story, that the drop which is ever dropping will wear the stone. And after all why should your faith in me be as hard even as a stone?"

"Do you believe that what he said had any such effect?"

"It is very hard to look into another person's heart; and the dearer and nearer that heart is to your own, the greater, I think, is the difficulty. I know that man's heart,—what he calls his heart; but I don't know yours."

For a moment or two Clavering made no answer, and then, when he did speak, he went back from himself to the count.

" If what you surmise of him be true, he must be a very devil.   He cannot be a man—"

" Man or devil, what matters which he be ?   Which is the worst, Harry, and what is the difference ?   The Fausts of this day want no Mephistopheles to teach them guile or to harden their hearts."

" I do not believe that there are such men.   There may be one."

" One, Harry !   What was Lord Ongar ?   What is your cousin Hugh ? What is this Count Pateroff?   Are they not all of the same nature ; hard as stone, desirous simply of indulging their own appetites, utterly without one generous feeling, incapable even of the idea of caring for any one ? Is it not so ?   In truth this count is the best of the three I have named. With him a woman would stand a better chance than with either of the others."

" Nevertheless, if that was his motive, he is a devil."

" He shall be a devil if you say so.   He shall be anything you please, so long as he has not made you think evil of me."

" No ; he has not done that."

" Then I don't care what he has done, or what he may do.   You would not have me see him, would you ? "   This she asked with a sudden energy, throwing herself forward from her seat with her elbows on the table, and resting her face on her hands, as she had already done more than once when he had been there ; so that the attitude, which became her well, was now customary in his eyes.

" You will hardly be guided by my opinion in such a matter."

" By whose, then, will I be guided ?   Nay, Harry, since you put me to a promise, I will make the promise.   I will be guided by your opinion. If you bid me see him, I will do it,—though, I own, it would be distressing to me."

" Why should you see him, if you do not wish it ? "

" I know no reason.   In truth there is no reason.   What he says about Lord Ongar is simply some part of his scheme.   You see what his scheme is, Harry ? "

" What is his scheme ? "

" Simply this—that I should be frightened into becoming his wife. My darling bosom friend Sophie, who, as I take it, has not quite managed to come to satisfactory terms with her brother,—and I have no doubt her price for assistance has been high,—has informed me more than once that her brother desires to do me so much honour. The count, perhaps, thinks that he can manage such a bagatelle without any aid from his sister ; and my dearest Sophie seems to feel that she can do better with me herself in my widowed state, than if I were to take another husband.   They are so kind and so affectionate ; are they not ? "

At this moment tea was brought in, and Clavering sat for a time silent with his cup in his hand.   She, the meanwhile, had resumed the old position with her face upon her hands, which she had abandoned when the servant entered the room, and was now sitting looking at him as he sipped his tea with his eyes averted from her. " I cannot understand," at last he said, " why you should persist in your intimacy with such a woman."

" You have not thought about it, Harry, or you would understand it. It is, I think, very easily understood."

" You know her to be treacherous, false, vulgar, covetous, unprincipled. You cannot like her. You say she is a dragon."

" A dragon to you, I said."

" You cannot pretend that she is a lady, and yet you put up with her society."

" Exactly. And now tell me what you would have me do."

" I would have you part from her."

" But how ? It is so easy to say, part. Am I to bar my door against her when she has given me no offence ? Am I to forget that she did me great service, when I sorely needed such services ? Can I tell her to her face that she is all these things that you say of her, and that therefore I will for the future dispense with her company ? Or do you believe that people in this world associate only with those they love and esteem ? "

" I would not have one for my intimate friend whom I did not love and esteem."

" But, Harry, suppose that no one loved and esteemed you; that you had no home down at Clavering with a father that admires you and a mother that worships you; no sisters that think you to be almost perfect, no comrades with whom you can work with mutual regard and emulation, no self-confidence, no high hopes of your own, no power of choosing companions whom you can esteem and love;— suppose with you it was Sophie Gordeloup or none,—how would it be with you then ? "

His heart must have been made of stone if this had not melted it. He got up and coming round to her stood over her. " Julia," he said, " it is not so with you."

" But it is so with Julia," she said. " That is the truth. How am I better than her, and why should I not associate with her ? "

" Better than her ! As women you are poles asunder."

" But as dragons," she said, smiling, " we come together."

" Do you mean that you have no one to love you ? "

" Yes, Harry ; that is just what I do mean. I have none to love me. In playing my cards I have won my stakes in money and rank, but have lost the amount ten times told in affection, friendship, and that general unpronounced esteem which creates the fellowship of men and women in the world. I have a carriage and horses, and am driven about with grand servants ; and people, as they see me, whisper and say that is

Lady Ongar, whom nobody knows. I can see it in their eyes till I fancy that I can hear their words."

"But it is all false."

"What is false? It is not false that I have deserved this. I have done that which has made me a fitting companion for such a one as Sophie Gordeloup, though I have not done that which perhaps these people think."

He paused again before he spoke, still standing near her on the rug. "Lady Ongar——" he said.

"Nay, Harry; not Lady Ongar when we are together thus. Let me feel that I have one friend who can dare to call me by my name,—from whose mouth I shall be pleased to hear my name. You need not fear that I shall think that it means too much. I will not take it as meaning what it used to mean."

He did not know how to go on with his speech, or in truth what to say to her. Florence Burton was still present to his mind, and from minute to minute he told himself that he would not become a villain. But now it had come to that with him, that he would have given all that he had in the world that he had never gone to Stratton. He sat down by her in silence, looking away from her at the fire, swearing to himself that he would not become a villain, and yet wishing, almost wishing, that he had the courage to throw his honour overboard. At last, half turning round towards her he took her hand, or rather took her first by the wrist till he could possess himself of her hand. As he did so he touched her hair and her cheek, and she let her hand drop till it rested in his. "Julia," he said, "what can I do to comfort you?" She did not answer him, but looked away from him as she sat, across the table into vacancy. "Julia," he said again, "is there anything that will comfort you?" But still she did not answer him.

He understood it all as well as the reader will understand it. He knew how it was with her, and was aware that he was at this instant false almost equally to her and to Florence. He knew that the question he had asked was one to which there could be made a true and satisfactory answer, but that his safety lay in the fact that that answer was all but impossible for her to give. Could she say, "Yes, you can comfort me. Tell me that you yet love me, and I will be comforted?" But he had not designed to bring her into such difficulty as this. He had not intended to be cruel. He had drifted into treachery unawares, and was torturing her, not because he was wicked, but because he was weak. He had held her hand now for some minute or two, but still she did not speak to him. Then he raised it and pressed it warmly to his lips.

"No, Harry," she said, jumping from her seat and drawing her hand rapidly from him; "no; it shall not be like that. Let it be Lady Ongar again if the sound of the other name brings back too closely the memory of other days. Let it be Lady Ongar again. I can understand that it will be better." As she spoke she walked away from him across the room, and he followed her.

"Are you angry?" he asked her.

"No, Harry; not angry. How should I be angry with you who alone are left to me of my old friends? But, Harry, you must think for me, and spare me in my difficulty."

"Spare you, Julia?"

"Yes, Harry, spare me; you must be good to me and considerate, and make yourself like a brother to me. But people will know you are not a brother, and you must remember all that, for my sake. But you must not leave me or desert me. Anything that people might say would be better than that."

"Was I wrong to kiss your hand?"

"Yes, wrong, certainly wrong;—that is, not wrong, but unmindful."

"I did it," he said, "because I love you." And as he spoke the tears stood in both his eyes.

"Yes; you love me, and I you; but not with love that may show itself in that form. That was the old love, which I threw away, and which has been lost. That was at an end when I—jilted you. I am not angry; but you will remember that that love exists no longer? You will remember that, Harry?"

He sat himself down in a chair in a far part of the room, and two tears coursed their way down his cheeks. She stood over him and watched him as he wept. "I did not mean to make you sad," she said. "Come, we will be sad no longer. I understand it all. I know how it is with you. The old love is lost, but we will not the less be friends." Then he rose suddenly from his chair, and taking her in his arms, and holding her closely to his bosom, pressed his lips to hers.

He was so quick in this that she had not the power, even if she had the wish, to restrain him. But she struggled in his arms, and held her face aloof from him as she gently rebuked his passion. "No, Harry, no; not so," she said, "it must not be so."

"Yes, Julia, yes; it shall be so; ever so,—always so." And he was still holding her in his arms, when the door opened, and with stealthy, cat-like steps Sophie Gordeloup entered the room. Harry immediately retreated from his position, and Lady Ongar turned upon her friend, and glared upon her with angry eyes.

"Ah," said the little Franco-Pole, with an expression of infinite delight on her detestable visage, "ah, my dears, is it not well that I thus announce myself?"

"No," said Lady Ongar, "it is not well. It is anything but well."

"And why not well, Julie? Come, do not be foolish. Mr. Clavering is only a cousin, and a very handsome cousin, too. What does it signify before me?"

"It signifies nothing before you," said Lady Ongar.

"But before the servant, Julie——?"

"It would signify nothing before anybody."

"Come, come, Julie, dear; that is nonsense."

"Nonsense or no nonsense, I would wish to be private when I please. Will you tell me, Madame Gordeloup, what is your pleasure at the present moment?"

"My pleasure is to beg your pardon and to say you must forgive your poor friend. Your fine man-servant is out, and Bessy let me in. I told Bessy I would go up by myself, and that is all. If I have come too late I beg pardon."

"Not too late, certainly,—as I am still up."

"And I wanted to ask you about the pictures to-morrow? You said, perhaps you would go to-morrow,—perhaps not."

Clavering had found himself to be somewhat awkwardly situated while Madame Gordeloup was thus explaining the causes of her having come unannounced into the room ; as soon, therefore, as he found it practicable, he took his leave. "Julia," he said, "as Madame Gordeloup is with you, I will now go."

"But you will let me see you soon?"

"Yes, very soon; that is, as soon as I return from Clavering. I leave town early to-morrow morning."

"Good-by, then," and she put out her hand to him frankly, smiling sweetly on him. As he felt the warm pressure of her hand he hardly knew whether to return it or to reject it. But he had gone too far now for retreat, and he held it firmly for a moment in his own. She smiled again upon him, oh! so passionately, and nodded her head at him. He had never, he thought, seen a woman look so lovely, or more light of heart. How different was her countenance now from that she had worn when she told him, earlier on that fatal evening, of all the sorrows that made her wretched! That nod of hers said so much. "We understand each other now,—do we not? Yes; although this spiteful woman has for the moment come between us, we understand each other. And is it not sweet? Ah! the troubles of which I told you ;—you, you have cured them all." All that had been said plainly in her farewell salutation, and Harry had not dared to contradict it by any expression of his countenance.

"By, by, Mr. Clavering," said Sophie.

"Good evening, Madame Gordeloup," said Harry, turning upon her a look of bitter anger. Then he went, leaving the two women together, and walked home to Bloomsbury Square,—not with the heart of a joyous thriving lover.

CHAPTER XXII.

The Day of the Funeral.

ARRY CLAVERING, when he walked away from Bolton Street after the scene in which he had been interrupted by Sophie Gordeloup, was not in a happy frame of mind, nor did he make his journey down to Clavering with much comfort to himself. Whether or no he was now to be regarded as a villain, at any rate he was not a villain capable of doing his villany without extreme remorse and agony of mind. It did not seem to him to be even yet possible that he should be altogether untrue to Florence. It hardly occurred to him to think that he could free himself from the contract by which he was bound to her. No; it was towards Lady Ongar that his treachery must be exhibited;—towards the woman whom he had sworn to befriend, and whom he now, in his distress, imagined to be the dearer to him of the two. He should, according to his custom, have written to Florence a day or two before he left London, and, as he went to Bolton Street, had determined to do so that evening on his return home; but when he reached his rooms he found it impossible to write such a letter. What could he say to her that would not be false? How could he tell her that he loved her, and speak as he was wont to do of his impatience, after that which had just occurred in Bolton Street?

But what was he to do in regard to Julia? He was bound to let her know at once what was his position, and to tell her that in treating her as he had treated her, he had simply insulted her. That look of gratified contentment with which she had greeted him as he was leaving her, clung to his memory and tormented him. Of that contentment he must now rob her, and he was bound to do so with as little delay as was possible. Early in the morning before he started on his journey he did make an attempt, a vain attempt, to write, not to Florence but to Julia. The letter would not get itself written. He had not the hardihood to inform her that he had amused himself with her sorrows, and that he had injured her by the exhibition of his love. And then that horrid Franco-Pole, whose prying eyes Julia had dared to disregard, because she had been proud of his love! If she had not been there, the case might have been easier. Harry, as he thought of this, forgot to remind himself that if Sophie had not interrupted him he would have floundered on from one danger to another till he would have committed himself more thoroughly even than he had done, and have made promises which it would have been as shameful to break as it would be to keep them. But even as it was, had he not made such promises? Was there not such a promise in that embrace, in the half-forgotten word or two which he had spoken while she was in his arms, and in the parting grasp of his hand? He could not write that letter then, on that morning, hurried as he was with the necessity of his journey; and he started for Clavering resolving that it should be written from his father's house.

It was a tedious, sad journey to him, and he was silent and out of spirits when he reached his home; but he had gone there for the purpose of his cousin's funeral, and his mood was not at first noticed, as it might have been had the occasion been different. His father's countenance wore that well-known look of customary solemnity which is found to be necessary on such occasions, and his mother was still thinking of the sorrows of Lady Clavering who had been at the rectory for the last day or two.

"Have you seen Lady Ongar since she heard of the poor child's death?" his mother asked.

"Yes, I was with her yesterday evening."

"Do you see her often?" Fanny inquired.

"What do you call often? No; not often. I went to her last night because she had given me a commission. I have seen her three or four times altogether."

"Is she as handsome as she used to be?" said Fanny.

"I cannot tell; I do not know."

"You used to think her very handsome, Harry."

"Of course she is handsome. There has never been a doubt about that; but when a woman is in deep mourning one hardly thinks about her beauty." Oh, Harry, Harry, how could you be so false?

"I thought young widows were always particularly charming," said Fanny; "and when one remembers about Lord Ongar one does not think of her being a widow so much as one would do if he had been different."

"I don't know anything about that," said he. He felt that he was stupid, and that he blundered in every word, but he could not help himself. It was impossible that he should talk about Lady Ongar with proper composure. Fanny saw that the subject annoyed him and that it made him cross, and she therefore ceased. "She wrote a very nice letter to your mother about the poor child, and about her sister," said the rector. "I wish with all my heart that Hermione could go to her for a time."

"I fear that he will not let her," said Mrs. Clavering. "I do not understand it all, but Hermione says that the rancour between Hugh and her sister is stronger now than ever."

"And Hugh will not be the first to put rancour out of his heart," said the rector.

On the following day was the funeral and Harry went with his father and cousins to the child's grave. When he met Sir Hugh in the dining-room in the Great House the baronet hardly spoke to him. "A sad occasion; is it not?" said Archie; "very sad; very sad." Then Harry could see that Hugh scowled at his brother angrily, hating his humbug, and hating it the more because in Archie's case it was doubly humbug. Archie was now heir to the property and to the title.

After the funeral Harry went to see Lady Clavering, and again had to endure a conversation about Lady Ongar. Indeed, he had been specially commissioned by Julia to press upon her sister the expediency of leaving Clavering for a while. This had been early on that last evening in Bolton Street, long before Madame Gordeloup had made her appearance. "Tell her from me," Lady Ongar had said, "that I will go anywhere that she may wish if she will go with me,—she and I alone; and, Harry, tell her this as though I meant it. I do mean it. She will understand why I do not write myself. I know that he sees all her letters when he is with her." This task Harry was now to perform, and the result he was bound to communicate to Lady Ongar. The message he might give; but delivering the answer to Lady Ongar would be another thing.

Lady Clavering listened to what he said, but when he pressed her for a reply she shook her head. "And why not, Lady Clavering?"

"People can't always leave their houses and go away, Harry."

"But I should have thought that you could have done so now;—that is before long. Will Sir Hugh remain here at Clavering?"

" He has not told me that he means to go."

" If he stays, I suppose you will stay ; but if he goes up to London again, I cannot see why you and your sister should not go away together. She mentioned Tenby as being very quiet, but she would be guided by you in that altogether."

" I do not think it will be possible, Harry. Tell her with my love, that I am truly obliged to her, but that I do not think it will be possible. She is free, you know, to do what she pleases."

" Yes, she is free. But do you mean——? "

" I mean, Harry, that I had better stay where I am. What is the use of a scene, and of being refused at last? Do not say more about it, but tell her that it cannot be so." This Harry promised to do, and after a while was rising to go, when she suddenly asked him a question. " Do you remember what I was saying about Julia and Archie when you were here last? "

" Yes ; I remember."

" Well, would he have a chance? It seems that you see more of her now than any one else."

" No chance at all, I should say." And Harry, as he answered, could not repress a feeling of most unreasonable jealousy.

" Ah, you have always thought little of Archie. Archie's position is changed now, Harry, since my darling was taken from me. Of course he will marry, and Hugh, I think, would like him to marry Julia. It was he proposed it. He never likes anything unless he has proposed it himself."

" It was he proposed the marriage with Lord Ongar. Does he like that ? "

" Well ; you know, Julia has got her money." Harry as he heard this, turned away, sick at heart. The poor baby whose mother was now speaking to him, had only been buried that morning, and she was already making fresh schemes for family wealth. Julia has got her money ! That had seemed to her, even in her sorrow, to be sufficient compensation for all that her sister had endured and was enduring. Poor soul ! Harry did not reflect as he should have done, that in all her schemes she was only scheming for that peace which might perhaps come to her if her husband were satisfied. " And why should not Julia take him ? " she asked.

" I cannot tell why, but she never will," said Harry, almost in anger. At that moment the door was opened, and Sir Hugh came into the room. " I did not know that you were here," Sir Hugh said, turning to the visitor.

" I could not be down here without saying a few words to Lady Clavering."

" The less said the better, I suppose, just at present," said Sir Hugh. But there was no offence in the tone of his voice, or in his countenance, and Harry took the words as meaning none.

" I was telling Lady Clavering that as soon as she can, she would be better if she left home for awhile."

"And why should you tell Lady Clavering that?"

"I have told him that I would not go," said the poor woman.

"Why should she go, and where; and why have you proposed it? And how does it come to pass that her going or not going, should be a matter of solicitude to you?" Now, as Sir Hugh asked these questions of his cousin, there was much of offence in his tone,—of intended offence,—and in his eye, and in all his bearing. He had turned his back upon his wife, and was looking full into Harry's face. "Lady Clavering, no doubt, is much obliged to you," he said, "but why is it that you specially have interfered to recommend her to leave her home at such a time as this?"

Harry had not spoken as he did to Sir Hugh without having made some calculation in his own mind as to the result of what he was about to say. He did not, as regarded himself, care for his cousin or his cousin's anger. His object at present was simply that of carrying out Lady Ongar's wish, and he had thought that perhaps Sir Hugh might not object to the proposal which his wife was too timid to make to him.

"It was a message from her sister," said Harry, "sent by me."

"Upon my word she is very kind. And what was the message,— unless it be a secret between you three?"

"I have had no secret, Hugh," said his wife.

"Let me hear what he has to say," said Sir Hugh.

"Lady Ongar thought that it might be well that her sister should leave Clavering for a short time, and has offered to go anywhere with her for a few weeks. That is all."

"And why the devil should Hermione leave her own house? And if she were to leave it, why should she go with a woman that has misconducted herself?"

"Oh, Hugh!" exclaimed Lady Clavering.

"Lady Ongar has never misconducted herself," said Harry.

"Are you her champion?" asked Sir Hugh.

"As far as that, I am. She has never misconducted herself; and what is more, she has been cruelly used since she came home."

"By whom; by whom?" said Sir Hugh, stepping close up to his cousin and looking with angry eyes into his face.

But Harry Clavering was not a man to be intimidated by the angry eyes of any man. "By you," he said, "her brother-in-law;—by you, who made up her wretched marriage, and who, of all others, were the most bound to protect her."

"Oh, Harry, don't, don't!" shrieked Lady Clavering.

"Hermione, hold your tongue," said the imperious husband; "or, rather, go away and leave us. I have a word or two to say to Harry Clavering, which had better be said in private."

"I will not go if you are going to quarrel."

"Harry," said Sir Hugh, "I will trouble you to go downstairs before me. If you will step into the breakfast-room I will come to you."

Harry Clavering did as he was bid, and in a few minutes was joined by his cousin in the breakfast-room.

"No doubt you intended to insult me by what you said upstairs." The baronet began in this way after he had carefully shut the door, and had slowly walked up to the rug before the fire, and had there taken his position.

"Not at all; I intended to take the part of an ill-used woman whom you had calumniated."

"Now look here, Harry, I will have no interference on your part in my affairs, either here or elsewhere. You are a very fine fellow, no doubt, but it is not part of your business to set me or my house in order. After what you have just said before Lady Clavering you will do well not to come here in my absence."

"Neither in your absence nor in your presence."

"As to the latter you may do as you please. And now touching my sister-in-law, I will simply recommend you to look after your own affairs."

"I shall look after what affairs I please."

"Of Lady Ongar and her life since her marriage I daresay you know as little as anybody in the world, and I do not suppose it likely that you will learn much from her. She made a fool of you once, and it is on the cards that she may do so again."

"You said just now that you would brook no interference in your affairs. Neither will I."

"I don't know that you have any affairs in which any one can interfere. I have been given to understand that you are engaged to marry that young lady whom your mother brought here one day to dinner. If that be so, I do not see how you can reconcile it to yourself to become the champion, as you called it, of Lady Ongar."

"I never said anything of the kind."

"Yes, you did."

"No; it was you who asked me whether I was her champion."

"And you said you were."

"So far as to defend her name when I heard it traduced by you."

"By heavens, your impudence is beautiful. Who knows her best, do you think,—you or I? Whose sister-in-law is she? You have told me I was cruel to her. Now to that I will not submit, and I require you to apologize to me."

"I have no apology to make, and nothing to retract."

"Then I shall tell your father of your gross misconduct, and shall warn him that you have made it necessary for me to turn his son out of my house. You are an impertinent, overbearing puppy, and if your name were not the same as my own, I would tell the grooms to horsewhip you off the place."

"Which order, you know, the grooms would not obey. They would a deal sooner horsewhip you. Sometimes I think they will, when I hear you speak to them."

" Now go ! "

" Of course I shall go.   What would keep me here ? "

Sir Hugh then opened the door, and Harry passed through it, not without a cautious look over his shoulder, so that he might be on his guard if any violence were contemplated.   But Hugh knew better than that, and allowed his cousin to walk out of the room, and out of the house, unmolested.

And this had happened on the day of the funeral !   Harry Clavering had quarrelled thus with the father within a few hours of the moment in which they two had stood together over the grave of that father's only child ! As he thought of this while he walked across the park he became sick at heart.   How vile, wretched and miserable was the world around him ! How terribly vicious were the people with whom he was dealing !   And what could he think of himself,—of himself, who was engaged to Florence Burton, and engaged also, as he certainly was, to Lady Ongar ?   Even his cousin had rebuked him for his treachery to Florence ; but what would his cousin have said had he known all ?   And then what good had he done ;—or rather what evil had he not done ?   In his attempt on behalf of Lady Clavering had he not, in truth, interfered without proper excuse, and fairly laid himself open to anger from his cousin ?   And he felt that he had been an ass, a fool, a conceited ass, thinking that he could produce good, when his interference could be efficacious only for evil. Why could he not have held his tongue when Sir Hugh came in, instead of making that vain suggestion as to Lady Clavering ?   But even this trouble was but an addition to the great trouble that overwhelmed him. How was he to escape the position which he had made for himself in reference to Lady Ongar ?   As he had left London he had promised to himself that he would write to her that same night and tell her every-thing as to Florence ; but the night had passed, and the next day was nearly gone, and no such letter had been written.

As he sat with his father that evening, he told the story of his quarrel with his cousin.   His father shrugged his shoulders and raised his eyebrows.   " You are a bolder man than I am," he said.   " I certainly should not have dared to advise Hugh as to what he should do with his wife."

" But I did not advise him.   I only said that I had been talking to her about it.   If he were to say to you that he had been recommending my mother to do this or that, you would not take it amiss ? "

" But Hugh is a peculiar man."

" No man has a right to be peculiar.   Every man is bound to accept such usage as is customary in the world."

" I don't suppose that it will signify much," said the rector.   " To have your cousin's doors barred against you, either here or in London, will not injure you."

" Oh, no ; it will not injure me ; but I do not wish you to think that I have been unreasonable."

The night went by and so did the next day, and still the letter did not get itself written. On the third morning after the funeral he heard that Sir Hugh had gone away; but he, of course, did not go up to the house, remembering well that he had been warned by the master not to do so in the master's absence. His mother, however, went to Lady Clavering, and some intercourse between the families was renewed. He had intended to stay but one day after the funeral, but at the end of a week he was still at the rectory. It was Whitsuntide he said, and he might as well take his holiday as he was down there. Of course they were glad that he should remain with them, but they did not fail to perceive that things with him were not altogether right; nor had Fanny failed to perceive that he had not once mentioned Florence's name since he had been at the rectory.

"Harry," she said, "there is nothing wrong between you and Florence?"

"Wrong! what should there be wrong? What do you mean by wrong?"

"I had a letter from her to-day and she asks where you are."

"Women expect such a lot of letter-writing! But I have been remiss I know. I got out of my business way of doing things when I came down here and have neglected it. Do you write to her to-morrow, and tell her that she shall hear from me directly I get back to town."

"But why should you not write to her from here?"

"Because I can get you to do it for me."

Fanny felt that this was not at all like a lover, and not at all like such a lover as her brother had been. While Florence had been at Clavering he had been most constant with his letters, and Fanny had often heard Florence boast of them as being perfect in their way. She did not say anything further at the present moment, but she knew that things were not altogether right. Things were by no means right. He had written neither to Lady Ongar nor to Florence, and the longer he put off the task the more burdensome did it become. He was now telling himself that he would write to neither till he got back to London.

On the day before he went, there came to him a letter from Stratton. Fanny was with him when he received it, and observed that he put it into his pocket without opening it. In his pocket he carried it unopened half the day, till he was ashamed of his own weakness. At last, almost in despair with himself, he broke the seal and forced himself to read it. There was nothing in it that need have alarmed him. It contained hardly a word that was intended for a rebuke.

"I wonder why you should have been two whole weeks without writing," she said. "It seems so odd to me, because you have spoiled me by your customary goodness. I know that other men when they are engaged do not trouble themselves with constant letter-writing. Even Theodore, who according to Cecilia is perfect, would not write to her then very often; and now, when he is away, his letters are only three

MEE

H.Harral

"HARRY," SHE SAID, "THERE IS NOTHING WRONG BETWEEN YOU AND FLORENCE?"

lines. I suppose you are teaching me not to be exacting. If so, I will kiss the rod like a good child; but I feel it the more because the lesson has not come soon enough."

Then she went on in her usual strain, telling him of what she had done, what she had read, and what she had thought. There was no suspicion in her letter, no fear, no hint at jealousy. And she should have no further cause for jealousy! One of the two must be sacrificed, and it was most fitting that Julia should be the sacrifice. Julia should be sacrificed,—Julia and himself! But still he could not write to Florence till he had written to Julia. He could not bring himself to send soft, pretty, loving words to one woman while the other was still regarding him as her affianced lover.

"Was your letter from Florence this morning?" Fanny asked him.

"Yes; it was."

"Had she received mine?"

"I don't know. Of course she had. If you sent it by post of course she got it."

"She might have mentioned it, perhaps."

"I daresay she did. I don't remember."

"Well, Harry; you need not be cross with me because I love the girl who is going to be your wife. You would not like it if I did not care about her."

"I hate being called cross."

"Suppose I were to say that I hated your being cross. I'm sure I do;—and you are going away to-morrow, too. You have hardly said a nice word to me since you have been home."

Harry threw himself back into a chair almost in despair. He was not enough a hypocrite to say nice words when his heart within him was not at ease. He could not bring himself to pretend that things were pleasant.

"If you are in trouble, Harry, I will not go on teasing you."

"I am in trouble," he said.

"And cannot I help you?"

"No; you cannot help me. No one can help me. But do not ask any questions."

"Oh, Harry! is it about money?"

"No, no; it has nothing to do with money."

"You have not really quarrelled with Florence?"

"No; I have not quarrelled with her at all. But I will not answer more questions. And, Fanny, do not speak of this to my father or mother. It will be over before long, and then, if possible, I will tell you."

"Harry, you are not going to fight with Hugh?"

"Fight with Hugh! no. Not that I should mind it; but he is not fool enough for that. If he wanted fighting done, he would do it by deputy. But there is nothing of that kind."

She asked him no more questions, and on the next morning

he returned to London. On his table he found a note which he at once knew to be from Lady Ongar, and which had come only that afternoon.

"Come to me at once;—at once." That was all that the note contained.

CHAPTER XXIII.

CUMBERLY LANE WITHOUT THE MUD.

FANNY CLAVERING, while she was inquiring of her brother about his troubles, had not been without troubles of her own. For some days past she had been aware,—almost aware,—that Mr. Saul's love was not among the things that were past. I am not prepared to say that this conviction on her part was altogether an unalloyed trouble, or that there might have been no faint touch of sadness, of silent melancholy about her, had it been otherwise. But Mr. Saul was undoubtedly a trouble to her; and Mr. Saul with his love in activity would be more troublesome than Mr. Saul with his love in abeyance. "It would be madness either in him or in me," Fanny had said to herself very often; "he has not a shilling in the world." But she thought no more in these days of the awkwardness of his gait, or of his rusty clothes, or his abstracted manner; and for his doings as a clergyman her admiration had become very great. Her mother saw something of all this, and cautioned her; but Fanny's demure manner deceived Mrs. Clavering. "Oh, mamma, of course I know that anything of the kind must be impossible; and I am sure he does not think of it himself any longer." When she had said this, Mrs. Clavering had believed that it was all right. The reader must not suppose that Fanny had been a hypocrite. There had been no hypocrisy in her words to her mother. At that moment the conviction that Mr. Saul's love was not among past events had not reached her; and as regarded herself, she was quite sincere when she said that anything of the kind must be impossible.

It will be remembered that Florence Burton had advised Mr. Saul to try again, and that Mr. Saul had resolved that he would do so,—resolving, also, that should he try in vain he must leave Clavering, and seek another home. He was a solemn, earnest, thoughtful man; to whom such a matter as this was a phase of life very serious, causing infinite present trouble, nay, causing tribulation, and, to the same extent, capable of causing infinite joy. From day to day he went about his work, seeing her amidst his ministrations almost daily. And never during these days did he say a word to her of his love,—never since that day in which he had plainly pleaded his cause in the muddy lane. To no one but Florence Burton had he since spoken of it, and Florence had certainly been true to her trust; but, notwithstanding all that, Fanny's conviction was very strong.

Florence had counselled Mr. Saul to try again, and Mr. Saul was prepared to make the attempt; but he was a man who allowed himself to do nothing in a hurry. He thought much of the matter before he could prepare himself to recur to the subject; doubting, sometimes, whether he would be right to do so without first speaking to Fanny's father; doubting, afterwards, whether he might not best serve his cause by asking the assistance of Fanny's mother. But he resolved at last that he would depend on himself alone. As to the rector, if his suit to Fanny were a fault against Mr. Clavering as Fanny's father, that fault had been already committed. But Mr. Saul would not admit to himself that it was a fault. I fancy that he considered himself to have, as a gentleman, a right to address himself to any lady with whom he was thrown into close contact. I fancy that he ignored all want of worldly preparation,—never for a moment attempting to place himself on a footing with men who were richer than himself, and, as the world goes, brighter, but still feeling himself to be in no way lower than they. If any woman so lived as to show that she thought his line better than their line, it was open to him to ask such woman to join her lot to his. If he failed, the misfortune was his; and the misfortune, as he well knew, was one which it was hard to bear. And as to the mother, though he had learned to love Mrs. Clavering dearly,—appreciating her kindness to all those around her, her conduct to her husband, her solicitude in the parish, all her genuine goodness, still he was averse to trust to her for any part of his success. Though Mr. Saul was no knight, though he had nothing knightly about him, though he was a poor curate in very rusty clothes and with manner strangely unfitted for much communion with the outer world, still he had a feeling that the spoil which he desired to win should be won by his own spear, and that his triumph would lose half its glory if it were not achieved by his own prowess. He was no coward, either in such matter as this or in any other. When circumstances demanded that he should speak he could speak his mind freely, with manly vigour, and sometimes not without a certain manly grace.

How did Fanny know that it was coming? She did know it, though he had said nothing to her beyond his usual parish communications. He was often with her in the two schools; often returned with her in the sweet spring evenings along the lane that led back to the rectory from Cumberly Green; often inspected with her the little amounts of parish charities and entries of pence collected from such parents as could pay. He had never reverted to that other subject. But yet Fanny knew that it was coming, and when she had questioned Harry about his troubles she had been thinking also of her own.

It was now the middle of May, and the spring was giving way to the early summer almost before the spring had itself arrived. It is so, I think, in these latter years. The sharpness of March prolongs itself almost through April; and then, while we are still hoping for the spring, there falls upon us suddenly a bright, dangerous, delicious gleam of summer. The lane from Cumberly Green was no longer muddy, and Fanny could go backwards and forwards between the parsonage and her distant school without that wading for which feminine apparel is so unsuited. One evening, just as she had finished her work, Mr. Saul's head appeared at the school-door, and he asked her whether she were about to return home. As soon as she saw his eye and heard his voice, she feared that the day was come. She was prepared with no new answer, and could only give the answer that she had given before. She had always told herself that it was impossible ; and as to all other questions, about her own heart or such like, she had put such questions away from her as being unnecessary, and, perhaps, unseemly. The thing was impossible, and should therefore be put away out of thought, as a matter completed and at an end. But now the time was come, and she almost wished that she had been more definite in her own resolutions.

" Yes, Mr. Saul, I have just done."

" I will walk with you, if you will let me." Then Fanny spoke some words of experienced wisdom to two or three girls, in order that she might show to them, to him, and to herself that she was quite collected. She lingered in the room for a few minutes, and was very wise and very experienced. " I am quite ready now, Mr. Saul." So saying, she came forth upon the green lane, and he followed her.

They walked on in silence for a little way, and then he asked her some question about Florence Burton. Fanny told him that she had heard from Stratton two days since, and that Florence was well.

" I liked her very much," said Mr. Saul.

" So did we all. She is coming here again in the autumn ; so it will not be very long before you see her again."

" How that may be I cannot tell, but if you see her that will be of more consequence."

" We shall all see her, of course."

" It was here, in this lane, that I was with her last, and wished her good-by. She did not tell you of my having parted with her, then ? "

" Not especially, that I remember."

" Ah, you would have remembered if she had told you ; but she was quite right not to tell you." Fanny was now a little confused, so that she could not exactly calculate what all this meant. Mr. Saul walked on by her side, and for some moments nothing was said. After a while he recurred again to his parting from Florence. " I asked her advice on that occasion, and she gave it me clearly,—with a clear purpose and an assured voice. I like a person who will do that. You are sure then that you are getting the truth out of your friend, even if it be a simple negative, or a refusal to give any reply to the question asked."

" Florence Burton is always clear in what she says."

" I had asked her if she thought that I might venture to hope for a more favourable answer if I urged my suit to you again."

"She cannot have said yes to that, Mr. Saul; she cannot have done so!"

"She did not do so. She simply bade me ask yourself. And she was right. On such a matter there is no one to whom I can with propriety address myself, but to yourself. Therefore I now ask you the question. May I venture to have any hope?"

His voice was so solemn, and there was so much of eager seriousness in his face that Fanny could not bring herself to answer him with quickness. The answer that was in her mind was in truth this: "How can you ask me to try to love a man who has but seventy pounds a year in the world, while I myself have nothing?" But there was something in his demeanour,—something that was almost grand in its gravity,—which made it quite impossible that she should speak to him in that tone. But he, having asked his question, waited for an answer; and she was well aware that the longer she delayed it, the weaker became the ground on which she was standing.

"It is quite impossible," she said at last.

"If it really be so,—if you will say again that it is so after hearing me out to an end, I will desist. In that case I will desist and leave you, —and leave Clavering."

"Oh, Mr. Saul, do not do that,—for papa's sake, and because of the parish."

"I would do much for your father, and as to the parish I love it well. I do not think I can make you understand how well I love it. It seems to me that I can never again have the same feeling for any place that I have for this. There is not a house, a field, a green lane, that is not dear to me. It is like a first love. With some people a first love will come so strongly that it makes a renewal of the passion impossible." He did not say that it would be so with himself, but it seemed to her that he intended that she should so understand him.

"I do not see why you should leave Clavering," she said.

"If you knew the nature of my regard for yourself, you would see why it should be so. I do not say that there ought to be any such necessity. If I were strong there would be no such need. But I am weak,—weak in this; and I could not hold myself under such control as is wanted for the work I have to do." When he had spoken of his love for the place,—for the parish, there had been something of passion in his language; but now in the words which he spoke of himself and of his feeling for her, he was calm and reasonable and tranquil, and talked of his going away from her as he might have talked had some change of air been declared necessary for his health. She felt that this was so, and was almost angry with him.

"Of course you must know what will be best for yourself," she said.

"Yes; I know now what I must do, if such is to be your answer. I have made up my mind as to that. I cannot remain at Clavering, if I am told that I may never hope that you will become my wife."

"But, Mr. Saul——"

"Well ; I am listening. But before you speak, remember how all-important your words will be to me."

"No ; they cannot be all-important."

"As regards my present happiness and rest in this world they will be so. Of course I know that nothing you can say or do will hurt me beyond that. But you might help me even to that further and greater bliss. You might help me too in that,—as I also might help you."

"But, Mr. Saul——" she began again, and then, feeling that she must go on, she forced herself to utter words which at the time she felt to be commonplace. "People cannot marry without an income. Mr. Fielding did not think of such a thing till he had a living assured to him."

"But, independently of that, might I hope ? " She ventured for an instant to glance at his face, and saw that his eyes were glistening with a wonderful brightness.

"How can I answer you further ? Is not that reason enough why such a thing should not be even discussed ? "

"No, Miss Clavering, it is not reason enough. If you were to tell me that you could never love me,—me, personally,—that you could never regard me with affection, that would be reason why I should desist ;—why I should abandon all my hope here, and go away from Clavering for ever. Nothing else can be reason enough. My being poor ought not to make you throw me aside if you loved me. If it were so that you loved me, I think you would owe it me to say so, let me be ever so poor."

"I do not like you the less because you are poor."

"But do you like me at all? Can you bring yourself to love me ? Would you make the effort if I had such an income as you thought necessary ? If I had such riches, could you teach yourself to regard me as him whom you were to love better than all the world beside ? I call upon you to answer me that question truly ; and if you tell me that it could be so, I will not despair, and I will not go away."

As he said this they came to a turn in the road which brought the parsonage gate within their view. Fanny knew that she would leave him there and go in alone, but she knew also that she must say something further to him before she could thus escape. She did not wish to give him an assurance of her positive indifference to him,—and still less did she wish to tell him that he might hope. It could not be possible that such an engagement should be approved by her father, nor could she bring herself to think that she could be quite contented with a lover such as Mr. Saul. When he had first proposed to her she had almost ridiculed his proposition in her heart. Even now there was something in it that was almost ridiculous ;—and yet there was something in it also that touched her as being sublime. The man was honest, good, and true,—perhaps the best and truest man that she had ever known. She could not bring herself to say to him any word that should banish him for ever from the place he loved so well.

"If you knew your own heart well enough to answer me, you should do so," he went on to say. "If you do not, say so, and I will be content to wait your own time."

"It would be better, Mr. Saul, that you should not think of this any more."

"No, Miss Clavering; that would not be better,—not for me; for it would prove me to be utterly heartless. I am not heartless. I love you dearly. I will not say that I cannot live without you; but it is my one great hope as regards this world, that I should have you at some future day as my own. It may be that I am too prone to hope; but surely, if that were altogether beyond hope, you would have found words to tell me so by this time." They had now come to the gateway, and he paused as she put her trembling hand upon the latch.

"I cannot say more to you now," she said.

"Then let it be so. But, Miss Clavering, I shall not leave this place till you have said more than that. And I will speak the truth to you, even though it may offend you. I have more of hope now than I have ever had before,—more hope that you may possibly learn to love me. In a few days I will ask you again whether I may be allowed to speak upon the subject to your father. Now I will say farewell, and may God bless you; and remember this,—that my only earthly wish and ambition is in your hands." Then he went on his way towards his own lodgings, and she entered the parsonage garden by herself.

What should she now do, and how should she carry herself? She would have gone to her mother at once, were it not that she could not resolve what words she would speak to her mother. When her mother should ask her how she regarded the man, in what way should she answer that question? She could not tell herself that she loved Mr. Saul; and yet, if she surely did not love him,—if such love were impossible,—why had she not said as much to him? We, however, may declare that that inclination to ridicule his passion, to think of him as a man who had no right to love, was gone for ever. She conceded to him clearly that right, and knew that he had exercised it well. She knew that he was good and true, and honest, and recognized in him also manly courage and spirited resolution. She would not tell herself that it was impossible that she should love him.

She went up at last to her room doubting, unhappy, and ill at ease. To have such a secret long kept from her mother would make her life unendurable to her. But she felt that, in speaking to her mother, only one aspect of the affair would be possible. Even though she loved him, how could she marry a curate whose only income was seventy pounds a year?

CHAPTER XXIV.

The Russian Spy.

When the baby died at Clavering Park, somebody hinted that Sir Hugh would certainly quarrel with his brother as soon as Archie should become the father of a presumptive heir to the title and property. That such would be the case those who best knew Sir Hugh would not doubt. That Archie should have that of which he himself had been robbed, would of itself be enough to make him hate Archie. But, nevertheless, at this present time, he continued to instigate his brother in that matter of the proposed marriage with Lady Ongar. Hugh, as well as others, felt that Archie's prospects were now improved, and that he could demand the hand of a wealthy lady with more of seeming propriety than would have belonged to such a proposition while the poor child was living. No one would understand this better than Lady Ongar, who knew so well all the circumstances of the family. The day after the funeral the two brothers returned to London together, and Hugh spoke his mind in the railway carriage. " It will be no good for you to hang on about Bolton Street, off and on, as though she were a girl of seventeen," he said.

" I'm quite up to that," said Archie. " I must let her know I'm there of course. I understand all that."

" Then why don't you do it? I thought you meant to go to her at once when we were talking about it before in London."

" So I did go to her, and got on with her very well, too, considering that I hadn't been there long when another woman came in."

" But you didn't tell her what you had come about?"

" No; not exactly. You see it doesn't do to pop at once to a widow like her. Ongar, you know, hasn't been dead six months. One has to be a little delicate in these things."

" Believe me, Archie, you had better give up all notions of being delicate, and tell her what you want at once,—plainly and fairly. You may be sure that she will not think of her former husband, if you don't."

" Oh! I don't think about him at all."

" Who was the woman you say was there?"

" That little Frenchwoman,—the sister of the man ;—Sophie she calls her. Sophie Gordeloup is her name. They are bosom friends."

" The sister of that count?"

" Yes; his sister. Such a woman for talking! She said ever so much about your keeping Hermione down in the country."

" The devil she did. What business was that of hers? That is Julia's doing."

" Well; no, I don't think so. Julia didn't say a word about it. In fact, I don't know how it came up. But you never heard such a woman to talk,—an ugly, old, hideous little creature! But the two are always together."

"If you don't take care you'll find that Julia is married to the count while you are thinking about it."

Then Archie began to consider whether he might not as well tell his brother of his present scheme with reference to Julia. Having discussed the matter at great length with his confidential friend, Captain Boodle, he had come to the conclusion that his safest course would be to bribe Madame Gordeloup, and creep into Julia's favour by that lady's aid. Now, on his return to London, he was about at once to play that game, and had already provided himself with funds for the purpose. The parting with ready money was a grievous thing to Archie, though in this case the misery would be somewhat palliated by the feeling that it was a bonâ fide sporting transaction. He would be lessening the odds against himself by a judicious hedging of his bets. "You must stand to lose something always by the horse you mean to win," Doodles had said to him, and Archie had recognized the propriety of the remark. He had, therefore, with some difficulty, provided himself with funds, and was prepared to set about his hedging operations as soon as he could find Madame Gordeloup on his return to London. He had already ascertained her address through Doodles, and had ascertained by the unparalleled acuteness of his friend that the lady was—a Russian spy. It would have been beautiful to have seen Archie's face when this information was whispered into his ear, in private, at the club. It was as though he had then been made acquainted with some great turf secret, unknown to the sporting world in general.

"Ah!" he said, drawing a long breath, "no;—by George, is she?"

The same story had been told everywhere in London of the little woman for the last half dozen years, whether truly or untruly I am not prepared to say; but it had not hitherto reached Archie Clavering; and now, on hearing it, he felt that he was becoming a participator in the deepest diplomatic secrets of Europe.

"By George," said he, "is she really?"

And his respect for the little woman rose a thousand per cent.

"That's what she is," said Doodles, "and it's a doosed fine thing for you, you know! Of course you can make her safe, and that will be everything."

Archie resolved at once that he would use the great advantage which chance and the ingenuity of his friend had thrown in his way; but that necessity of putting money in his purse was a sore grievance to him, and it occurred to him that it would be a grand thing if he could induce his brother to help him in this special matter. If he could only make Hugh see the immense advantage of an alliance with the Russian spy, Hugh could hardly avoid contributing to the expense,—of course on the understanding that all such moneys were to be repaid when the Russian spy's work had been brought to a successful result. Russian spy! There was in the very sound of the words something so charming that it almost made Archie in love with the outlay. A female Russian spy too ! Sophie Gordeloup certainly retained but very few of the charms of womanhood, nor had her presence as a lady affected Archie with any special pleasure; but yet he felt infinitely more pleased with the affair than he would have been had she been a man spy. The intrigue was deeper. His sense of delight in the mysterious wickedness of the thing was enhanced by an additional spice. It is not given to every man to employ the services of a political Russian lady-spy in his love-affairs ! As he thought of it in all its bearings, he felt that he was almost a Talleyrand, or, at any rate, a Palmerston.

Should he tell his brother ? If he could represent the matter in such a light to his brother as to induce Hugh to produce the funds for purchasing the spy's services, the whole thing would be complete with a completeness that has rarely been equalled. But he doubted. Hugh was a hard man,—a hard, unimaginative man, and might possibly altogether refuse to believe in the Russian spy. Hugh believed in little but what he himself saw, and usually kept a very firm grasp upon his money.

" That Madame Gordeloup is always with Julia," Archie said, trying the way, as it were, before he told his plan.

" Of course she will help her brother's views."

" I'm not so sure of that. Some of these foreign women ain't like other women at all. They go deeper;—a doosed sight deeper."

" Into men's pockets, you mean."

" They play a deep game altogether. What do you suppose she is, now ? " This question Archie asked in a whisper, bending his head forward towards his brother, though there was no one else in the carriage with them.

" What she is ? A thief of some kind probably. I've no doubt she's up to any roguery."

" She's a—Russian spy."

" Oh, I've heard of that for the last dozen years. All the ugly old Frenchwomen in London are Russian spies, according to what people say ; but the Russians know how to use their money better than that. If they employ spies, they employ people who can spy something."

Archie felt this to be cruel,—very cruel, but he said nothing further about it. His brother was stupid, pigheaded, obstinate, and quite unfitted by nature for affairs of intrigue. It was, alas, certain that his brother would provide no money for such a purpose as that he now projected ; but, thinking of this, he found some consolation in the reflection that Hugh would not be a participator with him in his great secret. When he should have bought the Russian spy, he and Doodles would rejoice together in privacy without any third confederate. Triumviri might be very well; Archie also had heard of triumviri ; but two were company, and three were none. Thus he consoled himself when his pigheaded brother expressed his disbelief in the Russian spy.

There was nothing more said between them in the railway carriage,

and, as they parted at the door in Berkeley Square, Hugh swore to himself that this should be the last season in which he would harbour his
brother in London. After this he must have a house of his own there,
or have no house at all. Then Archie went down to his club, and finally
arranged with Doodles that the first visit to the Spy should be made on
the following morning. After much consultation it was agreed between
them that the way should be paved by a diplomatic note. The diplomatic
note was therefore written by Doodles and copied by Archie.

"Captain Clavering presents his compliments to Madame Gordeloup,
and proposes to call upon her to-morrow morning at twelve o'clock, if
that hour will be convenient. Captain Clavering is desirous of consulting
Madame Gordeloup on an affair of much importance." "Consult me!"
said Sophie to herself, when she got the letter. "For what should he
consult me? It is that stupid man I saw with Julie. Ah, well; never
mind. The stupid man shall come." The commissioner, therefore, who
had taken the letter to Mount Street, returned to the club with a note
in which Madame Gordeloup expressed her willingness to undergo the
proposed interview. Archie felt that the letter,—a letter from a Russian
spy addressed positively to himself,—gave him already diplomatic rank,
and he kept it as a treasure in his breastcoat-pocket.

It then became necessary that he and his friend should discuss the
manner in which the Spy should be managed. Doodles had his misgivings that Archie would be awkward, and almost angered his friend
by the repetition of his cautions. "You mustn't chuck your money at
her head, you know," said Doodles.

"Of course not; but when the time comes I shall slip the notes into
her hand,—with a little pressure perhaps."

"It would be better to leave them near her on the table."

"Do you think so?"

"Oh, yes ; a great deal. It's always done in that way."

"But perhaps she wouldn't see them,—or wouldn't know where they
came from."

"Let her alone for that."

"But I must make her understand what I want of her,—in return,
you know. I ain't going to give her twenty pounds for nothing."

"You must explain that at first; tell her that you expect her aid, and
that she will find you a grateful friend,—a grateful friend, say ;—mind
you remember that."

"Yes ; I'll remember that. I suppose it would be as good a way
as any."

"It's the only way, unless you want her to ring for the servant to
kick you out of the house. It's as well understood as A B C, among the
people who do these things. I should say take jewellery instead of
money if she were anything but a Russian spy ; but they understand the
thing so well, that you may go farther with them than with others."

Archie's admiration for Sophie became still higher as he heard this.

"I do like people," said he, "who understand what's what, and no mistake."

"But even with her you must be very careful."

"Oh, yes ; that's a matter of course."

"When I was declaring for the last time that she would find me a grateful friend, just at the word grateful, I would put down the four fivers on the table, smoothing them with my hand like that." Then Doodles acted the part, putting a great deal of emphasis on the word grateful, as he went through the smoothing ceremony with two or three sheets of club notepaper. "That's your game, you may be sure. If you put them into her hand she may feel herself obliged to pretend to be angry ; but she can't be angry simply because you put your money on her table. Do you see that, old fellow ?" Archie declared that he did see it very plainly. "If she does not choose to undertake the job, she'll merely have to tell you that you have left something behind you."

"But there's no fear of that, I suppose ?"

"I can't say. Her hands may be full, you know, or she may think you don't go high enough."

"But I mean to tip her again, of course."

"Again ! I should think so. I suppose she must have about a couple of hundred before the end of next month if she's to do any good. After a bit you'll be able to explain that she shall have a sum down when the marriage has come off."

"She won't take the money and do nothing ; will she ? "

"Oh, no; they never sell you like that. It would spoil their own business if they were to play that game. If you can make it worth her while, she'll do the work for you. But you must be careful ;—do remember that." Archie shook his head, almost in anger, and then went home for his night's rest.

On the next morning he dressed himself in his best, and presented himself at the door in Mount Street, exactly as the clock struck twelve. He had an idea that these people were very punctilious as to time. Who could say but that the French ambassador might have an appointment with Madame Gordeloup at half-past one,—or perhaps some emissary from the Pope ! He had resolved that he would not take his left glove off his hand, and he had thrust the notes in under the palm of his glove, thinking he could get at them easier from there, should they be wanted in a moment, than he could do from his waistcoat pocket. He knocked at the door, knowing that he trembled as he did so, and felt considerable relief when he found himself to be alone in the room to which he was shown. He knew that men conversant with intrigues always go to work with their eyes open, and, therefore, at once he began to look about him. Could he not put the money into some convenient hiding-place,—now at once ? There, in one corner, was the spot in which she would seat herself upon the sofa. He saw plainly enough, as with the eye of a Talleyrand, the marks thereon of her constant sitting. So he seized the moment to place a chair suitable for himself, and cleared a few inches on the table near to it, for the smoothing of the bank-notes,—feeling, while so employed, that he was doing great things. He had almost made up his mind to slip one note between the pages of a book, not with any well-defined plan as to the utility of such a measure, but because it seemed to be such a diplomatic thing to do! But while this grand idea was still flashing backwards and forwards across his brain, the door opened, and he found himself in the presence of—the Russian spy.

He at once saw that the Russian spy was very dirty, and that she wore a nightcap, but he liked her the better on that account. A female Russian spy should, he felt, differ much in her attire from other women. If possible, she should be arrayed in diamonds, and pearl ear-drops, with as little else upon her as might be; but failing that costume, which might be regarded as the appropriate evening Spy costume,—a tumbled nightcap, and a dirty white wrapper, old cloth slippers, and objectionable stockings were just what they should be.

"Ah!" said the lady, "you are Captain Clavering. ‾Yes, I remember."

"I am Captain Clavering. I had the honour of meeting you at Lady Ongar's."

"And now you wish to consult me on an affair of great importance. Very well. You may consult me. Will you sit down—there." And Madame Gordeloup indicated to him a chair just opposite to herself, and far removed from that convenient spot which Archie had prepared for the smoothing of the bank-notes. Near to the place now assigned to him there was no table whatever, and he felt that he would in that position be so completely raked by the fire of her keen eyes, that he would not be able to carry on his battle upon good terms. In spite, therefore, of the lady's very plain instructions, he made an attempt to take possession of the chair which he had himself placed; but it was an ineffectual attempt, for the Spy was very peremptory with him. "There, Captain Clavering; there; there; you will be best there." Then he did as he was bid, and seated himself, as it were, quite out at sea, with nothing but an ocean of carpet around him, and with no possibility of manipulating his notes except under the raking fire of those terribly sharp eyes. "And now," said Madame Gordeloup, "you can commence to consult me. What is the business?"

Ah; what was the business? That was now the difficulty? In discussing the proper way of tendering the bank-notes, I fear the two captains had forgotten the nicest point of the whole negotiation. How was he to tell her what it was that he wanted to do himself, and what that she was to be required to do for him? It behoved him above all things not to be awkward! That he remembered. But how not to be awkward? "Well!" she said; and there was something almost of crossness in her tone. Her time, no doubt, was valuable. The French ambassador might even now be coming. "Well?"

"I think, Madame Gordeloup, you know my brother's sister-in-law, Lady Ongar?"

"What, Julie? Of course I know Julie. Julie and I are dear friends."

"So I supposed. That is the reason why I have come to you."

"Well;—well;—well?"

"Lady Ongar is a person whom I have known for a long time, and for whom I have a great,—I may say a very deep regard."

"Ah! yes. What a jointure she has! and what a park! Thousands and thousands of pounds,—and so beautiful! If I was a man I should have a very deep regard too. Yes."

"A most beautiful creature;—is she not?"

"Ah; if you had seen her in Florence, as I used to see her, in the long summer evenings! Her lovely hair was all loose to the wind, and she would sit hour after hour looking, oh, at the stars! Have you seen the stars in Italy?"

Captain Clavering couldn't say that he had, but he had seen them uncommon bright in Norway, when he had been fishing there.

"Or the moon?" continued Sophie, not regarding his answer. "Ah; that is to live! And he, her husband, the rich lord, he was dying,—in a little room just inside, you know. It was very melancholy, Captain Clavering. But when she was looking at the moon, with her hair all dishevelled," and Sophie put her hands up to her own dirty nightcap, "she was just like a Magdalen; yes, just the same;—just the same."

The exact strength of the picture, and the nature of the comparison drawn, were perhaps lost upon Archie; and indeed, Sophie herself probably trusted more to the tone of her words, than to any idea which they contained; but their tone was perfect, and she felt that if anything could make him talk, he would talk now.

"Dear me! you don't say so. I have always admired her very much, Madame Gordeloup."

"Well?"

The French ambassador was probably in the next street already, and if Archie was to tell his tale at all he must do it now.

"You will keep my secret if I tell it you?" he asked.

"Is it me you ask that? Did you ever hear of me that I tell a gentleman's secret. I think not. If you have a secret, and will trust me, that will be good; if you will not trust me,—that will be good also."

"Of course I will trust you. That is why I have come here."

"Then out with it. I am not a little girl. You need not be bashful. Two and two make four. I know that. But some people want them to make five. I know that too. So speak out what you have to say."

"I am going to ask Lady Ongar to—to—to—marry me."

"Ah, indeed; with all the thousands of pounds and the beautiful park ! But the beautiful hair is more than all the thousands of pounds. Is it not so ? "

" Well, as to that, they all go together, you know."

" And that is so lucky ! If they was to be separated, which would you take ? "

The little woman grinned as she asked this question, and Archie, had he at all understood her character, might at once have put himself on a pleasant footing with her ; but he was still confused and ill at ease, and only muttered something about the truth of his love for Julia.

" And you want to get her to marry you ? "

" Yes; that's just it."

" And you want me to help you ? "

" That's just it again."

" Well ? "

" Upon my word, if you'll stick to me, you know, and see me through it, and all that kind of thing, you'll find in me a most grateful friend;— indeed, a most grateful friend." And Archie, as from his position he was debarred from attempting the smoothing process, began to work with his right forefinger under the glove on his left hand.

" What have you got there ? " said Madame Gordeloup, looking at him with all her eyes.

Captain Clavering instantly discontinued the work with his finger, and became terribly confused. Her voice on asking the question had become very sharp ; and it seemed to him that if he brought out his money in that awkward, barefaced way which now seemed to be necessary, she would display all the wrath of which a Russian spy could be capable. Would it not be better that he should let the money rest for the present, and trust to his promise of gratitude ? Ah, how he wished that he had slipped at any rate one note between the pages of a book.

" What have you got there ? " she demanded again, very sharply.

" Oh, nothing."

" It is not nothing. What have you got there ? If you have got nothing, take off your glove. Come."

Captain Clavering became very red in the face, and was altogether at a loss what to say or do. " Is it money you have got there ? " she asked. " Let me see how much. Come."

" It is just a few bank-notes I put in here to be handy," he said.

" Ah ; that is very handy, certainly. I never saw that custom before. Let me look." Then she took his hand, and with her own hooked finger clawed out the notes. " Ah ! five, ten, fifteen, twenty pounds. Twenty pounds is not a great deal, but it is very nice to have even that always handy. I was wanting so much money as that myself ; perhaps you will make it handy to me."

" Upon my word I shall be most happy. Nothing on earth would give me more pleasure."

" Fifty pounds would give me more pleasure ; just twice as much pleasure." Archie had begun to rejoice greatly at the safe disposition of the money, and to think how excellently well this Spy did her business; but now there came upon him suddenly an idea that spies perhaps might do their business too well. "Twenty pounds in this country goes a very little way; you are all so rich," said the Spy.

"By George, I ain't. I ain't rich, indeed."

"But you mean to be—with Julie's money?"

"Oh—ah—yes; and you ought to know, Madame Gordeloup, that I am now the heir to the family estate and title."

"Yes; the poor little baby is dead, in spite of the pills and the powders, the daisies and the buttercups! Poor little baby! I had a baby of my own once, and that died also." Whereupon Madame Gordeloup, putting up her hand to her eyes, wiped away a real tear with the bank-notes which she still held. "And I am to remind Julie that you will be the heir?"

"She will know all about that already."

"But I will tell her. It will be something to say, at any rate,—and that, perhaps, will be the difficulty."

"Just so! I didn't look at it in that light before."

"And am I to propose it to her first?"

"Well; I don't know. Perhaps as you are so clever, it might be as well."

"And at once?"

"Yes, certainly; at once. You see, Madame Gordeloup, there may be so many buzzing about her."

"Exactly; and some of them perhaps will have more than twenty pounds handy. Some will buzz better than that."

"Of course I didn't mean that for anything more than just a little compliment to begin with."

"Oh, ah; just a little compliment for beginning. And when will it be making a progress and going on?"

"Making a progress!"

"Yes; when will the compliment become a little bigger? Twenty pounds! Oh! it's just for a few gloves, you know; nothing more."

"Nothing more than that, of course," said poor Archie.

"Well; when will the compliment grow bigger? Let me see. Julie has seven thousands of pounds, what you call, per annum. And have you seen that beautiful park? Oh! And if you can make her to look at the moon with her hair down,—oh! When will that compliment grow bigger? Twenty pounds! I am ashamed, you know."

"When will you see her, Madame Gordeloup?"

"See her! I see her every day, always. I will be there to-day, and to-morrow, and the next day."

"You might say a word then at once,—this afternoon."

"What! for twenty pounds! Seven thousands of pounds per annum; and you give me twenty pounds! Fie, Captain Clavering. It is only just for me to speak to you,—this! That is all. Come; when will you bring me fifty?"

"By George,—fifty!"

"Yes, fifty;—for another beginning. What; seven thousands of pounds per annum, and make difficulty for fifty pounds! You have a handy way with your glove. Will you come with fifty pounds to-morrow?" Archie, with the drops of perspiration standing on his brow, and now desirous of getting out again into the street, promised that he would come again on the following day with the required sum.

"Just for another beginning! And now, good-morning, Captain Clavering. I will do my possible with Julie. Julie is very fond of me, and I think you have been right in coming here. But twenty pounds was too little, even for a beginning." Mercenary wretch; hungry, greedy, ill-conditioned woman,—altogether of the harpy breed! As Archie Clavering looked into her grey eyes, and saw there her greed and her hunger, his flesh crept upon his bones. Should he not succeed with Julia, how much would this excellent lady cost him?

As soon as he was gone the excellent lady made an intolerable grimace, shaking herself and shrugging her shoulders, and walking up and down the room with her dirty wrapper held close round her. "Bah," she said. "Bah!" And as she thought of the heavy stupidity of her late visitor she shrugged herself and shook herself again violently, and clutched up her robe still more closely. "Bah!" It was intolerable to her that a man should be such a fool, even though she was to make money by him. And then, that such a man should conceive it to be possible that he should become the husband of a woman with seven thousand pounds a year! Bah!

Archie, as he walked away from Mount Street, found it difficult to create a triumphant feeling within his own bosom. He had been awk-ward, slow, and embarrassed, and the Spy had been too much for him. He was quite aware of that, and he was aware also that even the sagacious Doodles had been wrong. There had, at any rate, been no necessity for making a difficulty about the money. The Russian Spy had known her business too well to raise troublesome scruples on that point. That she was very good at her trade he was prepared to acknowledge; but a fear came upon him that he would find the article too costly for his own pur-poses. He remembered the determined tone in which she had demanded the fifty pounds merely as a further beginning.

And then he could not but reflect how much had been said at the interview about money,—about money for her, and how very little had been said as to the assistance to be given,—as to the return to be made for the money. No plan had been laid down, no times fixed, no facilities for making love suggested to him. He had simply paid over his twenty pounds, and been desired to bring another fifty. The other fifty he was to take to Mount Street on the morrow. What if she were to require fifty pounds every day, and declare that she could not stir in the matter for less? Doodles, no doubt, had told him that these first-class Russian spies did well the work for which they were paid; and no doubt, if paid according to her own tariff, Madame Gordeloup would work well for him; but such a tariff as that was altogether beyond his means! It would be imperatively necessary that he should come to some distinct settlement with her as to price. The twenty pounds, of course, were gone; but would it not be better that he should come to some final understanding with her before he gave her the further fifty? But then, as he thought of this, he was aware that she was too clever to allow him to do as he desired. If he went into that room with the fifty pounds in his pockets, or in his glove, or, indeed, anywhere about his person, she would have it from him, let his own resolution to make a previous bargain be what it might. His respect for the woman rose almost to veneration, but with the veneration was mixed a strong feeling of fear.

But, in spite of all this, he did venture to triumph a little when he met Doodles at the club. He had employed the Russian spy, and had paid her twenty pounds, and was enrolled in the corps of diplomatic and mysterious personages, who do their work by mysterious agencies. He did not tell Doodles anything about the glove, or the way in which the money was taken from him; but he did say that he was to see the Spy again to-morrow, and that he intended to take with him another present of fifty pounds.

"By George, Clavey, you are going it!" said Doodles, in a voice that was delightfully envious to the ears of Captain Archie. When he heard that envious tone he felt that he was entitled to be triumphant.

CHAPTER XXV.

What would Men say of You?

ARRY, tell me the truth,—
tell me all the truth." Harry
Clavering was thus greeted
when in obedience to the
summons from Lady Ongar,
he went to her almost im-
mediately on his return to
London.

It will be remembered that
he had remained at Clavering
some days after the departure
of Hugh and Archie, lacking
the courage to face his misfortunes boldly. But though
his delay had been cowardly,
it had not been easy to him
to be a coward. He despised
himself for not having written
with warm full-expressed
affection to Florence and with
honest clear truth to Julia.
Half his misery rose from
this feeling of self-abasement, and from the consciousness that he was weak,
—piteously weak, exactly in that in which he had often boasted to himself
that he was strong. But such inward boastings are not altogether bad.
They preserve men from succumbing, and make at any rate some attempt

to realize themselves. The man who tells himself that he is brave, will struggle much before he flies; but the man who never does so tell himself, will find flying easy unless his heart be of nature very high. Now had come the moment either for flying, or not flying; and Harry swearing that he would stand his ground, resolutely took his hat and gloves, and made his way to Bolton Street with a sore heart.

But as he went he could not keep himself from arguing the matter within his own breast. He knew what was his duty. It was his duty to stick to Florence, not only with his word and his hand, but with his heart. It was his duty to tell Lady Ongar that not only his word was at Stratton, but his heart also, and to ask her pardon for the wrong that he had done her by that caress. For some ten minutes as he walked through the streets his resolve was strong to do this manifest duty; but, gradually, as he thought of that caress, as he thought of the difficulties of the coming inter- view, as he thought of Julia's high-toned beauty,—perhaps something also of her wealth and birth,—and more strongly still as he thought of her love for him, false, treacherous, selfish arguments offered themselves to his mind,—arguments which he knew to be false and selfish. Which of them did he love? Could it be right for him to give his hand without his heart? Could it really be good for Florence,—poor injured Florence, that she should be taken by a man who had ceased to regard her more than all other women? Were he to marry her now, would not that deceit be worse than the other deceit? Or, rather, would not that be deceitful, whereas the other course would simply be unfortunate,—unfortunate through cir- cumstances for which he was blameless? Damnable arguments! False, cowardly logic, by which all male jilts seek to excuse their own treachery to themselves and to others!

Thus during the second ten minutes of his walk, his line of conduct became less plain to him, and as he entered Piccadilly he was racked with doubts. But instead of settling them in his mind he unconsciously allowed himself to dwell upon the words with which he would seek to excuse his treachery to Florence. He thought how he would tell her,—not to her face with spoken words, for that he could not do,—but with written skill, that he was unworthy of her goodness, that his love for her had fallen off through his own unworthiness, and had returned to one who was in all respects less perfect than she, but who in old days, as she well knew, had been his first love. Yes! he would say all this, and Julia, let her anger be what it might, should know that he had said it. As he planned this, there came to him a little comfort, for he thought there was something grand in such a resolution. Yes; he would do that, even though he should lose Julia also.

Miserable clap-trap! He knew in his heart that all his logic was false, and his arguments baseless. Cease to love Florence Burton! He had not ceased to love her, nor is the heart of any man made so like a weather- cock that it needs must turn itself hither and thither, as the wind directs, and be altogether beyond the man's control. For Harry, with all his

faults, and in spite of his present falseness, was a man. No man ceases
to love without a cause. No man need cease to love without a
cause. A man may maintain his love, and nourish it, and keep it
warm by honest manly effort, as he may his probity, his courage,
or his honour. It was not that he had ceased to love Florence ; but that
the glare of the candle had been too bright for him and he had scorched
his wings. After all, as to that embrace of which he had thought so much,
and the memory of which was so sweet to him and so bitter,—it had
simply been an accident. Thus, writing in his mind that letter to
Florence which he knew, if he were an honest man, he would never allow
himself to write, he reached Lady Ongar's door without having arranged
for himself any special line of conduct.

We must return for a moment to the fact that Hugh and Archie had
returned to town before Harry Clavering. How Archie had been engaged
on great doings, the reader, I hope, will remember ; and he may as well
be informed here that the fifty pounds were duly taken to Mount Street,
and were extracted from him by the spy without much difficulty. I do
not know that Archie in return obtained any immediate aid or valuable
information from Sophie Gordeloup ; but Sophie did obtain some information from him which she found herself able to use for her own purposes.
As his position with reference to love and marriage was being discussed,
and the position also of the divine Julia, Sophie hinted her fear of another
Clavering lover. What did Archie think of his cousin Harry ? " Why ;
he's engaged to another girl," said Archie, opening wide his eyes and his
mouth, and becoming very free with his information. This was a matter
to which Sophie found it worth her while to attend, and she soon learned
from Archie all that Archie knew about Florence Burton. And this was
all that could be known. No secret had been made in the family of
Harry's engagement. Archie told his fair assistant that Miss Burton had
been received at Clavering Park openly as Harry's future wife, and, " by
Jove, you know, he can't be coming it with Julia after that, you know."
Sophie made a little grimace, but did not say much. She, remembering
that she had caught Lady Ongar in Harry's arms, thought that, " by
Jove," he might be coming it with Julia, even after Miss Burton's
reception at Clavering Park. Then, too, she remembered some few words
that had passed between her and her dear Julia after Harry's departure on
the evening of the embrace, and perceived that Julia was in ignorance of
the very existence of Florence Burton, even though Florence had been
received at the Park. This was information worth having,—information
to be used ! Her respect for Harry rose immeasurably. She had not
given him credit for so much audacity, so much gallantry, and so much
skill. She had thought him to be a pigheaded Clavering, like the rest
of them. He was not pigheaded ; he was a promising young man ; she
could have liked him and perhaps aided him,—only that he had shown so
strong a determination to have nothing to do with her. Therefore the
information should be used ;—and it was used.

The reader will now understand what was the truth which Lady Ongar demanded from Harry Clavering. "Harry, tell me the truth; tell me all the truth." She had come forward to meet him in the middle of the room when she spoke these words, and stood looking him in the face, not having given him her hand.

"What truth?" said Harry. "Have I ever told you a lie?" But he knew well what was the truth required of him.

"Lies can be acted as well as told. Harry, tell me all at once. Who is Florence Burton; who and what?" She knew it all, then, and things had settled themselves for him without the necessity of any action on his part. It was odd enough that she should not have learned it before, but at any rate she knew it now. And it was well that she should have been told; —only how was he to excuse himself for that embrace? "At any rate speak to me," she said, standing quite erect, and looking as a Juno might have looked. "You will acknowledge at least that I have a right to ask the question. Who is this Florence Burton?"

"She is the daughter of Mr. Burton of Stratton."

"And is that all that you can tell me? Come, Harry, be braver than that. I was not such a coward once with you. Are you engaged to marry her?"

"Yes, Lady Ongar, I am."

"Then you have had your revenge on me, and now we are quits." So saying, she stepped back from the middle of the room, and sat herself down on her accustomed seat. He was left there standing, and it seemed as though she intended to take no further notice of him. He might go if he pleased, and there would be an end of it all. The difficulty would be over, and he might at once write to Florence in what language he liked. It would simply be a little episode in his life, and his escape would not have been arduous.

But he could not go from her in that way. He could not bring himself to leave the room without some further word. She had spoken of revenge. Was it not incumbent on him to explain to her that there had been no revenge ; that he had loved, and suffered, and forgiven without one thought of anger ;—and that then he had unfortunately loved again? Must he not find some words in which to tell her that she had been the light, and he simply the poor moth that had burned his wings?

"No, Lady Ongar," said he, "there has been no revenge."

"We will call it justice, if you please. At any rate I do not mean to complain."

"If you ever injured me ——" he began.

"I did injure you," said she, sharply.

"If you ever injured me, I forgave you freely."

"I did injure you ——" As she spoke she rose again from her seat, showing how impossible to her was that tranquillity which she had attempted to maintain. "I did injure you, but the injury came to you early in life, and sat lightly on you. Within a few months you had learned to love this young lady at the place you went to,—the first young lady you saw ! I had not done you much harm, Harry. But that which you have done me, cannot be undone."

"Julia," he said, coming up to her.

"No ; not Julia. When you were here before I asked you to call me so, hoping, longing, believing,—doing more, so much more than I could have done, but that I thought my love might now be of service to you. You do not think that I had heard of this then ? "

"Oh, no."

"No. It is odd that I should not have known it, as I now hear that she was at my sister's house; but all others have not been as silent as you have been. We are quits, Harry ; that is all that I have to say. We are quits now."

"I have intended to be true to you ;—to you and to her."

"Were you true when you acted as you did the other night ? " He could not explain to her how greatly he had been tempted. "Were you true when you held me in your arms as that woman came in ? Had you not made me think that I might glory in loving you, and that I might show her that I scorned her when she thought to promise me her secrecy ;—her secrecy, as though I were ashamed of what she had seen. I was not ashamed,—not then. Had all the world known it, I should not have been ashamed. 'I have loved him long,' I should have said, 'and him only. He is to be my husband, and now at last I need not be ashamed.' " So much she spoke, standing up, looking at him with firm face, and uttering her syllables with a quick clear voice; but at the last word there came a quiver in her tone, and the strength of her countenance quailed, and there was a tear which made dim her eye, and she knew that she could no longer stand before him. She endeavoured to seat herself with composure ; but the attempt failed, and as she fell back upon the sofa he just heard the sob which had cost her so great and vain an effort to restrain. In an instant he was kneeling at her feet, and grasping at the hand with which she was hiding her face. "Julia," he said, "look at me ; let us at any rate understand each other at last."

"No, Harry ; there must be no more such knowledge,—no more such understanding. You must go from me, and come here no more. Had it not been for that other night, I would still have endeavoured to regard you as a friend. But I have no right to such friendship. I have sinned and gone astray, and am a thing vile and polluted. I sold myself, as a beast is sold, and men have treated me as I treated myself."

"Have I treated you so ? "

"Yes, Harry ; you, you. How did you treat me when you took me in your arms and kissed me,—knowing, knowing that I was not to be your wife ? O God, I have sinned. I have sinned, and I am punished."

"No, no," said he, rising from his knees, "it was not as you say."

"Then how was it, sir ? Is it thus that you treat other women ;—your friends, those to whom you declare friendship ? What did you mean me to think ? "

"That I loved you."

"Yes; with a love that should complete my disgrace,—that should finish my degradation. But I had not heard of this Florence Burton; and, Harry, that night I was so happy in my bed. And in that next week when you were down there for that sad ceremony, I was happy here, happy and proud. Yes, Harry, I was so proud when I thought that you still loved me,—loved me in spite of my past sin, that I almost forgot that I was polluted. You have made me remember it, and I shall not forget it again."

It would have been better for him had he gone away at once. Now he was sitting in a chair sobbing violently, and pressing away the tears from his cheeks with his hands. How could he make her understand that he had intended no insult when he embraced her? Was it not incumbent on him to tell her that the wrong he then did was done to Florence Burton, and not to her? But his agony was too much for him at present, and he could find no words in which to speak to her.

"I said to myself that you would come when the funeral was over, and I wept for poor Hermy as I thought that my lot was so much happier than hers. But people have what they deserve, and Hermy, who has done no such wrong as I have done, is not crushed as I am crushed. It was just, Harry, that the punishment should come from you, but it has come very heavily."

"Julia, it was not meant to be so."

"Well; we will let that pass. I cannot unsay, Harry, all that I have said;—all that I did not say, but which you must have thought and known when you were here last. I cannot bid you believe that I do not—love you."

"Not more tenderly or truly than I love you."

"Nay, Harry, your love to me can be neither true nor tender,—nor will I permit it to be offered to me. You do not think I would rob that girl of what is hers. Mine for you may be both tender and true; but, alas, truth has come to me when it can avail me no longer."

"Julia, if you will say that you love me, it shall avail you."

"In saying that, you are continuing to ill-treat me. Listen to me now. I hardly know when it began, for, at first, I did not expect that you would forgive me and let me be dear to you as I used to be; but as you sat here, looking up into my face in the old way, it came on me gradually,—the feeling that it might be so; and I told myself that if you would take me I might be of service to you, and I thought that I might forgive myself at last for possessing this money if I could throw it into your lap, so that you might thrive with it in the world; and I said to myself that it might be well to wait awhile, till I should see whether you really loved me; but then came that burst of passion, and though I knew that you were wrong, I was proud to feel that I was still so dear to you. It is all over. We understand each other at last, and you may go. There is nothing to be forgiven between us."

He had now resolved that Florence must go by the board. If Julia would still take him she should be his wife, and he would face Florence and all the Burtons, and his own family, and all the world in the matter of his treachery. What would he care what the world might say? His treachery to Florence was a thing completed. Now, at this moment, he felt himself to be so devoted to Julia as to make him regard his engagement to Florence as one which must, at all hazards, be renounced. He thought of his mother's sorrow, of his father's scorn,—of the dismay with which Fanny would hear concerning him a tale which she would believe to be so impossible; he thought of Theodore Burton, and the deep, unquenchable anger of which that brother was capable, and of Cecilia and her outraged kindness; he thought of the infamy which would be attached to him, and resolved that he must bear it all. Even if his own heart did not move him so to act, how could he hinder himself from giving comfort and happiness to this woman who was before him? Injury, wrong, and broken-hearted wretchedness, he could not prevent; but, therefore, this part was as open to him as the other. Men would say that he had done this for Lady Ongar's money; and the indignation with which he was able to regard this false accusation,—for his mind declared such accusation to be damnably false,—gave him some comfort. People might say of him what they pleased. He was about to do the best within his power. Bad, alas, was the best, but it was of no avail now to think of that.

"Julia," he said, "between us at least there shall be nothing to be forgiven."

"There is nothing," said she.

"And there shall be no broken love. I am true to you now,—as ever."

"And, what, then, of your truth to Miss Florence Burton?"

"It will not be for you to rebuke me with that. We have, both of us, played our game badly, but not for that reason need we both be ruined and broken-hearted. In your folly you thought that wealth was better than love; and I, in my folly,—I thought that one love blighted might be mended by another. When I asked Miss Burton to be my wife you were the wife of another man. Now that you are free again I cannot marry Miss Burton."

"You must marry her, Harry."

"There shall be no must in such a case. You do not know her, and cannot understand how good, how perfect she is. She is too good to take a hand without a heart."

"And what would men say of you?"

"I must bear what men say. I do not suppose that I shall be all happy,—not even with your love. When things have once gone wrong they cannot be mended without showing the patches. But yet men stay the hand of ruin for a while, tinkering here and putting in a nail there, stitching and cobbling; and so things are kept together. It must be so for you and me. Give me your hand, Julia, for I have never deceived you, and you need not fear that I shall do so now. Give me your hand, and say that you will be my wife."

"No, Harry; not your wife. I do not, as you say, know that perfect girl, but I will not rob one that is so good."

"You are bound to me, Julia. You must do as I bid you. You have told me that you love me; and I have told you,—and I tell you now, that I love none other as I love you;—have never loved any other as I have loved you. Give me your hand." Then, coming to her, he took her hand, while she sat with her face averted from him. "Tell me that you will be my wife." But she would not say the words. She was less selfish than he, and was thinking,—was trying to think what might be best for them all, but, above all, what might be best for him. "Speak to me," he said, "and acknowledge that you wronged me when you thought that the expression of my love was an insult to you."

"It is easy to say, speak. What shall I say?"

"Say that you will be my wife."

"No,—I will not say it." She rose again from her chair, and took her hand away from him. "I will not say it. Go now and think over all that you have done; and I also will think of it. God help me. What evil comes, when evil has been done! But, Harry, I understand you now, and I at least will blame you no more. Go and see Florence Burton; and if, when you see her, you find that you can love her, take her to your heart, and be true to her. You shall never hear another reproach from me. Go now, go; there is nothing more to be said."

He paused a moment as though he were going to speak, but he left the room without another word. As he went along the passage and turned on the stairs he saw her standing at the door of the room, looking at him, and it seemed that her eyes were imploring him to be true to her in spite of the words that she had spoken. "And I will be true to her," he said to himself. "She was the first that I ever loved, and I will be true to her."

He went out, and for an hour or two wandered about the town, hardly knowing whither his steps were taking him. There had been a tragic seriousness in what had occurred to him this evening, which seemed to cover him with care, and make him feel that his youth was gone from him. At any former period of his life his ears would have tingled with pride to hear such a woman as Lady Ongar speak of her love for him in such terms as she had used; but there was no room now for pride in his bosom. Now at least he thought nothing of her wealth or rank. He thought of her as a woman between whom and himself there existed so strong a passion as to make it impossible that he should marry another, even though his duty plainly required it. The grace and graciousness of his life were over; but love still remained to him, and of that he must make the most. All others whom he regarded would revile him, and now he must live for this woman alone. She had said that she had injured him.

Yes, indeed, she had injured him! She had robbed him of his high character, of his unclouded brow, of that self-pride which had so often told him that he was living a life without reproach among men. She had brought him to a state in which misery must be his bedfellow, and disgrace his companion ;—but still she loved him, and to that love he would be true.

And as to Florence Burton ;—how was he to settle matters with her? That letter for which he had been preparing the words as he went to Bolton Street, before the necessity for it had become irrevocable, did not now appear to him to be very easy. At any rate he did not attempt it on that night.

CHAPTER XXVI.

The Man who dusted his Boots with his Handkerchief.

When Florence Burton had written three letters to Harry without receiving a word in reply to either of them, she began to be seriously unhappy. The last of these letters, received by him after the scene described in the last chapter, he had been afraid to read. It still remained unopened in his pocket. But Florence, though she was unhappy, was not even yet jealous. Her fears did not lie in that direction, nor had she naturally any tendency to such uneasiness. He was ill, she thought; or if not ill in health, then ill at ease. Some trouble afflicted him of which he could not bring himself to tell her the facts, and as she thought of this she remembered her own stubbornness on the subject of their marriage, and blamed herself in that she was not now with him, to comfort him. If such comfort would avail him anything now, she would be stubborn no longer. When the third letter brought no reply she wrote to her sister-in-law, Mrs. Burton, confessing her uneasiness, and begging for comfort. Surely Cecilia could not but see him occasionally, —or at any rate have the power of seeing him. Or Theodore might do so,—as of course he would be at the office. If anything ailed him would Cecilia tell her all the truth? But Cecilia, when she began to fear that something did ail him, did not find it very easy to tell Florence all the truth.

But there was jealousy at Stratton, though Florence was not jealous. Old Mrs. Burton had become alarmed, and was ready to tear the eyes out of Harry Clavering's head if Harry should be false to her daughter. This was a misfortune of which, with all her brood, Mrs. Burton had as yet known nothing. No daughter of hers had been misused by any man, and no son of hers had ever misused any one's daughter. Her children had gone out into the world steadily, prudently, making no brilliant marriages, but never falling into any mistakes. She heard of such misfortunes around her,—that a young lady here had loved in vain, and that a young lady there had been left to wear the willow; but such sorrows had never visited her roof, and she was disposed to think,—and perhaps to say,—that the fault lay chiefly in the imprudence of mothers. What if at last, when her work in this line had been so nearly brought to a successful close, misery and disappointment should come also upon her lamb! In such case Mrs. Burton, we may say, was a ewe who would not see her lamb suffer without many bleatings and considerable exercise of her maternal energies.

And tidings had come to Mrs. Burton which had not as yet been allowed to reach Florence's ears. In the office at the Adelphi was one Mr. Walliker, who had a younger brother now occupying that desk in Mr. Burton's office which had belonged to Harry Clavering. Through Bob Walliker, Mrs. Burton learned that Harry did not come to the office even when it was known that he had returned to London from Clavering; —and she also learned at last that the young men in the office were connecting Harry Clavering's name with that of the rich and noble widow, Lady Ongar. Then Mrs. Burton wrote to her son Theodore, as Florence had written to Theodore's wife.

Mrs. Burton, though she had loved Harry dearly, and had perhaps in many respects liked him better than any of her sons-in-law, had, nevertheless, felt some misgivings from the first. Florence was brighter, better educated, and cleverer than her elder sisters, and therefore when it had come to pass that she was asked in marriage by a man somewhat higher in rank and softer in manners than they who had married her sisters, there had seemed to be some reason for the change;—but Mrs. Burton had felt that it was a ground for apprehension. High rank and soft manners may not always belong to a true heart. At first she was unwilling to hint this caution even to herself; but at last, as her suspicions grew, she spoke the words very frequently, not only to herself but also to her husband. Why, oh why, had she let into her house any man differing in mode of life from those whom she had known to be honest and good? How would her gray hairs be made to go in sorrow to the grave, if, after all her old prudence and all her old success, her last pet lamb should be returned to the mother's side, ill-used, maimed, and blighted!

Theodore Burton, when he received his mother's letter, had not seen Harry since his return from Clavering. He had been inclined to be very angry with him for his long and unannounced absence from the office. "He will do no good," he had said to his wife. "He does not know what real work means." But his anger turned to disgust as regarded Harry, and almost to despair as regarded his sister, when Harry had been a week in town, and yet had not shown himself at the Adelphi. But at this time Theodore Burton had heard no word of Lady Ongar, though the clerks in the office had that name daily in their mouths. "Cannot you go to him, Theodore?" said his wife. "It is very easy to say go to him," he replied. "If I made it my business I could, of course, go to him, and no doubt find him if I was determined to do so;—but what more could I do? I can lead a horse to the water, but I cannot make him drink." "You could speak to him of Florence." "That is such a woman's idea," said the husband. "When every proper incentive to duty and ambition has failed him, he is to be brought into the right way by the mention of a girl's name!" "May I see him?" Cecilia urged. "Yes,—if you can catch him; but I do not advise you to try."

After that came the two letters for the husband and wife, each of which was shown to the other; and then for the first time did either of them receive the idea that Lady Ongar with her fortune might be a cause of misery to their sister. "I don't believe a word of it," said Cecilia, whose cheeks were burning, half with shame and half with anger. Harry had been such a pet with her,—had already been taken so closely to her heart as a brother! "I should not have suspected him of that kind of baseness," said Theodore, very slowly. "He is not base," said Cecilia. "He may be idle and foolish, but he is not base."

"I must at any rate go after him now," said Theodore. "I don't believe this;—I won't believe it. I do not believe it. But if it should be true —— !"

"Oh, Theodore."

"I do not think it is true. It is not the kind of weakness I have seen in him. He is weak and vain, but I should have said that he was true."

"I am sure he is true."

"I think so. I cannot say more than that I think so."

"You will write to your mother?"

"Yes."

"And may I ask Florence to come up? Is it not always better that people should be near to each other when they are engaged?"

"You can ask her, if you like. I doubt whether she will come."

"She will come if she thinks that anything is amiss with him."

Cecilia wrote immediately to Florence, pressing her invitation in the strongest terms that she could use. "I tell you the whole truth," she said. "We have not seen him, and this, of course, has troubled us very greatly. I feel quite sure he would come to us if you were here; and this, I think, should bring you, if no other consideration does so. Theodore imagines that he has become simply idle, and that he is ashamed to show himself here because of that. It may be that he has some trouble with reference to his own home, of which we know nothing. But if he has any such trouble, you ought to be made aware of it, and I feel sure that he would tell you if you were here." Much more she said, arguing in the same way, and pressing Florence to come to London.

Mr. Burton did not at once send a reply to his mother, but he wrote the following note to Harry:—

Adelphi·——, May, 186—

"MY DEAR CLAVERING,—I have been sorry to notice your continued absence from the office, and both Cecilia and I have been very sorry that

you have discontinued coming to us. But I should not have written to
you on this matter, not wishing to interfere in your own concerns, had I
not desired to see you specially with reference to my sister. As I have
that to say to you concerning her which I can hardly write, will you make
an appointment with me here, or at my house? Or, if you cannot do
that, will you say when I shall find you at home? If you will come and
dine with us we shall like that best, and leave you to name an early day :
to-morrow, or the next day, or the day after.

"Very truly yours,
"THEODORE BURTON."

When Cecilia's letter reached Stratton, and another post came without
any letter from Harry, poor Florence's heart sank low in her bosom.
"Well, my dear," said Mrs. Burton, who watched her daughter anxiously
while she was reading the letter. Mrs. Burton had not told Florence of
her own letter to her son; and now, having herself received no answer,
looked to obtain some reply from that which her daughter-in-law had
sent.

"Cecilia wants me to go to London," said Florence.

"Is there anything the matter that you should go just now ? "

"Not exactly the matter, mamma ; but you can see the letter."

Mrs. Burton read it slowly, and felt sure that much was the matter.
She knew that Cecilia would have written in that strain only under
the influence of some great alarm. At first she was disposed to think
that she herself would go to London. She was eager to know the
truth,—eager to utter her loud maternal bleatings if any wrong were
threatened to her lamb. Florence might go with her, but she longed
herself to be on the field of action. She felt that she could almost
annihilate any man by her words and looks who would dare to ill-treat
a girl of hers.

"Well, mamma ;—what do you think ? "

"I don't know yet, my dear. I will speak to your papa before dinner."
But as Mrs. Burton had been usually autocratic in the management of her
own daughters, Florence was aware that her mother simply required a little
time before she made up her mind. "It is not that I want to go to London
—for the pleasure of it, mamma."

"I know that, my dear."

"Nor yet merely to see him !—though of course I do long to see
him ! "

"Of course you do ;—why shouldn't you ? "

"But Cecilia is so very prudent, and she thinks that it will be better.
And she would not have pressed it, unless Theodore had thought so too ! "

"I thought Theodore would have written to me ! "

"But he writes so seldom."

"I expected a letter from him now, as I had written to him."

"About Harry, do you mean ? "

" Well ;—yes. I did not mention it, as I was aware I might make
you uneasy. But I saw that you were unhappy at not hearing from him."

" Oh, mamma, do let me go."

" Of course you shall go if you wish it ;—but let me speak to papa
before anything is quite decided."

Mrs. Burton did speak to her husband, and it was arranged that
Florence should go up to Onslow Crescent. But Mrs. Burton, though she
had been always autocratic about her unmarried daughters, had never
been autocratic about herself. When she hinted that she also might go,
she saw that the scheme was not approved, and she at once abandoned it.
" It would look as if we were all afraid," said Mr. Burton, " and after all
what does it come to ?—a young gentleman does not write to his sweetheart for two or three weeks. I used to think myself the best lover in the
world, if I wrote once a month."

" There was no penny post then, Mr. Burton."

" And I often wish there was none now," said Mr. Burton. That
matter was therefore decided, and Florence wrote back to her sister-in-law,
saying that she would go up to London on the third day from that. In
the meantime, Harry Clavering and Theodore Burton had met.

Has it ever been the lot of any unmarried male reader of these pages,
to pass three or four days in London, without anything to do,—to have
to get through them by himself,—and to have that burden on his shoulder,
with the additional burden of some terrible, wearing misery, away from
which there seems to be no road, and out of which there is apparently no
escape? That was Harry Clavering's condition for some few days after
the evening which he last passed in the company of Lady Ongar,—and I
will ask any such unmarried man whether, in such a plight, there was for
him any other alternative, but to wish himself dead ? In such a condition,
a man can simply walk the streets by himself, and declare to himself that
everything is bad, and rotten, and vile, and worthless. He wishes himself dead, and calculates the different advantages of prussic acid and pistols.
He may the while take his meals very punctually at his club, may smoke
his cigars, and drink his bitter beer, or brandy-and-water ;—but he is all
the time wishing himself dead, and making that calculation as to the best
way of achieving that desirable result. Such was Harry Clavering's
condition now. As for his office, the doors of that place were absolutely
closed against him, by the presence of Theodore Burton. When he
attempted to read he could not understand a word, or sit for ten minutes
with a book in his hand. No occupation was possible to him. He longed
to go again to Bolton Street, but he did not even do that. If there, he
could act only as though Florence had been deserted for ever ;—and if
he so acted he would be infamous for life. And yet he had sworn to
Julia that such was his intention. He hardly dared to ask himself which
of the two he loved. The misery of it all had become so heavy upon
him, that he could take no pleasure in the thought of his love. It must
always be all regret, all sorrow, and all remorse. Then there came upon

him the letter from Theodore Burton, and he knew that it was necessary that he should see the writer.

Nothing could be more disagreeable than such an interview, but he could not allow himself to be guilty of the cowardice of declining it. Of a personal quarrel with Burton he was not afraid. He felt, indeed, that he might almost find relief in the capability of being himself angry with any one. But he must positively make up his mind before such an interview. He must devote himself either to Florence or to Julia;—and he did not know how to abandon the one or the other. He had allowed himself to be so governed by impulse that he had pledged himself to Lady Ongar, and had sworn to her that he would be entirely hers. She, it is true, had not taken him altogether at his word, but not the less did he know,—did he think that he knew,—that she looked for the performance of his promise. And she had been the first that he had sworn to love!

In his dilemma he did at last go to Bolton Street, and there found that Lady Ongar had left town for three or four days. The servant said that she had gone, he believed, to the Isle of Wight; and that Madame Gordeloup had gone with her. She was to be back in town early in the following week. This was on a Thursday, and he was aware that he could not postpone his interview with Burton till after Julia's return. So he went to his club, and nailing himself as it were to the writing-table, made an appointment for the following morning. He would be with Burton at the Adelphi at twelve o'clock. He had been in trouble, he said, and that trouble had kept him from the office and from Onslow Crescent. Having written this, he sent it off, and then played billiards and smoked and dined, played more billiards and smoked and drank till the usual hours of the night had come. He was not a man who liked such things. He had not become what he was by passing his earlier years after this fashion. But his misery required excitement,—and billiards with tobacco were better than the desolation of solitude.

On the following morning he did not breakfast till near eleven. Why should he get up as long as it was possible to obtain the relief which was to be had from dozing? As far as possible he would not think of the matter till he had put his hat upon his head to go to the Adelphi. But the time for taking his hat soon came, and he started on his short journey. But even as he walked, he could not think of it. He was purposeless, as a ship without a rudder, telling himself that he could only go as the winds might direct him. How he did hate himself for his one weakness! And yet he hardly made an effort to overcome it. On one point only did he seem to have a resolve. If Burton attempted to use with him anything like a threat he would instantly resent it.

Punctually at twelve he walked into the outer office, and was told that Mr. Burton was in his room.

"Halloa, Clavering," said Walliker, who was standing with his back to the fire, "I thought we had lost you for good and all. And here you are come back again !"

Harry had always disliked this man, and now hated him worse than ever. "Yes; I am here," said he, "for a few minutes; but I believe I need not trouble you."

"All right, old fellow," said Walliker; and then Harry passed through into the inner room.

"I am very glad to see you, Harry," said Burton, rising and giving his hand cordially to Clavering. "And I am sorry to hear that you have been in trouble. Is it anything in which we can help you?"

"I hope,—Mrs. Burton is well," said Harry, hesitating.

"Pretty well."

"And the children?"

"Quite well. They say you are a very bad fellow not to go and see them."

"I believe I am a bad fellow," said Harry.

"Sit down, Harry. It will be best to come at the point at once;—will it not? Is there anything wrong between you and Florence?"

"What do you mean by wrong?"

"I should call it very wrong,—hideously wrong, if after all that has passed between you, there should now be any doubt as to your affection for each other. If such doubt were now to arise with her, I should almost disown my sister."

"You will never have to blush for her."

"I think not. I thank God that hitherto there have been no such blushes among us. And I hope, Harry, that my heart may never have to bleed for her. Come, Harry, let me tell you all at once like an honest man. I hate subterfuges and secrets. A report has reached the old people at home,—not Florence, mind,—that you are untrue to Florence, and are passing your time with that lady who is the sister of your cousin's wife."

"What right have they to ask how I pass my time?"

"Do not be unjust, Harry. If you simply tell me that your visits to that lady imply no evil to my sister, I, knowing you to be a gentleman, will take your word for all that it can mean." He paused, and Harry hesitated and could not answer. "Nay, dear friend,—brother as we both of us have thought you,—come once more to Onslow Crescent and kiss the bairns, and kiss Cecilia, too, and sit with us at our table, and talk as you used to do, and I will ask no further question;—nor will she. Then you will come back here to your work, and your trouble will be gone, and your mind will be at ease; and, Harry, one of the best girls that ever gave her heart into a man's keeping will be there to worship you, and to swear when your back is turned that any one who says a word against you shall be no brother and no sister and no friend of hers."

And this was the man who had dusted his boots with his pocket-handkerchief, and whom Harry had regarded as being on that account hardly fit to be his friend! He knew that the man was noble, and good, and generous, and true;—and knew also that in all that Burton said he simply did his duty as a brother. But not on that account was it the easier for him to reply.

"Say that you will come to us this evening," said Burton. "Even if you have an engagement, put it off."

"I have none," said Harry.

"Then say that you will come to us, and all will be well."

Harry understood of course that his compliance with this invitation would be taken as implying that all was right. It would be so easy to accept the invitation, and any other answer was so difficult! But yet he would not bring himself to tell the lie.

"Burton," he said, "I am in trouble."

"What is the trouble?" The man's voice was now changed, and so was the glance of his eye. There was no expression of anger,—none as yet; but the sweetness of his countenance was gone,—a sweetness that was unusual to him, but which still was at his command when he needed it.

"I cannot tell you all here. If you will let me come to you this evening I will tell you everything,—to you and to Cecilia too. Will you let me come?"

"Certainly. Will you dine with us?"

"No;—after dinner; when the children are in bed." Then he went, leaving on the mind of Theodore Burton an impression that though something was much amiss, his mother had been wrong in her fears respecting Lady Ongar.

CHAPTER XXVII.

FRESHWATER GATE.

COUNT PATEROFF, Sophie's brother, was a man who, when he had taken a thing in hand, generally liked to carry it through. It may perhaps be said that most men are of this turn of mind; but the count was, I think, especially eager in this respect. And as he was not one who had many irons in the fire, who made either many little efforts, or any great efforts after things altogether beyond his reach, he was justified in expecting success. As to Archie's courtship, any one who really knew the man and the woman, and who knew anything of the nature of women in general, would have predicted failure for him. Even with Doodle's aid he could not have a chance in the race. But when Count Pateroff entered himself for the same prize, those who knew him would not speak of his failure as a thing certain.

The prize was too great not to be attempted by so very prudent a gentleman. He was less impulsive in his nature than his sister, and did not open his eyes and talk with watering mouth of the seven thousands of pounds a year; but in his quiet way he had weighed and calculated all the advantages to be gained, had even ascertained at what rate he could insure the lady's life, and had made himself certain that nothing in the deed of Lord Ongar's marriage-settlement entailed any pecuniary penalty on his widow's second marriage. Then he had gone down, as we know, to Ongar Park, and as he had walked from the lodge to the house and back again, he had looked around him complacently, and told himself that the place would do very well. For the English character, in spite of the pigheadedness of many Englishmen, he had,—as he would have said himself,—much admiration, and he thought that the life of a country gentleman, with a nice place of his own,—with such a very nice place of his own as was Ongar Park,—and so very nice an income, would suit him well in his declining years.

And he had certain advantages, certain aids towards his object, which had come to him from circumstances;—as, indeed, he had also certain disadvantages. He knew the lady, which was in itself much. He knew much of the lady's history, and had that cognisance of the saddest circumstances of her life, which in itself creates an intimacy. It is not necessary now to go back to those scenes which had disfigured the last months of Lord Ongar's life, but the reader will understand that what had then occurred gave the count a possible footing as a suitor. And the reader will also understand the disadvantages which had at this time already shown themselves in the lady's refusal to see the count.

It may be thought that Sophie's standing with Lady Ongar would be a great advantage to her brother; but I doubt whether the brother trusted either the honesty or the discretion of his sister. He would have been willing to purchase such assistance as she might give,—not in Archie's pleasant way, with bank-notes hidden under his glove,—but by acknowledgments for services to be turned into solid remuneration when the marriage should have taken place, had he not feared that Sophie might communicate the fact of such acknowledgments to the other lady, —making her own bargain in doing so. He had calculated all this, and had come to the conclusion that he had better make no direct proposal to Sophie; and when Sophie made a direct proposal to him, pointing out to him in glowing language all the fine things which such a marriage would give him, he had hardly vouchsafed to her a word of answer. "Very well," said Sophie to herself;—"very well. Then we both know what we are about."

Sophie herself would have kept Lady Ongar from marrying any one had she been able. Not even a brother's gratitude would be so serviceable to her as the generous kindness of a devoted friend. That she might be able both to sell her services to a lover, and also to keep Julie from marrying, was a lucky combination of circumstances which did not occur to her till Archie came to her with the money in his glove. That complicated game she was now playing, and was aware that Harry Clavering was the great stumbling-block in her way. A woman even less clever than Sophie would have perceived that Lady Ongar was violently attached to Harry; and Sophie, when she did see it, thought that there was nothing left for her but to make her hay while the sun was yet shining. Then she heard the story of Florence Burton; and again she thought that Fortune was on her side. She told the story of Florence Burton, —with what result we know; and was quite sharp enough to perceive afterwards that the tale had had its intended effect,—even though her Julie had resolutely declined to speak either of Harry Clavering or of Florence Burton.

Count Pateroff had again called in Bolton Street, and had again been refused admittance. It was plain to him to see by the servant's manner that it was intended that he should understand that he was not to be admitted. Under such circumstances, it was necessary that he must either abandon his pursuit, or that he must operate upon Lady Ongar through some other feeling than her personal regard for himself. He might, perhaps, have trusted much to his own eloquence if he could have seen her; but how is a man to be eloquent in his wooing if he cannot see the lady whom he covets ? There is, indeed, the penny post, but in these days of legal restraints, there is no other method of approaching an unwilling beauty. Forcible abduction is put an end to as regards Great Britain and Ireland. So the count had resort to the post.

His letter was very long, and shall not, therefore, be given to the reader. He began by telling Lady Ongar that she owed it to him for the good services he had done her, to read what he might say, and to answer him. He then gave her various reasons why she should see him, pleading, among other things, in language which she could understand, though the words were purposely as ambiguous as they could be made, that he had possessed and did possess the power of doing her a grievous injury, and that he had abstained, and—hoped that he might be able to abstain for the future. She knew that the words contained no threat,—that taken literally they were the reverse of a threat, and amounted to a promise,—but she understood also all that he had intended to imply. Long as his own letter was, he said nothing in it as to his suit, confining himself to a request that she should see him. But with his letter he sent her an enclosure longer than the letter itself, in which his wishes were clearly explained.

This enclosure purported to be an expression of Lord Ongar's wishes on many subjects, as they had been communicated to Count Pateroff in the latter days of the lord's life ; but as the manuscript was altogether in the count's writing, and did not even pretend to have been subjected to Lord Ongar's eye, it simply amounted to the count's own story of their alleged conversations. There might have been no such conversations, or their tenour might have been very different from that which the count represented, or the statements and opinions, if expressed at all by Lord Ongar, might have been expressed at times when no statements or opinions coming from him could be of any value. But as to these conversations, if they could have been verified as having come from Lord Ongar's mouth when he was in full possession of such faculties as he possessed,—all that would have amounted to nothing with Lady Ongar. To Lord Ongar alive she had owed obedience, and had been obedient. To Lord Ongar dead she owed no obedience, and would not be obedient.

Such would have been her feelings as to any document which could have reached her, purporting to contain Lord Ongar's wishes; but this document was of a nature which made her specially antagonistic to the exercise of any such marital authority from the grave. It was very long, and went into small details,—details which were very small; but the upshot of it all was a tendering of great thanks to Count Pateroff, and the expression of a strong wish that the count should marry his widow. "O. said that this would be the only thing for J.'s name." "O. said that this would be the safest course for his own honour." "O. said, as he took my hand, that in promising to take this step I gave him great comfort." "O. commissioned me to speak to J. in his name to this effect." The O. was of course Lord Ongar, and the J. was of course Julia. It was all in French, and went on in the same strain for many pages. Lady Ongar answered the letter as follows:—

"Lady Ongar presents her compliments to Count Pateroff, and begs to return the enclosed manuscript, which is, to her, perfectly valueless. Lady Ongar must still decline, and now more strongly than before, to receive Count Pateroff.

"*Bolton Street, May* 186—.

She was quite firm as she did this. She had no doubt at all on the matter. She did not feel that she wanted to ask for any advice. But she did feel that this count might still work her additional woe, that her cup of sorrow might not even yet be full, and that she was sadly,—sadly in want of love and protection. For aught she knew, the count might publish the whole statement, and people might believe that those words came from her husband, and that her husband had understood what would be best for her fame and for his honour. The whole thing was a threat, and not to save herself from any misery, would she have succumbed to a menace; but still it was possible that the threat might be carried out.

She was sorely in want of love and protection. At this time, when the count's letter reached her, Harry had been with her; and we know what had passed between them. She had bid him go to Florence,—and love Florence,—and marry Florence,—and leave her in her desolation. That had been her last command to him. But we all know what such commands mean. She had not been false in giving him these orders. She had intended it at the moment. The glow of self-sacrifice had been warm in her bosom,—and she had resolved to do without that which she wanted in order that another might have it. But when she thought of it afterwards in her loneliness, she told herself that Florence Burton could not want Harry's love as she wanted it. There could not be such need to this girl, who possessed father and mother, and brothers, and youth, as there was to her, who had no other arm on which she could lean, besides that of the one man for whom she had acknowledged her love, and who had also declared his passion for her. She made no scheme to deprive Florence of her lover. In the long hours of her own solitude she never revoked, even within her own bosom, the last words she had said to Harry Clavering. But not the less did she hope that he might come to her again, and that she might learn from him that he had freed himself from that unfortunate engagement into which her falseness to him had driven him.

It was after she had answered Count Pateroff's letter that she resolved to go out of town for three or four days. For some short time she had been minded to go away altogether, and not to return till after the autumn; but this scheme gradually diminished itself and fell away, till she determined that she would come back after three or four days. Then came to her Sophie,—her devoted Sophie,—Sophie whom she despised and hated; Sophie of whom she was so anxious to rid herself that in all her plans there was some little under-plot to that effect ; Sophie whom she knew to be dishonest to her in any way that might make dishonesty profitable ; and before Sophie had left her, Sophie had engaged herself to go with her dear friend to the Isle of Wight ! As a matter of course, Sophie was to be franked on this expedition. On such expeditions Sophies are always franked as a matter of course. And Sophie would travel with all imaginable luxury,—a matter to which Sophie was by no means indifferent, though her own private life was conducted with an economy that was not luxurious. But, although all these good things came in Sophie's way, she contrived to make it appear that she was devoting herself in a manner that was almost sacrificial to the friend of her bosom. At the same time Lady Ongar sent a few words, as a message, to the count by his sister. Lady Ongar, having told to Madame Gordeloup the story of the document which had reached her, and having described her own answer, was much commended by her friend.

"You are quite right, dear, quite. Of course I am fond of my brother. Edouard and I have always been the best of friends. But that does not make me think you ought to give yourself to him. Bah ! Why should a woman give away everything? Edouard is a fine fellow. But what is that ? Fine fellows like to have all the money themselves."

"Will you tell him,—from me," said Lady Ongar, "that I will take it as a kindness on his part if he will abstain from coming to my house. I certainly shall not see him with my own consent."

Sophie promised,—and probably gave the message ; but when she also informed Edouard of Lady Ongar's intended visit to the Isle of Wight, telling him the day on which they were going and the precise spot, with the name of the hotel at which they were to stay, she went a little beyond the commission which her dearest friend had given her.

At the western end of the Isle of Wight, and on the further shore, about three miles from the point of the island which we call the Needles, there is a little break in the cliff, known to all stay-at-home English travellers as Freshwater Gate. Here there is a cluster of cottages and two inns, and a few bathing-boxes, and ready access by easy ascents to the breezy downs on either side, over which the sea air blows with all its salt and wholesome sweetness. At one of these two inns Lady Ongar located herself and Sophie ; and all Freshwater, and all Yarmouth, and all that end of the island were alive to the fact that the rich widowed countess respecting whom such strange tales were told, had come on a visit to these parts. Innkeepers like such visitors. The more venomous are the stories told against them, the more money are they apt to spend, and the less likely are they to examine their bills. A rich woman altogether with-out a character is a mine of wealth to an innkeeper. In the present case no such godsend had come in the way,—but there was supposed to be a something a little odd, and the visitor was on that account the more welcome.

Sophie was not the most delightful companion in the world for such a place. London was her sphere, as she herself had understood when declaiming against those husbands who keep their wives in the country. And she had no love for the sea specially, regarding all winds as nuisances excepting such as had been raised by her own efforts, and thinking that salt from a saltcellar was more convenient than that brought to her on the breezes. It was now near the end of May, but she had not been half an hour at the inn before she was loud in demanding a fire,—and when the fire came she was unwilling to leave it. Her gesture was magnificent when Lady Ongar proposed to her that she should bathe. What,—put her own dear little dry body, by her own will, into the cold sea ! She shrugged herself, and shook herself, and without speaking a word declined with so much eloquence that it was impossible not to admire her. Nor would she walk. On the first day, during the warmest part of the day, she allowed herself to be taken out in a carriage belonging to the inn ; but after her drive she clung to the fire, and consumed her time with a French novel.

Nor was Lady Ongar much more comfortable in the Isle of Wight than she had been in London. The old poet told us how Black Care sits behind the horseman, and some modern poet will some day describe to us that terrible goddess as she takes her place with the stoker close to the fire of the locomotive engine. Sitting with Sophie opposite to her, Lady Ongar was not happy, even though her eye rested on the lines of that magnificent coast. Once indeed, on the evening of their first day,

Sophie left her, and she was alone for nearly an hour. Ah, how happy could she have been if Harry Clavering might have been there with her. Perhaps a day might come in which Harry might bring her there. In such a case Atra Cura would be left behind, and then she might be altogether happy. She sat dreaming of this for above an hour, and Sophie was still away. When Sophie returned, which she did all too soon, she explained that she had been in her bedroom. She had been very busy, and now had come down to make herself comfortable.

On the next evening Lady Ongar declared her intention of going up on the downs by herself. They had dined at five, so that she might have a long evening, and soon after six she started. " If I do not break down I will get as far as the Needles," she said. Sophie, who had heard that the distance was three miles, lifted up her hands in despair. " If you are not back before nine I shall send the people after you." Consenting to this with a laugh, Lady Ongar made her way up to the downs, and walked steadily on towards the extreme point of the island. To the Needles themselves she did not make her way. These rocks are now approached, as all the stay-at-home travellers know, through a fort, and down to the fort she did not go. But turning a little from the highest point of the hill towards the cliffs on her left hand, she descended till she reached a spot from which she could look down on the pebbly beach lying some three hundred feet below her, and on the soft shining ripple of the quiet waters as they moved themselves with a pleasant sound on the long strand which lay stretched in a line from the spot beneath her out to the point of the island. The evening was warm, and almost transparent in its clearness, and very quiet. There was no sound even of a breeze. When she seated herself close upon the margin of the cliff, she heard the small waves moving the stones which they washed, and the sound was as the sound of little children's voices, very distant. Looking down, she could see through the wonderful transparency of the water, and the pebbles below it were bright as diamonds, and the sands were burnished like gold. And each tiny silent wavelet as it moved up towards the shore and lost itself at last in its own effort, stretched itself the whole length of the strand. Such brightness on the sea-shore she had never seen before, nor had she ever listened as now she listened to that infantine babble of the baby waves. She sat there close upon the margin, on a seat of chalk which the winds had made, looking, listening, and forgetting for a while that she was Lady Ongar whom people did not know, who lived alone in the world with Sophie Gordeloup for her friend,—and whose lover was betrothed to another woman. She had been there perhaps half-an-hour, and had learned to be at home on her perch, sitting there in comfort, with no desire to move, when a voice which she well knew at the first sound startled her, and she rose quickly to her feet. " Lady Ongar," said the voice, " are you not rather near the edge ? " As she turned round there was Count Pateroff with his

"LADY ONGAR, ARE YOU NOT RATHER NEAR THE EDGE?"

hand already upon her dress, so that no danger might be produced by the suddenness of his speech.

"There is nothing to fear," she said, stepping back from her seat. As she did so, he dropped his hand from her dress, and, raising it to his head, lifted his hat from his forehead. "You will excuse me, I hope, Lady Ongar," he said, "for having taken this mode of speaking to you."

"I certainly shall not excuse you ; nor, further than I can help it, shall I listen to you."

"There are a few words which I must say."

"Count Pateroff, I beg that you will leave me. This is treacherous and unmanly,—and can do you no good. By what right do you follow me here ? "

"I follow you for your own good, Lady Ongar; I do it that you may hear me say a few words that are necessary for you to hear."

"I will hear no words from you,—that is, none willingly. By this time you ought to know me and to understand me." She had begun to walk up the hill very rapidly, and for a moment or two he had thought that she would escape him ; but her breath had soon failed her, and she found herself compelled to stand while he regained his place beside her. This he had not done without an effort, and for some minutes they were both silent. "It is very beautiful," at last he said, pointing away over the sea.

"Yes ;—it is very beautiful," she answered. "Why did you disturb me when I was so happy ? " But the count was still recovering his breath and made no answer to this question. When, however, she attempted to move on again, still breasting the hill, he put his hand upon her arm very gently.

"Lady Ongar," he said, "you must listen to me for a moment. Why not do it without a quarrel ? "

"If you mean that I cannot escape from you, it is true enough."

"Why should you want to escape ? Did I ever hurt you ? Before this have I not protected you from injury ? "

"No ;—never. You protect me ! "

"Yes ;—I ; from your husband, from yourself, and from the world. You do not know,—not yet, all that I have done for you. Did you read what Lord Ongar had said ? "

"I read what it pleased you to write."

"What it pleased me ! Do you pretend to think that Lord Ongar did not speak as he speaks there ? Do you not know that those were his own words ? Do you not recognize them ? Ah, yes, Lady Ongar ; you know them to be true."

"Their truth or falsehood is nothing to me. They are altogether indifferent to me either way."

"That would be very well if it were possible ; but it is not. There ;

now we are at the top, and it will be easier. Will you let me have the honour to offer you my arm? No! Be it so; but I think you would walk the easier. It would not be for the first time."

"That is a falsehood." As she spoke she stepped before him, and looked into his face with eyes full of passion. "That is a positive false-hood. I never walked with a hand resting on your arm."

There came over his face the pleasantest smile as he answered her. "You forget everything," he said; — "everything. But it does not matter. Other people will not forget. Julie, you had better take me for your husband. You will be better as my wife, and happier, than you can be otherwise."

"Look down there, Count Pateroff; — down to the edge. If my misery is too great to be borne, I can escape from it there on better terms than you propose to me."

"Ah! That is what we call poetry. Poetry is very pretty, and in saying this as you do, you make yourself divine. But to be dashed over the cliffs and broken on the rocks;—in prose it is not so well."

"Sir, will you allow me to pass on while you remain; or will you let me rest here, while you return alone?"

"No, Julie; not so. I have found you with too much difficulty. In London, you see, I could not find you. Here, for a minute, you must listen to me. Do you not know, Julie, that your character is in my hands?"

"In your hands? No;—never; thank God, never. But what if it were?"

"Only this,—that I am forced to play the only game that you leave open to me. Chance brought you and me together in such a way that nothing but marriage can be beneficial to either of us;—and I swore to Lord Ongar that it should be so. I mean that it shall be so,—or that you shall be punished for your misconduct to him and to me."

"You are both insolent and false. But listen to me, since you are here and I cannot avoid you. I know what your threats mean."

"I have never threatened you. I have promised you my aid, but have used no threats."

"Not when you tell me that I shall be punished? But to avoid no punishment, if any be in your power, will I ever willingly place myself in your company. You may write of me what papers you please, and repeat of me whatever stories you may choose to fabricate, but you will not frighten me into compliance by doing so. I have, at any rate, spirit enough to resist such attempts as that."

"As you are living at present, you are alone in the world?"

"And I am content to remain alone."

"You are thinking, then, of no second marriage?"

"If I were, does that concern you? But I will speak no further word to you. If you follow me into the inn, or persecute me further by forcing yourself upon me, I will put myself under the protection of the police."

Having said this, she walked on as quickly as her strength would permit, while he walked by her side, urging upon her his old arguments as to Lord Ongar's expressed wishes, as to his own efforts on her behalf,— and at last as to the strong affection with which he regarded her. But she kept her promise, and said not a word in answer to it all. For more than an hour they walked side by side, and during the greater part of that time not a syllable escaped from her. From moment to moment she kept her eye warily on him, fearing that he might take her by the arm, or attempt some violence with her. But he was too wise for this, and too fully conscious that no such proceeding on his part could be of any service to him. He continued, however, to speak to her words which she could not avoid hearing,—hoping rather than thinking that he might at last frighten her by a description of all the evil which it was within his power to do her. But in acting thus he showed that he knew nothing of her character. She was not a woman whom any prospect of evil could possibly frighten into a distasteful marriage.

Within a few hundred yards of the hotel there is another fort, and at this point the path taken by Lady Ongar led into the private grounds of the inn at which she was staying. Here the count left her, raising his hat as he did so, and saying that he hoped to see her again before she left the island.

"If you do so," said she, "it shall be in presence of those who can protect me." And so they parted.

CHAPTER XXVIII.

What Cecilia Burton did for her Sister-in-Law.

A S soon as Harry Clavering had made his promise to Mr. Burton, and had declared that he would be in Onslow Crescent that same evening, he went away from the offices at the Adelphi, feeling it to be quite impossible that he should recommence his work there at that moment, even should it ever be within his power to do so. Nor did Burton expect that he should stay. He understood, from what had passed, much of Harry's trouble, if not the whole of it; and though he did not despair on behalf of his sister, he was aware that her lover had fallen into a difficulty, from which he could not extricate himself without great suffering and much struggling. But Burton was a man who, in spite of something cynical on the surface of his character, believed well of mankind generally, and well also of men as individuals. Even though Harry had done amiss, he might be saved And though Harry's conduct to Florence might have been bad, nay, might have been false, still, as Burton believed, he was too good to be cast aside, or spurned out of the way, without some further attempt to save him.

When Clavering had left him Burton went back to his work, and after a while succeeded in riveting his mind on the papers before him. It was a hard struggle with him, but he did it, and did not leave his business till his usual hour. It was past five when he took down his hat and his umbrella, and, as I fear, dusted his boots before he passed out of the office on to the passage. As he went he gave sundry directions to porters and clerks, as was his wont, and then walked off intent upon his usual exercise before he should reach his home.

But he had to determine on much with reference to Florence and Harry before he saw his wife. How was the meeting of the evening to take place, and in what way should it be commenced? If there were indispensable cause for his anger, in what way should he show it, and if necessity for vengeance, how should his sister be avenged? There is nothing more difficult for a man than the redressing of injuries done to a woman who is very near to him and very dear to him. The whole theory of Christian meekness and forgiveness becomes broken to pieces and falls to the ground, almost as an absurd theory, even at the idea of such wrong. What man ever forgave an insult to his wife or an injury to his sister, because he had taught himself that to forgive trespasses is a religious duty? Without an argument, without a moment's thought, the man declares to himself that such trespasses as those are not included in the general order. But what is he to do? Thirty years since his course was easy, and unless the sinner were a clergyman, he could in some sort satisfy his craving for revenge by taking a pistol in his hand, and having a shot at the offender. That method was doubtless barbarous and unreasonable, but it was satisfactory and sufficed. But what can he do now? A thoughtful, prudent, painstaking man, such as was Theodore Burton, feels that it is not given to him to attack another with his fists, to fly at his enemy's throat, and carry out his purpose after the manner of dogs. Such a one has probably something round his heart which tells him that if so attacked he could defend himself; but he knows that he has no aptitude for making such onslaught, and is conscious that such deeds of arms would be unbecoming to him. In many, perhaps in most of such cases, he may, if he please, have recourse to the laws. But any aid that the law can give him is altogether distasteful to him. The name of her that is so dear to him should be kept quiet as the grave under such misfortune, not blazoned through ten thousand columns for the amusement of all the crowd. There is nothing left for him but to spurn the man,—not with his foot but with his thoughts; and the bitter consciousness that to such spurning the sinner will be indifferent. The old way was barbarous certainly, and unreasonable,—but there was a satisfaction in it that has been often wanting since the use of pistols went out of fashion among us.

All this passed through Burton's mind as he walked home. One would not have supposed him to be a man eager for bloodshed,—he with a wife whom he deemed to be perfect, with children who in his eyes were gracious as young gods, with all his daily work which he loved as good workers always do; but yet, as he thought of Florence, as he thought of the possibility of treachery on Harry's part, he regarded almost with dismay the conclusion to which he was forced to come,—that there could be no punishment. He might proclaim the offender to the world as false, and the world would laugh at the proclaimer, and shake hands with the

offender.   To sit together with such a man on a barrel of powder, or fight
him over a handkerchief, seemed to him to be reasonable, nay salutary,
under such a grievance.   There are sins, he felt, which the gods should
punish with instant thunderbolts, and such sins as this was of such nature.
His Florence,—pure, good, loving, true, herself totally void of all suspicion, faultless in heart as well as mind, the flower of that Burton flock
which had prospered so well,—that she should be sacrificed through the
treachery of a man who, at his best, had scarcely been worthy of her !
The thought of this was almost too much for him, and he gnashed his
teeth as he went on his way.

But yet he had not given up the man.   Though he could not restrain
himself from foreshadowing the misery that would result from such baseness, yet he told himself that he would not condemn before condemnation
was necessary.   Harry Clavering might not be good enough for Florence.
What man was good enough for Florence ?   But still, if married, Harry,
he thought, would not make a bad husband.   Many a man who is prone
enough to escape from the bonds which he has undertaken to endure,—to
escape from them before they are riveted,—is mild enough under their
endurance, when they are once fastened upon him.   Harry Clavering was
not of such a nature that Burton could tell himself that it would be
well that his sister should escape even though her way of escape must
lie through the fire and water of outraged love.   That Harry Clavering
was a gentleman, that he was clever, that he was by nature affectionate,
soft in manner, tender of heart, anxious to please, good-tempered, and of
high ambition, Burton knew well; and he partly recognized the fact that
Harry had probably fallen into his present fault more by accident than
by design.   Clavering was not a skilled and practical deceiver.   At last,
as he drew near to his own door, he resolved on the line of conduct he
would pursue.   He would tell his wife everything, and she should receive
Harry alone.

He was weary when he reached home, and was a little cross with his
fatigue.   Good man as he was, he was apt to be fretful on the first moment
of his return to his own house, hot with walking, tired with his day's
labour, and in want of his dinner.   His wife understood this well, and
always bore with him at such moments, coming down to him in the
dressing-room behind the back parlour, and ministering to his wants.   I
fear he took some advantage of her goodness, knowing that at such moments
he could grumble and scold without danger of contradiction.   But the
institution was established, and Cecilia never rebelled against its traditional
laws.   On the present day he had much to say to her, but even that he
could not say without some few symptoms of petulant weariness.

" I'm afraid you've had a terrible long day," she said.

" I don't know what you call terribly long.   I find the days terribly
short.   I have had Harry with me, as I told you I should."

" Well, well.   Say in one word, dear, that it is all right,—if it is so."

" But it is not all right.   I wonder what on earth the men do to the boots, that I can never get a pair that do not hurt me in walking." At this moment she was standing over him with his slippers.

"Will you have a glass of sherry before dinner, dear; you are so tired?"

"Sherry—no!"

"And what about Harry? You don't mean to say——"

"If you'll listen, I'll tell you what I do mean to say." Then he described to her as well as he could, what had really taken place between him and Harry Clavering at the office.

"He cannot mean to be false, if he is coming here," said the wife.

"He does not mean to be false; but he is one of those men who can be false without meaning it,—who allow themselves to drift away from their anchors, and to be carried out into seas of misery and trouble, because they are not careful in looking to their tackle. I think that he may still be held to a right course, and therefore I have begged him to come here."

"I am sure that you are right, Theodore. He is so good and so affectionate, and he made himself so much one of us!"

"Yes; too easily by half. That is just the danger. But look here, Cissy. I'll tell you what I mean to do. I will not see him myself;—at any rate, not at first. Probably I had better not see him at all. You shall talk to him."

"By myself!"

"Why not? You and he have always been great friends, and he is a man who can speak more openly to a woman than to another man."

"And what shall I say as to your absence?"

"Just the truth. Tell him that I am remaining in the dining-room because I think his task will be easier with you in my absence. He has got himself into some mess with that woman."

"With Lady Ongar?"

"Yes; not that her name was mentioned between us, but I suppose it is so."

"Horrible woman;—wicked, wretched creature!"

"I know nothing about that, nor, as I suppose, do you."

"My dear, you must have heard."

"But if I had,—and I don't know that I have,—I need not have believed. I am told that she married an old man who is now dead, and I suppose she wants a young husband."

"My dear!"

"If I were you, Cissy, I would say as little as might be about her. She was an old friend of Harry's——"

"She jilted him when he was quite a boy; I know that;—long before he had seen our Florence."

"And she is connected with him through his cousin. Let her be ever so bad, I should drop that."

"You can't suppose, Theodore, that I want even to mention her name. I'm told that nobody ever visits her."

"She needn't be a bit the worse on that account. Whenever I hear that there is a woman whom nobody visits, I always feel inclined to go and pay my respects to her."

"Theodore, how can you say so?"

"And that, I suppose, is just what Harry has done. If the world and his wife had visited Lady Ongar, there would not have been all this trouble now."

Mrs. Burton of course undertook the task which her husband assigned to her, though she did so with much nervous trepidation, and many fears lest the desired object should be lost through her own maladroit management. With her, there was at least no doubt as to the thing to be done,—no hesitation as to the desirability of securing Harry Clavering for the Burton faction. Everything in her mind was to be forgiven to Harry, and he was to be received by them all with open arms and loving caresses, if he would only abandon Lady Ongar altogether. To secure her lover for Florence, was Mrs. Burton's single and simple object. She raised no questions now within her own breast as to whether Harry would make a good husband. Any such question as that should have been asked and answered before he had been accepted at Stratton. The thing to be done now was to bring Harry and Florence together, and,—since such terrible dangers were intervening,—to make them man and wife with as little further delay as might be possible. The name of Lady Ongar was odious to her. When men went astray in matters of love it was within the power of Cecilia Burton's heart to forgive them; but she could not pardon women that so sinned. This countess had once jilted Harry, and that was enough to secure her condemnation. And since that what terrible things had been said of her! And dear, uncharitable Cecilia Burton was apt to think, when evil was spoken of women,—of women whom she did not know,—that there could not be smoke without fire. And now this woman was a widow with a large fortune, and wanted a husband! What business had any widow to want a husband? It is so easy for wives to speak and think after that fashion when they are satisfied with their own ventures.

It was arranged that when Harry came to the door, Mrs. Burton should go up alone to the drawing-room and receive him there, remaining with her husband in the dining-room till he should come. Twice while sitting downstairs after the cloth was gone she ran upstairs with the avowed purpose of going into the nursery, but in truth that she might see that the room was comfortable, that it looked pretty, and that the chairs were so arranged as to be convenient. The two eldest children were with them in the parlour, and when she started on her second errand, Cissy reminded her that baby would be asleep. Theodore, who understood the little manœuvre, smiled but said nothing, and his wife, who in such matters was resolute, went and made her further little changes in the furniture. At last there came the knock at the door,— the expected knock, a knock which told something of the hesitating unhappy mind of him who had rapped, and Mrs. Burton started on her business. " Tell him just simply why you are there alone," said her husband.

" Is it Harry Clavering? " Cissy asked, " and mayn't I go? "

" It is Harry Clavering," her father said, " and you may not go. Indeed, it is time you went somewhere else."

It was Harry Clavering. He had not spent a pleasant day since he had left Mr. Beilby's offices in the morning, and, now that he had come to Onslow Crescent, he did not expect to spend a pleasant evening. When I declare that as yet he had not come to any firm resolution, I fear that he will be held as being too weak for the rôle of hero even in such pages as these. Perhaps no terms have been so injurious to the profession of the novelist as those two words, hero and heroine. In spite of the latitude which is allowed to the writer in putting his own interpretation upon these words, something heroic is still expected ; whereas, if he attempt to paint from Nature, how little that is heroic should he describe ! How many young men, subjected to the temptations which had befallen Harry Clavering,—how many young men whom you, delicate reader, number among your friends,—would have come out from them unscathed ? A man, you say, delicate reader, a true man can love but one woman,—but one at a time. So you say, and are so convinced ; but no conviction was ever more false. When a true man has loved with all his heart and all his soul,—does he cease to love,—does he cleanse his heart of that passion when circumstances run against him, and he is forced to turn elsewhere for his life's companion ? Or is he untrue as a lover in that he does not waste his life in desolation, because he has been disappointed ? Or does his old love perish and die away, because another has crept into his heart ? No ; the first love, if that was true, is ever there ; and should she and he meet after many years, though their heads be gray and their cheeks wrinkled, there will still be a touch of the old passion as their hands meet for a moment. Methinks that love never dies, unless it be murdered by downright ill-usage. It may be so murdered, but even ill-usage will more often fail than succeed in that enterprise. How, then, could Harry fail to love the woman whom he had loved first, when she returned to him still young, still beautiful, and told him, with all her charms and all her flattery, how her heart stood towards him ?

But it is not to be thought that I excuse him altogether. A man, though he may love many, should be devoted only to one. The man's feeling to the woman whom he is to marry should be this ;—that not from love only, but from chivalry, from manhood, and from duty, he will be prepared always, and at all hazards, to defend her from every misadventure, to struggle ever that she may be happy, to see that no wind blows upon her with needless severity, that no ravening wolf of a misery shall come near her, that her path be swept clean for her,—as clean as may be, and that her roof-tree be made firm upon a rock. There is much of this which is quite independent of love,—much of it that may be done without love. This is devotion, and it is this which a man owes to the woman who has once promised to be his wife, and has not forfeited her right. Doubtless Harry Clavering should have remembered this at the first moment of his weakness in Lady Ongar's drawing-room. Doubtless he should have known at once that his duty to Florence made it necessary that he should declare his engagement,—even though, in doing so, he might have seemed to caution Lady Ongar on that point on which no woman can endure a caution. But the fault was hers, and the caution was needed. No doubt he should not have returned to Bolton Street. He should not have cozened himself by trusting himself to her assurances of friendship; he should have kept warm his love for the woman to whom his hand was owed, not suffering himself to make comparisons to her injury. He should have been chivalric, manly, full of high duty. He should have been all this, and full also of love, and then he would have been a hero. But men as I see them are not often heroic.

As he entered the room he saw Mrs. Burton at once, and then looked round quickly for her husband. "Harry," said she, "I am so glad to see you once again," and she gave him her hand, and smiled on him with that sweet look which used to make him feel that it was pleasant to be near her. He took her hand and muttered some word of greeting, and then looked round again for Mr. Burton. "Theodore is not here," she said; "he thought it better that you and I should have a little talk together. He said you would like it best so; but perhaps I ought not to tell you that."

"I do like it best so,—much best. I can speak to you as I could hardly speak to him."

"What is it, Harry, that ails you? What has kept you away from us? Why do you leave poor Flo so long without writing to her? She will be here on Monday. You will come and see her then; or perhaps you will go with me and meet her at the station?"

"Burton said that she was coming, but I did not understand that it was so soon."

"You do not think it too soon, Harry; do you?"

"No," said Harry, but his tone belied his assertion. At any rate he had not pretended to display any of a lover's rapture at this prospect of seeing the lady whom he loved.

"Sit down, Harry. Why do you stand like that and look so comfortless? Theodore says that you have some trouble at heart. Is it a trouble that you can tell to a friend such as I am?"

"It is very hard to tell. Oh, Mrs. Burton, I am broken-hearted. For the last two weeks I have wished that I might die."

"Do not say that, Harry; that would be wicked."

"Wicked or not, it is true. I have been so wretched that I have not known how to hold myself. I could not bring myself to write to Florence."

"But why not? You do not mean that you are false to Florence. You cannot mean that. Harry, say at once that it is not so, and I will promise you her forgiveness, Theodore's forgiveness, all our forgiveness for anything else. Oh, Harry, say anything but that." In answer to this Harry Clavering had nothing to say, but sat with his head resting on his arm and his face turned away from her. "Speak, Harry; if you are a man, say something. Is it so? If it be so, I believe that you will have killed her. Why do you not speak to me? Harry Clavering, tell me what is the truth."

Then he told her all his story, not looking her once in the face, not changing his voice, suppressing his emotion till he came to the history of the present days. He described to her how he had loved Julia Brabazon, and how his love had been treated by her; how he had sworn to himself, when he knew that she had in truth become that lord's wife, that for her sake he would keep himself from loving any other woman. Then he spoke of his first days at Stratton and of his early acquaintance with Florence, and told her how different had been his second love,—how it had grown gradually and with no check to his confidence, till he felt sure that the sweet girl who was so often near him would, if he could win her, be to him a source of joy for all his life. "And so she shall," said Cecilia, with tears running down her cheeks; "she shall do so yet." And he went on with his tale, saying how pleasant it had been for him to find himself at home in Onslow Crescent; how he had joyed in calling her Cecilia, and having her infants in his arms, as though they were already partly belonging to him. And he told her how he had met the young widow at the station, having employed himself on her behalf at her sister's instance; and how cold she had been to him, offending him by her silence and sombre pride. "False woman!" exclaimed Mrs. Burton. "Oh, Cecilia, do not abuse her,—do not say a word till you know all." "I know that she is false," said Mrs. Burton, with vehement indignation. "She is not false," said Harry; "if there be falsehood, it is mine." Then he went on, and said how different she was when next he saw her. How then he understood that her solemn and haughty manner had been almost forced on her by the mode of her return, with no other friend to meet her. "She has deserved no friend," said Mrs. Burton. "You wrong her," said Harry; "you do not know her. If any woman has been ever sinned against, it is she." "But was she not false from the very first,—false, that she might become rich by marrying a man that she did not love? Will you speak up for her after that? Oh, Harry, think of it."

"I will speak up for her," said Harry; and now it seemed for the first time that something of his old boldness had returned to him. "I will speak up for her, although she did as you say, because she has suffered as few women have been made to suffer, and because she has repented in ashes as few women are called on to repent." And now as he warmed with his feeling for her, he uttered his words faster and with less of shame in his voice. He described how he had gone again and again to Bolton Street, thinking no evil, till—till—till something of the old feeling had come back upon him. He meant to be true in his story, but I doubt whether he told all the truth. How could he tell it all? How could he confess that the blaze of the woman's womanhood, the flame of her beauty, and the fire engendered by her mingled rank and suffering, had singed him and burned him up, poor moth that he was? "And then at last I learned," said he, "that—that she had loved me more than I had believed."

"And is Florence to suffer because she has postponed her love of you to her love of money?"

"Mrs. Burton, if you do not understand it now, I do not know that I can tell you more. Florence alone in this matter is altogether good. Lady Ongar has been wrong, and I have been wrong. I sometimes think that Florence is too good for me."

"It is for her to say that, if it be necessary."

'I have told you all now, and you will know why I have not come to you."

"No, Harry; you have not told me all. Have you told that—woman that she should be your wife?" To this question he made no immediate answer, and she repeated it. "Tell me; have you told her you would marry her?"

"I did tell her so."

"And you will keep your word to her?" Harry, as he heard the words, was struck with awe that there should be such vehemence, such anger, in the voice of so gentle a woman as Cecilia Burton. "Answer me, sir, do you mean to marry this—countess?" But still he made no answer. "I do not wonder that you cannot speak," she said. "Oh, Florence,—oh, my darling; my lost, broken-hearted angel!" Then she turned away her face and wept.

"Cecilia," he said, attempting to approach her with his hand, without rising from his chair.

"No, sir; when I desired you to call me so, it was because I thought you were to be a brother. I did not think that there could be a thing so weak as you. Perhaps you had better go now, lest you should meet my husband in his wrath, and he should spurn you."

But Harry Clavering still sat in his chair, motionless,—motionless, and without a word. After a while he turned his face towards her, and even in her own misery she was stricken by the wretchedness of his countenance. Suddenly she rose quickly from her chair, and coming close to him, threw herself on her knees before him. "Harry," she said, "Harry; it is not yet too late. Be our own Harry again; our dearest Harry. Say that it shall be so. What is this woman to you? What has she done for you, that for her you should throw aside such a one as our Florence? Is she noble, and good, and pure and spotless as Florence is? Will she love you with such love as Florence's? Will she believe in you as Florence believes? Yes, Harry, she believes yet. She knows nothing of this, and shall know nothing, if you will only say that you will be true. No one shall know, and I will remember it only to remember your goodness afterwards. Think of it, Harry; there can be no falseness to one who has been so false to you. Harry, you will not destroy us all at one blow ? "

Never before was man so supplicated to take into his arms youth and beauty and feminine purity ! And in truth he would have yielded, as indeed, what man would not have yielded,—had not Mrs. Burton been interrupted in her prayers. The step of her husband was heard upon the stairs, and she, rising from her knees, whispered quickly, " Do not tell him that it is settled. Let me tell him when you are gone."

" You two have been a long time together,"said Theodore, as he came in.

" Why did you leave us, then, so long?" said Mrs. Burton, trying to smile, though the signs of tears were, as she well knew, plain enough.

" I thought you would have sent for me."

" Burton," said Harry, " I take it kindly of you that you allowed me to see your wife alone."

" Women always understand these things best," said he.

" And you will come again to-morrow, Harry, and answer me my question ?"

" Not to-morrow."

" Florence will be here on Monday."

" And why should he not come when Florence is here ? " asked Theodore, in an angry tone.

" Of course he will come, but I want to see him again first. Do I not, Harry ? "

" I hate mysteries," said Burton.

" There shall be no mystery," said his wife. " Why did you send him to me, but that there are some things difficult to discuss among three ? Will you come to-morrow, Harry ? "

" Not to-morrow ; but I will write to-morrow,—early to-morrow. I will go now, and of course you will tell Burton everything that I have said. Good night." They both took his hand, and Cecilia pressed it as she looked with beseeching eyes into his face. What would she not have done to secure the happiness of the sister whom she loved ? On this occasion she had descended low that she might do much.

CHAPTER XXIX.

How Damon parted from Pythias.

Lady Ongar, when she left Count Pateroff at the little fort on the cliff and entered by herself the gardens belonging to the hotel, had long since made up her mind that there should at last be a positive severance between herself and her devoted Sophie. For half-an-hour she had been walking in silence by the count's side ; and though, of course, she had heard all that he had spoken, she had been able in that time to consider much. It must have been through Sophie that the count had heard of her journey to the Isle of Wight; and, worse than that, Sophie must, as she thought, have instigated this pursuit. In that she wronged her poor friend. Sophie had been simply paid by her brother for giving such information as enabled him to arrange this meeting. She had not even counselled him to follow Lady Ongar. But now Lady Ongar, in blind wrath, determined that Sophie should be expelled from her bosom. Lady Ongar would find this task of expulsion the less difficult in that she had come to loathe her devoted friend, and to feel it to be incumbent on her to rid herself of such devotion. Now had arrived the moment in which it might be done.

And yet there were difficulties. Two ladies living together in an inn cannot, without much that is disagreeable, send down to the landlord saying that they want separate rooms, because they have taken it into their minds to hate each other. And there would, moreover, be something awkward in saying to Sophie that, though she was discarded, her bill should be paid—for this last and only time. No; Lady Ongar had already perceived that that would not do. She would not quarrel with Sophie after that fashion. She would leave the Isle of Wight on the following morning early, informing Sophie why she did so, and would offer money to the little Franco-Pole, presuming that it might not be agreeable to the Franco-Pole to be hurried away from her marine or rural happiness so quickly. But in doing this she would be careful to make Sophie understand that Bolton Street was to be closed against her for ever afterwards. With neither Count Pateroff nor his sister would she ever again willingly place herself in contact.

It was dark as she entered the house,—the walk out, her delay there, and her return having together occupied her three hours. She had hardly felt the dusk growing on her as she progressed steadily on her way, with that odious man beside her. She had been thinking of other things, and her eyes had accustomed themselves gradually to the fading twilight. But now, when she saw the glimmer of the lamps from the inn-windows, she knew that the night had come upon her, and she began to fear that she had been imprudent in allowing herself to be out so late,—imprudent, even had she succeeded in being alone. She went direct to her own room, that, woman-like, she might consult her own face as to the effects of the insult she had received, and then having, as it were, steadied herself, and prepared herself for the scene that was to follow, she descended to the sitting-room and encountered her friend. The friend was the first to speak; and the reader will kindly remember that the friend had ample reason for knowing what companion Lady Ongar had been likely to meet upon the downs.

"Julie, dear, how late you are," said Sophie, as though she were rather irritated in having been kept so long waiting for her tea.

"I am late," said Lady Ongar.

"And don't you think you are imprudent,—all alone, you know, dear; just a leetle imprudent."

"Very imprudent, indeed. I have been thinking of that now as I crossed the lawn, and found how dark it was. I have been very imprudent; but I have escaped without much injury."

"Escaped! escaped what? Have you escaped a cold, or a drunken man?"

"Both, as I think." Then she sat down, and, having rung the bell, she ordered tea.

"There seems to be something very odd with you," said Sophie. "I do not quite understand you."

"When did you see your brother last?" Lady Ongar asked.

"My brother?"

"Yes, Count Pateroff. When did you see him last?"

"Why do you want to know?"

"Well, it does not signify, as of course you will not tell me. But will you say when you will see him next."

"How can I tell?"

"Will it be to-night?"

"Julie, what do you mean?"

"Only this, that I wish you would make him understand that if he has anything to do concerning me, he might as well do it out of hand. For the last hour——"

"Then you have seen him?"

"Yes; is not that wonderful? I have seen him."

"And why could you not tell him yourself what you had to say? He and I do not agree about certain things, and I do not like to carry messages to him. And you have seen him here on this sacré sea-coast?"

"Exactly so; on this sacré sea-coast. Is it not odd that he should have known that I was here,—known the very inn we were at,—and known, too, whither I was going to-night?"

"He would learn that from the servants, my dear."

"No doubt. He has been good enough to amuse me with mysterious threats as to what he would do to punish me if I would not——"

"Become his wife?" suggested Sophie.

"Exactly. It was very flattering on his part. I certainly do not intend to become his wife."

"Ah, you like better that young Clavering who has the other sweetheart. He is younger. That is true."

"Upon my word, yes. I like my cousin, Harry Clavering, much better than I like your brother; but, as I take it, that has not much to do with it. I was speaking of your brother's threats. I do not understand them; but I wish he could be made to understand that if he has anything to do, he had better go and do it. As for marriage, I would sooner marry the first ploughboy I could find in the fields."

"Julie,—you need not insult him."

"I will have no more of your Julie; and I will have no more of you." As she said this she rose from her chair, and walked about the room. "You have betrayed me, and there shall be an end of it."

"Betrayed you! what nonsense you talk. In what have I betrayed you?"

"You set him upon my track here, though you knew I desired to avoid him."

"And is that all? I was coming here to this detestable island, and I told my brother. That is my offence,—and then you talk of betraying! Julie, you sometimes are a goose."

"Very often, no doubt; but, Madame Gordeloup, if you please we will be geese apart for the future."

"Oh, certainly;—if you wish it."

"I do wish it."

"It cannot hurt me. I can choose my friends anywhere. The world is open to me to go where I please into society. I am not at a loss."

All this Lady Ongar well understood, but she could bear it without injury to her temper. Such revenge was to be expected from such a woman. "I do not want you to be at a loss," she said. "I only want you to understand that after what has this evening occurred between your brother and me, our acquaintance had better cease."

"And I am to be punished for my brother?"

"You said just now that it would be no punishment, and I was glad to hear it. Society is, as you say, open to you, and you will lose nothing."

"Of course society is open to me. Have I committed myself? I am not talked about for my lovers by all the town. Why should I be at a loss? No."

"I shall return to London to-morrow by the earliest opportunity. I have already told them so, and have ordered a carriage to go to Yarmouth at eight."

"And you leave me here, alone!"

"Your brother is here, Madame Gordeloup."

"My brother is nothing to me. You know well that. He can come and he can go when he please. I come here to follow you,—to be companion to you, to oblige you,—and now you say you go and leave me in this detestable barrack. If I am here alone, I will be revenged."

"You shall go back with me if you wish it."

"At eight o'clock in the morning,—and see, it is now eleven; while you have been wandering about alone with my brother in the dark! No; I will not go so early morning as that. To-morrow is Saturday—you was to remain till Tuesday."

"You may do as you please. I shall go at eight to-morrow."

"Very well. You go at eight, very well. And who will pay for the 'beels' when you are gone, Lady Ongar?"

"I have already ordered the bill up to-morrow morning. If you will allow me to offer you twenty pounds, that will bring you to London when you please to follow."

"Twenty pounds! What is twenty pounds? No; I will not have

H. Harral, Sc

MEE

How Damon parted from Pythias.

your twenty pounds." And she pushed away from her the two notes which Lady Ongar had already put upon the table. "Who is to pay me for the loss of all my time? Tell me that. I have devoted myself to you. Who will pay me for that?"

"Not I certainly, Madame Gordeloup."

"Not you! You will not pay me for my time;—for a whole year I have been devoted to you! You will not pay me, and you send me away in this way? By Gar, you will be made to pay,—through the nose."

As the interview was becoming unpleasant, Lady Ongar took her candle and went away to bed, leaving the twenty pounds on the table. As she left the room she knew that the money was there, but she could not bring herself to pick it up and restore it to her pocket. It was improbable, she thought, that Madame Gordeloup would leave it to the mercy of the waiters; and the chances were that the notes would go into the pocket for which they were intended.

And such was the result. Sophie, when she was left alone, got up from her seat, and stood for some moments on the rug, making her calculations. That Lady Ongar should be very angry about Count Pateroff's presence Sophie had expected; but she had not expected that her friend's anger would be carried to such extremity that she would pronounce a sentence of banishment for life. But, perhaps, after all, it might be well for Sophie herself that such sentence should be carried out. This fool of a woman with her income, her park, and her rank, was going to give herself,—so said Sophie to herself,—to a young, handsome, proud pig of a fellow,—so Sophie called him,—who had already shown himself to be Sophie's enemy, and who would certainly find no place for Sophie Gordeloup within his house. Might it not be well that the quarrel should be consummated now,—such compensation being obtained as might possibly be extracted. Sophie certainly knew a good deal, which it might be for the convenience of the future husband to keep dark—or convenient for the future wife that the future husband should not know. Terms might be yet had, although Lady Ongar had refused to pay anything beyond that trumpery twenty pounds. Terms might be had; or, indeed, it might be that Lady Ongar herself, when her anger was over, might sue for a reconciliation. Or Sophie,—and this idea occurred as Sophie herself became a little despondent after long calculation,—Sophie herself might acknowledge herself to be wrong, begging pardon, and weeping on her friend's neck. Perhaps it might be worth while to make some further calculation in bed. Then Sophie, softly drawing the notes towards her as a cat might have done, and hiding them somewhere about her person, also went to her room.

In the morning Lady Ongar prepared herself for starting at eight o'clock, and, as a part of that preparation, had her breakfast brought to her upstairs. When the time was up, she descended to the sitting-room on the way to the carriage, and there she found Sophie also prepared for a journey.

"I am going too. You will let me go?" said Sophie.

"Certainly," said Lady Ongar. "I proposed to you to do so yesterday."

"You should not be so hard upon your poor friend," said Sophie. This was said in the hearing of Lady Ongar's maid and of two waiters, and Lady Ongar made no reply to it. When they were in the carriage together, the maid being then stowed away in a dickey or rumble behind, Sophie again whined and was repentant. "Julie, you should not be so hard upon your poor Sophie."

"It seems to me that the hardest things said were spoken by you."

"Then I will beg your pardon. I am impulsive. I do not restrain myself. When I am angry I say I know not what. If I said any words that were wrong, I will apologize, and beg to be forgiven,—there,—on my knees." And, as she spoke, the adroit little woman contrived to get herself down upon her knees on the floor of the carriage. "There; say that I am forgiven; say that Sophie is pardoned." The little woman had calculated that even should her Julie pardon her, Julie would hardly condescend to ask for the two ten-pound notes.

But Lady Ongar had stoutly determined that there should be no further intimacy, and had reflected that a better occasion for a quarrel could hardly be vouchsafed to her than that afforded by Sophie's treachery in bringing her brother down to Freshwater. She was too strong, and too much mistress of her will, to be cheated now out of her advantage. "Madame Gordeloup, that attitude is absurd;—I beg you will get up."

"Never; never till you have pardoned me." And Sophie crouched still lower, till she was all among the dressing-cases and little bags at the bottom of the carriage. "I will not get up till you say the words, ' Sophie, dear, I forgive you.' "

"Then I fear you will have an uncomfortable drive. Luckily it will be very short. It is only half-an-hour to Yarmouth."

"And I will kneel again on board the packet; and on the—what you call, platform,—and in the railway carriage,—and in the street. I will kneel to my Julie everywhere, till she say, ' Sophie, dear, I forgive you!' "

"Madame Gordeloup, pray understand me; between you and me there shall be no further intimacy."

"No!"

"Certainly not. No further explanation is necessary, but our intimacy has certainly come to an end."

"It has."

"Undoubtedly."

"Julie!"

"That is such nonsense. Madame Gordeloup, you are disgracing yourself by your proceedings."

"Oh! disgracing myself, am I?" In saying this, Sophie picked herself up from among the dressing-cases, and recovered her seat. "I am disgracing myself! Well, I know very well whose disgrace is the most talked about in the world, yours or mine. Disgracing myself;—and from you? What did your husband say of you himself?"

Lady Ongar began to feel that even a very short journey might be too long. Sophie was now quite up, and was wriggling herself on her seat, adjusting her clothes which her late attitude had disarranged, not in the most graceful manner.

"You shall see," she continued. "Yes, you shall see. Tell me of disgrace! I have only disgraced myself by being with you. Ah,—very well. Yes; I will get out. As for being quiet, I shall be quiet whenever I like it. I know when to talk and when to hold my tongue. Disgrace!" So saying, she stepped out of the carriage, leaning on the arm of a boatman who had come to the door, and who had heard her last words.

It may be imagined that all this did not contribute much to the comfort of Lady Ongar. They were now on the little pier at Yarmouth, and in five minutes every one there knew who she was, and knew also that there had been some disagreement between her and the little foreigner. The eyes of the boatmen, and of the drivers, and of the other travellers, and of the natives going over to the market at Lymington, were all on her, and the eyes also of all the idlers of Yarmouth who had congregated there to watch the despatch of the early boat. But she bore it well, seating herself, with her maid beside her, on one of the benches on the deck, and waiting there with patience till the boat should start. Sophie once or twice muttered the word "disgrace!" but beyond that she remained silent.

They crossed over the little channel without a word, and without a word made their way up to the railway-station. Lady Ongar had been too confused to get tickets for their journey at Yarmouth, but had paid on board the boat for the passage of the three persons—herself, her maid, and Sophie. But, at the station at Lymington, the more important business of taking tickets for the journey to London became necessary. Lady Ongar had thought of this on her journey across the water, and, when at the railway-station, gave her purse to her maid, whispering her orders. The girl took three first-class tickets, and then going gently up to Madame Gordeloup, offered one to that lady. "Ah, yes; very well; I understand," said Sophie, taking the ticket. "I shall take this;" and she held the ticket up in her hand, as though she had some specially mysterious purpose in accepting it.

She got into the same carriage with Lady Ongar and her maid, but spoke no word on her journey up to London. At Basingstoke she had a glass of sherry, for which Lady Ongar's maid paid. Lady Ongar had telegraphed for her carriage, which was waiting for her, but Sophie betook herself to a cab. "Shall I pay the cabman, ma'am?" said the maid. "Yes," said Sophie, "or stop. It will be half-a-crown. You had better give me the half-crown." The maid did so, and in this way the careful Sophie added another shilling to her store,—over and above the twenty pounds,—knowing well that the fare to Mount Street was eighteen-pence.

CHAPTER XXX.

DOODLES IN MOUNT STREET.

CAPTAIN CLAVERING and Captain Boodle had, as may be imagined, discussed at great length and with much frequency the results of the former captain's negotiations with the Russian spy, and it had been declared strongly by the latter captain, and ultimately admitted by the former, that those results were not satisfactory. Seventy pounds had been expended, and, so to say, nothing had been accomplished. It was in vain that Archie, unwilling to have it thought that he had been worsted in diplomacy, argued that with these political personages, and especially with Russian political personages, the ambages were everything,—that the preliminaries were in fact the whole, and that when they were arranged, the thing was done. Doodles proved to demonstration that the thing was not done, and that seventy pounds was too much for mere preliminaries. "My dear fellow," he said, speaking I fear with some scorn in his voice, "where are you? That's what I want to know. Where are you? Just nowhere." This was true. All that Archie had received from Madame Gordeloup in return for his last payment, was an intimation that no immediate day could be at present named for a renewal of his personal attack upon the countess; but that a day might be named when he should next come to Mount Street,—provision, of course, being made that he should come with a due qualification under his glove. Now the original basis on which Archie was to carry on his suit had been arranged to be this, —that Lady Ongar should be made to know that he was there; and the way in which Doodles had illustrated this precept by the artistic and allegorical use of his heel was still fresh in Archie's memory. The meeting in which they had come to that satisfactory understanding had taken place early in the spring, and now June was coming on, and the countess certainly did not as yet know that her suitor was there! If anything was to be done by the Russian spy it should be done quickly, and Doodles did not refrain from expressing his opinion that his friend was " putting his foot into it," and " making a mull of the whole thing." Now Archie Clavering was a man not eaten up by the vice of self-confidence, but prone rather to lean upon his friends and anxious for the aid of counsel in difficulty.

"What the devil is a fellow to do?" he asked. "Perhaps I had better give it all up. Everybody says that she is as proud as Lucifer; and, after all, nobody knows what rigs she has been up to."

But this was by no means the view which Doodles was inclined to take. He was a man who in the field never gave up a race because he was thrown out at the start, having perceived that patience would achieve as much, perhaps, as impetuosity. He had ridden many a waiting race, and had won some of them. He was never so sure of his hand at billiards as when the score was strong against him. " Always fight whilst there's any fight left in you," was a maxim with him. He never surrendered a bet as lost, till the evidence as to the facts was quite conclusive, and had taught himself to regard any chance, be it ever so remote, as a kind of property.

"Never say die," was his answer to Archie's remark. "You see, Clavvy, you have still a few good cards, and you can never know what a woman really means till you have popped yourself. As to what she did when she was away, and all that, you see when a woman has got seven thousand a year in her own right, it covers a multitude of sins.''

"Of course, I know that."

"And why should a fellow be uncharitable? If a man is to believe all that he hears, by George, they're all much of a muchness. For my part I never believe anything. I always suppose every horse will run to win ; and though there may be a cross now and again, that's the surest line to go upon. D'you understand me now?" Archie said that of course he understood him ; but I fancy that Doodles had gone a little too deep for Archie's intellect.

"I should say, drop this woman, and go at the widow yourself at once."

"And lose all my seventy pounds for nothing!"

"You're not soft enough to suppose that you'll ever get it back again, I hope?" Archie assured his friend that he was not soft enough for any such hope as that, and then the two remained silent for a while, deeply considering the posture of the affair. "I'll tell you what I'll do for you," said Doodles ; "and upon my word I think it will be the best thing."

"And what's that?"

"I'll go to this woman myself."

"What ; to Lady Ongar?"

"No ; but to the spy, as you call her. Principals are never the best for this kind of work. When a man has to pay the money himself he can never make so good a bargain as another can make for him. That stands to reason. And I can be blunter with her about it than you can ; —can go straight at it, you know ; and you may be sure of this, she won't get any money from me, unless I get the marbles for it."

"You'll take some with you, then?"

"Well, yes ; that is, if it's convenient. We were talking of going two or three hundred pounds, you know, and you've only gone seventy as yet. Suppose you hand me over the odd thirty. If she gets it out of me easy, tell me my name isn't Boodle."

There was much in this that was distasteful to Captain Clavering, but at last he submitted, and handed over the thirty pounds to his friend. Then there was considerable doubt whether the ambassador should announce himself by a note, but it was decided at last that his arrival should not be expected. If he did not find the lady at home or disengaged on the first visit, or on the second, he might on the third or the fourth. He was a persistent, patient little man, and assured his friend that he would certainly see Madame Gordeloup before a week had passed over their heads.

On the occasion of his first visit to Mount Street, Sophie Gordeloup was enjoying her retreat in the Isle of Wight. When he called the second time she was in bed, the fatigue of her journey on the previous day,—the day on which she had actually risen at seven o'clock in the morning,—having oppressed her much. She had returned in the cab alone, and had occupied herself much on the same evening. Now that she was to be parted from her Julie, it was needful that she should be occupied. She wrote a long letter to her brother,—much more confidential than her letters to him had lately been,—telling him how much she had suffered on his behalf, and describing to him with great energy the perverseness, malignity, and general pigheadedness of her late friend. Then she wrote an anonymous letter to Mrs. Burton, whose name and address she had learned, after having ascertained from Archie the fact of Harry Clavering's engagement. In this letter she described the wretched wiles by which that horrid woman Lady Ongar was struggling to keep Harry and Miss Burton apart. "It is very bad, but it is true," said the diligent little woman. "She has been seen in his embrace; I know it." After that she dressed and went out into society,—the society of which she had boasted as being open to her,—to the house of some hanger-on of some embassy, and listened, and whispered, and laughed when some old sinner joked with her, and talked poetry to a young man who was foolish and lame, but who had some money, and got a glass of wine and a cake for nothing, and so was very busy; and on her return home calculated that her cab-hire for the evening had been judiciously spent. But her diligence had been so great that when Captain Boodle called the next morning at twelve o'clock she was still in bed. Had she been in dear Paris, or in dearer Vienna, that would have not hindered her from receiving the visit; but in pigheaded London this could not be done; and, therefore, when she had duly scrutinized Captain Boodle's card, and had learned from the servant that Captain Boodle desired to see herself on very particular business, she made an appointment with him for the following day.

On the following day at the same hour Doodles came and was shown up into her room. He had scrupulously avoided any smartness of apparel, calculating that a Newmarket costume would be, of all dresses, the most efficacious in filling her with an idea of his smartness; whereas Archie had probably injured himself much by his polished leather boots, and general newness of clothing. Doodles, therefore, wore a cut-away coat, a coloured shirt with a fogle round his neck, old brown trowsers that fitted very tightly round his legs, and was careful to take no gloves with him. He was a man with a small bullet head, who wore his hair cut very short, and had no other beard than a slight appendage on his lower chin. He certainly did possess a considerable look of smartness, and when he would knit his brows and nod his head, some men were apt to think that it was not easy to get on the soft side of him.

Sophie on this occasion was not arrayed with that becoming negligence which had graced her appearance when Captain Clavering had called. She knew that a visitor was coming, and the questionably white wrapper had been exchanged for an ordinary dress. This was regretted, rather than otherwise, by Captain Boodle, who had received from Archie a description of the lady's appearance, and who had been anxious to see the spy in her proper and peculiar habiliments. It must be remembered that Sophie knew nothing of her present visitor, and was altogether unaware that he was in any way connected with Captain Clavering.

"You are Captain Boddle," she said, looking hard at Doodles, as he bowed to her on entering the room.

"Captain Boodle, ma'am; at your service."

"Oh, Captain Bood-dle; it is English name, I suppose?"

"Certainly, ma'am, certainly. Altogether English, I believe. Our Boodles come out of Warwickshire; small property near Leamington,—doosed small, I'm sorry to say."

She looked at him very hard, and was altogether unable to discover what was the nature or probable mode of life of the young man before her. She had lived much in England, and had known Englishmen of many classes, but she could not remember that she had ever become conversant with such a one as he who was now before her. Was he a gentleman, or might he be a housebreaker? "A doosed small property near Leamington," she said, repeating the words after him. "Oh!"

"But my visit to you, ma'am, has nothing to do with that."

"Nothing to do with the small property."

"Nothing in life."

"Then, Captain Bood-dle, what may it have to do with?"

Hereupon Doodles took a chair, not having been invited to go through that ceremony. According to the theory created in her mind at the instant, this man was not at all like an English captain. Captain is an unfortunate title, somewhat equivalent to the foreign count,—unfortunate in this respect, that it is easily adopted by many whose claims to it are very slight. Archie Clavering, with his polished leather boots, had looked like a captain,—had come up to her idea of a captain,—but this man! The more she regarded him, the stronger in her mind became the idea of the housebreaker.

"My business, ma'am, is of a very delicate nature,—of a nature very delicate indeed. But I think that you and I, who understand the world, may soon come to understand each other."

"Oh, you understand the world. Very well, sir. Go on."

"Now, ma'am, money is money, you know."

"And a goose is a goose; but what of that?"

"Yes; a goose is a goose, and some people are not geese. Nobody, ma'am, would think of calling you a goose."

"I hope not. It would be so uncivil, even an Englishman would not say it. Will you go on?"

"I think you have the pleasure of knowing Lady Ongar?"

"Knowing who?" said Sophie, almost shrieking.

"Lady Ongar."

During the last day or two Sophie's mind had been concerned very much with her dear Julie, but had not been concerned at all with the affairs of Captain Clavering, and, therefore, when Lady Ongar's name was mentioned, her mind went away altogether to the quarrel, and did not once refer itself to the captain. Could it be that this was an attorney, and was it possible that Julie would be mean enough to make claims upon her? Claims might be made for more than those twenty pounds. "And you," she said, "do you know Lady Ongar?"

"I have not that honour myself."

"Oh, you have not; and do you want to be introduced?"

"Not exactly,—not at present; at some future day I shall hope to have the pleasure. But I am right in believing that she and you are very intimate? Now what are you going to do for my friend Archie Clavering?"

"Oh-h-h!" exclaimed Sophie.

"Yes. What are you going to do for my friend Archie Clavering? Seventy pounds, you know, ma'am, is a smart bit of money!"

"A smart bit of money, is it? That is what you think on your leetle property down in Warwickshire."

"It isn't my property, ma'am, at all. It belongs to my uncle."

"Oh, it is your uncle that has the leetle property. And what had your uncle to do with Lady Ongar? What is your uncle to your friend Archie?"

"Nothing at all, ma'am; nothing on earth."

"Then why do you tell me all this rigmarole about your uncle and his leetle property, and Warwickshire? What have I to do with your uncle? Sir, I do not understand you,—not at all. Nor do I know why I have the honour to see you here, Captain Bood-dle."

Even Doodles, redoubtable as he was—even he, with all his smartness, felt that he was overcome, and that this woman was too much for him. He was altogether perplexed, as he could not perceive whether in all her tirade about the little property she had really misunderstood him, and had in truth thought that he had been talking about his uncle, or whether the whole thing was cunning on her part. The reader, perhaps, will have a more correct idea of this lady than Captain Boodle had been able to obtain. She had now risen from her sofa, and was standing as though she expected him to go; but he had not as yet opened the budget of his business.

"I am here, ma'am," said he, "to speak to you about my friend, Captain Clavering."

"Then you can go back to your friend, and tell him I have nothing to say. And, more than that, Captain Booddle "—the woman intensified the name in a most disgusting manner, with the evident purpose of annoying him; of that he had become quite sure—" more than that, his sending you here is an impertinence. Will you tell him that?"

"No, ma'am, I will not."

"Perhaps you are his laquais," continued the inexhaustible Sophie, "and are obliged to come when he send you?"

"I am no man's laquais, ma'am."

"If so, I do not blame you; or, perhaps, it is your way to make your love third or fourth hand down in Warwickshire?"

"Damn Warwickshire!" said Doodles, who was put beyond himself.

"With all my heart. Damn Warwickshire." And the horrid woman grinned at him as she repeated his words. "And the leetle property, and the uncle, if you wish it; and the leetle nephew,—and the leetle nephew,—and the leetle nephew!" She stood over him as she repeated the last words with wondrous rapidity, and grinned at him, and grimaced and shook herself, till Doodles was altogether bewildered. If this was a Russian spy he would avoid such in future, and keep himself for the milder acerbities of Newmarket, and the easier chaff of his club. He looked up into her face at the present moment, striving to think of some words by which he might assist himself. He had as yet performed no part of his mission, but any such performance was now entirely out of the question. The woman had defied him, and had altogether thrown Clavering overboard. There was no further question of her services, and therefore he felt himself to be quite entitled to twit her with the payment she had taken.

"And how about my friend's seventy pounds?" said he.

"How about seventy pounds! a leetle man comes here and tells me he is a Booddle in Warwickshire, and says he has an uncle with a very leetle property, and asks me how about seventy pounds! Suppose I ask you how about the policeman, what will you say then?"

"You send for him and you shall hear what I say."

"No; not to take away such a leetle man as you. I send for a policeman when I am afraid. Booddle in Warwickshire is not a terrible man. Suppose you go to your friend and tell him from me that he have chose a very bad Mercury in his affairs of love;—the worst Mercury I ever see. Perhaps the Warwickshire Mercuries are not very good. Can you tell me, Captain Booddle, how they make love down in Warwickshire?"

"And that is all the satisfaction I am to have?"

"Who said you was to have satisfaction? Very little satisfaction I should think you ever have, when you come as a Mercury."

"My friend means to know something about that seventy pounds."

"Seventy pounds! If you talk to me any more of seventy pounds, I will fly at your face." As she spoke this she jumped across at him as though she were really on the point of attacking him with her nails, and he, in dismay, retreated to the door. "You, and your seventy pounds!

Oh, you English ! What mean mens you are ! Oh ! a Frenchman would despise to do it. Yes ; or a Russian or a Pole. But you,—you want it all down in black and white, like a butcher's beel. You know nothing, and understand nothing, and can never speak, and can never hold your tongues. You have no head, but the head of a bull. A bull can break all the china in a shop,—dash, smash, crash,—all the pretty things gone in a minute ! So can an Englishman. Your seventy pounds ! You will come again to me for seventy pounds, I think." In her energy she had acted the bull, and had exhibited her idea of the dashing, the smashing and the crashing, by the motion of her head and the waving of her hands.

"And you decline to say anything about the seventy pounds ?" said Doodles, resolving that his courage should not desert him.

Whereupon the divine Sophie laughed. "Ha, ha, ha ! I see you have not got on any gloves, Captain Booddle."

"Gloves ; no. I don't wear gloves."

"Nor your uncle with the leetle property in Warwickshire ? Captain Clavering, he wears a glove. He is a handy man." Doodles stared at her, understanding nothing of this. "Perhaps it is in your waistcoat pocket," and she approached him fearlessly, as though she were about to deprive him of his watch.

"I don't know what you mean," said he, retreating.

"Ah, you are not a handy man, like my friend the other captain, so you had better go away. Yes ; you had better go to Warwickshire. In Warwickshire, I suppose, they make ready for your Michaelmas dinners. You have four months to get fat. Suppose you go away and get fat."

Doodles understood nothing of her sarcasm, but began to perceive that he might as well take his departure. The woman was probably a lunatic, and his friend Archie had no doubt been grossly deceived when he was sent to her for assistance. He had some faint idea that the seventy pounds might be recovered from such a madwoman ; but in the recovery his friend would be exposed, and he saw that the money must be abandoned. At any rate, he had not been soft enough to dispose of any more treasure.

"Good-morning, ma'am," he said, very curtly.

"Good-morning to you, Captain Booddle. Are you coming again another day ?"

"Not that I know of, ma'am."

"You are very welcome to stay away. I like your friend the better. Tell him to come and be handy with his glove. As for you,—suppose you go to the leetle property."

Then Captain Boodle went, and, as soon as he had made his way out into the open street, stood still and looked around him, that by the aspect of things familiar to his eyes he might be made certain that he was in a world with which he was conversant. While in that room with the spy he had ceased to remember that he was in London,—his own London, within a mile of his club, within a mile of Tattersall's. He had been, as it were, removed to some strange world in which the tact, and courage, and acuteness natural to him had not been of avail to him. Madame Gordeloup had opened a new world to him,—a new world of which he desired to make no further experience. Gradually he began to understand why he had been desired to prepare himself for Michaelmas eating. Gradually some idea about Archie's glove glimmered across his brain. A wonderful woman certainly was the Russian spy,—a phenomenon which in future years he might perhaps be glad to remember that he had seen in the flesh. The first race-horse which he might ever own and name himself he would certainly call the Russian Spy. In the meantime, as he slowly walked across Berkeley Square he acknowledged to himself that she was not mad, and acknowledged also that the less said about that seventy pounds the better. From thence he crossed Piccadilly, and sauntered down St. James's Street into Pall Mall, revolving in his mind how he would carry himself with Clavvy. He, at any rate, had his ground for triumph. He had parted with no money, and had ascertained by his own wit that no available assistance from that quarter was to be had in the matter which his friend had in hand.

It was some hours after this when the two friends met, and at that time Doodles was up to his eyes in chalk and the profitable delights of pool. But Archie was too intent on his business to pay much regard to his friend's proper avocation. "Well, Doodles," he said, hardly waiting till his ambassador had finished his stroke and laid his ball close waxed to one of the cushions. "Well; have you seen her?"

"Oh, yes; I've seen her," said Doodles, seating himself on an exalted bench which ran round the room, while Archie, with anxious eyes, stood before him.

"Well?" said Archie.

"She's a rum 'un. Thank 'ee, Griggs; you always stand to me like a brick." This was said to a young lieutenant who had failed to hit the captain's ball, and now tendered him a shilling with a very bitter look.

"She is queer," said Archie,—"certainly."

"Queer! By George, I'll back her for the queerest bit of horseflesh going any way about these diggings. I thought she was mad at first, but I believe she knows what she's about."

"She knows what she's about well enough. She's worth all the money if you can only get her to work."

"Bosh, my dear fellow."

"Why bosh? What's up now?"

"Bosh! Bosh! Bosh! Me to play, is it?" Down he went, and not finding a good open for a hazard, again waxed himself to the cushion, to the infinite disgust of Griggs, who did indeed hit the ball this time, but in such a way as to make the loss of another life from Griggs' original three a matter of certainty. "I don't think it's hardly fair," whispered Griggs to a friend, "a man playing always for safety. It's not the game I like, and I shan't play at the same table with Doodles any more."

"It's all bosh," repeated Doodles, coming back to his seat. "She don't mean to do anything, and never did. I've found her out."

"Found out what ?"

"She's been laughing at you. She got your money out from under your glove, didn't she ?"

"Well, I did put it there."

"Of course you did. I knew that I should find out what was what if I once went there. I got it all out of her. But, by George, what a woman she is ! She swore at me to my very face."

"Swore at you ! In French you mean ?"

"No ; not in French at all, but damned me in downright English. By George, how I did laugh !—me and everybody belonging to me. I'm blessed if she didn't."

"There was nothing like that about her when I saw her."

"You didn't turn her inside out as I've done; but stop half a moment." Then he descended, chalked away at his cue hastily, pocketed a shilling or two, and returned. "You didn't turn her inside out as I've done. I tell you, Clavvy, there's nothing to be done there, and there never was. If you'd kept on going yourself she'd have drained you as dry,—as dry as that table. There's your thirty pounds back, and, upon my word, old fellow, you ought to thank me."

Archie did thank him, and Doodles was not without his triumph. Of the frequent references to Warwickshire which he had been forced to endure, he said nothing, nor yet of the reference to Michaelmas dinners ; and, gradually, as he came to talk frequently to Archie of the Russian spy, and perhaps also to one or two others of his more intimate friends, he began to convince himself that he really had wormed the truth out of Madame Gordeloup, and got altogether the better of that lady, in a very wonderful way.

CHAPTER XXXI.

HARRY CLAVERING'S CONFESSION.

 HARRY Clavering, when he went away from Onslow Crescent, after his interview with Cecilia Burton, was a wretched, pitiable man. He had told the truth of himself, as far as he was able to tell it, to a woman whom he thoroughly esteemed, and having done so was convinced that she could no longer entertain any respect for him. He had laid bare to her all his weakness, and for a moment she had spurned him. It was true that she had again reconciled herself to him, struggling to save both him and her sister from future misery,—that she had even condescended to implore him to be gracious to Florence, taking that which to her mind seemed then to be the surest path to her object ; but not the less did he feel that she must despise him. Having promised his hand to one woman,—to a woman whom he still professed that he loved dearly,—he had allowed himself to be cheated into offering it to another. And he knew that the cheating had been his own. It was he who had done the evil. Julia, in showing her affection for him, had tendered her love to a man whom she believed to be free. He had intended to walk straight. He had not allowed himself to be enamoured of the wealth possessed by this woman who had thrown herself at his feet. But he had been so weak that he had fallen in his own despite.

There is, I suppose, no young man possessed of average talents and average education, who does not early in life lay out for himself some career with more or less precision,—some career which is high in its tendencies and noble in its aspirations, and to which he is afterwards com-

pelled to compare the circumstances of the life which he shapes for himself.
In doing this he may not attempt, perhaps, to lay down for himself any
prescribed amount of success which he will endeavour to reach, or even
the very pathway by which he will strive to be successful; but he will
tell himself what are the vices which he will avoid, and what the virtues
which he will strive to attain. Few young men ever did this with more
precision than it had been done by Harry Clavering, and few with more
self-confidence. Very early in life he had been successful,—so successful
as to enable him to emancipate himself not only from his father's absolute
control, but almost also from any interference on his father's part. It
had seemed to be admitted that he was a better man than his father, better
than the other Claverings,—the jewel of the race, the Clavering to whom
the family would in future years look up, not as their actual head, but
as their strongest prop and most assured support. He had said to himself
that he would be an honest, truthful, hard-working man, not covetous
after money, though conscious that a labourer was worthy of his hire, and
conscious also that the better the work done the better should be his wages.
Then he had encountered a blow,—a heavy blow from a false woman,—
and he had boasted to himself that he had borne it well, as a man should
bear all blows. And now, after all these resolves and all these boastings,
he found himself brought by his own weakness to such a pass that he
hardly dared to look in the face any of his dearest and most intimate
friends.

He was not remiss in telling himself all this. He did draw the comparison ruthlessly between the character which he had intended to make
his own and that which he now had justly earned. He did not excuse
himself. We are told to love others as ourselves, and it is hard to do so.
But I think that we never hate others, never despise others, as we are
sometimes compelled by our own convictions and self-judgment to hate
and to despise ourselves. Harry, as he walked home on this evening, was
lost in disgust at his own conduct. He could almost have hit his head
against the walls, or thrown himself beneath the waggons as he passed
them, so thoroughly was he ashamed of his own life. Even now, on
this evening, he had escaped from Onslow Crescent,—basely escaped,—
without having declared any purpose. Twice on this day he had escaped,
almost by subterfuges; once from Burton's office, and now again from
Cecilia's presence. How long was this to go on, or how could life be
endurable to him under such circumstances?

In parting from Cecilia, and promising to write at once, and promising
to come again in a few days, he had had some idea in his head that he
would submit his fate to the arbitrament of Lady Ongar. At any rate he
must, he thought, see her, and finally arrange with her what the fate of
both of them should be, before he could make any definite statement of
his purpose in Onslow Crescent. The last tender of his hand had been
made to Julia, and he could not renew his former promises on Florence's
behalf, till he had been absolved by Julia.

This may at any rate be pleaded on his behalf,—that in all the workings of his mind at this time there was very little of personal vanity. Very personally vain he had been when Julia Brabazon,—the beautiful and noble-born Julia,—had first confessed at Clavering that she loved him; but that vanity had been speedily knocked on the head by her conduct to him. Men when they are jilted can hardly be vain of the conquest which has led to such a result. Since that there had been no vanity of that sort. His love to Florence had been open, honest, and satisfactory, but he had not considered himself to have achieved a wonderful triumph at Stratton. And when he found that Lord Ongar's widow still loved him,—that he was still regarded with affection by the woman who had formerly wounded him,—there was too much of pain, almost of tragedy, in his position, to admit of vanity. He would say to himself that, as far as he knew his own heart, he thought he loved Julia the best; but, nevertheless, he thoroughly wished that she had not returned from Italy, or that he had not seen her when she had so returned.

He had promised to write, and that he would do this very night. He had failed to make Cecilia Burton understand what he intended to do, having, indeed, hardly himself resolved; but before he went to bed he would both resolve and explain to her his resolution. Immediately, therefore, on his return home he sat down at his desk with the pen in his hand and the paper before him.

At last the words came. I can hardly say that they were the product of any fixed resolve made before he commenced the writing. I think that his mind worked more fully when the pen was in his hands than it had done during the hour through which he sat listless, doing nothing, struggling to have a will of his own, but failing. The letter when it was written was as follows :—

Bloomsbury Square, May, 186—.

DEAREST MRS. BURTON,—I said that I would write to-morrow, but I am writing now, immediately on my return home. Whatever else you may think of me, pray be sure of this, that I am most anxious to make you know and understand my own position at any rate as well as I do myself. I tried to explain it to you when I was with you this evening, but I fear that I failed ; and when Mr. Burton came in I could not say anything farther.

I know that I have behaved very badly to your sister,—very badly, even though she should never become aware that I have done so. Not that that is possible, for if she were to be my wife to-morrow I should tell her everything. But badly as you must think of me, I have never for a moment had a premeditated intention to deceive her. I believe you do know on what terms I had stood with Miss Brabazon before her marriage, and that when she married, whatever my feelings might be, there was no self-accusation. And after that you know all that took place between me and Florence till the return of Lord Ongar's widow. Up to that time everything had been fair between us. I had told Florence of my former attachment, and she probably thought but little of it. Such things are so common with men ! Some change happens as had happened with me, and a man's second love is often stronger and more worthy of a woman's acceptance than the first. At any rate, she knew it, and there was, so far, an end of it. And you understood, also, how very anxious I was to avoid delay in our marriage. No one knows that better than you,—not even Florence,—for I have talked it over with you so often ; and you will remember how I have begged you to assist me. I don't blame my darling Florence. She was doing what she deemed best ; but oh, if she had only been guided by what you once said to her !

Then Lord Ongar's widow returned ; and dear Mrs. Burton, though I fear you think ill of her, you must remember that as far as you know, or I, she has done nothing wrong, has been in no respect false, since her marriage. As to her early conduct to me, she did what many women have done, but what no woman should do. But how can I blame her, knowing how terrible has been my own weakness ! But as to her conduct since her marriage, I implore you to believe with me that she has been sinned against grievously, and has not sinned. Well ; as you know, I met her. It was hardly unnatural that I should do so, as we are connected. But whether natural or unnatural, foolish or wise, I went to her often. I thought at first that she must know of my engagement as her sister knew it well, and had met Florence. But she did not know it ; and so, having none near her that she could love, hardly a friend but myself, grievously wronged by the world and her own relatives, thinking that with her wealth she could make some amend to me for her former injury, she——. Dear Mrs. Burton, I think you will understand it now, and will see that she at least is free from blame.

I am not defending myself ; of course all this should have been without effect on me. But I had loved her so dearly ! I do love her still so dearly ! Love like that does not die. When she left me it was natural that I should seek some one else to love. When she returned to me,—when I found that in spite of her faults she had loved me through it all, I—I yielded and became false and a traitor.

I say that I love her still ; but I know well that Florence is far the nobler woman of the two. Florence never could have done what she did. In nature, in mind, in acquirement, in heart, Florence is the better. The man who marries Florence must be happy if any woman can make a man happy. Of her of whom I am now speaking, I know well that I cannot say that. How then, you will ask, can I be fool enough, having had such a choice, to doubt between the two ! How is it that man doubts between vice and virtue, between honour and dishonour, between heaven and hell ?

But all this is nothing to you. I do not know whether Florence would take me now. I am well aware that I have no right to expect that she should. But if I understood you aright this evening, she, as yet, has heard nothing of all this. What must she think of me for not writing to her ! But I could not bring myself to write in a false spirit ; and how could I tell her all that I have now told to you ?

I know that you wish that our engagement should go on. Dear Mrs. Burton, I love you so dearly for wishing it ! Mr. Burton, when he shall have heard everything, will, I fear, think differently. For me, I feel that I must see Lady Ongar before I can again go to your house, and I write now chiefly to tell you that this is what I have determined to do. I believe she is now away, in the Isle of Wight, but I will see her as soon as she returns. After that I will either come to Onslow Crescent or send. Florence will be with you then. She of course must know everything, and you have my permission to show this letter to her if you think well to do so.—Most sincerely and affectionately yours, HARRY CLAVERING.

This he delivered himself the next morning at the door in Onslow Crescent, taking care not to be there till after Theodore Burton should have gone from home. He left a card also, so that it might be known, not only that he had brought it himself, but that he had intended Mrs. Burton to be aware of that fact. Then he went and wandered about, and passed his day in misery, as such men do when they are thoroughly discontented with their own conduct. This was the Saturday on which Lady Ongar returned with her Sophie from the Isle of Wight ; but of that premature return Harry knew nothing, and therefore allowed the Sunday to pass by without going to Bolton Street. On the Monday morning he received a letter from home which made it necessary,—or induced him to suppose it to be necessary, that he should go home to Clavering, at any rate for one day. This he did on the Monday, sending a line to Mrs. Burton to say whither he was gone, and that he should be back by Wednesday night or Thursday morning,—and imploring her to give his love to Florence, if she would venture to do so. Mrs. Burton would know what must be his first business in London on his return, and she might be sure he would come or send to Onslow Crescent as soon as that was over.

Harry's letter,—the former and longer letter, Cecilia had read over, till she nearly knew it by heart, before her husband's return. She well understood that he would be very hard upon Harry. He had been inclined to forgive Clavering for what had been remiss,—to forgive the silence, the absence from the office, and the want of courtesy to his wife, till Harry had confessed his sin;—but he could not endure that his sister should seek the hand of a man who had declared himself to be in doubt whether he would take it, or that any one should seek it for her, in her ignorance of all the truth. His wife, on the other hand, simply looked to Florence's comfort and happiness. That Florence should not suffer the pang of having been deceived and rejected was all in all to Cecilia. "Of course she must know it some day," the wife had pleaded to her husband. "He is not the man to keep anything secret. But if she is told when he has returned to her, and is good to her, the happiness of the return will cure the other misery." But Burton would not submit to this. "To be comfortable at present is not everything," he said. "If the man be so miserably weak that he does not even now know his own mind, Florence had better take her punishment, and be quit of him."

Cecilia had narrated to him with passable fidelity what had occurred upstairs, while he was sitting alone in the dining-room. That she, in her anger, had at one moment spurned Harry Clavering, and that in the next she had knelt to him, imploring him to come back to Florence,—those two little incidents she did not tell to her husband. Harry's adventures with Lady Ongar, as far as she knew them, she described accurately. "I can't make any apology for him; upon my life I can't," said Burton. "If I know what it is for a man to behave ill, falsely, like a knave in such matters, he is so behaving." So Theodore Burton spoke as he took his candle to go away to his work; but his wife had induced him to promise that he would not write to Stratton or take any other step in the matter till they had waited twenty-four hours for Harry's promised letter.

The letter came before the twenty-four hours were expired, and Burton, on his return home on the Saturday, found himself called upon to read and pass judgment upon Harry's confession. "What right has he to speak of her as his darling Florence," he exclaimed, "while he is confessing his own knavery?"

" But if she is his darling—— ? " pleaded his wife.

" Trash ! But the word from him in such a letter is simply an additional insult. And what does he know about this woman who has come back ? He vouches for her, but what can he know of her ? Just what she tells him. He is simply a fool."

" But you cannot dislike him for believing her word."

" Cecilia," said he, holding down the letter as he spoke,—" you are so carried away by your love for Florence, and your fear lest a marriage which has been once talked of should not take place, that you shut your eyes to this man's true character. Can you believe any good of a man who tells you to your face that he is engaged to two women at once ? "

" I think I can," said Cecilia, hardly venturing to express so dangerous an opinion above her breath.

" And what would you think of a woman who did so ? "

" Ah, that is so different ! I cannot explain it, but you know that it is different."

" I know that you would forgive a man anything, and a woman nothing." To this she submitted in silence, having probably heard the reproof before, and he went on to finish the letter. " Not defending himself ! " he exclaimed,—" then why does he not defend himself ? When a man tells me that he does not, or cannot defend himself, I know that he is a sorry fellow, without a spark of spirit."

" I don't think that of Harry. Surely that letter shows a spirit."

" Such a one as I should be ashamed to see in a dog. No man should ever be in a position in which he cannot defend himself. No man, at any rate, should admit himself to be so placed. Wish that he should go on with his engagement ! I do not wish it at all. I am sorry for Florence. She will suffer terribly. But the loss of such a lover as that is infinitely a lesser loss than would be the gain of such a husband. You had better write to Florence, and tell her not to come."

" Oh, Theodore ! "

" That is my advice."

" But there is no post between this and Monday," said Cecilia temporizing.

" Send her a message by the wires."

" You cannot explain this by a telegram, Theodore. Besides, why should she not come ? Her coming can do no harm. If you were to tell your mother now of all this, it would prevent the possibility of things ever being right."

" Things,—that is, this thing, never will be right," said he.

" But let us see. She will be here on Monday, and if you think it best you can tell her everything. Indeed, she must be told when she is here, for I could not keep it from her. I could not smile and talk to her about him and make her think that it is all right."

" Not you ! I should be very sorry if you could."

"But I think I could make her understand that she should not decide upon breaking with him altogether."

"And I think I could make her understand that she ought to do so."

"But you wouldn't do that, Theodore?"

"I would if I thought it my duty."

"But at any rate, she must come, and we can talk of that to-morrow."

As to Florence's coming, Burton had given way, beaten, apparently, by that argument about the post. On the Sunday very little was said about Harry Clavering. Cecilia studiously avoided the subject, and Burton had not so far decided on dropping Harry altogether, as to make him anxious to express any such decision. After all, such dropping or not dropping must be the work of Florence herself. On the Monday morning Cecilia had a further triumph. On that day her husband was very fully engaged, —having to meet a synod of contractors, surveyors, and engineers, to discuss which of the remaining thoroughfares of London should not be knocked down by the coming railways,—and he could not absent himself from the Adelphi. It was, therefore, arranged that Mrs. Burton should go to the Paddington Station to meet her sister-in-law. She therefore would have the first word with Florence, and the earliest opportunity of impressing the new-comer with her own ideas. "Of course, you must say something to her of this man," said her husband, "but the less you say the better. After all she must be left to judge for herself." In all matters such as this,—in all affairs of tact, of social intercourse, and of conduct between man and man, or man and woman, Mr. Burton was apt to be eloquent in his domestic discussion, and sometimes almost severe;—but the final arrangement of them was generally left to his wife. He enunciated principles of strategy,—much, no doubt, to her benefit; but she actually fought the battles.

CHAPTER XXXII.

FLORENCE BURTON PACKS UP A PACKET.

THOUGH nobody had expressed to Florence at Stratton any fear of Harry Clavering's perfidy, that young lady was not altogether easy in her mind. Weeks and weeks had passed, and she had not heard from him. Her mother was manifestly uneasy, and had announced some days before Florence's departure, her surprise and annoyance in not having heard from her eldest son. When Florence inquired as to the subject of the expected letter, her mother put the question aside, saying, with a little assumed irritability, that of course she liked to get an answer to her letters when she took the trouble to write them. And when the day for Florence's journey drew nigh, the old lady became more and more uneasy,—showing plainly that she wished her daughter was not going to London. But Florence, as she was quite determined to go, said nothing to all this. Her father also was uneasy, and neither of them had for some days named her lover in her hearing. She knew that there was something wrong, and felt that it was better that she should go to London and learn the truth.

No female heart was ever less prone to suspicion than the heart of Florence Burton. Among those with whom she had been most intimate nothing had occurred to teach her that men could be false, or women either. When she had heard from Harry Clavering the story of Julia Brabazon, she had, not making much accusation against the sinner in speech, put Julia down in the books of her mind as a bold, bad woman who could forget her sex, and sell her beauty and her womanhood for money. There might be such a woman here and there, or such a man. There were murderers in the world,—but the bulk of mankind is not made subject to murderers. Florence had never considered the possibility that she herself could become liable to such a misfortune. And then, when the day came that she was engaged, her confidence in the man chosen by her was unlimited. Such love as hers rarely suspects. He with whom she had to do was Harry Clavering, and therefore she could not be deceived. Moreover she was supported by a self-respect and a self-confidence which did not at first allow her to dream that a man who had once loved her would ever wish to leave her. It was to her as though a sacrament as holy as that of the church had passed between them, and she could not easily bring herself to think that that sacrament had been as nothing to Harry Clavering. But nevertheless there was something wrong, and when she left her father's house at Stratton, she was well aware that she must prepare herself for tidings that might be evil. She could bear anything, she thought, without disgracing herself; but there were tidings which might send her back to Stratton a broken woman, fit perhaps to comfort the declining years of her father and mother, but fit for nothing else.

Her mother watched her closely as she sat at her breakfast that morning, but much could not be gained by watching Florence Burton when Florence wished to conceal her thoughts. Many messages were sent to Theodore, to Cecilia, and to the children, messages to others of the Burton clan who were in town, but not a word was said of Harry Clavering. The very absence of his name was enough to make them all wretched, but Florence bore it as the Spartan boy bore the fox beneath his tunic. Mrs. Burton could hardly keep herself from a burst of indignation; but she had been strongly warned by her husband, and restrained herself till Florence was gone. "If he is playing her false," said she, as soon as she was alone with her old husband, "he shall suffer for it, though I have to tear his face with my own fingers."

"Nonsense, my dear; nonsense."

"It is not nonsense, Mr. Burton. A gentleman, indeed! He is to be allowed to be dishonest to my girl because he is a gentleman! I wish there was no such thing as a gentleman;—so I do. Perhaps there would be more honest men then." It was unendurable to her that a girl of hers should be so treated.

Immediately on the arrival of the train at the London platform, Florence espied Cecilia, and in a minute was in her arms. There was a special tenderness in her sister-in-law's caress, which at once told Florence that her fears had not been without cause. Who has not felt the evil tidings conveyed by the exaggerated tenderness of a special kiss? But while on the platform and among the porters she said nothing of herself. She asked after Theodore and heard of the railway confederacy with a shew of delight. "He'd like to make a line from Hyde Park Corner to the Tower of London," said Florence, with a smile. Then she asked after the children, and specially for the baby; but as yet she spoke no word of Harry Clavering. The trunk and the bag were at last found; and the two ladies were packed into a cab, and had started. Cecilia, when they were seated, got hold of Florence's hand, and pressed it warmly. "Dearest," she said, "I am so glad to have you with us once again." "And now," said Florence, speaking with a calmness that was almost unnatural, "tell me all the truth."

All the truth! What a demand it was. And yet Cecilia had expected that none less would be made upon her. Of course Florence must have known that there was something wrong. Of course she would ask as to her lover immediately upon her arrival. "And now tell me all the truth."

"Oh, Florence!"

"The truth, then, is very bad?" said Florence, gently. "Tell me first of all whether you have seen him. Is he ill?"

"He was with us on Friday. He is not ill."

"Thank God for that. Has anything happened to him? Has he lost money?"

"No; I have heard nothing about money."

"Then he is tired of me. Tell me at once, my own one. You know me so well. You know I can bear it. Don't treat me as though I were a coward."

"No; it is not that. It is not that he is tired of you. If you had heard him speak of you on Friday,—that you were the noblest, purest, dearest, best of women——" This was imprudent on her part; but what loving woman could at such a moment have endured to be prudent.

"Then what is it?" asked Florence, almost sternly. "Look here, Cecilia; if it be anything touching himself or his own character, I will put up with it, in spite of anything my brother may say. Though he had been a murderer, if that were possible, I would not leave him. I will never leave him unless he leaves me. Where is he now, at this moment?"

"He is in town." Mrs. Burton had not received Harry's note, telling her of his journey to Clavering, before she had left home. Now at this moment it was waiting for her in Onslow Crescent.

"And am I to see him? Cecilia, why cannot you tell me how it is? In such a case I should tell you,—should tell you everything at once; because I know that you are not a coward. Why cannot you do so to me?"

"You have heard of Lady Ongar?"

"Heard of her;—yes. She treated Harry very badly before her marriage."

"She has come back to London, a widow."

"I know she has. And Harry has gone back to her! Is that it? Do you mean to tell me that Harry and Lady Ongar are to be married."

"No; I cannot say that. I hope it is not so. Indeed, I do not think it."

"Then what have I to fear? Does she object to his marrying me? What has she to do between us?"

"She wishes that Harry should come back to her, and Harry has been unsteady. He has been with her often, and he has been very weak. It may be all right yet, Flo; it may indeed,—if you can forgive his weakness."

Something of the truth had now come home to Florence, and she sat thinking of it long before she spoke again. This widow, she knew, was very wealthy, and Harry had loved her before he had come to Stratton. Harry's first love had come back free,—free to wed again, and able to make the fortune of the man she might love and marry. What had Florence to give to any man that could be weighed with this? Lady Ongar was very rich. Florence had already heard all this from Harry,—was very rich, was clever, and was beautiful; and moreover she had been Harry's first love. Was it reasonable that she with her little claims, her puny attractions, should stand in Harry's way when such a prize as that came across him! And as for his weakness;—might it not be strength, rather than weakness;—the strength of an old love which he could not quell, now that the woman was free to take him? For herself,—had she not known that she had only come second? As she thought of him with his noble bride and that bride's great fortune, and of her own insignificance, her low birth, her doubtful prettiness,—prettiness that had ever been doubtful to herself, of her few advantages, she told herself that she had no right to stand upon her claims. "I wish I had known it sooner," she said, in a voice so soft that Cecilia strained her ears to catch the words. "I wish I had known it sooner. I would not have come up to be in his way."

"But you will be in no one's way, Flo, unless it be in hers."

"And I will not be in hers," said Florence, speaking somewhat louder, and raising her head in pride as she spoke. "I will be neither in hers nor in his. I think I will go back at once."

Cecilia upon this ventured to look round at her, and saw that she was very pale, but that her eyes were dry and her lips pressed close together. It had not occurred to Mrs. Burton that her sister-in-law would take it in this way,—that she would express herself as being willing to give way, and that she would at once surrender her lover to her rival. The married woman, she who was already happy with a husband, having enlisted all her sympathies on the side of a marriage between Florence and Harry Clavering, could by no means bring herself to agree to this view. No one liked success better than Cecilia Burton, and to her success would consist in rescuing Harry from Lady Ongar and securing him for Florence. In fighting this battle she had found that she would have against her Lady Ongar—of course, and then her husband, and Harry himself too, as she feared; and now also she must reckon Florence also among her opponents. But she could not endure the idea of failing in such a cause. "Oh, Florence, I think you are so wrong," she said.

"You would feel as I do, if you were in my place."

"But people cannot always judge best when they feel the most. What you should think of is his happiness."

"So I do ;—and of his future career."

"Career! I hate to hear of careers. Men do not want careers, or should not want them. Could it be good for him to marry a woman who has been false—who has done as she has, simply because she has made herself rich by her wickedness? Do you believe so much in riches yourself?"

"If he loves her best, I will not blame him," said Florence. "He knew her before he had seen me. He was quite honest and told me all the story. It is not his fault if he still likes her the best."

When they reached Onslow Crescent, the first half-hour was spent with the children, as to whom Florence could not but observe that even from their mouths the name of Harry Clavering was banished. But she played with Cissy and Sophie, giving them their little presents from Stratton ; and sat with the baby in her lap, kissing his pink feet and making little soft noises for his behoof, sweetly as she might have done if no terrible crisis in her own life had now come upon her. Not a tear as yet had moistened her eyes, and Cecilia was partly aware that Florence's weeping would be done in secret. "Come up with me into my own room;—I have something to show you," she said, as the nurse took the baby at last; and Cissy and Sophie were at the same time sent away with their brother. "As I came in I got a note from Harry, but, before you see that, I must show you the letter which he wrote to me on Friday. He has gone down to Clavering,—on some business,—for one day." Mrs. Burton, in her heart, could hardly acquit him of having run out of town at the moment to avoid the arrival of Florence.

They went upstairs, and the note was, in fact, read before the letter. "I hope there is nothing wrong at the parsonage," said Florence.

"You see he says he will be back after one day."

"Perhaps he has gone to tell them,—of this change in his prospects."

"No, dear, no ; you do not yet understand his feelings. Read his letter, and you will know more. If there is to be a change, he is at any rate too much ashamed of it to speak of it. He does not wish it himself. It is simply this,—that she has thrown herself in his way, and he has not known how to avoid her."

Then Florence read the letter very slowly, going over most of the sentences more than once, and struggling to learn from them what were really the wishes of the writer. When she came to Harry's exculpation of Lady Ongar, she believed it thoroughly, and said so,—meeting, however, a direct contradiction on that point from her sister-in-law. When she had finished it, she folded it up and gave it back. "Cissy," she said, "I know that I ought to go back. I do not want to see him, and I am glad that he has gone away."

"But you do not mean to give him up?"

"Yes, dearest."

"But you said you would never leave him, unless he left you."

"He has left me."

"No, Florence; not so. Do you not see what he says;—that he knows you are the only woman that can make him happy?"

"He has not said that; but if he had, it would make no matter. He understands well how it is. He says that I could not take him now,— even if he came to me; and I cannot. How could I? What! wish to marry a man who does not love me, who loves another, when I know that I am regarded simply as a barrier between them; when by doing so I should mar his fortunes? Cissy, dear, when you think of it, you will not wish it."

"Mar his fortunes! It would make them. I do wish it,—and he wishes it too. I tell you that I had him here, and I know it. Why should you be sacrificed?"

"What is the meaning of self-denial, if no one can bear to suffer?"

"But he will suffer too,—and all for her caprices! You cannot really think that her money would do him any good. Who would ever speak to him again, or even see him? What would the world say of him? Why, his own father and mother and sisters would disown him, if they are such as you say they are."

Florence would not argue it further, but went to her room, and remained there alone till Cecilia came to tell her that her brother had returned. What weeping there may have been there, need not be told. Indeed, as I think, there was not much, for Florence was a girl whose education had not brought her into the way of hysterical sensations. The Burtons were an active, energetic people who sympathized with each other in labour and success,—and in endurance also; but who had little sympathy to express for the weaknesses of grief. When her children had stumbled in their play, bruising their little noses, and barking their little shins, Mrs. Burton, the elder, had been wont to bid them rise, asking them what their legs were for, if they could not stand. So they had dried their own little eyes with their own little fists, and had learned to understand that the rubs of the world were to be borne in silence. This rub that had come to Florence was of grave import, and had gone deeper than the outward skin; but still the old lesson had its effect.

Florence rose from the bed on which she was lying, and prepared to come down. "Do not commit yourself to him, as 'to anything," said Cecilia.

"I understand what that means," Florence answered. "He thinks as I do. But never mind. He will not say much, and I shall say less. It is bad to talk of this to any man,—even to a brother."

Burton also received his sister with that exceptional affection which declares pity for some overwhelming misfortune. He kissed her lips, which was rare with him, for he would generally but just touch her forehead, and he put his hand behind her waist and partly embraced her. "Did Cissy manage to find you at the station?"

"Oh, yes;—easily."

"Theodore thinks that a woman is no good for any such purpose as that," said Cecilia. "It is a wonder to him, no doubt, that we are not now wandering about London in search of each other,—and of him."

"I think she would have got home quicker if I could have been there," said Burton.

"We were in a cab in one minute;—weren't we, Florence? The difference would have been that you would have given a porter sixpence,—and I gave him a shilling, having bespoken him before."

"And Theodore's time was worth the sixpence, I suppose," said Florence.

"That depends," said Cecilia. "How did the synod go on?"

"The synod made an ass of itself;—as synods always do. It is necessary to get a lot of men together, for the show of the thing,—otherwise the world will not believe. That is the meaning of committees. But the real work must always be done by one or two men. Come;—I'll go and get ready for dinner."

The subject,—the one real subject, had thus been altogether avoided at this first meeting with the man of the house, and the evening passed without any allusion to it. Much was made of the children, and much was said of the old people at home; but still there was a consciousness over them all that the one matter of importance was being kept in the background. They were all thinking of Harry Clavering, but no one mentioned his name. They all knew that they were unhappy and heavy-hearted through his fault, but no one blamed him. He had been received in that house with open arms, had been warmed in their bosom, and had stung them; but though they were all smarting from the sting, they uttered no complaint. Burton had made up his mind that it would be better to pass over the matter thus in silence,—to say nothing further of Harry Clavering. A misfortune had come upon them. They must bear it, and go on as before. Harry had been admitted into the London office on the footing of a paid clerk,—on the same footing, indeed, as Burton himself, though with a much smaller salary and inferior work. This position had been accorded to him of course through the Burton interest, and it was understood that if he chose to make himself useful, he could rise in the business as Theodore had risen. But he could only do so as one of the

Burtons. For the last three months he had declined to take his salary, alleging that private affairs had kept him away from the office. It was to the hands of Theodore Burton himself that such matters came for management, and therefore there had been no necessity for further explanation. Harry Clavering would of course leave the house, and there would be an end of him in the records of the Burton family. He would have come and made his mark,—a terrible mark, and would have passed on. Those whom he had bruised by his cruelty, and knocked over by his treachery, must get to their feet again as best they could, and say as little as might be of their fall. There are knaves in this world, and no one can suppose that he has a special right to be exempted from their knavery because he himself is honest. It is on the honest that the knaves prey. That was Burton's theory in this matter. He would learn from Cecilia how Florence was bearing herself; but to Florence herself he would say little or nothing if she bore with patience and dignity, as he believed she would, the calamity which had befallen her.

But he must write to his mother. The old people at Stratton must not be left in the dark as to what was going on. He must write to his mother, unless he could learn from his wife that Florence herself had communicated to them at home the fact of Harry's iniquity. But he asked no question as to this on the first night, and on the following morning he went off, having simply been told that Florence had seen Harry's letter, that she knew all, and that she was carrying herself like an angel.

"Not like an angel that hopes?" said Theodore.

"Let her alone for a day or two," said Cecilia. "Of course she must have a few days to think of it. I need hardly tell you that you will never have to be ashamed of your sister."

The Tuesday and the Wednesday passed by, and though Cecilia and Florence when together discussed the matter, no change was made in the wishes or thoughts of either of them. Florence, now that she was in town, had consented to remain till after Harry should return, on the understanding that she should not be called upon to see him. He was to be told that she forgave him altogether,—that his troth was returned to him and that he was free, but that in such circumstances a meeting between them could be of no avail. And then a little packet was made up, which was to be given to him. How was it that Florence had brought with her all his presents and all his letters? But there they were in her box upstairs, and sitting by herself, with weary fingers, she packed them, and left them packed under lock and key, addressed by herself to Harry Clavering, Esq. Oh, the misery of packing such a parcel! The feeling with which a woman does it is never encountered by a man. He chucks the things together in wrath,—the lock of hair, the letters in the pretty Italian hand that have taken so much happy care in the writing, the jewelled shirt-studs, which were first put in by the fingers that gave them. They are thrown together, and given to some other woman to deliver. But the girl lingers over her torture. She reads the letters

MEE

J.H.Harral.sc

FLORENCE BURTON MAKES UP A PACKET.

again. She thinks of the moments of bliss which each little toy has given. She is loth to part with everything. She would fain keep some one thing,—the smallest of them all. She doubts,—till a feeling of maidenly reserve constrains her at last, and the coveted trifle, with careful, painstaking fingers, is put with the rest, and the parcel is made complete, and the address is written with precision.

"Of course I cannot see him," said Florence. "You will hand to him what I have to send to him; and you must ask him, if he has kept any of my letters, to return them." She said nothing of the shirt-studs, but he would understand that. As for the lock of hair,—doubtless it had been burned.

Cecilia said but little in answer to this. She would not as yet look upon the matter as Florence looked at it, and as Theodore did also. Harry was to be back in town on Thursday morning. He could not, probably, be seen or heard of on that day, because of his visit to Lady Ongar. It was absolutely necessary that he should see Lady Ongar before he could come to Onslow Terrace, with possibility of becoming once more the old Harry Clavering whom they were all to love. But Mrs. Burton would by no means give up all hope. It was useless to say anything to Florence, but she still hoped that good might come.

And then, as she thought of it all, a project came into her head. Alas, and alas ! Was she not too late with her project? Why had she not thought of it on the Tuesday or early on the Wednesday, when it might possibly have been executed? But it was a project which she must have kept secret from her husband, of which he would by no means have approved ; and as she remembered this, she told herself that perhaps it was as well that things should take their own course without such interference as she had contemplated.

On the Thursday morning there came to her a letter in a strange hand. It was from Clavering,—from Harry's mother. Mrs. Clavering wrote, as she said, at her son's request, to say that he was confined to his bed, and could not be in London as soon as he expected. Mrs. Burton was not to suppose that he was really ill, and none of the family were to be frightened. From this Mrs. Burton learned that Mrs. Clavering knew nothing of Harry's apostasy. The letter went on to say that Harry would write as soon as he himself was able, and would probably be in London early next week,—at any rate before the end of it. He was a little feverish, but there was no cause for alarm. Florence, of course, could only listen and turn pale. Now at any rate she must remain in London.

Mrs. Burton's project might, after all, be feasible; but then what if her husband should really be angry with her ? That was a misfortune which never yet had come upon her.

———

CHAPTER XXXIII.

Showing why Harry Clavering was wanted at the Rectory.

The letter which had summoned Harry to the parsonage had been from his mother, and had begged him to come to Clavering at once, as trouble had come upon them from an unexpected source. His father had quarrelled with Mr. Saul. The rector and the curate had had an interview, in which there had been high words, and Mr. Clavering had refused to see Mr. Saul again. Fanny also was in great trouble,—and the parish was, as it were, in hot water. Mrs. Clavering thought that Harry had better run down to Clavering, and see Mr. Saul. Harry, not unwillingly, acceded to his mother's request, much wondering at the source of this new misfortune. As to Fanny, she, as he believed, had held out no encouragement to Mr. Saul's overtures. When Mr. Saul had proposed to her,— making that first offer of which Harry had been aware,—nothing could have been more steadfast than her rejection of the gentleman's hand. Harry had regarded Mr. Saul as little less than mad to think of such a thing, but, thinking of him as a man very different in his ways and feelings from other men, had believed that he might go on at Clavering comfortably as curate in spite of that little accident. It appeared, however, that he was not going on comfortably; but Harry, when he left London, could not quite imagine how such violent discomfort should have arisen that the rector and the curate should be unable to meet each other. If the reader will allow me, I will go back a little and explain this.

The reader already knows what Fanny's brother did not know,— namely, that Mr. Saul had pressed his suit again, and had pressed it very strongly ; and he also knows that Fanny's reception of the second offer was very different from her reception of the first. She had begun to doubt ;—to doubt whether her first judgment as to Mr. Saul's character had not been unjust,—to doubt whether, in addressing her, he was not right, seeing that his love for her was so strong,—to doubt whether she did not like him better than she had thought she did,—to doubt whether an engagement with a penniless curate was in truth a position utterly to be reprehended and avoided. Young penniless curates must love somebody as well as young beneficed vicars and rectors. And then Mr. Saul pleaded his cause so well !

She did not at once speak to her mother on the matter, and the fact that she had a secret made her very wretched. She had left Mr. Saul in doubt, giving him no answer, and he had said that he would ask her again in a few days what was to be his fate. She hardly knew how to tell her mother of this till she had told herself what were her own wishes. She thoroughly desired to have her mother in her confidence, and promised herself that it should be so before Mr. Saul renewed his suit. He was a man who was never hurried or impatient in his doings. But Fanny put off the interview with her mother,—put off her own final resolution, till it was too late, and Mr. Saul came upon her again, when she was but ill-prepared for him.

A woman, when she doubts whether she loves or does not love, is inclined five parts out of six towards the man of whom she is thinking. When a woman doubts she is lost, the cynics say. I simply assert, being no cynic, that when a woman doubts she is won. The more Fanny thought of Mr. Saul, the more she felt that he was not the man for which she had first taken him,—that he was of larger dimensions as regarded spirit, manhood, and heart, and better entitled to a woman's love. She would not tell herself that she was attached to him; but in all her arguments with herself against him, she rested her objection mainly on the fact, that he had but seventy pounds a year. And then the threatened attack, the attack that was to be final, came upon her before she was prepared for it!

They had been together as usual during the intervening time. It was, indeed, impossible that they should not be together. Since she had first begun to doubt about Mr. Saul, she had been more diligent than heretofore in visiting the poor and in attending to her school, as though she were recognizing the duty which would specially be hers if she were to marry such a one as he. And thus they had been brought together more than ever. All this her mother had seen, and seeing, had trembled; but she had not thought it wise to say anything till Fanny should speak. Fanny was very good and very prudent. It could not be but that Fanny should know how impossible must be such a marriage. As to the rector he had no suspicions on the matter. Saul had made himself an ass on one occasion, and there had been an end of it. As a curate Saul was invaluable, and therefore the fact of his having made himself an ass had been forgiven him. It was thus that the rector looked at it.

It was hardly more than ten days since the last walk in Cumberly Lane when Mr. Saul renewed the attack. He did it again on the same spot, and at the same hour of the day. Twice a week, always on the same days, he was in the chapel up at this end of the parish, and on these days he could always find Fanny on her way home. When he put his head in at the little school door and asked for her, her mind misgave her. He had not walked home with her since, and though he had been in the school with her often, had always left her there, going about his own business, as though he were by no means desirous of her company. Now the time had come, and Fanny felt that she was not prepared. But she took up her hat, and went out to him, knowing that there was no escape.

"Miss Clavering," said he, "have you thought of what I was saying to you?" To this she made no answer, but merely played with the point of the parasol which she held in her hand. "You cannot but have thought of it," he continued. "You could not dismiss it altogether from your thoughts."

"I have thought about it, of course," she said.

"And what does your mind say? Or rather what does your heart say? Both should speak, but I would sooner hear the heart first."

"I am sure, Mr. Saul, that it is quite impossible."

"In what way impossible?"

"Papa would not allow it."

"Have you asked him?"

"Oh, dear, no."

"Or Mrs. Clavering?"

Fanny blushed as she remembered how she had permitted the days to go by without asking her mother's counsel. "No; I have spoken to no one. Why should I, when I knew that it is impossible?"

"May I speak to Mr. Clavering?" To this Fanny made no immediate answer, and then Mr. Saul urged the question again. "May I speak to your father?"

Fanny felt that she was assenting, even in that she did not answer such a question by an immediate refusal of her permission; and yet she did not mean to assent. "Miss Clavering," he said, "if you regard me with affection, you have no right to refuse me this request. I tell you so boldly. If you feel for me that love which would enable you to accept me as your husband, it is your duty to tell me so,—your duty to me, to yourself, and to your God."

Fanny did not quite see the thing in this light, and yet she did not wish to contradict him. At this moment she forgot that in order to put herself on perfectly firm ground, she should have gone back to the first hypothesis, and assured him that she did not feel any such regard for him. Mr. Saul, whose intellect was more acute, took advantage of her here, and chose to believe that that matter of her affection was now conceded to him. He knew what he was doing well, and is open to a charge of some jesuitry. "Mr. Saul," said Fanny, with grave prudence, "it cannot be right for people to marry when they have nothing to live upon." When she had shown him so plainly that she had no other piece left on the board to play than this, the game may be said to have been won on his side.

"If that be your sole objection," said he, "you cannot but think it right that I and your father should discuss it." To this she made no reply whatever, and they walked along the lane for a considerable way in silence. Mr. Saul would have been glad to have had the interview over now, feeling that at any future meeting he would have stronger power of assuming the position of an accepted lover than he would do now. Another man would have desired to get from her lips a decided word of love,—to take her hand, perhaps, and to feel some response from it,—to go further than this, as is not unlikely, and plead for the happy indulgences of an accepted lover. But Mr. Saul abstained, and was wise in abstaining. She had not so far committed herself, but that she might even now have drawn back, had he pressed her too hard. For hand-pressing, and the titillations of love-making, Mr. Saul was not adapted; but he was a man, who having once loved, would love on to the end.

The way, however, was too long to be completed without further speech. Fanny, as she walked, was struggling to find some words by which she might still hold her ground, but the words were not forthcoming. It seemed to herself that she was being carried away by this man, because she had suddenly lost her remembrance of all negatives. The more she struggled the more she failed, and at last gave it up in despair. Let Mr. Saul say what he would, it was impossible that they should be married. All his arguments about duty were nonsense. It could not be her duty to marry a man who would have to starve in his attempt to keep her. She wished she had told him at first that she did not love him, but that seemed to be too late now. The moment that she was in the house she would go to her mother and tell her everything.

"Miss Clavering," said he, "I shall see your father to-morrow."

"No, no," she ejaculated.

"I shall certainly do so in any event. I shall either tell him that I must leave the parish,—explaining to him why I must go; or I shall ask him to let me remain here in the hope that I may become his son-in-law. You will not now tell me that I am to go?" Fanny was again silent, her memory failing her as to either negative or affirmative that would be of service. "To stay here hopeless would be impossible to me. Now I am not hopeless. Now I am full of hope. I think I could be happy, though I had to wait as Jacob waited."

"And perhaps have Jacob's consolation," said Fanny. She was lost by the joke and he knew it. A grim smile of satisfaction crossed his thin face as he heard it, and there was a feeling of triumph at his heart. "I am hardly fitted to be a patriarch, as the patriarchs were of old," he said. "Though the seven years should be prolonged to fourteen I do not think I should seek any Leah."

They were soon at the gate, and his work for that evening was done. He would go home to his solitary room at a neighbouring farm-house, and sit in triumph as he eat his morsel of cold mutton by himself. He, without any advantage of a person to back him, poor, friendless, hitherto conscious that he was unfitted to mix even in ordinary social life—he had won the heart of the fairest woman he had ever seen. "You will give me your hand at parting," he said, whereupon she tendered it to him with her eyes fixed upon the ground. "I hope we understand each other," he continued. "You may at any rate understand this, that I love you with all my heart and all my strength. If things prosper with me, all my prosperity shall be for you. If there be no prosperity for me, you shall be my only consolation in this world. You are my Alpha and my Omega, my first and last, my beginning and end,—my everything, my all." Then he turned away and left her, and there had come no negative from her lips. As far as her lips were concerned no negative was any longer possible to her.

She went into the house knowing that she must at once seek her mother; but she allowed herself first to remain for some half-hour in her own bedroom, preparing the words that she would use. The interview she knew would be difficult,—much more difficult than it would have been before her last walk with Mr. Saul; and the worst of it was that she could not quite make up her mind as to what it was that she wished to say. She waited till she should hear her mother's step on the stairs. At last Mrs. Clavering came up to dress, and then Fanny following her quickly into her bedroom, abruptly began.

"Mamma," she said, "I want to speak to you very much."

"Well, my dear?"

"But you mustn't be in a hurry, mamma." Mrs. Clavering looked at her watch, and declaring that it still wanted three-quarters of an hour to dinner, promised that she would not be very much in a hurry.

"Mamma, Mr. Saul has been speaking to me again."

"Has he, my dear? You cannot, of course, help it if he chooses to speak to you, but he ought to know that it is very foolish. It must end in his having to leave us."

"That is what he says, mamma. He says he must go away unless——"

"Unless what?"

"Unless I will consent that he shall remain here as——"

"As your accepted lover. Is that it, Fanny?"

"Yes, mamma."

"Then he must go, I suppose. What else can any of us say? I shall be sorry both for his sake and for your papa's." Mrs. Clavering as she said this looked at her daughter, and saw at once that this edict on her part did not settle the difficulty. There was that in Fanny's face which showed trouble and the necessity of further explanation. "Is not that what you think yourself, my dear?" Mrs. Clavering asked.

"I should be very sorry if he had to leave the parish on my account."

"We all shall feel that, dearest; but what can we do? I presume you don't wish him to remain as your lover?"

"I don't know, mamma," said Fanny.

It was then as Mrs. Clavering had feared. Indeed from the first word that Fanny had spoken on the present occasion, she had almost been sure of the facts, as they now were. To her father it would appear wonderful that his daughter should have come to love such a man as Mr. Saul, but Mrs. Clavering knew better than he how far perseverance will go with women,—perseverance joined with high mental capacity, and with high spirit to back it. She was grieved but not surprised, and would at once have accepted the idea of Mr. Saul becoming her son-in-law, had not the poverty of the man been so much against him. "Do you mean, my dear, that you wish him to remain here after what he has said to you? That would be tantamount to accepting him. You understand that, Fanny;—eh, dear?"

"I suppose it would, mamma."

"And is that what you mean? Come, dearest, tell me the whole of it. What have you said to him yourself? What has he been led to think from the answer you have given him to-day?"

"He says that he means to see papa to-morrow."

"But is he to see him with your consent?" Fanny had hitherto placed herself in the nook of a bow-window which looked out into the garden, and there, though she was near to the dressing-table at which her mother was sitting, she could so far screen herself as almost to hide her face when she was speaking. From this retreat her mother found it necessary to withdraw her; so she rose, and going to a sofa in the room, bade her daughter come and sit beside her. "A doctor, my dear, can never do any good," she said, "unless the patient will tell him every-thing. Have you told Mr. Saul that he may see papa,—as coming from you, you know?"

"No, mamma;—I did not tell him that. I told him that it would be altogether impossible, because we should be so poor."

"He ought to have known that himself."

"But I don't think he ever thinks of such things as that, mamma. I can't tell you quite what he said, but it went to show that he didn't regard money at all."

"But that is nonsense; is it not, Fanny?"

"What he means is, not that people if they are fond of each other ought to marry at once when they have got nothing to live upon, but that they ought to tell each other so and then be content to wait. I suppose he thinks that some day he may have a living."

"But, Fanny, are you fond of him;—and have you ever told him so?"

"I have never told him so, mamma."

"But you are fond of him?" To this question Fanny made no answer, and now Mrs. Clavering knew it all. She felt no inclination to scold her daughter, or even to point out in very strong language how foolish Fanny had been in allowing a man to engage her affections merely by asking for them. The thing was a misfortune, and should have been avoided by the departure of Mr. Saul from the parish after his first decla-ration of love. He had been allowed to remain for the sake of the rector's comfort, and the best must now be made of it. That Mr. Saul must now go was certain, and Fanny must endure the weariness of an attachment with an absent lover to which her father would not consent. It was very bad, but Mrs. Clavering did not think that she could make it better by attempting to scold her daughter into renouncing the man.

"I suppose you would like me to tell papa all this before Mr. Saul comes to-morrow?"

"If you think it best, mamma."

"And you mean, dear, that you would wish to accept him, only that he has no income?"

"I think so, mamma."

"Have you told him so?"

"I did not tell him so, but he understands it."

"If you did not tell him so, you might still think of it again."

But Fanny had surrendered herself now, and was determined to make no further attempt at sending the garrison up to the wall. "I am sure, mamma, that if he were well off, like Edward, I should accept him. It is only because he has no income."

"But you have not told him that?"

"I would not tell him anything without your consent and papa's. He said he should go to papa to-morrow, and I could not prevent that. I did say that I knew it was quite impossible."

The mischief was done and there was no help for it. Mrs. Clavering told her daughter that she would talk it all over with the rector that night, so that Fanny was able to come down to dinner without fearing any further scene on that evening. But on the following morning she did not appear at prayers, nor was she present at the breakfast table. Her mother went to her early, and she immediately asked if it was considered necessary that she should see her father before Mr. Saul came. But this was not required of her. "Papa says that it is out of the question," said Mrs. Clavering. "I told him so myself," said Fanny, beginning to whimper. "And there must be no engagements," said Mrs. Clavering. "No, mamma. I haven't engaged myself. I told him it was impossible." "And papa thinks that Mr. Saul must leave him," continued Mrs. Clavering. "I knew papa would say that;—but, mamma, I shall not forget him for that reason." To this Mrs. Clavering made no reply, and Fanny was allowed to remain upstairs till Mr. Saul had come and gone.

Very soon after breakfast Mr. Saul did come. His presence at the rectory was so common that the servants were not generally summoned to announce his arrivals, but his visits were made to Mrs. Clavering and Fanny more often than to the rector. On this occasion he rang the bell, and asked for Mr. Clavering, and was shown into the rector's so-called study, in a way that the maid-servant felt to be unusual. And the rector was sitting uncomfortably prepared for the visit, not having had his after-breakfast cigar. He had been induced to declare that he was not, and would not be, angry with Fanny; but Mr. Saul was left to such indignation as he thought it incumbent on himself to express. In his opinion, the marriage was impossible, not only because there was no money, but because Mr. Saul was Mr. Saul, and because Fanny Clavering was Fanny Clavering. Mr. Saul was a gentleman; but that was all that could be said of him. There is a class of country clergymen in England, of whom Mr. Clavering was one, and his son-in-law, Mr. Fielding, another, which is so closely allied to the squirearchy, as to possess a double identity. Such clergymen are not only clergymen, but they are country gentlemen also. Mr. Clavering regarded clergymen of his class,—of the country gentlemen class, as being quite distinct from all others,—and as being, I may say, very much higher than all others, without reference to any money question. When meeting his brother rectors and vicars, he had quite a different tone in addressing them,—as they might belong to his class, or to another. There was no offence in this. The clerical country-gentlemen understood it all as though there were some secret sign or shibboleth between them; but the outsiders had no complaint to make of arrogance, and did not feel themselves aggrieved. They hardly knew that there was an inner clerical familiarity to which they were not admitted. But now that there was a young curate from the outer circle demanding Mr. Clavering's daughter in marriage, and that without a shilling in his pocket, Mr. Clavering felt that the eyes of the offender must be opened. The nuisance to him was very great, but this opening of Mr. Saul's eyes was a duty from which he could not shrink.

He got up when the curate entered, and greeted his curate, as though he were unaware of the purpose of the present visit. The whole burden of the story was to be thrown upon Mr. Saul. But that gentleman was not long in casting the burden from his shoulders. "Mr. Clavering," he said, "I have come to ask your permission to be a suitor for your daughter's hand."

The rector was almost taken aback by the abruptness of the request. "Quite impossible, Mr. Saul," he said—"quite impossible. I am told by Mrs. Clavering that you were speaking to Fanny again about this yesterday, and I must say, that I think you have been behaving very badly."

"In what way have I behaved badly?"

"In endeavouring to gain her affections behind my back."

"But, Mr. Clavering, how otherwise could I gain them? How otherwise does any man gain any woman's love. If you mean—— "

"Look here, Mr. Saul. I don't think that there is any necessity for an argument between you and me on this point. That you cannot marry Miss Clavering is so self-evident that it does not require to be discussed. If there were nothing else against it, neither of you have got a penny. I have not seen my daughter since I heard of this madness,—hear me out if you please, sir,—since I heard of this madness, but her mother tells me that she is quite aware of that fact. Your coming to me with such a proposition is an absurdity if it is nothing worse. Now you must do one of two things, Mr. Saul. You must either promise me that this shall be at an end altogether, or you must leave the parish."

"I certainly shall not promise you that my hopes as they regard your daughter will be at an end."

"Then, Mr. Saul, the sooner you go the better."

A dark cloud came across Mr. Saul's brow as he heard these last words. "That is the way in which you would send away your groom, if he had offended you," he said.

"I do not wish to be unnecessarily harsh," said Mr. Clavering, "and what I say to you now I say to you not as my curate, but as to a most unwarranted suitor for my daughter's hand. Of course I cannot turn you out of the parish at a day's notice. I know that well enough. But your feelings as a gentleman ought to make you aware that you should go at once."

" And that is to be my only answer ? "

" What answer did you expect ? "

" I have been thinking so much lately of the answers I might get from your daughter, that I have not made other calculations. Perhaps I had no right to expect any other than that you have now given me."

" Of course you had not. And now I ask you again to give her up."

" I shall not do that certainly."

" Then, Mr. Saul, you must go ; and, inconvenient as it will be to myself,—terribly inconvenient, I must ask you to go at once. Of course I cannot allow you to meet my daughter any more. As long as you remain she will be debarred from going to her school, and you will be debarred from coming here."

" If I say that I will not seek her at the school ? "

" I will not have it. It is out of the question that you should remain in the parish. You ought to feel it."

" Mr. Clavering, my going,—I mean my instant going,—is a matter of which I have not yet thought. I must consider it before I give you an answer."

" It ought to require no consideration," said Mr. Clavering, rising from his chair,—" none at all; not a moment's. Heavens and earth ! Why, what did you suppose you were to live upon ? But I won't discuss it. I will not say one more word upon a subject which is so distasteful to me. You must excuse me if I leave you."

Mr. Saul then departed, and from this interview had arisen that state of things in the parish which had induced Mrs. Clavering to call Harry to their assistance. The rector had become more energetic on the subject than any of them had expected. He did not actually forbid his wife to see Mr. Saul, but he did say that Mr. Saul should not come to the rectory. Then there arose a question as to the Sunday services, and yet Mr. Clavering would have no intercourse with his curate. He would have no intercourse with him unless he would fix an immediate day for going, or else promise that he would think no more of Fanny. Hitherto he had done neither, and therefore Mrs. Clavering had sent for her son.

CHAPTER XXXIV.

MR. SAUL'S ABODE.

WHEN Harry Clavering left London he was not well, though he did not care to tell himself that he was ill. But he had been so harassed by his position, was so ashamed of himself, and as yet so unable to see any escape from his misery, that he was sore with fatigue and almost worn out with trouble. On his arrival at the parsonage, his mother at once asked him if he was ill, and received his petulant denial with an ill-satisfied countenance. That there was something wrong between him and Florence she suspected, but at the present moment she was not disposed to inquire into that matter. Harry's love-affairs had for her a great interest, but Fanny's love-affairs at the present moment were paramount in her bosom. Fanny, indeed, had become very troublesome since Mr. Saul's visit to her father. On the evening of her conversation with her mother, and on the following morning, Fanny had carried herself with bravery, and Mrs. Clavering had been disposed to think that her daughter's heart was not wounded deeply. She had admitted the impossibility of her marriage with Mr. Saul, and had never insisted on the strength of her attachment. But no sooner was she told that Mr. Saul had been banished from the house, than she took upon herself to mope in the most love-lorn fashion, and behaved herself as though she were the victim of an all-absorbing passion. Between her and her father no word on the subject had been spoken, and even to her mother she was silent, respectful, and subdued, as it becomes daughters to be who are hardly used when they are in love. Now, Mrs. Clavering felt that in this her daughter was not treating her well.

"But you don't mean to say that she cares for him?" Harry said to his mother, when they were alone on the evening of his arrival.

"Yes, she cares for him, certainly. As far as I can tell, she cares for him very much."

"It is the oddest thing I ever knew in my life. I should have said he was the last man in the world for success of that kind."

"One never can tell, Harry. You see he is a very good young man."

"But girls don't fall in love with men because they're good, mother."

"I hope they do,—for that and other things together."

"But he has got none of the other things. What a pity it was that he was let to stay here after he first made a fool of himself."

"It's too late to think of that now, Harry. Of course she can't marry him. They would have nothing to live on. I should say that he has no prospect of a living."

"I can't conceive how a man can do such a wicked thing," said Harry, moralizing, and forgetting for a moment his own sins. "Coming into a house like this, and in such a position, and then undermining a girl's affections, when he must know that it is quite out of the question that he should marry her! I call it downright wicked. It is treachery of the worst sort, and coming from a clergyman is of course the more to be condemned. I shan't be slow to tell him my mind."

"You will gain nothing by quarrelling with him."

"But how can I help it, if I am to see him at all?"

"I mean that I would not be rough with him. The great thing is to make him feel that he should go away as soon as possible, and renounce all idea of seeing Fanny again. You see, your father will have no conversation with him at all, and it is so disagreeable about the services. They'll have to meet in the vestry-room on Sunday, and they won't speak. Will not that be terrible? Anything will be better than that he should remain here."

"And what will my father do for a curate?"

"He can't do anything till he knows when Mr. Saul will go. He talks of taking all the services himself."

"He couldn't do it, mother. He must not think of it. However, I'll see Saul the first thing to-morrow."

The next day was Tuesday, and Harry proposed to leave the rectory at ten o'clock for Mr. Saul's lodgings. Before he did so, he had a few words with his father, who professed even deeper animosity against Mr. Saul than his son. "After that," he said, "I'll believe that a girl may fall in love with any man! People say all manner of things about the folly of girls; but nothing but this,—nothing short of this,—would have convinced me that it was possible that Fanny should have been such a fool. An ape of a fellow,—not made like a man,—with a thin hatchet face, and unwholesome stubbly chin. Good heavens!"

"He has talked her into it."

"But he is such an ass. As far as I know him, he can't say Bo! to a goose."

"There I think you are perhaps wrong."

"Upon my word, I've never been able to get a word from him except about the parish. He is the most uncompanionable fellow. There's Edward Fielding is as active a clergyman as Saul; but Edward Fielding has something to say for himself."

"Saul is a cleverer man than Edward is; but his cleverness is of a different sort."

"It is of a sort that is very invisible to me. But what does all that matter? He hasn't got a shilling. When I was a curate, we didn't think of doing such things as that." Mr. Clavering had only been a curate for twelve months, and during that time had become engaged to his present wife with the consent of every one concerned. "But clergy-men were gentlemen then. I don't know what the Church will come to; I don't indeed."

After this Harry went away upon his mission. What a farce it was that he should be engaged to make straight the affairs of other people, when his own affairs were so very crooked! As he walked up to the old farmhouse in which Mr. Saul was living, he thought of this, and acknow-ledged to himself that he could hardly make himself in earnest about his sister's affairs, because of his own troubles. He tried to fill himself with a proper feeling of dignified wrath and high paternal indignation against the poor curate; but under it all, and at the back of it all, and in front of it all, there was ever present to him his own position. Did he wish to escape from Lady Ongar; and if so, how was he to do it? And if he did not escape from Lady Ongar, how was he ever to hold up his head again?

He had sent a note to Mr. Saul on the previous evening giving notice of his intended visit, and had received an answer, in which the curate had promised that he would be at home. He had never before been in Mr. Saul's room, and as he entered it, felt more strongly than ever how incongruous was the idea of Mr. Saul as a suitor to his sister. The Claverings had always had things comfortable around them. They were a people who had ever lived on Brussels carpets, and had seated themselves in capacious chairs. Ormolu, damask hangings, and Sèvres china were not familiar to them ; but they had never lacked anything that is needed for the comfort of the first-class clerical world. Mr. Saul in his abode boasted but few comforts. He inhabited a big bed-room, in which there was a vast fireplace, and a very small grate,—the grate being very much more modern than the fireplace. There was a small rag of a carpet near the hearth, and on this stood a large deal table,—a table made of un-alloyed deal, without any mendacious paint, putting forward a pretence in the direction of mahogany. One wooden Windsor arm-chair—very comfortable in its way—was appropriated to the use of Mr. Saul himself, and two other small wooden chairs flanked the other side of the fireplace. In one distant corner stood Mr. Saul's small bed, and in another distant corner stood his small dressing-table. Against the wall stood a rickety deal press in which he kept his clothes. Other furniture there was none. One of the large windows facing towards the farmyard had been permanently closed, and in the wide embrasure was placed a portion of Mr. Saul's library,—books which he had brought with him from college ; and on the ground under this closed window were arranged the others, making a long row, which stretched from the bed to the dressing-table, very pervious, I fear, to the attacks of mice. The big table near the fireplace was covered with books and papers,—and, alas, with dust ; for he had fallen into that terrible habit which prevails among bachelors, of allowing his work to remain ever open, never finished, always confused,—with papers above books, and books above papers,—looking as though no useful product could ever be made to come forth from such chaotic elements. But there Mr. Saul composed his sermons, and studied his Bible, and followed up, no doubt, some special darling pursuit which his ambition dictated. But there he did not eat his meals ; that had been made impossible by the pile of papers and dust ; and his chop, therefore, or his broiled rasher, or bit of pig's fry was deposited for him on the little dressing-table, and there consumed.

Such was the solitary apartment of the gentleman who now aspired to the hand of Miss Clavering ; and for this accommodation, including attendance, he paid the reasonable sum of 10*l.* per annum. He then had 60*l.* left, with which to feed himself, clothe himself like a gentleman,—a duty somewhat neglected,—and perform his charities !

Harry Clavering, as he looked around him, felt almost ashamed of his sister. The walls were whitewashed, and stained in many places ; and the floor in the middle of the room seemed to be very rotten. What young man who has himself dwelt ever in comfort would like such a house for his sister ? Mr. Saul, however, came forward with no marks of visible shame on his face, and greeted his visitor frankly with an open hand. "You came down from London yesterday, I suppose ? " said Mr. Saul.

"Just so," said Harry.

"Take a seat ; " and Mr. Saul suggested the arm-chair, but Harry contented himself with one of the others. "I hope Mrs. Clavering is well ? " "Quite well," said Harry, cheerfully. "And your father,—and sister?" "Quite well, thank you," said Harry, very stiffly. "I would have come down to you at the rectory," said Mr. Saul, "instead of bringing you up here; only, as you have heard, no doubt, I and your father have unfortunately had a difference." This Mr. Saul said without any apparent effort, and then left Harry to commence the further conversation.

"Of course, you know what I'm come here about?" said Harry.

"Not exactly; at any rate not so clearly but what I would wish you to tell me."

"You have gone to my father as a suitor for my sister's hand."

"Yes, I have."

"Now you must know that that is altogether impossible,—a thing not to be even talked of."

"So your father says. I need not tell you that I was very sorry to hear him speak in that way."

"But, my dear fellow, you can't really be in earnest? You can't suppose it possible that he would allow such an engagement?"

"As to the latter question, I have no answer to give; but I certainly was,—and certainly am in earnest."

"Then I must say that I think you have a very erroneous idea of what the conduct of a gentleman should be."

"Stop a moment, Clavering," said Mr. Saul, rising, and standing with ris back to the big fireplace. "Don't allow yourself to say in a hurry words which you will afterwards regret. I do not think you can have intended to come here and tell me that I am not a gentleman."

"I don't want to have an argument with you; but you must give it up; that's all."

"Give what up? If you mean give up your sister, I certainly shall never do that. She may give me up, and if you have anything to say on that head, you had better say it to her."

"What right can you have,—without a shilling in the world—— ?"

"I should have no right to marry her in such a condition,—with your father's consent or without it. It is a thing which I have never proposed to myself for a moment,—or to her."

"And what have you proposed to yourself?"

Mr. Saul paused a moment before he spoke, looking down at the dusty heap upon his table, as though hoping that inspiration might come to him from them. "I will tell you what I have proposed," said he at last, "as nearly as I can put it into words. I propose to myself to have the image in my heart of one human being whom I can love above all the world beside; I propose to hope that I, as others, may some day marry, and that she whom I so love may become my wife; I propose to bear with such courage as I can much certain delay, and probable absolute failure in all this; and I propose also to expect,—no, hardly to expect,—that that which I will do for her, she will do for me. Now you know all my mind, and you may be sure of this, that I will instigate your sister to no disobedience."

" Of course she will not see you again."

" I shall think that hard after what has passed between us ; but I certainly shall not endeavour to see her clandestinely."

" And under these circumstances, Mr. Saul, of course you must leave us."

" So your father says."

" But leave us at once, I mean. It cannot be comfortable that you and my father should go on in the parish together in this way."

" What does your father mean by ' at once ? ' "

" The sooner the better ; say in two months' time at furthest."

" Very well. I will go in two months' time. I have no other home to go to, and no other means of livelihood ; but as your father wishes it, I will go at the end of two months. As I comply with this, I hope my request to see your sister once before I go will not be refused."

" It could do no good, Mr. Saul."

" To me it would do great good,—and, as I think, no harm to her."

" My father, I am sure, will not allow it. Indeed, why should he ? Nor, as I understand, would my sister wish it."

" Has she said so ? "

" Not to me ; but she has acknowledged that any idea of a marriage between herself and you is quite impossible, and after that I'm sure she'll have too much sense to wish for an interview. If there is anything further that I can do for you, I shall be most happy." Mr. Saul did not see that Harry Clavering could do anything for him, and then Harry took his leave. The rector, when he heard of the arrangement, expressed himself as in some sort satisfied. One month would have been better than two, but then it could hardly be expected that Mr. Saul could take himself away instantly, without looking for a hole in which to lay his head. " Of course it is understood that he is not to see her ? " the rector said. In answer to this, Harry explained what had taken place, expressing his opinion that Mr. Saul would, at any rate, keep his word. " Interview, indeed ! " said the rector. " It is the man's audacity that most astonishes me. It passes me to think how such a fellow can dare to propose such a thing. What is it that he expects as the end of it ? " Then Harry endeavoured to repeat what Mr. Saul had said as to his own expectations, but he was quite aware that he failed to make his father understand those expectations as he had understood them when the words came from Mr. Saul's own mouth. Harry Clavering had acknowledged to himself that it was impossible not to respect the poor curate.

To Mrs. Clavering, of course, fell the task of explaining to Fanny what had been done, and what was going to be done. " He is to go away, my dear, at the end of two months."

" Very well, mamma."

" And, of course, you and he are not to meet before that."

" Of course not, if you and papa say so."

" I have told your papa that it will only be necessary to tell you this, and that then you can go to your school just as usual, if you please. Neither papa nor I would doubt your word for a moment."

"But what can I do if he comes to me?" asked Fanny, almost whimpering.

"He has said that he will not, and we do not doubt his word either."

"That I am sure you need not. Whatever anybody may say, Mr. Saul is as much a gentleman as though he had the best living in the diocese. No one ever knew him break his word,—not a hair's breadth,—or do— anything else—that he ought—not to do." And Fanny, as she pronounced this rather strong eulogium, began to sob. Mrs. Clavering felt that Fanny was headstrong, and almost ill-natured, in speaking in this tone of her lover, after the manner in which she had been treated; but there could be no use in discussing Mr. Saul's virtues, and therefore she let the matter drop. "If you will take my advice," she said, "you will go about your occupations just as usual. You'll soon recover your spirits in that way."

"I don't want to recover my spirits," said Fanny; "but if you wish it I'll go on with the schools."

It was quite manifest now that Fanny intended to play the rôle of a broken-hearted young lady, and to regard the absent Mr. Saul with passionate devotion. That this should be so Mrs. Clavering felt to be the more cruel, because no such tendencies had been shown before the paternal sentence against Mr. Saul had been passed. Fanny in telling her own tale had begun by declaring that any such an engagement was an impossibility. She had not asked permission to have Mr. Saul for a lover. She had given no hint that she even hoped for such permission. But now when that was done which she herself had almost dictated, she took upon herself to live as though she were ill-used as badly as a heroine in a castle among the Apennines! And in this way she would really become deeply in love with Mr. Saul;—thinking of all which Mrs. Clavering almost regretted that the edict of banishment had gone forth. It would, perhaps, have been better to have left Mr. Saul to go about the parish, and to have laughed Fanny out of her fancy. But it was too late now for that, and Mrs. Clavering said nothing further on the subject to any one.

On the day following his visit to the farm house, Harry Clavering was unwell,—too unwell to go back to London; and on the next day he was ill in bed. Then it was that he got his mother to write to Mrs. Burton;— and then also he told his mother a part of his troubles. When the letter was written he was very anxious to see it, and was desirous that it should be specially worded, and so written as to make Mrs. Burton certain that he was in truth too ill to come to London, though not ill enough to create alarm. "Why not simply let me say that you are kept here for a day or two?" asked Mrs. Clavering.

"Because I promised that I would be in Onslow Terrace to-morrow, and she must not think that I would stay away if I could avoid it."

Then Mrs. Clavering closed the letter and directed it. When she had done that, and put on it the postage-stamp, she asked in a voice that was intended to be indifferent whether Florence was in London; and, hearing that she was so, expressed her surprise that the letter should not be written to Florence.

"My engagement was with Mrs. Burton," said Harry.

"I hope there is nothing wrong between you and Florence?" said his mother. To this question, Harry made no immediate answer, and Mrs. Clavering was afraid to press it. But after a while he recurred to the subject himself. "Mother," he said, "things are wrong between Florence and me."

"Oh, Harry;—what has she done?"

"It is rather what have I done? As for her, she has simply trusted herself to a man who has been false to her."

"Dear Harry, do not say that. What is it that you mean? It is not true about Lady Ongar?"

"Then you have heard, mother. Of course I do not know what you have heard, but it can hardly be worse than the truth. But you must not blame her. Whatever fault there may be, is all mine." Then he told her much of what had occurred in Bolton Street. We may suppose that he said nothing of that mad caress,—nothing, perhaps, of the final promise which he made to Julia as he last passed out of her presence; but he did give her to understand that he had in some way returned to his old passion for the woman whom he had first loved.

I should describe Mrs. Clavering in language too highly eulogistic were I to lead the reader to believe that she was altogether averse to such advantages as would accrue to her son from a marriage so brilliant as that which he might now make with the grandly dowered widow of the late earl. Mrs. Clavering by no means despised worldly goods; and she had, moreover, an idea that her highly gifted son was better adapted to the spending than to the making of money. It had come to be believed at the rectory that though Harry had worked very hard at college,—as is the case with many highly born young gentlemen,—and though he would, undoubtedly, continue to work hard if he were thrown among congenial occupations,—such as politics and the like,—nevertheless, he would never excel greatly in any drudgery that would be necessary for the making of money. There had been something to be proud of in this, but there had, of course, been more to regret. But now if Harry were to marry Lady Ongar, all trouble on that score would be over. But poor Florence! When Mrs. Clavering allowed herself to think of the matter she knew that Florence's claims should be held as paramount. And when she thought further and thought seriously, she knew also that Harry's honour and Harry's happiness demanded that he should be true to the girl to whom his hand had been promised. And, then, was not Lady Ongar's name tainted? It might be that she had suffered cruel ill-usage in this. It might be that no such taint had been deserved. Mrs. Clavering could plead the injured woman's cause when speaking of it without any close reference to her own belongings ; but it would have been very grievous to her, even had there been no Florence Burton in the case, that her son should make his fortune by marrying a woman as to whose character the world was in doubt.

She came to him late in the evening when his sister and father had just left him, and sitting with her hand upon his, spoke one word, which perhaps had more weight with Harry than any word that had yet been spoken. "Have you slept, dear?" she said.

"A little before my father came in."

"My darling," she said,—"you will be true to Florence ; will you not?" Then there was a pause. "My own Harry, tell me that you will be true where your truth is due."

"I will, mother," he said.

"My own boy ; my darling boy ; my own true gentleman !" Harry felt that he did not deserve the praise ; but praise undeserved, though it may be satire in disguise, is often very useful.

CHAPTER XXXV.

PARTING.

On the next day Harry was not better, but the doctor still said that there was no cause for alarm. He was suffering from a low fever, and his sister had better be kept out of his room. He would not sleep, and was restless, and it might be some time before he could return to London.

Early in the day the rector came into his son's bedroom, and told him and his mother, who was there, the news which he had just heard from the great house. "Hugh has come home," he said, "and is going out yachting for the rest of the summer. They are going to Norway in Jack Stuart's yacht. Archie is going with them." Now Archie was known to be a great man in a yacht, cognizant of ropes, well up in booms and spars, very intimate with bolts, and one to whose hands a tiller came as naturally as did the saddle of a steeple-chase horse to the legs of his friend Doodles. "They are going to fish," said the rector.

But Jack Stuart's yacht is only a river-boat,—or just big enough for Cowes harbour, but nothing more," said Harry, roused in his bed to some excitement by the news.

"I know nothing about Jack Stuart or his boat either," said the rector ; "but that's what they told me. He's down here, at any rate, for I saw the servant that came with him."

"What a shame it is," said Mrs. Clavering,—"a scandalous shame."

"You mean his going away?" said the rector.

"Of course I do ;—his leaving her here by herself, all alone. He can have no heart ;—after losing her child and suffering as she has done. It makes me ashamed of my own name."

" You can't alter him, my dear. He has his good qualities and his bad,—and the bad ones are by far the more conspicuous."

" I don't know any good qualities he has."

" He does not get into debt. He will not destroy the property. He will leave the family after him as well off as it was before him,—and though he is a hard man, he does nothing actively cruel. Think of Lord Ongar, and then you'll remember that there are worse men than Hugh. Not that I like him. I am never comfortable for a moment in his presence. I always feel that he wants to quarrel with me, and that I almost want to quarrel with him."

" I detest him," said Harry, from beneath the bedclothes.

" You won't be troubled with him any more this summer, for he means to be off in less than a week."

" And what is she to do ? " asked Mrs. Clavering.

" Live here as she has done ever since Julia married. I don't see that it will make much difference to her. He's never with her when he's in England, and I should think she must be more comfortable without him than with him."

" It's a great catch for Archie," said Harry.

" Archie Clavering is a fool," said Mrs. Clavering.

" They say he understands a yacht," said the rector, who then left the room.

The rector's news was all true. Sir Hugh Clavering had come down to the Park, and had announced his intention of going to Norway in Jack Stuart's yacht. Archie also had been invited to join the party. Sir Hugh intended to leave the Thames in about a week, and had not thought it necessary to give his wife any intimation of the fact, till he told her himself of his intention. He took, I think, a delight in being thus over-harsh in his harshness to her. He proved to himself thus not only that he was master, but that he would be master without any let or drawback, without compunctions, and even without excuses for his ill-conduct. There should be no plea put in by him in his absences, that he had only gone to catch a few fish, when his intentions had been other than piscatorial. He intended to do as he liked now and always,—and he intended that his wife should know that such was his intention. She was now childless, and therefore he had no other terms to keep with her than those which appertained to her necessities for bed and board. There was the house, and she might live in it; and there were the butchers and the bakers, and other tradesmen to supply her wants. Nay ; —there were the old carriage and the old horses at her disposal, if they could be of any service to her. Such were Sir Hugh Clavering's ideas as to the bonds inflicted upon him by his marriage vows.

" I'm going to Norway next week." It was thus Sir Hugh communicated his intention to his wife within five minutes of their first greeting.

" To Norway, Hugh ? "

" Yes ;—why not to Norway ? I and one or two others have got some fishing there. Archie is going too. It will keep him from spending his money;—or rather from spending money which isn't his."

" And for how long will you be gone ? "

It was part of Sir Hugh Clavering's theory as to these matters that there should be no lying in the conduct of them. He would not condescend to screen any part of his doings by a falsehood;—so he answered this question with exact truth.

" I don't suppose we shall be back before October."

" Not before October ? "

" No. We are talking of putting in on the coast of Normandy somewhere; and probably may run down to Brittany. I shall be back, at any rate, for the hunting. As for the partridges, the game has gone so much to the devil here, that they are not worth coming for."

" You'll be away four months ! "

" I suppose I shall if I don't come back till October." Then he left her, calculating that she would have considered the matter before he returned, and have decided that no good could come to her from complaint. She knew his purpose now, and would no doubt reconcile herself to it quickly;—perhaps with a few tears, which would not hurt him if he did not see them.

But this blow was almost more than Lady Clavering could bear,—was more than she could bear in silence. Why she should have grudged her husband his trip abroad, seeing that his presence in England could hardly have been a solace to her, it is hard to understand. Had he remained in England, he would rarely have been at Clavering Park; and when he was at the Park he would rarely have given her the benefit of his society. When they were together he was usually scolding her, or else sitting in gloomy silence, as though that phase of his life was almost insupportable to him. He was so unusually disagreeable in his intercourse with her, that his absence, one would think, must be preferable to his presence. But women can bear anything better than desertion. Cruelty is bad, but neglect is worse than cruelty, and desertion worse even than neglect. To be treated as though she were not in existence, or as though her existence were a nuisance simply to be endured, and, as far as possible, to be forgotten, was more than even Lady Clavering could bear without complaint. When her husband left her, she sat meditating how she might turn against her oppressor. She was a woman not apt for fighting,—unlike her sister, who knew well how to use the cudgels in her own behalf; she was timid, not gifted with a full flow of words, prone to sink and become dependent; but she,—even she,—with all these deficiencies,—felt that she must make some stand against the outrage to which she was now to be subjected.

" Hugh," she said, when next she saw him, " you can't really mean that you are going to leave me from this time till the winter ? "

" I said nothing about the winter."

" Well,—till October ? "

" I said that I was going, and I usually mean what I say."

"I cannot believe it, Hugh; I cannot bring myself to think that you will be so cruel."

"Look here, Hermy, if you take to calling names I won't stand it."

"And I won't stand it, either. What am I to do? Am I to be here in this dreadful barrack of a house all alone? How would you like it? Would you bear it for one month, let alone four or five? I won't remain here; I tell you that fairly."

"Where do you want to go?"

"I don't want to go anywhere, but I'll go away somewhere and die; —I will indeed. I'll destroy myself, or something."

"Psha!"

"Yes; of course it's a joke to you. What have I done to deserve this? Have I ever done anything that you told me not? It's all because of Hughy,—my darling,—so it is; and it's cruel of you, and not like a husband; and it's not manly. It's very cruel. I didn't think anybody would have been so cruel as you are to me." Then she broke down and burst into tears.

"Have you done, Hermy?" said her husband.

"No; I've not done."

"Then go on again," said he.

But in truth she had done, and could only repeat her last accusation. "You're very, very cruel."

"You said that before."

"And I'll say it again. I'll tell everybody; so I will. I'll tell your uncle at the rectory, and he shall speak to you."

"Look here, Hermy; I can bear a deal of nonsense from you because some women are given to talk nonsense; but if I find you telling tales about me out of this house, and especially to my uncle, or indeed to any-body, I'll let you know what it is to be cruel."

"You can't be worse than you are."

"Don't try me; that's all. And as I suppose you have now said all that you've got to say, if you please we will regard that subject as finished." The poor woman had said all that she could say, and had no further means of carrying on the war. In her thoughts she could do so; in her thoughts she could wander forth out of the gloomy house in the night, and perish in the damp and cold, leaving a paper behind her to tell the world that her husband's cruelty had brought her to that pass. Or she would go to Julia and leave him for ever. Julia, she thought, would still receive her. But as to one thing she had certainly made up her mind; she would go with her complaint to Mrs. Clavering at the rectory, let her lord and master show his anger in whatever form he might please.

The next day Sir Hugh himself made her a proposition which some-what softened the aspect of affairs. This he did in his usual voice, with something of a smile on his face, and speaking as though he were altogether oblivious of the scenes of yesterday. "I was thinking, Hermy," he said, "that you might have Julia down here while I am away."

" Have Julia here ? "

" Yes ; why not ? She'll come, I'm sure, when she knows that my back is turned."

" I've never thought about asking her,—at least not lately."

" No ; of course. But you might as well do so now. It seems that she never goes to Ongar Park, and, as far as I can learn, never will. I'm going to see her myself."

" You going to see her ? "

" Yes ; Lord Ongar's people want to know whether she can be induced to give up the place ; that is, to sell her interest in it. I have promised to see her. Do you write her a letter first, and tell her that I want to see her ; and ask her also to come here as soon as she can leave London."

" But wouldn't the lawyers do it better than you ? "

" Well ;—one would think so ; but I am commissioned to make her a kind of apology from the whole Courton family. They fancy they've been hard upon her ; and, by George, I believe they have. I may be able to say a word for myself too. If she isn't a fool she'll put her anger in her pocket, and come down to you."

Lady Clavering liked the idea of having her sister with her, but she was not quite meek enough to receive the permission now given her as full compensation for the injury done. She said that she would do as he had bidden her, and then went back to her own grievances. " I don't suppose Julia, even if she would come for a little time, would find it very pleasant to live in such a place as this, all alone."

" She wouldn't be all alone when you are with her," said Hugh, gruffly, and then again went out, leaving his wife to become used to her misfortune by degrees.

It was not surprising that Lady Clavering should dislike her solitude at Clavering Park house, nor surprising that Sir Hugh should find the place disagreeable. The house was a large, square, stone building, with none of the prettinesses of modern country-houses about it. The gardens were away from the house, and the cold desolate flat park came up close around the windows. The rooms were large and lofty,—very excellent for the purpose of a large household, but with nothing of that snug, pretty comfort which solitude requires for its solace. The furniture was old and heavy, and the hangings were dark in colour. Lady Clavering when alone there,—and she generally was alone,—never entered the rooms on the ground-floor. Nor did she ever pass through the wilderness of a hall by which the front-door was to be reached. Throughout more than half her days she never came downstairs at all ; but when she did so, preparatory to being dragged about the parish lanes in the old family carriage, she was let out at a small side-door ; and so it came to pass that during the absences of the lord of the mansion, the shutters were not even moved from any of the lower windows. Under such circumstances there can be no wonder that Lady Clavering regarded the place as a prison. " I wish you could come upon it unawares, and see how gloomy it is," she said to him. "I don't think you'd stand it alone for two days, let alone all your life."

"I'll shut it up altogether if you like," said he.

"And where am I to go?" she asked.

"You can go to Moor Hall if you please." Now Moor Hall was a small house, standing on a small property belonging to Sir Hugh, in that part of Devonshire which lies north of Dartmoor, somewhere near the Holsworthy region, and which is perhaps as ugly, as desolate, and as remote as any part of England. Lady Clavering had heard much of Moor Hall, and dreaded it as the heroine, made to live in the big grim castle low down among the Apennines, dreads the smaller and grimmer castle which is known to exist somewhere higher up in the mountains.

"Why couldn't I go to Brighton?" said Lady Clavering boldly.

"Because I don't choose it," said Sir Hugh. After that she did go to the rectory, and told Mrs. Clavering all her troubles. She had written to her sister, having, however, delayed the doing of this for two or three days, and she had not at this time received an answer from Lady Ongar. Nor did she hear from her sister till after Sir Hugh had left her. It was on the day before his departure that she went to the rectory, finding herself driven to this act of rebellion by his threat of Moor Hall. "I will never go there unless I am dragged there by force," she said to Mrs. Clavering.

"I don't think he means that," said Mrs. Clavering. "He only wants to make you understand that you'd better remain at the Park."

"But if you knew what a house it is to be all alone in!"

"Dear Hermione, I do know! But you must come to us oftener, and let us endeavour to make it better for you."

"But how can I do that? How can I come to his uncle's house, just because my own husband has made my own home so wretched that I cannot bear it. I'm ashamed to do that. I ought not to be telling you all this, of course. I don't know what he'd do if he knew it; but it is so hard to bear it all without telling some one."

"My poor dear!"

"I sometimes think I'll ask Mr. Clavering to speak to him, and to tell him at once that I will not submit to it any longer. Of course he would be mad with rage, but if he were to kill me, I should like it better than having to go on in this way. I'm sure he is only waiting for me to die."

Mrs. Clavering said all that she could to comfort the poor woman, but there was not much that she could say. She had strongly advocated the plan of having Lady Ongar at the Park, thinking perhaps that Harry would be more safe while that lady was at Clavering, than he might perhaps be if she remained in London. But Mrs. Clavering doubted much whether Lady Ongar would consent to make such a visit. She regarded Lady Ongar as a hard, worldly, pleasure-seeking woman,—sinned against perhaps in much, but also sinning in much herself,—to whom the desolation of the Park would be even more unendurable than it was to the elder sister. But of this, of course, she said nothing. Lady Clavering left her, somewhat quieted, if not comforted; and went back to pass her last evening with her husband.

"Upon second thought, I'll go by the first train," he said, as he saw her for a moment before she went up to dress. "I shall have to be off from here a little after six, but I don't mind that in summer." Thus she was to be deprived of such gratification as there might have been in breakfasting with him on the last morning! It might be hard to say in what that gratification would have consisted. She must by this time have learned that his presence gave her none of the pleasures usually expected from society. He slighted her in everything. He rarely vouchsafed to her those little attentions which all women expect from all gentlemen. If he handed her a plate, or cut for her a morsel of bread from the loaf, he showed by his manner and by his brow that the doing so was a nuisance to him. At their meals he rarely spoke to her,—having always at breakfast a paper or a book before him, and at dinner devoting his attention to a dog at his feet. Why should she have felt herself cruelly ill-used in this matter of his last breakfast,—so cruelly ill-used that she wept afresh over it as she dressed herself,—seeing that she would lose so little? Because she loved the man;—loved him, though she now thought that she hated him. We very rarely, I fancy, love those whose love we have not either possessed or expected,—or at any rate for whose love we have not hoped; but when it has once existed, ill-usage will seldom destroy it. Angry as she was with the man, ready as she was to complain of him, to rebel against him,—perhaps to separate herself from him for ever, nevertheless she found it to be a cruel grievance that she should not sit at table with him on the morning of his going. "Jackson shall bring me a cup of coffee as I'm dressing," he said, "and I'll breakfast at the club." She knew that there was no reason for this, except that breakfasting at his club was more agreeable to him than breakfasting with his wife.

She had got rid of her tears before she came down to dinner, but still she was melancholy and almost lachrymose. This was the last night, and she felt that something special ought to be said; but she did not know what she expected, or what it was that she herself wished to say. I think that she was longing for an opportunity to forgive him,—only that he would not be forgiven. If he would have spoken one soft word to her, she would have accepted that one word as an apology; but no such word came. He sat opposite to her at dinner, drinking his wine and feeding his dog; but he was no more gracious to her at this dinner than he had been on any former day. She sat there pretending to eat, speaking a dull word now and then, to which his answer was a monosyllable, looking out at him from under her eyes, through the candlelight, to see whether any feeling was moving him; and then having pretended to eat a couple of strawberries she left him to himself. Still, however, this was not the last. There would come some moment for an embrace,—for some cold half-embrace, in which he would be forced to utter something of a farewell.

He, when he was left alone, first turned his mind to the subject of Jack Stuart and his yacht. He had on that day received a letter from a noble friend,—a friend so noble that he was able to take liberties even with Sir Hugh Clavering,—in which his noble friend had told him that he was a fool to trust himself on so long an expedition in Jack Stuart's little boat. Jack, the noble friend said, knew nothing of the matter, and as for the masters who were hired for the sailing of such crafts, their only object was to keep out as long as possible, with an eye to their wages and perquisites. It might be all very well for Jack Stuart, who had nothing in the world to lose but his life and his yacht; but his noble friend thought that any such venture on the part of Sir Hugh was simple tomfoolery. But Sir Hugh was an obstinate man, and none of the Claverings were easily made afraid by personal danger. Jack Stuart might know nothing about the management of a boat, but Archie did. And as for the smallness of the craft,—he knew of a smaller craft which had been out on the Norway coast during the whole of the last season. So he drove that thought away from his mind, with no strong feelings of gratitude towards his noble friend.

And then for a few moments he thought of his own home. What had his wife done for him, that he should put himself out of his way to do much for her? She had brought him no money. She had added nothing either by her wit, beauty, or rank to his position in the world. She had given him no heir. What had he received from her that he should endure her commonplace conversation, and washed-out, dowdy prettinesses? Perhaps some momentary feeling of compassion, some twang of conscience, came across his heart, as he thought of it all; but if so he checked it instantly, in accordance with the teachings of his whole life. He had made his reflections on all these things, and had tutored his mind to certain resolutions, and would not allow himself to be carried away by any womanly softness. She had her house, her carriage, her bed, her board, and her clothes; and seeing how very little she herself had contributed to the common fund, her husband determined that in having those things she had all that she had a right to claim. Then he drank a glass of sherry, and went into the drawing-room with that hard smile upon his face, which he was accustomed to wear when he intended to signify to his wife that she might as well make the best of existing things, and not cause unnecessary trouble, by giving herself airs or assuming that she was unhappy.

He had his cup of coffee, and she had her cup of tea, and she made one or two little attempts at saying something special,—something that might lead to a word or two as to their parting; but he was careful and crafty, and she was awkward and timid,—and she failed. He had hardly been there an hour, when looking at his watch he declared that it was ten o'clock, and that he would go to bed. Well; perhaps it might be best to bring it to an end, and to go through this embrace, and have done with it! Any tender word that was to be spoken on either side, it

HUSBAND AND WIFE.

was now clear to her, must be spoken in that last farewell. There was a tear in her eye as she rose to kiss him; but the tear was not there of her own good will, and she strove to get rid of it without his seeing it. As he spoke he also rose, and having lit for himself a bed-candle was ready to go. "Good-by, Hermy," he said, submitting himself, with the candle in his hand, to the inevitable embrace.

"Good-by, Hugh; and God bless you," she said, putting her arms round his neck. "Pray,—pray take care of yourself."

"All right," he said. His position with the candle was awkward, and he wished that it might be over.

But she had a word prepared which she was determined to utter,—poor weak creature that she was. She still had her arm round his shoulders, so that he could not escape without shaking her off, and her forehead was almost resting on his bosom. "Hugh," she said, "you must not be angry with me for what I said to you."

"Very well," said he;—"I won't."

"And, Hugh," said she; "of course I can't like your going."

"Oh, yes, you will," said he.

"No;—I can't like it; but, Hugh, I will not think ill of it any more. Only be here as much as you can when you come home."

"All right," said he; then he kissed her forehead and escaped from her, and went his way, telling himself, as he went, that she was a fool.

That was the last he saw of her,—before his yachting commenced; but she,—poor fool,—was up by times in the morning, and, peeping out between her curtains as the early summer sun glanced upon her eyelids, saw him come forth from the porch and descend the great steps, and get into his dog-cart and drive himself away. Then, when the sound of the gig could be no longer heard, and when her eyes could no longer catch the last expiring speck of his hat, the poor fool took herself to bed again and cried herself to sleep.

CHAPTER XXXVI.

Captain Clavering makes his last Attempt.

The yachting scheme was first proposed to Archie by his brother Hugh. "Jack says that he can make a berth for you, and you'd better come," said the elder brother, understanding that when his edict had thus gone forth, the thing was as good as arranged. "Jack finds the boat and men, and I find the grub and wine,—and pay for the fishing," said Hugh; "so you need not make any bones about it." Archie was not disposed to make any bones about it as regarded his acceptance either of the berth or of the grub and wine, and as he would be expected to earn his passage by his work, there was no necessity for any scruple; but there arose the question whether he had not got more important fish to fry. He had not as yet made his proposal to Lady Ongar, and although he now knew that he had nothing to hope from the Russian Spy,—nevertheless he thought that he might as well try his own hand at the venture. His resolution on this head was always stronger after dinner than before, and generally became stronger and more strong as the evening advanced;—so that he usually went to bed with a firm determination " to pop," as he called it to his friend Doodles, early on the next day; but distance affected him as well as the hour of the day, and his purpose would become surprisingly cool in the neighbourhood of Bolton Street. When, however, his brother suggested that he should be taken altogether away from the scene of action, he thought of the fine income and of Ongar Park with pangs of regret, and ventured upon a mild remonstrance. " But there's this affair of Julia, you know," said he.

" I thought that was all off," said Hugh.

" O dear, no ; not off at all. I haven't asked her yet."

" I know you've not ; and I don't suppose you ever will."

" Yes, I shall ;—that is to say, I mean it. I was advised not to be in too much of a hurry ; that is to say, I thought it best to let her settle down a little after her first seeing me."

" To recover from her confusion ? "

" Well, not exactly that. I don't suppose she was confused."

" I should say not. My idea is that you haven't a ghost of chance, and that as you haven't done anything all this time, you need not trouble yourself now."

" But I have done something," said Archie, thinking of his seventy pounds.

" You may as well give it up, for she means to marry Harry."

" No ! "

" But I tell you she does. While you've been thinking he's been doing. From what I hear he may have her to-morrow for the asking."

" But he's engaged to that girl whom they had with them down at the rectory," said Archie, in a tone which showed with what horror he should regard any inconstancy towards Florence Burton on the part of Harry Clavering.

" What does that matter ? You don't suppose he'll let seven thousand a year slip through his fingers because he had promised to marry a little girl like her ? If her people choose to proceed against him they'll make him pay swinging damages ; that is all."

Archie did not like this idea at all, and became more than ever intent on his own matrimonial prospects. He almost thought that he had a right to Lady Ongar's money, and he certainly did think that a monstrous injustice was done to him by this idea of a marriage between her and his cousin. " I mean to ask her as I've gone so far, certainly," said he.

" You can do as you like about that."

" Yes ; of course I can do as I like ; but when a fellow has gone in for a thing, he likes to see it through." He was still thinking of the

seventy pounds which he had invested, and which he could now recover
only out of Lady Ongar's pocket.

"And you mean to say you won't come to Norway?"

"Well; if she accepts me——"

"If she accepts you," said Hugh, "of course you can't come; but
supposing she don't?"

"In that case, I might as well do that as anything else," said
Archie. Whereupon Sir Hugh signified to Jack Stuart that Archie would
join the party, and went down to Clavering with no misgiving on that
head.

Some few days after this there was another little dinner at the
military club, to which no one was admitted but Archie and his friend
Doodles. Whenever these prandial consultations were held, Archie paid
the bill. There were no spoken terms to that effect, but the regulation
seemed to come naturally to both of them. Why should Doodles be taken
from his billiards half-an-hour earlier than usual, and devote a portion of
the calculating powers of his brain to Archie's service without compensation? And a richer vintage was needed when so much thought was
required, the burden of which Archie would not of course allow to fall on
his friend's shoulders. Were not this explained, the experienced reader
would regard the devoted friendship of Doodles as exaggerated.

"I certainly shall ask her to-morrow," said Archie, looking with
a thoughtful cast of countenance through the club window into the street.
"It may be hurrying the matter a little, but I can't help that." He
spoke in a somewhat boastful tone, as though he were proud of himself
and had forgotten that he had said the same words once or twice before.

"Make her know that you're there; that's everything," said Doodles.
"Since I fathomed that woman in Mount Street, I've felt that you must
make the score off your own bat, if you're to make it at all."

"You did that well," said Archie, who knew that the amount of
pleasing encouragement which he might hope to get from his friend, must
depend on the praise which he himself should bestow. "Yes; you certainly did bowl her over uncommon well."

"That kind of thing just comes within my line," said Doodles, with
conscious pride. "Now, as to asking Lady Ongar downright to marry me,
—upon my word I believe I should be half afraid of doing it myself."

"I've none of that kind of feeling," said Archie.

"It comes more in your way, I daresay," said Doodles. "But for
me, what I like is a little bit of management,—what I call a touch of the
diplomatic. You'll be able to see her to-morrow?"

"I hope so. I shall go early,—that is, as soon as I've looked through
the papers and written a few letters. Yes, I think she'll see me. And as
for what Hugh says about Harry Clavering, why, d—— it, you know, a
fellow can't go on in that way; can he?"

"Because of the other girl, you mean?"

"He has had her down among all our people, just as though they were going to be married to-morrow. If a man is to do that kind of thing, what woman can be safe?"

"I wonder whether she likes him?" asked the crafty Doodles.

"She did like him, I fancy, in her calf days; but that means nothing. She knows what she's at now, bless you, and she'll look to the future. It's my son who'll have the Clavering property and be the baronet, not his. You see what a string to my bow that is."

When this banquet was over, Doodles made something of a resolution that it should be the last to be eaten on that subject. The matter had lost its novelty, and the price paid to him was not sufficient to secure his attention any longer. "I shall be here to-morrow at four," he said, as he rose from his chair with the view of retreating to the smoking-room, "and then we shall know all about it. Whichever way it's to be, it isn't worth your while keeping such a thing as that in hand any longer. I should say give her her chance to-morrow, and then have done with it." Archie in reply to this declared that those were exactly his sentiments, and then went away to prepare himself in silence and solitude for the next day's work.

On the following day at two o'clock Lady Ongar was sitting alone in the front room on the ground-floor in Bolton Street. Of Harry Clavering's illness she had as yet heard nothing, nor of his absence from London. She had not seen him since he had parted from her on that evening when he had asked her to be his wife, and the last words she had heard from his lips had made this request. She, indeed, had then bade him be true to her rival,—to Florence Burton. She had told him this in spite of her love,—of her love for him and of his for her. They two, she had said, could not now become man and wife;—but he had not acknowledged the truth of what she had said. She could not write to him. She could make no overtures. She could ask no questions. She had no friend in whom she could place confidence. She could only wait for him, till he should come to her or send to her, and let her know what was to be her fate.

As she now sat she held a letter in her hand which had just been brought to her from Sophie,—from her poor famished, but indefatigable Sophie. Sophie she had not seen since they had parted on the railway platform, and then the parting was supposed to be made in lasting enmity. Desolate as she was, she had congratulated herself much on her escape from Sophie's friendship, and was driven by no qualms of her heart to long for a renewal of the old ties. But it was not so with the more affectionate Sophie; and Sophie therefore had written,— as follows:—

Mount Street—Friday morning.

DEAREST DEAREST JULIE,—My heart is so sad that I cannot keep my silence longer. What; can such friendship as ours has been be made to die all in a minute? Oh, no;—not at least in my bosom, which is filled with love for my Julie. And my Julie will not turn from her friend, who has been so true to her,—ah, at such moments too,—oh, yes, at such moments!—just for an angry word, or a little indiscretion. What was it after all about my brother? Bah! He is a fool; that is all. If you shall wish it, I will never speak to him again. What is my brother to me, compared to my Julie? My brother is nothing to me. I tell him we go to that accursed island,—accursed island because my Julie has quarrelled with me there,— and he arranges himself to follow us. What could I do? I could not tie him up by the leg in his London club. He is a man whom no one can tie up by the leg. Mon Dieu, no. He is very hard to tie up.

Do I wish him for your husband? Never! Why should I wish him for your husband? If I was a man, my Julie, I should wish you for myself. But I am not, and why should you not have him whom you like the best? If I was you, with your beauty and money and youth, I would have any man that I liked,—everything. I know, of course,—for did I not see? It is that young Clavering to whom your little heart wishes to render itself;—not the captain who is a fool,—such a fool! but the other who is not a fool, but a fine fellow;—and so handsome! Yes; there is no doubt as to that. He is beautiful as a Phœbus. [This was good-natured on the part of Sophie, who, as the reader may remember, hated Harry Clavering herself.]

Well,—why should he not be your own? As for your poor Sophie, she would do all in her power to assist the friend whom she love. There is that little girl,—yes; it is true as I told you. But little girls cannot have all they want always. He is a gay deceiver. These men who are so beautiful as Phœbus are always deceivers. But you need not be the one deceived;—you with your money and your beauty and your —what you call rank. No, I think not; and I think that little girl must put up with it, as other little girls have done, since the men first learned how to tell lies. That is my advice, and if you will let me I can give you good assistance.

Dearest Julie, think of all this, and do not banish your Sophie. I am so true to you, that I cannot live without you. Send me back one word of permission, and I will come to you, and kneel at your feet. And in the meantime, I am

Your most devoted friend,
SOPHIE.

Lady Ongar, on the receipt of this letter, was not at all changed in her purpose with reference to Madame Gordeloup. She knew well enough where her Sophie's heart was placed, and would yield to no further pressure from that quarter; but Sophie's reasoning, nevertheless, had its effect. She, Lady Ongar, with her youth, her beauty, her wealth, and her rank, why should she not have that one thing which alone could make her happy, seeing, as she did see, or as she thought she saw, that in making herself happy she could do so much, could confer such great blessings on him she loved? She had already found that the money she had received as the price of herself had done very little towards making her happy in her present state. What good was it to her that she had a carriage and horses and two footmen six feet high? One pleasant word from lips that she could love,—from the lips of man or woman that she could esteem,— would be worth it all. She had gone down to her pleasant place in the country,—a place so pleasant that it had a fame of its own among the luxuriantly pleasant seats of the English country gentry; she had gone there, expecting to be happy in the mere feeling that it was all her own; and the whole thing had been to her so unutterably sad, so wretched in the severity of its desolation, that she had been unable to endure her life amidst the shade of her own trees. All her apples hitherto had turned to ashes between her teeth, because her fate had forced her to attempt the eating of them alone. But if she could give the fruit to him,—if she could make the apples over, so that they should all be his, and not hers, then would there not come to her some of the sweetness of the juice of them ?

She declared to herself that she would not tempt this man to be untrue to his troth, were it not that in doing so she would so greatly benefit himself. Was it not manifest that Harry Clavering was a gentleman, qualified to shine among men of rank and fashion, but not qualified to make his way by his own diligence ? In saying this of him, she did not know how heavy was the accusation that she brought against him ; but what woman, within her own breast, accuses the man she loves ? Were he to marry Florence Burton, would he not ruin himself, and probably ruin her also ? But she could give him all that he wanted. Though Ongar Park to her alone was, with its rich pastures and spreading oaks and lowing cattle, desolate as the Dead Sea shore, for him,—and for her with him,—would it not be the very paradise suited to them ? Would it not be the heaven in which such a Phœbus should shine amidst the gyrations of his satellites ? A Phœbus going about his own field in knickerbockers, and with attendant satellites, would possess a divinity which, as she thought, might make her happy. As she thought of all this, and asked herself these questions, there was an inner conscience which told her that she had no right to Harry's love or Harry's hand ; but still she could not cease to long that good things might come to her, though those good things had not been deserved. Alas, good things not deserved too often lose their goodness when they come ! As she was sitting with Sophie's letter in her hand the door was opened, and Captain Clavering was announced.

Captain Archibald Clavering was again dressed in his very best, but he did not even yet show by his demeanour that aptitude for the business now in hand of which he had boasted on the previous evening to his friend. Lady Ongar, I think, partly guessed the object of his visit. She had perceived, or perhaps had unconsciously felt, on the occasion of his former coming, that the visit had not been made simply from motives of civility. She had known Archie in old days, and was aware that the splendour of his vestments had a significance. Well, if anything of that kind was to be done, the sooner it was done the better.

" Julia," he said, as soon as he was seated, " I hope I have the pleasure of seeing you quite well ? "

" Pretty well, I thank you," said she.

" You have been out of town, I think ? " She told him that she had been in the Isle of Wight for a day or two, and then there was a short silence. " When I heard that you were gone," he said, " I feared that perhaps you were ill ! "

" O dear, no ; nothing of that sort."

" I am so glad," said Archie ; and then he was silent again. He had, however, as he was aware, thrown a great deal of expression into his inquiries after her health, and he had now to calculate how he could best use the standing-ground that he had made for himself.

" Have you seen my sister lately ? " she asked.

" Your sister ? no. She is always at Clavering. I think it doosed wrong of Hugh, the ways he goes on, keeping her down there, while he is up here in London. It isn't at all my idea of what a husband ought to do."

" I suppose she likes it," said Lady Ongar.

" Oh, if she likes it, that's a different thing, of course," said Archie. Then there was another pause.

" Don't you find yourself rather lonely here sometimes ? " he asked.

Lady Ongar felt that it would be better for all parties that it should be over, and that it would not be over soon unless she could help him. " Very lonely indeed," she said ; " but then I suppose that it is the fate of widows to be lonely."

" I don't see that at all," said Archie, briskly ; " —unless they are old and ugly, and that kind of thing. When a widow has become a widow after she has been married ever so many years, why then I suppose she looks to be left alone ; and I suppose they like it."

" Indeed, I can't say. I don't like it."

" Then you would wish to change ? "

" It is a very intricate subject, Captain Clavering, and one which I do not think I am quite disposed to discuss at present. After a year or two, perhaps I shall go into society again. Most widows do, I believe."

" But I was thinking of something else," said Archie, working himself up to the point with great energy, but still with many signs that he was ill at ease at his work. " I was, by Jove ! "

" And of what were you thinking, Captain Clavering ? "

" I was thinking,—of course you know, Julia, that since poor little Hughy's death, I am the next in for the title ? "

" Poor Hughy ! I'm sure you are too generous to rejoice at that."

" Indeed I am. When two fellows offered me a dinner at the club on the score of my chances, I wouldn't have it. But there's the fact ;— isn't it ? "

" There is no doubt of that, I believe."

" None on earth ; and the most of it is entailed, too ; not that Hugh would leave an acre away from the title. I'm as safe as wax as far as that is concerned. I don't suppose he ever borrowed a shilling or mortgaged an acre in his life."

" I should think he was a prudent man."

" We are both of us prudent. I will say that of myself, though I oughtn't to say it. And now, Julia,—a few words are the best after all. Look here,—if you'll take me just as I am, I'm blessed if I shan't be the happiest fellow in all London. I shall indeed. I've always been uncommon fond of you, though I never said anything about it in the old days, because,—because you see, what's the use of a man asking a girl to marry him if they haven't got a farthing between them. I think it's wrong ; I do indeed ; but it's different now, you know." It certainly was very different now.

"Captain Clavering," she said, "I'm sorry you should have troubled yourself with such an idea as this."

"Don't say that, Julia. It's no trouble ; it's a pleasure."

"But such a thing as you mean never can take place."

"Yes, it can. Why can't it ? I ain't in a hurry. I'll wait your own time, and do just whatever you wish all the while. Don't say no without thinking about it, Julia."

"It is one of those things, Captain Clavering, which want no more thinking than what a woman can give to it at the first moment."

"Ah,—you think so now, because you're surprised a little."

"Well ; I am surprised a little, as our previous intercourse was never of a nature to make such a proposition as this at all probable."

"That was merely because I didn't think it right," said Archie, who, now that he had worked himself into the vein, liked the sound of his own voice. "It was indeed."

"And I don't think it right now. You must listen to me for a moment, Captain Clavering—for fear of a mistake. Believe me, any such plan as this is quite out of the question ;—quite." In uttering that last word she managed to use a tone of voice which did make an impression on him. "I never can, under any circumstances, become your wife. You might as well look upon that as altogether decided, because it will save us both annoyance."

"You needn't be so sure yet, Julia."

"Yes, I must be sure. And unless you will promise me to drop the matter, I must,—to protect myself,—desire my servants not to admit you into the house again. I shall be sorry to do that, and I think you will save me from the necessity."

He did save her from that necessity, and before he went he gave her the required promise. "That's well," said she, tendering him her hand ; "and now we shall part friends."

"I shall like to be friends," said he, in a crestfallen voice, and with that he took his leave. It was a great comfort to him that he had the scheme of Jack Stuart's yacht and the trip to Norway for his immediate consolation.

CHAPTER XXXVII.

What Lady Ongar thought about it.

MRS. BURTON, it may perhaps be remembered, had formed in her heart a scheme of her own— a scheme of which she thought with much trepidation, and in which she could not request her husband's assistance, knowing well that he would not only not assist it, but that he would altogether disapprove of it. But yet she could not put it aside from her thoughts, believing that it might be the means of bringing Harry Clavering and Florence together. Her husband had now thoroughly condemned poor Harry, and had passed sentence against him,—not indeed openly to Florence herself, but very often in the hearing of his wife. Cecilia, womanlike, was more angry with circumstances than with the offending man,—with circumstances and with the woman who stood in Florence's way. She was perfectly willing to forgive Harry, if Harry could only be made to go right at last. He was good-looking and pleasant, and had nice ways in a house, and was altogether too valuable as a lover to be lost without many struggles. So she kept to her scheme, and at last she carried it into execution.

She started alone from her house one morning, and getting into an omnibus at Brompton had herself put down on the rising ground in Piccadilly, opposite to the Green Park. Why she had hesitated to tell the omnibus-man to stop at Bolton Street can hardly be explained; but she had felt that there would be almost a declaration of guilt in naming that locality. So she got out on the little hill, and walked up in front of the Prime Minister's house,—as it was then,—and of the yellow palace built by one of our merchant princes, and turned into the street that was all but interdicted to her by her own conscience. She turned up Bolton Street, and with a trembling hand knocked at Lady Ongar's door.

Florence in the meantime was sitting alone in Onslow Terrace. She knew now that Harry was ill at Clavering,—that he was indeed very ill, though Mrs. Clavering had assured her that his illness was not dangerous. For Mrs. Clavering had written to herself,—addressing her with all the old familiarity and affection,—with a warmth of affection that was almost more than natural. It was clear that Mrs. Clavering knew nothing of Harry's sins. Or, might it not be possible, Cecilia had suggested, that Mrs. Clavering might have known, and have resolved potentially that those sins should be banished, and become ground for some beautifully sincere repentance? Ah, how sweet it would be to receive that wicked sheep back again into the sheepfold, and then to dock him a little of his wandering powers, to fix him with some pleasant clog, to tie him down as a prudent domestic sheep should be tied, and make him the pride of the flock! But all this had been part of Cecilia's scheme, and of that scheme poor Florence knew nothing. According to Florence's view Mrs. Clavering's letter was written under a mistake. Harry had kept his secret at home, and intended to keep it for the present. But there was the letter, and Florence felt that it was impossible for her to answer it without telling the whole truth. It was very painful to her to leave unanswered so kind a letter as that, and it was quite impossible that she should write of Harry in the old strain. "It will be best that I should tell her the whole," Florence had said, "and then I shall be saved the pain of any direct communication with him." Her brother, to whom Cecilia had repeated this, applauded his sister's resolution. "Let her face it and bear it, and live it down," he had said. "Let her do it at once, so that all this maudlin sentimentality may be at an end." But Cecilia would not accede to this, and as Florence was in truth resolved, and had declared her purpose plainly, Cecilia was driven to the execution of her scheme more quickly than she had intended. In the meantime, Florence took out her little desk and wrote her letter. In tears and an agony of spirit which none can understand but women who have been driven to do the same, was it written. Could she have allowed herself to express her thoughts with passion, it would have been comparatively easy; but it behoved her to be calm, to be very quiet in her words,—

almost reticent even in the language which she chose, and to abandon her claim not only without a reproach, but almost without an allusion to her love. Whilst Cecilia was away, the letter was written, and re-written and copied; but Mrs. Burton was safe in this, that her sister-in-law had promised that the letter should not be sent till she had seen it.

Mrs. Burton, when she knocked at Lady Ongar's door, had a little note ready for the servant between her fingers. Her compliments to Lady Ongar, and would Lady Ongar oblige her by an interview. The note contained simply that, and nothing more; and when the servant took it from her, she declared her intention of waiting in the hall till she had received an answer. But she was shown into the dining-room, and there she remained for a quarter of an hour, during which time she was by no means comfortable. Probably Lady Ongar might refuse to receive her; but should that not be the case,—should she succeed in making her way into that lady's presence, how should she find the eloquence wherewith to plead her cause? At the end of the fifteen minutes, Lady Ongar herself opened the door and entered the room. "Mrs. Burton," she said, smiling, "I am really ashamed to have kept you so long; but open confession, they say, is good for the soul, and the truth is that I was not dressed. Then she led the way upstairs, and placed Mrs. Burton on a sofa, and placed herself in her own chair,—from whence she could see well, but in which she could not be well seen,—and stretched out the folds of her morning dress gracefully, and made her visitor thoroughly understand that she was at home and at her ease.

We may, I think, surmise that Lady Ongar's open confession would do her soul but little good, as it lacked truth, which is the first requisite for all confessions. Lady Ongar had been sufficiently dressed to receive any visitor, but had felt that some special preparation was necessary for the reception of the one who had now come to her. She knew well who was Mrs. Burton, and surmised accurately the purpose for which Mrs. Burton had come. Upon the manner in which she now carried herself might hang the decision of the question which was so important to her,—whether that Phœbus in knickerbockers should or should not become lord of Ongar Park. To effect success now, she must maintain an ascendancy during this coming interview, and in the maintenance of all ascendancy, much depends on the outward man or woman; and she must think a little of the words she must use, and a little, too, of her own purpose. She was fully minded to get the better of Mrs. Burton if that might be possible, but she was not altogether decided on the other point. She wished that Harry Clavering might be her own. She would have wished to pension off that Florence Burton with half her wealth, had such pensioning been possible. But not the less did she entertain some half doubts whether it would not be well that she could abandon her own wishes, and give up her own hope of happiness. Of Mrs. Burton personally she had known nothing, and having expected to see a somewhat strong-featured and perhaps rather vulgar woman, and to hear a voice painfully indicative of a strong mind, she was agreeably surprised to find a pretty, mild lady, who from the first showed that she was half afraid of what she herself was doing. "I have heard your name, Mrs. Burton," said Lady Ongar, "from our mutual friend, Mr. Clavering, and I have no doubt you have heard mine from him also." This she said in accordance with the little plan which during those fifteen minutes she had laid down for her own guidance.

Mrs. Burton was surprised, and at first almost silenced, by this open mentioning of a name which she had felt that she would have the greatest difficulty in approaching. She said, however, that it was so. She had heard Lady Ongar's name from Mr. Clavering. "We are connected, you know," said Lady Ongar. "My sister is married to his first-cousin, Sir Hugh; and when I was living with my sister at Clavering, he was at the rectory there. That was before my own marriage." She was perfectly easy in her manner, and flattered herself that the ascendancy was complete.

"I have heard as much from Mr. Clavering," said Cecilia.

"And he was very civil to me immediately on my return home. Perhaps you may have heard that also. He took this house for me, and made himself generally useful, as young men ought to do. I believe he is in the same office with your husband; is he not? I hope I may not have been the means of making him idle?"

This was all very well and very pretty, but Mrs. Burton was already beginning to feel that she was doing nothing towards the achievement of her purpose. "I suppose he has been idle," she said, "but I did not mean to trouble you about that." Upon hearing this, Lady Ongar smiled. This supposition that she had really intended to animadvert upon Harry Clavering's idleness was amusing to her as she remembered how little such idleness would signify if she could only have her way.

"Poor Harry!" she said. "I supposed his sins would be laid at my door. But my idea is, you know, that he never will do any good at such work as that."

"Perhaps not;—that is, I really can't say. I don't think Mr. Burton has ever expressed any such opinion; and if he had —— "

"If he had, you wouldn't mention it."

"I don't suppose I should, Lady Ongar;—not to a stranger."

"Harry Clavering and I are not strangers," said Lady Ongar, changing the tone of her voice altogether as she spoke.

"No; I know that. You have known him longer than we have. I am aware of that."

"Yes; before he ever dreamed of going into your husband's business, Mrs. Burton; long before he had ever been to—Stratton."

The name of Stratton was an assistance to Cecilia, and seemed to have been spoken with the view of enabling her to commence her work. "Yes," she said, "but nevertheless he did go to Stratton. He went to Stratton, and there he became acquainted with my sister-in-law, Florence Burton."

"I am aware of it, Mrs. Burton."

" And he also became engaged to her."

" I am aware of that too. He has told me as much himself."

" And has he told you whether he means to keep, or to break that engagement ? "

" Ah, Mrs. Burton, is that question fair ? Is it fair either to him, or to me ? If he has taken me into his confidence and has not taken you, should I be doing well to betray him ? Or if there can be anything in such a secret specially interesting to myself, why should I be made to tell it to you ? "

" I think the truth is always the best, Lady Ongar."

" Truth is always better than a lie ;—so at least people say, though they sometimes act differently ; but silence may be better than either."

" This is a matter, Lady Ongar, in which I cannot be silent. I hope you will not be angry with me for coming to you,—or for asking you these questions—— "

" O dear, no."

" But I cannot be silent. My sister-in-law must at any rate know what is to be her fate."

" Then why do you not ask him ? "

" He is ill at present."

" Ill ! Where is he ill ? Who says he is ill ? " And Lady Ongar, though she did not quite leave her chair, raised herself up and forgot all her preparations. " Where is he, Mrs. Burton ? I have not heard of his illness."

" He is at Clavering ;—at the parsonage."

" I have heard nothing of this. What ails him ? If he be really ill, dangerously ill, I conjure you to tell me. But pray tell me the truth. Let there be no tricks in such a matter as this."

" Tricks, Lady Ongar ! "

" If Harry Clavering be ill, tell me what ails him. Is he in danger ? "

" His mother in writing to Florence says that he is not in danger ; but that he is confined to the house. He has been taken by some fever." On that very morning Lady Ongar had received a letter from her sister, begging her to come to Clavering Park during the absence of Sir Hugh ; but in the letter no word had been said as to Harry's illness. Had he been seriously, or at least dangerously ill, Hermione would certainly have mentioned it. All this flashed across Julia's mind as these tidings about Harry reached her. If he were not really in danger, or even if he were, why should she betray her feeling before this woman ? " If there had been much in it," she said, resuming her former position and manners, " I should no doubt have heard of it from my sister."

" We hear that it is not dangerous," continued Mrs. Burton ; " but he is away, and we cannot see him. And, in truth, Lady Ongar, we cannot see him any more until we know that he means to deal honestly by us."

" Am I the keeper of his honesty ?"

" From what I have heard, I think you are. If you will tell me that I have heard falsely, I will go away and beg your pardon for my intrusion.

But if what I have heard be true, you must not be surprised that I show this anxiety for the happiness of my sister. If you knew her, Lady Ongar, you would know that she is too good to be thrown aside with indifference."

"Harry Clavering tells me that she is an angel,—that she is perfect."

"And if he loves her, will it not be a shame that they should be parted?"

"I said nothing about his loving her. Men are not always fond of perfection. The angels may be too angelic for this world."

"He did love her."

"So I suppose;—or at any rate he thought that he did."

"He did love her, and I believe he loves her still."

"He has my leave to do so, Mrs. Burton."

Cecilia, though she was somewhat afraid of the task which she had undertaken, and was partly awed by Lady Ongar's style of beauty and demeanour, nevertheless felt that if she still hoped to do any good, she must speak the truth out at once. She must ask Lady Ongar whether she held herself to be engaged to Harry Clavering. If she did not do this, nothing could come of the present interview.

"You say that, Lady Ongar, but do you mean it?" she asked. "We have been told that you also are engaged to marry Mr. Clavering."

"Who has told you so?"

"We have heard it. I have heard it, and have been obliged to tell my sister that I had done so."

"And who told you? Did you hear it from Harry Clavering himself?"

"I did. I heard it in part from him."

"Then why have you come beyond him to me? He must know. If he has told you that he is engaged to marry me, he must also have told you that he does not intend to marry Miss Florence Burton. It is not for me to defend him or to accuse him. Why do you come to me?"

"For mercy and forbearance," said Mrs. Burton, rising from her seat and coming over to the side of the room in which Lady Ongar was seated.

"And Miss Burton has sent you?"

"No; she does not know that I am here; nor does my husband know it. No one knows it. I have come to tell you that before God this man is engaged to become the husband of Florence Burton. She has learned to love him, and has now no other chance of happiness."

"But what of his happiness?"

"Yes; we are bound to think of that. Florence is bound to think of that above all things."

"And so am I. I love him too;—as fondly, perhaps, as she can do. I loved him first, before she had even heard his name."

"But, Lady Ongar——"

"Yes; you may ask the question if you will, and I will answer it truly." They were both standing now and confronting each other. "Or

A PLEA FOR MERCY.

I will answer it without your asking it. I was false to him. I would not marry him because he was poor ; and then I married another because he was rich. All that is true. But it does not make me love him the less now. I have loved him through it all. Yes ; you are shocked, but it is true. I have loved him through it all. And what am I to do now, if he still loves me ? I can give him wealth now."

" Wealth will not make him happy."

" It has not made me happy ; but it may help to do so with him. But with me at any rate there can be no doubt. It is his happiness to which I am bound to look. Mrs. Burton, if I thought that I could make him happy, and if he would come to me, I would marry him to-morrow, though I broke your sister's heart by doing so. But if I felt that she could do so more than I, I would leave him to her, though I broke my own. I have spoken to you very openly. Will she say as much as that ? "

" She would act in that way. I do not know what she would say."

" Then let her do so, and leave him to be the judge of his own happiness. Let her pledge herself that no reproaches shall come from her, and I will pledge myself equally. It was I who loved him first, and it is I who have brought him into this trouble. I owe him everything. Had I been true to him, he would never have thought of, never have seen, Miss Florence Burton."

All that was, no doubt, true, but it did not touch the question of Florence's right. The fact on which Mrs. Burton wished to insist, if only she knew how, was this, that Florence had not sinned at all, and that Florence therefore ought not to bear any part of the punishment. It might be very true that Harry's fault was to be excused in part because of Lady Ongar's greater and primary fault ;—but why should Florence be the scapegoat ?

" You should think of his honour as well as his happiness," said Mrs. Burton at last.

" That is rather severe, Mrs. Burton, considering that it is said to me in my own house. Am I so low as that, that his honour will be tarnished if I become his wife ? " But she, in saying this, was thinking of things of which Mrs. Burton knew nothing.

" His honour will be tarnished," said she, " if he do not marry her whom he has promised to marry. He was welcomed by her father and mother to their house, and then he made himself master of her heart. But it was not his till he had asked for it, and had offered his own and his hand in return for it. Is he not bound to keep his promise ? He cannot be bound to you after any such fashion as that. If you are solicitous for his welfare, you should know that if he would live with the reputation of a gentleman, there is only one course open to him."

" It is the old story," said Lady Ongar ; " the old story ! Has not somebody said that the gods laugh at the perjuries of lovers ? I do not know that men are inclined to be much more severe than the gods. These broken hearts are what women are doomed to bear."

" And that is to be your answer to me, Lady Ongar ? "

" No ; that is not my answer to you. That is the excuse that I make for Harry Clavering. My answer to you has been very explicit. Pardon me if I say that it has been more explicit than you had any right to expect. I have told you that I am prepared to take any step that may be most conducive to the happiness of the man whom I once injured, but whom I have always loved. I will do this, let it cost myself what it may ; and I will do this let the cost to any other woman be what it may. You cannot expect that I should love another woman better than myself." She said this, still standing, not without something more than vehemence in her tone. In her voice, in her manner, and in her eye there was that which amounted almost to ferocity. She was declaring that some sacrifice must be made, and that she recked little whether it should be of herself or of another. As she would immolate herself without hesitation, if the necessity should exist, so would she see Florence Burton destroyed without a twinge of remorse, if the destruction of Florence would serve the purpose which she had in view. You and I, O reader, may feel that the man for whom all this was to be done was not worth the passion. He had proved himself to be very far from such worth. But the passion, nevertheless, was there, and the woman was honest in what she was saying.

After this Mrs. Burton got herself out of the room as soon as she found an opening which allowed her to go. In making her farewell speech, she muttered some indistinct apology for the visit which she had been bold enough to make. " Not at all," said Lady Ongar. " You have been quite right ;—you are fighting your battle for the friend you love bravely ; and were it not that the cause of the battle must, I fear, separate us hereafter, I should be proud to know one who fights so well for her friends. And when all this is over and has been settled, in whatever way it may be settled, let Miss Burton know from me that I have been taught to hold her name and character in the highest possible esteem." Mrs. Burton made no attempt at further speech, but left the room with a low curtsey.

Till she found herself out in the street, she was unable to think whether she had done most harm or most good by her visit to Bolton Street,—whether she had in any way served Florence, or whether she had simply confessed to Florence's rival the extent of her sister's misery. That Florence herself would feel the latter to be the case, when she should know it all, Mrs. Burton was well aware. Her own ears had tingled with shame as Harry Clavering had been discussed as a grand prize for which her sister was contending with another woman,—and contending with so small a chance of success. It was terrible to her that any woman dear to her should seem to seek for a man's love. And the audacity with which Lady Ongar had proclaimed her own feelings had been terrible also to Cecilia. She was aware that she was meddling with things which were foreign to her nature, and which would be odious to her husband. But yet, was not the battle worth fighting ? It was not to be endured that Florence should seek after this thing ; but, after all, the possession of the thing in question was the only earthly good that could give any comfort to poor Florence. Even Cecilia, with all her partiality for Harry, felt that he was not worth the struggle; but it was for her now to estimate him at the price which Florence might put upon him,—not at her own price.

But she must tell Florence what had been done, and tell her on that very day of her meeting with Lady Ongar. In no other way could she stop that letter which she knew that Florence would have already written to Mrs. Clavering. And could she now tell Florence that there was ground for hope? Was it not the fact that Lady Ongar had spoken the simple and plain truth when she had said that Harry must be allowed to choose the course which appeared to him to be the best for him? It was hard, very hard, that it should be so. And was it not true also that men, as well as gods, excuse the perjuries of lovers? She wanted to have back Harry among them as one to be forgiven easily, to be petted much, and to be loved always; but, in spite of the softness of her woman's nature, she wished that he might be punished sorely if he did not so return. It was grievous to her that he should any longer have a choice in the matter. Heavens and earth! was he to be allowed to treat a woman as he had treated Florence, and was nothing to come of it? In spite both of gods and men, the thing was so grievous to Cecilia Burton, that she could not bring herself to acknowledge that it was possible. Such things had not been done in the world which she had known.

She walked the whole way home to Brompton, and had hardly perfected any plan when she reached her own door. If only Florence would allow her to write the letter to Mrs. Clavering, perhaps something might be done in that way. So she entered the house prepared to tell the story of her morning's work.

And she must tell it also to her husband in the evening! It had been hard to do the thing without his knowing of it beforehand; but it would be impossible to her to keep the thing a secret from him, now that it was done.

CHAPTER XXXVIII.

HOW TO DISPOSE OF A WIFE.

WHEN Sir Hugh came up to town there did not remain to him quite a week before the day on which he was to leave the coast of Essex in Jack Stuart's yacht for Norway, and he had a good deal to do in the meantime in the way of provisioning the boat. Fortnum and Mason, no doubt, would have done it all for him without any trouble on his part, but he was not a man to trust any Fortnum or any Mason as to the excellence of the article to be supplied, or as to the price. He desired to have good wine,—very good wine; but he did not desire to pay a very high price. No one knew better than Sir Hugh that good wine cannot be bought cheap,—but things may be costly and yet not dear; or they may be both. To such matters Sir Hugh was wont to pay very close attention himself. He had done something in that line before he left London, and immediately on his return he went to the work again, summoning Archie to his assistance, but never asking Archie's opinion,—as though Archie had been his head-butler.

Immediately on his arrival in London he cross-questioned his brother as to his marriage prospects. "I suppose you are going with us?" Hugh said to Archie, as he caught him in the hall of the house in Berkeley Square on the morning after his arrival.

"O dear, yes," said Archie. "I thought that was quite understood. I have been getting my traps together." The getting of his traps together had consisted in the ordering of a sailor's jacket with brass buttons, and three pair of white duck trousers.

"All right," said Sir Hugh. "You had better come with me into the City this morning. I am going to Boxall's in Great Thames Street."

"Are you going to breakfast here?" asked Archie.

"No; you can come to me at the Union in about an hour. I suppose you have never plucked up courage to ask Julia to marry you?"

"Yes, I did," said Archie.

"And what answer did you get?" Archie had found himself obliged to repudiate with alacrity the attack upon his courage which his brother had so plainly made; but, beyond that, the subject was one which was not pleasing to him. "Well, what did she say to you?" asked his brother, who had no idea of sparing Archie's feelings in such a matter.

"She said;—indeed I don't remember exactly what it was that she did say."

"But she refused you?"

"Yes;—she refused me. I think she wanted me to understand that I had come to her too soon after Ongar's death."

"Then she must be an infernal hypocrite;—that's all." But of any hypocrisy in this matter the reader will acquit Lady Ongar, and will understand that Archie had merely lessened the severity of his own fall by a clever excuse. After that the two brothers went to Boxall's in the City, and Archie, having been kept fagging all day, was sent in the evening to dine by himself at his own club.

Sir Hugh also was desirous of seeing Lady Ongar, and had caused his wife to say as much in that letter which she wrote to her sister. In this way an appointment had been made without any direct intercourse between Sir Hugh and his sister-in-law. They two had never met since the day on which Sir Hugh had given her away in Clavering Church. To Hugh Clavering, who was by no means a man of sentiment, this signified little or nothing. When Lady Ongar had returned a widow, and when evil stories against her had been rife, he had thought it expedient to have nothing to do with her. He did not himself care much about his sister-in-law's morals; but should his wife become much complicated with a sister damaged in character, there might come of it trouble and annoyance. Therefore, he had resolved that Lady Ongar should be dropped. But during the last few months things had in some respects changed. The Courton people,—that is to say, Lord Ongar's family,—had given Hugh Clavering to understand that, having made inquiry, they were disposed to acquit Lady Ongar, and to declare their belief that she was subject to no censure. They did not wish themselves to know her, as no intimacy between them could now be pleasant; but they had felt it to be incumbent on them to say as much as that to Sir Hugh. Sir Hugh had not even told his wife, but he had twice suggested that Lady Ongar should be asked to Clavering Park. In answer to both these invitations, Lady Ongar had declined to go to Clavering Park.

And now Sir Hugh had a commission on his hands from the same Courton people, which made it necessary that he should see his sister-in-law, and Julia had agreed to receive him. To him, who was very hard in such matters, the idea of his visit was not made disagreeable by any remembrance of his own harshness to the woman whom he was going to see. He cared nothing about that, and it had not occurred to him that she would care much. But, in truth, she did care very much, and when the hour was coming on which Sir Hugh was to appear, she thought much of the manner in which it would become her to receive him. He had condemned her in that matter as to which any condemnation is an insult to a woman; and he had so condemned her, being her brother-in-law and her only natural male friend. In her sorrow she should have been able to lean upon him; but from the first, without any inquiry, he had believed the worst of her, and had withdrawn from her altogether his support, when the slightest support from him would have been invaluable to her. Could she forgive this? Never; never! She was not a woman to wish to forgive such an offence. It was an offence which it would be despicable in her to forgive. Many had offended her, some had injured her, one or two had insulted her; but to her thinking, no one had so offended her, had so injured her, had so grossly insulted her, as he had done. In what way then would it become her to receive him? Before his arrival she had made up her mind on this subject, and had resolved that she would, at least, say no word of her own wrongs.

"How do you do, Julia?" said Sir Hugh, walking into the room with a step which was perhaps unnaturally quick, and with his hand extended. Lady Ongar had thought of that too. She would give much to escape the touch of his hand, if it were possible; but she had told herself that she would best consult her own dignity by declaring no actual quarrel. So she put out her fingers and just touched his palm.

"I hope Hermy is well?" she said.

"Pretty well, thank you. She is rather lonely since she lost her poor little boy, and would be very glad if you would go to her."

"I cannot do that; but if she would come to me I should be delighted."

"You see it would not suit her to be in London so soon after Hughy's death."

"I am not bound to London. I would go anywhere else,—except to Clavering."

"You never go to Ongar Park, I am told?"

"I have been there."

"But they say you do not intend to go again?"

"Not at present, certainly. Indeed, I do not suppose I shall ever go there. I do not like the place."

"That's just what they have told me. It is about that—partly—that I want to speak to you. If you don't like the place, why shouldn't you sell your interest in it back to the family? They'd give you more than the value for it."

"I do not know that I should care to sell it."

"Why not, if you don't mean to use the house? I might as well explain at once what it is that has been said to me. John Courton, you know, is acting as guardian for the young earl, and they don't want to keep up so large a place as the Castle. Ongar Park would just suit Mrs. Courton,"—Mrs. Courton was the widowed mother of the young earl,—"and they would be very happy to buy your interest."

"Would not such a proposition come best through a lawyer?" said Lady Ongar.

"The fact is this,—they think they have been a little hard on you."

"I have never accused them."

"But they feel it themselves, and they think that you might take it perhaps amiss if they were to send you a simple message through an attorney. Courton told me that he would not have allowed any such proposition to be made, if you had seemed disposed to use the place. They wish to be civil, and all that kind of thing."

"Their civility or incivility is indifferent to me," said Julia.

"But why shouldn't you take the money?"

"The money is equally indifferent to me."

"You mean then to say that you won't listen to it? Of course they can't make you part with the place if you wish to keep it."

"Not more than they can make you sell Clavering Park. I do not, however, wish to be uncivil, and I will let you know through my lawyer what I think about it. All such matters are best managed by lawyers."

After that Sir Hugh said nothing further about Ongar Park. He was well aware, from the tone in which Lady Ongar answered him, that she was averse to talk to him on that subject; but he was not conscious that his presence was otherwise disagreeable to her, or that she would resent any interference from him on any subject because he had been cruel to her. So after a little while he began again about Hermione. As the world had determined upon acquitting Lady Ongar, it would be convenient to him that the two sisters should be again intimate, especially as Julia was a rich woman. His wife did not like Clavering Park, and he certainly did not like Clavering Park himself. If he could once get the house shut up, he might manage to keep it shut for some years to come.

His wife was now no more than a burden to him, and it would suit him well to put off the burden on to his sister-in-law's shoulders. It was not that he intended to have his wife altogether dependent on another person, but he thought that if they two were established together, in the first instance merely as a summer arrangement, such establishment might be made to assume some permanence. This would be very pleasant to him. Of course he would pay a portion of the expense,—as small a portion as might be possible,—but such a portion as might enable him to live with credit before the world.

"I wish I could think that you and Hermy might be together while I am absent," he said.

"I shall be very happy to have her if she will come to me," Julia replied.

"What,—here, in London? I am not quite sure that she wishes to come up to London at present."

"I have never understood that she had any objection to being in town," said Lady Ongar.

"Not formerly, certainly ; but now since her boy's death——"

"Why should his death make more difference to her than to you? " To this question Sir Hugh made no reply. "If you are thinking of society, she could be nowhere safer from any such necessity than with me. I never go out anywhere. I have never dined out, or even spent an evening in company since Lord Ongar's death. And no one would come here to disturb her."

"I didn't mean that."

"I don't quite know what you did mean. From different causes she and I are left pretty nearly equally without friends."

"Hermione is not left without friends," said Sir Hugh with a tone of offence.

"Were she not, she would not want to come to me. Your society is in London, to which she does not come, or in other country-houses than your own, to which she is not taken. She lives altogether at Clavering, and there is no one there, except your uncle."

"Whatever neighbourhood there is she has,—just like other women."

"Just like some other women, no doubt. I shall remain in town for another month, and after that I shall go somewhere ; I don't much care where. If Hermy will come to me as my guest I shall be most happy to have her. And the longer she will stay with me the better. Your coming home need make no difference, I suppose."

There was a keenness of reproach in her tone as she spoke, which even he could not but feel and acknowledge. He was very thick-skinned to such reproaches, and would have left this unnoticed had it been possible. Had she continued speaking he would have done so. But she remained silent, and sat looking at him, saying with her eyes the same thing that she had already spoken with her words. Thus he was driven to speak.

"I don't know," said he, "whether you intend that for a sneer."

She was perfectly indifferent whether or no she offended him. Only that she had believed that the maintenance of her own dignity forbade it, she would have openly rebuked him, and told him that he was not welcome in her house. No treatment from her could, as she thought, be worse than he had deserved from her. His first enmity had injured her, but she could afford to laugh at his present anger. "It is hard to talk to you about Hermy without what you are pleased to call a sneer. You simply wish to rid yourself of her."

"I wish no such thing, and you have no right to say so."

"At any rate you are ridding yourself of her society; and if under those circumstances she likes to come to me I shall be glad to receive her. Our life together will not be very cheerful, but neither she nor I ought to expect a cheerful life."

He rose from his chair now with a cloud of anger upon his brow. "I can see how it is," said he; "because everything has not gone smooth with yourself you choose to resent it upon me. I might have expected that you would not have forgotten in whose house you met Lord Ongar."

"No, Hugh; I forget nothing; neither when I met him, nor how I married him, nor any of the events that have happened since. My memory, unfortunately, is very good."

"I did all I could for you, and should have been safe from your insolence."

"You should have continued to stay away from me, and you would have been quite safe. But our quarrelling in this way is foolish. We can never be friends,—you and I; but we need not be open enemies. Your wife is my sister, and I say again that if she likes to come to me, I shall be delighted to have her."

"My wife," said he, "will go to the house of no person who is insolent to me." Then he took his hat, and left the room without further word or sign of greeting. In spite of his calculations and caution as to money,—in spite of his well-considered arrangements and the comfortable provision for his future ease which he had proposed to himself, he was a man who had not his temper so much under control as to enable him to postpone his anger to his prudence. That little scheme for getting rid of his wife was now at an end. He would never permit her to go to her sister's house after the manner in which Julia had just treated him!

When he was gone Lady Ongar walked about her own room smiling, and at first was well pleased with herself. She had received Archie's overture with decision, but at the same time with courtesy, for Archie was weak, and poor, and powerless. But she had treated Sir Hugh with scorn, and had been enabled to do so without the utterance of any actual reproach as to the wrongs which she herself had endured from him. He had put himself in her power, and she had not thrown away the opportunity. She had told him that she did not want his friendship, and would not be his friend; but she had done this without any loud abuse unbecoming to her either as a countess, a widow, or a lady. For

Hermione she was sorry. Hermione now could hardly come to her. But even as to that she did not despair. As things were going on, it would become almost necessary that her sister and Sir Hugh should be parted. Both must wish it; and if this were arranged, then Hermione should come to her.

But from this she soon came to think again about Harry Clavering. How was that matter to be decided, and what steps would it become her to take as to its decision? Sir Hugh had proposed to her that she should sell her interest in Ongar Park, and she had promised that she would make known her decision on that matter through her lawyer. As she had been saying this she was well aware that she would never sell the property; —but she had already resolved that she would at once give it back, without purchase-money, to the Ongar family, were it not kept that she might hand it over to Harry Clavering as a fitting residence for his lordship. If he might be there, looking after his cattle, going about with the steward subservient at his heels, ministering justice to the Enoch Gubbys and others, she would care nothing for the wants of any of the Courton people. But if such were not to be the destiny of Ongar Park,— if there were to be no such Adam in that Eden,—then the mother of the little lord might take herself thither, and revel among the rich blessings of the place without delay, and with no difficulty as to price. As to price,— had she not already found the money-bag that had come to her to be too heavy for her hands?

But she could do nothing till that question was settled; and how was she to settle it? Every word that had passed between her and Cecilia Burton had been turned over and over in her mind, and she could only declare to herself as she had then declared to her visitor, that it must be as Harry should please. She would submit, if he required her submission; but she could not bring herself to take steps to secure her own misery.

CHAPTER XXXIX.

FAREWELL TO DOODLES.

AT last came the day on which the two Claverings were to go down to Harwich, and put themselves on board Jack Stuart's yacht. The hall of the house in Berkeley Square was strewed with portmanteaus, gun-cases, and fishing-rods, whereas the wine and packets of preserved meat, and the bottled beer and fish in tins, and the large box of cigars, and the pre-pared soups, had been sent down by Boxall, and were by this time on board the boat. Hugh and Archie were to leave London this day by train at 5 P.M., and were to sleep on board. Jack Stuart was already there, having assisted in working the yacht round from Brightlingsea.

On that morning Archie had a farewell breakfast at his club with Doodles, and after that, having spent the intervening hours in the billiard-

room, a farewell luncheon. There had been something of melancholy in
this last day between the friends, originating partly in the failure of
Archie's hopes as to Lady Ongar, and partly perhaps in the bad character
which seemed to belong to Jack Stuart and his craft. "He has been at
it for years, and always coming to grief," said Doodles. "He is just like
a man I know, who has been hunting for the last ten years, and can't sit a
horse at a fence yet. He has broken every bone in his skin, and I don't
suppose he ever saw a good thing to a finish. He never knows whether
hounds are in cover, or where they are. His only idea is to follow another
man's red coat till he comes to grief;—and yet he will go on hunting.
There are some people who never will understand what they can do, and
what they can't." In answer to this, Archie reminded his friend that on
this occasion Jack Stuart would have the advantage of an excellent dry-
nurse, acknowledged to be very great on such occasions. Would not he,
Archie Clavering, be there to pilot Jack Stuart and his boat? But, nevertheless, Doodles was melancholy, and went on telling stories about that
unfortunate man who would continue to break his bones, though he had
no aptitude for out-of-door sports. "He'll be carried home on a stretcher
some day, you know," said Doodles.

"What does it matter if he is," said Archie, boldly, thinking of himself and of the danger predicted for him. "A man can only die once."

"I call it quite a tempting of Providence," said Doodles.

But their conversation was chiefly about Lady Ongar and the Spy.
It was only on this day that Doodles had learned that Archie had in truth
offered his hand, and been rejected; and Captain Clavering was surprised
by the extent of his friend's sympathy. "It's a doosed disagreeable thing,—
a very disagreeable thing indeed," said Doodles. Archie, who did not
wish to be regarded as specially unfortunate, declined to look at the matter
in this light; but Doodles insisted. "It would cut me up like the very
mischief," he said. "I know that; and the worst of it is, that perhaps
you wouldn't have gone on, only for me. I meant it all for the best, old
fellow. I did, indeed. There; that's the game to you. I'm playing
uncommon badly this morning; but the truth is, I'm thinking of those
women," Now as Doodles was playing for a little money, this was really
civil on his part.

And he would persevere in talking about the Spy, as though there
were something in his remembrance of the lady which attracted him
irresistibly to the subject. He had always boasted that in his interview
with her he had come off with the victory, nor did he now cease to make
such boasts; but still he spoke of her and her powers with an awe which
would have completely opened the eyes of any one a little more sharp on
such matters than Archie Clavering. He was so intent on this subject that
he sent the marker out of the room so that he might discuss it with more
freedom, and might plainly express his views as to her influence on his
friend's fate.

"By George! she's a wonderful woman. Do you know I can't help thinking of her at night. She keeps me awake ;—she does, upon my honour."

"I can't say she keeps me awake, but I wish I had my seventy pounds back again."

"Do you know, if I were you, I shouldn't grudge it. I should think it worth pretty nearly all the money to have had the dealing with her."

"Then you ought to go halves."

"Well, yes ;—only that I ain't flush, I would. When one thinks of it, her absolutely taking the notes out of your waistcoat-pocket, upon my word it's beautiful ! She'd have had it out of mine, if I hadn't been doosed sharp."

"She understood what she was about, certainly."

"What I should like to know is this ; did she or did she not tell Lady Ongar what she was to do ;—about you I mean ? I daresay she did after all."

"And took my money for nothing ? "

"Because you didn't go high enough, you know."

"But that was your fault. I went as high as you told me."

"No, you didn't, Clavvy ; not if you remember. But the fact is, I don't suppose you could go high enough. I shouldn't be surprised if such a woman as that wanted—thousands ! I shouldn't indeed. I shall never forget the way in which she swore at me ;—and how she abused me about my family. I think she must have had some special reason for disliking Warwickshire, she said such awful hard things about it."

"How did she know that you came from Warwickshire ? "

"She did know it. If I tell you something don't you say anything about it. I have an idea about her."

"What is it ? "

"I didn't mention it before, because I don't talk much of those sort of things. I don't pretend to understand them, and it is better to leave them alone."

"But what do you mean ? "

Doodles looked very solemn as he answered. "I think she's a medium —or a media, or whatever it ought to be called."

"What! one of those spirit-rapping people ? " And Archie's hair almost stood on end as he asked the question.

"They don't rap now,—not the best of them, that is. That was the old way, and seems to have been given up."

"But what do you suppose she did ? "

"How did she know that the money was in your waistcoat-pocket, now ? How did she know that I came from Warwickshire ? And then she had a way of going about the room as though she could have raised herself off her feet in a moment if she had chosen. And then her swearing, and the rest of it,—so unlike any other woman, you know."

"But do you think she could have made Julia hate me ? "

"Ah, I can't tell that. There are such lots of things going on now-a-days that a fellow can understand nothing about! But I've no doubt of this,—if you were to tie her up with ropes ever so, I don't in the least doubt but what she'd get out."

Archie was awe-struck, and made two or three strokes after this; but then he plucked up his courage and asked a question,—

"Where do you suppose they get it from, Doodles?"

"That's just the question."

"Is it from—— the devil, do you think?" said Archie, whispering the name of the evil one in a very low voice.

"Well, yes; I suppose that's most likely."

"Because they don't seem to do a great deal of harm with it after all. As for my money, she would have had that any way, for I intended to give it to her."

"There are people who think," said Doodles, "that the spirits don't come from anywhere, but are always floating about."

"And then one person catches them, and another doesn't?" asked Archie.

"They tell me that it depends upon what the mediums or medias eat and drink," said Doodles, "and upon what sort of minds they have. They must be cleverish people, I fancy, or the spirits wouldn't come to them."

"But you never hear of any swell being a medium. Why don't the spirits go to a prime minister or some of those fellows? Only think what a help they'd be."

"If they come from the devil," suggested Doodles, "he wouldn't let them do any real good."

"I've heard a deal about them," said Archie, "and it seems to me that the mediums are always poor people, and that they come from nobody knows where. The Spy is a clever woman I daresay——"

"There isn't much doubt about that," said the admiring Doodles.

"But you can't say she's respectable, you know. If I was a spirit I wouldn't go to a woman who wore such dirty stockings as she had on."

"That's nonsense, Clavvy. What does a spirit care about a woman's stockings?"

"But why don't they ever go to the wise people? that's what I want to know." And as he asked the question boldly he struck his ball sharply, and, lo, the three balls rolled vanquished into three different pockets. "I don't believe about it," said Archie, as he readjusted the score. "The devil can't do such things as that or there'd be an end of everything; and as to spirits in the air, why should there be more spirits now than there were four-and-twenty years ago?"

"That's all very well, old fellow," said Doodles, "but you and I ain't clever enough to understand everything." Then that subject was dropped, and Doodles went back for a while to the perils of Jack Stuart's yacht.

After the lunch, which was in fact Archie's early dinner, Doodles was going to leave his friend, but Archie insisted that his brother captain should walk with him up to Berkeley Square, and see the last of him into his cab. Doodles had suggested that Sir Hugh would be there, and that Sir Hugh was not always disposed to welcome his brother's friends to his own house after the most comfortable modes of friendship; but Archie explained that on such an occasion as this there need be no fear on that head; he and his brother were going away together, and there was a certain feeling of jollity about the trip which would divest Sir Hugh of his roughness. "And besides," said Archie, "as you will be there to see me off, he'll know that you're not going to stay yourself." Convinced by this, Doodles consented to walk up to Berkeley Square.

Sir Hugh had spent the greatest part of this day at home, immersed among his guns and rods, and their various appurtenances. He also had breakfasted at his club, but had ordered his luncheon to be prepared for him at home. He had arranged to leave Berkeley Square at four, and had directed that his lamb chops should be brought to him exactly at three. He was himself a little late in coming downstairs, and it was ten minutes past the hour when he desired that the chops might be put on the table, saying that he himself would be in the drawing-room in time to meet them. He was a man solicitous about his lamb chops, and careful that the asparagus should be hot; solicitous also as to that bottle of Lafitte by which those comestibles were to be accompanied and which was, of its own nature, too good to be shared with his brother Archie. But as he was on the landing, by the drawing-room door, descending quickly, conscious that in obedience to his orders the chops had been already served, he was met by a servant who, with disturbed face and quick voice, told him that there was a lady waiting for him in the hall.

"D—— it!" said Sir Hugh.

"She has just come, Sir Hugh, and says that she specially wants to see you."

"Why the devil did you let her in?"

"She walked in when the door was opened, Sir Hugh, and I couldn't help it. She seemed to be a lady, Sir Hugh, and I didn't like not to let her inside the door."

"What's the lady's name?" asked the master.

"It's a foreign name, Sir Hugh. She said she wouldn't keep you five minutes." The lamb chops, and the asparagus, and the Lafitte were in the dining-room, and the only way to the dining-room lay through the hall to which the foreign lady had obtained an entrance. Sir Hugh, making such calculations as the moments allowed, determined that he would face the enemy, and pass on to his banquet over her prostrate body. He went quickly down into the hall, and there was encountered by Sophie Gordeloup, who, skipping over the gun-cases, and rushing through the portmanteaus, caught the baronet by the arm before he had been able to approach the dining-room door. "Sir 'Oo," she said, "I am so glad to have caught you. You are going away, and I have things to tell you which you must hear—yes; it is well for you I have caught you, Sir 'Oo." Sir Hugh looked as though he by no means participated in this feeling, and saying something about his great hurry begged that he might be allowed to go to his food. Then he added that, as far as his memory served him, he had not the honour of knowing the lady who was addressing him.

"You come in to your little dinner," said Sophie, "and I will tell you everything as you are eating. Don't mind me. You shall eat and drink, and I will talk. I am Madame Gordeloup,—Sophie Gordeloup. Ah,— you know the name now. Yes. That is me. Count Pateroff is my brother. You know Count Pateroff. He knowed Lord Ongar, and I knowed Lord Ongar. We know Lady Ongar. Ah,—you understand now that I can have much to tell. It is well you was not gone without seeing me? Eh; yes! You shall eat and drink, but suppose you send that man into the kitchen?"

Sir Hugh was so taken by surprise that he hardly knew how to act on the spur of the moment. He certainly had heard of Madame Gordeloup, though he had never before seen her. For years past her name had been familiar to him in London, and when Lady Ongar had returned as a widow it had been, to his thinking, one of her worst offences that this woman had been her friend. Under ordinary circumstances his judgment would have directed him to desire the servant to put her out into the street as an impostor, and to send for the police if there was any difficulty. But it certainly might be possible that this woman had something to tell with reference to Lady Ongar which it would suit his purposes to hear. At the present moment he was not very well inclined to his sister-in-law, and was disposed to hear evil of her. So he passed on into the dining-room and desired Madame Gordeloup to follow him. Then he closed the room door, and standing up with his back to the fireplace, so that he might be saved from the necessity of asking her to sit down, he declared himself ready to hear anything that his visitor might have to say.

"But you will eat your dinner, Sir 'Oo? You will not mind me. I shall not care."

"Thank you, no;—if you will just say what you have got to say, I will be obliged to you."

"But the nice things will be so cold! Why should you mind me? Nobody minds me."

"I will wait, if you please, till you have done me the honour of leaving me."

"Ah, well,—you Englishmen are so cold and ceremonious. But Lord Ongar was not with me like that. I knew Lord Ongar so well."

"Lord Ongar was more fortunate than I am."

"He was a poor man who did kill himself. Yes. It was always that bottle of Cognac. And there was other bottles was worser still. Never mind; he has gone now, and his widow has got the money. It is she has been a fortunate woman! Sir 'Oo, I will sit down here in the arm-chair." Sir Hugh made a motion with his hand, not daring to forbid her to do as she was minded. "And you, Sir 'Oo;—will not you sit down also?"

" I will continue to stand if you will allow me.

" Very well ; you shall do as most pleases you. As I did walk here, and shall walk back, I will sit down."

" And now if you have anything to say, Madame Gordeloup," said Sir Hugh, looking at the silver covers which were hiding the chops and the asparagus, and looking also at his watch, " perhaps you will be good enough to say it."

" Anything to say ! Yes, Sir 'Oo, I have something to say. It is a pity you will not sit at your dinner."

" I will not sit at my dinner till you have left me. So now, if you will be pleased to proceed——"

" I will proceed. Perhaps you don't know that Lord Ongar died in these arms ?" And Sophie, as she spoke, stretched out her skinny hands, and put herself as far as possible into the attitude in which it would be most convenient to nurse the head of a dying man upon her bosom. Sir Hugh, thinking to himself that Lord Ongar could hardly have received much consolation in his fate from this incident, declared that he had not heard the fact before. " No ; you have not heard it. She have tell nothing to her friends here. He die abroad, and she has come back with all the money ; but she tell nothing to anybody here, so I must tell."

" But I don't care how he died, Madame Gordeloup. It is nothing to me."

" But yes, Sir 'Oo. The lady, your wife, is the sister to Lady Ongar. Is not that so ? Lady Ongar did live with you before she was married. Is not that so ? Your brother and your cousin both wishes to marry her and have all the money. Is not that so ? Your brother has come to me to help him, and has sent the little man out of Warwickshire. Is not that so ? "

" What the d—— is all that to me ? " said Sir Hugh, who did not quite understand the story as the lady was telling it.

" I will explain, Sir 'Oo, what the d—— it is to you ; only I wish you were eating the nice things on the table. This Lady Ongar is treating me very bad. She treat my brother very bad too. My brother is Count Pateroff. We have been put to—oh, such expenses for her ! It have nearly ruined me. I make a journey to your London here altogether for her. Then, for her, I go down to that accursed little island ;—what you call it ?—where she insult me. Oh ! all my time is gone. Your brother and your cousin, and the little man out of Warwickshire, all coming to my house,—just as it please them."

" But what is this to me ? " shouted Sir Hugh.

" A great deal to you," screamed back Madame Gordeloup. " You see I know everything,—everything. I have got papers."

" What do I care for your papers ? Look here, Madame Gordeloup, you had better go away."

" Not yet, Sir 'Oo ; not yet. You are going away to Norway—I know ; and I am ruined before you come back."

" Look here, madame ; do you mean that you want money from me ? "

" I want my rights, Sir 'Oo. Remember, I know everything ;—every-thing ; oh, such things ! If they were all known,—in the newspapers, you understand, or that kind of thing, that lady in Bolton Street would lose all her money to-morrow. Yes. There is uncles to the little lord ; yes ! Ah, how much would they give me, I wonder ? They would not tell me to go away."

Sophie was perhaps justified in the estimate she had made of Sir Hugh's probable character from the knowledge which she had acquired of his brother Archie ; but, nevertheless, she had fallen into a great mistake. There could hardly have been a man then in London less likely to fall into her present views than Sir Hugh Clavering. Not only was he too fond of his money to give it away without knowing why he did so ; but he was subject to none of that weakness by which some men are prompted to submit to such extortions. Had he believed her story, and had Lady Ongar been really dear to him, he would never have dealt with such a one as Madame Gordeloup otherwise than through the police.

" Madame Gordeloup," said he, " if you don't immediately take your-self off, I shall have you put out of the house."

He would have sent for a constable at once, had he not feared that by doing so, he would retard his journey.

" What ! " said Sophie, whose courage was as good as his own. " Me put out of the house ! Who shall touch me ? "

" My servant shall ; or if that will not do, the police. Come, walk." And he stepped over towards her as though he himself intended to assist in her expulsion by violence.

" Well, you are there ; I see you ; and what next ? " said Sophie. " You, and your valk ! I can tell you things fit for you to know, and you say, Valk. If I valk, I will valk to some purpose. I do not often valk for nothing when I am told—Valk ! " Upon this, Sir Hugh rang the bell with some violence. " I care nothing for your bells, or for your servants, or for your policemen. I have told you that your sister owe me a great deal of money, and you say,—Valk. I vill valk." Thereupon the servant came into the room, and Sir Hugh, in an angry voice, desired him to open the front door. " Yes,—open vide," said Sophie, who, when anger came upon her, was apt to drop into a mode of speaking English which she was able to avoid in her cooler moments. " Sir 'Oo, I am going to valk, and you shall hear of my valking."

" Am I to take that as a threat ? " said he.

" Not a tret at all," said she ; " only a promise. Ah, I am good to keep my promises ! Yes, I make a promise. Your poor wife,—down with the daises ; I know all, and she shall hear too. That is another promise. And your brother, the captain. Oh ! here he is, and the little man out of Warwickshire." She had got up from her chair, and had moved towards the door with the intention of going ; but just as she was passing out into the hall, she encountered Archie and Doodles. Sir Hugh, who had been altogether at a loss to understand what she had meant by the man out of Warwickshire, followed her into the hall, and became more angry than before at finding that his brother had brought a friend to his house at so very inopportune a moment. The wrath in his face was so plainly expressed that Doodles could perceive it, and wished himself away. The presence also of the Spy was not pleasant to the gallant captain. Was the wonderful woman ubiquitous, that he should thus encounter her again, and that so soon after all the things that he had spoken of her on this morning? "How do you do, gentlemen?" said Sophie. "There is a great many boxes here, and I with my crinoline have not got room." Then she shook hands, first with Archie, and then with Doodles; and asked the latter why he was not as yet gone to Warwickshire. Archie, in almost mortal fear, looked up into his brother's face. Had his brother learned the story of that seventy pounds? Sir Hugh was puzzled beyond measure at finding that the woman knew the two men; but having still an eye to his lamb chops, was chiefly anxious to get rid of Sophie and Doodles together.

"This is my friend Boodle,—Captain Boodle," said Archie, trying to put a bold face upon the crisis. "He has come to see me off."

"Very kind of him," said Sir Hugh. "Just make way for this lady, will you? I want to get her out of the house if I can. Your friend seems to know her; perhaps he'll be good enough to give her his arm?"

"Who;—I?" said Doodles. "No; I don't know her particularly. I did meet her once before, just once,—in a casual way."

"Captain Booddle and me is very good friends," said Sophie. "He come to my house and behave himself very well; only he is not so handy a man as your brother, Sir 'Oo."

Archie trembled, and he trembled still more when his brother, turning to him, asked him if he knew the woman.

"Yes; he know the woman very well," said Sophie. "Why do you not come any more to see me? You send your little friend; but I like you better yourself. You come again when you return, and all that shall be made right."

But still she did not go. She had now seated herself on a gun-case which was resting on a portmanteau, and seemed to be at her ease. The time was going fast, and Sir Hugh, if he meant to eat his chops, must eat them at once.

"See her out of the hall, into the street," he said to Archie; "and if she gives trouble, send for the police. She has come here to get money from me by threats, and only that we have no time, I would have her taken to the lock-up house at once." Then Sir Hugh retreated into the dining-room and shut the door.

"Lock-up-ouse!" said Sophie, scornfully. "What is dat?"

"He means a prison," said Doodles.

"Prison! I know who is most likely be in a prison. Tell me of a prison! Is he a minister of state that he can send out order for me to be made prisoner ? Is there lettres de cachet now in England ? I think not. Prison, indeed ! "

" But really, Madame Gordeloup, you had better go; you had, indeed," said Archie.

" You, too—you bid me go ? Did I bid you go when you came to me ? Did I not tell you, sit down ? Was I not polite ? Did I send for a police ? or talk of lock-up-ouse to you ? No. It is English that do these things ; only English."

Archie felt that it was incumbent on him to explain that his visit to her house had been made under other circumstances,—that he had brought money instead of seeking it ; and had, in fact, gone to her simply in the way of her own trade. He did begin some preliminaries to this explanation ; but as the servant was there, and as his brother might come out from the dining-room,—and as also he was aware that he could hardly tell the story much to his own advantage, he stopped abruptly, and, looking piteously at Doodles, implored him to take the lady away.

" Perhaps you wouldn't mind just seeing her into Mount Street," said Archie.

" Who ; I ? " said Doodles, electrified.

" It is only just round the corner," said Archie.

"Yes, Captain Booddle, we will go," said Sophie. "This is a bad house ; and your Sir 'Oo,—I do not like him at all. Lock-up, indeed ! I tell you he shall very soon be locked up himself. There is what you call Davy's locker. I know;—yes."

Doodles also trembled when he heard this anathema, and thought once more of the character of Jack Stuart and his yacht.

" Pray go with her," said Archie.

" But I had come to see you off."

" Never mind," said Archie. " He is in such a taking, you know. God bless you, old fellow ; good-by ! I'll write and tell you what fish we get, and mind you tell me what Turriper does for the Bedfordshire. Good-by, Madame Gordeloup—good-by."

There was no escape for him, so Doodles put on his hat and prepared to walk away to Mount Street with the Spy under his arm,—the Spy as to whose avocations, over and beyond those of her diplomatic profession, he had such strong suspicions ! He felt inclined to be angry with his friend, but the circumstances of his parting hardly admitted of any expression of anger.

" Good-by, Clavvy," he said. " Yes ; I'll write ; that is, if I've got anything to say."

" Take care of yourself, captain," said Sophie.

" All right," said Archie.

" Mind you come and see me when you come back," said Sophie.

" Of course I will," said Archie.

" And we'll make that all right for you yet. Gentlemen, when they have so much to gain, shouldn't take a No too easy. You come with your

handy glove, and we'll see about it again." Then Sophie walked off
leaning upon the arm of Captain Boodle, and Archie stood at the door
watching them till they turned out of sight round the corner of the
square. At last he saw them no more, and then he returned to his
brother.

And as we shall see Doodles no more,—or almost no more,—we will
now bid him adieu civilly. The pair were not ill-matched, though the
lady perhaps had some advantage in acuteness, given to her no doubt by
the experience of a longer life. Doodles, as he walked along two sides of
the square with the fair burden on his arm, felt himself to be in some sort
proud of his position, though it was one from which he would not have
been sorry to escape, had escape been possible. A remarkable phenomenon
was the Spy, and to have walked round Berkeley Square with such a woman
leaning on his arm, might in coming years be an event to remember with
satisfaction. In the meantime he did not say much to her, and did not
quite understand all that she said to him. At last he came to the door
which he well remembered, and then he paused. He did not escape even
then. After a while the door was opened, and those who were passing
might have seen Captain Boodle, slowly and with hesitating steps, enter
the narrow passage before the lady. Then Sophie followed, and closed
the door behind her. As far as this story goes, what took place at that
interview cannot be known. Let us bid farewell to Doodles, and wish him
a happy escape.

"How did you come to know that woman?" said Hugh to his brother,
as soon as Archie was in the dining-room.

"She was a friend of Julia's," said Archie.

"You haven't given her money?" Hugh asked.

"O dear, no," said Archie.

Immediately after that they got into their cab; the things were
pitched on the top; and,—for a while,—we may bid adieu to them also.

CHAPTER XL.

SHEWING HOW MRS. BURTON FOUGHT HER BATTLE.

"FLORENCE, I have been to Bolton Street and I have seen Lady Ongar." Those were the first words which Cecilia Burton spoke to her sister-in-law, when she found Florence in the drawing-room on her return from the visit which she had made to the countess. Florence had still before her the desk on which she had been writing; and the letter in its envelope addressed to Mrs. Clavering, but as yet unclosed, was lying beneath her blotting-paper. Florence, who had never dreamed of such an undertaking on Cecilia's part, was astounded at the tidings which she heard. Of course her first effort was made to learn from her sister's tone and countenance what had been the result of this interview;—but she could learn nothing from either. There was no radiance as of joy in Mrs. Burton's face, nor was there written there anything of despair. Her voice was serious and almost solemn, and her manner was very grave ;—but that was all. "You have seen her ? " said Florence, rising up from her chair.

"Yes, dear. I may have done wrong. Theodore, I know, will say so. But I thought it best to try to learn the truth before you wrote to Mrs. Clavering."

"And what is the truth ? But perhaps you have not learned it ? "

"I think I have learned all that she could tell me. She has been very frank."

"Well ;—what is the truth ? Do not suppose, dearest, that I cannot bear it. I hope for nothing now. I only want to have this settled, that I may be at rest."

Upon this Mrs. Burton took the suffering girl in her arms and caressed her tenderly. "My love," said she, "it is not easy for us to be at rest. You cannot be at rest as yet."

"I can. I will be so, when I know that this is settled. I do not wish to interfere with his fortune. There is my letter to his mother, and now I will go back to Stratton."

"Not yet, dearest ; not yet," said Mrs. Burton, taking the letter in her hand, but refraining from withdrawing it at once from the envelope. "You must hear what I have heard to-day."

"Does she say that she loves him ? "

"Ah, yes ;—she loves him. We must not doubt that."

"And he ;—what does she say of him ? "

"She says what you also must say, Florence ;—though it is hard that it should be so. It must be as he shall decide."

"No," said Florence, withdrawing herself from the arm that was still around her. "No ; it shall not be as he may choose to decide. I will not so submit myself to him. It is enough as it is. I will never see him more ;—never. To say that I do not love him would be untrue, but I will never see him again."

"Stop, dear ; stop. What if it be no fault of his ? "

"No fault of his that he went to her when we—we—we—he and I— were, as we were, together ! "

"Of course there has been some fault ; but, Flo dearest, listen to me. You know that I would ask you to do nothing from which a woman should shrink."

"I know that you would give your heart's blood for me ;—but nothing will be of avail now. Do not look at me with melancholy eyes like that. Cissy, it will not kill me. It is only the doubt that kills one."

"I will not look at you with melancholy eyes, but you must listen to me. She does not herself know what his intention is."

"But I know it,—and I know my own. Read my letter, Cissy. There is not one word of anger in it, nor will I ever utter a reproach. He knew her first. If he loved her through it all, it was a pity he could not be constant to his love, even though she was false to him."

"But you won't hear me, Flo. As far as I can learn the truth,—

as I myself most firmly believe,—when he went to her on her return
to England, he had no other intention than that of visiting an old
friend."

"But what sort of friend, Cissy?"

"He had no idea then of being untrue to you. But when he saw
her the old intimacy came back. That was natural. Then he was dazzled
by her beauty."

"Is she then so beautiful?"

"She is very beautiful."

"Let him go to her," said Florence, tearing herself away from her
sister's arm, and walking across the room with a quick and almost angry
step. "Let her have him. Cissy, there shall be an end of it. I will not
condescend to solicit his love. If she is such as you say, and if beauty
with him goes for everything,—what chance could there be for such
as me?"

"I did not say that beauty with him went for everything."

"Of course it does. I ought to have known that it would be so with
such a one as him. And then she is rich also,—wonderfully rich! What
right can I have to think of him?"

"Florence, you are unjust. You do not even suspect that it is her
money."

"To me it is the same thing. I suppose that a woman who is so
beautiful has a right to everything. I know that I am plain, and I will
be—content—in future—to think no more——" Poor Florence, when she
had got as far as that, broke down, and could go on no further with the
declaration which she had been about to make as to her future prospects.
Mrs. Burton, taking advantage of this, went on with her story, struggling,
not altogether unsuccessfully, to assume a calm tone of unimpassioned
reason.

"As I said before, he was dazzled——"

"Dazzled!—oh!"

"But even then he had no idea of being untrue to you."

"No; he was untrue without an idea. That is worse."

"Florence, you are perverse, and are determined to be unfair. I
must beg that you will hear me to the end, so that then you may be able
to judge what course you ought to follow." This Mrs. Burton said with
the air of a great authority; after which she continued in a voice something
less stern—"He thought of doing no injury to you when he went to see
her; but something of the feeling of his old love grew upon him when he
was in her company, and he became embarrassed by his position before he
was aware of his own danger. He might, of course, have been stronger."
Here Florence exhibited a gesture of strong impatience, though she did
not speak. "I am not going to defend him altogether, but I think you
must admit that he was hardly tried. Of course I cannot say what passed
between them, but I can understand how easily they might recur to the
old scenes;—how naturally she would wish for a renewal of the love

which she had been base enough to betray! She does not, however, consider herself as at present engaged to him. That you may know for certain. It may be that she has asked him for such a promise, and that he has hesitated. If so, his staying away from us, and his not writing to you, can be easily understood."

"And what is it you would have me do?"

"He is ill now. Wait till he is well. He would have been here before this, had not illness prevented him. Wait till he comes."

"I cannot do that, Cissy. Wait I must, but I cannot wait without offering him, through his mother, the freedom which I have so much reason to know that he desires."

"We do not know that he desires it. We do not know that his mother even suspects him of any fault towards you. Now that he is there,—at home,—away from Bolton Street——"

"I do not care to trust to such influences as that, Cissy. If he could not spend this morning with her in her own house, and then as he left her feel that he preferred me to her, and to all the world, I would rather be as I am than take his hand. He shall not marry me from pity, nor yet from a sense of duty. We know the old story,—how the devil would be a monk when he was sick. I will not accept his sick-bed allegiance, or have to think that I owe my husband to a mother's influence over him while he is ill."

"You will make me think, Flo, that you are less true to him than she is."

"Perhaps it is so. Let him have what good such truth as hers can do him. For me, I feel that it is my duty to be true to myself. I will not condescend to indulge my heart at the cost of my pride as a woman."

"Oh, Florence, I hate that word pride."

"You would not hate it for yourself, in my place."

"You need take no shame to love him."

' Have I taken shame to love him?" said Florence, rising again from her chair. "Have I been missish or coy about my love? From the moment in which I knew that it was a pleasure to myself to regard him as my future husband, I have spoken of my love as being always proud of it. I have acknowledged it as openly as you can do yours for Theodore. I acknowledge it still, and will never deny it. Take shame that I have loved him! No. But I should take to myself great shame should I ever be brought so low as to ask him for his love, when once I had learned to think that he had transferred it from myself to another woman." Then she walked the length of the room, backwards and forwards, with hasty steps, not looking at her sister-in-law, whose eyes were now filled with tears. "Come, Cissy," she then said, "we will make an end of this. Read my letter if you choose to read it,—though indeed it is not worth the reading, and then let me send it to the post."

Mrs. Burton now opened the letter and read it very slowly. It was stern and almost unfeeling in the calmness of the words chosen: but in those words her proposed marriage with Harry Clavering was absolutely abandoned. "I know," she said, "that your son is more warmly attached to another lady than he is to me, and under those circumstances, for his sake as well as for mine, it is necessary that we should part. Dear Mrs. Clavering, may I ask you to make him understand that he and I are never to recur to the past? If he will send me back any letters of mine,—should any have been kept,—and the little present which I once gave him, all will have been done which need be done, and all have been said which need be said. He will receive in a small parcel his own letters and the gifts which he has made me." There was in this a tone of completeness,—as of a business absolutely finished,—of a judgment admitting no appeal, which did not at all suit Mrs. Burton's views. A letter, quite as becoming on the part of Florence, might, she thought, be written, which would still leave open a door for reconciliation. But Florence was resolved, and the letter was sent.

The part which Mrs. Burton had taken in this conversation had surprised even herself. She had been full of anger with Harry Clavering,— as wrathful with him as her nature permitted her to be; and yet she had pleaded his cause with all her eloquence, going almost so far in her defence of him as to declare that he was blameless. And in truth she was prepared to acquit him of blame,—to give him full absolution without penance, —if only he could be brought back again into the fold. Her wrath against him would be very hot should he not so return;—but all should be more than forgiven if he would only come back, and do his duty with affectionate and patient fidelity. Her desire was, not so much that justice should be done, as that Florence should have the thing coveted, and that Florence's rival should not have it. According to the arguments, as arranged by her feminine logic, Harry Clavering would be all right or all wrong according as he might at last bear himself. She desired success, and, if she could only be successful, was prepared to forgive everything. And even yet she would not give up the battle, though she admitted to herself that Florence's letter to Mrs. Clavering made the contest more difficult than ever. It might, however, be that Mrs. Clavering would be good enough, just enough, true enough, clever enough, to know that such a letter as this, coming from such a girl and written under such circumstances, should be taken as meaning nothing. Most mothers would wish to see their sons married to wealth, should wealth throw itself in their way;—but Mrs. Clavering, possibly, might not be such a mother as that.

In the meantime there was before her the terrible necessity of explaining to her husband the step which she had taken without his knowledge, and of which she knew that she must tell him the history before she could sit down to dinner with him in comfort. "Theodore," she said, creeping in out of her own chamber to his dressing-room, while he was washing his hands, "you mustn't be angry with me, but I have done something to-day."

"And why must I not be angry with you?"

"You know what I mean. You mustn't be angry—especially about this,—because I don't want you to be."

"That's conclusive," said he. It was manifest to her that he was in a good humour, which was a great blessing. He had not been tried with his work as he was often wont to be, and was therefore willing to be playful.

"What do you think I've done?" said she. "I have been to Bolton Street and have seen Lady Ongar."

"No!"

"I have, Theodore, indeed."

Mr. Burton had been rubbing his face vehemently with a rough towel at the moment in which the communication had been made to him, and so strongly was he affected by it that he was stopped in his operation and brought to a stand in his movement, looking at his wife over the towel as he held it in both his hands. "What on earth has made you do such a thing as that?" he said.

"I thought it best. I thought that I might hear the truth,—and so I have. I could not bear that Florence should be sacrificed whilst anything remained undone that was possible."

"Why didn't you tell me that you were going?"

"Well, my dear; I thought it better not. Of course I ought to have told you, but in this instance I thought it best just to go without the fuss of mentioning it."

"What you really mean is, that if you had told me I should have asked you not to go."

"Exactly."

"And you were determined to have your own way?"

"I don't think, Theodore, I care so much about my own way as some women do. I am sure I always think your opinion is better than my own;—that is, in most things."

"And what did Lady Ongar say to you?" He had now put down the towel, and was seated in his arm-chair, looking up into his wife's face.

"It would be a long story to tell you all that she said."

"Was she civil to you?"

"She was not uncivil. She is a handsome, proud woman, prone to speak out what she thinks and determined to have her own way when it is possible; but I think that she intended to be civil to me personally."

"What is her purpose now?"

"Her purpose is clear enough. She means to marry Harry Clavering if she can get him. She said so. She made no secret of what her wishes are."

"Then, Cissy, let her marry him, and do not let us trouble ourselves further in the matter."

"But Florence, Theodore! Think of Florence!"

"I am thinking of her, and I think that Harry Clavering is not worth her acceptance. She is as the traveller that fell among thieves. She is hurt and wounded, but not dead. It is for you to be the Good Samaritan, but the oil which you should pour into her wounds is not a renewed hope as to that worthless man. Let Lady Ongar have him. As far as I can see, they are fit for each other."

Then she went through with him, diligently, all the arguments which she had used with Florence, palliating Harry's conduct, and explaining the circumstances of his disloyalty, almost as those circumstances had in truth occurred. "I think you are too hard on him," she said. "You can't be too hard on falsehood," he replied. "No, not while it exists. But you would not be angry with a man for ever, because he should once have been false? But we do not know that he is false." "Do we not?" said he. "But never mind; we must go to dinner now. Does Florence know of your visit?" Then, before she would allow him to leave his room, she explained to him what had taken place between herself and Florence, and told him of the letter that had been written to Mrs. Clavering. "She is right," said he. "That way out of her difficulty is the best that is left to her." But, nevertheless, Mrs. Burton was resolved that she would not as yet surrender.

Theodore Burton, when he reached the drawing-room, went up to his sister and kissed her. Such a sign of the tenderness of love was not common with him, for he was one of those who are not usually demonstrative in their affection. At the present moment he said nothing of what was passing in his mind, nor did she. She simply raised her face to meet his lips, and pressed his hand as she held it. What need was there of any further sign between them than this? Then they went to dinner, and their meal was eaten almost in silence. Almost every moment Cecilia's eye was on her sister-in-law. A careful observer, had there been one there, might have seen this; but, while they remained together downstairs, there occurred among them nothing else to mark that all was not well with them.

Nor would the brother have spoken a word during the evening on the subject that was so near to all their hearts had not Florence led the way. When they were at tea, and when Cecilia had already made up her mind that there was to be no further discussion that night, Florence suddenly broke forth.

"Theodore," she said, "I have been thinking much about it, and I believe I had better go home, to Stratton, to-morrow."

"Oh, no," said Cecilia, eagerly.

"I believe it will be better that I should," continued Florence. "I suppose it is very weak in me to own it; but I am unhappy, and, like the wounded bird, I feel that it will be well that I should hide myself."

Cecilia was at her feet in a moment. "Dearest Flo," she said. "Is not this your home as well as Stratton?"

"When I am able to be happy it is. Those who have light hearts may have more homes than one; but it is not so with those whose hearts are heavy. I think it will be best for me to go."

"You shall do exactly as you please," said her brother. "In such a matter I will not try to persuade you. I only wish that we could tend to comfort you."

"You do comfort me. If I know that you think I am doing right, that will comfort me more than anything. Absolute and immediate comfort is not to be had when one is sorrowful."

"No, indeed," said her brother. "Sorrow should not be killed too quickly. I always think that those who are impervious to grief must be impervious also to happiness. If you have feelings capable of the one, you must have them capable also of the other!"

"You should wait at any rate, till you get an answer from Mrs. Clavering," said Cecilia.

"I do not know that she has any answer to send to me."

"Oh, yes; she must answer you, if you will think of it. If she accepts what you have said——"

"She cannot but accept it."

"Then she must reply to you. There is something which you have asked her to send to you; and I think you should wait, at any rate, till it reaches you here. Mind I do not think her answer will be of that nature; but it is clear that you should wait for it whatever it may be." Then Florence, with the concurrence of her brother's opinion, consented to remain in London for a few days, expecting the answer which would be sent by Mrs. Clavering;—and after that no further discussion took place as to her trouble.

CHAPTER XLI.

THE SHEEP RETURNS TO THE FOLD.

HARRY CLAVERING had spoken solemn words to his mother, during his illness, which both he and she regarded as a promise that Florence should not be deserted by him. After that promise nothing more was said between them on the subject for a few days. Mrs. Clavering was contented that the promise had been made, and Harry himself, in the weakness consequent upon his illness, was willing enough to accept the excuse which his illness gave him for postponing any action in the matter. But the fever had left him, and he was sitting up in his mother's room, when Florence's letter reached the parsonage,—and, with the letter, the little parcel which she herself had packed up so carefully. On the day before that a few words had passed between the rector and his wife, which will explain the feelings of both of them in the matter.

"Have you heard," said he,—speaking in a voice hardly above a whisper, although no third person was in the room—"that Harry is again thinking of making Julia his wife?"

"He is not thinking of doing so," said Mrs. Clavering. "They who say so, do him wrong."

"It would be a great thing for him as regards money."

"But he is engaged,—and Florence Burton has been received here as his future wife. I could not endure to think that it should be so. At any rate, it is not true."

"I only tell you what I heard," said the rector, gently sighing, partly in obedience to his wife's implied rebuke, and partly at the thought that so grand a marriage should not be within his son's reach. The rector was beginning to be aware that Harry would hardly make a fortune at the profession which he had chosen, and that a rich marriage would be an easy way out of all the difficulties which such a failure promised. The rector was a man who dearly loved easy ways out of difficulties. But in such matters as these his wife he knew was imperative and powerful, and he lacked the courage to plead for a cause that was prudent, but ungenerous.

When Mrs. Clavering received the letter and parcel on the next morning, Harry Clavering was still in bed. With the delightful privilege of a convalescent invalid, he was allowed in these days to get up just when getting up became more comfortable than lying in bed, and that time did not usually come till eleven o'clock was past;—but the postman reached the Clavering parsonage by nine. The letter, as we know, was addressed to Mrs. Clavering herself, as was also the outer envelope which contained the packet; but the packet itself was addressed in Florence's clear hand-writing to Harry Clavering, Esq. "That is a large parcel to come by post, mamma," said Fanny.

"Yes, my dear; but it is something particular."

"It's from some tradesman, I suppose?" said the rector.

"No; it's not from a tradesman," said Mrs. Clavering. But she said nothing further, and both husband and daughter perceived that it was not intended that they should ask further questions.

Fanny, as usual, had taken her brother his breakfast, and Mrs. Clavering did not go up to him till that ceremony had been completed and removed. Indeed it was necessary that she should study Florence's letter in her own room before she could speak to him about it. What the parcel contained she well knew, even before the letter had been thoroughly read; and I need hardly say that the treasure was sacred in her hands. When she had finished the perusal of the letter there was a tear,—a gentle tear, in each eye. She understood it all, and could fathom the strength and weakness of every word which Florence had written. But she was such a woman,— exactly such a woman, — as Cecilia Burton had pictured to herself. Mrs. Clavering was good enough, great enough, true enough, clever enough to know that Harry's love for Florence should be sustained, and his fancy for Lady Ongar overcome. At no time would she have been proud to see her son prosperous only in the prosperity of a wife's fortune; but she would have been thoroughly ashamed of him, had he resolved to pursue such prosperity under his present circumstances.

But her tears,—though they were there in the corners of her eyes,— were not painful tears. Dear Florence! She was suffering bitterly now.

This very day would be a day of agony to her. There had been for her, doubtless, many days of agony during the past month. That the letter was true in all its words Mrs. Clavering did not doubt. That Florence believed that all was over between her and Harry, Mrs. Clavering was as sure as Florence had intended that she should be. But all should not be over, and the days of agony should soon be at an end. Her boy had promised her, and to her he had always been true. And she understood, too, the way in which these dangers had come upon him, and her judgment was not heavy upon her son ;—her gracious boy, who had ever been so good to her ! It might be that he had been less diligent at his work than he should have been,—that on that account further delay would still be necessary ; but Florence would forgive that, and he had promised that Florence should not be deserted.

Then she took the parcel in her hands, and considered all its circumstances,—how precious had once been its contents, and how precious doubtless they still were, though they had been thus repudiated ! And she thought of the moments,—nay, rather of the hours,—which had been passed in the packing of that little packet. She well understood how a girl would linger over such dear pain, touching the things over and over again, allowing herself to read morsels of the letters at which she had already forbidden herself even to look,—till every word had been again seen and weighed, again caressed and again abjured. She knew how those little trinkets would have been fondled ! How salt had been the tears that had fallen on them, and how carefully the drops would have been removed. Every fold in the paper of the two envelopes, with the little morsels of wax just adequate for their purpose, told of the lingering painful care with which the work had been done. Ah ! the parcel should go back at once with words of love that should put an end to all that pain ! She, who had sent these loved things away, should have her letters again, and should touch her little treasures with fingers that should take pleasure in the touching. She should again read her lover's words with an enduring delight. Mrs. Clavering understood it all, as though she also were still a girl with a lover of her own.

Harry was beginning to think that the time had come in which getting up would be more comfortable than lying in bed, when his mother knocked at his door and entered his room. " I was just going to make a move, mother," he said, having reached that stage of convalescence in which some shame comes upon the idler.

" But I want to speak to you first, my dear," said Mrs. Clavering. " I have got a letter for you, or rather a parcel." Harry held out his hand, and taking the packet, at once recognized the writing of the address.

" You know from whom it comes, Harry ? "

" Oh, yes, mother."

" And do you know what it contains ? " Harry, still holding the packet, looked at it, but said nothing. " I know," said his mother ; " for she has written and told me. Will you see her letter to me ? " Again Harry held out his hand, but his mother did not at once give him the letter. " First of all, my dear, let us know that we understand each other. This dear girl,—to me she is inexpressibly dear,—is to be your wife ? "

" Yes, mother ;—it shall be so."

" That is my own boy ! Harry, I have never doubted you ;—have never doubted that you would be right at last. Now you shall see her letter. But you must remember that she has had cause to make her unhappy."

" I will remember."

" Had you not been ill, everything would of course have been all right before now." As to the correctness of this assertion the reader probably will have doubts of his own. Then she handed him the letter, and sat on his bed-side while he read it. At first he was startled, and made almost indignant at the firmness of the girl's words. She gave him up as though it were a thing quite decided, and uttered no expression of her own regret in doing so. There was no soft woman's wail in her words. But there was in them something which made him unconsciously long to get back the thing which he had so nearly thrown away from him. They inspired him with a doubt whether he might yet succeed, which very doubt greatly increased his desire. As he read the letter for the second time, Julia became less beautiful in his imagination, and the charm of Florence's character became stronger.

" Well, dear ? " said his mother, when she saw that he had finished the second reading of the epistle.

He hardly knew how to express, even to his mother, all his feelings,— the shame that he felt, and with the shame something of indignation that he should have been so repulsed. And of his love, too, he was afraid to speak. He was willing enough to give the required assurance, but after that he would have preferred to have been left alone. But his mother could not leave him without some further word of agreement between them as to the course which they would pursue.

" Will you write to her, mother, or shall I ? "

" I shall write, certainly,—by to-day's post. I would not leave her an hour if I could help it, without an assurance of your unaltered affection."

" I could go to town to-morrow, mother ;—could I not ? "

" Not to-morrow, Harry. It would be foolish. Say on Monday."

" And you will write to-day ? "

" Certainly."

" I will send a line also,—just a line."

" And the parcel ? "

" I have not opened it yet."

" You know what it contains. Send it back at once, Harry ;—at once. If I understand her feelings, she will not be happy till she gets it into her hands again. We will send Jem over to the post-office, and have it registered."

When so much was settled, Mrs. Clavering went away about the affairs

THE SHEEP RETURNS TO THE FOLD.

of her house, thinking as she did so of the loving words with which she would strive to give back happiness to Florence Burton.

Harry, when he was alone, slowly opened the parcel. He could not resist the temptation of doing this, and of looking again at the things which she had sent back to him. And he was not without an idea,—perhaps a hope—that there might be with them some short note,—some scrap containing a few words for himself. If he had any such hope he was disappointed. There were his own letters, all scented with lavender from the casket in which they had been preserved; there was the rich bracelet which had been given with some little ceremony, and the cheap brooch which he had thrown to her as a joke, and which she had sworn that she would value the most of all because she could wear it every day; and there was the pencil-case which he had fixed on to her watch-chain, while her fingers were touching his fingers, caressing him for his love while her words were rebuking him for his awkwardness. He remembered it all as the things lay strewed upon his bed. And he re-read every word of his own words. "What a fool a man makes of himself," he said to himself at last, with something of the cheeriness of laughter about his heart. But as he said so he was quite ready to make himself a fool after the same fashion again,—if only there were not in his way that difficulty of recommencing. Had it been possible for him to write again at once in the old strain,—without any reference to his own conduct during the last month, he would have begun his fooling without waiting to finish his dressing.

"Did you open the parcel?" his mother asked him, some hour or so before it was necessary that Jem should be started on his mission.

"Yes; I thought it best to open it."

"And have you made it up again?"

"Not yet, mother."

"Put this with it, dear." And his mother gave him a little jewel, a cupid in mosaic surrounded by tiny diamonds, which he remembered her to wear ever since he had first noticed the things she had worn. "Not from me, mind. I give it to you. Come;—will you trust me to pack them?" Then Mrs. Clavering again made up the parcel, and added the trinket which she had brought with her.

Harry at last brought himself to write a few words. "Dearest, dearest Florence,—They will not let me out, or I would go to you at once. My mother has written, and though I have not seen her letter, I know what it contains. Indeed, indeed you may believe it all. May I not venture to return the parcel? I do send it back and implore you to keep it. I shall be in town, I think, on Monday, and will go to Onslow Crescent,— instantly. Your own, H. C." Then there was scrawled a postscript which was worth all the rest put together,—was better than his own note, better than his mother's letter, better than the returned packet. "I love no one better than you;—no one half so well,—neither now, nor ever did." These words, whether wholly true or only partially so, were at least to the point; and were taken by Cecilia Burton, when she heard of them, as a confession of faith that demanded instant and plenary absolution.

The trouble which had called Harry down to Clavering remained, I regret to say, almost in full force now that his prolonged visit had been brought so near its close. Mr. Saul, indeed, had agreed to resign his curacy, and was already on the look-out for similar employment in some other parish. And since his interview with Fanny's father he had never entered the rectory, or spoken to Fanny. Fanny had promised that there should be no such speaking, and indeed no danger of that kind was feared. Whatever Mr. Saul might do he would do openly,—nay, audaciously. But though there existed this security, nevertheless things as regarded Fanny were very unpleasant. When Mr. Saul had commenced his court-ship, she had agreed with her family in almost ridiculing the idea of such a lover. There had been a feeling with her as with the others that poor Mr. Saul was to be pitied. Then she had come to regard his overtures as matters of grave import,—not indeed avowing to her mother anything so strong as a return of his affection, but speaking of his proposal as one to which there was no other objection than that of a want of money. Now, however, she went moping about the house as though she were a victim of true love, condemned to run unsmoothly for ever; as though her passion for Mr. Saul were too much for her, and she were waiting in patience till death should relieve her from the cruelty of her parents. She never com-plained. Such victims never do complain. But she moped and was wretched, and when her mother questioned her, struggling to find out how strong this feeling might in truth be, Fanny would simply make her dutiful promises,—promises which were wickedly dutiful,—that she would never mention the name of Mr. Saul any more. Mr. Saul in the meantime went about his parish duties with grim energy, supplying the rector's short-comings without a word. He would have been glad to preach all the sermons and read all the services during these six months, had he been allowed to do so. He was constant in the schools,—more constant than ever in his visitings. He was very courteous to Mr. Clavering when the necessities of their position brought them together. For all this Mr. Claver-ing hated him,—unjustly. For a man placed as Mr. Saul was placed a line of conduct exactly level with that previously followed is impossible, and it was better that he should become more energetic in his duties than less so. It will be easily understood that all these things interfered much with the general happiness of the family at the rectory at this time.

The Monday came, and Harry Clavering, now convalescent and simply interesting from the remaining effects of his illness, started on his journey from London. There had come no further letters from Onslow Terrace to the parsonage, and, indeed, owing to the intervention of Sunday, none could have come unless Florence had written by return of post. Harry made his journey, beginning it with some promise of happiness to himself, —but becoming somewhat uneasy as his train drew near to London. He

had behaved badly, and he knew that in the first place he must own that
he had done so. To men such a necessity is always grievous. Women
not unfrequently like the task. To confess, submit, and be accepted as
confessing and submitting, comes naturally to the feminine mind. The
cry of peccavi sounds soft and pretty when made by sweet lips in a loving
voice. But a man who can own that he has done amiss without a pang,
—who can so own it to another man, or even to a woman,—is usually but
a poor creature. Harry must now make such confession, and therefore
he became uneasy. And then, for him, there was another task behind the
one which he would be called upon to perform this evening,—a task which
would have nothing of pleasantness in it to redeem its pain. He must
confess not only to Florence,—where his confession might probably have its
reward,—but he must confess also to Julia. This second confession would,
indeed, be a hard task to him. That, however, was to be postponed till
the morrow. On this evening he had pledged himself that he would go
direct to Onslow Terrace; and this he did as soon after he had reached
his lodgings as was possible. It was past six when he reached London,
and it was not yet eight when, with palpitating heart, he knocked at
Mr. Burton's door.

I must take the reader back with me for a few minutes, in order that
we may see after what fashion the letters from Clavering were received by
the ladies in Onslow Terrace. On that day Mr. Burton had been required
to go out of London by one of the early trains, and had not been in the
house when the postman came. Nothing had been said between Cecilia
and Florence as to their hopes or fears in regard to an answer from
Clavering;—nothing at least since that conversation in which Florence
had agreed to remain in London for yet a few days; but each of them was
very nervous on the matter. Any answer, if sent at once from Clavering,
would arrive on this morning; and therefore, when the well-known knock
was heard, neither of them was able to maintain her calmness perfectly.
But yet nothing was said, nor did either of them rise from her seat at the
breakfast-table. Presently the girl came in with apparently a bundle of
letters, which she was still sorting when she entered the room. There
were two or three for Mr. Burton, two for Cecilia, and then two besides
the registered packet for Florence. For that a receipt was needed, and
as Florence had seen the address and recognized the writing, she was
hardly able to give her signature. As soon as the maid was gone, Cecilia
could keep her seat no longer. "I know those are from Clavering," she
said, rising from her chair, and coming round to the side of the table.
Florence instinctively swept the packet into her lap, and, leaning forward,
covered the letters with her hands. "Oh, Florence, let us see them; let
us see them at once. If we are to be happy let us know it." But Florence
paused, still leaning over her treasures, and hardly daring to show her
burning face. Even yet it might be that she was rejected. Then Cecilia
went back to her seat, and simply looked at her sister with beseeching
eyes. "I think I'll go upstairs," said Florence. "Are you afraid of me,

Flo?" Cecilia answered reproachfully. "Let me see the outside of them." Then Florence brought them round the table, and put them into her sister's hands. "May I open this one from Mrs. Clavering?" Florence nodded her head. Then the seal was broken, and in one minute the two women were crying in each other's arms. "I was quite sure of it," said Cecilia, through her tears,—"perfectly sure. I never doubted it for a moment. How could you have talked of going to Stratton?" At last Florence got herself away up to the window, and gradually mustered courage to break the envelope of her lover's letter. It was not at once that she showed the postscript to Cecilia, nor at once that the packet was opened. That last ceremony she did perform in the solitude of her own room. But before the day was over the postscript had been shown, and the added trinket had been exhibited. "I remember it well," said Florence. "Mrs. Clavering wore it on her forehead when we dined at Lady Clavering's." Mrs. Burton in all this saw something of the gentle persuasion which the mother had used, but of that she said nothing. That he should be back again, and should have repented, was enough for her.

Mr. Burton was again absent, when Harry Clavering knocked in person at the door; but on this occasion his absence had been specially arranged by him with a view to Harry's comfort. "He won't want to see me this evening," he had said. "Indeed you'll all get on a great deal better without me." He therefore had remained away from home, and not being a club man, had dined most uncomfortably at an eating-house. "Are the ladies at home?" Harry asked, when the door was opened. Oh, yes; they were at home. There was no danger that they should be found out on such an occasion as this. The girl looked at him pleasantly, calling him by his name as she answered him, as though she too desired to show him that he had again been taken into favour,—into her favour as well as that of her mistress.

He hardly knew what he was doing as he ran up the steps to the drawing-room. He was afraid of what was to come; but nevertheless he rushed at his fate as some young soldier rushes at the trench in which he feels that he may probably fall. So Harry Clavering hurried on, and before he had looked round upon the room which he had entered, found his fate with Florence on his bosom.

Alas, alas! I fear that justice was outraged in the welcome that Harry received on that evening. I have said that he would be called upon to own his sins, and so much, at least, should have been required of him. But he owned no sin! I have said that a certain degradation must attend him in that first interview after his reconciliation. Instead of this the hours that he spent that evening in Onslow Terrace were hours of one long ovation. He was, as it were, put upon a throne as a king who had returned from his conquest, and those two women did him honour, almost kneeling at his feet. Cecilia was almost as tender with him as Florence, pleading to her own false heart the fact of his illness as his excuse. There was something of the pallor of the sick-room left with him,—a slight tenuity in his hands and brightness in his eye which did him yeoman's service. Had he been quite robust, Cecilia might have felt that she could not justify to herself the peculiar softness of her words. After the first quarter of an hour he was supremely happy. His awkwardness had gone, and as he sat with his arm round Florence's waist, he found that the little pencil-case had again been attached to her chain, and as he looked down upon her he saw that the cheap brooch was again on her breast. It would have been pretty, could an observer have been there, to see the skill with which they both steered clear of any word or phrase which could be disagreeable to him. One might have thought that it would have been impossible to avoid all touch of a rebuke. The very fact that he was forgiven would seem to imply some fault that required pardon. But there was no hint at any fault. The tact of women excels the skill of men ; and so perfect was the tact of these women that not a word was said which wounded Harry's ear. He had come again into their fold, and they were rejoiced and showed their joy. He who had gone astray had repented, and they were beautifully tender to the repentant sheep.

CHAPTER XLII.

RESTITUTION.

HARRY stayed a little too long with his love,—a little longer at least than had been computed, and in consequence met Theodore Burton in the Crescent as he was leaving it. This meeting could hardly be made without something of pain, and perhaps it was well for Harry that he should have such an opportunity as this for getting over it quickly. But when he saw Mr. Burton under the bright gas-lamp he would very willingly have avoided him, had it been possible.

" Well, Harry ? " said Burton, giving his hand to the repentant sheep.

" How are you, Burton ? " said Harry, trying to speak with an unconcerned voice. Then in answer to an inquiry as to his health, he told of his own illness, speaking of that confounded fever having made him very low. He intended no deceit, but he made more of the fever than was necessary.

" When will you come back to the shop ? " Burton asked. It must be remembered that though the brother could not refuse to welcome back to his home his sister's lover, still he thought that the engagement was a misfortune. He did not believe in Harry as a man of business, and had almost rejoiced when Florence had been so nearly quit of him. And now there was a taint of sarcasm in his voice as he asked as to Harry's return to the chambers in the Adelphi.

" I can hardly quite say as yet," said Harry, still pleading his illness. " They were very much against my coming up to London so soon. Indeed I should not have done it had I not felt so very—very anxious to see

Florence. I don't know, Burton, whether I ought to say anything to you about that."

" I suppose you have said what you had to say to the women ? "

" Oh, yes. I think they understand me completely, and I hope that I understand them."

" In that case I don't know that you need say anything to me. Come to the Adelphi as soon as you can ; that's all. I never think myself that a man becomes a bit stronger after an illness by remaining idle." Then Harry passed on, and felt that he had escaped easily in that interview.

But as he walked home he was compelled to think of the step which he must next take. When he had last seen Lady Ongar he had left her with a promise that Florence was to be deserted for her sake. As yet that promise would by her be supposed to be binding. Indeed he had thought it to be binding on himself till he had found himself under his mother's influence at the parsonage. During his last few weeks in London he had endured an agony of doubt; but in his vacillations the pendulum had always veered more strongly towards Bolton Street than to Onslow Crescent. Now the swinging of the pendulum had ceased altogether. From henceforth Bolton Street must be forbidden ground to him, and the sheepfold in Onslow Crescent must be his home till he should have established a small peculiar fold for himself. But, as yet, he had still before him the task of communicating his final decision to the lady in Bolton Street. As he walked home he determined that he had better do so in the first place by letter, and so eager was he as to the propriety of doing this at once, that on his return to his lodgings he sat down, and wrote the letter before he went to his bed. It was not very easily written. Here, at any rate, he had to make those confessions of which I have before spoken ;—confessions which it may be less difficult to make with pen and ink than with spoken words, but which when so made are more degrading. The word that is written is a thing capable of permanent life, and lives frequently to the confusion of its parent. A man should make his confessions always by word of mouth if it be possible. Whether such a course would have been possible to Harry Clavering may be doubtful. It might have been that in a personal meeting the necessary confession would not have got itself adequately spoken. Thinking, perhaps, of this he wrote his letter as follows on that night.

Bloomsbury Square, July, 186—.

The date was easily written, but how was he to go on after that ? In what form of affection or indifference was he to address her whom he had at that last meeting called his own, his dearest Julia ? He got out of his difficulty in the way common to ladies and gentlemen under such stress, and did not address her by any name or any epithet. The date he allowed to remain, and then he went away at once to the matter of his subject.

I feel that I owe it you at once to tell you what has been my history during the last few weeks. I came up from Clavering to-day, and have since that been with Mrs. and Miss Burton. Immediately on my return from them I sit down to write you.

After having said so much, Harry probably felt that the rest of his letter would be surplusage. Those few words would tell her all that it was required that she should know. But courtesy demanded that he should say more, and he went on with his confession.

You know that I became engaged to Miss Burton soon after your own marriage. I feel now that I should have told you this when we first met; but yet, had I done so, it would have seemed as though I told it with a special object. I don't know whether I make myself understood in this. I can only hope that I do so.

Understood! Of course she understood it all. She required no blundering explanation from him to assist her intelligence.

I wish now that I had mentioned it. It would have been better for both of us. I should have been saved much pain; and you, perhaps, some uneasiness. I was called down to Clavering a few weeks ago, about some business in the family, and then became ill,—so that I was confined to my bed instead of returning to town. Had it not been for this I should not have left you so long in suspense,—that is if there has been suspense. For myself, I have to own that I have been very weak, —worse than weak, I fear you will think. I do not know whether your old regard for me will prompt you to make any excuse for me, but I am well sure that I can make none for myself which will not have suggested itself to you without my urging it. If you choose to think that I have been heartless,—or rather, if you are able so to think of me, no words of mine, written or spoken now, will remove that impression from your mind.

I believe that I need write nothing further. You will understand from what I have said all that I should have to say were I to refer at length to that which has passed between us. All that is over now, and it only remains for me to express a hope that you may be happy. Whether we shall ever see each other again who shall say?—but if we do I trust that we may not meet as enemies. May God bless you here and hereafter.

HARRY CLAVERING.

When the letter was finished Harry sat for a while by his open window looking at the moon, over the chimney-pots of his square, and thinking of his career in life as it had hitherto been fulfilled. The great promise of his earlier days had not been kept. His plight in the world was now poor enough, though his hopes had been so high! He was engaged to be married, but had no income on which to marry. He had narrowly escaped great wealth. Ah!—It was hard for him to think of that without a regret; but he did strive so to think of it. Though he told himself that it would have been evil for him to have depended on money which had been procured by the very act which had been to him an injury,—to have dressed himself in the feathers which had been plucked from Lord Ongar's wings,—it was hard for him to think of all that he had missed, and rejoice thoroughly that he had missed it. But he told himself that he so rejoiced, and endeavoured to be glad that he had not soiled his hands with riches which never would have belonged to the woman he had loved had she not earned them by being false to him. Early on the following morning he sent off his letter, and then, putting himself into a cab, bowled down to Onslow Crescent. The sheepfold now was very pleasant to him when the head shepherd was away, and so much gratification it was natural that he should allow himself.

That evening, when he came from his club, he found a note from Lady Ongar. It was very short, and the blood rushed to his face as he felt ashamed at seeing with how much apparent ease she had answered him. He had written with difficulty, and had written awkwardly. But there was nothing awkward in her words.

DEAR HARRY,—We are quits now. I do not know why we should ever meet as enemies. I shall never feel myself to be an enemy of yours. I think it would be well that we should see each other, and if you have no objection to seeing me, I will be at home any evening that you may call. Indeed I am at home always in the evening. Surely, Harry, there can be no reason why we should not meet. You need not fear that there will be danger in it.

Will you give my compliments to Miss Florence Burton, with my best wishes for her happiness. Your Mrs. Burton I have seen,—as you may have heard, and I congratulate you on your friend.

Yours always, J. O.

The writing of this letter seemed to have been easy enough, and certainly there was nothing in it that was awkward; but I think that the writer had suffered more in the writing than Harry had done in producing his longer epistle. But she had known how to hide her suffering, and had used a tone which told no tale of her wounds. We are quits now, she had said, and she had repeated the words over and over again to herself as she walked up and down her room. Yes! they were quits now,— if the reflection of that fact could do her any good. She had ill-treated him in her early days; but, as she had told herself so often, she had served him rather than injured him by that ill-treatment. She had been false to him; but her falsehood had preserved him from a lot which could not have been fortunate. With such a clog as she would have been round his neck,—with such a wife, without a shilling of fortune, how could he have risen in the world? No! Though she had deceived him, she had served him. Then,—after that,—had come the tragedy of her life, the terrible days in thinking of which she still shuddered, the days of her husband and Sophie Gordeloup,—that terrible deathbed, those attacks upon her honour, misery upon misery, as to which she never now spoke a word to any one, and as to which she was resolved that she never would speak again. She had sold herself for money, and had got the price; but the punishment of her offence had been very heavy. And now, in these latter days, she had thought to compensate the man she had loved for the treachery with which she had used him. That treachery had been serviceable to him, but not the less should the compensation be very rich. And she would love him too. Ah, yes; she had always loved him! He should have it all now,—everything, if only he would consent to forget that terrible episode in her life, as she would strive to forget it. All that should remain to remind them of Lord Ongar would be the wealth that should henceforth belong to Harry Clavering. Such had been her dream, and

Harry had come to her with words of love which made it seem to be a reality. He had spoken to her words of love which he was now forced to withdraw, and the dream was dissipated. It was not to be allowed to her to escape her penalty so easily as that! As for him, they were now quits. That being the case, there could be no reason why they should quarrel.

But what now should she do with her wealth, and especially how should she act in respect to that place down in the country? Though she had learned to hate Ongar Park during her solitary visit there, she had still looked forward to the pleasure the property might give her, when she should be able to bestow it upon Harry Clavering. But that had been part of her dream, and the dream was now over. Through it all she had been conscious that she might hardly dare to hope that the end of her punishment should come so soon,—and now she knew that it was not to come. As far as she could see, there was no end to her punishment in prospect for her. From her first meeting with Harry Clavering on the platform of the railway station his presence, or her thoughts of him, had sufficed to give some brightness to her life,—had enabled her to support the friendship of Sophie Gordeloup, and also to support her solitude when poor Sophie had been banished. But now she was left without any resource. As she sat alone, meditating on all this, she endeavoured to console herself with the reflection that, after all, she was the one whom Harry loved,—whom Harry would have chosen, had he been free to choose. But the comfort to be derived from that was very poor. Yes; he had loved her once,—nay, perhaps he loved her still. But when that love was her own she had rejected it. She had rejected it, simply declaring to him, to her friends, and to the world at large, that she preferred to be rich. She had her reward, and, bowing her head upon her hands, she acknowledged that the punishment was deserved.

Her first step after writing her note to Harry was to send for Mr. Turnbull, her lawyer. She had expected to see Harry on the evening of the day on which she had written, but instead of that she received a note from him in which he said that he would come to her before long. Mr. Turnbull was more instant in obeying her commands, and was with her on the morning after he received her injunction. He was almost a perfect stranger to her, having only seen her once and that for a few moments after her return to England. Her marriage settlements had been prepared for her by Sir Hugh's attorney; but during her sojourn in Florence it had become necessary that she should have some one in London to look after her own affairs, and Mr. Turnbull had been recommended to her by lawyers employed by her husband. He was a prudent, sensible man, who recognized it to be his imperative interest to look after his client's interest. And he had done his duty by Lady Ongar in that trying time immediately after her return. An offer had then been made by the Courton family to give Julia her income without opposition if she would surrender Ongar Park. To this she had made objections with indignation, and Mr. Turnbull, though he had at first thought that she would be wise to comply with the terms proposed, had done her work for her with satisfactory expedition. Since those days she had not seen him, but now she had summoned him, and he was with her in Bolton Street.

"I want to speak to you, Mr. Turnbull," she said, "about that place down in Surrey. I don't like it."

"Not like Ongar Park?" he said. "I have always heard that it is so charming."

"It is not charming to me. It is a sort of property that I don't want, and I mean to give it up."

"Lord Ongar's uncles would buy your interest in it, I have no doubt."

"Exactly. They have sent to me, offering to do so. My brother-in-law, Sir Hugh Clavering, called on me with a message from them saying so. I thought that he was very foolish to come, and so I told him. Such things should be done by one's lawyers. Don't you think so, Mr. Turnbull?" Mr. Turnbull smiled as he declared that, of course, he, being a lawyer, was of that opinion. "I am afraid they will have thought me uncivil," continued Julia, "as I spoke rather brusquely to Sir Hugh Clavering. I am not inclined to take any steps through Sir Hugh Clavering; but I do not know that I have any reason to be angry with the little lord's family."

"Really, Lady Ongar, I think not. When your ladyship returned there was some opposition thought of for a while, but I really do not think it was their fault."

"No; it was not their fault."

"That was my feeling at the time; it was indeed."

"It was the fault of Lord Ongar,—of my husband. As regards all the Courtons I have no word of complaint to make. It is not to be expected,—it is not desirable that they and I should be friends. It is impossible, after what has passed, that there should be such friendship. But they have never injured me, and I wish to oblige them. Had Ongar Park suited me I should, doubtless, have kept it; but it does not suit me, and they are welcome to have it back again."

"Has a price been named, Lady Ongar?"

"No price need be named. There is to be no question of a price. Lord Ongar's mother is welcome to the place,—or rather to such interest as I have in it."

"And to pay a rent?" suggested Mr. Turnbull.

"To pay no rent! Nothing would induce me to let the place, or to sell my right in it. I will have no bargain about it. But as nothing also will induce me to live there, I am not such a dog in the manger as to wish to keep it. If you will have the kindness to see Mr. Courton's lawyer and to make arrangements about it."

"But, Lady Ongar; what you call your right in the estate is worth over twenty thousand pounds. It is indeed. You could borrow twenty thousand pounds on the security of it to-morrow."

"But I don't want to borrow twenty thousand pounds."

"No, no ; exactly. Of course you don't. But I point out that fact to show the value. You would be making a present of that sum of money to people who do not want it,—who have no claim upon you. I really don't see how they could take it."

"Mrs. Courton wishes to have the place very much."

"But, my lady, she has never thought of getting it without paying for it. Lady Ongar, I really cannot advise you to take any such step as that. Indeed, I cannot. I should be wrong, as your lawyer, if I did not point out to you that such a proceeding would be quite romantic,—quite so ; what the world would call Quixotic. People don't expect such things as that. They don't, indeed."

"People don't often have such reasons as I have," said Lady Ongar. Mr. Turnbull sat silent for a while, looking as though he were unhappy. The proposition made to him was one which, as a lawyer, he felt to be very distasteful to him. He knew that his client had no male friends in whom she confided, and he felt that the world would blame him if he allowed this lady to part with her property in the way she had suggested. "You will find that I am in earnest," she continued, smiling. "And you may as well give way to my vagaries with a good grace."

"They would not take it, Lady Ongar."

"At any rate we can try them. If you will make them understand that I don't at all want the place, and that it will go to rack and ruin because there is no one to live there, I am sure they will take it."

Then Mr. Turnbull again sat silent and unhappy, thinking with what words he might best bring forward his last and strongest argument against this rash proceeding.

"Lady Ongar," he said, "in your peculiar position there are double reasons why you should not act in this way."

"What do you mean, Mr. Turnbull ? What is my peculiar position ? "

"The world will say that you have restored Ongar Park, because you were afraid to keep it. Indeed, Lady Ongar, you had better let it remain as it is."

"I care nothing for what the world says," she exclaimed, rising quickly from her chair ;—"nothing ; nothing ! "

"You should really hold by your rights ; you should, indeed. Who can possibly say what other interests may be concerned ? You may marry, and live for the next fifty years, and have a family. It is my duty, Lady Ongar, to point out these things to you."

"I am sure you are quite right, Mr. Turnbull," she said, struggling to maintain a quiet demeanour. "You, of course, are only doing your duty. But whether I marry or whether I remain as I am, I shall give up this place. And as for what the world, as you call it, may say, I will not deny that I cared much for that on my immediate return. What people said then made me very unhappy. But I care nothing for it now. I have established my rights, and that has been sufficient. To me it seems that the world, as you call it, has been civil enough in its usage of me lately. It is only of those who should have been my friends that I have a right to complain. If you will please to do this thing for me, I will be obliged to you."

"If you are quite determined about it——"

"I am quite determined. What is the use of the place to me? I never shall go there. What is the use even of the money that comes to me? I have no purpose for it. I have nothing to do with it."

There was something in her tone as she said this which well filled him with pity.

"You should remember," he said, "how short a time it is since you became a widow. Things will be different with you soon."

"My clothes will be different, if you mean that," she answered; "but I do not know that there will be any other change in me. But I am wrong to trouble you with all this. If you will let Mr. Courton's lawyer know, with my compliments to Mrs. Courton, that I have heard that she would like to have the place, and that I do not want it, I will be obliged to you." Mr. Turnbull having by this time perceived that she was quite in earnest, took his leave, having promised to do her bidding.

In this interview, she had told her lawyer only a part of the plan which was now running in her head. As for giving up Ongar Park, she took to herself no merit for that. The place had been odious to her ever since she had endeavoured to establish herself there and had found that the clergyman's wife would not speak to her,—that even her own housekeeper would hardly condescend to hold converse with her. She felt that she would be a dog in the manger to keep the place in her own possession. But she had thoughts beyond this,—resolutions only as yet half-formed as to a wider surrender. She had disgraced herself, ruined herself, robbed herself of all happiness by the marriage she had made. Her misery had not been simply the misery of that lord's lifetime. As might have been expected, that was soon over. But an enduring wretchedness had come after that from which she saw no prospect of escape. What was to be her future life, left as she was and would be, in desolation? If she were to give it all up,—all the wealth that had been so ill-gotten,—might there not then be some hope of comfort for her?

She had been willing enough to keep Lord Ongar's money, and use it for the purposes of her own comfort, while she had still hoped that comfort might come from it. The remembrance of all that she had to give had been very pleasant to her, as long as she had hoped that Harry Clavering would receive it at her hands. She had not at once felt that the fruit had all turned to ashes. But now,—now that Harry was gone from her,—now that she had no friend left to her whom she could hope to make happy by her munificence,—the very knowledge of her wealth was a burden to her. And as she thought of her riches in these first days of her desertion, as she had indeed been thinking since Cecilia Burton had been with her, she came to understand that she was degraded by their acquisition. She had done that which had been unpardonably bad, and she felt like Judas when he stood with the price of his treachery in his hand. He had given up his money, and would not she do as much? There had been a moment in which she had nearly declared all her purpose to the lawyer, but she was held back by the feeling that she ought to make her plans certain before she communicated them to him.

She must live. She could not go out and hang herself as Judas had done. And then there was her title and rank, of which she did not know whether it was within her power to divest herself. She sorely felt the want of some one from whom in her present need she might ask counsel; of some friend to whom she could trust to tell her in what way she might now best atone for the evil she had done. Plans ran through her head which were thrown aside almost as soon as made, because she saw that they were impracticable. She even longed in these days for her sister's aid, though of old she had thought but little of Hermy as a counsellor. She had no friend whom she might ask;—unless she might still ask Harry Clavering.

If she did not keep it all might she still keep something,—enough for decent life,—and yet comfort herself with the feeling that she had expiated her sin? And what would be said of her when she had made this great surrender? Would not the world laugh at her instead of praising her,—that world as to which she had assured Mr. Turnbull that she did not care what its verdict about her might be? She had many doubts. Ah! why had not Harry Clavering remained true to her? But her punishment had come upon her with all its severity, and she acknowledged to herself now that it was not to be avoided.

CHAPTER XLIII.

LADY ONGAR'S REVENGE.

A T last came the night which Harry had fixed for his visit to Bolton Street. He had looked forward certainly with no pleasure to the interview, and now that the time for it had come, was disposed to think that Lady Ongar had been unwise in asking for it. But he had promised that he would go, and there was no possible escape.

He dined that evening in Onslow Crescent, where he was now again established with all his old comfort. He had again gone up to the children's nursery with Cecilia, had kissed them all in their cots, and made himself quite at home in the establishment. It was with them there as though there had been no dreadful dream about Lady Ongar. It was so altogether with Cecilia and Florence, and even Mr. Burton was allowing himself to be brought round to a charitable view of Harry's character. Harry on this day had gone to the chambers in the Adelphi for an hour, and walking away with Theodore Burton had declared his intention of working like a horse. "If you were to say like a man, it would perhaps be better," said Burton. "I must leave you to say that," answered Harry; "for the present I will content myself with the horse." Burton was willing to hope, and allowed himself once more to fall into his old pleasant way of talking about the business as though there were no other subject under the sun so full of manifold interest. He was very keen at the present moment about Metropolitan railways, and was ridiculing the folly of those who feared that the railway projectors were going too fast. "But we shall never get any thanks," he said. "When the thing has been done, and thanks are our due, people will look upon all our work so much as a matter of course that it will never occur to them to think that they owe us anything. They will have forgotten all their cautions, and will take what they get as though it were simply their due. Nothing astonishes me so much as the fear people feel before a thing is done when I join it with their want of surprise or admiration afterwards." In this way even Theodore Burton had resumed his terms of intimacy with Harry Clavering.

Harry had told both Cecilia and Florence of his intended visit to Bolton Street, and they had all become very confidential on the subject. In most such cases we may suppose that a man does not say much to one woman of the love which another woman has acknowledged for himself. Nor was Harry Clavering at all disposed to make any such boast. But in this case, Lady Ongar herself had told everything to Mrs. Burton. She had declared her passion, and had declared also her intention of making Harry her husband if he would take her. Everything was known, and there was no possibility of sparing Lady Ongar's name.

"If I had been her I would not have asked for such a meeting," Cecilia said. The three were at this time sitting together, for Mr. Burton rarely joined them in their conversation.

"I don't know," said Florence. "I do not see why she and Harry should not remain as friends."

"They might be friends without meeting now," said Cecilia.

"Hardly. If the awkwardness were not got over at once it would never be got over. I almost think she is right, though if I was her I should long to have it over." That was Florence's judgment in the matter. Harry sat between them, like a sheep as he was, very meekly,— not without some enjoyment of his sheepdom, but still feeling that he was a sheep. At half-past eight he started up, having already been told that a cab was waiting for him at the door. He pressed Cecilia's hand as he went, indicating his feeling that he had before him an affair of some magnitude, and then of course had a word or two to say to Florence in private on the landing. Oh, those delicious private words the need for which comes so often during those short halcyon days of one's lifetime! They were so pleasant that Harry would fain have returned to repeat them

HARRY SAT BETWEEN THEM, LIKE A SHEEP AS HE WAS, VERY MEEKLY.

after he was seated in his cab; but the inevitable wheels carried him onwards with cruel velocity, and he was in Bolton Street before the minutes had sufficed for him to collect his thoughts.

Lady Ongar, when he entered the room, was sitting in her accustomed chair, near a little work-table which she always used, and did not rise to meet him. It was a pretty chair, soft and easy, made with a back for lounging, but with no arms to impede the circles of a lady's hoop. Harry knew the chair well and had spoken of its graceful comfort in some of his visits to Bolton Street. She was seated there when he entered; and though he was not sufficiently experienced in the secrets of feminine attire to know at once that she had dressed herself with care, he did perceive that she was very charming, not only by force of her own beauty, but by the aid also of her dress. And yet she was in deep mourning,—in the deepest mourning; nor was there anything about her of which complaint might fairly be made by those who do complain on such subjects. Her dress was high round her neck, and the cap on her head was indisputably a widow's cap; but enough of her brown hair was to be seen to tell of its rich loveliness; and the black dress was so made as to show the full perfection of her form; and with it all there was that graceful feminine brightness that care and money can always give, and which will not come without care and money. It might be well, she had thought, to surrender her income, and become poor and dowdy hereafter, but there could be no reason why Harry Clavering should not be made to know all that he had lost.

"Well, Harry," she said, as he stepped up to her and took her offered hand. "I am glad that you have come that I may congratulate you. Better late than never; eh, Harry?"

How was he to answer her when she spoke to him in this strain? "I hope it is not too late," he said, hardly knowing what the words were which were coming from his mouth.

"Nay; that is for you to say. I can do it heartily, Harry, if you mean that. And why not? Why should I not wish you happy? I have always liked you,—have always wished for you happiness. You believe that I am sincere when I congratulate you;—do you not?"

"Oh, yes; you are always sincere."

"I have always been so to you. As to any sincerity beyond that we need say nothing now. I have always been your good friend,—to the best of my ability. Ah, Harry; you do not know how much I have thought of your welfare; how much I do think of it. But never mind that. Tell me something now of this Florence Burton of yours. Is she tall?" I believe that Lady Ongar, when she asked this question, knew well that Florence was short of stature.

"No; she is not tall," said Harry.

"What,—a little beauty? Upon the whole I think I agree with your taste. The most lovely women that I have ever seen have been small, bright, and perfect in their proportions. It is very rare that a tall woman has a perfect figure." Julia's own figure was quite perfect. "Do you remember Constance Vane? Nothing ever exceeded her beauty." Now Constance Vane,—she at least who had in those days been Constance Vane, but who now was the stout mother of two or three children,—had been a waxen doll of a girl, whom Harry had known, but had neither liked nor admired. But she was highly bred, and belonged to the cream of English fashion; she had possessed a complexion as pure in its tints as are the interior leaves of a blush rose,—and she had never had a thought in her head, and hardly ever a word on her lips. She and Florence Burton were as poles asunder in their differences. Harry felt this at once, and had an indistinct notion that Lady Ongar was as well aware of the fact as was he himself. "She is not a bit like Constance Vane," he said.

"Then what is she like? If she is more beautiful than what Miss Vane used to be, she must be lovely indeed."

"She has no pretensions of that kind," said Harry, almost sulkily.

"I have heard that she was so very beautiful!" Lady Ongar had never heard a word about Florence's beauty;—not a word. She knew nothing personally of Florence beyond what Mrs. Burton had told her. But who will not forgive her the little deceit that was necessary to her little revenge?

"I don't know how to describe her," said Harry. "I hope the time may soon come when you will see her, and be able to judge for yourself."

"I hope so too. It shall not be my fault if I do not like her."

"I do not think you can fail to like her. She is very clever, and that will go further with you than mere beauty. Not but what I think her very,—very pretty."

"Ah,—I understand. She reads a great deal, and that sort of thing. Yes; that is very nice. But I shouldn't have thought that that would have taken you. You used not to care much for talent and learning,—not in women I mean."

"I don't know about that," said Harry, looking very foolish.

"But a contrast is what you men always like. Of course I ought not to say that, but you will know of what I am thinking. A clever, highly-educated woman like Miss Burton will be a much better companion to you than I could have been. You see I am very frank, Harry." She wished to make him talk freely about himself, his future days, and his past days, while he was simply anxious to say on these subjects as little as possible. Poor woman! The excitement of having a passion which she might indulge was over with her,—at any rate for the present. She had played her game and had lost wofully; but before she retired altogether from the gaming-table she could not keep herself from longing for a last throw of the dice.

"These things, I fear, go very much by chance," said Harry.

"You do not mean me to suppose that you are taking Miss Burton by chance. That would be as uncomplimentary to her as to yourself."

" Chance, at any rate, has been very good to me in this instance."

" Of that I am sure. Do not suppose that I am doubting that. It is not only the paradise that you have gained, but the pandemonium that you have escaped ! " Then she laughed slightly, but the laughter was uneasy, and made her angry with herself. She had especially determined to be at ease during this meeting, and was conscious that any falling off in that respect on her part would put into his hands the power which she was desirous of exercising.

" You are determined to rebuke me, I see," said he. " If you choose to do so, I am prepared to bear it. My defence, if I have a defence, is one that I cannot use."

" And what would be your defence ? "

" I have said that I cannot use it."

" As if I did not understand it all ! What you mean to say is this,— that when your good stars sent you in the way of Florence Burton, you had been ill-treated by her who would have made your pandemonium for you, and that she therefore,—she who came first and behaved so badly—can have no right to find fault with you in that you have obeyed your good stars and done so well for yourself. That is what you call your defence. It would be perfect, Harry,—perfect, if you had only whispered to me a word of Miss Burton when I first saw you after my return home. It is odd to me that you should not have written to me and told me when I was abroad with my husband. It would have comforted me to have known that the wound which I had given had been cured ;—that is, if there was a wound."

" You know that there was a wound."

" At any rate, it was not mortal. But when are such wounds mortal ? When are they more than skin-deep ? "

" I can say nothing as to that now."

" No, Harry ; of course you can say nothing. Why should you be made to say anything ? You are fortunate and happy, and have all that you want. I have nothing that I want."

There was a reality in the tone of sorrow in which this was spoken which melted him at once ;—and the more so in that there was so much in her grief which could not but be flattering to his vanity. " Do not say that, Lady Ongar," he exclaimed.

" But I do say it. What have I got in the world that is worth having ? My possessions are ever so many thousands a year,—and a damaged name."

" I deny that. I deny it altogether. I do not think that there is one who knows of your story who believes ill of you."

" I could tell you of one, Harry, who thinks very ill of me ;—nay, of two ; and they are both in this room. Do you remember how you used to teach me that terribly conceited bit of Latin,—Nil conscire sibi ? Do you suppose that I can boast that I never grow pale as I think of my own fault ? I am thinking of it always, and my heart is ever becoming paler and paler. And as to the treatment of others ;—I wish I could make you know what I suffered when I was fool enough to go to that place in Surrey. The coachman who drives me no doubt thinks that I poisoned my husband, and the servant who let you in just now supposes me to be an abandoned woman because you are here."

"You will be angry with me, perhaps, if I say that these feelings are morbid and will die away. They show the weakness which has come from the ill-usage you have suffered."

"You are right in part, no doubt. I shall become hardened to it all, and shall fall into some endurable mode of life in time. But I can look forward to nothing. What future have I? Was there ever any one so utterly friendless as I am? Your kind cousin has done that for me ;—and yet he came here to me the other day, smiling and talking as though he were sure that I should be delighted by his condescension. I do not think that he will ever come again."

"I did not know you had seen him."

"Yes; I saw him ;—but I did not find much relief from his visit. We won't mind that, however. We can talk about something better than Hugh Clavering during the few minutes that we have together ;—can we not? And so Miss Burton is very learned and very clever?"

"I did not quite say that."

"But I know she is. What a comfort that will be to you! I am not clever, and I never should have become learned. Oh, dear! I had but one merit, Harry ;—I was fond of you."

"And how did you show it?" He did not speak these words, because he would not triumph over her, nor was he willing to express that regret on his own part which these words would have implied ;—but it was impossible for him to avoid a thought of them. He remained silent, therefore, taking up some toy from the table into his hands, as though that would occupy his attention.

"But what a fool I am to talk of it ;—am I not? And I am worse than a fool. I was thinking of you when I stood up in church to be married ;—thinking of that offer of your little savings. I used to think of you at every harsh word that I endured ;—of your modes of life when I sat through those terrible nights by that poor creature's bed ;—of you when I knew that the last day was coming. I thought of you always, Harry, when I counted up my gains. I never count them up now. Ah, how I thought of you when I came to this house in the carriage which you had provided for me, when I had left you at the station almost without speaking a word to you! I should have been more gracious had I not had you in my thoughts throughout my whole journey home from Florence. And after that I had some comfort in believing that the price of my shame might make you rich without shame. Oh, Harry, I have been disappointed! You will never understand what I felt when first that evil woman told me of Miss Burton."

"Oh, Julia, what am I to say?"

"You can say nothing; but I wonder that you had not told me."

"How could I tell you? Would it not have seemed that I was vain enough to have thought of putting you on your guard."

"And why not? But never mind. Do not suppose that I am rebuking you. As I said in my letter, we are quits now, and there is no place for scolding on either side. We are quits now; but I am punished and you are rewarded."

Of course he could not answer this. Of course he was hard pressed for words. Of course he could neither acknowledge that he had been rewarded, nor assert that a share of the punishment of which she spoke had fallen upon him also. This was the revenge with which she had intended to attack him. That she should think that he had in truth been punished and not rewarded, was very natural. Had he been less quick in forgetting her after her marriage, he would have had his reward without any punishment. If such were her thoughts, who shall quarrel with her on that account?

"I have been very frank with you," she continued. "Indeed, why should I not be so? People talk of a lady's secret, but my secret has been no secret from you? That I was made to tell it under,—under, —what I will call an error,—was your fault; and it is that that has made us quits."

"I know that I have behaved badly to you."

"But then unfortunately you know also that I had deserved bad treatment. Well; we will say no more about it. I have been very candid with you, but then I have injured no one by my candour. You have not said a word to me in reply; but then your tongue is tied by your duty to Miss Burton,—your duty and your love together, of course. It is all as it should be, and now I will have done. When are you to be married, Harry?"

"No time has been fixed. I am a very poor man, you know."

"Alas, alas,—yes. When mischief is done, how badly all the things turn out. You are poor and I am rich, and yet we cannot help each other."

"I fear not."

"Unless I could adopt Miss Burton, and be a sort of mother to her. You would shrink, however, from any such guardianship on my part. But you are clever, Harry, and can work when you please, and will make your way. If Miss Burton keeps you waiting now by any prudent fear on her part, I shall not think so well of her as I am inclined to do."

"The Burtons are all prudent people."

"Tell her, from me, with my love,—not to be too prudent. I thought to be prudent, and see what has come of it."

"I will tell her what you say."

"Do, please; and, Harry, look here. Will she accept a little present from me? You, at any rate, for my sake, will ask her to do so. Give her this,—it is only a trifle,"—and she put her hand on a small jeweller's box, which was close to her arm upon the table, " and tell her,—of course she knows all our story, Harry ? "

" Yes ; she knows it all."

" Tell her that she whom you have rejected sends it with her kindest wishes to her whom you have taken."

" No ; I will not tell her that."

" Why not ? It is all true. I have not poisoned the little ring, as the ladies would have done some centuries since. They were grander then than we are now, and perhaps hardly worse, though more cruel. You will bid her take it,—will you not ? "

" I am sure she will take it without bidding on my part."

" And tell her not to write me any thanks. She and I will both understand that that had better be omitted. If, when I shall see her at some future time as your wife, it shall be on her finger, I shall know that I am thanked." Then Harry rose to go. " I did not mean by that to turn you out, but perhaps it may be as well. I have no more to say,— and as for you, you cannot but wish that the penance should be over." Then he pressed her hand, and with some muttered farewell, bade her adieu. Again she did not rise from her chair, but nodding at him with a sweet smile, let him go without another word.

CHAPTER XLIV.

SHEWING WHAT HAPPENED OFF HELIGOLAND.

DURING the six weeks after this, Harry Clavering settled down to his work at the chambers in the Adelphi with exemplary diligence. Florence, having remained a fortnight in town after Harry's return to the sheepfold, and having accepted Lady Ongar's present,—not without a long and anxious consultation with her sister-in-law on the subject,—had returned in fully restored happiness to Stratton. Mrs. Burton was at Ramsgate with the children, and Mr. Burton was in Russia with reference to a line of railway which was being projected from Moscow to Astracan. It was now September, and Harry, in his letters home, declared that he was the only person left in London. It was hard upon him,—much harder than it was upon the Wallikers and other young men whom fate retained in town, for Harry was a man given to shooting,—a man accustomed to pass the autumnal months in a country house. And then, if things had chanced to go one way instead of another, he would have had his own shooting down at Ongar Park with his own friends,—admiring him at his heels ; or if not so this year, he would have been shooting elsewhere with the prospect of these rich joys for years to come. As it was, he had promised to stick to the shop, and was sticking to it manfully. Nor do I think that he allowed his mind to revert to those privileges which might have been his, at all more frequently than any of my readers would have done

in his place. He was sticking to the shop, and though he greatly disliked
the hot desolation of London in those days, being absolutely afraid to
frequent his club at such a period of the year,—and though he hated
Walliker mortally,—he was fully resolved to go on with his work. Who
could tell what might be his fate ? Perhaps in another ten years he
might be carrying that Russian railway on through the deserts of Siberia.
Then there came to him suddenly tidings which disturbed all his resolutions, and changed the whole current of his life.

At first there came a telegram to him from the country, desiring him
to go down at once to Clavering, but not giving him any reason. Added
to the message were these words,—" We are all well at the parsonage ; "—
words evidently added in thoughtfulness. But before he had left the office
there came to him there a young man from the bank at which his cousin
Hugh kept his account, telling him the tidings to which the telegram
no doubt referred. Jack Stuart's boat had been lost, and his two cousins
had gone to their graves beneath the sea ! The master of the boat, and
Stuart himself, with a boy, had been saved. The other sailors whom they
had with them, and the ship's steward, had perished with the Claverings.
Stuart, it seemed, had caused tidings of the accident to be sent to the
rector of Clavering and to Sir Hugh's bankers. At the bank they had
ascertained that their late customer's cousin was in town, and their messenger had thereupon been sent, first to Bloomsbury Square, and from
thence to the Adelphi.

Harry had never loved his cousins. The elder he had greatly disliked,
and the younger he would have disliked had he not despised him. But
not the less on that account was he inexpressibly shocked when he first
heard what had happened. The lad said that there could, as he imagined,
be no mistake. The message had come, as he believed, from Holland,
but of that he was not certain. There could, however, be no doubt about
the fact. It distinctly stated that both brothers had perished. Harry
had known when he received the message from home, that no train would
take him till three in the afternoon, and had therefore remained at the
office ; but he could not remain now. His head was confused, and he
could hardly bring himself to think how this matter would affect himself.
When he attempted to explain his absence to an old serious clerk there,
he spoke of his own return to the office as certain. He should be back,
he supposed, in a week at the furthest. He was thinking then of his
promises to Theodore Burton, and had not begun to realize the fact that
his whole destiny in life would be changed. He said something, with a
long face, of the terrible misfortune which had occurred, but gave no hint
that that misfortune would be important in its consequences to himself.
It was not till he had reached his lodgings in Bloomsbury Square that he
remembered that his own father was now the baronet, and that he was his
father's heir. And then for a moment he thought about the property.
He believed that it was entailed, but even of that he was not certain.
But if it were unentailed, to whom could his cousin have left it ? He

endeavoured, however, to expel such thoughts from his mind, as though there was something ungenerous in entertaining them. He tried to think of the widow, but even in doing that he could not tell himself that there was much ground for genuine sorrow. No wife had ever had less joy from her husband's society than Lady Clavering had had from that of Sir Hugh. There was no child to mourn the loss,—no brother, no unmarried sister. Sir Hugh had had friends,—as friendship goes with such men; but Harry could not but doubt whether among them all there would be one who would feel anything like true grief for his loss. And it was the same with Archie. Who in the world would miss Archie Clavering? What man or woman would find the world to be less bright because Archie Clavering was sleeping beneath the waves? Some score of men at his club would talk of poor Clavvy for a few days,—would do so without any pretence at the tenderness of sorrow; and then even of Archie's memory there would be an end. Thinking of all this as he was carried down to Clavering, Harry could not but acknowledge that the loss to the world had not been great; but, even while telling himself this, he would not allow himself to take comfort in the prospect of his heirship. Once, perhaps, he did speculate how Florence should bear her honours as Lady Clavering; but this idea he swept away from his thoughts as quickly as he was able.

The tidings had reached the parsonage very late on the previous night; so late that the rector had been disturbed in his bed to receive them. It was his duty to make known to Lady Clavering the fact that she was a widow, but this he could not do till the next morning. But there was little sleep that night for him or for his wife! He knew well enough that the property was entailed. He felt with sufficient strength what it was to become a baronet at a sudden blow, and to become also the owner of the whole Clavering property. He was not slow to think of the removal to the great house, of the altered prospects of his son, and of the mode of life which would be fitting for himself in future. Before the morning came he had meditated who should be the future rector of Clavering, and had made some calculations as to the expediency of resuming his hunting. Not that he was a heartless man,—or that he rejoiced at what had happened. But a man's ideas of generosity change as he advances in age, and the rector was old enough to tell himself boldly that this thing that had happened could not be to him a cause of much grief. He had never loved his cousins, or pretended to love them. His cousin's wife he did love, after a fashion, but in speaking to his own wife of the way in which this tragedy would affect Hermione, he did not scruple to speak of her widowhood as a period of coming happiness.

"She will be cut to pieces," said Mrs. Clavering. "She was attached to him as earnestly as though he had treated her always well."

"I believe it; but not the less will she feel her release, unconsciously; and her life, which has been very wretched, will gradually become easy to her."

Even Mrs. Clavering could not deny that this would be so, and then

they reverted to matters which more closely concerned themselves. " I
suppose Harry will marry at once now," said the mother.

"No doubt;—it is almost a pity; is it not?" The rector,—as we
will still call him,—was thinking that Florence was hardly a fitting wife
for his son with his altered prospects. Ah, what a grand thing it would
have been if the Clavering property and Lady Ongar's jointure could have
gone together!

"Not a pity at all," said Mrs. Clavering. "You will find that
Florence will make him a very happy man."

"I dare say;—I dare say. Only he would hardly have taken her had
this sad accident happened before he saw her. But if she will make him
happy that is everything. I have never thought much about money
myself. If I find any comfort in these tidings it is for his sake, not for
my own. I would sooner remain as I am." This was not altogether untrue,
and yet he was thinking of the big house and the hunting.

"What will be done about the living?" It was early in the morning
when Mrs. Clavering asked this question. She had thought much about
the living during the night. And so had the rector;—but his thoughts had
not run in the same direction as hers. He made no immediate answer,
and then she went on with her question. "Do you think that you will
keep it in your own hands?"

"Well,—no; why should I? I am too idle about it as it is. I should
be more so under these altered circumstances."

"I am sure you would do your duty if you resolved to keep it, but I
don't see why you should do so."

"Clavering is a great deal better than Humbleton," said the rector.
Humbleton was the name of the parish held by Mr. Fielding, his son-
in-law.

But the idea here put forward did not suit the idea which was running
in Mrs. Clavering's mind. "Edward and Mary are very well off," she
said. "His own property is considerable, and I don't think they want
anything. Besides, he would hardly like to give up a family living."

"I might ask him at any rate."

"I was thinking of Mr. Saul," said Mrs. Clavering boldly.

"Of Mr. Saul!" The image of Mr. Saul, as rector of Clavering,
perplexed the new baronet egregiously.

"Well;—yes. He is an excellent clergyman. No one can deny
that." Then there was silence between them for a few moments. "In
that case he and Fanny would of course marry. It is no good concealing
the fact that she is very fond of him."

"Upon my word I can't understand it," said the rector.

"It is so,—and as to the excellence of his character there can be no
doubt." To this the rector made no answer, but went away into his
dressing-room, that he might prepare himself for his walk across the park
to the great house. While they were discussing who should be the future
incumbent of the living, Lady Clavering was still sleeping in unconscious-

ness of her fate. Mr. Clavering greatly dreaded the task which was before him, and had made a little attempt to induce his wife to take the office upon herself; but she had explained to him that it would be more seemly that he should be the bearer of the tidings. "It would seem that you were wanting in affection for her if you do not go yourself," his wife had said to him. That the rector of Clavering was master of himself and of his own actions, no one who knew the family ever denied, but the instances in which he declined to follow his wife's advice were not many.

It was about eight o'clock when he went across the park. He had already sent a messenger with a note to beg that Lady Clavering would be up to receive him. As he would come very early, he had said, perhaps she would see him in her own room. The poor lady had, of course, been greatly frightened by this announcement; but this fear had been good for her, as they had well understood at the rectory; the blow, dreadfully sudden as it must still be, would be somewhat less sudden under this pre-paration. When Mr. Clavering reached the house the servant was in waiting to show him upstairs to the sitting-room which Lady Clavering usually occupied when alone. She had been there waiting for him for the last half-hour.

"Mr. Clavering, what is it?" she exclaimed, as he entered with tidings of death written on his visage. "In the name of heaven, what is it? You have something to tell me of Hugh."

"Dear Hermione," he said, taking her by the hand.

"What is it? Tell me at once. Is he still alive?"

The rector still held her by the hand, but spoke no word. He had been trying as he came across the park to arrange the words in which he should tell his tale, but now it was told without any speech on his part.

"He is dead. Why do you not speak? Why are you so cruel?"

"Dearest Hermione, what am I to say to comfort you?"

What he might say after this was of little moment, for she had fainted. He rang the bell, and then, when the servants were there,—the old house-keeper and Lady Clavering's maid,—he told to them, rather than to her, what had been their master's fate.

"And Captain Archie?" asked the housekeeper.

The rector shook his head, and the housekeeper knew that the rector was now the baronet. Then they took the poor widow to her own room, —should I not rather call her, as I may venture to speak the truth, the enfranchised slave than the poor widow?—and the rector, taking up his hat, promised that he would send his wife across to their mistress. His morning's task had been painful, but it had been easily accomplished. As he walked home among the oaks of Clavering Park, he told himself, no doubt, that they were now all his own.

That day at the rectory was very sombre, if it was not actually sad. The greater part of the morning Mrs. Clavering passed with the widow, and sitting near her sofa she wrote sundry letters to those who were connected

with the family. The longest of these was to Lady Ongar, who was now
at Tenby ; and in that there was a pressing request from Hermione that
her sister would come to her at Clavering Park. "Tell her," said Lady
Clavering, "that all her anger must be over now." But Mrs. Clavering
said nothing of Julia's anger. She merely urged the request that Julia
would come to her sister. "She will be sure to come," said Mrs.
Clavering. "You need have no fear on that head."

"But how can I invite her here, when the house is not my own?"

"Pray do not talk in that way, Hermione. The house will be your
own for any time that you may want it. Your husband's relations are
your dear friends; are they not?" But this allusion to her husband
brought her to another fit of hysterical tears. "Both of them gone," she
said. "Both of them gone!" Mrs. Clavering knew well that she was
not alluding to the two brothers, but to her husband and to her baby. Of
poor Archie no one had said a word,—beyond that one word spoken by the
housekeeper. For her, it had been necessary that she should know who
was now the master of Clavering Park.

Twice in the day Mrs. Clavering went over to the big house, and on
her second return, late in the evening, she found her son. When she
arrived, there had already been some few words on the subject between
him and his father.

"You have heard of it, Harry?"

"Yes ; a clerk came to me from the banker's."

"Dreadful ; is it not? Quite terrible to think of!"

"Indeed it is, sir. I was never so shocked in my life."

"He would go in that cursed boat, though I know that he was advised
against it," said the father, holding up his hands and shaking his head.
"And now both of them gone ;—both gone at once!"

"How does she bear it?"

"Your mother is with her now. When I went in the morning,—I
had written a line, and she expected bad news,—she fainted. Of course,
I could do nothing. I can hardly say that I told her. She asked the question, and then saw by my face that her fears were well-founded. Upon
my word, I was glad when she did faint ;—it was the best thing for her."

"It must have been very painful for you."

"Terrible ;—terrible ;" and the rector shook his head. "It will make
a great difference in your prospects, Harry."

"And in your life, sir! So to say, you are as young a man as
myself."

"Am I? I believe I was about as young when you were born. But
I don't think at all about myself in this matter. I am too old to care to
change my manner of living. It won't affect me very much. Indeed, I
hardly know yet how it may affect me. Your mother thinks I ought to
give up the living. If you were in orders, Harry——"

"I'm very glad, sir, that I am not."

"I suppose so. And there is no need ; certainly, there is no need.

You will be able to do pretty nearly what you like about the property. I shall not care to interfere."

"Yes, you will, sir. It feels strange now, but you will soon get used to it. I wonder whether he left a will."

"It can't make any difference to you, you know. Every acre of the property is entailed. She has her settlement. Eight hundred a year, I think it is. She'll not be a rich woman like her sister. I wonder where she'll live. As far as that goes, she might stay at the house, if she likes it. I'm sure your mother wouldn't object."

Harry on this occasion asked no question about the living, but he also had thought of that. He knew well that his mother would befriend Mr. Saul, and he knew also that his father would ultimately take his mother's advice. As regarded himself he had no personal objection to Mr. Saul, though he could not understand how his sister should feel any strong regard for such a man.

Edward Fielding would make a better neighbour at the parsonage, and then he thought whether an exchange might not be made. After that, and before his mother's return from the great house, he took a stroll through the park with Fanny. Fanny altogether declined to discuss any of the family prospects, as they were affected by the accident which had happened. To her mind the tragedy was so terrible that she could only feel its tragic element. No doubt she had her own thoughts about Mr. Saul as connected with it. "What would he think of this sudden death of the two brothers? How would he feel it? If she could be allowed to talk to him on the matter, what would he say of their fate here and hereafter? Would he go to the great house to offer the consolations of religion to the widow?" Of all this she thought much; but no picture of Mr. Saul as rector of Clavering, or of herself as mistress in her mother's house, presented itself to her mind. Harry found her to be a dull companion, and he, perhaps, consoled himself with some personal attention to the oak trees. The trees loomed larger upon him now than they had ever done before.

On the third day, the rector went up to London, leaving Harry at the parsonage. It was necessary that lawyers should be visited, and that such facts as to the loss should be proved as were capable of proof. There was no doubt at all as to the fate of Sir Hugh and his brother. The escape of Mr. Stuart and of two of those employed by him prevented the possibility of a doubt. The vessel had been caught in a gale off Heligoland, and had foundered. They had all striven to get into the yacht's boat, but those who had succeeded in doing so had gone down. The master of the yacht had seen the two brothers perish. Those who were saved had been picked up off the spars to which they had attached themselves. There was no doubt in the way of the new baronet, and no difficulty.

Nor was there any will made either by Sir Hugh or his brother. Poor Archie had nothing to leave, and that he should have left no will was not remarkable. But neither had there been much in the power of Sir Hugh to bequeath, nor was there any great cause for a will on his part. Had he left a son, his son would have inherited everything. He had, however, died childless, and his wife was provided for by her settlement. On his marriage he had made the amount settled as small as his wife's friends would accept, and no one who knew the man expected that he would increase the amount after his death. Having been in town for three days the rector returned,—being then in full possession of the title; but this he did not assume till after the second Sunday from the date of the telegram which brought the news.

In the meantime Harry had written to Florence, to whom the tidings were as important as to any one concerned. She had left London very triumphant,—quite confident that she had nothing now to fear from Lady Ongar or from any other living woman, having not only forgiven Harry his sins, but having succeeded also in persuading herself that there had been no sins to forgive,—having quarrelled with her brother half-a-dozen times in that he would not accept her arguments on this matter. He too would forgive Harry,—had forgiven him; was quite ready to omit all further remark on the matter; but could not bring himself when urged by Florence to admit that her Apollo had been altogether godlike. Florence had thus left London in triumph, but she had gone with a conviction that she and Harry must remain apart for some indefinite time, which probably must be measured by years. "Let us see at the end of two years," she had said; and Harry had been forced to be content. But how would it be with her now?

Harry of course began his letter by telling her of the catastrophe, with the usual amount of epithets. It was very terrible, awful, shocking,— the saddest thing that had ever happened! The poor widow was in a desperate state, and all the Claverings were nearly beside themselves. But when this had been duly said, he allowed himself to go into their own home question. "I cannot fail," he wrote, "to think of this chiefly as it concerns you,—or rather, as it concerns myself in reference to you. I suppose I shall leave the business now. Indeed, my father seems to think that my remaining there would be absurd, and my mother agrees with him. As I am the only son, the property will enable me to live easily without a profession. When I say 'me,' of course you will understand what 'me' means. The better part of 'me' is so prudent, that I know she will not accept this view of things without ever so much consideration, and, therefore, she must come to Clavering to hear it discussed by the elders. For myself, I cannot bear to think that I should take delight in the results of this dreadful misfortune; but how am I to keep myself from being made happy by the feeling that we may now be married without further delay? After all that has passed, nothing will make me happy or even permanently comfortable till I can call you fairly my own. My mother has already said that she hopes you will come here in about a fortnight,—that is, as soon as we shall have fallen tolerably into our places again; but she will write herself before that time. I have written a line to your brother addressed to the office, which I suppose will find him. I have written also to Cecilia. Your brother, no doubt, will hear the news first through the French newspapers." Then he said a little, but a very little, as to their future modes of life, just intimating to her, and no more, that her destiny might probably call upon her to be the mother of a future baronet.

The news had reached Clavering on a Saturday. On the following Sunday every one in the parish had no doubt heard of it, but nothing on the subject was said in church on that day. The rector remained at home during the morning, and the whole service was performed by Mr. Saul. But on the second Sunday Mr. Fielding had come over from Humbleton, and he preached a sermon on the loss which the parish had sustained in the sudden death of the two brothers. It is, perhaps, well that such sermons should be preached. The inhabitants of Clavering would have felt that their late lords had been treated like dogs, had no word been said of them in the house of God. The nature of their fate had forbidden even the common ceremony of a burial service. It is well that some respect should be maintained from the low in station towards those who are high, even when no respect has been deserved. And, for the widow's sake, it was well that some notice should be taken in Clavering of this death of the head of the Claverings. But I should not myself have liked the duty of preaching an eulogistic sermon on the lives and death of Hugh Clavering and his brother Archie. What had either of them ever done to merit a good word from any man, or to earn the love of any woman? That Sir Hugh had been loved by his wife had come from the nature of the woman, not at all from the qualities of the man. Both of the brothers had lived on the unexpressed theory of consuming, for the benefit of their own backs and their own bellies, the greatest possible amount of those good things which fortune might put in their way. I doubt whether either of them had ever contributed anything willingly to the comfort or happiness of any human being. Hugh, being powerful by nature and having a strong will, had tyrannized over all those who were subject to him. Archie, not gifted as was his brother, had been milder, softer, and less actively hateful; but his principle of action had been the same. Everything for himself! Was it not well that two such men should be consigned to the fishes, and that the world,—especially the Clavering world, and that poor widow, who now felt herself to be so inexpressibly wretched when her period of comfort was in truth only commencing,—was it not well that the world and Clavering should be well quit of them? That idea is the one which one would naturally have felt inclined to put into one's sermon on such an occasion; and then to sing some song of rejoicing;—either to do that, or to leave the matter alone.

But not so are such sermons preached; and not after that fashion did the young clergyman who had married the first-cousin of these Claverings buckle himself to the subject. He indeed had, I think, but little difficulty, either inwardly with his conscience, or outwardly with his subject. He possessed the power of a pleasant, easy flow of words, and of producing tears, if not from other eyes, at any rate from his own. He drew a picture of the little ship amidst the storm, and of God's hand as it moved in its anger upon the waters; but of the cause of that divine wrath and its direction he said nothing. Then, of the suddenness of death and its awfulness he said much, not insisting as he did so on the necessity of repentance for salvation, as far as those two poor sinners were concerned. No, indeed;—how could any preacher have done that? But he improved the occasion by telling those around him that they should so live as to be ever ready for the hand of death. If that were possible, where then indeed would be the victory of the grave? And at last he came to the master and lord whom they had lost. Even here there was no difficulty for him. The heir had gone first, and then the father and his brother. Who among them would not pity the bereaved mother and the widow? Who among them would not remember with affection the babe whom they had seen at that font, and with respect the landlord under whose rule they had lived? How pleasant it must be to ask those questions which no one can rise to answer! Farmer Gubbins as he sat by, listening with what power of attention had been vouchsafed to him, felt himself to be somewhat moved, but soon released himself from the task, and allowed his mind to run away into other ideas. The rector was a kindly man and a generous. The rector would allow him to enclose that little bit of common land, that was to be taken in, without adding anything to his rent. The rector would be there on audit days, and things would be very pleasant. Farmer Gubbins, when the slight murmuring gurgle of the preacher's tears was heard, shook his own head by way of a responsive wail; but at that moment he was congratulating himself on the coming comfort of the new reign. Mr. Fielding, however, got great credit for his sermon; and it did, probably, more good than harm,—unless, indeed, we should take into our calculation, in giving our award on this subject, the permanent utility of all truth, and the permanent injury of all falsehood.

Mr. Fielding remained at the parsonage during the greater part of the following week, and then there took place a great deal of family conversation, respecting the future incumbent of the living. At these family conclaves, however, Fanny was not asked to be present. Mrs. Clavering, who knew well how to do such work, was gradually bringing her husband round to endure the name of Mr. Saul. Twenty times had he asserted that he could not understand it; but, whether or no such understanding might ever be possible, he was beginning to recognize it as true that the thing not understood was a fact. His daughter Fanny was positively in love with Mr. Saul, and that to such an extent that her mother believed her happiness to be involved in it. "I can't understand it;—upon my word I can't," said the rector for the last time, and then he gave way. There was now the means of giving an ample provision for the lovers, and that provision was to be given.

Mr. Fielding shook his head,—not in this instance as to Fanny's predilection for Mr. Saul; though in discussing that matter with his own wife he had shaken his head very often; but he shook it now with reference to the proposed change. He was very well where he was. And although Clavering was better than Humbleton, it was not so much better as to induce him to throw his own family over by proposing to send Mr. Saul among them. Mr. Saul was an excellent clergyman, but perhaps his uncle, who had given him his living, might not like Mr. Saul. Thus it was decided in these conclaves that Mr. Saul was to be the future rector of Clavering.

In the meantime poor Fanny moped,—wretched in her solitude, anticipating no such glorious joys as her mother was preparing for her; and Mr. Saul was preparing with energy for his departure into foreign parts.

CHAPTER XLV.

Is She Mad?

LADY ONGAR was at Tenby when she received Mrs. Clavering's letter, and had not heard of the fate of her brother-in-law till the news reached her in that way. She had gone down to a lodging at Tenby with no attendant but one maid, and was preparing herself for the great surrender of her property which she meditated. Hitherto she had heard nothing from the Courtons or their lawyer as to the offer she had made about Ongar Park; but the time had been short, and lawyers' work, as she knew, was never done in a hurry. She had gone to Tenby, flying, in truth, from the loneliness of London to the loneliness of the sea-shore,—but expecting she knew not what comfort from the change. She would take with her no carriage, and there would, as she thought, be excitement even in that. She would take long walks by herself;—she would read;—nay, if possible, she would study and bring herself to some habits of industry. Hitherto she had failed in everything, but now she would try if some mode of success might not be open to her. She would ascertain, too, on what smallest sum she could live respectably and without penury, and would keep only so much out of Lord Ongar's wealth.

But hitherto her life at Tenby had not been successful. Solitary days were longer there even than they had been in London. People stared at her more; and, though she did not own it to herself, she missed greatly the comforts of her London house. As for reading, I doubt whether she did much better by the seaside than she had done in the town. Men and women say that they will read, and think so,—those, I mean, who have acquired no habit of reading,—believing the work to be, of all works, the easiest. It may be work, they think, but of all works it must be the easiest of achievement. Given the absolute faculty of reading, the task of going through the pages of a book must be, of all tasks, the most certainly within the grasp of the man or woman who attempts it! Alas, no;—if the habit be not there, of all tasks it is the most difficult. If a man have not acquired the habit of reading till he be old, he shall sooner in his old age learn to make shoes than learn the adequate use of a book. And worse again;—under such circumstances the making of shoes shall be more pleasant to him than the reading of a book. Let those who are not old,— who are still young, ponder this well. Lady Ongar, indeed, was not old, by no means too old to clothe herself in new habits. But even she was old enough to find that the doing so was a matter of much difficulty. She had her books around her; but, in spite of her books, she was sadly in want of some excitement when the letter from Clavering came to her relief.

It was indeed a relief. Her brother-in-law dead, and he also who had so lately been her suitor! These two men whom she had so lately seen in lusty health,—proud with all the pride of outward life,—had both, by a stroke of the winds, been turned into nothing. A terrible retribution had fallen upon her enemy,—for as her enemy she had ever regarded Hugh Clavering since her husband's death. She took no joy in this retribution. There was no feeling of triumph at her heart in that he had perished. She did not tell herself that she was glad,—either for her own sake or for her sister's. But mingled with the awe she felt there was a something of unexpressed and inexpressible relief. Her present life was very grievous to her,—and now had occurred that which would open to her new hopes and a new mode of living. Her brother-in-law had oppressed her by his very existence, and now he was gone. Had she had no brother-in-law who ought to have welcomed her, her return to England would not have been terrible to her as it had been. Her sister would be now restored to her, and her solitude would probably be at an end. And then the very excitement occasioned by the news was salutary to her. She was, in truth, shocked. As she said to her maid, she felt it to be very dreadful. But, nevertheless, the day on which she received those tidings was less wearisome to her than any other of the days that she had passed at Tenby.

Poor Archie! Some feeling of a tear, some half-formed drop that was almost a tear, came to her eye as she thought of his fate. How foolish he had always been, how unintelligent, how deficient in all those qualities which recommend men to women! But the very memory of his deficiencies created something like a tenderness in his favour. Hugh was disagreeable, nay hateful, by reason of the power which he possessed; whereas Archie was not hateful at all, and was disagreeable simply because nature had been a niggard to him. And then he had professed himself to be her lover. There had not been much in this; for he had come, of course, for her money; but even when that is the case a woman will feel something for the man who has offered to link his lot with hers. Of all those to whom the fate of the two brothers had hitherto been matter of moment, I think that Lady Ongar felt more than any other for the fate of poor Archie.

And how would it affect Harry Clavering? She had desired to give Harry all the good things of the world, thinking that they would become him well,—thinking that they would become him very well as reaching him from her hand. Now he would have them all, but would not have them from her. Now he would have them all, and would share them with Florence Burton. Ah,—if she could have been true to him in those early days,—in those days when she had feared his poverty,—would it not have been well now with her also? The measure of her retribution was come full home to her at last! Sir Harry Clavering! She tried the name and found that it sounded very well. And she thought of the figure of the man and of his nature, and she knew that he would bear it with a becoming manliness. Sir Harry Clavering would be somebody in his county,—would be a husband of whom his wife would be proud as he went about among his tenants and his gamekeepers,—and perhaps on wider and better journeys, looking up the voters of his neighbourhood. Yes; happy would be the wife of Sir Harry Clavering. He was a man who would delight in sharing his house, his hopes, his schemes and councils with his wife. He would find a companion in his wife. He would do honour to his wife, and make much of her. He would like to see her go bravely. And then, if children came, how tender he would be to them! Whether Harry could ever have become a good head to a poor household might be doubtful, but no man had ever been born fitter for the position which he was now called upon to fill. It was thus that Lady Ongar thought of Harry Clavering as she owned to herself that the full measure of her just retribution had come home to her.

Of course she would go at once to Clavering Park. She wrote to her sister saying so, and the next day she started. She started so quickly on her journey that she reached the house not very many hours after her own letter. She was there when the rector started for London, and there when Mr. Fielding preached his sermon; but she did not see Mr. Clavering before he went, nor was she present to hear the eloquence of the younger clergyman. Till after that Sunday the only member of the family she had seen was Mrs. Clavering, who spent some period of every day up at the great house. Mrs. Clavering had not hitherto seen Lady Ongar since her return, and was greatly astonished at the change which so short a time had made. "She is handsomer than ever she was," Mrs. Clavering said to the rector; "but it is that beauty which some women carry into middle life, and not the loveliness of youth." Lady Ongar's manner was cold and stately when first she met Mrs. Clavering. It was on the morning of her marriage when they had last met,—when Julia Brabazon was resolving that she would look like a countess, and that to be a countess should be enough for her happiness. She could not but remember this now, and was unwilling at first to make confession of her failure by any meekness of conduct. It behoved her to be proud, at any rate till she should know how this new Lady Clavering would receive her. And then it was more than probable that this new Lady Clavering knew all that had taken place between her and Harry. It behoved her, therefore, to hold her head on high.

But before the week was over, Mrs. Clavering,—for we will still call her so,—had broken Lady Ongar's spirit by her kindness; and the poor woman who had so much to bear had brought herself to speak of the weight of her burden. Julia had, on one occasion, called her Lady Clavering, and for the moment this had been allowed to pass without observation. The widowed lady was then present, and no notice of the name was possible. But soon afterwards Mrs. Clavering made her little request on the subject. "I do not quite know what the custom may be," she said, "but do not call me so just yet. It will only be reminding Hermy of her bereavement."

"She is thinking of it always," said Julia.

"No doubt she is; but still the new name would wound her. And, indeed, it perplexes me also. Let it come by-and-by, when we are more settled."

Lady Ongar had truly said that her sister was as yet always thinking of her bereavement. To her now it was as though the husband she had lost had been a paragon among men. She could only remember of him his manliness, his power,—a dignity of presence which he possessed,—and the fact that to her he had been everything. She thought of that last and vain caution which she had given him, when with her hardly permitted last embrace she had besought him to take care of himself. She did not remember now how coldly that embrace had been received, how completely those words had been taken as meaning nothing, how he had left her not only without a sign of affection, but without an attempt to repress the evidences of his indifference. But she did remember that she had had her arm upon his shoulder, and tried to think of that embrace as though it had been sweet to her. And she did remember how she had stood at the window, listening to the sounds of the wheels which took him off, and watching his form as long as her eye could rest upon it. Ah! what falsehoods she told herself now of her love to him, and of his goodness to her; pious falsehoods which would surely tend to bring some comfort to her wounded spirit.

But her sister could hardly bear to hear the praises of Sir Hugh. When she found how it was to be, she resolved that she would bear them, —bear them, and not contradict them; but her struggle in doing so was great, and was almost too much for her.

"He had judged me and condemned me," she said at last, "and therefore, as a matter of course, we were not such friends when we last met as we used to be before my marriage."

"But, Julia, there was much for which you owed him gratitude."

"We will say nothing about that now, Hermy."

"I do not know why your mouth should be closed on such a subject because he has gone. I should have thought that you would be glad to acknowledge his kindness to you. But you were always hard."

" Perhaps I am hard."

" And twice he asked you to come here since you returned,—but you would not come."

" I have come now, Hermy, when I have thought that I might be of use."

" He felt it when you would not come before. I know he did." Lady Ongar could not but think of the way in which he had manifested his feelings on the occasion of his visit to Bolton Street. " I never could understand why you were so bitter."

" I think, dear, we had better not discuss that. I also have had much to bear,—I, as well as you. What you have borne has come in no wise from your own fault."

" No, indeed ; I did not want him to go. I would have given anything to keep him at home."

Her sister had not been thinking of the suffering which had come to her from the loss of her husband, but of her former miseries. This, however, she did not explain. " No," Lady Ongar continued to say. " You have nothing for which to blame yourself, whereas I have much,— indeed everything. If we are to remain together, as I hope we may, it will be better for us both that bygones should be bygones."

" Do you mean that I am never to speak of Hugh ? "

" No ;—I by no means intend that. But I would rather that you should not refer to his feelings towards me. I think he did not quite understand the sort of life that I led while my husband was alive, and that he judged me amiss. Therefore I would have bygones be bygones."

Three or four days after this, when the question of leaving Clavering Park was being mooted, the elder sister started a difficulty as to money matters. An offer had been made to her by Mrs. Clavering to remain at the great house, but this she had declined, alleging that the place would be distasteful to her after her husband's death. She, poor soul, did not allege that it had been made distasteful to her for ever by the solitude which she had endured there during her husband's lifetime ! She would go away somewhere, and live as best she might upon her jointure. It was not very much, but it would be sufficient. She did not see, she said, how she could live with her sister, because she did not wish to be dependent. Julia, of course, would live in a style to which she could make no pretence.

Mrs. Clavering, who was present,—as was also Lady Ongar,—declared that she saw no such difficulty. " Sisters together," she said, " need hardly think of a difference in such matters."

Then it was that Lady Ongar first spoke to either of them of her half-formed resolution about her money, and then too, for the first time, did she come down altogether from that high horse on which she had been, as it were, compelled to mount herself while in Mrs. Clavering's presence. " I think I must explain," said she, " something of what I mean to do,—about my money that is. I do not think that there will be much difference between me and Hermy in that respect."

"That is nonsense," said her sister, fretfully.

"There will be a difference in income certainly," said Mrs. Clavering, "but I do not see that that need create any uncomfortable feeling."

"Only one doesn't like to be dependent," said Hermione.

"You shall not be asked to give up any of your independence," said Julia, with a smile,—a melancholy smile, that gave but little sign of pleasantness within. Then on a sudden her face became stern and hard. "The fact is," she said, "I do not intend to keep Lord Ongar's money."

"Not to keep your income!" said Hermione.

"No;—I will give it back to them,—or at least the greater part of it. Why should I keep it?"

"It is your own," said Mrs. Clavering.

"Yes; legally it is my own. I know that. And when there was some question whether it should not be disputed I would have fought for it to the last shilling. Somebody,—I suppose it was the lawyer,—wanted to keep from me the place in Surrey. I told them then that I would not abandon my right to an inch of it. But they yielded,—and now I have given them back the house."

"You have given it back!" said her sister.

"Yes;—I have said they may have it. It is of no use to me. I hate the place."

"You have been very generous," said Mrs. Clavering.

"But that will not affect your income," said Hermione.

"No;—that would not affect my income." Then she paused, not knowing how to go on with the story of her purpose.

"If I may say so, Lady Ongar," said Mrs. Clavering, "I would not if I were you, take any steps in so important a matter without advice."

"Who is there that can advise me? Of course the lawyer tells me that I ought to keep it all. It is his business to give such advice as that. But what does he know of what I feel? How can he understand me? How, indeed, can I expect that any one shall understand me?"

"But it is possible that people should misunderstand you," said Mrs. Clavering.

"Exactly. That is just what he says. But, Mrs. Clavering, I care nothing for that. I care nothing for what anybody says or thinks. What is it to me what they say?"

"I should have thought it was everything," said her sister.

"No,—it is nothing;—nothing at all." Then she was again silent, and was unable to express herself. She could not bring herself to declare in words that self-condemnation of her own conduct which was now weighing so heavily upon her. It was not that she wished to keep back her own feelings, either from her sister or from Mrs. Clavering; but that the words in which to express them were wanting to her.

"And have they accepted the house?" Mrs. Clavering asked.

"They must accept it. What else can they do? They cannot make me call it mine if I do not choose. If I refuse to take the income which Mr. Courton's lawyer pays in to my bankers', they cannot compel me to have it."

"But you are not going to give that up too?" said her sister.

"I am. I will not have his money,—not more than enough to keep me from being a scandal to his family. I will not have it. It is a curse to me, and has been from the first. What right have I to all that money, because,—because,—because—" She could not finish her sentence, but turned away from them, and walked by herself to the window.

Lady Clavering looked at Mrs. Clavering as though she thought that her sister was mad. "Do you understand her?" said Lady Clavering in a whisper.

"I think I do," said the other. "I think I know what is passing in her mind." Then she followed Lady Ongar across the room, and taking her gently by the arm tried to comfort her,—to comfort her, and to argue with her as to the rashness of that which she proposed to do. She endeavoured to explain to the poor woman how it was that she should at this moment be wretched, and anxious to do that which, if done, would put it out of her power afterwards to make herself useful in the world. It shocked the prudence of Mrs. Clavering,—this idea of abandoning money, the possession of which was questioned by no one. "They do not want it, Lady Ongar," she said.

"That has nothing to do with it," answered the other.

"And nobody has any suspicion but what it is honourably and fairly your own."

"But does anybody ever think how I got it?" said Lady Ongar, turning sharply round upon Mrs. Clavering. "You,—you,—you,—do you dare to tell me what you think of the way in which it became mine? Could you bear it, if it had become yours after such a fashion? I cannot bear it, and I will not." She was now speaking with so much violence that her sister was awed into silence, and Mrs. Clavering herself found a difficulty in answering her.

"Whatever may have been the past," said she, "the question now is how to do the best for the future."

"I had hoped," continued Lady Ongar without noticing what was said to her, "I had hoped to make everything straight by giving his money to another. You know to whom I mean, and so does Hermy. I thought, when I returned, that bad as I had been I might still do some good in the world. But it is as they tell us in the sermons. One cannot make good come out of evil. I have done evil, and nothing but evil has come from the evil which I have done. Nothing but evil will come from it. As for being useful in the world,—I know of what use I am! When women hear how wretched I have been they will be unwilling to sell themselves as I did." Then she made her way to the door, and left the room, going out with quiet steps, and closing the lock behind her without a sound.

"I did not know that she was such as that," said Mrs. Clavering.

"Nor did I. She has never spoken in that way before."

"Poor soul! Hermione, you see there are those in the world whose sufferings are worse than yours."

"I don't know," said Lady Clavering. "She never lost what I have lost,—never."

"She has lost what I am sure you never will lose, her own self-esteem. But, Hermy, you should be good to her. We must all be good to her. Will it not be better that you should stay with us for a while,—both of you?"

"What, here at the park?"

"We will make room for you at the rectory, if you would like it."

"Oh, no; I will go away. I shall be better away. I suppose she will not be like that often; will she?"

"She was much moved just now."

"And what does she mean about her income? She cannot be in earnest."

"She is in earnest now."

"And cannot it be prevented? Only think,—if after all she were to give up her jointure! Mrs. Clavering, you do not think she is mad; do you?"

Mrs. Clavering said what she could to comfort the elder and weaker sister on this subject, explaining to her that the Courtons would not be at all likely to take advantage of any wild generosity on the part of Lady Ongar, and then she walked home across the park, meditating on the character of the two sisters.

CHAPTER XLVI.

MADAME GORDELOUP RETIRES FROM BRITISH DIPLOMACY.

THE reader must be asked to accompany me once more to that room in Mount Street in which poor Archie practised diplomacy, and whither the courageous Doodles was carried prisoner in those moments in which he was last seen of us. The Spy was now sitting alone before her desk, scribbling with all her energy,—writing letters on foreign policy, no doubt, to all the courts of Europe, but especially to that Russian court to which her services were more especially due. She was hard at work, when there came the sound of a step upon the stairs. The practised ear of the Spy became erect, and she at once knew who was her visitor. It was not one with whom diplomacy would much avail, or who was likely to have money ready under his glove for her behoof. "Ah, Edouard, is that you ? I am glad you have come," she said, as Count Pateroff entered the room.

"Yes, it is I. I got your note yesterday."

"You are good,—very good. You are always good." Sophie as she said this went on very rapidly with her letter,—so rapidly that her hand seemed to run about the paper wildly. Then she flung down her pen, and folded the paper on which she had been writing with marvellous quickness. There was an activity about the woman, in all her movements, which was wonderful to watch. "There," she said, "that is done ; now we can talk. Ah ! I have nearly written off my fingers this morning." Her brother smiled, but said nothing about the letters. He never allowed himself to allude in any way to her professional duties.

"So you are going to St. Petersburg ? " he said.

"Well,—yes, I think. Why should I remain here spending money with both hands and through the nose ? " At this idea, the brother again smiled pleasantly. He had never seen his sister to be culpably extravagant as she now described herself. "Nothing to get and everything to lose," she went on saying.

"You know your own affairs best," he answered.

"Yes ; I know my own affairs. If I remained here, I should be taken away to that black building there ; " and she pointed in the direction of the workhouse, which fronts so gloomily upon Mount Street. "You would not come to take me out."

The count smiled again. "You are too clever for that, Sophie, I think."

"Ah, it is well for a woman to be clever, or she must starve,—yes, starve ! Such a one as I must starve in this accursed country, if I were not what you call, clever." The brother and sister were talking in French, and she spoke now almost as rapidly as she had written. "They are beasts and fools, and as awkward as bulls,—yes, as bulls. I hate them. I hate them all. Men, women, children,—they are all alike. Look at the street out there. Though it is summer, I shiver when I look out at its blackness. It is the ugliest nation ! And they understand nothing. Oh, how I hate them ! "

"They are not without merit. They have got money."

"Money,—yes. They have got money ; and they are so stupid, you may take it from under their eyes. They will not see you. But of their own hearts, they will give you nothing. You see that black building,—the workhouse. I call it Little England. It is just the same. The naked, hungry, poor wretches lie at the door, and the great fat beadles swell about like turkey-cocks inside."

"You have been here long enough to know, at any rate."

"Yes ; I have been here long,—too long. I have made my life a wilderness, staying here in this country of barracks. And what have I got for it ? I came back because of that woman, and she has thrown me over. That is your fault,—yours,—yours ! "

" And you have sent for me to tell me that again ? "

" No, Edouard. I sent for you that you might see your sister once more,—that I might once more see my brother." This she said leaning forward on the table, on which her arms rested, and looking steadfastly into his face with eyes moist,—just moist, with a tear in each. Whether Edouard was too unfeeling to be moved by this show of affection, or whether he gave more credit to his sister's histrionic powers than to those of her heart, I will not say ; but he was altogether irresponsive to her appeal. " You will be back again before long," he said.

" Never ! I shall come back to this accursed country never again. No ; I am going once and for all. I will soil myself with the mud of its gutters no more. I came for the sake of Julie ; and now,—how has she treated me ? " Edouard shrugged his shoulders. " And you,—how has she treated you ? "

" Never mind me."

" Ah, but I must mind you. Only that you would not let me manage, it might be yours now,—yes, all. Why did you come down to that accursed island ? "

" It was my way to play my game. Leave that alone, Sophie." And there came a frown over the brother's brow.

" Your way to play your game ! Yes ; and what has become of mine ? You have destroyed mine ; but you think nothing of that. After all that I have gone through, to have nothing ; and through you,—my brother ! Ah, that is the hardest of all,—when I was putting all things in train for you ! "

" You are always putting things in train. Leave your trains alone, where I am concerned."

" But why did you come to that place in the accursed island ? I am ruined by that journey. Yes ; I am ruined. You will not help me to get a shilling from her,—not even for my expenses."

" Certainly not. You are clever enough to do your own work without my aid."

" And is that all from a brother ? Well ! And now that they have drowned themselves,—the two Claverings,—the fool and the brute ; and she can do what she pleases——"

" She could always do as she pleased since Lord Ongar died."

" Yes ; but she is more lonely than ever now. That cousin who is the greatest fool of all, who might have had everything,—mon Dieu ! yes, everything ;—she would have given it all to him with a sweep of her hand, if he would have taken it. He is to marry himself to a little brown girl, who has not a shilling. No one but an Englishman could make follies so abominable as these. Ah, I am sick,—I am sick when I remember it ! " And Sophie gave unmistakeable signs of a grief which could hardly have been self-interested. But in truth she suffered pain at seeing a good game spoilt. It was not that she had any wish for Harry Clavering's welfare. Had he gone to the bottom of the sea in the same boat with his cousins, the tidings of his fate would have been pleasurable to her rather than otherwise. But when she saw such cards thrown away as he had held in his hand, she encountered that sort of suffering which a good player feels when he sits behind the chair of one who plays up to his adversary's trump, and makes no tricks of his own kings and aces.

"He may marry himself to the devil, if he please;—it is nothing to me," said the count.

"But she is there;—by herself,—at that place;—what is it called? Ten—bie. Will you not go now, when you can do no harm?"

"No; I will not go now."

"And in a year she will have taken some other one for her husband."

"What is that to me? But look here, Sophie, for you may as well understand me at once. If I were ever to think of Lady Ongar again as my wife, I should not tell you."

"And why not tell me,—your sister?"

"Because it would do me no good. If you had not been there she would have been my wife now."

"Edouard!"

"What I say is true. But I do not want to reproach you because of that. Each of us was playing his own game; and your game was not my game. You are going now, and if I play my game again I can play it alone."

Upon hearing this Sophie sat awhile in silence, looking at him. "You will play it alone?" she said at last. "You would rather do that?"

"Much rather, if I play any game at all."

"And you will give me something to go?"

"Not one sou."

"You will not;—not a sou?"

"Not half a sou,—for you to go or stay. Sophie, are you not a fool to ask me for money?"

"And you are a fool,—a fool who knows nothing. You need not look at me like that. I am not afraid. I shall remain here. I shall stay and do as the lawyer tells me. He says that if I bring my action she must pay me for my expenses. I will bring my action. I am not going to leave it all to you. No. Do you remember those days in Florence? I have not been paid yet, but I will be paid. One hundred and seventy-five thousand francs a year,—and after all I am to have none of it! Say;—should it become yours, will you do something for your sister?"

"Nothing at all;—nothing. Sophie, do you think I am fool enough to bargain in such a matter?"

"Then I will stay. Yes;—I will bring my action. All the world shall hear, and they shall know how you have destroyed me and yourself.

Ah;—you think I am afraid; that I will not spend my money. I will spend all,—all,—all; and I will be revenged."

"You may go or stay; it is the same thing to me. Now, if you please, I will take my leave." And he got up from his chair to leave her.

"It is the same thing to you?"

"Quite the same."

"Then I will stay, and she shall hear my name every day of her life; —every hour. She shall be so sick of me and of you, that,—that—that—— Oh, Edouard!" This last appeal was made to him because he was already at the door, and could not be stopped in any other way.

"What else have you to say, my sister?"

"Oh, Edouard, what would I not give to see all those riches yours? Has it not been my dearest wish? Edouard, you are ungrateful. All men are ungrateful." Now, having succeeded in stopping him, she buried her face in the corner of the sofa and wept plentifully. It must be presumed that her acting before her brother must have been altogether thrown away; but the acting was, nevertheless, very good.

"If you are in truth going to St. Petersburg," he said, "I will bid you adieu now. If not,—au revoir."

"I am going. Yes, Edouard, I am. I cannot bear this country longer. My heart is being torn to pieces. All my affections are outraged. Yes, I am going;—perhaps on Monday;—perhaps on Monday week. But I go in truth. My brother, adieu." Then she got up, and putting a hand on each of his shoulders, lifted up her face to be kissed. He embraced her in the manner proposed, and turned to leave her. But before he went she made to him one other petition, holding him by the arm as she did so. "Edouard, you can lend me twenty napoleons till I am at St. Petersburg?"

"No, Sophie; no."

"Not lend your sister twenty napoleons!"

"No, Sophie. I never lend money. It is a rule."

"Will you give me five? I am so poor. I have almost nothing."

"Things are not so bad with you as that, I hope?"

"Ah, yes; they are very bad. Since I have been in this accursed city,—now, this time, what have I got? Nothing,—nothing. She was to be all in all to me,—and she has given me nothing! It is very bad to be so poor. Say that you will give me five napoleons;—O my brother!" She was still hanging by his arm, and, as she did so, she looked up into his face with tears in her eyes. As he regarded her, bending down his face over hers, a slight smile came upon his countenance. Then he put his hand into his pocket, and taking out his purse, handed to her five sovereigns.

"Only five?" she said.

"Only five," he answered.

"A thousand thanks, O my brother." Then she kissed him again, and after that he went. She accompanied him to the top of the stairs, and from thence showered blessings on his head, till she heard the lock of the door closed behind him. When he was altogether gone she unlocked an inner drawer in her desk, and, taking out an uncompleted rouleau of gold, added her brother's sovereigns thereto. The sum he had given her was exactly wanted to make up the required number of twenty-five. She counted them half-a-dozen times, to be quite sure, and then rolled them carefully in paper, and sealed the little packet at each end. " Ah," she said, speaking to herself, " they are very nice. Nothing else English is nice, but only these." There were many rolls of money there before her in the drawer of the desk;—some ten, perhaps, or twelve. These she took out one after another, passing them lovingly through her fingers, looking at the little seals at the ends of each, weighing them in her hand as though to make sure that no wrong had been done to them in her absence, standing them up one against another to see that they were of the same length. We may be quite sure that Sophie Gordeloup brought no sovereigns with her to England when she came over with Lady Ongar after the earl's death, and that the hoard before her contained simply the plunder which she had collected during this her latest visit to the " accursed " country which she was going to leave.

But before she started she was resolved to make one more attempt upon that mine of wealth which, but a few weeks ago, had seemed to lie open before her. She had learned from the servants in Bolton Street that Lady Ongar was with Lady Clavering, at Clavering Park, and she addressed a letter to her there. This letter she wrote in English, and she threw into her appeal all the pathos of which she was capable. —

Mount Street, October, 186—.

DEAREST JULIE,—I do not think you would wish me to go away from this country for ever,—for ever, without one word of farewell to her I love so fondly. Yes ; I have loved you with all my heart,—and now I am going away,—for ever. Shall we not meet each other once, and have one embrace? No trouble will be too much to me for that. No journey will be too long. Only say, Sophie, come to your Julie.

I must go, because I am so poor. Yes; I cannot live longer here without having the means. I am not ashamed to say to my Julie, who is rich, that I am poor. No; nor would I be ashamed to wait on my Julie like a slave if she would let me. My Julie was angry with me, because of my brother ! Was it my fault that he came upon us in our little retreat, where we was so happy ? Oh, no. I told him not to come. I knew his coming was for nothing,—nothing at all. I knew where was the heart of my Julie !—my poor Julie ! But he was not worth that heart, and the pearl was thrown before a pig. But my brother—! Ah, he has ruined me. Why am I separated from my Julie but for him ? Well; I can go away, and in my own countries there are those who will not wish to be separated from Sophie Gordeloup.

May I now tell my Julie in what condition is her poor friend ? She will remember how it was that my feet brought me to England,—to England, to which I had said farewell for ever,—to England, where people must be rich like my Julie before they can eat and drink. I thought nothing then but of my Julie. I stopped not on the road to make merchandise,—what you call a bargain,—about my coming. No ; I came at once, leaving all things,—my little affairs,—in confusion, because my

Julie wanted me to come! It was in the winter. Oh, that winter! My poor bones shall never forget it. They are racked still with the pains which your savage winds have given them. And now it is autumn. Ten months have I been here, and I have eaten up my little substance. Oh, Julie, you, who are so rich, do not know what is the poverty of your Sophie !

A lawyer have told me,—not a French lawyer, but an English,—that somebody should pay me everything. He says the law would give it me. He have offered me the money himself,—just to let him make an action. But I have said,—No. No ; Sophie will not have an action with her Julie. She would scorn that ; and so the lawyer went away. But if my Julie will think of this, and will remember her Sophie,—how much she have expended, and now at last there is nothing left. She must go and beg among her friends. And why ? Because she have loved her Julie too well. You, who are so rich, would miss it not at all. What would two,—three hundred pounds be to my Julie?

Shall I come to you ? Say so; say so, and I will go at once, if I did crawl on my knees. Oh, what a joy to see my Julie! And do not think I will trouble you about money. No ; your Sophie will be too proud for that. Not a word will I say, but to love you. Nothing will I do, but to print one kiss on my Julie's forehead, and then to retire for ever; asking God's blessing for her dear head.

Thine,—always thine,

Sophie.

Lady Ongar, when she received this letter, was a little perplexed by it, not feeling quite sure in what way she might best answer it. It was the special severity of her position that there was no one to whom, in such difficulties, she could apply for advice. Of one thing she was quite sure,— that, willingly, she would never again see her devoted Sophie. And she knew that the woman deserved no money from her ; that she had deserved none, but had received much. Every assertion in her letter was false. No one had wished her to come, and the expense of her coming had been paid for her over and over again. Lady Ongar knew that she had money,—and knew also that she would have had immediate recourse to law, if any lawyer would have suggested to her with a probability of success that he could get more for her. No doubt she had been telling her story to some attorney, in the hope that money might thus be extracted, and had been dragging her Julie's name through the mud, telling all she knew of that wretched Florentine story. As to all that Lady Ongar had no doubt ; and yet she wished to send the woman money !

There are services for which one is ready to give almost any amount of money payment,—if only one can be sure that that money payment will be taken as sufficient recompence for the service in question. Sophie Gordeloup had been useful. She had been very disagreeable,—but she had been useful. She had done things which nobody else could have done, and she had done her work well. That she had been paid for her work over and over again, there was no doubt ; but Lady Ongar was willing to give her yet further payment, if only there might be an end of it. But she feared to do this, dreading the nature and cunning of the little woman,— lest she should take such payment as an acknowledgment of services for which secret compensation must be made,—and should then proceed to further threats. Thinking much of all this, Julie at last wrote to her Sophie as follows :—

> Lady Ongar presents her compliments to Madame Gordeloup, and must decline to see Madame Gordeloup again after what has passed. Lady Ongar is very sorry to hear that Madame Gordeloup is in want of funds. Whatever assistance Lady Ongar might have been willing to afford, she now feels that she is prohibited from giving any by the allusion which Madame Gordeloup has made to legal advice. If Madame Gordeloup has legal demands on Lady Ongar which are said by a lawyer to be valid, Lady Ongar would strongly recommend Madame Gordeloup to enforce them.
>
> Clavering Park, October, 186—.

This she wrote, acting altogether on her own judgment, and sent off by return of post. She almost wept at her own cruelty after the letter was gone, and greatly doubted her own discretion. But of whom could she have asked advice ? Could she have told all the story of Madame Gordeloup to the rector or to the rector's wife ? The letter no doubt was a discreet letter ; but she greatly doubted her own discretion, and when she received her Sophie's rejoinder, she hardly dared to break the envelope.

Poor Sophie ! Her Julie's letter nearly broke her heart. For sincerity little credit was due to her ;—but some little was perhaps due. That she should be called Madame Gordeloup, and have compliments presented to her by the woman,—by the countess with whom and with whose husband she had been on such closely familiar terms, did in truth wound some tender feelings within her bosom. Such love as she had been able to give, she had given to her Julie. That she had always been willing to rob her Julie, to make a milch-cow of her Julie, to sell her Julie, to threaten her Julie, to quarrel with her Julie if aught might be done in that way,—to expose her Julie ; nay, to destroy her Julie if money was to be so made ; —all this did not hinder her love. She loved her Julie, and was broken-hearted that her Julie should have written to her in such a strain.

But her feelings were much more acute when she came to perceive that she had damaged her own affairs by the hint of a menace which she had thrown out. Business is business, and must take precedence of all sentiment and romance in this hard world in which bread is so necessary. Of that Madame Gordeloup was well aware. And therefore, having given herself but two short minutes to weep over her Julie's hardness, she applied her mind at once to the rectification of the error she had made. Yes ; she had been wrong about the lawyer, certainly wrong. But then these English people were so pig-headed ! A slight suspicion of a hint, such as that she had made, would have been taken by a Frenchman, by a Russian, by a Pole, as meaning no more than it meant. " But these English are bulls ; the men and the women are all like bulls,—bulls ! "

She at once sat down and wrote another letter ; another in such an ecstasy of eagerness to remove the evil impressions which she had made, that she wrote it almost with the natural effusion of her heart.—

DEAR FRIEND,—Your coldness kills me,—kills me ! But perhaps I have deserved it. If I said there were legal demands I did deserve it. No; there are none. Legal

demands! Oh, no. What can your poor friend demand legally? The lawyer—
he knows nothing; he was a stranger. It was my brother spoke to him. What
should I do with a lawyer? Oh, my friend, do not be angry with your poor servant.
I write now not to ask for money,—but for a kind word; for one word of kindness
and love to your Sophie before she have gone for ever! Yes; for ever. Oh, Julie,
oh, my angel; I would lie at your feet and kiss them if you were here.

Yours till death, even though you should still be hard to me,

SOPHIE.

To this appeal Lady Ongar sent no direct answer, but she commissioned Mr. Turnbull, her lawyer, to call upon Madame Gordeloup and pay to
that lady one hundred pounds, taking her receipt for the same. Lady Ongar,
in her letter to the lawyer, explained that the woman in question had been
useful in Florence; and explained also that she might pretend that she
had further claims. " If so," said Lady Ongar, " I wish you to tell her
that she can prosecute them at law if she pleases. The money I now give
her is a gratuity made for certain services rendered in Florence during the
illness of Lord Ongar." This commission Mr. Turnbull executed, and
Sophie Gordeloup, when taking the money, made no demand for any further
payment.

Four days after this a little woman, carrying a very big bandbox in her
hands, might have been seen to scramble with difficulty out of a boat in
the Thames up the side of a steamer bound from thence for Boulogne.
And after her there climbed up an active little man, who, with peremptory
voice, repulsed the boatman's demand for further payment. He also had
a bandbox on his arm,—belonging, no doubt, to the little woman. And it
might have been seen that the active little man, making his way to the
table at which the clerk of the boat was sitting, out of his own purse paid
the passage-money for two passengers,—through to Paris. And the head
and legs and neck of that little man were like to the head and legs and
neck of — our friend Doodles, alias Captain Boodle, of Warwickshire.

CHAPTER XLVII.

SHOWING HOW THINGS SETTLED THEMSELVES AT THE RECTORY.

WHEN Harry's letter, with the tidings of the fate of his cousins, reached
Florence at Stratton, the whole family was, not unnaturally, thrown into
great excitement. Being slow people, the elder Burtons had hardly as yet
realized the fact that Harry was again to be accepted among the Burton
Penates as a pure divinity. Mrs. Burton, for some weeks past, had
grown to be almost sublime in her wrath against him. That a man
should live and treat her daughter as Florence was about to be treated!
Had not her husband forbidden such a journey, as being useless in regard
to the expenditure, she would have gone up to London that she might
have told Harry what she thought of him. Then came the news that

Harry was again a divinity,—an Apollo, whom the Burton Penates ought only to be too proud to welcome to a seat among them !

And now came this other news that this Apollo was to be an Apollo indeed ! When the god first became a god again, there was still a cloud upon the minds of the elder Burtons as to the means by which the divinity was to be sustained. A god in truth, but a god with so very moderate an annual income ;—unless indeed those old Burtons made it up to an extent which seemed to them to be quite unnatural ! There was joy among the Burtons, of course, but the joy was somewhat dimmed by these reflections as to the slight means of their Apollo. A lover who was not an Apollo might wait; but, as they had learned already, there was danger in keeping such a god as this suspended on the tenter-hooks of expectation.

But now there came the further news ! This Apollo of theirs had really a place of his own among the gods of Olympus. He was the eldest son of a man of large fortune, and would be a baronet ! He had already declared that he would marry at once ;—that his father wished him to do so, and that an abundant income would be forthcoming. As to his eagerness for an immediate marriage, no divinity in or out of the heavens could behave better. Old Mrs. Burton, as she went through the process of taking him again to her heart, remembered that that virtue had been his, even before the days of his backsliding had come. A warm-hearted, eager, affectionate divinity,—with only this against him, that he wanted some careful looking after in these, his unsettled days. " I really do think that he'll be as fond of his own fireside as any other man, when he has once settled down," said Mrs. Burton.

It will not, I hope, be taken as a blot on the character of this mother that she was much elated at the prospect of the good things which were to fall to her daughter's lot. For herself she desired nothing. For her daughters she had coveted only good, substantial, painstaking husbands, who would fear God and mind their business. When Harry Clavering had come across her path and had demanded a daughter from her, after the manner of the other young men who had learned the secrets of their profession at Stratton, she had desired nothing more than that he and Florence should walk in the path which had been followed by her sisters and their husbands. But then had come that terrible fear ; and now had come these golden prospects. That her daughter should be Lady Clavering, of Clavering Park ! She could not but be elated at the thought of it. She would not live to see it, but the consciousness that it would be so was pleasant to her in her old age. Florence had ever been regarded as the flower of the flock, and now she would be taken up into high places,—according to her deserts.

First had come the letter from Harry, and then, after an interval of a week, another letter from Mrs. Clavering, pressing her dear Florence to go to the parsonage. " We think that at present we all ought to be together," said Mrs. Clavering, " and therefore we want you to be with us." It was very flattering, "I suppose I ought to go, mamma?" said Florence. Mrs. Burton was of opinion that she certainly ought to go. "You should write to her ladyship at once," said Mrs. Burton, mindful of the change which had taken place. Florence, however, addressed her letter, as heretofore, to Mrs. Clavering, thinking that a mistake on that side would be better than a mistake on the other. It was not for her to be over-mindful of the rank with which she was about to be connected. "You won't forget your old mother now that you are going to be so grand?" said Mrs. Burton, as Florence was leaving her.

"You only say that to laugh at me," said Florence. "I expect no grandness, and I am sure you expect no forgetfulness."

The solemnity consequent upon the first news of the accident had worn itself off, and Florence found the family at the parsonage happy and comfortable. Mrs. Fielding was still there, and Mr. Fielding was expected again after the next Sunday. Fanny also was there, and Florence could see during the first half-hour that she was very radiant. Mr. Saul, however, was not there, and it may as well be said at once that Mr. Saul as yet knew nothing of his coming fortune. Florence was received with open arms by them all, and by Harry with arms which were almost too open. "I suppose it may be in about three weeks from now?" he said at the first moment in which he could have her to himself.

"Oh, Harry,—no," said Florence.

"No;—why no? That's what my mother proposes."

"In three weeks!—She could not have said that. Nobody has begun to think of such a thing yet at Stratton."

"They are so very slow at Stratton!"

"And you are so very fast at Clavering! But, Harry, we don't know where we are going to live."

"We should go abroad at first, I suppose."

"And what then? That would only be for a month or so."

"Only for a month? I mean for all the winter,—and the spring. Why not? One can see nothing in a month. If we are back for the shooting next year that would do,—and then of course we should come here. I should say next winter,—that is the winter after the next,— we might as well stay with them at the big house, and then we could look about us, you know. I should like a place near to this, because of the hunting!"

Florence, when she heard all this, became aware that in talking about a month she had forgotten herself. She had been accustomed to holidays of a month's duration,—and to honeymoon trips fitted to such vacations. A month was the longest holiday ever heard of in the Chambers in the Adelphi,—or at the house in Onslow Crescent. She had forgotten herself. It was not to be the lot of her husband to earn his bread, and fit himself to such periods as business might require. Then Harry went on describing the tour which he had arranged;—which as he said he only suggested. But it was quite apparent that in this matter he intended to be paramount.

Florence indeed made no objection. To spend a fortnight in Paris;—to hurry over the Alps before the cold weather came ; to spend a month in Florence, and then go on to Rome ;—it would all be very nice. But she declared that it would suit the next year better than this.

" Suit ten thousand fiddlesticks," said Harry.

" But it is October now."

" And therefore there is no time to lose."

" I haven't a dress in the world but the one I have on, and a few others like it. Oh, Harry, how can you talk in that way ? "

" Well, say four weeks then from now. That will make it the seventh of November, and we'll only stay a day or two in Paris. We can do Paris next year,—in May. If you'll agree to that, I'll agree."

But Florence's breath was taken away from her, and she could agree to nothing. She did agree to nothing till she had been talked into doing so by Mrs. Clavering.

" My dear," said her future mother-in-law, " what you say is undoubtedly true. There is no absolute necessity for hurrying. It is not an affair of life and death. But you and Harry have been engaged quite long enough now, and I really don't see why you should put it off. If you do as he asks you, you will just have time to make yourselves comfortable before the cold weather begins."

" But mamma will be so surprised."

" I'm sure she will wish it, my dear. You see Harry is a young man of that sort,—so impetuous I mean, you know, and so eager,— and so—you know what I mean,—that the sooner he is married the better. You can't but take it as a compliment, Florence, that he is so eager."

" Of course I do."

" And you should reward him. Believe me it will be best that it should not be delayed." Whether or no Mrs. Clavering had present in her imagination the possibility of any further danger that might result from Lady Ongar, I will not say, but if so, she altogether failed in communicating her idea to Florence.

" Then I must go home at once," said Florence, driven ·almost to bewail the terrors of her position.

" You can write home at once and tell your mother. You can tell her all that I say, and I am sure she will agree with me. If you wish it, I will write a line to Mrs. Burton myself." Florence said that she would wish it. " And we can begin, you know, to get your things ready here. People don't take so long about all that now-a-days as they used to do." When Mrs. Clavering had turned against her, Florence knew that she had no hope, and surrendered, subject to the approval of the higher authorities at Stratton. The higher authorities at Stratton approved also, of course, and Florence found herself fixed to a day with a suddenness that bewildered her. Immediately,—almost as soon as the consent had been extorted from her,—she began to be surrounded with incipient preparation for the event, as to which, about three weeks since, she had made up her mind that it would never come to pass.

On the second day of her arrival, in the privacy of her bedroom, Fanny communicated to her the decision of her family in regard to Mr. Saul. But she told the story at first as though this decision referred to the living only,—as though the rectory were to be conferred on Mr. Saul without any burden attached to it. "He has been here so long, dear," said Fanny, "and understands the people so well."

"I am so delighted," said Florence.

"I am sure it is the best thing papa could do ;—that is if he quite makes up his mind to give up the parish himself."

This troubled Florence, who did not know that a baronet could hold a living.

"I thought he must give up being a clergyman now that Sir Hugh is dead ?"

"O dear, no." And then Fanny, who was great on ecclesiastical subjects, explained it all. "Even though he were to be a peer, he could hold a living if he pleased. A great many baronets are clergymen, and some of them do hold preferments. As to papa, the doubt has been with him whether he would wish to give up the work. But he will preach sometimes, you know ; though of course he will not be able to do that unless Mr. Saul lets him. No one but the rector has a right to his own pulpit except the bishop ; and he can preach three times a year if he likes it."

"And suppose the bishop wanted to preach four times ?"

"He couldn't do it ; at least, I believe not. But you see he never wants to preach at all,—not in such a place as this,—so that does not signify."

"And will Mr. Saul come and live here, in this house ?"

"Some day I suppose he will," said Fanny, blushing.

"And you, dear ?"

"I don't know how that may be."

"Come, Fanny."

"Indeed I don't, Florence, or I would tell you. Of course Mr. Saul has asked me. I never had any secret with you about that ; have I ?"

"No ; you were very good."

"Then he asked me again ; twice again. And then there came,— oh, such a quarrel between him and papa. It was so terrible. Do you know, I believe they wouldn't speak in the vestry ! Not but what each of them has the highest possible opinion of the other. But of course Mr. Saul couldn't marry on a curacy. When I think of it it really seems that he must have been mad."

"But you don't think him so mad now, dear ?"

"He doesn't know a word about it yet ; not a word. He hasn't been in the house since, and papa and he didn't speak,—not in a friendly way,

—till the news came of poor Hugh's being drowned. Then he came up to papa, and, of course, papa took his hand. But he still thinks he is going away."

"And when is he to be told that he needn't go?"

"That is the difficulty. Mamma will have to do it, I believe. But what she will say, I'm sure I for one can't think."

"Mrs. Clavering will have no difficulty."

"You mustn't call her Mrs. Clavering."

"Lady Clavering then."

"That's a great deal worse. She's your mamma now,—not quite so much as she is mine, but the next thing to it."

"She'll know what to say to Mr. Saul."

"But what is she to say?"

"Well, Fanny,—you ought to know that. I suppose you do—love him?"

"I have never told him so."

"But you will?"

"It seems so odd. Mamma will have to —— Suppose he were to turn round and say he didn't want me?"

"That would be awkward."

"He would in a minute if that was what he felt. The idea of having the living would not weigh with him a bit."

"But when he was so much in love before, it won't make him out of love;—will it?"

"I don't know," said Fanny. "At any rate, mamma is to see him to-morrow, and after that I suppose;—I'm sure I don't know,—but I suppose he'll come to the rectory as he used to do."

"How happy you must be," said Florence, kissing her. To this Fanny made some unintelligible demur. It was undoubtedly possible that, under the altered circumstances of the case, so strange a being as Mr. Saul might have changed his mind.

There was a great trial awaiting Florence Burton. She had to be taken up to call on the ladies at the great house,—on the two widowed ladies who were still remaining there when she came to Clavering. It was only on the day before her arrival that Harry had seen Lady Ongar. He had thought much of the matter before he went across to the house, doubting whether it would not be better to let Julia go without troubling her with a further interview. But he had not then seen even Lady Clavering since the tidings of her bereavement had come, and he felt that it would not be well that he should let his cousin's widow leave Clavering without offering her his sympathy. And it might be better, also, that he should see Julia once again, if only that he might show himself capable of meeting her without the exhibition of any peculiar emotion. He went, therefore, to the house, and having asked for Lady Clavering, saw both the sisters together. He soon found that the presence of the younger one was a relief to him. Lady Clavering was so sad, and so peevish in her sadness,—so broken-spirited, so far as yet from recognizing the great enfranchisement that had come to her, that with her alone he would have found himself almost unable to express the sympathy which he felt. But with Lady Ongar he had no difficulty. Lady Ongar, her sister being with them in the room, talked to him easily, as though there had never been anything between them two to make conversation difficult. That all words between them should, on such an occasion as this, be sad, was a matter of course; but it seemed to Harry that Julia had freed herself from all the effects of that feeling which had existed between them, and that it would become him to do this as effectually as she had done it. Such an idea, at least, was in his mind for a moment; but when he left her she spoke one word which dispelled it. "Harry," she said, "you must ask Miss Burton to come across and see me. I hear that she is to be at the rectory to-morrow." Harry of course said that he would send her. "She will understand why I cannot go to her, as I should do,—but for poor Hermy's position. You will explain this, Harry." Harry, blushing up to his forehead, declared that Florence would require no explanation, and that she would certainly make the visit as proposed. "I wish to see her, Harry,—so much. And if I do not see her now, I may never have another chance."

It was nearly a week after this that Florence went across to the great house with Mrs. Clavering and Fanny. I think that she understood the nature of the visit she was called upon to make, and no doubt she trembled much at the coming ordeal. She was going to see her great rival,—her rival, who had almost been preferred to her,—nay, who had been preferred to her for some short space of time, and whose claims as to beauty and wealth were so greatly superior to her own. And this woman whom she was to see had been the first love of the man whom she now regarded as her own,—and would have been about to be his wife at this moment had it not been for her own treachery to him. Was she so beautiful as people said? Florence, in the bottom of her heart, wished that she might have been saved from this interview.

The three ladies from the rectory found the two ladies at the great house sitting together in the small drawing-room. Florence was so confused that she could hardly bring herself to speak to Lady Clavering, or so much as to look at Lady Ongar. She shook hands with the elder sister, and knew that her hand was then taken by the other. Julia at first spoke a very few words to Mrs. Clavering, and Fanny sat herself down beside Hermione. Florence took a chair at a little distance, and was left there for a few minutes without notice. For this she was very thankful, and by degrees was able to fix her eyes on the face of the woman whom she so feared to see, and yet on whom she so desired to look. Lady Clavering was a mass of ill-arranged widow's weeds. She had assumed in all its grotesque ugliness those paraphernalia of outward woe which women have been condemned to wear, in order that for a time they may be shorn of all the charms of their sex. Nothing could be more proper or unbecoming than the heavy, drooping, shapeless blackness in which Lady Clavering had enveloped herself. But Lady Ongar, though also a widow, though as yet a widow of not twelve months' standing, was dressed,—in weeds, no doubt,—but in weeds which had been so cultivated that they were as good as flowers. She was very beautiful. Florence owned to herself as she sat there in silence, that Lady Ongar was the most beautiful woman that she had ever seen. But hers was not the beauty by which, as she would have thought, Harry Clavering would have been attached. Lady Ongar's form, bust, and face were, at this period of her life, almost majestic; whereas the softness and grace of womanhood were the charms which Harry loved. He had sometimes said to Florence that, to his taste, Cecilia Burton was almost perfect as a woman. And there could be no contrast greater than that between Cecilia Burton and Lady Ongar. But Florence did not remember that the Julia Brabazon of three years' since had not been the same as the Lady Ongar whom now she saw.

When they had been there some minutes Lady Ongar came and sat beside Florence, moving her seat as though she were doing the most natural thing in the world. Florence's heart came to her mouth, but she made a resolution that she would, if possible, bear herself well. " You have been at Clavering before, I think ? " said Lady Ongar. Florence said that she had been at the parsonage during the last Easter. " Yes,—I heard that you dined here with my brother-in-law." This she said in a low voice, having seen that Lady Clavering was engaged with Fanny and Mrs. Clavering. " Was it not terribly sudden ? "

" Terribly sudden," said Florence.

" The two brothers ! Had you not met Captain Clavering ? "

" Yes,—he was here when I dined with your sister."

" Poor fellow ! Is it not odd that they should have gone, and that their friend, whose yacht it was, should have been saved ? They say, however, that Mr. Stuart behaved admirably, begging his friends to get into the boat first. He stayed by the vessel when the boat was carried away, and he was saved in that way. But he meant to do the best he could for them. There's no doubt of that."

" But how dreadful his feelings must be ! "

" Men do not think so much of these things as we do. They have so much more to employ their minds. Don't you think so ? " Florence did not at the moment quite know what she thought about men's feelings, but said that she supposed that such was the case. " But I think that after all they are juster than we are," continued Lady Ongar,—" juster and truer, though not so tender-hearted. Mr. Stuart, no doubt, would have been willing to drown himself to save his friends, because the fault was in some degree his. I don't know that I should have been able to do so much."

" In such a moment it must have been so difficult to think of what ought to be done."

" Yes, indeed ; and there is but little good in speculating upon it now. You know this place, do you not;—the house, I mean, and the gardens?"

"Not very well." Florence, as she answered this question, began again to tremble. "Take a turn with me, and I will show you the garden. My hat and cloak are in the hall." Then Florence got up to accompany her, trembling very much inwardly. "Miss Burton and I are going out for a few minutes," said Lady Ongar, addressing herself to Mrs. Clavering. "We will not keep you waiting very long."

"We are in no hurry," said Mrs. Clavering. Then Florence was carried off, and found herself alone with her conquered rival.

"Not that there is much to show you," said Lady Ongar; "indeed nothing; but the place must be of more interest to you than to any one else; and if you are fond of that sort of thing, no doubt you will make it all that is charming."

"I am very fond of a garden," said Florence.

"I don't know whether I am. Alone, by myself, I think I should care nothing for the prettiest Eden in all England. I don't think I would care for a walk through the Elysian fields by myself. I am a chamelion, and take the colour of those with whom I live. My future colours will not be very bright as I take it. It's a gloomy place enough; is it not? But there are fine trees, you see, which are the only things which one cannot by any possibility command. Given good trees, taste and money may do anything very quickly; as I have no doubt you'll find."

"I don't suppose I shall have much to do with it—at present."

"I should think that you will have everything to do with it. There, Miss Burton; I brought you here to show you this very spot, and to make to you my confession here,—and to get from you, here, one word of confidence, if you will give it me." Florence was trembling now outwardly as well as inwardly. "You know my story; as far, I mean, as I had a story once, in conjunction with Harry Clavering?"

"I think I do," said Florence.

"I am sure you do," said Lady Ongar. "He has told me that you do; and what he says is always true. It was here, on this spot, that I gave him back his troth to me, and told him that I would have none of his love, because he was poor. That is barely two years ago. Now he is poor no longer. Now, had I been true to him, a marriage with him would have been, in a prudential point of view, all that any woman could desire. I gave up the dearest heart, the sweetest temper, ay, and the truest man that, that—— Well, you have won him instead, and he has been the gainer. I doubt whether I ever should have made him happy; but I know that you will do so. It was just here that I parted from him."

"He has told me of that parting," said Florence.

"I am sure he has. And, Miss Burton, if you will allow me to say one word further,—do not be made to think any ill of him because of what happened the other day."

LADY ONGAR AND FLORENCE.

"I think no ill of him," said Florence proudly.

"That is well. But I am sure you do not. You are not one to think evil, as I take it, of anybody; much less of him whom you love. When he saw me again, free as I am, and when I saw him, thinking him also to be free, was it strange that some memory of old days should come back upon us? But the fault, if fault there has been, was mine."

"I have never said that there was any fault."

"No, Miss Burton; but others have said so. No doubt I am foolish to talk to you in this way; and I have not yet said that which I desired to say. It is simply this;—that I do not begrudge you your happiness. I wished the same happiness to be mine; but it is not mine. It might have been, but I forfeited it. It is past; and I will pray that you may enjoy it long. You will not refuse to receive my congratulations?"

"Indeed, I will not."

"Or to think of me as a friend of your husband's?"

"Oh, no."

"That is all then. I have shown you the gardens, and now we may go in. Some day, perhaps, when you are Lady Paramount here, and your children are running about the place, I may come again to see them; —if you and he will have me."

"I hope you will, Lady Ongar. In truth, I hope so."

"It is odd enough that I said to him once that I would never go to Clavering Park again till I went there to see his wife. That was long before those two poor brothers perished,—before I had ever heard of Florence Burton. And yet, indeed, it was not very long ago. It was since my husband died. But that was not quite true, for here I am, and he has not yet got a wife. But it was odd; was it not?"

"I cannot think what should have made you say that."

"A spirit of prophecy comes on one sometimes, I suppose. Well; shall we go in? I have shown you all the wonders of the garden, and told you all the wonders connected with it of which I know aught. No doubt there would be other wonders, more wonderful, if one could ransack the private history of all the Claverings for the last hundred years. I hope, Miss Burton, that any marvels which may attend your career here may be happy marvels." She then took Florence by the hand, and drawing close to her, stooped over and kissed her. "You will think me a fool, of course," said she; "but I do not care for that." Florence now was in tears, and could make no answer in words; but she pressed the hand which she still held, and then followed her companion back into the house. After that, the visit was soon brought to an end, and the three ladies from the rectory returned across the park to their house.

CHAPTER XLVIII.

CONCLUSION.

FLORENCE BURTON had taken upon herself to say that Mrs. Clavering would have no difficulty in making to Mr. Saul the communication which was now needed before he could be received at the rectory, as the rector's successor and future son-in-law; but Mrs. Clavering was by no means so confident of her own powers. To her it seemed as though the undertaking which she had in hand, was one surrounded with difficulties. Her husband, when the matter was being discussed, at once made her understand that he would not relieve her by an offer to perform the task. He had been made to break the bad news to Lady Clavering, and, having been submissive in that matter, felt himself able to stand aloof altogether as to this more difficult embassy. "I suppose it would hardly do to ask Harry to see him again," Mrs. Clavering had said. "You would do it much better, my dear," the rector had replied. Then Mrs. Clavering had submitted in her turn; and when the scheme was fully matured, and the time had come in which the making of the proposition could no longer be delayed with prudence, Mr. Saul was summoned by a short note. "Dear Mr. Saul,—If you are disengaged would you come to me at the rectory at eleven to-morrow?—Yours ever, M. C." Mr. Saul of course said that he would come. When the to-morrow had arrived and breakfast was over, the rector and Harry took themselves off, somewhere about the grounds of the great house,—counting up their treasures of proprietorship, as we can fancy that men so circumstanced would do,—while Mary Fielding with Fanny and Florence retired upstairs, so that they might be well out of the way. They knew, all of them, what was about to be done, and Fanny behaved herself like a white lamb decked with bright ribbons for the sacrificial altar. To her it was a sacrificial morning,—very sacred, very solemn, and very trying to the nerves. "I don't think that any girl was ever in such a position before," she said to her sister. "A great many girls would be glad to be in the same position," Mrs. Fielding replied. "Do you think so? To me there is something almost humiliating in the idea that he should be asked to take me." "Fiddlestick, my dear," replied Mrs. Fielding.

Mr. Saul came, punctual as the church clock,—of which he had the regulating himself,—and was shown into the rectory dining-room, where Mrs. Clavering was sitting alone. He looked, as he ever did, serious, composed, ill-dressed, and like a gentleman. Of course he must have supposed that the present rector would make some change in his mode of living, and could not be surprised that he should have been summoned to the rectory;—but he was surprised that the summons should have come from Mrs. Clavering, and not from the rector himself. It appeared to him that the old enmity must be very enduring, if, even now, Mr.

Clavering could not bring himself to see his curate on a matter of business.

"It seems a long time since we have seen you here, Mr. Saul," said Mrs. Clavering.

"Yes ;—when I have remembered how often I used to be here, my absence has seemed long and strange."

"It has been a source of great grief to me."

"And to me, Mrs. Clavering."

"But, as circumstances then were, in truth it could not be avoided. Common prudence made it necessary. Don't you think so, Mr. Saul ? "

"If you ask me I must answer, according to my own ideas. Common prudence should not have made it necessary,—at least not according to my view of things. Common prudence, with different people, means such different things ! But I am not going to quarrel with your ideas of common prudence, Mrs. Clavering."

Mrs. Clavering had begun badly, and was aware of it. She should have said nothing about the past. She had foreseen, from the first, the danger of doing so ; but had been unable to rush at once into the golden future. "I hope we shall have no more quarrelling at any rate," she said.

"There shall be none on my part. Only, Mrs. Clavering, you must not suppose from my saying so that I intend to give up my pretensions. A word from your daughter would make me do so, but no words from any one else."

"She ought to be very proud of such constancy on your part, Mr. Saul, and I have no doubt she will be." Mr. Saul did not understand this, and made no reply to it. "I don't know whether you have heard that Mr. Clavering intends to—give up the living."

"I have not heard it. I have thought it probable that he would do so."

"He has made up his mind that he will. The fact is, that if he held it, he must neglect either that or the property." We will not stop at this moment to examine what Mr. Saul's ideas must have been as to the exigencies of the property, which would leave no time for the performance of such clerical duties as had fallen for some years past to the share of the rector himself. "He hopes that he may be allowed to take some part in the services,—but he means to resign the living."

"I suppose that will not much affect me for the little time that I have to remain ? "

"We think it will affect you,—and hope that it may. Mr. Clavering wishes you to accept the living."

"To accept the living ? " And for a moment even Mr. Saul looked as though he were surprised.

"Yes, Mr. Saul."

"To be rector of Clavering ? "

"If you see no objection to such an arrangement."

"It is a most munificent offer,—but as strange as it is munificent.

Unless indeed——" And then some glimpse of the truth made its way into the chinks of Mr. Saul's mind.

"Mr. Clavering would, no doubt, have made the offer to you himself, had it not been that I can, perhaps, speak to you about dear Fanny better than he could do. Though our prudence has not been quite to your mind, you can at any rate understand that we might very much object to her marrying you when there was nothing for you to live on, even though we had no objection to yourself personally."

"But Mr. Clavering did object on both grounds."

"I was not aware that he had done so; but, if so, no such objection is now made by him,—or by me. My idea is that a child should be allowed to consult her own heart, and to indulge her own choice,—provided that in doing so she does not prepare for herself a life of indigence, which must be a life of misery; and of course providing also that there be no strong personal objection."

"A life of indigence need not be a life of misery," said Mr. Saul, with that obstinacy which formed so great a part of his character.

"Well, well."

"I am very indigent, but I am not at all miserable. If we are to be made miserable by that, what is the use of all our teaching?"

"But, at any rate, a competence is comfortable."

"Too comfortable!" As Mr. Saul made this exclamation, Mrs. Clavering could not but wonder at her daughter's taste. But the matter had gone too far now for any possibility of receding.

"You will not refuse it, I hope, as it will be accompanied by what you say you still desire."

"No; I will not refuse it. And may God give her and me grace so to use the riches of this world that they become not a stumbling-block to us, and a rock of offence. It is possible that the camel should be made to go through the needle's eye. It is possible."

"The position, you know, is not one of great wealth."

"It is to me, who have barely hitherto had the means of support. Will you tell your husband from me that I will accept, and endeavour not to betray the double trust he proposes to confer on me. It is much that he should give to me his daughter. She shall be to me bone of my bone, and flesh of my flesh. If God will give me his grace thereto, I will watch over her, so that no harm shall come nigh her. I love her as the apple of my eye; and I am thankful,—very thankful that the rich gift should be made to me."

"I am sure that you love her, Mr. Saul."

"But," continued he, not marking her interruption, "that other trust is one still greater, and requiring a more tender care and even a closer sympathy. I shall feel that the souls of these people will be, as it were, in my hand, and that I shall be called upon to give an account of their welfare. I will strive,—I will strive. And she, also, will be with me, to help me."

When Mrs. Clavering described this scene to her husband, he shook his head; and there came over his face a smile, in which there was much of melancholy, as he said, "Ah, yes,—that is all very well now. He will settle down as other men do, I suppose, when he has four or five children around him." Such were the ideas which the experience of the outgoing and elder clergyman taught him to entertain as to the ecstatic piety of his younger brother.

It was Mrs. Clavering who suggested to Mr. Saul that perhaps he would like to see Fanny. This she did when her story had been told, and he was preparing to leave her. "Certainly, if she will come to me."

"I will make no promise," said Mrs. Clavering, "but I will see." Then she went upstairs to the room where the girls were sitting, and the sacrificial lamb was sent down into the drawing-room. "I suppose if you say so, mamma——"

"I think, my dear, that you had better see him. You will meet then more comfortably afterwards." So Fanny went into the drawing-room, and Mr. Saul was sent to her there. What passed between them all readers of these pages will understand. Few young ladies, I fear, will envy Fanny Clavering her lover; but they will remember that Love will still be lord of all; and they will acknowledge that he had done much to deserve the success in life which had come in his way.

It was long before the old rector could reconcile himself either to the new rector or his new son-in-law. Mrs. Clavering had now so warmly taken up Fanny's part, and had so completely assumed a mother's interest in her coming marriage, that Mr. Clavering, or Sir Henry, as we may now call him, had found himself obliged to abstain from repeating to her the wonder with which he still regarded his daughter's choice. But to Harry he could still be eloquent on the subject. "Of course it's all right now," he said. "He's a very good young man, and nobody would work harder in the parish. I always thought I was very lucky to have such an assistant. But upon my word I cannot understand Fanny; I cannot indeed."

"She has been taken by the religious side of her character," said Harry.

"Yes, of course. And no doubt it is very gratifying to me to see that she thinks so much of religion. It should be the first consideration with all of us at all times. But she has never been used to men like Mr. Saul."

"Nobody can deny that he is a gentleman."

"Yes; he is a gentleman. God forbid that I should say he was not; especially now that he is going to marry your sister. But—— I don't know whether you quite understand what I mean?"

"I think I do. He isn't quite one of our sort."

"How on earth she can ever have brought herself to look at him in that light!"

"There's no accounting for tastes, sir. And, after all, as he's to have the living, there will be nothing to regret."

"No; nothing to regret. I suppose he'll be up at the other house occasionally. I never could make anything of him when he dined at the rectory; perhaps he'll be better there. Perhaps, when he's married, he'll get into the way of drinking a glass of wine like anybody else. Dear Fanny; I hope she'll be happy. That's everything." In answer to this Harry took upon himself to assure his father that Fanny would be happy; and then they changed the conversation, and discussed the alterations which they would make in reference to the preservation of pheasants.

Mr. Saul and Fanny remained long together on that occasion, and when they parted he went off about his work, not saying a word to any other person in the house, and she betook herself as fast as her feet could carry her to her own room. She said not a word either to her mother, or to her sister, or to Florence as to what had passed at that interview; but, when she was first seen by any of them, she was very grave in her demeanour, and very silent. When her father congratulated her, which he did with as much cordiality as he was able to assume, she kissed him and thanked him for his care and kindness; but even this she did almost solemnly. "Ah, I see how it is to be," said the old rector to his wife. "There are to be no more cakes and ale in the parish." Then his wife reminded him of what he himself had said of the change which would take place in Mr. Saul's ways when he should have a lot of children running about his feet. "Then I can only hope that they'll begin to run about very soon," said the old rector.

To her sister, Mary Fielding, Fanny said little or nothing of her coming marriage, but to Florence, who, as regarded that event, was in the same position as herself, she frequently did express her feelings,—declaring how awful to her was the responsibility of the thing she was about to do. "Of course that's quite true," said Florence, "but it doesn't make one doubt that one is right to marry."

"I don't know," said Fanny. "When I think of it, it does almost make me doubt."

"Then if I were Mr. Saul I would not let you think of it at all."

"Ah;—that shows that you do not understand him. He would be the first to advise me to hesitate if he thought that,—that—that;—I don't know that I can quite express what I mean."

"Under those circumstances Mr. Saul won't think that,—that—that —that——"

"Oh, Florence, it is too serious for laughing. It is indeed." Then Florence also hoped that a time might come, and that shortly, in which Mr. Saul might moderate his views,—though she did not express herself exactly as the rector had done.

Immediately after this Florence went back to Stratton, in order that she might pass what remained to her of her freedom with her mother and father, and that she might prepare herself for her wedding. The affair with her was so much hurried that she had hardly time to give her mind to those considerations which were weighing so heavily on Fanny's mind. It was felt by all the Burtons,—especially by Cecilia,—that there was need for extension of their views in regard to millinery, seeing that Florence was to marry the eldest son and heir of a baronet. And old Mrs. Burton was awed almost into quiescence by the reflections which came upon her when she thought of the breakfast, and of the presence of Sir Henry Clavering. She at once summoned her daughter-in-law from Ramsgate to her assistance, and felt that all her experience, gathered from the wedding breakfasts of so many elder daughters, would hardly carry her through the difficulties of the present occasion.

The two widowed sisters were still at the great house when Sir Henry Clavering with Harry and Fanny went to Stratton, but they left it on the following day. The father and son went up together to bid them farewell, on the eve of their departure, and to press upon them, over and over again, the fact that they were still to regard the Claverings of Clavering Park as their nearest relations and friends. The elder sister simply cried when this was said to her,—cried easily with plenteous tears, till the weeds which enveloped her seemed to be damp from the ever-running fountain. Hitherto, to weep had been her only refuge ; but I think that even this had already become preferable to her former life. Lady Ongar assured Sir Henry, or Mr. Clavering, as he was still called till after their departure,—that she would always remember and accept his kindness. " And you will come to us ? " said he. " Certainly ; when I can make Hermy come. She will be better when the summer is here. And then, after that, we will think about it." On this occasion she seemed to be quite cheerful herself, and bade Harry farewell with all the frank affection of an old friend.

" I have given up the house in Bolton Street," she said to him.

" And where do you mean to live ? "

" Anywhere ; just as it may suit Hermy. What difference does it make ? We are going to Tenby now, and though Tenby seems to me to have as few attractions as any place I ever knew, I daresay we shall stay there, simply because we shall be there. That is the consideration which weighs most with such old women as we are. Good-by, Harry."

" Good-by, Julia. I hope that I may yet see you,—you and Hermy, happy before long."

" I don't know much about happiness, Harry. There comes a dream of it sometimes,—such as you have got now. But I will answer for this : you shall never hear of my being down-hearted. At least not on my own account," she added in a whisper. " Poor Hermy may sometimes drag me down. But I will do my best. And, Harry, tell your wife that I shall write to her occasionally,—once a year, or something like that ; so that she need not be afraid. Good-by, Harry."

" Good-by, Julia." And so they parted.

Immediately on her arrival at Tenby, Lady Ongar communicated to Mr. Turnbull her intention of giving back to the Courton family, not only the place called Ongar Park, but also the whole of her income with the exception of eight hundred a year, so that in that respect she might be equal to her sister. This brought Mr. Turnbull down to Tenby, and there was interview after interview between the countess and the lawyer. The proposition, however, was made to the Courtons, and was absolutely refused by them. Ongar Park was accepted on behalf of the mother of the present earl; but as regarded the money, the widow of the late earl was assured by the elder surviving brother that no one doubted her right to it, or would be a party to accepting it from her. "Then," said Lady Ongar, "it will accumulate in my hands, and I can leave it as I please in my will."

"As to that, no one can control you," said her brother-in-law—who went to Tenby to see her; "but you must not be angry, if I advise you not to make any such resolution. Such hoards never have good results." This good result, however, did come from the effort which the poor broken-spirited woman was making,—that an intimacy, and at last a close friendship, was formed between her and the relatives of her deceased lord.

And now my story is done. My readers will easily understand what would be the future life of Harry Clavering and his wife after the completion of that tour in Italy, and the birth of the heir,—the preparations for which made the tour somewhat shorter than Harry had intended. His father, of course, gave up to him the shooting, and the farming of the home farm,—and after a while, the management of the property. Sir Henry preached occasionally,—believing himself to preach much oftener than he did,—and usually performed some portion of the morning service.

"Oh, yes," said Theodore Burton, in answer to some comfortable remark from his wife; "Providence has done very well for Florence. And Providence has done very well for him also;—but Providence was making a great mistake when she expected him to earn his bread."

A CATALOG OF SELECTED
DOVER BOOKS
IN ALL FIELDS OF INTEREST

A CATALOG OF SELECTED DOVER
BOOKS IN ALL FIELDS OF INTEREST

LASERS AND HOLOGRAPHY, Winston E. Kock. Sound introduction to burgeoning field, expanded (1981) for second edition. 84 illustrations. 160pp. 5⅜ × 8¼. (EUK)   24041-X Pa. $3.50

FLORAL STAINED GLASS PATTERN BOOK, Ed Sibbett, Jr. 96 exquisite floral patterns—irises, poppie, lilies, tulips, geometrics, abstracts, etc.—adaptable to innumerable stained glass projects. 64pp. 8¼ × 11.   24259-5 Pa. $3.50

THE HISTORY OF THE LEWIS AND CLARK EXPEDITION, Meriwether Lewis and William Clark. Edited by Eliott Coues. Great classic edition of Lewis and Clark's day-by-day journals. Complete 1893 edition, edited by Eliott Coues from Biddle's authorized 1814 history. 1508pp. 5⅜ × 8½.
21268-8, 21269-6, 21270-X Pa. Three-vol. set $22.50

ORLEY FARM, Anthony Trollope. Three-dimensional tale of great criminal case. Original Millais illustrations illuminate marvelous panorama of Victorian society. Plot was author's favorite. 736pp. 5⅜ × 8½.   24181-5 Pa. $10.95

THE CLAVERINGS, Anthony Trollope. Major novel, chronicling aspects of British Victorian society, personalities. 16 plates by M. Edwards; first reprint of full text. 412pp. 5⅜ × 8½.   23464-9 Pa. $6.00

EINSTEIN'S THEORY OF RELATIVITY, Max Born. Finest semi-technical account; much explanation of ideas and math not readily available elsewhere on this level. 376pp. 5⅜ × 8½.   60769-0 Pa. $5.00

COMPUTABILITY AND UNSOLVABILITY, Martin Davis. Classic graduate-level introduction th theory of computability, usually referred to as theory of recurrent functions. New preface and appendix. 288pp. 5⅜ × 8½. 61471-9 Pa. $6.50

THE GODS OF THE EGYPTIANS, E.A. Wallis Budge. Never excelled for richness, fullness: all gods, goddesses, demons, mythical figures of Ancient Egypt; their legends, rites, incarnations, etc. Over 225 illustrations, plus 6 color plates. 988pp. 6⅛ × 9¼. (EBE)   22055-9, 22056-7 Pa., Two-vol. set $20.00

THE I CHING (THE BOOK OF CHANGES), translated by James Legge. Most penetrating divination manual ever prepared. Indispensable to study of early Oriental civilizations, to modern inquiring reader. 448pp. 5⅜ × 8½.
21062-6 Pa. $6.50

THE CRAFTSMAN'S HANDBOOK, Cennino Cennini. 15th-century handbook, school of Giotto, explains applying gold, silver leaf; gesso; fresco painting, grinding pigments, etc. 142pp. 6⅛ × 9¼.   20054-X Pa. $3.50

AN ATLAS OF ANATOMY FOR ARTISTS, Fritz Schider. Finest text, working book. Full text, plus anatomical illustrations; plates by great artists showing anatomy. 593 illustrations. 192pp. 7⅛ × 10¼.   20241-0 Pa. $6.50

EASY-TO-MAKE STAINED GLASS LIGHTCATCHERS, Ed Sibbett, Jr. 67 designs for most enjoyable ornaments: fruits, birds, teddy bears, trumpet, etc. Full size templates. 64pp. 8¼ × 11.   24081-9 Pa. $3.95

TRIAD OPTICAL ILLUSIONS AND HOW TO DESIGN THEM, Harry Turner. Triad explained in 32 pages of text, with 32 pages of Escher-like patterns on coloring stock. 92 figures. 32 plates. 64pp. 8¼ × 11.   23549-1 Pa. $2.95

SMOCKING: TECHNIQUE, PROJECTS, AND DESIGNS, Dianne Durand. Foremost smocking designer provides complete instructions on how to smock. Over 10 projects, over 100 illustrations. 56pp. 8¼ × 11. 23788-5 Pa. $2.00

AUDUBON'S BIRDS IN COLOR FOR DECOUPAGE, edited by Eleanor H. Rawlings. 24 sheets, 37 most decorative birds, full color, on one side of paper. Instructions, including work under glass. 56pp. 8¼ × 11. 23492-4 Pa. $3.95

THE COMPLETE BOOK OF SILK SCREEN PRINTING PRODUCTION, J.I. Biegeleisen. For commercial user, teacher in advanced classes, serious hobbyist. Most modern techniques, materials, equipment for optimal results. 124 illustrations. 253pp. 5⅜ × 8½. 21100-2 Pa. $4.50

A TREASURY OF ART NOUVEAU DESIGN AND ORNAMENT, edited by Carol Belanger Grafton. 577 designs for the practicing artist. Full-page, spots, borders, bookplates by Klimt, Bradley, others. 144pp. 8⅜ × 11¼. 24001-0 Pa. $5.95

ART NOUVEAU TYPOGRAPHIC ORNAMENTS, Dan X. Solo. Over 800 Art Nouveau florals, swirls, women, animals, borders, scrolls, wreaths, spots and dingbats, copyright-free. 100pp. 8⅛ × 11. 24366-4 Pa. $4.00

HAND SHADOWS TO BE THROWN UPON THE WALL, Henry Bursill. Wonderful Victorian novelty tells how to make flying birds, dog, goose, deer, and 14 others, each explained by a full-page illustration. 32pp. 6½ × 9¼. 21779-5 Pa. $1.50

AUDUBON'S BIRDS OF AMERICA COLORING BOOK, John James Audubon. Rendered for coloring by Paul Kennedy. 46 of Audubon's noted illustrations: red-winged black-bird, cardinal, etc. Original plates reproduced in full-color on the covers. Captions. 48pp. 8¼ × 11. 23049-X Pa. $2.25

SILK SCREEN TECHNIQUES, J.I. Biegeleisen, M.A. Cohn. Clear, practical, modern, economical. Minimal equipment (self-built), materials, easy methods. For amateur, hobbyist, 1st book. 141 illustrations. 185pp. 6⅛ × 9¼. 20433-2 Pa. $3.95

101 PATCHWORK PATTERNS, Ruby S. McKim. 101 beautiful, immediately useable patterns, full-size, modern and traditional. Also general information, estimating, quilt lore. 140 illustrations. 124pp. 7⅞ × 10¾. 20773-0 Pa. $3.50

READY-TO-USE FLORAL DESIGNS, Ed Sibbett, Jr. Over 100 floral designs (most in three sizes) of popular individual blossoms as well as bouquets, sprays, garlands. 64pp. 8¼ × 11. 23976-4 Pa. $2.95

AMERICAN WILD FLOWERS COLORING BOOK, Paul Kennedy. Planned coverage of 46 most important wildflowers, from Rickett's collection; instructive as well as entertaining. Color versions on covers. Captions. 48pp. 8¼ × 11. 20095-7 Pa. $2.50

CARVING DUCK DECOYS, Harry V. Shourds and Anthony Hillman. Detailed instructions and full-size templates for constructing 16 beautiful, marvelously practical decoys according to time-honored South Jersey method. 70pp. 9¼ × 12¼. 24083-5 Pa. $4.95

TRADITIONAL PATCHWORK PATTERNS, Carol Belanger Grafton. Cardboard cut-out pieces for use as templates to make 12 quilts: Buttercup, Ribbon Border, Tree of Paradise, nine more. Full instructions. 57pp. 8¼ × 11. 23015-5 Pa. $3.50

25 KITES THAT FLY, Leslie Hunt. Full, easy-to-follow instructions for kites made from inexpensive materials. Many novelties. 70 illustrations. 110pp. 5⅜ × 8½.
22550-X Pa. $2.25

PIANO TUNING, J. Cree Fischer. Clearest, best book for beginner, amateur. Simple repairs, raising dropped notes, tuning by easy method of flattened fifths. No previous skills needed. 4 illustrations. 201pp. 5⅜ × 8½.
23267-0 Pa. $3.50

EARLY AMERICAN IRON-ON TRANSFER PATTERNS, edited by Rita Weiss. 75 designs, borders, alphabets, from traditional American sources. 48pp. 8¼ × 11.
23162-3 Pa. $1.95

CROCHETING EDGINGS, edited by Rita Weiss. Over 100 of the best designs for these lovely trims for a host of household items. Complete instructions, illustrations. 48pp. 8¼ × 11.
24031-2 Pa. $2.25

FINGER PLAYS FOR NURSERY AND KINDERGARTEN, Emilie Poulsson. 18 finger plays with music (voice and piano); entertaining, instructive. Counting, nature lore, etc. Victorian classic. 53 illustrations. 80pp. 6½ × 9¼. 22588-7 Pa. $1.95

BOSTON THEN AND NOW, Peter Vanderwarker. Here in 59 side-by-side views are photographic documentations of the city's past and present. 119 photographs. Full captions. 122pp. 8¼ × 11.
24312-5 Pa. $6.95

CROCHETING BEDSPREADS, edited by Rita Weiss. 22 patterns, originally published in three instruction books 1939-41. 39 photos, 8 charts. Instructions. 48pp. 8¼ × 11.
23610-2 Pa. $2.00

HAWTHORNE ON PAINTING, Charles W. Hawthorne. Collected from notes taken by students at famous Cape Cod School; hundreds of direct, personal *apercus*, ideas, suggestions. 91pp. 5⅜ × 8½.
20653-X Pa. $2.50

THERMODYNAMICS, Enrico Fermi. A classic of modern science. Clear, organized treatment of systems, first and second laws, entropy, thermodynamic potentials, etc. Calculus required. 160pp. 5⅜ × 8½.
60361-X Pa. $4.00

TEN BOOKS ON ARCHITECTURE, Vitruvius. The most important book ever written on architecture. Early Roman aesthetics, technology, classical orders, site selection, all other aspects. Morgan translation. 331pp. 5⅜ × 8½. 20645-9 Pa. $5.50

THE CORNELL BREAD BOOK, Clive M. McCay and Jeanette B. McCay. Famed high-protein recipe incorporated into breads, rolls, buns, coffee cakes, pizza, pie crusts, more. Nearly 50 illustrations. 48pp. 8¼ × 11.
23995-0 Pa. $2.00

THE CRAFTSMAN'S HANDBOOK, Cennino Cennini. 15th-century handbook, school of Giotto, explains applying gold, silver leaf; gesso; fresco painting, grinding pigments, etc. 142pp. 6⅛ × 9¼.
20054-X Pa. $3.50

FRANK LLOYD WRIGHT'S FALLINGWATER, Donald Hoffmann. Full story of Wright's masterwork at Bear Run, Pa. 100 photographs of site, construction, and details of completed structure. 112pp. 9¼ × 10.
23671-4 Pa. $6.95

OVAL STAINED GLASS PATTERN BOOK, C. Eaton. 60 new designs framed in shape of an oval. Greater complexity, challenge with sinuous cats, birds, mandalas framed in antique shape. 64pp. 8¼ × 11.
24519-5 Pa. $3.50

THE MURDER BOOK OF J.G. REEDER, Edgar Wallace. Eight suspenseful stories by bestselling mystery writer of 20s and 30s. Features the donnish Mr. J.G. Reeder of Public Prosecutor's Office. 128pp. 5⅜ × 8½. (Available in U.S. only) 24374-5 Pa. $3.50

ANNE ORR'S CHARTED DESIGNS, Anne Orr. Best designs by premier needlework designer, all on charts: flowers, borders, birds, children, alphabets, etc. Over 100 charts, 10 in color. Total of 40pp. 8¼ × 11. 23704-4 Pa. $2.50

BASIC CONSTRUCTION TECHNIQUES FOR HOUSES AND SMALL BUILDINGS SIMPLY EXPLAINED, U.S. Bureau of Naval Personnel. Grading, masonry, woodworking, floor and wall framing, roof framing, plastering, tile setting, much more. Over 675 illustrations. 568pp. 6½ × 9¼. 20242-9 Pa. $8.95

MATISSE LINE DRAWINGS AND PRINTS, Henri Matisse. Representative collection of female nudes, faces, still lifes, experimental works, etc., from 1898 to 1948. 50 illustrations. 48pp. 8⅜ × 11¼. 23877-6 Pa. $2.50

HOW TO PLAY THE CHESS OPENINGS, Eugene Znosko-Borovsky. Clear, profound examinations of just what each opening is intended to do and how opponent can counter. Many sample games. 147pp. 5⅜ × 8½. 22795-2 Pa. $2.95

DUPLICATE BRIDGE, Alfred Sheinwold. Clear, thorough, easily followed account: rules, etiquette, scoring, strategy, bidding; Goren's point-count system, Blackwood and Gerber conventions, etc. 158pp. 5⅜ × 8½. 22741-3 Pa. $3.00

SARGENT PORTRAIT DRAWINGS, J.S. Sargent. Collection of 42 portraits reveals technical skill and intuitive eye of noted American portrait painter, John Singer Sargent. 48pp. 8¼ × 11⅛. 24524-1 Pa. $2.95

ENTERTAINING SCIENCE EXPERIMENTS WITH EVERYDAY OBJECTS, Martin Gardner. Over 100 experiments for youngsters. Will amuse, astonish, teach, and entertain. Over 100 illustrations. 127pp. 5⅜ × 8½. 24201-3 Pa. $2.50

TEDDY BEAR PAPER DOLLS IN FULL COLOR: A Family of Four Bears and Their Costumes, Crystal Collins. A family of four Teddy Bear paper dolls and nearly 60 cut-out costumes. Full color, printed one side only. 32pp. 9¼ × 12¼. 24550-0 Pa. $3.50

NEW CALLIGRAPHIC ORNAMENTS AND FLOURISHES, Arthur Baker. Unusual, multi-useable material: arrows, pointing hands, brackets and frames, ovals, swirls, birds, etc. Nearly 700 illustrations. 80pp. 8⅜ × 11¼. 24095-9 Pa. $3.75

DINOSAUR DIORAMAS TO CUT & ASSEMBLE, M. Kalmenoff. Two complete three-dimensional scenes in full color, with 31 cut-out animals and plants. Excellent educational toy for youngsters. Instructions; 2 assembly diagrams. 32pp. 9¼ × 12¼. 24541-1 Pa. $4.50

SILHOUETTES: A PICTORIAL ARCHIVE OF VARIED ILLUSTRATIONS, edited by Carol Belanger Grafton. Over 600 silhouettes from the 18th to 20th centuries. Profiles and full figures of men, women, children, birds, animals, groups and scenes, nature, ships, an alphabet. 144pp. 8⅜ × 11¼. 23781-8 Pa. $4.95

SURREAL STICKERS AND UNREAL STAMPS, William Rowe. 224 haunting, hilarious stamps on gummed, perforated stock, with images of elephants, geisha girls, George Washington, etc. 16pp. one side. 8¼ × 11.   24371-0 Pa. $3.50

GOURMET KITCHEN LABELS, Ed Sibbett, Jr. 112 full-color labels (4 copies each of 28 designs). Fruit, bread, other culinary motifs. Gummed and perforated. 16pp. 8¼ × 11.   24087-8 Pa. $2.95

PATTERNS AND INSTRUCTIONS FOR CARVING AUTHENTIC BIRDS, H.D. Green. Detailed instructions, 27 diagrams, 85 photographs for carving 15 species of birds so life-like, they'll seem ready to fly! 8¼ × 11.   24222-6 Pa. $2.75

FLATLAND, E.A. Abbott. Science-fiction classic explores life of 2-D being in 3-D world. 16 illustrations. 103pp. 5⅜ × 8.   20001-9 Pa. $2.00

DRIED FLOWERS, Sarah Whitlock and Martha Rankin. Concise, clear, practical guide to dehydration, glycerinizing, pressing plant material, and more. Covers use of silica gel. 12 drawings. 32pp. 5⅜ × 8½.   21802-3 Pa. $1.00

EASY-TO-MAKE CANDLES, Gary V. Guy. Learn how easy it is to make all kinds of decorative candles. Step-by-step instructions. 82 illustrations. 48pp. 8¼ × 11.
                                23881-4 Pa. $2.50

SUPER STICKERS FOR KIDS, Carolyn Bracken. 128 gummed and perforated full-color stickers: GIRL WANTED, KEEP OUT, BORED OF EDUCATION, X-RATED, COMBAT ZONE, many others. 16pp. 8¼ × 11.   24092-4 Pa. $2.50

CUT AND COLOR PAPER MASKS, Michael Grater. Clowns, animals, funny faces...simply color them in, cut them out, and put them together, and you have 9 paper masks to play with and enjoy. 32pp. 8¼ × 11.   23171-2 Pa. $2.25

A CHRISTMAS CAROL: THE ORIGINAL MANUSCRIPT, Charles Dickens. Clear facsimile of Dickens manuscript, on facing pages with final printed text. 8 illustrations by John Leech, 4 in color on covers. 144pp. 8⅜ × 11¼.
                                20980-6 Pa. $5.95

CARVING SHOREBIRDS, Harry V. Shourds & Anthony Hillman. 16 full-size patterns (all double-page spreads) for 19 North American shorebirds with step-by-step instructions. 72pp. 9¼ × 12¼.   24287-0 Pa. $4.95

THE GENTLE ART OF MATHEMATICS, Dan Pedoe. Mathematical games, probability, the question of infinity, topology, how the laws of algebra work, problems of irrational numbers, and more. 42 figures. 143pp. 5⅜ × 8½. (EBE)
                                22949-1 Pa. $3.50

READY-TO-USE DOLLHOUSE WALLPAPER, Katzenbach & Warren, Inc. Stripe, 2 floral stripes, 2 allover florals, polka dot; all in full color. 4 sheets (350 sq. in.) of each, enough for average room. 48pp. 8¼ × 11.   23495-9 Pa. $2.95

MINIATURE IRON-ON TRANSFER PATTERNS FOR DOLLHOUSES, DOLLS, AND SMALL PROJECTS, Rita Weiss and Frank Fontana. Over 100 miniature patterns: rugs, bedspreads, quilts, chair seats, etc. In standard dollhouse size. 48pp. 8¼ × 11.   23741-9 Pa. $1.95

THE DINOSAUR COLORING BOOK, Anthony Rao. 45 renderings of dinosaurs, fossil birds, turtles, other creatures of Mesozoic Era. Scientifically accurate. Captions. 48pp. 8¼ × 11.   24022-3 Pa. $2.50

CHANCERY CURSIVE STROKE BY STROKE, Arthur Baker. Instructions and illustrations for each stroke of each letter (upper and lower case) and numerals. 54 full-page plates. 64pp. 8¼ × 11. 24278-1 Pa. $2.50

THE ENJOYMENT AND USE OF COLOR, Walter Sargent. Color relationships, values, intensities; complementary colors, illumination, similar topics. Color in nature and art. 7 color plates, 29 illustrations. 274pp. 5⅜ × 8½. 20944-X Pa. $4.95

SCULPTURE PRINCIPLES AND PRACTICE, Louis Slobodkin. Step-by-step approach to clay, plaster, metals, stone; classical and modern. 253 drawings, photos. 255pp. 8⅛ × 11. 22960-2 Pa. $7.50

VICTORIAN FASHION PAPER DOLLS FROM HARPER'S BAZAR, 1867-1898, Theodore Menten. Four female dolls with 28 elegant high fashion costumes, printed in full color. 32pp. 9¼ × 12¼. 23453-3 Pa. $3.50

FLOPSY, MOPSY AND COTTONTAIL: A Little Book of Paper Dolls in Full Color, Susan LaBelle. Three dolls and 21 costumes (7 for each doll) show Peter Rabbit's siblings dressed for holidays, gardening, hiking, etc. Charming borders, captions. 48pp. 4¼ × 5½. 24376-1 Pa. $2.25

NATIONAL LEAGUE BASEBALL CARD CLASSICS, Bert Randolph Sugar. 83 big-leaguers from 1909-69 on facsimile cards. Hubbell, Dean, Spahn, Brock plus advertising, info, no duplications. Perforated, detachable. 16pp. 8¼ × 11.
24308-7 Pa. $2.95

THE LOGICAL APPROACH TO CHESS, Dr. Max Euwe, et al. First-rate text of comprehensive strategy, tactics, theory for the amateur. No gambits to memorize, just a clear, logical approach. 224pp. 5⅜ × 8½. 24353-2 Pa. $4.50

MAGICK IN THEORY AND PRACTICE, Aleister Crowley. The summation of the thought and practice of the century's most famous necromancer, long hard to find. Crowley's best book. 436pp. 5⅜ × 8½. (Available in U.S. only)
23295-6 Pa. $6.50

THE HAUNTED HOTEL, Wilkie Collins. Collins' last great tale; doom and destiny in a Venetian palace. Praised by T.S. Eliot. 127pp. 5⅜ × 8½.
24333-8 Pa. $3.00

ART DECO DISPLAY ALPHABETS, Dan X. Solo. Wide variety of bold yet elegant lettering in handsome Art Deco styles. 100 complete fonts, with numerals, punctuation, more. 104pp. 8⅛ × 11. 24372-9 Pa. $4.50

CALLIGRAPHIC ALPHABETS, Arthur Baker. Nearly 150 complete alphabets by outstanding contemporary. Stimulating ideas; useful source for unique effects. 154 plates. 157pp. 8⅜ × 11¼. 21045-6 Pa. $5.95

ARTHUR BAKER'S HISTORIC CALLIGRAPHIC ALPHABETS, Arthur Baker. From monumental capitals of first-century Rome to humanistic cursive of 16th century, 33 alphabets in fresh interpretations. 88 plates. 96pp. 9 × 12.
24054-1 Pa. $4.50

LETTIE LANE PAPER DOLLS, Sheila Young. Genteel turn-of-the-century family very popular then and now. 24 paper dolls. 16 plates in full color. 32pp. 9¼ × 12¼. 24089-4 Pa. $3.50

TOLL HOUSE TRIED AND TRUE RECIPES, Ruth Graves Wakefield. Pop-overs, veal and ham loaf, baked beans, much more from the famous Mass. restaurant. Nearly 700 recipes. 376pp. 5⅜ × 8½.   23560-2 Pa. $4.95

FAVORITE CHRISTMAS CAROLS, selected and arranged by Charles J.F. Cofone. Title, music, first verse and refrain of 34 traditional carols in handsome calligraphy; also subsequent verses and other information in type. 79pp. 8⅜ × 11.
                                                              20445-6 Pa. $3.50

CAMERA WORK: A PICTORIAL GUIDE, Alfred Stieglitz. All 559 illustrations from most important periodical in history of art photography. Reduced in size but still clear, in strict chronological order, with complete captions. 176pp. 8⅜ × 11¼.
                                                              23591-2 Pa. $6.95

FAVORITE SONGS OF THE NINETIES, edited by Robert Fremont. 88 favorites: "Ta-Ra-Ra-Boom-De-Aye," "The Band Played On," "Bird in a Gilded Cage," etc. 401pp. 9 × 12.   21536-9 Pa. $12.95

STRING FIGURES AND HOW TO MAKE THEM, Caroline F. Jayne. Fullest, clearest instructions on string figures from around world: Eskimo, Navajo, Lapp, Europe, more. Cat's cradle, moving spear, lightning, stars. 950 illustrations. 407pp. 5⅜ × 8½.   20152-X Pa. $5.95

LIFE IN ANCIENT EGYPT, Adolf Erman. Detailed older account, with much not in more recent books: domestic life, religion, magic, medicine, commerce, and whatever else needed for complete picture. Many illustrations. 597pp. 5⅜ × 8½.
                                                              22632-8 Pa. $7.95

ANCIENT EGYPT: ITS CULTURE AND HISTORY, J.E. Manchip White. From pre-dynastics through Ptolemies: scoiety, history, political structure, religion, daily life, literature, cultural heritage. 48 plates. 217pp. 5⅜ × 8½. (EBE)
                                                              22548-8 Pa. $4.95

KEPT IN THE DARK, Anthony Trollope. Unusual short novel about Victorian morality and abnormal psychology by the great English author. Probably the first American publication. Frontispiece by Sir John Millais. 92pp. 6½ × 9¼.
                                                              23609-9 Pa. $2.95

MAN AND WIFE, Wilkie Collins. Nineteenth-century master launches an attack on out-moded Scottish marital laws and Victorian cult of athleticism. Artfully plotted. 35 illustrations. 239pp. 6⅛ × 9¼.   24451-2 Pa. $5.95

RELATIVITY AND COMMON SENSE, Herman Bondi. Radically reoriented presentation of Einstein's Special Theory and one of most valuable popular accounts available. 60 illustrations. 177pp. 5⅜ × 8. (EUK)   24021-5 Pa. $3.95

THE EGYPTIAN BOOK OF THE DEAD, E.A. Wallis Budge. Complete reproduction of Ani's papyrus, finest ever found. Full hieroglyphic text, interlinear transliteration, word-for-word translation, smooth translation. 533pp. 6½ × 9¼.
                                                          (USO) 21866-X Pa. $8.95

COUNTRY AND SUBURBAN HOMES OF THE PRAIRIE SCHOOL PERIOD, H.V. von Holst. Over 400 photographs floor plans, elevations, detailed drawings (exteriors and interiors) for over 100 structures. Text. Important primary source. 128pp. 8⅜ × 11¼.   24373-7 Pa. $5.95

KEYBOARD WORKS FOR SOLO INSTRUMENTS, G.F. Handel. 35 neglected works from Handel's vast oeuvre, originally jotted down as improvisations. Includes Eight Great Suites, others. New sequence. 174pp. 9⅜ × 12¼.
24338-9 Pa. $7.50

AMERICAN LEAGUE BASEBALL CARD CLASSICS, Bert Randolph Sugar. 82 stars from 1900s to 60s on facsimile cards. Ruth, Cobb, Mantle, Williams, plus advertising, info, no duplications. Perforated, detachable. 16pp. 8¼ × 11.
24286-2 Pa. $2.95

A TREASURY OF CHARTED DESIGNS FOR NEEDLEWORKERS, Georgia Gorham and Jeanne Warth. 141 charted designs: owl, cat with yarn, tulips, piano, spinning wheel, covered bridge, Victorian house and many others. 48pp. 8¼ × 11.
23558-0 Pa. $1.95

DANISH FLORAL CHARTED DESIGNS, Gerda Bengtsson. Exquisite collection of over 40 different florals: anemone, Iceland poppy, wild fruit, pansies, many others. 45 illustrations. 48pp. 8¼ × 11. 23957-8 Pa. $1.75

OLD PHILADELPHIA IN EARLY PHOTOGRAPHS 1839-1914, Robert F. Looney. 215 photographs: panoramas, street scenes, landmarks, President-elect Lincoln's visit, 1876 Centennial Exposition, much more. 230pp. 8⅜ × 11¼.
23345-6 Pa. $9.95

PRELUDE TO MATHEMATICS, W.W. Sawyer. Noted mathematician's lively, stimulating account of non-Euclidean geometry, matrices, determinants, group theory, other topics. Emphasis on novel, striking aspects. 224pp. 5⅜ × 8½.
24401-6 Pa. $4.50

ADVENTURES WITH A MICROSCOPE, Richard Headstrom. 59 adventures with clothing fibers, protozoa, ferns and lichens, roots and leaves, much more. 142 illustrations. 232pp. 5⅜ × 8½. 23471-1 Pa. $3.95

IDENTIFYING ANIMAL TRACKS: MAMMALS, BIRDS, AND OTHER ANIMALS OF THE EASTERN UNITED STATES, Richard Headstrom. For hunters, naturalists, scouts, nature-lovers. Diagrams of tracks, tips on identification. 128pp. 5⅜ × 8. 24442-3 Pa. $3.50

VICTORIAN FASHIONS AND COSTUMES FROM HARPER'S BAZAR, 1867-1898, edited by Stella Blum. Day costumes, evening wear, sports clothes, shoes, hats, other accessories in over 1,000 detailed engravings. 320pp. 9⅜ × 12¼.
22990-4 Pa. $10.95

EVERYDAY FASHIONS OF THE TWENTIES AS PICTURED IN SEARS AND OTHER CATALOGS, edited by Stella Blum. Actual dress of the Roaring Twenties, with text by Stella Blum. Over 750 illustrations, captions. 156pp. 9 × 12.
24134-3 Pa. $8.50

HALL OF FAME BASEBALL CARDS, edited by Bert Randolph Sugar. Cy Young, Ted Williams, Lou Gehrig, and many other Hall of Fame greats on 92 full-color, detachable reprints of early baseball cards. No duplication of cards with *Classic Baseball Cards*. 16pp. 8¼ × 11. 23624-2 Pa. $3.50

THE ART OF HAND LETTERING, Helm Wotzkow. Course in hand lettering, Roman, Gothic, Italic, Block, Script. Tools, proportions, optical aspects, individual variation. Very quality conscious. Hundreds of specimens. 320pp. 5⅜ × 8½.
21797-3 Pa. $4.95

TWENTY-FOUR ART NOUVEAU POSTCARDS IN FULL COLOR FROM CLASSIC POSTERS, Hayward and Blanche Cirker. Ready-to-mail postcards reproduced from rare set of poster art. Works by Toulouse-Lautrec, Parrish, Steinlen, Mucha, Cheret, others. 12pp. 8¼× 11. 24389-3 Pa. $2.95

READY-TO-USE ART NOUVEAU BOOKMARKS IN FULL COLOR, Carol Belanger Grafton. 30 elegant bookmarks featuring graceful, flowing lines, foliate motifs, sensuous women characteristic of Art Nouveau. Perforated for easy detaching. 16pp. 8¼ × 11. 24305-2 Pa. $2.95

FRUIT KEY AND TWIG KEY TO TREES AND SHRUBS, William M. Harlow. Fruit key covers 120 deciduous and evergreen species; twig key covers 160 deciduous species. Easily used. Over 300 photographs. 126pp. 5⅜ × 8½. 20511-8 Pa. $2.25

LEONARDO DRAWINGS, Leonardo da Vinci. Plants, landscapes, human face and figure, etc., plus studies for Sforza monument, *Last Supper*, more. 60 illustrations. 64pp. 8¼ × 11⅛. 23951-9 Pa. $2.75

CLASSIC BASEBALL CARDS, edited by Bert R. Sugar. 98 classic cards on heavy stock, full color, perforated for detaching. Ruth, Cobb, Durocher, DiMaggio, H. Wagner, 99 others. Rare originals cost hundreds. 16pp. 8¼ × 11. 23498-3 Pa. $3.25

TREES OF THE EASTERN AND CENTRAL UNITED STATES AND CANADA, William M. Harlow. Best one-volume guide to 140 trees. Full descriptions, woodlore, range, etc. Over 600 illustrations. Handy size. 288pp. 4½ × 6⅜. 20395-6 Pa. $3.95

JUDY GARLAND PAPER DOLLS IN FULL COLOR, Tom Tierney. 3 Judy Garland paper dolls (teenager, grown-up, and mature woman) and 30 gorgeous costumes highlighting memorable career. Captions. 32pp. 9¼ × 12¼. 24404-0 Pa. $3.50

GREAT FASHION DESIGNS OF THE BELLE EPOQUE PAPER DOLLS IN FULL COLOR, Tom Tierney. Two dolls and 30 costumes meticulously rendered. Haute couture by Worth, Lanvin, Paquin, other greats late Victorian to WWI. 32pp. 9¼ × 12¼. 24425-3 Pa. $3.50

FASHION PAPER DOLLS FROM GODEY'S LADY'S BOOK, 1840-1854, Susan Johnston. In full color: 7 female fashion dolls with 50 costumes. Little girl's, bridal, riding, bathing, wedding, evening, everyday, etc. 32pp. 9¼ × 12¼. 23511-4 Pa. $3.95

THE BOOK OF THE SACRED MAGIC OF ABRAMELIN THE MAGE, translated by S. MacGregor Mathers. Medieval manuscript of ceremonial magic. Basic document in Aleister Crowley, Golden Dawn groups. 268pp. 5⅜ × 8½. 23211-5 Pa. $5.00

PETER RABBIT POSTCARDS IN FULL COLOR: 24 Ready-to-Mail Cards, Susan Whited LaBelle. Bunnies ice-skating, coloring Easter eggs, making valentines, many other charming scenes. 24 perforated full-color postcards, each measuring 4¼ × 6, on coated stock. 12pp. 9 × 12. 24617-5 Pa. $2.95

CELTIC HAND STROKE BY STROKE, A. Baker. Complete guide creating each letter of the alphabet in distinctive Celtic manner. Covers hand position, strokes, pens, inks, paper, more. Illustrated. 48pp. 8¼ × 11. 24336-2 Pa. $2.50

YUCATAN BEFORE AND AFTER THE CONQUEST, Diego de Landa. Only significant account of Yucatan written in the early post-Conquest era. Translated by William Gates. Over 120 illustrations. 162pp. 5⅜ × 8½.   23622-6 Pa. $3.50

ORNATE PICTORIAL CALLIGRAPHY, E.A. Lupfer. Complete instructions, over 150 examples help you create magnificent "flourishes" from which beautiful animals and objects gracefully emerge. 8⅛ × 11.   21957-7 Pa. $2.95

DOLLY DINGLE PAPER DOLLS, Grace Drayton. Cute chubby children by same artist who did Campbell Kids. Rare plates from 1910s. 30 paper dolls and over 100 outfits reproduced in full color. 32pp. 9¼ × 12¼.   23711-7 Pa. $3.50

CURIOUS GEORGE PAPER DOLLS IN FULL COLOR, H. A. Rey, Kathy Allert. Naughty little monkey-hero of children's books in two doll figures, plus 48 full-color costumes: pirate, Indian chief, fireman, more. 32pp. 9¼ × 12¼.
24386-9 Pa. $3.50

GERMAN: HOW TO SPEAK AND WRITE IT, Joseph Rosenberg. Like *French, How to Speak and Write It.* Very rich modern course, with a wealth of pictorial material. 330 illustrations. 384pp. 5⅜ × 8½. (USUKO)   20271-2 Pa. $4.75

CATS AND KITTENS: 24 Ready-to-Mail Color Photo Postcards, D. Holby. Handsome collection; feline in a variety of adorable poses. Identifications. 12pp. on postcard stock. 8¼ × 11.   24469-5 Pa. $2.95

MARILYN MONROE PAPER DOLLS, Tom Tierney. 31 full-color designs on heavy stock, from *The Asphalt Jungle, Gentlemen Prefer Blondes,* 22 others. 1 doll. 16 plates. 32pp. 9⅜ × 12¼.   23769-9 Pa. $3.50

FUNDAMENTALS OF LAYOUT, F.H. Wills. All phases of layout design discussed and illustrated in 121 illustrations. Indispensable as student's text or handbook for professional. 124pp. 8⅛ × 11.   21279-3 Pa. $4.50

FANTASTIC SUPER STICKERS, Ed Sibbett, Jr. 75 colorful pressure-sensitive stickers. Peel off and place for a touch of pizzazz: clowns, penguins, teddy bears, etc. Full color. 16pp. 8¼ × 11.   24471-7 Pa. $2.95

LABELS FOR ALL OCCASIONS, Ed Sibbett, Jr. 6 labels each of 16 different designs—baroque, art nouveau, art deco, Pennsylvania Dutch, etc.—in full color. 24pp. 8¼ × 11.   23688-9 Pa. $2.95

HOW TO CALCULATE QUICKLY: RAPID METHODS IN BASIC MATHE-MATICS, Henry Sticker. Addition, subtraction, multiplication, division, checks, etc. More than 8000 problems, solutions. 185pp. 5 × 7¼.   20295-X Pa. $2.95

THE CAT COLORING BOOK, Karen Baldauski. Handsome, realistic renderings of 40 splendid felines, from American shorthair to exotic types. 44 plates. Captions. 48pp. 8¼ × 11.   24011-8 Pa. $2.25

THE TALE OF PETER RABBIT, Beatrix Potter. The inimitable Peter's terrifying adventure in Mr. McGregor's garden, with all 27 wonderful, full-color Potter illustrations. 55pp. 4¼ × 5½. (Available in U.S. only)   22827-4 Pa. $1.75

BASIC ELECTRICITY, U.S. Bureau of Naval Personnel. Batteries, circuits, conductors, AC and DC, inductance and capacitance, generators, motors, trans-formers, amplifiers, etc. 349 illustrations. 448pp. 6½ × 9¼.   20973-3 Pa. $7.95

REASON IN ART, George Santayana. Renowned philosopher's provocative, seminal treatment of basis of art in instinct and experience. Volume Four of *The Life of Reason*. 230pp. 5⅜ × 8. 24358-3 Pa. $4.50

LANGUAGE, TRUTH AND LOGIC, Alfred J. Ayer. Famous, clear introduction to Vienna, Cambridge schools of Logical Positivism. Role of philosophy, elimination of metaphysics, nature of analysis, etc. 160pp. 5⅜ × 8½. (USCO) 20010-8 Pa. $2.75

BASIC ELECTRONICS, U.S. Bureau of Naval Personnel. Electron tubes, circuits, antennas, AM, FM, and CW transmission and receiving, etc. 560 illustrations. 567pp. 6½ × 9¼. 21076-6 Pa. $8.95

THE ART DECO STYLE, edited by Theodore Menten. Furniture, jewelry, metalwork, ceramics, fabrics, lighting fixtures, interior decors, exteriors, graphics from pure French sources. Over 400 photographs. 183pp. 8⅜ × 11¼. 22824-X Pa. $6.95

THE FOUR BOOKS OF ARCHITECTURE, Andrea Palladio. 16th-century classic covers classical architectural remains, Renaissance revivals, classical orders, etc. 1738 Ware English edition. 216 plates. 110pp. of text. 9½ × 12¾. 21308-0 Pa. $11.50

THE WIT AND HUMOR OF OSCAR WILDE, edited by Alvin Redman. More than 1000 ripostes, paradoxes, wisecracks: Work is the curse of the drinking classes, I can resist everything except temptations, etc. 258pp. 5⅜ × 8½. (USCO) 20602-5 Pa. $3.95

THE DEVIL'S DICTIONARY, Ambrose Bierce. Barbed, bitter, brilliant witticisms in the form of a dictionary. Best, most ferocious satire America has produced. 145pp. 5⅜ × 8½. 20487-1 Pa. $2.50

ERTÉ'S FASHION DESIGNS, Erté. 210 black-and-white inventions from *Harper's Bazar*, 1918-32, plus 8pp. full-color covers. Captions. 88pp. 9 × 12. 24203-X Pa. $6.50

ERTÉ GRAPHICS, Erté. Collection of striking color graphics: *Seasons, Alphabet, Numerals, Aces* and *Precious Stones*. 50 plates, including 4 on covers. 48pp. 9⅜ × 12¼. 23580-7 Pa. $6.95

PAPER FOLDING FOR BEGINNERS, William D. Murray and Francis J. Rigney. Clearest book for making origami sail boats, roosters, frogs that move legs, etc. 40 projects. More than 275 illustrations. 94pp. 5⅜ × 8½. 20713-7 Pa. $2.25

ORIGAMI FOR THE ENTHUSIAST, John Montroll. Fish, ostrich, peacock, squirrel, rhinoceros, Pegasus, 19 other intricate subjects. Instructions. Diagrams. 128pp. 9 × 12. 23799-0 Pa. $4.95

CROCHETING NOVELTY POT HOLDERS, edited by Linda Macho. 64 useful, whimsical pot holders feature kitchen themes, animals, flowers, other novelties. Surprisingly easy to crochet. Complete instructions. 48pp. 8¼ × 11. 24296-X Pa. $1.95

CROCHETING DOILIES, edited by Rita Weiss. Irish Crochet, Jewel, Star Wheel, Vanity Fair and more. Also luncheon and console sets, runners and centerpieces. 51 illustrations. 48pp. 8¼ × 11. 23424-X Pa. $2.50

DECORATIVE NAPKIN FOLDING FOR BEGINNERS, Lillian Oppenheimer and Natalie Epstein. 22 different napkin folds in the shape of a heart, clown's hat, love knot, etc. 63 drawings. 48pp. 8¼ × 11. 23797-4 Pa. $1.95

DECORATIVE LABELS FOR HOME CANNING, PRESERVING, AND OTHER HOUSEHOLD AND GIFT USES, Theodore Menten. 128 gummed, perforated labels, beautifully printed in 2 colors. 12 versions. Adhere to metal, glass, wood, ceramics. 24pp. 8¼ × 11. 23219-0 Pa. $2.95

EARLY AMERICAN STENCILS ON WALLS AND FURNITURE, Janet Waring. Thorough coverage of 19th-century folk art: techniques, artifacts, surviving specimens. 166 illustrations, 7 in color. 147pp. of text. 7⅞ × 10¾. 21906-2 Pa. $9.95

AMERICAN ANTIQUE WEATHERVANES, A.B. & W.T. Westervelt. Extensively illustrated 1883 catalog exhibiting over 550 copper weathervanes and finials. Excellent primary source by one of the principal manufacturers. 104pp. 6⅛ × 9¼. 24396-6 Pa. $3.95

ART STUDENTS' ANATOMY, Edmond J. Farris. Long favorite in art schools. Basic elements, common positions, actions. Full text, 158 illustrations. 159pp. 5⅜ × 8½. 20744-7 Pa. $3.95

BRIDGMAN'S LIFE DRAWING, George B. Bridgman. More than 500 drawings and text teach you to abstract the body into its major masses. Also specific areas of anatomy. 192pp. 6½ × 9¼. (EA) 22710-3 Pa. $4.50

COMPLETE PRELUDES AND ETUDES FOR SOLO PIANO, Frederic Chopin. All 26 Preludes, all 27 Etudes by greatest composer of piano music. Authoritative Paderewski edition. 224pp. 9 × 12. (Available in U.S. only) 24052-5 Pa. $7.50

PIANO MUSIC 1888-1905, Claude Debussy. Deux Arabesques, Suite Bergamesque, Masques, 1st series of Images, etc. 9 others, in corrected editions. 175pp. 9⅜ × 12¼. (ECE) 22771-5 Pa. $5.95

TEDDY BEAR IRON-ON TRANSFER PATTERNS, Ted Menten. 80 iron-on transfer patterns of male and female Teddys in a wide variety of activities, poses, sizes. 48pp. 8¼ × 11. 24596-9 Pa. $2.25

A PICTURE HISTORY OF THE BROOKLYN BRIDGE, M.J. Shapiro. Profusely illustrated account of greatest engineering achievement of 19th century. 167 rare photos & engravings recall construction, human drama. Extensive, detailed text. 122pp. 8¼ × 11. 24403-2 Pa. $7.95

NEW YORK IN THE THIRTIES, Berenice Abbott. Noted photographer's fascinating study shows new buildings that have become famous and old sights that have disappeared forever. 97 photographs. 97pp. 11⅜ × 10. 22967-X Pa. $7.50

MATHEMATICAL TABLES AND FORMULAS, Robert D. Carmichael and Edwin R. Smith. Logarithms, sines, tangents, trig functions, powers, roots, reciprocals, exponential and hyperbolic functions, formulas and theorems. 269pp. 5⅜ × 8½. 60111-0 Pa. $4.95

HANDBOOK OF MATHEMATICAL FUNCTIONS WITH FORMULAS, GRAPHS, AND MATHEMATICAL TABLES, edited by Milton Abramowitz and Irene A. Stegun. Vast compendium: 29 sets of tables, some to as high as 20 places. 1,046pp. 8 × 10½. 61272-4 Pa. $19.95

THE RIME OF THE ANCIENT MARINER, Gustave Doré, S.T. Coleridge. Doré's finest work, 34 plates capture moods, subtleties of poem. Full text. 77pp. 9¼ × 12.
22305-1 Pa. $4.95

SONGS OF INNOCENCE, William Blake. The first and most popular of Blake's famous "Illuminated Books," in a facsimile edition reproducing all 31 brightly colored plates. Additional printed text of each poem. 64pp. 5¼ × 7.
22764-2 Pa. $3.50

AN INTRODUCTION TO INFORMATION THEORY, J.R. Pierce. Second (1980) edition of most impressive non-technical account available. Encoding, entropy, noisy channel, related areas, etc. 320pp. 5⅜ × 8½.
24061-4 Pa. $4.95

THE DIVINE PROPORTION: A STUDY IN MATHEMATICAL BEAUTY, H.E. Huntley. "Divine proportion" or "golden ratio" in poetry, Pascal's triangle, philosophy, psychology, music, mathematical figures, etc. Excellent bridge between science and art. 58 figures. 185pp. 5⅜ × 8½.
22254-3 Pa. $3.95

THE DOVER NEW YORK WALKING GUIDE: From the Battery to Wall Street, Mary J. Shapiro. Superb inexpensive guide to historic buildings and locales in lower Manhattan: Trinity Church, Bowling Green, more. Complete Text; maps. 36 illustrations. 48pp. 3⅞ × 9¼.
24225-0 Pa. $2.50

NEW YORK THEN AND NOW, Edward B. Watson, Edmund V. Gillon, Jr. 83 important Manhattan sites: on facing pages early photographs (1875-1925) and 1976 photos by Gillon. 172 illustrations. 171pp. 9¼ × 10.
23361-8 Pa. $7.95

HISTORIC COSTUME IN PICTURES, Braun & Schneider. Over 1450 costumed figures from dawn of civilization to end of 19th century. English captions. 125 plates. 256pp. 8⅜ × 11¼.
23150-X Pa. $7.50

VICTORIAN AND EDWARDIAN FASHION: A Photographic Survey, Alison Gernsheim. First fashion history completely illustrated by contemporary photographs. Full text plus 235 photos, 1840-1914, in which many celebrities appear. 240pp. 6½ × 9¼.
24205-6 Pa. $6.00

CHARTED CHRISTMAS DESIGNS FOR COUNTED CROSS-STITCH AND OTHER NEEDLECRAFTS, Lindberg Press. Charted designs for 45 beautiful needlecraft projects with many yuletide and wintertime motifs. 48pp. 8¼ × 11.
24356-7 Pa. $2.50

101 FOLK DESIGNS FOR COUNTED CROSS-STITCH AND OTHER NEEDLE-CRAFTS, Carter Houck. 101 authentic charted folk designs in a wide array of lovely representations with many suggestions for effective use. 48pp. 8¼ × 11.
24369-9 Pa. $2.25

FIVE ACRES AND INDEPENDENCE, Maurice G. Kains. Great back-to-the-land classic explains basics of self-sufficient farming. The one book to get. 95 illustrations. 397pp. 5⅜ × 8½.
20974-1 Pa. $4.95

A MODERN HERBAL, Margaret Grieve. Much the fullest, most exact, most useful compilation of herbal material. Gigantic alphabetical encyclopedia, from aconite to zedoary, gives botanical information, medical properties, folklore, economic uses, and much else. Indispensable to serious reader. 161 illustrations. 888pp. 6½ × 9¼. (Available in U.S. only)
22798-7, 22799-5 Pa., Two-vol. set $16.45

READY-TO-USE BORDERS, Ted Menten. Both traditional and unusual inter-changeable borders in a tremendous array of sizes, shapes, and styles. 32 plates. 64pp. 8¼ × 11. 23782-6 Pa. $3.50

THE WHOLE CRAFT OF SPINNING, Carol Kroll. Preparing fiber, drop spindle, treadle wheel, other fibers, more. Highly creative, yet simple. 43 illus-trations. 48pp. 8¼ × 11. 23968-3 Pa. $2.50

HIDDEN PICTURE PUZZLE COLORING BOOK, Anna Pomaska. 31 delightful pictures to color with dozens of objects, people and animals hidden away to find. Captions. Solutions. 48pp. 8¼ × 11. 23909-8 Pa. $2.25

QUILTING WITH STRIPS AND STRINGS, H.W. Rose. Quickest, easiest way to turn left-over fabric into handsome quilt. 46 patchwork quilts; 31 full-size templates. 48pp. 8¼ × 11. 24357-5 Pa. $3.25

NATURAL DYES AND HOME DYEING, Rita J. Adrosko. Over 135 specific recipes from historical sources for cotton, wool, other fabrics. Genuine premodern handicrafts. 12 illustrations. 160pp. 5⅜ × 8½. 22688-3 Pa. $2.95

CARVING REALISTIC BIRDS, H.D. Green. Full-sized patterns, step-by-step instructions for robins, jays, cardinals, finches, etc. 97 illustrations. 80pp. 8¼ × 11. 23484-3 Pa. $3.00

GEOMETRY, RELATIVITY AND THE FOURTH DIMENSION, Rudolf Rucker. Exposition of fourth dimension, concepts of relativity as Flatland characters continue adventures. Popular, easily followed yet accurate, profound. 141 illustrations. 133pp. 5⅜ × 8½. 23400-2 Pa. $3.00

READY-TO-USE SMALL FRAMES AND BORDERS, Carol B. Grafton. Graphic message? Frame it graphically with 373 new frames and borders in many styles: Art Nouveau, Art Deco, Op Art. 64pp. 8¼ × 11. 24375-3 Pa. $3.50

CELTIC ART: THE METHODS OF CONSTRUCTION, George Bain. Simple geometric techniques for making Celtic interlacements, spirals, Kellstype initials, animals, humans, etc. Over 500 illustrations. 160pp. 9 × 12. (Available in U.S. only) 22923-8 Pa. $6.00

THE TALE OF TOM KITTEN, Beatrix Potter. Exciting text and all 27 vivid, full-color illustrations to charming tale of naughty little Tom getting into mischief again. 58pp. 4¼ × 5½. (USO) 24502-0 Pa. $1.75

WOODEN PUZZLE TOYS, Ed Sibbett, Jr. Transfer patterns and instructions for 24 easy-to-do projects: fish, butterflies, cats, acrobats, Humpty Dumpty, 19 others. 48pp. 8¼ × 11. 23713-3 Pa. $2.50

MY FAMILY TREE WORKBOOK, Rosemary A. Chorzempa. Enjoyable, easy-to-use introduction to genealogy designed specially for children. Data pages plus text. Instructive, educational, valuable. 64pp. 8¼ × 11. 24229-3 Pa. $2.50

Prices subject to change without notice.

Available at your book dealer or write for free catalog to Dept. GI, Dover Publications, Inc., 31 East 2nd St. Mineola, N.Y. 11501. Dover publishes more than 175 books each year on science, elementary and advanced mathematics, biology, music, art, literary history, social sciences and other areas.